SAM SILVER: UNDERCOVER PIRATE

THE DEADLY TRAP

Collect all the Sam Silver: Undercover Pirate *books*

THE
DEADLY TRAP

Jan Burchett and Sara Vogler

Illustrated by Leo Hartas

Orion
Children's Books

First published in Great Britain in 2013
by Orion Children's Books
a division of the Orion Publishing Group Ltd
Orion House
5 Upper St Martin's Lane
London WC2H 9EA
An Hachette UK company

The Orion Publishing Group's policy is to use papers that are
natural, renewable and recyclable products and made from wood grown
in sustainable forests. The logging and manufacturing processes are expected
to conform to the environmental regulations of the country of origin.

A catalogue record for this book is available from the British Library.

Printed in Great Britain by Clays Ltd, St Ives plc

For Sally May,
without whom we wouldn't be
where we are today!

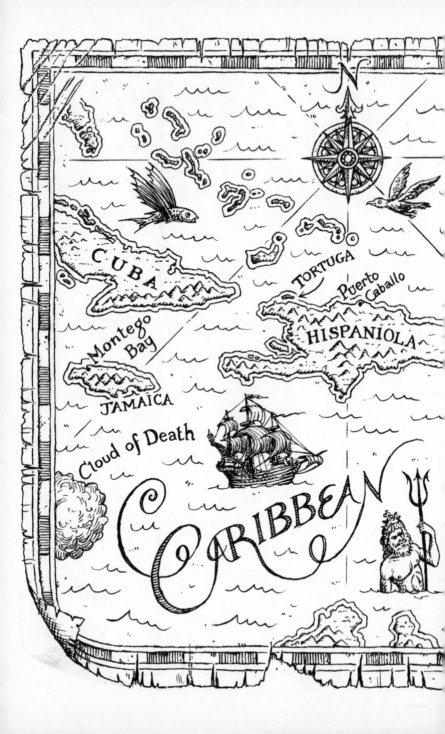

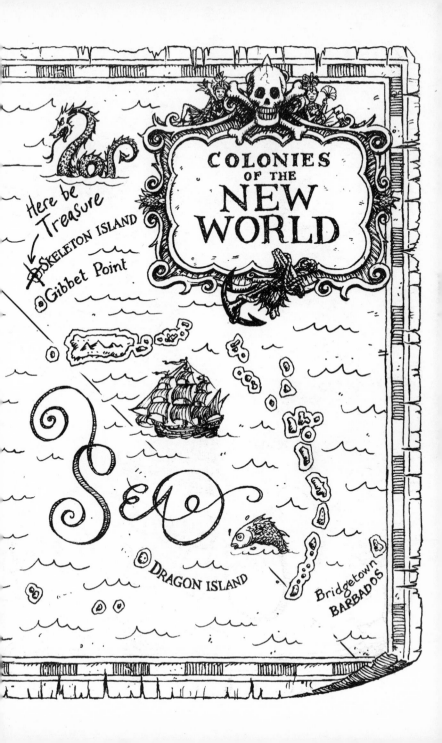

The
SEA
WOLF

Captain's
Cabin
Hammocks
Gun Deck
Galley
Ship's Stores

CHAPTER ONE

"Take that, you villain!" yelled Sam Silver, stabbing viciously at his reflection with a ruler.

He fought his imaginary enemy over his duvet and round a chair and trapped him in the wardrobe. His super sword skill had saved the day! But then, he'd had lessons from experts – a bunch of fierce Caribbean pirates.

It sounded impossible. His home in Backwater Bay was thousands of miles from the Caribbean, and the pirate crew of the *Sea Wolf* had lived three hundred years ago. But Sam had an amazing magic coin to take him there whenever he wanted.

Sam had never forgotten the day he'd found the gold doubloon in a bottle washed up on the beach. It had been sent to him by a pirate ancestor of his, Joseph Silver. When he spat on it and rubbed it, it whisked him back in time to the *Sea Wolf* and its crew of brave buccaneers. The coin was his most prized possession and he kept it in its bottle on a shelf in his bedroom.

Sam swished his ruler wildly in the air, knocking the bottle flying. It hit the lampshade, bounced off his pillow and landed on the floor at his feet. He snatched it up and checked for cracks.

No, it seemed to be OK, but the cork was missing and the coin that should have been inside had gone.

"Disaster!" he cried, scrabbling about on the floor, searching for the precious doubloon.

There was no sign of it. Shining his torch under the bed, he could see something glinting near the wall. He fished it out with a coat hanger. It was only a lump of silver foil. He feverishly searched his bin in case the coin had fallen into it. He found a sock, two apple cores and a squashed sandwich, but no gold doubloon. This was serious. The magic coin seemed to have vanished into thin air! Without it Sam couldn't travel back to the *Sea Wolf*. He gulped at the idea of never seeing his friends, Charlie and Fernando, and the pirate crew ever again.

"Sam!" His mum was calling from their fish and chip shop below the flat. "Can you pop to the supermarket for me? We need some milk."

Sam groaned. How could he concentrate on buying milk when he'd lost his magic doubloon? But he knew he'd be in trouble if he didn't go.

He kept glancing round the room as he slipped his left foot into his trainer.

"Ow!" There was something hard in there. He pulled his foot out and tipped the trainer upside down. The doubloon tumbled out onto the carpet!

Sam snatched it up and held it tightly

in his hands. That had been the worst moment of his life. Then he had a dreadful thought. Supposing the coin had lost its power now he'd dropped it. He'd better check it out. Then he'd go to the shops for his mum. That was the great thing about the magic doubloon. However long his pirate adventure lasted, he knew it would bring him back to exactly the same time in the present – if it still worked.

He pulled on the tatty jeans and T-shirt that he always wore when he went time travelling, and rammed on his trainers. Then he spat on the coin and rubbed it on his sleeve. At once his bedroom whooshed around him in a mad spin. He felt himself being sucked up as if he was in a giant vacuum cleaner.

Sam landed with a thump on the floor of a small wooden storeroom. He could hear the timbers creaking and feel the room swaying. Awesome! He was back on the *Sea Wolf*.

The shouts of the busy crew came from the main deck above. Sam jumped up. His pirate jerkin, belt and neckerchief were on a barrel, along with his spyglass. Charlie always put them there for him. She was the only one who knew he was a time traveller. Everyone else believed he popped home now and then to see his mum, which was true, of course. He just had a longer journey than they realised.

Stowing his coin safely in his jeans pocket, he threw on his pirate clothes and grabbed his spyglass. He ran up the stairway, bursting out onto the bright, sunlit deck. The blue ocean sparkled, the patched sails were tight in the wind and the flag with its snarling wolf's head and crossed bones fluttered merrily at the top of the mast.

Someone had hung some washing on a line strung across the deck. Ragged shirts and breeches flapped in the breeze.

I didn't know pirates had washday! thought Sam. *Hope I don't have to do the ironing!* He ducked under the line of clothes to find the crew and cannoned straight into someone coming the other way.

"Sorry," he gasped. "I was—" He stopped. He was looking up into a face he'd never seen before. What had happened? He was on the right ship, but where was the *Sea Wolf* crew?

CHAPTER TWO

For a moment the man looked astonished. Then he gave a deep laugh. "Where did you spring from, young'un. A stowaway, are you?" He gave Sam a friendly punch on the arm. "Have you been hiding in the hold?"

The man was tall and broad, with crinkly, smiling eyes. He seemed friendly enough but what was he doing here? Sam felt a dull ache in his stomach. Where were all his shipmates and Crow, his parrot friend? Was the coin damaged after all? Had it brought him back to the right ship but the wrong time?

"Sam!" came a cry. Sam knew that voice. A grin of relief spread over his face as Charlie, with her ragged hair and boy's shirt and breeches, rushed up beside him.

"I'm glad you're back!" she said, sliding her arm through his.

"And I'm glad to see you!" Sam burst out. "I didn't spot anyone I knew at first and I thought the coin must have brought me back to a different— Ouch!"

Charlie had stepped firmly on his toe. "This is Sam Silver," she said to the man. "We told you about him. He comes to join us when his mum doesn't need him, don't you Sam? And he never knows how long it will take him to get here."

"Er, that's right," agreed Sam, rubbing his foot. He could always rely on Charlie

to get him out of trouble. It would have
been a disaster to talk about time travel to
this man. He'd think Sam was possessed
by an evil demon.

"So you're Sam Silver," said the man,
beaming as he shook Sam's hand. "I'm Dick
Gudgeon. I've only been on this ship for two
weeks but I've heard all about you. Pleased
to make your acquaintance. The captain
thinks very highly of you, you know."

Sam felt his face turning
red with the praise.

"But you came
aboard without
anyone seeing!" Dick
went on, looking
keenly at him.
"You're a clever lad
to do that. Where
does your mum
live?"

"That's Sam's

business," said Charlie quickly. "He doesn't tell us and we don't ask."

"And that's all right with us!" came a deep voice. Captain Blade strode up, the weapons in his belts gleaming in the sun. "Glad to have you back," he told Sam. "I see you've met our new crew member. He came aboard in Tortuga when we stopped for supplies. Dick's been a doing a good job of lookout while you've been gone."

"Just doing my duty," said Dick modestly.

"Does that mean you won't need me up in the crow's nest, Captain?" asked Sam, disappointed. He loved being lookout boy, watching the seas from the wooden basket at the top of the mainmast with Crow on his shoulder, and warning the crew when he spied an enemy vessel. He could see a flash of green feathers, which meant the parrot was up there at this very moment, waiting for him.

"Of course I'll need you, Sam," Blade

told him. "You're a first-rate lookout. Besides, we could do with Dick's help on deck. He's an expert sailor and can turn his hand to anything."

"Shiver me timbers," declared Harry Hopp, his wooden leg thumping on the deck as he came to join them. "Dick's worth his weight in gold."

"He really is," came a Spanish voice from the rigging.

Fernando jumped down next to Sam and slapped him on the back in welcome. Sam noticed that a new earring shone in his ear under his wild curly hair. He'd ruined the last one picking a lock. "You've got here at the right time, my friend," Fernando told him. "Dick's going to lead us to a great hoard of treasure."

"Aye," agreed the new crew member, rubbing his hands. "I heard of a ship, the *Queen Bess*, that's setting sail from Barbados. There's gold on her like you've never seen! Seems a waste to let all that wealth go to England."

"So we wait till she's at sea and ambush her!" cried Sam eagerly.

"Not so fast, lad!" laughed Captain Blade. "She'll be heavily guarded by a fleet of men-o'-war."

"I suggested to your captain that we take her treasure while she's still at anchor in Bridgetown port," said Dick.

Sam felt a thrill of excitement. Then a doubt suddenly popped into his head. "But you must have come from another pirate crew," he said to Dick. "Won't they be after it, too?"

"I like a boy with a quick mind," replied Dick. "No, my last crew were lost in a terrible storm. I was the only survivor . . ." He broke off and Sam saw the sheen of tears in his eyes.

"Aye, but you've got new shipmates now," said Captain Blade gruffly, giving Dick a kindly pat on the shoulder. "Get to your posts, men. We'll be reaching Barbados in a few hours. Sam, you're on lookout." He turned abruptly and walked straight into a flapping shirt. "And someone get this washing off my deck!"

Dick Gudgeon was smiling again now. "This is a fine ship," he said. He looked Sam up and down. "And you've got the makings of a fine pirate. You're quick-witted and canny. You'll be a captain one day, I'll be bound!"

Sam glowed with pride as he climbed the rigging towards the crow's nest. This adventure might be the best yet!

CHAPTER THREE

That afternoon Sam sat with Dick on the foredeck. Dick was teaching him some new knots. The north coast of Barbados had been sighted an hour ago and now they were heading south for Bridgetown. Sam felt the excitement bubbling up and he had to fight to keep his hands steady. Not only did this treasure sound awesome, but they were going to sneak in and take it from under the noses of the authorities. It was like being in an adventure film.

While Sam practised his clove hitch knot, Dick whistled an old tune, *Greensleeves*, and made a loop on the end of a piece of rope. Sam stopped and watched in amazement. His new shipmate had enormous hands, but he worked the ropes together as if he were stitching the finest embroidery.

"That must have taken you a long time to learn," said Sam.

"Not if you've lived all your life on a ship, my lad," said Dick genially. "I could easily teach a clever boy like you to splice rope as well as I do." He picked up a wooden stick and pushed the sharp end through the rope. "See, I take my fid to make the hole and then—"

"Swab the decks!" came a hoarse cry and the ship's parrot flapped down to perch on Sam's shoulder.

"Hello there, Crow," said Dick, stroking his head. "He's kept me good company when I've been on lookout." He dug about in the pockets of his breeches. "I've got some maize seed somewhere." He pulled out a handful of yellow seeds and held them out. Crow gave a delighted squawk and tucked in. "They love sunflower seeds too, but you mustn't give him too many — they'll make him fat!"

"You know a lot about parrots," said Sam, impressed.

"I had one when I was a boy," Dick told him. "Beautiful bird. I called him Drake."

"Drake!" squawked Crow.

"What a fantastic pirate name!" laughed Sam. "We call this one Crow to keep the captain happy."

Dick looked confused. "Why would that make Captain Blade happy?"

"Because that way he can pretend Crow is a real crow," explained Sam. "Of course, he doesn't really think that, but it's the only way he'll allow Crow on board. He's scared of parrots, you see."

"Scared of parrots!" exclaimed Dick, dropping his rope. "I thought Blade was fearless. I did wonder that he never went near the bird."

He fell silent and Sam felt terrible. Everyone else on board knew about Captain Blade's one fear and it didn't bother them. But Dick was a new member of the crew. He might be disappointed in the captain of the *Sea Wolf* and decide not to stay. And that meant they wouldn't get the gold in Bridgetown.

Dick Gudgeon had a curious expression on his face. To Sam's surprise it wasn't disappointment. He was grinning! Dick seemed to find the captain's fear funny. But it wasn't a nice grin. It was a grin that sent a chill through Sam.

Dick saw Sam staring and the expression was gone in an instant. "Well, well," he said, shaking his head sympathetically. "Each of us has his faults. Blade's still a fine, brave man, for all that."

"The bravest!" declared Sam. "He'll outfight anyone who threatens the *Sea Wolf* and its men."

"I've no doubt of it," replied Dick thoughtfully. He stood up. "You've learned those knots mighty quick, Sam.

I'll be off to help the bosun with the new fore rail."

Sam watched him go in search of Ned. Dick Gudgeon was a great shipmate. He was a hard worker and everyone liked him. But something niggled inside Sam's brain: why had he looked pleased to hear of the captain's fear?

With Crow clinging tightly to his jerkin, Sam went to find Charlie. He'd tell her what he'd seen. She'd know what to do.

Charlie was sitting on the poop deck with a fishing rod, the line dangling over the side. Sinbad, the ship's cat, lay curled at her feet. Crow took one look, gave a squawk and flew up to the top of the mast. The cat watched him go then began to wash his paws.

"Who's the softest kitty in the world?" said Charlie. Sinbad rolled over and let her tickle his belly.

Sinbad adored Charlie but greeted everyone else with a flash of his claws.

Keeping his distance, Sam told his friend what he'd seen.

"I don't think you've given Dick a fair chance," said Charlie, when he'd finished. "He's helpful and friendly and really useful. Why would he tell us where to find gold if he meant us harm?"

"You're right," sighed Sam. "I can't explain what I saw. I only know that his smile made me go cold."

Charlie put her hand on Sam's forehead. "You haven't got a fever, have you?" she asked with a grin.

"I'm as well as you are," insisted Sam.

"Then I'm sure you were mistaken," said Charlie.

Sam frowned. He liked to think of himself as a cool detective, but he had to admit he did sometimes get a bit overexcited. He remembered reporting a suspicious-looking person in the school playground. It had turned out to be the new vicar who was very surprised when a policeman tried to arrest him. Sam certainly didn't want to make a fool of himself like that. He'd be too ashamed to visit the *Sea Wolf* ever again!

"Maybe I'm imagining things," he admitted, "but I'm going to keep my eye on Dick from now on."

"And so will I," Charlie assured him. "Just in case."

Sam walked across the deck, making for

the rigging. It was his turn up in the crow's nest. As he grasped the knotted rope ready to climb, he spotted Dick and Ned repairing a piece of broken rail. Dick was holding a length of wood as Ned sawed.

"I feel sorry for Captain Blade," Dick was saying. "I mean, I wouldn't like to be scared of parrots. There are so many around these parts."

Sam quickly hid by the galley door and watched.

"It could be worse," Ned answered as he cut into the wood. "We just keep Crow out of his way. I heard it's because one stole his porridge when he was a young 'un." Ned grinned. "We're lucky it's only them he's scared of and not ghosts, or storms — or the enemy!"

"Too right," agreed Dick. "But what happens if a parrot comes near him?"

"He goes as white as my shirt," said Ned. He glanced at his grimy clothes.

"That is, when my shirt was new!"

"Is that all?" laughed Dick. "It doesn't sound like any great fear."

"Not to you or me, I suppose," said Ned. "But the captain's always happier when Crow's not nearby."

"Good job there's only one parrot on board then," said Dick, looking thoughtful.

Sam pulled himself up the rigging and swung himself into the wooden crow's nest at the top. His mind was racing. Why was Dick Gudgeon so interested in the captain's fear of parrots?

"Scurvy sea dog!" squawked Crow, landing on his shoulder.

"You've hit the nail on the head there," Sam told the green parrot. "I reckon Dick's not the man the crew thinks he is."

But he had to prove it. And there was only one way — he'd have to make a plan to catch Dick out!

CHAPTER FOUR

Late that afternoon the *Sea Wolf* lay at anchor off the coast of Barbados. The crew were trying to eat a fish stew. At least that's what Peter the cook called it. Sam decided it tasted more like dirty dishwater with the dirty dishes still in it!

"Well, I'll polish the portholes with a piranha!" said Ned, spitting out a bone.

"This treasure will be a fine haul. We can stash it on Skeleton Island."

Sam watched Dick intently, but the new crew member was as cheerful and friendly as ever.

"The *Queen Bess* is carrying a lot of gold," he laughed. "I hope you've got plenty of room for it in that stronghold of yours."

The pirates rubbed their hands at the thought of all the booty.

"You'll be setting foot there yourself," Captain Blade told him. "But you'll understand that we'll need to blindfold you when we get near. We'll let you see where it is when we know you better."

"I wouldn't have it any other way, Captain," said Dick earnestly. "In my book, a man must prove himself worthy and I'll do anything to earn that trust."

"I reckon it won't be long!" called Harry.

"Aye!" chorused the crew enthusiastically.

Sam's brain was buzzing. Dick Gudgeon didn't know where the pirates' stronghold was. He said he was happy to wait until the captain chose to tell him, but was that true? If Dick wasn't the loyal shipmate everyone believed, then Sam was certain he'd want to know where the *Sea Wolf* treasure was stored right now! A plan began to form in his head. He'd make a false map of the location of Skeleton Island and hide it somewhere. Then he'd tell Dick where he'd put it and wait to see what happened.

The crew were astonished at the sight of Sam gulping his stew down and heading off to the galley with his tin plate.

"Surely the boy doesn't want seconds!" he heard Harry Hopp exclaim.

Once he was inside the small ship's kitchen, Sam put his plate down and took a burned stick from the cooking fire. Then he sneaked down to the storeroom. He found an old piece of sail and sketched a quick map of the Caribbean with the blackened end of the stick. He drew a blob of an island right in the middle of the western sea, as far away from Skeleton Island as he could – and put an X on it.

He looked around for a hiding place for his map – somewhere that no one else would discover unless they were told about it. But there seemed to be nowhere really safe. If he put it in a box or barrel someone might open it. As he wandered round the storeroom he caught his foot on a nail that was sticking up. He looked down. One of the floorboards was loose. Sam got his fingers under it and pulled until the wood came away. He pushed his map into the little gap below and placed the board back.

"Now to give Dick the bait," he muttered, "and see if he takes it." He grabbed some rope and went in search of the new crewman. He found him sitting by the bowsprit, carving an intricate pineapple shape into the round end of his wooden fid.

"I'm sorry to bother you," said Sam, holding out the rope, "but I can't remember the clove hitch you showed me. Can you help?"

"Of course," said Dick with a friendly grin. He took the rope, looped and threaded it round the rail, and pulled it tight. "See what I'm doing? It's simple, especially for a bright boy like you."

"I'm not bright," said Sam, looking down as if he was sad. "I'm no good at remembering things. Like that knot — and which side is port and which is starboard. Don't tell anyone, but I only remember the location of our secret hideout because I've made a map."

He studied Dick's face as he spoke, but the man's expression didn't change.

"Well," said Dick, untying the rope. "I hope you've got that map good and hidden. You wouldn't want it to fall into the wrong hands if an enemy boarded the *Sea Wolf*."

"They'd never find it," said Sam eagerly. "It's hidden under a loose plank in the storeroom floor."

Dick nodded. "Good place!"

Sam jumped up. "I'm on lookout in a minute," he said. "Thanks for your help with the knot."

"Happy to oblige, lad," said Dick. "I'll be heading off to my hammock."

Sam left the foredeck, but instead of making for the rigging he dived down the hatchway to the storeroom. He wasn't really on lookout duty.

He just wanted Dick to think he was as far away as possible. He hid behind an empty barrel. If Dick Gudgeon was as honourable as he pretended then he would go straight to bed and not seek out the map. Sam hoped that was exactly what would happen. The crew really liked Dick and it would be awful to disappoint them.

Sam waited. He wondered how long he was going to have to stay squashed behind the barrel. He'd need to come out eventually or the crew would come looking for him, and they'd think he was mad if he said he was playing hide-and-seek.

He was beginning to think he'd been wrong about his new shipmate, when . . . *Creak!*

The storeroom door slowly opened. Sam peeped round his barrel. Someone was coming in!

CHAPTER FIVE

A tall figure crept into the storeroom. He was holding a lantern. When he turned Sam could see his face in the flickering candlelight. It was Dick Gudgeon! He carefully closed the door behind him and crept across the floor, testing each board with his foot.

Sam tried to slow his breathing down,

terrified that he could be heard, but Dick was too busy searching. Sam stayed stock still as Dick moved towards the map's hiding place. Suddenly he dived down, placed the lantern beside him and put his fingers round the loose floorboard. In an instant he had the map in his hand. After a furtive look about him, he studied it in the lantern light and let out a low laugh.

Got him! thought Sam. Now to show the crew the truth about Dick Gudgeon.

"You villain!" he yelled, leaping up and sending the barrel rolling. "I knew you weren't to be trusted."

Dick turned on him. There was no sign of the friendly expression he always wore in front of the crew. His face was boiling with fury as he gripped the map in one hand and curled his other fist, ready to strike. "Shut your stupid mouth!" he hissed, aiming a vicious punch at Sam. "Or I'll shut it for you."

Sam dodged the blow. "We'll see what the captain has to say about this!" He flung open the storeroom door. "Help!" he shouted at the top of his voice. "Captain Blade! Harry! Everyone! Come here quickly!"

Footsteps thundered and Captain Blade appeared, cutlass drawn. Harry Hopp and Fernando were close behind.

"What in blazes is going on here?" demanded the captain.

"Dick Gudgeon's trying to find out where our hideout is," cried Sam, pointing accusingly at Dick. "He's no friend of the *Sea Wolf*!"

But the evil expression had completely vanished from Dick's face. He held out the piece of sail, smiling pityingly at Sam. "I think the poor lad is talking about this," he said. "He told me he'd made a chart of where your hideout lies."

"Blow me down!" exclaimed Harry Hopp, horrified.

"Don't be hard on him," Gudgeon went on in a pleading voice. "He's a bit simpleminded. I was going to destroy it before it fell into the wrong hands." As he spoke, he crushed the sail up, rubbing it between his palms to obliterate the charcoal drawing.

"That's not true!" yelled Sam. "He wanted to . . ."

He stopped as he realised that everyone

was staring at him. Harry was shaking his head.

"You put down where our stronghold is!" gasped Fernando. "But it's a sacred secret."

"I thought you knew that, Sam," snapped Captain Blade.

"Don't worry on my account," said Dick pleasantly. "I didn't so much as glance at it. I've told you, I don't want to know where it is until the captain thinks I'm worthy." He handed the piece of sail to Blade and left, whistling *Greensleeves* as if he didn't have a care in the world.

"You have to believe me, Captain," gabbled Sam. "I hid the map as a test to see if Dick would fall for it – and he did. But it was a false—"

"Avast your jabbering!" Blade's face looked sharp and stern in the lantern light. "I cannot believe you're accusing an honest man of treachery. Dick Gudgeon has done nothing to deserve that."

"But . . . I . . ." spluttered Sam.

"You're acting very strangely, Sam," said Fernando looking puzzled.

"I'll not have a crew member make trouble on board," roared the captain. "You are never to do that again. Do you understand?"

Sam hung his head. "Yes, sir," he muttered.

"Then we'll say no more about it."

The captain spun on his heel and left with Harry Hopp stomping behind him. Fernando opened his mouth as if to speak, then seemed to change his mind and left without a word. Sam found himself alone.

Charlie slipped in, Sinbad in her arms. The ship's cat stared at Sam as if he was accusing him as well.

Sam flopped miserably down onto the floor. "I suppose you've come to have a go at me too."

But to his surprise Charlie shook her head. "I know you must have had good reasons for accusing Dick," she said, settling down beside him. "But I don't understand. Why did you make a map of Skeleton Island? That was really stupid."

"I was trying to catch Dick out," sighed Sam. He told her about his plan. "And it worked," he finished bitterly, "but no one believes me."

Charlie put her hand on his arm. "*I* believe you," she said solemnly.

Sam gave her a grateful smile. "Dick Gudgeon's a dangerous man to have on board. He's after our gold and I reckon he'll stop at nothing to get it!"

Charlie gave a shiver. "This is serious. Dick's such a good actor that everyone else thinks he's an honest man."

"Then we've got to show them they're wrong," muttered Sam, "before it's too late!"

"I agree," said Charlie, "but we mustn't let Dick know we're working together."

"Then you have to pretend not to be my friend any more," said Sam, "and that's going to be horrible."

CHAPTER SIX

That night Sam lay in his hammock on the gun deck. He felt very lonely all on his own. No one had come near him after the map had been found, although he could tell that Dick Gudgeon was keeping a crafty eye on him and Fernando was throwing him puzzled looks. He realised it must be hard for the crew. Sam only sailed with them now and again. Dick had worked alongside them for two whole weeks, and he'd brought the promise of treasure.

Sam wondered how he was ever going to find evidence that the man was a villain. It wasn't as if he could overhear Dick having a conversation on a mobile, or read one of his emails. He decided it was much harder being a detective three hundred years ago, before those handy things had been invented.

Sam drifted into a dream where he was fighting a shark that had Dick Gudgeon's evil, grinning face. The shark kept coming at him, its teeth sharp and vicious, and no matter how fast he swam, it wouldn't go away.

Suddenly he woke with a start. He could hear a faint scuffling noise. At first he wondered if it was a rat – but he was used to them scurrying about. What was it then? Not someone going to bed, that was

for sure. The pirates always clumped around, throwing belts to the floor with a clatter, and yawning and belching loudly as they clambered into their hammocks. No, this sounded like someone who didn't want to be heard.

Sam cautiously opened one eye. Dick was standing on the other side of the deck. Something told Sam he'd better pretend to be asleep. He lay still and watched. A lantern swung at the far end of the gun deck. By its faint light Sam could see that Dick had laid his sailor's bag on his bed. He was carefully feeling inside it in the gloom. He swung round suddenly as if he knew he was being spied on. Sam shut his eyes just in time. He waited a few seconds until he could hear Dick searching in his bag again. He opened his eyes a sliver to see Dick pull out a long tube wrapped in oilskin. Dick looked furtively about, then made to stash the scroll in his shirt.

But there was a sudden noise above, as if someone was about to come down to the gun deck. Dick hurriedly thrust the roll under his pillow and was gone.

When Sam was sure it was safe to move he crept over to Dick's hammock, his heart thumping hard. He had to know what was so important about that tube. It must be precious to Dick or he wouldn't have been checking it so secretly and hiding it from the crew. Sam plunged his hand under the pillow and retrieved it. His fingers trembled with excitement as he undid the oilskin wrapping to reveal a parchment. He smoothed it out, but he was deep in the shadows and couldn't read any of the words. He crept silently along the deck, hoping none of the crew would choose that moment to come to bed. He stopped under the swinging lantern and read the beautifully written words in front of him.

The bearer of this letter is on secret official business and is to be given safe passage on the island of Barbados.

Bevil Granville, Governor

There was a red wax seal on the bottom, next to the signature.

Sam stared at the letter, his brain working furiously. Dick Gudgeon was on official business for the governor! And Sam knew that every governor of every Caribbean island was an enemy of the pirates.

What was Dick up to? The crew always

said that the authorities were no better than pirates themselves. So why had Dick come to the captain with the information about the gold? A worm of an idea wriggled in his brain. Could it be that the governor of Barbados was paying Dick to steal the gold from the *Queen Bess*? And that Dick had decided to use the *Sea Wolf* crew to do it for him? Then, when they thought they were safely away, the *Sea Wolf* would be captured and the gold would be taken by Dick and Governor Granville.

The pirates would be thrown into prison and Dick could then go to their hideout on Skeleton Island and pinch the booty stored there, too. That would also explain why he wanted to know where the stronghold could be found. But the villain wasn't going to get away with it. Sam looked at the parchment again. Here was the evidence to prove to the captain and crew that Dick was not to be trusted.

He spun round, ready to make for the steps up to the deck — and stopped dead. Dick Gudgeon was standing in his path. He wore a nasty smirk of delight on his face, and he held a knife out in front of him.

"You're not going anywhere," he snarled.

CHAPTER SEVEN

"That's my letter and for my eyes only," hissed Dick Gudgeon. "You're a little thief. And thieves deserve to die!" He lunged at Sam, the point of his dagger aiming straight at his heart.

Sam threw himself to the floor. He scuttled like a crab towards the cutlass store, but Dick had already barred the way.

Sam got to his feet to face him, the parchment gripped tightly in his hand. He mustn't let Gudgeon have it back. The angry man swished his dagger in front of Sam, weaving it skilfully like a cobra about to strike.

"You can't stab me and get away with it," said Sam desperately. He darted behind the nearest hammock. "The captain and the crew would find you standing over my body."

"What body?" said Dick nastily. "There won't be one. I'll dispose of it through a porthole. No one will wonder where you've gone. You're always popping off to see your mother." He lunged again, slashing the canvas bed between them. "And they won't miss you either. They all think you're stupid so they'll be glad to see the back of you."

Sam remembered how the captain and Harry Hopp had looked at him in the storeroom. Dick was probably right. But he wasn't going anywhere while his crew were in danger. He glanced around, but he couldn't see anything to defend himself with, just the mop and bucket for swabbing the deck.

He grabbed the mop and thrust the wet end into Dick's face, earning himself valuable seconds while his attacker tried to untangle himself.

But Sam knew he couldn't hold out for long. He had to get help. He snatched up the bucket and banged it hard against the hull. It gave out a tremendous clang and he yelled at the top of his voice at the same time. Dick launched himself at Sam with a furious roar.

Sam jumped aside and found himself staggering back against a pile of cannonballs. Before Dick could get to him he'd pushed the pile over, sending them thudding loudly on to the deck.

"You crafty little devil!" growled Dick. He caught Sam by the shirt. Sam tried to move but it was no good. Dick's knife was raised to strike.

At that moment there was a clattering of footsteps from the hold below. Dick let out an oath and relaxed his grip. "I'll deal with you later," he spat viciously, "when there's no one around."

Sam sprang to his feet. Even though Gudgeon was now pretending to look innocent, the crew would soon realise the truth when they saw the letter! "He was going to kill me!" he shouted as Fernando ran up to him with Ned and Ben close behind, carrying lanterns.

"What are you rambling about now, Sam Silver?" said Ben. His eyes fell on the cannonballs scattered over the floor. "We thought we heard thunder and it turns out to be you playing bowls with the ammunition!"

"Well, I'll go to Jamaica in a gin jug," declared Ned. "I think he's lost his wits. We must tell the captain."

"Aye," said Dick sorrowfully. "It's the only thing to do."

"You don't understand!" yelled Sam. "Dick's working for the governor of Barbados. I found this letter giving him safe passage."

"I'll have that!" came Captain Blade's stern voice. The captain strode along the length of the gun deck and took the paper with a flourish. As he read it a furious expression came over his face.

"I saw him take it out of his bag," insisted Sam, "and hide it under his pillow."

"Explain yourself, Dick Gudgeon," said the captain fiercely.

Good, thought Sam. *There's no way he can wriggle out of this now!*

"The boy *says* it was in my bag, but you'll notice he's the one holding it," said

Dick, with a wide-eyed expression. "I've never seen it before."

"Liar!" cried Sam. "You only want the *Sea Wolf* to steal the gold from the *Queen Bess* so that you and the governor can share it between you!"

But Dick was staring earnestly at the captain. "I came down to sleep and saw the boy with the paper. I just asked him, friendly-like, if it was a letter from his mother and he turned on me."

"That's not true," gasped Sam. "He attacked *me* with a knife."

Dick held up his hands. They were empty. Sam realised with a sinking heart that somehow he'd got rid of his dagger. "If my name is on that letter," Dick told the captain, "then throw me overboard now."

"There's no name written here," said Blade.

"But it really is his letter," pleaded Sam desperately. The pirates were looking at him as if he was something they'd emptied out of the bilge pump. "It was in his bag," Sam repeated, but the words sounded weak.

"I had the notion that this lad was a bit simple when he put down your stronghold on a map," said Dick, "but now I realise I was wrong. He's not simple at all. He's a nasty piece of work. He did that map to show the governor. And this letter of safe passage on Barbados proves it. He's a spy for Sir Bevil Granville." He looked at the grim faces round him. "And if I were you I'd check you've still got your weapons." He delved under the blanket in Sam's hammock and produced his own knife. "I saw him steal this from my bag."

"But I . . ." protested Sam.

"The foolish boy didn't know I was watching," Dick went on. "He'd have had us all without arms by the time we reached Bridgetown."

"Easy pickings for the governor's men!"

said Fernando. Sam could hear the shock in his voice. Fernando was looking at him as if he couldn't believe the things he was hearing. "What a false friend!" he murmured sadly.

"And happy enough to steal from a fellow crewmate," muttered Ben angrily.

Captain Blade's piercing blue eyes fixed Sam with a look that felt like a stab in the heart. "We'll deal with you later," he snapped. "We'll not delay our treasure plan. Lock Silver up, Ned, where he can't do any more harm."

"No!" Sam's cry echoed around the gun deck. "Please, Captain, you've got to believe me."

But Captain Blade merely folded the letter and shoved it in his pocket. "Everyone to your posts!" he barked as he spun on his heel and headed back up on deck, followed by Ben.

Ned's huge hand grabbed Sam's arm and held him fast. He pushed him towards the stairway.

Fernando looked away as Sam went past.

"I didn't do anything wrong," Sam told his friend desperately. "You believe me, don't you?"

"I wish I could," muttered Fernando. "But everything is telling me that you're a traitor to the crew."

Sam let Ned haul him up the stairs. He had never felt so awful in his life. He twisted back to try and plead with Fernando one last time, but Dick Gudgeon was standing in the way. He shot Sam a look of triumph.

Sam shivered. The man was evil, and he meant the *Sea Wolf* pirates harm. He was sure of it.

CHAPTER EIGHT

Sam shifted about, trying to get comfortable. He was locked in a wooden cage on the foredeck and his bottom had gone numb. The cage had been used for goats and it stank of dung and sour milk. The crew were going about their business, throwing him dirty looks.

Gazing round the lantern-lit deck,

Sam could see Charlie heading for the galley. He called to her in a low voice.

She looked up at him, tossed her head and moved on out of sight. Sam gulped. Was she pretending to hate him or did she believe Dick Gudgeon's story now? If she'd turned against him too then he didn't have a single friend on the *Sea Wolf*. Well, even if he had to act alone, one thing was certain – he was descended from a brave pirate and he wasn't going to give up!

"Bridgetown's just a mile up the coast from here," said a voice. It was Dick. He was walking with the captain across the main deck. They stopped under one of the lanterns.

"The *Sea Wolf* is too recognisable," answered Captain Blade. "We can't just sail into the harbour. We'll be shot out of the water."

"You're right, Captain," said Dick. Sam squirmed as he heard the falseness in the man's tone. "And my information is at least two weeks old. I can't be sure exactly where the *Queen Bess* will be anchored."

Sam peeped through his fingers and saw the captain pulling at the braids in his beard as he considered the matter. "We'll check that before we make our final plan," he said. "She doesn't sail for another day, I believe."

"Then I volunteer to go ashore," said Dick. "While it's still dark, I'll make my way along the coast on foot and see what I can spy in the harbour. There'll be plenty of soldiers about but, with luck,

I might manage to avoid them. Though, of course, it would be easier with two men . . ."

Blade stroked his beard as Dick went on.

"If I get through and report back we can decide how to lighten the *Queen Bess* of her load. If I don't return by the end of the day you'll know it was too risky, but you'll have time to make your escape from these waters. And only one man will have been lost."

Sam watched as the captain grasped Dick's shoulder. He wanted to call out for him not to trust the man, but he had to bite his tongue.

"I agree it's a job for two men," said Blade. "It's too dangerous for you to go alone. I will go with you."

"No, your life is more important to your men and your ship than mine," protested Dick, although Sam thought he saw a small smile playing round his lips in the lantern light. "Of course I would feel invincible with you by my side, but . . ."

Blade held up his hands. "I will hear no argument. It will be safer for two than one."

"Thank you, sir," said Dick humbly. "I'll be glad to have my captain as my companion. I can think of no one better."

"We'll take Fernando with us," said the captain. "He can slip aboard the *Queen Bess* like a cat and not be seen."

"No need," replied Dick quickly. "I can do that. We don't want to put the lad in danger."

Captain Blade nodded and looked up at the dark sky. "We'll leave within the half hour," he said. "That should give us enough of the night for cover. I'm going to give Harry Hopp his instructions before I go."

Sam watched as he strode away to

his cabin, calling to his first mate as he
went. Sam felt more helpless than ever.
The captain had complete trust in Dick
Gudgeon and was going ashore with him.
And Sam was certain that that was what
Dick had wanted all along, even though
he'd *said* he was happy to go alone. What
was the man up to?

Dick cast a furtive look around, then
took the lantern from its hook. He crept
to the rail and lifted it so it was shining

towards the shore. He raised his hand in front of the flame, held it there for a moment and then moved it away. Sam saw him make exactly the same action three more times.

He's giving a signal! he thought with alarm. He stared intently at the coastline, black against the starlit sky.

At that moment there was an answering light from somewhere along the dark shore further down the coast.

Sam was horrified. Dick must have an accomplice. There might even be more than one! And they were sure to be the governor's men. But that didn't make sense. Why would they show up now? If Sam was right and Dick wanted the *Sea Wolf* crew to steal the treasure, then surely the governor's troops wouldn't make an appearance until the booty was on board!

And then the truth hit Sam. Dick had

cleverly made sure that it was the captain who went ashore with him and no one else. It wasn't treasure that the governor and Dick were after – it was Captain Blade himself!

CHAPTER NINE

The door to the captain's cabin opened. Quick as a flash, Dick returned the lantern to its hook.

Blade and Harry Hopp joined him at the rail.

"Captain!" called Sam. "You mustn't go. It's a trap!"

The captain looked at him, his face hard as rock in the lanternlight. "I'll deal with you on my return," he said in a low, chilling voice. "If you take my advice, you'll keep your mouth closed until then. I doubt any of the crew will want to hear from you."

"But I'm telling the truth," pleaded Sam. "Mr Hopp, listen to me. The captain's in great danger."

"Aye, that's what you would want, I'll warrant!" snapped the first mate. "You scurvy snake. The captain's right. Keep your mouth shut or he'll return to find an empty cage and a shark with a full belly!"

Some of the crew came to see the shore party off. Sam spotted Fernando and Charlie among his shipmates at the rail, but they didn't even glance at him.

Splat! Something hit the side of the cage, spraying Sam with a stinking mess of rotten tomato. At last the crew went away, muttering curses under their breath. Sam saw a movement at the corner of his cage and heard a strange rumbling noise. It sounded like his electric toothbrush when its battery was running low. To his astonishment he realised it was Sinbad rubbing against the bars – and the surly ship's cat was purring! Sam stuck his hand through the cage to stroke him, too miserable to wonder if he'd lose a finger or two. "At least you're on my side," he told him as he scratched him under the chin.

"Don't go near that traitor!" came a shrill voice. Charlie stormed up to the cage, dropping the sack she was carrying.

"Charlie, please listen," pleaded Sam. "I know the captain's in danger."

She stooped to pick up the cat. "Sinbad's not the only one on your side," she whispered. "I believe that letter wasn't yours, but I can't be seen to be friendly."

Two of the crew came up onto the foredeck to secure some ropes. Charlie immediately rubbed her face against Sinbad's. "You are a very naughty puss to go near Sam Silver!" she told him sternly.

The men laughed, finished their task and went back down to the main deck.

"Quick, Sam," hissed Charlie. "Tell me what you know."

Sam told her about Dick's signalling. "I'm sure the captain's heading for a trap," he finished.

"Then we'll have to go after him!" declared Charlie. "He needs to be warned. We'll take the other rowing boat."

"Good thinking," said Sam. "He might believe *you*. But there's one little problem. How are you going to tow me along in my cage?"

Charlie pinned Sinbad under one

arm and delved into her pocket, pulling
out a small object that glinted in the
lantern light. "You won't need towing. I
'borrowed' this key from Harry's belt."

"Brilliant!" breathed Sam. He sniffed the
air. "But what's that awful smell? It's worse
than my prison."

"Just a fish head I've got in my pocket,"
said Charlie, airily. "I'll give it to Sinbad to
keep him busy while we go ashore. I don't
want him following us." She produced the
fish head and threw it to the deck. The cat
sprang out of her arms and onto it with a
delighted miaow.

Charlie turned the key in the padlock. It opened with a loud click. She paused, eyes darting over the deck in case someone had heard. Then she swung open the little door and Sam crawled out, stretching painfully and shaking tomato pips out of his hair. Charlie delved into the sack she'd dropped and produced a coconut. She arranged the sack in a pile on the floor of the cage and plonked the coconut next to it. "That looks enough like you to fool the crew for a little while," she whispered. "If anyone goes by they'll think you're asleep."

They crept to the steps that led down to the main deck. Harry Hopp and Ned were patrolling up and down, talking in low voices.

"Now!" hissed Charlie as the two men turned towards the stern. Sam and Charlie made a dash for the side rail. They slid silently over it and were halfway down the footholds to the rowing boat below when

Sam's foot suddenly slipped with a loud *bang!*

"What was that?" came a voice from the deck.

They flattened themselves to the side of the ship. Sam's heart was beating wildly. Were they about to get caught?

Chapter Ten

Sam and Charlie clung to the ship, not daring to move a muscle.

"Sounded like it came from below," they heard Ned call.

"But something's moving on the foredeck!" said Harry Hopp.

Footsteps crossed above their heads.

"It's only Sinbad up here," came Ned's voice. "He's chasing a fish head.

I don't dare tell him it's already dead!"

A spyglass opened with a snap. "The captain and Dick have almost reached land now," reported Harry. "I can just see the boat."

"As soon as we get word from the captain, we'll be aboard the *Queen Bess*." Ned chuckled. "I do hope Her Royal Majesty doesn't mind us dipping our fingers into her gold."

"She won't have a choice," laughed Harry. "And there'll be one less to share the booty with." Sam winced as he heard the sound of his cage being kicked. Would they discover that he wasn't inside? He held his breath. No, it was all right, the sack and coconut must be doing their job!

Harry was still talking. "Silver should get all the sleep he can before Captain Blade gets back and throws him off the ship!"

The voices moved away.

Sam and Charlie lowered themselves into the rowing boat. Sam untied the rope from the mooring ring on the hull and pushed off. Charlie kept her eyes firmly on the beach as he rowed swiftly for shore.

"The captain and Dick are still there," Charlie told Sam. "They've got a lantern. I think they're making sure their boat is well hidden."

"We'd better land a bit further along," said Sam, reversing the stroke of his left oar to change their course. "Then we'll stay out of sight until I can distract Dick and you can speak to the captain."

"Agreed," said Charlie. "And we'd better do it before Dick's accomplices get here."

As soon as the water was shallow enough, they leapt out and pulled the boat up the sand.

"We'll use those trees for cover," said
Sam, pointing to a dense grove of palms
growing along the shore.

They hid among the tall trunks of the
palm trees. The silence was broken now
and again by the night calls of animals
deep in the undergrowth.

"Get down!" whispered Charlie
suddenly. "I saw a light."

She and Sam dived into a thicket as a
bobbing lantern came into view.

They heard a deep voice. "Are you
certain this is the route? There was a much
clearer path back there."

"It's Captain Blade!" hissed Charlie.

"And I can see Dick behind him."

The two men came into view. They were a good ship's length away, walking across a clearing in the trees. Dick was carrying a lantern that cast a faint beam onto the tree trunks around. Sam and Charlie shrank back.

"But this way's quicker," Dick answered. "It goes directly to Bridgetown port."

At that moment Sam saw him spread out his free hand.

"What's he doing?" he whispered in Charlie's ear. "Do you think that's another signal?"

"No," replied Charlie, puzzled. "It looks like he's scattering something – but what?"

There was a loud squawking from among the palm leaves and parrots suddenly swooped out of the trees, flying round Dick and the captain in a swirling flock.

"It must be seed!" breathed Sam.

The captain was frozen to the spot as the flapping birds surrounded him. More and more parrots had appeared from the dark, filling the air in a whirlwind of feathers, then swooping down to fight for their share of the feast.

Dick Gudgeon gave a harsh laugh. From behind his back, he slipped his wooden fid out of his belt and raised it.

Sam went to shout a warning but he was too late. Dick brought it down on the back of the captain's head. Blade fell to his knees, swaying groggily.

Sam started forwards but Charlie grabbed his arm.

"We must help him," Sam said angrily, trying to shake her off.

"I agree," said Charlie in his ear. "But not yet. We must get close enough to take Dick by surprise."

Sam knew she was right. They crept

towards the clearing, using the bushes as cover.

"What a piece of luck." Dick was goading Blade as the captain tried to stand up. He lifted his foot and pushed him over. "When I found out you were scared of parrots, it gave me an idea of how to capture you."

"I should have listened to Sam Silver," muttered the captain. Dick kicked him hard in the ribs and Blade fell to the ground. "You're a slimy sea worm," he groaned.

"There's no treasure and no *Queen Bess* either," Dick went on. "There's just a nice big price on your head and I'm going to collect the reward."

Sam and Charlie were close now. Dick hadn't heard them coming. He was too busy gloating. Charlie looked at Sam and motioned with a nod for them to charge. Sam nodded back, then stopped in horror.

Dick Gudgeon had drawn a pistol. He was aiming it at Captain Blade's forehead, his finger on the trigger.

CHAPTER ELEVEN

Sam looked around desperately for a weapon of some kind. He had to stop Dick Gudgeon from shooting Captain Blade.

Just as Sam had decided he would have to rush Dick and knock the pistol away, Dick let out a cruel laugh and swung the barrel of his pistol upwards. He squeezed the trigger, firing a single bullet into the air.

"Just giving my signal," he said. "Now the soldiers will know exactly where to find us. That's why I took us on this path. It's not really quicker. I had to give them time to get here from Bridgetown." He pulled out a length of rope and tied the captain's arms behind his back. "And I'll get a bigger reward if I hand you over alive."

"You're nothing but a lily-livered coward!" gasped Blade. "To think that I trusted you."

Sam tried to get his brain to work. If soldiers were coming he and Charlie needed to rescue the captain now. He felt about the ground and found a stick.

"We must wait," Charlie whispered. "We can't risk Dick shooting the captain."

"I seem to have the sort of face that men trust," Dick told Blade pleasantly, as if they were having a friendly conversation. "You're the third pirate captain I've delivered to Governor Granville. And a very nice pile of gold I've made for myself. Of course, the reward for the great Captain Blade will be double the rest put together."

"By Jupiter, you'll regret this," snarled the captain, struggling against his ropes.

Dick aimed his pistol and shot twice, sending up two spurts of dust near the captain's feet. Blade stopped struggling.

"I'll hand you over dead if I have to," said Dick in his oily voice. "Now, where was I? Oh, yes, then I've got your stronghold to plunder. I remember enough of the map that boy was kind enough to draw for me. He was very useful. First the parrot information and then that."

Sam's blood boiled. He leapt to his feet. But Charlie threw herself at him and pulled him down again. Sam realised she was right. If he made a move, Dick would shoot the captain before they could get anywhere near.

Gudgeon didn't seem to have heard anything. "I won't be telling the governor about that. It's all for me. I'll buy myself a big house on Jamaica and live a life of luxury."

"You'll be for ever looking over your shoulder," snarled the captain, struggling against his bonds. "My men will hunt you down."

"Hunt down the brave Dick Gudgeon who nearly died trying to save you?" laughed the villain. "Surely not. They'll be so grateful, they'll make me captain."

He turned his head at the sound of feet pounding towards them. A second later, a group of armed soldiers burst into the clearing. Quick as a flash, Dick pulled the letter of safe passage from the captain's coat and showed it to their leader.

"I think you'll find this is in order," he said. "And here is your prisoner."

He pointed at his captive and, before Sam and Charlie's horrified eyes, Captain Blade was seized. His bonds were cut, his hands forced out in front of him and iron manacles slapped around his wrists.

The soldiers dragged him away. Dick Gudgeon sauntered along behind, swinging his arms and whistling *Greensleeves*.

The soldiers were taking a rough dirt track that led along the shoreline. Sam and Charlie followed, darting from tree to tree, keeping a safe distance.

"It'll be sunrise soon," Charlie told Sam, pulling him over to the side of the path. "We must be careful we're not seen."

"I wonder what's happening on the *Sea Wolf*," said Sam. "They must have noticed that I'm missing. They'll think I've gone to betray the captain." He gulped, remembering how awful it was to have the crew hating him.

"The captain will put them right," said Charlie, squeezing his arm, "when we've rescued him and got him back to the ship."

They walked on as the sun began to appear over the low hills to their left. Here and there, a house lay off the track, and soon there were more, lying closer together.

"We must be coming to Bridgetown," whispered Sam.

The dirt track joined a cobbled street. It was early, but people were already up and about carrying milk churns and baskets of bread. Stalls were being set up for a market. The soldiers pushed their way through the townsfolk, who gawped when they saw the captured pirate and hurled insults at him. Sam could see that, despite his manacled hands and the blow to his head, Blade was walking tall, ignoring the jibes and catcalls of the Bridgetown people.

As they followed the soldiers round a corner they found themselves in a central square. On the other side was a tall, stark building with grey stone walls.

"That's the fort," said Charlie. "That's where they'll take Captain Blade. We can't follow him in there."

Two big gates swung open to let in the soldiers and their prisoner. Dick Gudgeon followed. Sam got a glimpse of crowds of uniformed men inside before the gates were pulled shut.

There was a sudden noise of sliding bolts and a door, barely big enough for a man to pass through, opened in one of the huge gates. Two soldiers emerged.

"That Blade's not so scary when you see him in irons," one was saying.

"And we'll be giving *him* something to be scared of later this morning!" laughed the other. He hammered a large notice

to the gate. Then he spotted Sam and
Charlie. "Have a look at this," he told
them. "Not long to wait for a bit of
entertainment!"

As soon as the two men had disappeared
back inside the fort, Charlie slipped
forwards and read the notice. She turned
to Sam, her eyes huge and dark in her pale
face.

"What does it say?" he asked.

"It says that Captain Thomas Blade . . ."
Charlie gulped. ". . . it says that he'll hang
at nine o'clock!"

Chapter Twelve

"There's no time to get help from the crew," declared Sam. He took Charlie by the shoulders. "It's up to us. Somehow we've got to get into that fort and rescue him."

Charlie's forehead creased in concentration. "I've got a better idea. The notice says it's going to be a public hanging in the main square here. We'll free him when he's brought out."

"In full view of all the people and soldiers?" gasped Sam. "Not to mention the governor! How will we manage that?"

Charlie gave him a sudden grin. "Trust me!" she said. "Wait here!" The next second she'd vanished into the crowd.

Sam was bewildered. Where was his friend going? As he stood gazing at the heavy arched gates of the fort, he heard a familiar voice behind him.

"Found you at last!"

"Fernando!" exclaimed Sam. He spun round in delight. "Am I glad to see—" He stopped dead. Fernando's teeth were bared in an angry snarl and the blade of his knife flashed in front of Sam's eyes.

"Don't move a muscle!" Fernando pushed him up against the wall and thrust the knife against Sam's throat. "Where are the captain and Dick Gudgeon? You have

betrayed them to the governor, haven't you? And I expect Charlie is having a nice cosy chat to Granville right now. Admit it, before I kill you!"

Sam gulped. "You don't understand, Fernando. Charlie and I—"

"I understand perfectly!" snapped Fernando. "As soon as I found that the two of you had gone, I knew where you'd be. As you'd used the other boat I swam to shore to come after you. You're a dirty traitor, and so is Charlie!"

"It wasn't like that," said Sam desperately. "*We're* not the traitors. Dick Gudgeon is." He held his friend's gaze.

"You must believe me. Haven't I always been your friend – and loyal to the *Sea Wolf*?" He quickly told Fernando how they had watched Blade fall into Gudgeon's trap and how the captain was going to be hanged.

For a moment Fernando looked unsure. "I want to believe you, but how can I? The captain is going to be hanged because of you," he said desperately. "You're coming with me. I'm going to tie you up and then rescue him."

The gate to the fort opened again and someone slipped out, whistling. Sam recognised the tune. It was *Greensleeves*. The man strolled away between the stalls, inspecting the food for sale.

"See?" Sam spoke hoarsely. "It's Dick Gudgeon. He's free."

As he spoke, Fernando's eyes grew wide with amazement and then fury. The dagger dropped from Sam's throat.

"Captain Blade's execution is set for nine this morning," said Sam urgently. "Will you help us?"

"You have no need to ask!" declared Fernando, shoving his knife back into his belt. "I should never have doubted you, my friend."

"That's all right," said Sam. "I'm just glad that you believe me now. And listen, I believed Dick was a good 'un when I first met him, too."

"Well, I hope you will forgive me," said Fernando. "Though I'm not sure I can forgive myself."

"Of course I do," said Sam. "We're friends for ever."

Fernando held up his hand. "Let's high five to seal the deal!"

He gave Sam a ringing slap on his palm. Sam sometimes regretted that he'd taught him how to do this – Fernando didn't always know his own strength.

"Now, what's the plan?" Fernando went on.

"I wish I knew," Sam said, rubbing his hand. "Charlie told me to wait here. I'm hoping she's thought of something."

At that moment a small figure pushed through the crowd, carrying a bundle of clothes with a lady's feathered hat wobbling on top. To the boys' surprise it stopped in front of them. Charlie's face popped up between the feathers. She beamed as she saw Fernando.

"I'm so glad you found us!" she exclaimed. "I knew you'd be on our side!"

Fernando gave Sam an embarrassed glance. Sam grinned back. "What's all this for, Charlie?" he asked. "Are we putting on a play?"

"Don't be silly!" exclaimed Charlie, dropping the clothes on the ground. "I borrowed these from a big house down the road. The window was open and no one saw me pop in. I just grabbed what I could."

The boys looked at her, impressed.

"They're going to help us carry out my brilliant plan. We are going to be an elegant young girl attending the hanging with her two servants. An elegant but bad-tempered girl who will have an enormous tantrum just as the captain is brought out. Then, while everyone's looking at *her*, the two servants will whisk Captain Blade away to the *Sea Wolf*! Simple!" She picked out a long silky dress and held it against herself.

"But the soldiers aren't going to let us snatch the captain from under their noses," protested Sam.

"It might work!" said Fernando eagerly. "But we'll need something more to keep the soldiers busy. Sam and I will think of something."

"There's only one problem," Charlie interrupted, looking down at the fine red material. "This dress is too long for me. Fernando, you're tall. You'll have to be the elegant young girl."

Fernando gawped at her.

"Don't stand there looking like a dead fish!" laughed Charlie. She thrust the dress into her friend's arms. "We have to get changed!"

Fernando held the garment at arm's length and stared in disgust at the frills and lace. "I can't wear this!" he spluttered.

"Someone's got to," said Sam, trying to keep his face straight.

"You do it!" Fernando burst out.

"I'm sure Sam would love to help," said Charlie. Sam looked horrified. "But he's too short. You want to help save the captain, don't you, Fernando?"

"Of course I do! But—"

"That's settled then." Charlie passed Sam a blue jacket with brass buttons and a pair of white breeches. "Cheer up, Fernando. We'll be your servants. It'll give you a chance to boss us about. Follow me."

Fernando slunk along behind Charlie, muttering under his breath, as she led them to a quiet alley close to the town square. They hurriedly put on their disguises over their own clothes.

"It's lucky there's enough for three here," said Charlie, pulling on a long braided jerkin. She took her pirate bandana out of her hair and shoved it in her pocket. "Need any help, Fernando?"

Fernando had toppled over, his nose poking out of one of the gown's sleeves and his legs tied up in the folds of the stiff petticoats. Giggling helplessly, Sam and Charlie managed to untangle him and at last he was ready, the hat pulled low, with a feather dangling over his scowling face. Charlie tried to smooth and untangle his long black curls.

"No one will believe that I am a girl," growled Fernando. "Let alone a highborn one."

"They certainly won't if you look like that!" said Charlie. "Stand up straight and try to walk elegantly – and keep your bare feet out of sight. Remember, the captain is depending on you."

Fernando picked up the folds of his skirts and swept off towards the town square. He stopped and swirled round. "Stop dawdling, you good-for-nothing servants!" he called in a high-pitched voice.

"I'll have you whipped if you don't attend me properly."

Grinning, Sam and Charlie scampered after him.

"And I shall require food when I am seated," he went on. "And a drink!"

They came out into the open and stood staring at the scene in front of them. The town square was full of people. Two sides of the square looked out to sea, bounded by low walls with cannon placed at intervals along them. Stalls had been set up to sell beer, fruit and pastries and smoke rose from an ox roasting over an open fire. Chairs stood in rows, all facing a high platform with steps leading up to it. Well-dressed ladies and gentlemen sat eating and chatting cheerfully to each other. The people of Bridgetown were buzzing with the news that a famous pirate captain was soon to be hanged.

In the very centre of the platform stood a wooden framework, with a rope noose swinging in the breeze. It was the gallows. Sam shivered. It was ready for Captain Blade.

CHAPTER THIRTEEN

"Come on," muttered Fernando. He began to stride across the square and nearly tripped on his dress. With little mincing steps he approached the two sentries who stood by the gallows. Sam and Charlie hurried after him.

"You there!" Fernando called in his high girly voice. "I am Doña Francesca

Catolina Maria Montoya, daughter of the Spanish Ambassador, and I demand the best seat to watch this pirate hang."

The guards looked at each other, not bothering to keep the smiles from their faces.

Fernando stamped his foot. "I do not like to be kept waiting!" he screeched. "My father will be very angry if he hears that you have not shown me proper respect. He will tell the governor. And the governor does not like his wealthy friends to be upset."

The men looked nervous now and they glanced over at the seats where the well-dressed people were. Sam followed their gaze. He didn't need to be told which of the fine gentlemen was Sir Bevil Granville. A man sat in the middle seat, one hand on the ivory handle of a carved cane. He wore a fine coat and

waistcoat with gold buttonholes all the way down the front and a massive, curly brown wig on his head. In the seat next to the governor sat Dick Gudgeon, wearing a new hat and smart clothes. He had a smug look on his face as he waited to see Captain Blade hang. Sam quickly turned his head away.

"My father is very important!" snapped Fernando, his voice getting even shriller.

Some of the gentry started to look round.

"Find her a seat before she gets us into trouble," muttered one of the guards.

They bustled Fernando to the end of the line of chairs. Sam watched Dick out of the corner of his eye, but he was busy fawning over the governor.

Fernando made a great fuss of sorting out his petticoats as he sat down. Then he turned to Sam and Charlie. "Be off with you!" he said imperiously. "Go and sit with the common people!"

Sam and Charlie scampered away.

"It must be nearly nine," said Charlie. "We've got to hurry."

They mingled with the townsfolk round the stalls. The smell of the roasting ox reached his nostrils and Sam's stomach rumbled.

Charlie pointed to a horse and cart, tethered by the fort gate. "That's to take the body away," she gulped.

"No one's guarding it," said Sam. "I think we've found our getaway vehicle."

"What do you mean?" demanded Charlie. "What funny future thing is a 'getaway vehicle'?"

"We'll use it to 'get away' from here," Sam explained, "to make our escape. You know how to drive a cart, don't you?"

Charlie nodded. "Now, Fernando said we'd need to make a diversion after he's had his tantrum. Something that will send the soldiers running away from the captain."

Sam checked out the area. A pile of cannonballs and a keg of powder stood close to one of the cannon, guarded by two men. "You distract those two guards over there," he told Charlie, "and I'll grab some of the gunpowder. A bit of that thrown on the fire should make everyone sit up and take notice!"

Charlie ran towards the guards, holding her hands up to her face. "Help me," she wailed. "A thief just stole my penny and my mistress will beat me when I don't return with her ribbons, and I can't buy the ribbons because the thief stole my penny and my mistress will beat me." She broke into sobs, pulling at the men's jackets.

Sam took his chance. He slipped over to the keg behind them. The lid was loosely on. Keeping an eye on the men, he pushed it aside and scooped out a handful of powder. Then he slunk away.

Charlie felt in the pocket of her borrowed jerkin. "Oh!" she gasped. "Silly me. Here's my penny!" And she ran to join him, leaving the guards scratching their heads.

The church clock began to toll nine and a slow drumbeat could be heard from inside the fort. The large gates opened and a squad of soldiers marched out. The crowd gave a great cheer as they saw Captain Blade in the middle, chained and manacled. He turned and gave them all a defiant bow. The guards led him up the steps to the gallows.

Sir Bevil Granville stood and held out a scroll.

"As Her Majesty Queen Anne's representative in this fair island, I declare that this is Thomas Blade, known pirate, and he shall hang by the neck until he is dead."

The crowd cheered again, led by Dick Gudgeon. A man wearing a black mask

stepped up on to the platform and pushed the captain towards the noose. A priest came forwards and the crowd quietened as he began to murmur prayers.

"This is not to be borne!" A tremendous shriek filled the air and Fernando jumped to his feet. "I cannot see anything from here!"

The people nearest to him put their fingers to their lips but Fernando screamed again. Some of the sentries came over to him, trying to make him sit down. Fernando kicked out at his chair, sending it flying with a crash. "You expect me to sit on that as if I were a common kitchen maid. My father is Don Cristiano Montoya and he will have you all flogged!"

Fernando pushed the woman who'd been sitting next to him. She fell against her neighbour and the whole row toppled like dominos.

Sam could see that Blade had a smile on his lips. His heart leapt. The captain had recognised Fernando. He knew there was a rescue plot afoot. Now it was time for him and Charlie to carry out their part. There were still some guards around the captain and they had to draw them away.

With one hand, Sam whipped the kerchief from his neck and spread the cloth out. He tipped the gunpowder into the middle and swiftly tied the corners together.

While the crowd gawped at Fernando's tantrum, Sam lobbed the package at the roasting ox. It hit it on the nose and vanished into the flames. A second passed and then . . . *BOOM!*

Chapter Fourteen

Clouds of black smoke filled the square and lumps of sizzling beef rained down on the terrified spectators.

"Blackheart's attacking!" Sam shouted at the top of his voice.

"You get the captain, I'll get the cart!" Charlie yelled in his ear. A second later she'd disappeared into the crowd.

Women screamed, soldiers ran to

man the cannon, and dogs and urchins
fought for the pieces of falling meat.
Eyes stinging from the smoke, Sam wove
through the panicking townspeople
towards the gallows. Only one guard stood
next to the captain, fist firmly clamped
round his chains. There was no sign of
Fernando anywhere. Sam hoped he was all
right but he had no time to look for him
now. He had to focus on the captain.

He crept up the steps behind the soldier
and poked him hard in the back. The
soldier swung round and Sam put his
thumbs in his ears, waggled his fingers and
stuck his tongue out at him.

"Oi, you little varmint!" growled the guard, dropping his hold on Blade's chains. He advanced on Sam, his hand raised ready to strike him. Captain Blade immediately whacked him on the head with his heavy manacles. As the man tottered towards the edge of the platform, Sam promptly stuck out a foot and tipped him off into the crowd.

"By Satan, you're a sight for sore eyes!" exclaimed Blade. "Now it's time to run!"

"We can go a lot faster than that," said Sam. "Look!"

The crowd was parting in fresh panic as a horse and cart charged at top speed into the square.

Charlie was perched on the front, clutching the reins. "Out of the way!" she shrieked. "Runaway horse!" The cart swerved round the stalls, knocking apples, oranges and pastries all over the place and scattering the onlookers who ran in terror.

"Get ready to jump!" cried Sam.

As the horse thundered past the gallows, Sam and the captain sprang from the platform and landed with a thud in the back of the cart.

The wild-eyed horse reared up with a loud neigh at the sound and clattered off down a cobbled street. The cart jolted along behind.

Sam looked over his shoulder. A band of soldiers was running after them, shouting and firing as they made their escape. The horse galloped round a corner, sending the cart onto two wheels. For a moment Sam thought it would overturn. Then it righted itself and they were heading out of town. There was no sign of the soldiers now.

"That was brilliant, Charlie!" called Sam. "Everyone believed the horse was out of control!"

"It was!" shrieked Charlie, as they rattled along at top speed. "I can't stop it!"

Sam gripped the side of the cart. Had they saved the captain just to kill him in a road accident? Then he saw Charlie give a huge wink.

"I'm joking," she said, pulling on the reins. The horse began to slow to a canter. "I'm in charge – not Dobbin." The cart hit a rut and she was nearly thrown from the driver's seat.

"But not in charge of the road!" laughed Sam.

Then he remembered Fernando. Where was their friend? Was he safe? He tried not to worry. Fernando was wily and brave. He'd be OK.

"Sam Silver," said Captain Blade. He was looking at him intently, his manacled hands held out in front of him for balance. "I am truly sorry for believing that scoundrel and not you," he went on. "I let appearances blind me."

"Don't worry about it," said Sam, a bit embarrassed. "Dick seemed a great bloke and he was very clever. He knew how to say the right things."

"Well, I swear on the *Sea Wolf* that I will never doubt you again, no matter how strange things turn." The captain's face suddenly broke into a broad grin. "And talking of strange things, just wait until I tell Harry how you all turned up to rescue me with Fernando in a dress . . . Where is he?"

"We couldn't find him in all the rush," said Charlie anxiously.

"Then we must go back this instant!" demanded Blade.

"No, Captain, sir," Charlie replied without turning round. "I'm in control of this horse and we're not stopping until we reach our rowing boat."

"And then we're not stopping until you're safe on board," finished Sam. "You're a marked man. We'll come back for Fernando afterwards."

A loud cheer went up as the *Sea Wolf* crew caught sight of Captain Blade being rowed towards the ship. Sam moored the boat to the hull and Harry Hopp spotted the captain's chains.

"What has that villain Silver done?" he called down fiercely.

"He and Charlie have saved my life," the captain called back. "With a little help from Fernando. Sam Silver was right all along. It was Dick Gudgeon who was the villain."

He was helped on board and as Ned went off to fetch an axe to break the chains, the captain told the crew about the trap that had been set for him and how Sam, Charlie and Fernando had saved him.

Shuffling their feet and red in the face, the men of the *Sea Wolf* came one by one to apologise to Sam. He listened with half an ear. He was worrying about Fernando. Had he been hurt in the explosion? Or had Dick Gudgeon found him?

"Boat ahoy!" came a cry.

Sam rushed to the rail with the others. Had the governor sent soldiers after them? No, it was the *Sea Wolf*'s other rowing boat and the rower looked familiar. There was a heaped tarpaulin at the back of the boat.

"Sink me!" exclaimed Harry Hopp, stamping the end of his wooden leg on the deck. "That's Dick Gudgeon. I reckon he's done harm to Fernando. Where's me pistol?"

CHAPTER FIFTEEN

"Hold hard, Harry," declared the captain. "I'll not have a man shot in the back. Let him on board. Perhaps he doesn't know of my escape and is still pretending to be loyal to the *Sea Wolf*. He may have news of the young lad."

Sam watched as the tarpaulin began to wriggle and writhe. Then a grinning face popped out.

"It's Fernando!" Sam yelled in jubilation.

"And he's got Dick's own pistol trained on him," gasped Charlie. "He's taken the scoundrel prisoner!"

"No wonder Dick's rowing so well," said Ned cheerfully.

His face white with fear, Dick Gudgeon scrambled up onto the deck with Fernando close behind, still wearing the dress. At once Dick was seized in the strong grip of Ned and Harry Hopp.

"Captain Blade," he whimpered. "I'm so glad you're all right. I think there has been a misunderstanding." He suddenly set eyes on Sam. "What is that villain doing here? He will be your downfall, Captain, mark my words."

"Belay your cowardly talk or by Mars I'll run you through," thundered the captain. "He's brought about *your* downfall and I owe my life to him and his friends."

Sam and Charlie rushed over to Fernando.

"We were really worried about you," said Charlie. "What happened?"

"I got Dick to bring me here," said Fernando, airily smoothing down his petticoats. "It was the least he could do after all the trouble he's caused."

Sam saw the mischievous glint in his friend's eyes. "And how did you do that?"

"I'm glad you asked, my friend," said Fernando. "I saw him in the smoke and confusion. I believe he was trying to sneak off. So I ran up to him and put on my best girly voice . . ." Fernando carried on in a high-pitched whine. "Help me. I am Doña Francesca Catolina Maria Montoya and my father will pay you handsomely if you rescue me from the invasion."

Dick muttered angrily under his breath. "He was totally fooled by his own greed,"

Fernando told them. "But as soon as he had led me away from the square, I shoved my hat in his face and used the sash from that stupid dress to tie him up. Then I stole a mule and rode to the beach to see if I could find one of the *Sea Wolf* rowing boats. Dick had to lie over the beast's back and I'm sure he had a nice bumpy ride."

"It's no more than he deserves," growled Harry Hopp.

"But why were you under the tarpaulin?" asked the captain. "We could have turned the cannon on the boat when we saw this villain was rowing."

"We heard soldiers coming," said Fernando, "so I decided to hide and let this snivelling sea snail do all the work. He was happy to do so when I threatened him with his own gun." He untied a bag that was fastened to his belt. It was bulging with coins. "And I suggested that he might like to give us the reward money the governor gave him for capturing Captain Blade!"

"Excellent!" exclaimed Blade, slapping Fernando on the back. "The reward for my capture and death. It seems fitting that we should have it. But we mustn't tarry in these waters any longer. Let's dispose of Mr Gudgeon and be on our way. Fetch the plank, Ben!"

As the plank was fixed over the side of the ship, the captain turned to Dick. "You'll make it to shore, I've no doubt," he said, "but you may not want to linger there. The governor will believe that you're one of us. After all, how else did I escape after you'd been paid?"

Ben shoved Dick up onto the plank. The man turned and stared at them angrily. "Aye, I'll make it to shore," he spat. "And then, when you least expect it, I'll sail to your hideout and take everything you've got. You haven't enough men to keep it guarded for ever." He walked to the end of the plank and stared down at the water.

Harry Hopp stomped up on the plank to stop him, but with a triumphant laugh, Dick jumped. The crew looked accusingly at Sam.

"Don't worry," Sam said with a grin. "I'm not that stupid. I put a false location on the map. Dick will find himself heading for the Cloud of Death."

The crew cheered at the thought of Gudgeon finding himself lost in the thick bank of fog that sailors spoke of with terror.

"There's a fin following him," cried Charlie, pointing out towards the shore.

"It's probably just a dolphin," said Captain Blade. Sam could hear a tinge of disappointment in his voice.

"But hopefully it's a shark!" muttered Fernando. "One of his own kind."

"Aye to that!" declared Ned. The crew cheered again.

"Blast the blackguard!" squawked Crow, peering down at them from the top of the mast.

Captain Blade glanced up, then wiped

his forehead nervously as he strode over to take the wheel.

"Weigh anchor!" shouted Harry Hopp, and at once the deck was a bustle of activity. Sam realised that any minute now the coin would whisk him back to the future.

"I may need to check on my mum soon," he told the captain. "I don't want to leave, but I have to go to the supermarket for some milk . . ."

The captain stared at him.

"Supermarket is the name of his cow," said Charlie quickly. "Sam's got to go and milk her."

Captain Blade slapped him on the back. "Just make sure you hurry back, young Silver. This crew needs you."

"Aye, aye Captain!" said Sam, a huge smile on his face. He turned to Charlie. "Thank you for believing in me. You're a true friend."

Charlie's cheeks went pink.

Sinbad slunk out from behind a barrel and stared at him, unblinking.

Sam knelt down.

"And thank *you* for being friendly when I was locked in that cage," he said, holding out a hand to pet the cat.

Merow! Just in time, Sam snatched his hand out of the way of a vicious swipe.

He grinned happily at Charlie. "If Sinbad's back to normal then everything's back to normal!"

Sam suddenly felt his fingers and toes begin to tingle. The coin was about to take him home. He dived out of sight and into the storeroom as he felt himself sucked up into the dark, whirling tunnel that would carry him through time.

A moment later, Sam landed on his bedroom carpet. He jumped up and put the coin safely away in its bottle. Now he had to run to the supermarket for his mum. He was glad he didn't have to try and milk a cow! He had to admit that lots of things were much easier in his modern world – but not half as exciting as life on the *Sea Wolf*!

The Sea Wolf

Charlie Fleetwood
Deckhand

Ben Hudson
Quartermaster

Sam Silver
Lookout

Ned Wainwright
Bosun

Harry Hopp
First Mate

CREW MANIFEST

Sinbad

Crow

Thomas Blade
Captain

Peter Craddock
Ship's Cook

Fernando
Rigger

Don't miss the next exciting adventure in the
Sam Silver: Undercover Pirate series

DRAGON FIRE

Available in February 2013!
Read on for a special preview
of the first chapter.

CHAPTER ONE

Sam Silver opened his eyes and jumped out of bed. It was Saturday and Saturday meant a fantastic game of football down on the beach with his mates. But he could hear a spattering sound against his bedroom window. He pulled the curtains and groaned – rain was coming down in sheets! The high street was deserted and he could hardly

see the sand of Backwater Bay in the grey
mist. His heart sank to the bottom of
his pyjamas. There'd be no football this
morning.

He glanced over at the shelf on his
bedroom wall. It was covered in things he'd
found washed up by the sea. In the middle
stood the old sand-pitted bottle that was
more valuable to him than the World Cup!

Inside lay a gold doubloon, put there three hundred years ago by his pirate ancestor, Joseph Silver. The coin had the power to take him back in time to the *Sea Wolf*, a real pirate ship.

"Well, if I can't play footie," he said to the bottle, "I'll have an adventure instead — in the hot Caribbean sunshine."

Sam knew no one would miss him. No time ever passed in the present when he was back in 1706. He quickly dressed in the scruffy jeans and T-shirt that he always wore when he took up his buccaneer duties. He tipped the coin out of the bottle, spat on it and rubbed it on his sleeve.

Sam's bedroom walls began to spin. He caught a glimpse of his rain-soaked window rushing by before he was lifted into the dark tunnel of time and whooshed around. It was like being inside a monster vacuum cleaner. The next instant he found himself sitting on the floor of the storeroom of the *Sea Wolf*. But the ship was tipping violently from side to side. He was flung against a barrel then thrown onto a coil of rope. The ship's timbers creaked and groaned as if they were going to break.

"Batten down the hatches!" came a squawk and the ship's parrot, flew out from behind a chest and landed on his shoulder.

"Hello there, Crow," said Sam, delighted to see his feathery friend. "What's happening? Let's get up on deck and see."

He spotted his belt, spyglass and jerkin scattered across the floor. His friend Charlie had left them for him, as she always did when Sam was whisked home to the future. The bold girl pirate was the only one on board who knew his time-travelling secret. He was pleased to see that she'd found him a new neckerchief too – he'd blown the last one up. Sam put on his pirate gear and grabbed hold of the door handle. The tossing motion of the ship flung him against the door, but with the next roll, he forced it open and burst out. He staggered up the steps to the main deck.

There was no sign of the sparkling sea and blue Caribbean sky that he usually saw when he arrived in the past. Fierce black clouds raced overhead and waves crashed against the sides of the ship. Rain hammered the deck, drenching him instantly. Through the downpour he could see the captain struggling to keep the wheel steady.

Harry Hopp, a stocky pirate with a wooden leg, was hauling on a rope. "Someone help me get these sails round," he yelled.

With Crow clinging to his shoulder, Sam lurched across the streaming deck. He joined the first mate and seized the end of the rope.

"I'll help you, Mr Hopp," he bellowed over the wind, pulling with all his strength.

"Stap me!" cried Harry, his stubbly face breaking into a broad grin. "It's Sam Silver! How did you get here in this storm?"

Sam didn't know what to say. "Er . . . I . . . well . . ." he spluttered. Charlie usually got him out of this sort of pickle, but she was nowhere to be seen. Then it came to him. "I got here before the storm started!"

"I never saw you," shouted Harry.

"Never saw you," the parrot repeated helpfully.

"Of course not," panted Sam as he worked. "That's because, er . . . I was just coming up on deck when the storm began. Yes, that's it, and I got thrown about and bumped my head and . . ."

Two huge hands took hold of the rope behind him.

"Well, boil me up for breakfast!" It was

Ned the cheerful bosun. "The poor boy must have knocked himself out! And yet here he is, getting to work straight away."

"Aye," said Harry, lashing the rope to a strong wooden hook. "He's a true Silver, just like his grandfather, God rest his soul."

The pirates thought that Sam was Joseph Silver's grandson. Sam went along with this. He couldn't tell them just how many "greats" there really were in between.

"We're glad you're back!" called Captain Blade from the wheel. The weapons in the belts across his chest glistened with rain, and his dark hair and beard hung in rats' tails.

Sam battled through the wind to reach him.

"Keep your distance," ordered the captain, eyeing Crow who was still

on Sam's shoulder. Captain Blade was the bravest man Sam knew, but the sight of the green bird always made him go pale. Peter the cook claimed it was because a parrot had pooed on him in his pram, but every pirate on the *Sea Wolf* had a different story about the reason for the captain's one fear. However, they all agreed about one thing – when Captain Blade was around, the parrot was to be called a Caribbean crow. That way the captain could pretend he had nothing to be scared of.

Blade looked up at the sky. "By Orion, I think the storm's abating ahead," he said. "Those clouds don't look as heavy and I'd bet a bag of doubloons that the waves aren't as high."

"We'll soon be back on course," agreed Harry Hopp.

"Where were you heading?" asked Sam.

"Till this weather came along, we were

following a French treasure fleet," the captain told him.

"They'll be scattered in the storm by now," said Harry Hopp with a cunning grin. "Easier to make one of them a target."

Great! thought Sam. *A treasure hunt.*

"Set sail north-east," ordered the captain. "There's nothing can stop us now."

Someone came pounding up the steps from the gun deck below. One look at the long curly hair and bright bandana and Sam knew it was his friend Fernando.

He ran across to greet him, but Fernando was making straight for Captain Blade. He was muttering under his breath in Spanish.

"We're leaking, Captain!" he cried. "And it's bad!"

Find out how the adventures began in . . .

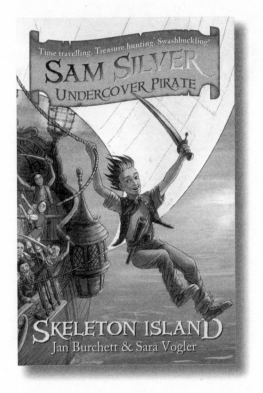

Join Sam Silver aboard the pirate ship,
Sea Wolf, for a rip-roaring adventure
on the high seas! Can Sam lead the crew
to buried treasure, or will he be forced
to walk the plank?

the
orion star

Sign up for **the orion star**
newsletter to get inside information
about your favourite children's authors
as well as exclusive competitions and
early reading copy giveaways.

www.orionbooks.co.uk/newsletters

Follow on

Orion
Children's Books

Praise for *Why Social Media is Ruining Your Life*:

'This book is a call to arms from the eye of the storm'
Emma Gannon, author of *The Multi-Hyphen Method*

'Enter Ormerod's vital manual, which will help you navigate
social media and turn it not into a weapon, but a useful tool'
Pandora Sykes

'It will come as no surprise that social media and the inclination
to compare our lives' to others is having a malign effect on
humans. But it might be slightly more alarming to discover
that it's not just bringing us down but rewiring our behavioural
patterns. Read this book and then carve out some for room
yourself and your brain' *Emerald Street*

'Katherine Ormerod investigates the worst aspects of being
constantly connected and how to offset the negative impact
on your life.' *Mail online*, Femail

'Ormerod's well-researched book is packed full of wisdom that
will not only make you feel less alone in your worries,
it offers advice and tips to help you armour up against the all-
consuming force that is social media' *Mashable*

'A statistic-packed investigation into a worldwide
phenomenon... It is no exaggeration to say this book
is essential reading for anyone' *Metro*

'Who better to help us wade through the muddy waters
of the great Insta-sham?' *Elle*

Katherine Ormerod has worked as a journalist for over a decade, starting her career as a fashion assistant at *Sunday Times Style*, moving to *Grazia* to become Senior Fashion News & Features Editor then on to *Glamour* where she was Fashion Features Editor at Large. Prior to her career, she graduated with a MA(Hons) in History from the University of Edinburgh and went on to get a Master's in Fashion History & Theory from the London College of Fashion. Katherine has written for the *FT*, the *Telegraph*, *Harper's Bazaar* and the *Mail on Sunday*.

As one of the first to recognise the changing landscape from traditional to digital media, Katherine set up her own consultancy in 2014 to accelerate fashion, beauty and lifestyle brands in editorialising their marketing messages across social platforms. A social media influencer in her own right, she has 55k followers, has been featured in a broad selection of press features and is a regular panellist with experience in TV and radio including Good Morning Britain, Sky News, LBC, ABC News Radio and Radio 5 Live.

In January 2017, she launched workworkwork.co, an anti-perfectionism platform where high-profile social media stars and women with aspirational careers share stories from their 'unedited' lives.

Why Social Media is Ruining Your Life

Katherine Ormerod

To Beth, Lauren, Ashley, Chloe and Nikki for inspiring this book

An Hachette UK Company
www.hachette.co.uk

First published in Great Britain in 2018 by Cassell,
an imprint of Octopus Publishing Group Ltd, Carmelite House,
50 Victoria Embankment, London EC4Y 0DZ
www.octopusbooks.co.uk
www.octopusbooksusa.com

This edition published in 2020

Text copyright © Katherine Ormerod 2018, 2020
Design and layout copyright © Octopus Publishing Group 2018, 2020

Distributed in the US by Hachette Book Group,
1290 Avenue of the Americas, 4th and 5th Floors, New York, NY 10104

Distributed in Canada by Canadian Manda Group,
664 Annette St, Toronto, Ontario, Canada M6S 2C8

Katherine Ormerod asserts the moral right to be identified as the
author of this work.

ISBN 978-1-78840-130-2

A CIP catalogue record for this book is available from the
British Library.

Printed and bound in the UK.

10 9 8 7 6 5 4 3 2 1

Senior Commissioning Editor: Romilly Morgan
Creative Director: Jonathan Christie
Senior Editor: Leanne Bryan
Senior Production Manager: Peter Hunt

Contents

Introduction

You shall not covet your neighbour's house. You shall not covet your neighbour's wife, or his male or female servant, his ox or donkey, or anything that belongs to your neighbour.
– EXODUS 20:17

Do you ever obsess about your body? Lament your belly size and lack of thigh – or even leg – gap? Do you sometimes lie awake at night, spinning about the state of your career? Is it perhaps a feeling that everyone else seems to go on endless holidays and live in perfect houses that you could never afford, filled with perfect décor and perfect, perfect children? Doesn't it just seem like everyone is living a life that's better than yours? Have you ever felt something like that? Because I definitely have, and the truth is that there's a major cause of this *holistic* life dissatisfaction.

Mention social media to any group of women – mums on the school run, girls in the common room or professionals at after-work drinks – and you'll hear the same thing: "I wish I could stop scrolling." Since its early infancy in the 1990s, social media has become part of the furniture, spanning all generations and all walks of life. It's estimated that *2.77 billion* of us will be using social media by the end of 2019. As with radio and TV before, we've welcomed these platforms into our homes, our workplaces and public spaces, ushering in a new era of community and social structures without much thought. As new social media applications have boomed hand in hand with the mobile phone explosion – 95 per cent of Americans own a phone and 77 per cent carry a smartphone – we have seen a complete and utter revolution in the way we consume news, products and, most importantly, each other. We did not wait or even pause momentarily to survey the fallout from such a significant shift; there's been no clear post-mortem on the long-term impacts of social media exposure from either the medical or academic professions. It's all too recent, too fresh and too pervasive. Yet, we're already at a point where unplugging from the system seems unthinkable for most. One thing's for sure: what has been done cannot be undone – the proverbial milk has been spilt and social media is now part of the fabric of modern life.

Offering opportunity, discovery and the chance to forge new relationships in one hand, and self-criticism, alienation and potential mental-health crises in the other, social media is a double-edged sword which cuts deeply both ways. And, while there's been plenty of cultural anxiety around the use of social media, research has been too mixed and limited to convincingly persuade the majority of us to actually alter our patterns of behaviour.

Humans have always struggled with too much technological change in too short a time, and we're currently stuck between a rock of headlines screaming loudly to predict digital doomsday and a hard place of inconclusive research which divides expert opinion. After all, there are countless studies which have established that social media has changed our lives as much for the better as for the worse.

It's worth remembering that, before social media, it was the internet that was considered the scourge of modern life. This new technology was supposed to herald the end of life as we knew it, causing isolation, alienation and the withdrawal of the next generation from the community and themselves. While it has certainly made an indelible impact, the internet has not, thus far, marked the death knell for the human race. Over time, government legislation has started to curb some of its worst (though by no means all) excesses, and school protocols and internet safety awareness have gone some way to protect the youngest from the world wide web's deepest cesspools. Simply put, we have come to understand that the internet offers both good and bad. Before the internet came along, it was television that was rotting children's brains, while computer games were desensitizing them to violence... No matter what the technology, change always comes with fear, and advancement with pitfalls. There is no such thing as perfect technology because it is *us*, fallible humans, who use it. But we mustn't forget that we're also the ones at the controls.

Like most forms of media or technology, it's easy to argue that the new social media platforms are more a mirror to a complex human psyche than fundamentally destructive. However, the idea that the new technology is entirely neutral is slowly being undermined, often by whistle-blowers from within the now multi-billion-dollar social media companies. Tech insiders have revealed the way programmers have exploited our brain's natural reward system to hook us to our feeds – what some call "brain hacking". And our compulsive need to stay engaged has so penetrated our lives that billions of us around the world are suffering from "nomophobia" – a dread of being separated from our phones and accounts, even for a few hours. Consequently, our lives have changed entirely, with far-reaching implications in how we build relationships, value ourselves and map out our life expectations. Whether the new technology has been engineered to manipulate human psychology or not, the ways in which we use it deserve more scrutiny.

It's a Woman's World

Tellingly, many of the adverse effects of social media use appear to be inherently gendered. Women make up the majority of audiences across all the visual platforms, notably Instagram and Pinterest, as well as Facebook and Twitter. They also post the most selfies, share more personal issues, log on more frequently and spend more time on social media overall. In the US, women use social media more than men – by a gap of 73 to 65 per cent. As Dr James A Roberts, a professor of marketing and an expert on consumer and technology behaviours, explains: "Women form deeper attachments to their devices than men. They score higher on the behavioural addiction scale, and we've found that's down to the reasons that women use smartphones – unlike men who are still in the main using their phones for traditional purposes like communication, information and entertainment – women often focus their use of technology on maintaining social relationships through social media".

If we can be certain of anything, it's that we haven't properly come to terms with the new world order. Many of us are grappling with the more challenging impacts of social media without any real idea of how to navigate the new waters. Instead, we're coping alone, consuming social media content from the moment we wake to the instant before we sleep and allowing the worst sides of it to slowly eat away at our self-esteem, sense of identity and happiness.

While privately and among friends, we women may discuss how social media makes us feel, or has changed our perspectives and the way we interact with each other, on a cultural level we're not openly acknowledging a fistful of issues. We don't want to sound like Luddites. We don't want to admit that looking at pictures of other people makes us feel bad about ourselves. We don't really want anyone else to know how much time we spend scrolling through our feeds. And, of course, underlying this is the desire to avoid anything which might, just might, mean we have to stop scrolling.

The Social Media Rap Sheet

So what proof do we have of the downsides of our collective social media habit? The facts are crystal clear: there's a barrage of cold and hard research pointing to correlations between social media use and mental health issues spanning anxiety and depression, which will be explored in depth throughout this book. A study in 2016 found that spending just one hour a day on social networks reduces the probability of a teenager being happy by around 14 per cent and that girls are more adversely affected than boys. At its worst, the UK charity NSPCC has gone so far as to blame social media for the dramatic increase in the number of children admitted to hospital for self-harm. There is no wriggle room here – social media is clearly linked to an increase in mental health problems and is depleting our children's happiness at a deeply worrying rate. Is it any wonder that French schools are planning a total ban of phones from all primary and secondary schools by the end of 2018?

And the concern is not just reserved for girls and young women. This is an undeniable cross-generational crisis, created in the main by the new "norms" presented by social networks. In 2017 more than 80 per cent of women in a UK survey said that Instagram and Facebook "added pressure to be the perfect mum", while Terri Smith, CEO of Australian perinatal depression helpline PANDA, has spoken about the damage caused by "social media representations of ideal families". Even when we've reached a level of maturity to know that these images *can't* be entirely reflective of real life, they can still get to us and undermine our happiness. A recent study reported that mothers who more frequently compared themselves on social media sites had a higher incidence than average of depression, were more likely to feel overloaded in their parental role and less competent as parents – the very last things that any mum juggling responsibilities needs. Women can feel just as inadequate viewing fantasy images of the "mommy glow" with kid-mess-free interiors in the backdrop as teenagers may feel when they see Kim Kardashian's plumped-up lips.

A 2017 Harvard Business Review report surveyed the academic literature to argue that social media may "detract from face-to-face relationships, reduce investment in meaningful activities, increase sedentary behaviour...and erode self-esteem". For mums, add in sleep deprivation, increased levels of anxiety, a massive reduction in attention span and, ironically, social isolation, and you've got a cocktail of crappy side effects. And those are just for starters.

Even Facebook has begrudgingly accepted that "passive" social media use (more on that later) has a negative impact on both mood and mental health. Citing both academic and internal enquiries, researchers for the social network admitted that, "in general, when people spend a lot of time passively consuming information – reading but not interacting with people – they report feeling worse afterward." When the world's biggest social media platform has conceded there's a problem and tech leaders have admitted they've barred their own children from logging on, it's time to have a calm look at the impact of our edited worlds.

Technology Addicts Anonymous

One of the biggest causes of concern among the parents, educators and care-givers across the world that I interviewed for this book is the amount of time we spend per day on our devices. Today we *live* on our screens, jumping from laptops to tablets to smartphones, seamlessly switching from games to social media platforms to smartphone apps to webpages. While it's not only social media that we're consuming, a 2016 Global Web Index survey of more than fifty thousand global internet users found that the average person has eight social media accounts and spends one hour and fifty-eight minutes a day – or a third of their entire internet time – browsing them. Smartphone and social media use are not synonymous but they are deeply linked, and a compulsion to check one often means a compulsion to check the other.

Drawing from his work on social media and smartphone addiction, Dr Roberts explains: "Generally people are reluctant to think of behaviours as addictions. We're programmed to believe that we could be addicted to alcohol or drugs, but when it comes to behaviours, we're certainly resistant to accepting that addiction could apply. With social media and smartphone use, what we're seeing in many cases certainly fits the definition of behavioural addiction – engaging in behaviour which you know will have negative consequences for both you and the people around you. It doesn't make logical sense for people to do things that harm them – unless they are addicted. Why else would so many Americans check their social media accounts while driving? Putting themselves and others at risk isn't in their self-interest, but the truth is they just can't stop themselves."

Highlighting the six core components of addiction, Dr Roberts presents a convincing description of the way many of us feel about our phones. "There's salience (how deeply ingrained is your smartphone in your life), tolerance (are you using your phone more and more? Checking your accounts endlessly?), euphoria (the excitement or anticipation you get just before or after you use your cell phone), conflict (is your phone causing trouble in your life with work or relationships?), withdrawal symptoms (do you panic when you're separated from your phone?) and relapse (have you tried to cut back and failed?). Relapse is one of the issues that a psychiatrist will go to first – because when you attempt to cut back you have made a clear decision that something is harmful, but if you are unable to stop, you can be pretty sure you're in an addictive situation." If you recognize any or all of the above, it's certainly worth starting to analyse your behaviour.

According to a report released by research firm Dscout in 2016, the typical mobile phone user touches his or her phone 2,617 times a day. For the top 10 per cent of users in the study, increase that to 5,427 touches a day. Data confirmed by Apple themselves indicates that the average user with Touch ID unlocks their phone every 11 minutes, 15 seconds. Most of us will spend a staggering *seven years* of our lives on our phones. For anyone who might suggest that smartphones' overuse has been blown out of proportion, I'll give you just over ten minutes to try to rationalize these mind-blowing figures. If you had to honestly count how often you reach for your device, where do you think you would rate on the scale? Does work get in the way of your phone time? What about your commute? Can you identify with the 75 per cent of other smartphone owners who admit to using their phones on the toilet? Perhaps 11 minutes and 15 seconds actually feels like a pretty long time?

Not only are we conspicuously and compulsively handling our phones, but we also believe them to be of utmost importance to our lives. In 2011, a McCann WorldGroup analysis of the youth market found that 53 per cent of millennials aged 16–22 (at the time) would rather lose their sense of *smell* than lose access to an item of technology (a phone or a computer). And that was seven years ago. Ask yourself, what would you be prepared to sacrifice in return for your connectivity? Imagine you couldn't log on to the web, or ever access your phone. What would you give up to get it back?

Forget life; choose your phone
The encroachment that phones have made into our rest time, and the resulting global decline in sleep quality and quantity, is one of the biggest charges against phone use. A 2017 survey by Accel and Qualtics revealed that 79 per cent of millennials keep their phones by or in their bed and over half check their phone in the middle of the night. Elsewhere, 55 per cent of British respondents in a 2015 Deloitte report said they look at their phone within 15 minutes of waking and 28 per cent checked within five minutes before going to sleep *every* night. The inability to actually switch off isn't a niche issue. When it starts intruding into your rest time, being connected 24/7 can be incredibly bad for your health. It's been conclusively proven that the longer your screen time during the day, the worse you sleep at night. And as well as having a massive impact on your quality of life, sleep deprivation has been associated with everything from weight gain to high blood pressure and lower life expectancy. If we're talking about self-care, no rational person would ever have their phone in their bedroom.

Social media can also erode our ability to be, well, social. Sherry Turkle, a leading professor in the field of the impact of technology on society, has warned of an "empathy gap", in which young people are unable to develop the social skill of empathy due to their need for constant stimulus and their increasingly distracted family interaction. "These days we find ways around conversation," she explains in *Reclaiming Conversation: The Power of Talk in a Digital Age*. "We hide from each other even, as we're constantly connected to each other."

A 2015 poll found that 89 per cent of Americans admitted they took out a phone at their last social encounter and 82 per cent said that they felt the conversation deteriorated after they did so. Research has proven that even a silent phone sitting innocently on the table inhibits conversation. Turkle also relates use of digital technologies to "simulation", saying that they offer "the illusion of friendship without the demands of intimacy".

Denial is a powerful force when it comes to social media use, but who hasn't been guilty of the occasional Saturday night binge on their favourite platform? The issue is how often you personally access your social media accounts and how that usage makes you feel. Even though I'm very conscious of my own use and try to spread the message about the dangers of social media at any opportunity, I'm certainly not immune to the pull of the scroll. More than anything, I can identify with the idea that social media use is a time drain, which takes me away from getting things done. There have been times when I've thought, "Right, I need to reduce my consumption of these pictures", but I've never been able to completely disengage, even when I know it's making me feel bad. One of the reasons we all keep coming back to social media is that we believe there will be a chance it will make us feel better, but in reality, when you're in a rut, it just makes you feel worse and traps you in a vicious cycle. Just like everyone else, I know it's time to take a break, but I just don't seem to be able to unplug.

A Social Me-Dia History

My social media story has been coloured by many factors, including my age and my job background. I remember the first time I ever heard about Facebook, back in March 2006. I was in my final year of university in Edinburgh, writing my dissertation, and suddenly there were these rumours of a new "exclusive" online club called Facebook. In its early days, the site targeted college students, choosing influential kingpins in specific social circles to spread the message – if I remember correctly, the first person who introduced it to me was a guy who put on "nights" at clubs in the city. To join, you needed a university email address, and it definitely felt like something intercollegiate rather than a platform that would soon capture the attention of every mum and her cat. There were plenty of discussions among my group of friends on the positives and negatives of signing up – at the time the cons surrounded issues of privacy and the fact that it was seen as a bit "uncool" to be showing off about what you were doing. How quaint and antiquated that all sounds now. It goes to show how much the world has changed since the advent of social media, or how much social media has changed our world.

I was an immediate convert. Whenever I needed a break from ten thousand words on the relationship between second- and third-wave feminism, I'd log on to Facebook. Soon I started to dread the days when I was in the library and I didn't have access to the internet (this was the Stone Age – aka the pre Google-on-your-phone era). Offering a brief, but effective, respite from the intense brainwork of my history degree, Facebook soon became one of my favourite pastimes. As an early adopter, I'd often meet people who had never heard of it – or didn't have an accepted university email address but really wanted to set up an account – so it definitely felt good to be part of the inner circle. In the early days, it felt as though Facebook was a diary of our after-dark escapades, and there were a host of seriously dodgy – and definitely unedited – pictures that were uploaded on to the site. Early messages were written directly on friends' walls, with invites to events with free or cheap booze seemingly a focus. It was basically "pure" and unfiltered from both a visual and a content point of view – a mix of cute messages and candid pictures taken on BlackBerry cameras. It was only later when I was building my career that I started to be conscious of the impression of myself I was projecting to the outside world and considered vetting the content.

Over time, of course, things changed and moved on. Looking through my timeline images, the shift started when I got a job at *Grazia* magazine in 2012 (five years after starting my career in fashion) and was instructed by my editor to upgrade to an iPhone and set up an Instagram account. Since then, fewer and fewer of the pictures I've posted feature friends or, indeed, any other people, and more and more are images of me on my own in exotic or exclusive places and locations. As my pictures have become more glamorous and aspirational, my interaction with my Facebook community has conversely plummeted and migrated to Instagram. Now I rarely log on to chat to people or even stalk their timelines, as I keep in touch with friends on WhatsApp and use social media as a platform not for socializing but for forming career-related contacts, building a community around causes that I'm passionate about and earning money as an influencer.

There's no doubt that starting to grow an Instagram audience has had a huge impact on the way I see myself and feel about my life. Initially I felt really reluctant to get involved and I wasn't comfortable with posting images of myself at all. My partner at the time was anti social media in general and constantly berated me for vanity and self-obsession. Even more troubling was the feeling among fashion-industry insiders that editors were "cheapening" themselves by sharing their personal lives. Again, it's now hard to believe, but anyone who was serious about a career in fashion journalism in 2012 needed to think carefully about whether or not they were going to "risk" their integrity by uploading pictures of themselves – as that was seen as something that bloggers (still a dirty word back then) did, not journalists on a reputable publication. Peers who had started to get involved were often ridiculed for their posts, and self-promotional content was equated with extreme narcissism. That feeling is still present in certain areas of the industry, but obviously the context has shifted somewhat.

My first handle was @katherine_grazia, which gives you an indication of how important my job role was to my content. The amount of people who thought the magazine title was my surname was concerning, but it provided protection from the "cringe factor": I was posting as *part of my job*, not because I thought I looked beautiful or wanted other people to see how wonderful my life was. Basically, it gave me carte blanche to build a following without feeling embarrassed about showing off. For Gen Z and younger millennials, the idea that starting a social media account is anything but a rite of passage may be difficult to grasp, but for older millennials like me, who cut their teeth in the old school yet were expected to adapt to the new technology, there was a lot of hand-wringing involved.

Since then, social media has provided me with so many #blessings. It's given me an independent income stream and enabled me to connect with thousands of other people and speak to them directly in one of the most supportive and genuine communities I've ever known. At times, I've legitimately *loved* taking pictures, felt creatively challenged and fulfilled, and experienced genuine happiness that I've finally found somewhere to express myself without anyone to tell me what I've done wrong. However, I've also dealt with the full gamut of emotion that social media can generate. It has made me worry about things like engagement and algorithms, made me question myself, and made me wonder what's wrong with me and why people don't like me. It's made me want to buy things that I can't afford, made me feel like I'm lazy in comparison to other people and, at times, made me feel very low. It's also made me feel overweight, unattractive, poor, unstylish, lonely, left out, unpopular and seriously devoid of a sense of humour.

However clued up on the "system" you are, however much you use social media for your business and however much you keep telling yourself not to be affected by what you consume online, no-one is immune. Whether it's the occasional pang of envy or jolt to your self-esteem caused by a single picture or a more sustained Saturday-night-in-on-your-own-scroll-mania, social media can make even a balanced and mentally well-adjusted person have severe moments of self-doubt and angst.

While this might all sound very doom-like, I do truly believe there are meaningful positives to take away from all of my experiences. The big questions are: what's the secret to filtering out the bad but keeping the good; and how can we make sure that we keep all this in perspective and consciously control our social media use – something which we can pass down to future generations?

Picture Perfect?

What does "perfect" look like to you? Is it about blemish-free skin and a straight smile? Or happy relationships and a beautiful home? Perhaps your idea of perfect is based on career success or a well-maintained six-pack? Or really do we mean all of the above and more? Perfection in its very definition is the state of being *or becoming* perfect, the process of refining something until it is flawless. In the age of social media, the action of perfecting is something we have quickly learned to master. If we aren't perfect to start off with, no matter... A flattering filter here, a retouch tweak there; a quick clear-up of one corner of a messy house, a smile which covers a tricky day. Each and every fault can be erased and replaced with new and increasingly homogenous upgrades to make you feel like the very best version of yourself – or, even better, more like someone else you admire. We can whiten our teeth, slim our thighs and blur our pimples to improve our genetics and supposedly our appeal to each other. We can also turn a miserable, rainy day into a summer classic and curate a schedule of images which not only show us in the best light but suggest a life of rounded perfection. And why not? That's what other people want to see, isn't it?

As a consumer journalist with a decade of experience working on women's magazines, I've been trained to see content as a mix of fantasy and reality – the fashion spreads, which inspire us to dream, but also the real-life stories, which allow us to empathize. Fashion titles have quite rightly had their fair share of criticism over the years, especially in relation to their promotion of an unrealistic body image and lack of diverse representation. These accusations are, in the main, entirely justified, and anyone who has worked in traditional magazine publishing will know that images of white – most likely blonde – thin women dominate any single magazine issue. While things are slowly shifting, there's no point pretending that the days of magazine dominance were a long-lost utopia of diversity.

What traditional magazines did have, however, was a huge focus on relatability, something which is now often painfully edited out of the social media sphere. Every issue of every title I ever worked on offered a mix of content that the reader could identify with – providing support for their struggles and challenges – as well as inspiration for their aspirational desires. We'd cover fertility, heartbreak and financial ruin, *as well as* the hottest new heels of the season. There was also often a light-heartedness and self-deprecation – the countless "test run" stories I wrote which involved me spending a week in 10-inch platforms, Google Glasses or waist-training corsets were always teed up for laughs. (Spoiler alert: they always made me look ridiculous, especially the Google Glasses. But that was the point.)

As the curated imagery of social media has become more and more prominent, the space devoted to real-life issues and collective empathy around life's challenges, both extraordinary and universal, has diminished. Scroll through Facebook or Instagram today and you'll find that lifestyles are a procession of idyllic holidays, "leaning-in" career promotions, material consumption and happy family moments, all captured in the most aesthetically attractive frame possible. Ill-health, failure, loss, sadness, struggle, hard work, setbacks – indeed anything not entirely positive – has become increasingly underrepresented in our discourse, because it doesn't fit the mould of the often image-focused world of social media. We also take ourselves *seriously* seriously, and the pressure to be immaculate has definitely come hand in hand with a new po-faced attitude, in which our personal brands can't be compromised by any lightweight or anecdotal content. Aside from the comedy-focused accounts (which are understandably hugely successful), the standard social media feed is so focused on self-promotion that we can't bear to look foolish in front of others.

According to a 2017 research paper, these days women rarely compare their appearance to women they see in billboards and magazines and only sometimes compare their appearance to others they see on TV. Instead it's social media comparisons which are making women feel unhappiest. Because these women are supposedly more accessible and "normal" – not A-list actresses or internationally famous pop stars – the standards they set feel like a bare minimum. If those in your community most like you can achieve a level of life success and perfect appearance, why can't you too?

And through these platforms we're also all looking up to new heroes. The status of these new "micro-celebrities" is key to the social media system. Super-users by nature, these "influencers" have the faces, bodies and wardrobes that we pore over as avatars of the new era. Their vast reach opens them up to the very good, very bad and everything in-between that social media has to offer. However, I've found that, whether it's a beautiful model on set or an Instagram star with a million followers, the women who seem to have everything are just like the rest of us: struggling, self-doubting and feeling under huge pressure to look and feel a certain way. For them there is often no escape from the strain of keeping up appearances. Though they're projecting a lifestyle which we're all hungrily aspiring to, the reality is that they are often addicted to their phones, deeply insecure and highly anxious about their social media profile.

However, in the new media moment, these women can also be potent agents of change. These are the women that other women listen to. Their advice, their philosophies and their styling tips guide the way that the social media community at large behaves. Through engagement with their, often unbelievably enormous, audiences, they are able to challenge cultural values, bring causes to the masses and undermine traditional structures of power. Contrary to popular opinion, influencers don't just make us buy things (though they're certainly very good at it). Instead, they have meaningfully influenced our attitudes. From providing role models for under-represented and marginal communities, busting taboos around hidden struggles like miscarriage and poor mental health, and promoting feminist and environmental issues (#FreeTheNipple, #SayNoToPlastic), they have enacted change on a global scale. Young women won't listen to their parents, teachers or researchers. But they will listen to those sitting on top of the new media pedestal. This is why this book has included the voices of female influencers across a broad array of social communities to help explore the biggest issues that we face online today. Between them they have an audience of almost 10 million followers, a particular experience with the highs and lows of the social media experience, and the capacity to help make us all wake up to the crisis we're sitting on. They are not just the new power players; they're also the experts. It is their words that will really help to burst the bubble.

Social media has inarguably set destructive standards of flawlessness and comparison, which continuously deplete millions of women's self-belief, every minute of every day. We're working so hard to live up to these new benchmarks that we're burning ourselves out, and we're striving so hard to maintain our image that we're self-perpetuating an unobtainable reality. Until girls and women alike see the social media fantasies for what they are – constructed realities – and stop comparing their lifestyles, bodies, partners and even families to those seen on their feeds and screens, they will never be able to realize their potential in the workplace, their relationships or in their quest for happiness.

I'm not attempting to be holier than thou or sanctimonious; we all like nice pictures of ourselves, and there's a reason social media is so popular. Glamour, fantasy and the creative worlds curated by social content-makers can be fun, artistic and beautiful, and there's nothing wrong with taking enjoyment and positives from social media consumption, creation and interaction. But the conversation *must* be re-framed, because if we continue projecting fantasy as reality and continue believing, or even semi-believing, in the make-believe, the dangers are both very real and very present. While my aim is to always err on the side of balance, the changes that social media have brought to our lives *are* sensational, therefore deserve to be probed and laid bare as such.

The Comparison Trap

When you look at other people's lives on social media, how does it make you feel about yours? If the answer is "a bit rubbish", rest assured you're not the only one. Social psychologist Leon Festinger's classic 1954 social comparison theory suggests that individuals evaluate their own abilities and success by gauging their position in the social pecking order. His argument is that we can only really rate our own position in life by comparing it to those of others within our communities, which means the boundaries of those communities really matter.

In times of yore, aka when we lived offline, there were two ways that social comparison could work: upward and downward. When we saw others we judged to be in a worse position than ourselves, it would often lead to an improvement in self-appraisal, however, when we saw people we deemed to be living superior lives to us, or having superior abilities and attributes, it had a tendency to create a sense of inadequacy and insecurity, and had an overall negative effect on our self-evaluation.

When all we see is the very, *very* best side of the people in our communities online, curated especially to exclusively highlight their best attributes, is it any wonder that most of us feel that we are on the back foot in relation to pretty much everyone we know? Instead of upward and downward comparisons, we are seeing exclusively those who appear to be superior to us, in every single way. Comparing ourselves to idealized versions of each other is, scroll by scroll, overexposing us to upward social comparison, which has a massive knock-on impact on body image, self-esteem, expectations and life satisfaction.

Of course, there is nothing new in the process of comparison itself, but social media puts it into hyper-drive – especially among young people. A 2017 poll of more than 1,900 girls and young women by the

UK charity Girlguiding found that 35 per cent of girls aged 11–21 said their biggest worry online was comparing themselves and their lives with others. But it's not just the kids. In a recent study by UK disability charity Scope, 60 per cent of adult Twitter and Facebook users reported feelings of jealousy when comparing themselves to other users too. As we consume more and more information about each other, we're finding it perilously easy to slip into the quicksand of comparison.

On social media, comparison breeds envy at every corner. Instead of feeling grateful for what we have, we believe we need to be more, just to come up to scratch. Our careers, our wardrobes, our lifestyles, even our children (let's not even get started on apps to make babies and children look "cuter") – none of them are enough. So, what's the solution? Aside from more honesty in our content creation, the more we accept that digital identities are simulations rather than true benchmarks from which to judge our own position in life, the kinder we can be to ourselves. The time is nigh to stop battering ourselves with comparisons to versions of others which just don't exist. We need to forget about coveting what our neighbours appear to have; the time is nigh to stop battering ourselves with comparisons to versions of others that just don't exist.

Every Voice Counts

On the positive side, during my research through the murky and addictive algorithms social media has been built from, I have heard plenty of accounts from followers as well as influencers, both micro and mega, explaining that the engagement they found online had increased their confidence hugely. Discovering that there are people out there who think and feel like you can make everyone, both old and young, feel less marginalized. One of social media's most positive contributions to modern life is that it can help you find "your people".

"Growing up I wasn't used to seeing successful women that looked like me," says Freddie Harrel, a fashion and lifestyle blogger, beauty entrepreneur, and confidence coach and speaker with 136k followers on Instagram. Born and raised in Paris to Cameroonian parents, she explains, "In France, if you open a fashion magazine you will not see a single, remotely 'tanned' face. There is no diversity. At all." One huge advancement that social media has facilitated is a democratization of the types of men and women we see in aspirational positions. Communities have been built around individuals whose stories would have been edited out of the traditional media environment, because of systemic prejudice.

On any social platform you will find groups which celebrate, inform and serve plus-size women, LGBT women, women of colour and women of faith. All shapes, all sizes, all shades and all creeds are welcome to join in. From a racial perspective, the proportion of white, black and Latino users across all social media sites is roughly the same, although more black and Latino people use Instagram in comparison to their white counterparts, while Pinterest is more popular among white users than other groups.

"Social media has really changed the landscape and I follow some incredible women of colour on Instagram – many of whom have built a huge following – who inspire me," Freddie continues. "There's now not [only] one version of what a successful woman looks like, and that is so important for younger generations coming up behind us."

Leandra Medine, founder of fashion and lifestyle platform ManRepeller.com (one of the first blogs to achieve fashion-industry recognition) explains that these relationships can make women feel both supported and empowered. "The notion of making women feel less alone and more understood is a cornerstone of Man Repeller. Social media can facilitate a community if you are open and vulnerable – and if the people you don't know come out to support you, care to listen to your story and dare to share their own. That's a really strong and impactful experience. The number of private messages I have received from strangers, and the outpour of their personal narratives that they've generously shared...it's a true connection."

Like Me So I Can Love Myself

However, what happens when no-one engages? When you don't receive any likes or comments on your posts? Or more likely "too few" likes against your own standards? We all know that adolescents are eager for peer validation. I can remember the threat of "peer pressure" being rammed down my throat through school, especially when it came to smoking (I completely caved and ended up with a 20-a-day habit – the moral of the story: listen to your parents). But a need for acceptance from our community isn't something most of us leave behind on graduation day. In today's digital age, a desire for validation has intensified for the straightforward reason that social media has made it quantifiable. Those little numbers under our captions and pictures, and the threat of eerie silence around our digital updates, give each and every one of us a clear indication of how liked we are. Instead of increasing our confidence in our own self-definition, we are becoming more and more aware of what our peers think of us, often "caving" to that pressure way into our adult lives.

Sean Parker, one of Facebook's earliest investors (Justin Timberlake in the film *The Social Network*) told news and information website Axios in an interview in 2017 that a social media site is a "social-validation feedback loop...exploiting a vulnerability in human psychology". He explained that he and other early social media pioneers built their platforms to "consume as much of your time and conscious attention as possible" with the "like" button devised to give users "a little dopamine hit", which in turn would fuel a desire to upload more content.

In a world where you can tangibly rate your popularity and see exactly who in your social circle cares, "chasing the likes" has become a collective interest which can veer into an obsession. The "like" function wasn't part of the original social media blueprint – indeed, Facebook only introduced it in 2009, five years after its initial launch. Almost a decade later, we tap out 4.5 billion likes each day on that platform alone, meaning there's a hell of a lot of validation out there to ensnare with what we share.

So how does that craving for endorsement impact our psyches? In 2014 Thailand's government psychiatrist Dr Panpimol Wipulakorn warned through the country's Department of Mental Health that young Thais were experiencing emotional problems when images they posted of themselves weren't receiving the desired level of likes. This lack of validation could, she argued, "affect their thoughts. They can lose self-confidence and have a negative attitude toward themselves, such as feeling dissatisfied with themselves or their body." In a far-reaching conclusion she finished, "This could affect the development of the country in the future as the number of new-generation leaders will fall short. It will hinder the country's creativity and innovation."

A 2016 study from UCLA (University of California, Los Angeles) used MRI scanning to examine the brains of teenagers aged 13–18 while they used social media. The results showed that viewing likes underneath a picture they had posted activated the same brain signals as eating chocolate or winning money. Another interesting finding was that teens were much more likely to click the "like" button on images that had already received lots of love from their peers, showing that endorsement from others made them more likely to offer validation to others. While the study highlighted the particularly sensitive reward circuitry in adolescents, it's not a reach for most adults to relate to. I can certainly identify with the feelings described. Anyone who says they don't feel good when an image or comment they've created clocks up lots of likes and comments is probably lying. The validation can feel like a rush, a sense of "something I've said or done matters to people". It's only natural to feel this way; after all, we are social beings at heart and we're hard-wired to feel good about approval from others. It's also not difficult to see why posts that have already gained lots of likes might inspire us to click our own little hearts. Aside from subconscious conformity, there's a sense that we must be "missing" something if we don't like it too. Did we not get the joke? Or aren't we quite up to speed with a new trend? If everyone else thinks it's so cool, why don't we?

When likes become an indicator of popularity and social standing, gaining approval from others can momentarily improve our self-esteem and release a hit of dopamine, which backs up that feel-good emotion. A *New Statesman* 2017 survey showed that for 89 per cent of social media users, getting a high level of likes makes them feel happy, but revealingly for 40 per cent of those people, the happiness only lasts as long as the likes keep coming in. For 12.5 per cent of people, they will still feel happy after an hour; for 10.2 per cent, they will feel it for the entire day; and only 3.1 per cent will be sustained for a week. Overall 62.7 per cent of respondents agreed or strongly agreed with the statement, "I feel a buzz when someone likes my post." No matter what, we all love to be liked.

Conversely, a perceived lack of engagement can create a huge dent in our self-esteem. Who hasn't posted a picture or comment on social media only to feel deflated minutes later when no-one has liked or commented on it? We don't need to be told it feels crap to be ignored, left hanging in digital time and space without that little pick-me-up that a "successful" post can offer. Is it any wonder that a whole industry exists to help individuals pay for likes, that so many of us ask friends to like our pictures to up our digital cred or that we end up deleting so many images and captions that haven't generated enough likes? But then...the allure of the dopamine high returns and you find yourself posting another image. This cycle can become a pathological obsession, and if you find yourself checking your likes every minute of the day, it's no surprise the process can have a huge impact on your mental state. A solid body of research has proven that the lower your self-esteem to start with, the more a lack of engagement on social media can impact you negatively, meaning those who feel the most need for validation are also the least able to cope with the effects of receiving low engagement.

Worryingly it was suggested in a 2018 article by the Canadian *Globe & Mail* that social media platforms are capitalizing on our hunger for validation by holding back likes to keep us checking our accounts. Quoting Matt Mayberry, who works at a California startup called Dopamine Labs, the article claims: "It's common knowledge in the industry that Instagram exploits this craving by strategically withholding 'likes' from certain users. If the photo-sharing app decides you need to use the service more often, it'll show only a fraction of the likes you've received on a given post at first, hoping you'll be disappointed with your haul and check back again in a minute or two."

In response, Mike Krieger, the CTO of Instagram, used Twitter to deny that there was any intention to withhold likes, but he did admit that there might be a replication lag and that the platform tries to "strike a balance of being timely + [and] not over-sending notifs [notifications]". The idea that our social media apps could be so calculatingly taking advantage of our human weaknesses is obviously abhorrent – but we have to remember that this is business and the more we connect, the more they profit. Ultimately it is in the interest of every social media platform to make us feel this way.

Disentangling our sense of worth from the numbers is one of the most important steps in moderating the impact that social media can have on our lives, but it's far trickier than it sounds. Sure, you can go cold turkey, delete your accounts or take a break (something which a 2015 study proved will increase your life satisfaction), but for many of us that's not always a practical solution. Social media can sometimes be part of our job, or we may need to stay connected or maintain a digital presence to be relevant for other professional reasons, such as networking. Unless your social media use is causing you relentless anxiety, depression or unhappiness, there is definitely a time and place for it and there are many positives to be taken away. It's just about knowing how to control that time and ensuring you're in the right frame of mind – two things we are often entirely unconscious of as we click on our apps and get ready to scroll.

Real or Fake? And Why It Matters

In the early days of the internet there was a utopian belief that anyone could be anyone they wanted to be online. It was suggested that the space would be non-gendered, without racial bias, and would offer individuals the chance to present themselves exactly as they wished, without prompting the assumptions people make, from our accents to body shapes, that colour all of our identities in real life. "On the internet no-one knows you're a dog", is an adage taken from a 1993 *New Yorker* cartoon by Paul Steiner featuring two computer-savvy canines. The point being made was that the internet was a plane of anonymity where individuals were liberated to redefine who they were to the world. Of course, now the biggest social media stars have their own accounts and the @DogsOfInstagram feed has over four million followers. Despite this, our understanding of identity in the digital space has certainly been transformed.

As time has gone on, internet obscurity has instead become associated with illegal activity. And research has proven that real-life preconceptions immediately bled over to the internet. Doctors are instantly presumed to be white men, for example, and judgements are made based on people's names, even without images, to determine either race, class or social status. While the internet has helped connect communities of all stripes, it certainly hasn't eradicated prejudice against those of non-white ethnicities or non-heterosexual sexualities, nor stopped those of differing religions judging each other – in fact there's little doubt that the internet has enabled and intensified hate speech against both mainstream and marginalized communities as well as given a platform for extremists.

However, a kernel of that concept of self-invention has continued to shape our understanding of the online world. Stretching the truth is part and parcel of the digital experience. Consider profile pictures or given ages on internet dating sites. A 2008 study found that 81 per cent of matchmaking site participants lied or misrepresented themselves in some, albeit often small, way. Not everyone online is catfishing (creating a fake identity online to impersonate someone entirely different), but then again, very few of us are always entirely honest. Without the non-verbal cues which we rely on to see if someone is telling the truth in real life, it can be all too easy to be fooled.

And being duped we are. Escapism is an entirely understandable drive, and social media can offer a platform to express and explore fantasy identities. However, we've failed to develop a collective understanding that many of the images and captions which make up many profiles are, at best, misrepresentations of the truth and, at worst, outright lies. Somehow our scepticism has been put on the backburner; we all seem happy to suspend disbelief. Only posting the beautiful side of our lives without mentioning the less photogenic parts, or even the daily grind, isn't "living in truth". None of these things are unlawful and they are entirely reasonable in the context of the games of micro-deception that everyone else is playing online. But even the little tweaks we're making to our realities are distorting our understanding of normality and making hundreds and thousands of people feel disappointed with the reality of their lives. In the era of fake news, the fact that so many people are living "fake" lives, photographing fake designer shoes and posting #IWokeUpLikeThis selfies with a full face of slap on, is perhaps no shocker. It is, however, having a massive influence on our perceptions of the world and ourselves.

For one thing, it's important to acknowledge that how we represent ourselves online can have a dramatic impact on our success in life. According to a 2017 CareerBuilder survey, 70 per cent of employers use social media to screen candidates before hiring, and three in ten HR departments have a member of staff dedicated solely to social recruiting. The study showed that a positive online persona was not only advantageous for job recruitment, but also that *more than half of all employers wouldn't hire a candidate that didn't have a social media account*. From excessive posting to provocative or inappropriate pictures, there are a range of obvious turn-offs for employers. But the fact it's also now almost a requirement to cultivate a certain image in the digital realm as part of your résumé is most significant.

What's more, the process doesn't finish after you've signed your contract – more than half of all bosses say they monitor the digital accounts of their current staff, so opening up about mental health issues, home-life struggles and relationship challenges online comes with definite risks. Basically, your future or current boss will probably read it, so you'd better think twice before you post anything. Judgements on what a "positive persona" is, of course, are subjective, but from a professional perspective it's obviously far "safer" to keep things upbeat, iron out the wrinkles of life and make everything seem fabulous. The sad truth is that you don't have a "personal" life on social media – even if your posts are private, things can slip through the net. Everything you publish in the online realm could potentially have a bearing on your professional success and reputation.

On the flipside, there is a vocal "authenticity police" force out there ready to jump on perceived fakery in an instant. Digitally naming and shaming others on social media has become a hot new pursuit, with followers calling out individuals with audiences both big and small. The *New Statesman* chronicled the case of a beauty blogger who was accused of Photoshopping her images to edit out crowds from iconic tourist destinations by creating a composite between two images and passing them off as authentic. Since the blogger made money from these constructed images through sponsored posts, many of her followers felt that she had lost her integrity. As the author of the article, Amelia Tait, says, "Though a Photoshopped sunset is not as damaging as the 'fake news' spread during and since the United States Presidential Election, it is still a worrying aspect of the erosion of authenticity online." While, in my personal opinion, much of the disgruntlement from the digital community was not much more than trolling – singling out one blogger when there are literally hundreds of thousands of people doing the same kind of thing seems patently unjust – Tait has a solid point. Social media's ability to stretch the truth in a way that we have accepted and internalized has permeated all areas of life, including our thoughts, our decisions and our votes. It's not a private or personal thing: it's a political attitude which can have a bearing on how we view both the superficial and essential organized structures of our society. To be anti-Trump and complain about governmental gaslighting seems somewhat disingenuous if you're publicly misrepresenting the truths of your life too.

Aren't we all complicit?

So what do I edit out of my life online? Well I definitely make my pictures look "prettier" by adjusting the light balance of the vast majority of my social media images – when you're shooting in London, for six months of the year you're basically in low- to no-light situations. I've definitely added saturation to colours in images and filters to make them look more jolly (bleak, rainy days are another London perk). I'm not a massive selfie-taker, but if I were I wouldn't flinch at taking out a massive zit, though personally I wouldn't touch my wrinkles (that poreless, smoothed plastic skin just looks freaky to me), my crooked teeth or any of my features because I would be embarrassed not to look like myself when people meet me in real life. Elsewhere I am a witch with removing things from the background of my images – cables, cigarette butts and green wheelie bins are my pet peeves and I have Photoshopped them out of lots of my pictures. I also really know how to take a flattering shot and generally choose the image that makes me look tallest and slimmest (I'm 5ft 3in/160cm). I don't obsess about the way my face looks (that doesn't mean I don't notice the flaws) but I wouldn't post a picture that I thought made me look squat.

The sum of all of this is that my pictures are probably about 90 per cent real and about 10 per cent "fake", but certainly 100 per cent the best that I can look. As an educated woman, a feminist and someone who considers the impact of my actions on others, it's worth questioning why I always want to project "acceptable" images of myself. Aside from the obvious answer of vanity – I wouldn't frame an unflattering photo and put it on my mantelpiece at home, so why should I do it online? – it's a mixture of different reasons. Firstly, if I posted entirely unfiltered, un-lightened, images, which were taken in one shot rather than the 50 or so I usually pick from, I probably wouldn't have built the same following on social media. The images would have looked grey, depressing and entirely uninspiring. Since I run a business which values the numbers of my audience, it's important to me that my images have appeal. Secondly, I don't think we have to rehash the argument that a feminist can wear lipstick and expensive shoes and still believe in equal pay, treatment and opportunity. I've worked as a fashion editor; I know the power and confidence that distinctive clothing can give you, and I'm entirely unashamed of showcasing that. Making an effort with my presentation is largely for me a question of self-respect and investment in myself. Images where I look put together and well dressed make me feel a sense of pride, whereas a picture of me in a sloppy tracksuit and unwashed hair would make me feel the reverse. It feels good to look good and I enjoy the theatre of putting a killer outfit together, even if I'm just at home on my own. And, finally, there is the right to artistic licence. The creativity in making a beautiful image with interesting clothes and considered make-up is arguably a case of self-expression.

The one area which I still tussle with is the way I choose to project my own body image. My desire to pick only images in which I look slimmest is definitely a product of social conditioning and deeply ingrained beliefs around what makes something or someone beautiful. Trying to leave these fixations behind is an uphill struggle – a challenge I wonder if I'll ever overcome. Perhaps not, but it's definitely a work in progress.

Of course, it could easily be claimed that what I'm doing, even at this low level of image manipulation, is helping fan those deceitful flames. If the tools are available on our chosen platforms (the in-app Snapchat filters have the power to make this 34-year-old woman look *literally* 12), by using them are we contributing to the problem?

Ultimately if the pictures look better than we do in real life, then we can't say we're not complicit in creating these unrealistic standards that are damaging the way women feel about themselves.

Walking the social media tightrope

So, how do you find the happy medium between representing yourself in a way that doesn't harm your prospects and ensuring you keep away from the darkest sides of digital deception? Where is that line? If a filter or enhanced lighting is fine, why isn't the injection of a pretty sunset in the window? Should doctored images come with a warning disclaimer? Or instead, is it about educating ourselves to doubt *everything* we see? Everyone can agree that wholesale misrepresentations of who you are, how you live and how you look don't do anyone favours. Although it is possible to fake your home, your job, your social life and your friends on social media, doing so not only raises the bar for everyone else but also makes you believe that your true life isn't good enough.

However, let's be real: most people aren't going to voluntarily start posting pictures they hate of themselves. While there is an increasingly vocal "real beauty" movement on social media, with women rebelling every day against aesthetic conformity, and burgeoning communities of posters who either for political or artistic reasons adamantly refuse to tweak any of their visuals, it isn't even close to the majority. Recommending total social media honesty is largely going to fall on deaf ears because our capitalist societies still lionize youth, slimness and financial success, and it's hugely difficult to escape that conditioning. However, surely there has to be a midway point that we can all sign up to – somewhere between still recognizing yourself and your life and endless pictures of grey skies, massive zits and green wheelie bins? And don't the social media companies who created the filters in the first place have to be part of finding that solution, rather than feeding young, impressionable minds more and more tools of mass fakery, mass perfection and identikit idealism?

How to Scroll to a Better Future

In this book I'll be exploring these difficult questions and more, and will look to carve out a new path for a healthy and beneficial relationship with social media. One where we are in the driving seat, controlling our intake and uptake of these digital platforms so they work for us, rather than being taken along for the bumpy ride. Over the course of the book I will examine several key areas of modern womanhood – identity, body image, health, relationships, motherhood, career and money, and politics – and will look at exactly how social media has impacted and penetrated each. There will be common themes throughout, but each topic will have its own specific approach, and I will provide useful takeaways at the end of each chapter to help you manage your own social media diet within that context. It's definitely not about absolutes or extremes. Social media is here to stay, as are our phones, and while "off-gridding" for a certain amount of time is gaining popularity, for most of us it's really a matter of conscious, mindful consumption rather than the unthinking binges many of us have become prone to.

The digital age has been the architect of a distinct crisis in self-worth among women. Everything looks so rosy through a social media lens, and the platforms which we're glued to have been fine-tuned to appeal to our natural desire to be accepted, admired and loved. But these worlds we're creating and consuming aren't ones which always serve our best interests – and through our addiction to them we've lost the ability to recognize that. The apps are just too entertaining, too exciting and too compelling for us to realize what they're doing to us. The tendency to compare and despair, the acceptance of inauthenticity, and the way our content can shape our real-life existence are just some of the ways that social media is redefining what it means to be a woman in the 21st century. But really, that's just the tip of the iceberg.

Chapter 1:
Why Social Media is
Ruining Your **Identity**

Who are you? What is it that defines you? Is it where you come from, or where you're going? Your parents or your music taste? Are you still trying to figure it out?

If so, don't sweat it, because social media is changing the landscape and nearly *everyone* is going through an identity crisis. Guiding how we see ourselves, and to an extent how others view us too, our identity can be shaped by nationality, social class, ethnicity, age, sexuality, wealth and gender, as well as differences ranging from political alignment to taste in books to breakfast food preference. Like a map of your experiences, these are the markers which make you "you".

Whether you're an emo avocado-toast lover or plus-size rainbow-hair aficionado, "who you are" truly matters in the digital context. Not only do we actively carve our identity, through finding communities of like-minded people and choosing to project a "personal brand" for others to judge us on, but we are also being surreptitiously categorized, as nearly every online action we take leaves a trail of "identity markers". Due to the way that the internet and social media sites are monetized, these markers or cookies inform Google, Facebook et al., what kind of content you might be interested in. From what you buy on Amazon, to the *New Yorker* article you commented on last night, to that puppy picture you sent to your sister, your on-screen actions help define your digital identity and therefore dictate the images, ads, entertainment and news which then stalk you around the internet. So the identity you formulate online actually becomes your personal key into this matrix.

To put it simply, in real life you walk down the street and consume a breadth of information geared to all kinds of people. Online, your identity is reduced by a combination of clicks and you only see things aimed at "people like you". Don't think you have a digital identity? Think again.

The Whole World's a Stage

Your digital self is your 21st-century calling card. In an age when more people own a mobile phone than a toothbrush, managing your online identity – and thus reputation – is hardly a niche activity. Whether you're updating your CV on LinkedIn or un-tagging unflattering pictures posted on Facebook, we're all making – often daily – decisions about how we want to project ourselves. In the same way we worry about looking "good on paper", we want to look good on screen too. On the whole, we emphasize our abilities, downplay anything which could cast aspersions on our character, and try at all costs to project an image of success. For example, my LinkedIn page doesn't mention that my last magazine job contract was reduced from full time to three days a week and my dating profiles definitely keep schtum about my divorce. It's all about selective disclosure.

Inspired by Erving Goffman's *The Presentation of Self in Everyday Life*, the idea that the internet is a stage and we are all in a sense performing on it has become a popular analogy. Goffman originally argued back in 1959 that our public life represents the "front stage" – a world where everyone is watching and impressions matter – but that there's also a "backstage" sanctuary where "the performer can relax; he can drop his front and step out of character." The all-seeing, all-knowing, 24/7 world of social media has ramped up the sheer volume of public information that we're all sharing, and the culture of Periscope, Instagram Stories and Snapchat, which encourage a near-live streamed existence, have significantly upped our "on stage" time. Messages and comments that are shared online are often public by default and are in a sense "on the record" – so even as we build relationships online we can never let our guard down. Today our "front stage", idealized personas are becoming more and more how we define ourselves. As our ability to maintain this supercharged good impression layer is fast-evolving, we have less and less time with the off-duty "backstage" side of ourselves.

Aside from being exhausting, keeping the show constantly on the road has proven to have a huge impact not only on *our* minds, but on our friends' as well. A 2013 paper coined a process known as the *self-promotion–envy spiral*. Triggered by a range of positive content uploaded by our friends, we end up using "even greater self-promotion and impression management" in reaction, to help cope with our feelings of envy. Basically, rampant sharing of positive information about our own lives and identities causes our friends to up the ante with their own posts, until we all feel under pressure to project a more and more impressive version of "who we are". "Of the seven deadly sins, only envy is no fun at all," said American writer Joseph Epstein, and anyone who spends their time scrolling through their friends' and acquaintances' happiness highlight reels will certainly, at some point, concur. Yes, you can feel happy for other people's success, but that doesn't mean you can't also feel slightly (and even sometimes deeply) bitter too.

Over the past eight years, Andrew Oswald, a professor of economics and behaviour at the University of Warwick, has been studying the power that envy has over our happiness, curious to find out if the new institutions of social media ("that make people feel inadequate and envious of others") are having an impact on our overall wellbeing. His findings: higher levels of envy lead to greater mental-health problems and have no power to motivate or lead to greater levels of financial success in the future. In summary, our increasingly impressive online identities equal bad news for our friends.

The process of presenting ever more admirable information online in turn leads to a temptation to misrepresent our lives. Tweaking the truth to present a slightly better version of who we are is something we consciously and subconsciously do offline too – who hasn't slightly exaggerated their job role at a party or glossed over the finer details of their relationship status when put on the spot by their family over the holidays? In the digital realm, however, the lines between harmless hyperbole and self-delusion are far easier to cross. IRL (in real life), there are limits to what we can make of ourselves, but online you can go waaaay further with self-invention: hello, catfish; hello, Facetune. Even if we don't go the whole hog, we're probably embellishing.

Camille Charrière, a French fashion blogger and podcast host, describes how she reinvented herself when she constructed her digital identity. "My fashion taste was not something I was raised or born with. Fashion wasn't a part of my upbringing at all. I read a comment on Reddit the other day which said, 'I just found out that someone I used to go to school with now has 600k followers on Instagram – just goes to show you shouldn't make fun of awkward, ginger weirdos.' The post was about me. Growing up I was a long way from being an it-kid. I really was not that girl in secondary school or even in university. When I set up my blog I basically decided to invent a new digital persona which was very different from the geeky real-life version."

There's little doubt that we are buying into these newly created digital selves, whether they're grounded in real life or not, and often embracing them wholesale. Chronic comparison anxieties generated by the ubiquity of social media imagery have come to define the lives of many women across all generations. Decisions we make about the ways in which we project our identities on social media are at the nub of this process, so the relationship between who we are online and who we are at home is in a sense political as well as personal. We all contribute to the community, and as such everyone has at least a small responsibility to define the rules of the game. As Professor Nicole Ellison, of the School of Information at the University of Michigan, explains, "When you're thinking of your own messy identity and you're comparing it to this very curated and to some extent fabricated version of what someone else's life is like, it's not a like-for-like measure." If half of us are exaggerating our wealth, success, happiness and achievements, the other half are left floundering and wondering what's gone wrong in their lives. Obviously, the answer is nothing; it's all just a question of presentation.

The Happiness Homogeneity

One of the biggest issues is that we aren't being open enough about the fact that social media is indeed a game – one where we play with ideas about our sense of self. While most people are aware, at least conceptually, that our digital identities aren't identical to our everyday realities, there is a disconnect. Many people have suggested this is down to the visual nature of many social media sites. Instagram and Snapchat have been found to be the most damaging platforms among 14–25 year olds, in terms of their impact on health and wellbeing issues such as anxiety, depression and self-identity, and this is said to be due to their image-focus. We all know the phrase "a picture speaks a thousand words", but there's rigorous scientific backup to prove that our brains process information gleaned from visuals in a different way to that from words. Back in the 1960s and 1970s, Allan Paivio developed "dual coding theory", which suggests we have two distinct cognitive processes – verbal and visual. He claimed that images have an advantage over text as they generate both verbal *and* image codes in our brains, meaning we are more likely to remember them and form more meaningful associations. By the 1980s, influential market researchers Terry Childers and Michael Houston had discovered that image-based advertisements required less exposure than verbal ads to resonate with the public, proving once again that we're more likely to take on board messages which we've consumed visually.

Even though we can write and talk about how much these images are embroidered, our minds still find it easy to recognize, and then internalize, what we see. Familiarity with certain visual cues also stimulates faster recognition, meaning the emotions that these images can generate have an increased potency.

This might go some way to explaining why social media "clichés" and trends like sliced avocado on toast or identical tourist shots continue to receive such high engagement – we like them, because we already know them. Whereas once avocado was just a fruit, now it automatically symbolizes status, relevance and consumerism, things that many of us aspire to. We've become so used to viewing images that we recognize and desire – identikit smiling shots of time-worn moments which overwhelmingly project the most positive sides of our identities. The more we see them, the more we believe them.

Our depictions of travel on social media have become an area in which homogeneity – or a relentless sameness – has started to be seriously discussed. Travel in the digital context is an important identity marker, especially for young people. Keen to display their worldly and curious characters, prove that they are wealthy enough to globetrot and affiliate themselves to the aspirational lifestyles they see their social media heroes living (some of whom appear to be in a constant state of motion around the globe), for millennials especially, travel has become about much more than a two-week summer break. When many won't be able to afford to buy their own home until they're in their sixties, travel becomes a far more tangible life goal to invest their savings in.

Importantly, where you choose to tour in a sense defines the kind of person you are. Whether it's a five-day circuit of Santorini's swanky infinity pools, a road trip to hipster-looking lake houses in upstate New York or a pilgrimage to the waterfalls of Bali, your spot on the social media trail reveals your tastes and says a lot about what you're trying to project from a personal brand point of view. Indeed, in 2017 a UK home insurance survey found that the "Instagrammability" of a destination was the primary booking motivator for 18–33 year olds – well ahead of cost and personal development.

The problem is that all the pictures have become identical: iconic tourist destination in the background, woman with her back to the camera wearing a cute dress from Réalisation or Reformation, clutching at a straw hat. When you travel to any picturesque spot in the world today you encounter lines of young women trying to recreate the same images. Even if you've never been to Italy, you've seen that picture before; *you know it, so you'd probably like it.*

"I often find myself feeling sick to my stomach when I have to post a new picture," Sara Melotti, an Italian travel photographer and blogger with over 40k followers on Instagram, explained to me. "In my field, you quickly realize that everyone's content is basically exactly the same. What people do is research which images have generated the most likes in the past and then they'll recreate a duplicate shot for their own feed. They don't care about travelling as an experience, they just want the picture to show everyone where they've been and make sure they get enough likes to feed the social media algorithms. Every time I post a picture of something a bit more unusual – but still beautiful – it doesn't get anywhere near the same engagement. It's depressing that it's only the images that people recognize that get the likes, and if you want to build your numbers, that's what you have to post. Creating this kind of soulless content doesn't just make you feel bad – it can completely destroy your self-esteem and sense of who you are."

Instead of diversity and originality, what the majority of people on social media appear to want is more of the same. Conformity is rewarded by both the community and the system – what we "like" most drives the algorithms, which in turn feed us more indistinguishable content which we happily consume. The general, appeal-to-all, lowest-common-denominator visuals are making our world view increasingly bland, and while there are other vantage points to be found – including all kinds of amazing rebellious and subcultural content – you have to actively seek them out. And it's not just travel, it's all aspects of how we express ourselves: décor, weddings, how we dress, the art we like, the food we eat, even our politics.

Social media has become an echo chamber of mainstream and predictable content through a process which has been described as the "memeification of human experience". For older users who have seen the world through different lenses, it's easy to dismiss the social media window as just one take on the world. When you're a teenager who spends every possible waking minute scrolling, the understanding of what exists outside these limited trends is increasingly lacking. The impact this can have on identity formation is obvious: expectations, benchmarks and important signifiers of individual identity are being channelled through a very narrow funnel.

Happiness and fulfilment also feature heavily in this funnelled vision. While not a traditional identity marker, in the same way as, say, sexuality or ethnic background, being identified as happy is one of social media's ultimate status symbols. Conversely, admitting struggles with contentment can lead to different character labels spanning "authentic" (to fans) to "difficult", "attention-seeking" and "unstable" (to trolls and, worryingly, life insurers). Happiness is something that nearly everyone wants to project, whether they feel it or not. The "smiling depressive", described as a person whose inner turmoil is masked by outer cheerfulness, has found a new platform to display a "winning at life" front. Nearly 20 per cent of two thousand women surveyed in a US mental illness report said the stigma they felt about their depression or anxiety had led them to share a photo on social media for which the caption didn't match what they felt inside. The procession of bright smiles, #blessed captions and blissful family shots are pretty much the exact opposite of what you see staring back at you on your Monday morning commute. But it's easy to believe that everyone else is joyful when you spend too much time scrolling and forget that another, somewhat bleaker, real-life context exists. Happiness is not a medal to be showcased; it ebbs and flows, and no-one can keep hold of it 100 per cent of the time. The fact that social media obscures this and treats happiness as if it's part of our personal brand is wildly misleading and sets a dangerous yardstick for those still seeking to discover who they are.

Multiple Identities in the Digital Era

Over the course of writing this book, I've spoken to scores of women who make their living from creating curated images and have heard countless accounts saying that *they too* find it difficult to take social media images with a pinch of salt. Lauren Alexander, LA-based fashion designer and co-founder of casualwear brand LNA, explains: "I know a huge proportion of images that I consume aren't real – I work in the business and I know how much gets retouched, edited and even Facetuned before it makes it on to social. But even though I know that, it's still difficult to remind yourself that those images you are comparing yourself to don't actually exist. It's like you know and don't know at the same time."

Questions around fakery are a huge theme of our zeitgeist, and how they affect our identities is intimately wrapped into the contemporary crisis of trust. As Sara Melotti expands, "The way my life looks on Instagram is not even a close approximation of my real life. It's the same for every other travel blogger too. As a photographer, I know what goes on behind the lens and I know that those pictures take hours to set up. They're planned, staged and not a reflection of anyone's holiday. We *make* these images. None of them are spontaneous shots of my real life. I'm creating them for art and I want to make things pretty. But that doesn't mean everything in my life is pretty – far from that. I know a lot of people are so clueless about what's behind a picture or how the whole social media industry works. A normal person is very vulnerable and it can be a dangerous space for them to be psychologically. When I wrote a post on my blog talking honestly about my experiences, I received something crazy like three thousand messages from my followers. Most of them said, 'I don't feel OK,' or 'I feel like shit.' 'When I open Instagram I want to cry.' There's a reason behind that."

One thing that's worth considering is the idea that these online personas are no less "real" than our offline selves. When discussing the difference between the on- and offline identity with Professor Nicole Ellison she raised a pertinent point: "The phrase 'in real life' always bothers me because the insinuation is that there is this authentic face-to-face embodied reality and then anything that happens through mediated channels is somehow fake or deceptive or un-connected to our offline self. The online realm is not a separate sphere of activity in the 'virtual' world, as distinct from the 'real' one. Rather, online activities are as 'real' as those that take place offline (face-to-face). After all it's a person sitting at the computer typing; it's not a robot."

This idea has plenty of research support. There are studies which prove we're unable to hide our personalities online in the long run, that extroverted or introverted tendencies can be determined from our Facebook likes, and emotional stability can be inferred from our tweets. Whether on- or offline, we can't entirely hide from who we are. As Tomas Chamorro-Premuzic, professor of business psychology at University College London and Columbia University, and an authority in psychological profiling, wrote in the *Guardian*, "Although our digital identity may be fragmented, it seems clear that our various online personas are all digital breadcrumbs of the same persona; different symptoms of our same core self."

When it comes to living multiple realities and struggling to locate this "core self", I can certainly relate. My twenties were a process of coming to terms with my current identity, which has really ended up being an amalgam of all the different versions of myself – a sum of constituent parts. It was also a time for shedding shame and embarrassment about where I'd come from and where I'd been in between. Like lots of upwardly mobile people, I've had my fair share of identities over the course of my 34 years. As a teenager living in suburban south-east London, I was constantly trying on tribal identities, desperate to find one that fitted. By the turn of the millennium, I was firmly part of the garage music scene, dressed every Friday in skin-tight jeans by Moschino, sparkly going-out tops and loafers with no socks. I could not wear enough gold, use enough gel in my fringe or make my acrylic French tips any squarer. My accent was heavily accented estuary and the guys I liked were all "bad boys done good". From a cultural and aesthetic perspective, my identity was firmly working class and very much related to my childhood and teenage experiences within my family context.

University changed all that almost immediately. A large part of it was because I was ready to shed my suburban skin and become a new version of myself. I definitely didn't want the same life as my contemporaries back home and in that vein quickly realized that certain social airs and graces would help me get closer to what I wanted in life. My accent changed. I was basically a mid-2000s Eliza Doolittle and I worked tirelessly and consciously to develop a new identity for myself. Whereas social mobility is seen as a positive – something politicians write lengthy manifestos about promoting – the idea of leaving your roots behind and trying to climb to the next rung of opportunity is conversely seen as something shameful and inauthentic. While we like to preach the idea that you can "be anything you want to be" in our real lives, the truth is that there is a social stigma attached to self-invention as if it's a con.

There's no doubt that along with my new identity came a fear of being found out. Of course, there was no digital trail in 2002 to point to my true beginnings and no online shots of all that gold jewellery I used to wear to suggest my previous identity. No-one really ever "found out" about where I grew up or what my family was like. As far as anyone I met in my new circle knew, I came from the same background as them and I was keen for them to continue to think that. I was definitely conflicted about the modesty of where I came from, mostly because at the time I felt it would close off the route to a future I aspired to. So, I exaggerated my skiing abilities and hid broad elements of my "true" identity from the rest of the world. It was, of course, a phase and, as I matured, several other versions of who I am were thrown into the mix. But ultimately, I truly believe there is nothing wrong with playing slightly loose and free with your personal history, especially when you are a young person incubating your adult sense of self – a little bit of creativity is totally normal rather than calculated or "fake".

Curating Yourself into Anxiety

Aside from the tensions in trying to conceal the trickier elements of our lives, there are other potential problems when you're not projecting your "offline self" online. For some, the differences between their "lived" life and their perceived life start to undermine their grasp on reality, leading, for example, to huge overspending to keep up the façade. For others, a perceived shortfall in the offline self in comparison to the online version can unravel their self-esteem: six in ten girls now say they feel prettier online than they do offline. I'd argue this is because they're so deeply involved with their digital projection that they've lost track of what *is* performance and what is *not*.

When you invent your own narrative, the issue of exposure also becomes an understandable anxiety and this is the case online as it is in offline life. Of all generations, millennials are those most likely to have feelings associated with inadequacy, and 70 per cent are said to display traits of what is known as impostor syndrome (the persistent feeling that you don't deserve your achievements or success). One of the reasons attributed to this prevalence is social media comparison; in a 2014 poll conducted by the UK disability charity Scope, 62 per cent of participants said that social media made them feel inadequate about their own lives and achievements. But these feelings of fraudulence are also being caused by the projections of our own relentless perfectionism. Comparing your offline self to the online self you've created has added yet another layer to self-critique, leading to what can only be described as "self-curation anxiety". This is a type of disquiet generated by attempts to live up to the edited version of ourselves we project online.

Professor Nicole Ellison notes, "When individuals ignore their face-to-face environment or community and pour all of their energies into ersatz, fake connections it can be problematic for their identity construction. And if, for instance, they feel like their online self is not authentic, it can also be deeply distressing." A blogger who asked to remain anonymous told me that scrolling through her feed made her feel deep feelings of worry because all she could see was the pretence; her "mediocre and uninteresting" offline life was so far away from what it seemed on social media that she felt constantly ill at ease whenever she posted in case someone "found her out".

As vast numbers of people are opening themselves up to unprecedented levels of public scrutiny, that "unmasking" can come from several corners of the web. "Calling out" people online has become a whole culture in itself. From comments boxes to internet forums, entire communities exist online to keep us in our place and reveal what we are "really" like.

"YouTube audiences are incredibly engaged and perceptive, but a lot of what people say about you and assume isn't accurate at all," explains Lizzy Hadfield, a British blogger and vlogger with over 190k followers on Instagram and over 110k subscribers on the video sharing site. "Of course, it's only natural to speculate, but it's definitely strange reading other people's ideas about your identity. As an example, I recently addressed a comment which accused me of having my lips 'done'. The comment accused me of lying to my audience and basically said that I wasn't a trustworthy person – and that really got to me because that's an important part of my identity. The idea that other people might think I was a liar made me feel really paranoid. When you read forums like Guru Gossip [a site for fans and haters to celebrate or take down YouTube stars] and see all these comments about who you 'really' are, it can be so hard not to respond when something has been said that's way off the mark. The truth is that you're allowed to create whatever persona you want online – there's no law about being a carbon copy of your offline self. When it comes to YouTube, the viewer is always two steps removed, in the sense the camera is the first removal then you have the editing process. There is so much that can be changed and altered about the way you want to present yourself, so people have to realize they don't actually know everything about you."

Cynthia Johnson, a personal branding specialist, says that it's virtually impossible to reflect an entirely accurate version of yourself online. "In the digital age, we have to consider the technology that can lead to miscommunication and misunderstanding about who we are and what we want". Feeling anxiety around other people's perceptions of us is entirely understandable, but more often than not it's something that is out of our control. And that's worth keeping in mind, whether you're on- or offline.

You Don't Own Me: The Evolution of Identity Perception

The idea of "familiar strangers" – people within your community who feel they have a claim to you, or that they know you *even when you haven't met* – was first introduced by American social psychologist Stanley Milgram in 1972. Back when he was writing, the concept was tied to the people that you regularly share a physical space with – your daily commuter train, for example. You wouldn't call them acquaintances, but if you ran into them out of context you'd feel a quasi connection and a sense of who they were. Today, his theory has been applied to the digital realm, with Theresa Senft, senior lecturer in social media at Macquarie University in Sydney, describing a related "strange familiarity" among those who have shared a *digital* space arising from "exchanging private information with people from whom we are otherwise remote". She suggests that social media connections with people we don't know offline, "rework the old question 'Who am I?' to read 'Who do you think I am?' Identity, once believed to be the property of the bearer, now belongs to the perceiver." Basically, other people who have consumed your identity in a public digital space feel a sense of ownership over who you are. They believe that they know you inherently and are both elated when their assessment of you rings true and deflated when you behave in a way they didn't expect. By performing for them you can also give up a sense of responsibility for who you are, instead leaning on a model of how others see you. This is our generation's version of living for your family's expectations rather than your true desires.

For me, personally, the early evolution of my identity didn't really happen on social media – sure, you can scroll back through my

Facebook, but by the time I'd signed up, I was in my final year of university and had tussled with lots of my demons. While the photos from my teens and early twenties might be a bit embarrassing, none of them have had any bearing on how people see me today or could be used to prove who I "really am". No-one can stalk my accounts and accuse me of having "changed" (as if that's a bad thing). Now I have the maturity and self-confidence to feel incredibly proud of where I come from and have no shame in the steps it took me to get from there to here. The fact that my parents grew up in council houses and that I'm the first of my family to go to university is something I wear on my sleeve, and the experiences and friends I've made through my different identity phases have enriched my life and created a truly eccentric circle of people from all walks.

It's easy to say that from this side of the journey, and I don't doubt that some of the doors that were opened to me might have stayed closed if I'd been less opaque about my background and identity at different stages of my social and working life. And there have been blips. For most of my twenties, my identity was wrapped up in my life with my ex-husband, and rebuilding who I was after our divorce was tricky. In some ways, I find it hard to identify with the young girl I was back then, and it does sometimes feel like it was a totally different person who walked down the aisle and struggled through an unhappy marriage. However, in lots of ways the early setbacks have enabled me to rebuild my identity as an adult, free from the misdemeanours of my youth.

Living with someone or being in a circle of people who have known you since you were an adolescent can hold you back from continuing to develop your identity. Everyone has friends who want to remind them of things they said or did back in the day. In a similar way, acting as an open record of our past identities, social media binds us to the previous incarnations of our former selves. Whereas once a battered photo album or yearbook would have been the only proof of who we once were, now the whole world can back-stalk and pass judgement on our "true" nature with a simple scroll of the thumb.

Ultimately, we are all products of our pasts, presents and futures, and our identities combine both our roots and aspirations. Very few of us are facsimiles of our parents and many of us want the ability to construct our own sense of self, liberated from the people we used to be and know. That process is something which happens throughout our lives. Indeed, Harvard psychologist Daniel Gilbert has gone so far as to suggest, in his 2014 TED Talk, that "human beings are works in progress that mistakenly think they're finished", and that our "who we are" is much more fluid than we could ever guess. Identity, in his reading, isn't a fixed point, but an ever-changing concept, which we tinker and tailor over our lifetimes. I'm lucky that my identity growing pains have had no lasting impact on how authentic I'm perceived to be, but children and young adults no longer have that luxury. Looking back, I just didn't know who I was yet in my twenties – for the majority of us it takes years of experimentation and introspection to come to any solid conclusions on our own identities, and that is a process we should all have the right to go through without others' perceptions muddying the waters.

LA-based blogger and influencer Courtney Trop is known for her originality, but she found the journey to self-expression on social media fraught with challenges: "When you change on social media people have a hard time accepting it, because they fell in love with you at one point – or who they thought you were – so they feel a sense that they can count on you to be the same. If something shifts, it's like they are almost offended by it, as if there's a sense of betrayal. For example, whenever I change my hair some of my followers freak out and I get people saying that they wish I would keep it the same or that they preferred who I was or how I looked before. From a social media perspective, if you change your identity you have to accept that you may lose some of your audience who no longer identify with you – that's the price you pay for being yourself. But the alternative is just doing what your followers want to see, which is basically living your life for other people. The idea that you can be consistent to one identity is crazy, and kids growing up now – even the ones with huge followings –

are going to change. Yes, with the internet things are there forever, but they shouldn't have to define you. The sad thing is that for some people it's hard to see past your past."

We all have reputations – within our industries or social spheres – whether we like it or not. What makes a personal brand different is the conscious projection and positive manipulation of our skills and achievements and the focus on consistency and repetition. The problem with commodifying your identity is that "personal brands" are subject to all the rules that normal brands are. Authenticity is established through consistent and reliable values; a flip-flop in attitude or aesthetic will lose audience trust and affection. When we construct a social media persona or brand, to be recognized as authentic means creating a very clear and unwavering USP. You're either a hippy, beachy girl with a penchant for vegan treats or a fitness fan with a proclivity for sharing gym gear. If you've built a personal brand on wellness then start posting about KFC, people won't believe in you. If we all only have this 15 minutes of fame, we can't be confused about what we stand for or how an audience perceives us.

Offline life, however, is consistently inconsistent and throws us curveballs along the way. Whether it's something negative or positive, your reality can change on a heel spin, and so can elements of your identity. You can fall pregnant or experience a change in financial circumstances. You might change religion or sexuality, split from a stable family unit or simply alter your hair colour. All these things could be seen to change your identity and your personal brand, and if that suggests inauthenticity to those who know or follow you, that's something that can "damage" both your digital reputation and your brand equity. The desire to be authentic yet appeal to as many people as possible seems to be inherently contradictory, and the pressure that "personal branding" is putting us all under is sure to shape identity construction over the next decade. As Cynthia Johnson rightly argues, "You cannot spend every day trying to be authentic. Trying to be authentic will push you to lose your authenticity, and your mind. Brands strive to be more like people and not the other way around. My advice is don't try to be a brand, because every person is already better than the best brand out there."

Incubating Identity:
How Social Media Can Foster Self-Expression

It would be remiss not to mention the ways in which social media can play a positive role in identity formation. The relative ease with which marginal groups can connect in comparison to the offline context has to be one of the digital world's biggest selling points. As Nicole Ellison says, "There's a clear case to be made for social media in terms of supporting young people doing identity work. A good example would be an adolescent struggling with coming to terms with their sexual orientation living in a small town with no-one to talk to. The fact that they can go online and access people who share elements of that identity and get questions answered has huge potential to be positive for identity construction. The ability to express an aspect of the self which may feel very important and fundamental to a person's identity but isn't able to be expressed in a face-to-face environment is a game-changer." There's no doubt that social media, and indeed the internet, has forged new bonds of subcultural and minority-culture belonging, bringing people from disparate backgrounds together and offering a sense of hope and understanding for those in a normative cultural environment.

The key to finding confidence in your identity through social media is all about vulnerability, as blogger Freddie Harrel explains. "When I started out, I wasn't immediately so honest and upfront about who I was. At the beginning, I shared less of my personal life and career, but this platform has encouraged me to speak up more about my personal experiences. It's very easy to let Instagram turn [your identity] into something which works against you. If you display a life or identity that isn't your own – that you're always happy and you have everything you could ever want – then you have to be able to maintain that. Obviously because you are human and have a normal life and have your mental health to look after, it's nearly impossible to keep up the lie and it's definitely not good for you. But by showing my vulnerability, I've found like-minded people who are going through the same things as me and their support has changed my life and how I feel about myself. If you are able to face your insecurities and your lows and your struggles, face them head-on and not feel ashamed by them; that's how you become stronger and more confident and truly start to find out who you are."

Research proves that having a high level of comfort with our weaknesses is fundamental to our happiness, yet in many ways social media can encourage a culture of invulnerability. Stepping outside that appears to be paramount in accessing the positive aspects these platforms can offer.

✖ ✖ ✖

Social media can offer a place to articulate who it is you want to be, and that should never be underestimated. But walking the new tightrope of digital identity can also lead to the creation of an online persona which highlights the mundane mediocrity of your everyday. As voyeurs into a realm of best-life scenarios, who doesn't feel that they need to focus on their best angles? The conclusion I hope we can all soon come to is that social media is not the place to go for a 360-degree insight into anyone's life. Struggling with how you define yourself on the new media platforms is something that everyone is grappling with, and worrying about how you are perceived digitally is part of the 21st-century human condition. Who you are is one of life's great questions, and no matter how many self-help books you may have read, the journey to that "core" self is a universal challenge in any and every environment.

Takeaways

1. You can never fully control people's perceptions of you
However aware and careful you are with what you share online, and however well-managed your digital portfolio might be, you can never

stop people forming their own opinions on your identity. Each and every single one of us has a unique lens on to the world, coloured by our personal experiences. Individuals have prejudices fostered over decades, and their attitudes to elements of your makeup often say more about them than you. We know that you cannot please everyone and we've heard that it's impossible to judge unless you've walked in another woman's shoes – but it can be hard to accept that no matter what you do and how you behave, people might form an inaccurate impression of you. This is as true in life as it is online, but the difference in the digital world is that your identity is up for public scrutiny.

Criticism in any form can be hard to take. When it seems entirely unjustified and it's coming from someone who has never met you, it can be even trickier. In the online environment, the key to dealing with judgement starts with separating the constructive from the plain mean. If someone replied to one of your Facebook posts touching on your identity with a thoughtful disagreement complete with considered merits, give it the time of day. If instead you get a barrage of criticism or messages which reveal discriminatory attitudes, ignore them. Either delete or disregard unconstructive criticism, because engaging with aggression will only fan the flames. Make sure you always respond to positive feedback and put the negativity into context – if you've received countless supportive messages, focus entirely on those.

2. Don't let your digital persona overwhelm you

How close is your online identity to your offline identity? Are you merely tinkering with the digital version of your life, or is it pure fiction? Take a long, calm look at what you are curating online and be honest with yourself. Does it feel like hard work to keep up the pretence? Does posting on social media make you feel stressed and under pressure to perform? Do you constantly feel like you have to emphasize some elements of your identity and hide others? Of course, there are benefits in being aware of your digital reputation and identity, but if maintaining a façade is coming at the expense of your mental health it's time to re-address what you are posting.

By all means share what you are passionate about and content that you can relate to. And it's worth reiterating there are no laws against the world you curate online. But if you look at your digital profile and have trouble connecting it with your real life, or, worse, prefer who you are online, this could be adversely impacting your happiness.

So, take time to consider what makes you feel discontented with your current life and identity and try to discover exactly what it is about the online version of you that is so appealing. That is your starting point for potential changes you need to make to your life in order to get to a place where you feel more fulfilled. If you have exaggerated your financial status, your qualifications or interest in certain areas, what can you do to square the circle between the "truth" and the projected reality? Perhaps look into taking a course which could bolster your diploma count or join an offline group to explore your interest. Does an over-emphasized image of your working life actually suggest that you're unhappy in your role and that it might be time to look for the next step? All of these idealized identities that we have created online are a useful window into our aspirations and can often give us pointers to our true goals.

However, if you do feel anxiety about the world you have created, remember you can do something about it, simply by being as true to yourself as possible. If you're going through a rocky moment with your other half, don't feel you have to post a smiling selfie of the two of you; if you're struggling with your career, perhaps rein in the #GirlBoss posts. To a certain extent, you are in control of the pressure that you put on yourself in the pursuit of perfection, so do yourself a favour and keep it real.

3. Cut yourself some slack

If you're only sharing the positives of your life and the socially attractive sides of your identity, you have to be aware that so are the vast majority of other people. It can be so hard to consciously consume other people's projections of their identities and very easy, especially when you're being inundated with imagery, which resonates much more deeply than words, to believe everything you see. But just remember how straightforward it was for you to be selective with what *you* shared and remember everyone else is under the same pressures to present the very best versions of themselves.

Consider interspersing your positive spin with occasional more realistic posts and admissions of challenges. Not only will the people who follow you be more likely to appreciate your candour, but having a more balanced profile will avoid anxiety around having to live up to a constructed ideal. Basically, cut yourself some slack. While I'm not suggesting that you use social media as a platform for a meltdown, showing your humanity won't suddenly make you an outcast either.

4. How to change your identity online

If something life-changing has happened and you wish to reflect it in your online persona, you have two choices. Firstly, you can address the shift and share the experiences which have led to your altered identity – a process which would be recommended by personal brand managers, as it conveys authenticity. "It would be naive to think that you could sweep something under the carpet and that your followers – whether they're friends, family or acquaintances – wouldn't notice," says Lizzy Hadfield. "Often if you don't say anything at all, you can promote more speculation and you do have to protect yourself from things like that getting out of hand." She advises, "If you introduce something online, you have to close the door online too. You don't have to share every detail, but you can be very clear about what's happened and then say, 'We're not talking about it again.'"

A second option is to apply Courtney Trop's school of thought: "My whole thing has always been to change and not even address it. You shouldn't feel that you owe anyone an explanation. Some people will hate on it, but you just have to ignore it and be confident with who you are. The people that are meant to come along with you will and the others... There's an unfollow button right there."

Whether you face an identity shift head-on or refuse to comment, you have to acknowledge that people will speculate and those who were naturally drawn to you may no longer be so interested. That is a natural, logical consequence and not something personal that should feel hurtful.

5. Remember you're only human – and that's *your* asset

What we do and say on the internet can last a lifetime and the ways in which we communicate our identities in the digital environment are definitely important. However, mistakes are a part of life and, for anyone actively engaging on a public platform, there will be times when you make a misstep. Protecting your digital identity from those slip-ups is a whole industry in itself, but if you do feel like you've screwed up and you want to clarify your position on something you've said, you can always apologize. Remember that the online world is only one facet of your existence; the offline world is still out there, and no matter what type of reaction you're experiencing in the digital world, it is not the be all and end all.

To avoid making missteps in the first place, aside from thinking before you tweet, it's worth having some kind of idea how *you* feel most comfortable projecting yourself. Rather than focusing on other people's reception to your posts, try to consciously consider if you are happy with your own digital contributions. What are the causes you are really engaged with? What are your personal values? Are you happy with who you are online? It's also worth considering common courtesy, empathy and not being entirely tone deaf to the context. If a close friend has just been made redundant and she shares it online, perhaps don't immediately post your promotion update. Instead reach out to her and see how she's doing – your news won't be any less impressive next week.

Kindness, whether on- or offline, never goes out of fashion.

Chapter 2:
Why Social Media is
Ruining Your **Body Image**

Of all the changes that social media has wrought on modern womanhood, it's the impact on our body image that gets the most press. And little wonder: who hasn't felt the often-daily sting of body inadequacy when scanning feeds chockablock with flawless examples of the female form. The inundation of "perfect" bodies and faces is probably the most prominent issue that any of us using social media has to deal with, and it's often the first issue that women will highlight when describing their social media anxieties. The fact that social media can make you feel bad about how you look is hardly a newsflash – in fact it's just assumed to be part of our new reality. And how could it not be when nearly everyone seems to have the body of a Victoria's Secret model, the wrinkle-free skin of a teenager and the facial features of an A-list leading lady?

In 2015 we uploaded approximately 24 billion selfies to Google's servers. According to recent research, teenage girls in the UK spend on average 84 minutes preparing for selfies every week, and it's estimated that the average millennial will turn their phone camera on themselves over *25,000* times over their lifetime. The impact of consuming and creating these hundreds, thousands, millions of images is only slowly being addressed, but the academic, medical and anecdotal consensus is that we are sitting on a huge health, sociological and psychological time bomb. The sheer scale and volume of images we now view and internalize is fundamentally altering our relationship with our bodies.

Traditional media was previously accused of increasing body image dissatisfaction with its persistent depiction of thin, attractive models –

and it was regularly blamed for the rise in eating disorders. However, the new social platforms have supercharged this situation – we are now so immersed in images of perfection that we have almost no realistic idea what other people look like. And, perhaps even more worrying, we've lost a grip on our own mirror image too.

The use of both in-app tools and Photoshop software to modify our appearance means that the images we upload bear increasingly little resemblance to our actual faces and bodies. How many of your friends do you not really recognize on social media? I'll bet you can list at least a handful who are either a completely different size, or have a different jawline, skin or facial features from the ones you'd find scrolling through their feed. The issue is endemic. When you factor in that it takes less than a second to scroll an image on Instagram and that in five minutes you can consume two to three hundred images, the fact that a good proportion of the pictures featuring a body or face has in some way been edited is obviously going to have an impact on our benchmarks. What we're creating through these images is a pressure cooker of comparison, with unreachable levels of perfection. Is it any surprise that all this self-documentation is sending us into a pit of self-loathing and body-dysmorphic despair?

But for some reason we aren't addressing the issue head-on. Somehow the crisis has become so normalized that, among the girls and women it affects, it's almost a cliché to mention the extent of its bearing – more likely to elicit a reaction of "obviously" than a critical appraisal. Conversely, among older generations, policy makers and those not au fait with these platforms the issue seems overblown. They think it can't really be that bad – after all it's only a few bikini pictures, isn't it? Neither of those vantage points enables us to tackle the very real problems which are having such a profound impact on women across the globe. It is neither normal nor exaggerated. It is in fact one of the biggest contemporary challenges that women in every country that has Wi-Fi are contending with. And it's time we all wake up to it.

You Must Love Yourself to Post That...

There's a common misconception that posting images of yourself – especially body shots and selfies – means you're a show off who thinks you're the shit. However, a slew of recent studies actually proves the opposite is more often the case. A 2017 research paper on the experience of taking and sharing a selfie lays bare the psychological factors at play: the actual act of snapping a selfie has been shown to make us immediately more self-conscious and more aware of how others view us. At the same time, respondents revealed a drop in self-esteem at the very moment of taking the image of themselves. The combination of increased feelings of pressure around how people view you and a process which dents your self-esteem makes for a complex cocktail of emotions far removed from "showing off".

While posting a provocative shot of your cleavage and abs may appear to be the height of vanity, it's often more a reflection of a shaky sense of self-esteem. Elsa Godart, author of *Je Selfie Donc Je Suis* ('I Selfie Therefore I Am'), writes that: "What may look like straight-forward narcissism can often be insecurity and a craving for reassurance: a reassurance that you can only ever get from 'likes'. But you're chasing the dragon, because far from calming any neuroses down (although it may do this for a second), posting another selfie will only amplify them." A narcissism which is about desperately *wanting* to feel good about yourself isn't the same as actually feeling good about yourself. And really isn't that what everyone's searching for when they post a picture of themselves? Isn't that truly the Holy selfie Grail?

Tune It All Out

How far can you really go with retouching your own images these days? The answer is as far as you want – and you don't even have to have any Photoshop skills, or a computer. Today you can do it all on your phone on the go. Up to 57 per cent of women say that they crop, filter or doctor their pictures, and Dr Pippa Hugo, a leading eating disorder consultant at Priory Hospital Roehampton, says as many as nine out of ten teenage girls now digitally enhance social media images of themselves – with filters or specially designed on-phone apps before they share them. With names like Perfect365, Facetune, ModiFace and Visage Lab, these apps can dramatically doctor body and face images, whitening your teeth, slimming your nose, smoothing your cellulite and nipping in your waist until you've created a Barbie-fied version of yourself.

The first time I saw the app Facetune, I thought it was a laugh – the kind of thing you'd play with to turn yourself into a Pokémon character. But I soon realized that it could be insanely dangerous. What could start out as a tweak here and there might soon evolve into a highly skilled operation of skin smoothing, waist trimming and leg lengthening until any average woman is suddenly transformed into a professional model with an Amazonian physique. Over six million people downloaded the first version of the app and it was the fourth highest seller in 2016. Facetune 2 allows you to enlarge or shrink your eyes, nose and mouth and reshape your entire face. You can change the colour of your irises, add studio lighting, while refining your figure in a manner which won't distort the backdrop (often a telltale sign of retouching). It is startling how much "better" you can make yourself look. As for how many people are using it, Facetune 2 costs £32.99/$20 for the year at the time of writing, so no-one's downloading it for a one-off giggle any more. It's an open secret among influencers that nearly *everyone* uses it to some extent, though admittedly some are more subtle and skilful in their use of it than others.

One issue is that the use of these apps is creating unrealistic "memories" of your own face and body. The images stored on your phones never actually happened. You never had thighs that slim or skin that glowing – but it can be easy to start believing that once upon a time you were that "perfect". This leads to a world where young women are holding themselves up to scrutiny not just against the images that other people have edited and posted, but also against the images of *themselves* which they have edited. In this context, it's no wonder that the consumption of these visuals can make women feel overweight and unattractive: the mirror can never compete. "Social media has made us want to look like other people – but those people don't even look like that," influencer and mental health campaigner Roxie Nafousi says. "What we're lusting over is so blurred and edited and, even though we know that to an extent, it can still distort our frame of reference."

The use of these "cosmetic surgery" apps is also creating a "list" of flaws in our physical attributes, and making us all hyperaware of what we feel we could change about our appearance. Lauren Alexander explained to me: "Social media has brought a lot of LA culture to the rest of the world. Here it's completely normalized to want to change your body and your face – we have a phrase, 'you're not ugly, you're just poor.' There is such an emphasis on self-improvement and striving for perfection. Growing up I would never sit around a table with friends and talk about Botox or peels or plastic surgery, and now that's entirely usual. When I first moved here, I remember being asked why I didn't do Botox, have a nutritionist or a personal trainer. Those things were just assumed, and now social media has made the rest of the world feel they need it all too. It's impossible not to wonder: if everyone else is doing it, why aren't I? When you add up the personal trainer, barre-method classes, gym membership, hair appointments, the supplements, Botox, facials and lasers, it becomes a full-time job just to keep up with it all."

Going one step further, Beverly Hills expert in rhinoplasty Dr Deepak Dugar (who was trained by Dr Raj Kanodia, the surgeon known for his work on A-listers, reportedly including Cameron Diaz and Jennifer Aniston) says, "social media has definitely normalized plastic surgery. Before, people used to think, 'Oh, plastic surgery is just for these LA people or London people, but that's not for us.' There was a sense that it was only for an elite. What these new platforms have done is pull back the veil to show that anyone can do it. You can see the pre and post videos and the before and after results on average people – not just celebrities. The entire world, from Russia to the Middle East to Europe and across the States, has seen a shift in accessibility and availability of procedures – simply because social media has made it seem more accessible and available. There's a new sense of democracy."

However, the selfie culture, particularly the use of editing apps, has also led to a worrying trend, Dr Dugar explains. "Apps like Facetune have given an unrealistic expectation of what we want to look like. We've all had times when a friend has taken a photo and we don't like the way we look. The problem is that if you take that to a deep level where you don't like any photo of yourself and you find yourself editing every single picture of yourself, you end up creating unrealistic expectations. And often surgery can't address that. There's no way to 'fix' a face. If you don't like your nose and lips – then I think it can be very healthy to address it, conquer it and move on and feel empowered. But the problem is that social media breeds a situation in which most people don't have a specific issue they can pinpoint – it's generally that they don't like the way they look *overall*. At that point, I truly believe it's unhealthy to be doing any procedures."

If She Can Have It, Why Can't I?

In the case of body image, social comparison certainly plays an important part: a 2014 study for US *Glamour* magazine found that 64 per cent of women said looking at pictures on sites like Facebook and Instagram made them have negative thoughts about their body. Comments from the study include this insight: "With actresses, I know they have a personal chef and trainer and it's their job to have the bodies they do – I don't have any real expectations of looking like them. With people I know, it's like, well, she did it. Why can't I?"

LA clinical psychologist Dr Jessica Zucker explains: "The anonymous woman [on social media] could be anyone, so your expectations change. It's hard not to go straight to 'I wish I looked like her,' or 'what can I do to look like her?' All the self-loathing and hatred this generates could even trigger issues around what someone is eating – or not eating – that day. It can be very complex. On social media, you'll also often find a focus on specific body parts. Women are chopped up in general in the media – and we're all aware that some areas of society only value women as tits and ass. But now it's thigh gaps, clavicles and bikini bridges under the microscope. We typically see images of flawless female body parts tailored to titillate the opposite sex as if they're not full people and we've internalized so many of these ideas. We live in such a patriarchal world, there's no way around the inherent bias. It's almost impossible not to soak up these viewpoints then express them in a way that leads us to survey ourselves and have negative feelings about our bodies."

And this is where the millennial experience is distinct from previous generation's issues around magazine retouching and altering. It is the omnipresence of these seemingly "relatable" images of myopic perfection which defines their consumption.

One of the most challenging aspects of digital body image is that these women with perfect figures that we're aspiring to are women and girls all around us. They go to our gyms, they work in our offices and they date our exes. For millennials, it's the girl next door who has the thigh gap, her BFF's sister who has the washboard abs. It is this systemic peer-to-peer comparison and false sense of reality that makes us feel we're failing if our life doesn't match up to what we see. The closeness which we often feel with our favourite YouTubers and Instagram stars, and the fact that they seem so resolutely "normal" and "just like us", further reiterates the fact that our lives and bodies are lacking in some way. Social media has created an intimate window into the female form, but those that rise to the "top" (gaining the most likes from their communities and thus boosted in feeds by the platform's algorithm architecture) are those that fulfil a popularized, mainstream idea of what a "good body" is. The bombardment of specific body types in the media is nothing new, but the reaffirmation of those often unattainable shapes via social media is more pernicious in its omnipresence than ever before.

Lucy Williams, a London-based blogger, is known for a particular brand of effortless cool with a side of wanderlust. But even as a #BikiniInspo pinup, she feels the pressures of perfection and comparison: "Like everyone else, I am totally impacted by what I consume on social media and I look at those girls on Instagram with minute waists and endless limbs, comparing myself and coming up short – it's impossible not to. There is no such thing as a perfect body, and I am 100 per cent not an owner of one, even if it did exist. The perfect that people usually think of is basically the Photoshop look: no stretchmarks, no cellulite, no rolls. I have rolls on my tummy, I have dimples on my thighs and the more women I hang out with the more I realize that everyone has the same to a certain degree. Confidence doesn't come from the numbers on the scales, it comes from acceptance – and social media can make that hard to find, no matter what your size."

So how deeply does this crisis penetrate? A 2016 study found that out of 1,765 Americans aged 19–32, those who spent more time on social media were 2.2 times more likely to report eating and body-image concerns. Among the most active users, that jumped to 2.6 times more issues. What's more, a study of 960 college women found that even *20 minutes* of scrolling on Facebook was associated with higher levels of disordered eating. Unsurprisingly, it was the women who placed greater importance on receiving comments and "likes" on their status updates and untagged photos of themselves who reported the highest levels of disordered eating.

Claire Mysko, CEO of the New York-based National Eating Disorders Association, said in *USA Today*, "We live in a culture where eating disorders thrive because of the messages we're exposed to. Social media heightens that exposure. Before [a girl or woman] would do [disordered eating behaviour] in isolation or with a classmate. Now you can log on and see what thousands of people are doing. It changes the game." In 2015 the UK's National Health Service released figures showing the number of teenage admissions into hospital for eating disorders had nearly doubled over the previous three years. When you consider that anorexia has the highest mortality rate for any mental illness – one in five anorexics will die either from physical complications associated with the disease or suicide and in the US every 62 minutes someone dies as a direct result of an eating disorder – the magnitude of the issue becomes apparent. And there's no fudge here; healthcare professionals are *directly* blaming social media for the increase in admissions. This is something that we should not just be aware of but should be actively campaigning to change.

A Personal Obsession

My list of newly adopted hang-ups is something that I've only developed because of looking at social media pictures of myself that bit too hard. I've actually never been one for too much mirror gazing – in fact I'll often get home in the evening and find a smear of newsprint across my cheek – but when you take so many pictures of yourself and have them stored on a reel of thousands of zoom-able shots on your phone, it's easy to start to identify "problem" body parts. From there it's a simple step to becoming consumed with tiny body and face features, which in the bigger picture are almost entirely inconsequential. But social media culture can make us ultra aware of all sorts of things we wouldn't have batted an eyelid at before, and if that imagery is the first thing we look at when we wake up in the morning and the last thing we see before we go to sleep, it takes a steely confidence not to be sucked into the vortex.

In truth, I have spent the vast majority of my life obsessed with my weight. Over the course of my 34 years there have been times when this preoccupation teetered over the edge into the abyss of self-destruction, at other times, especially during my thirties, it subsided to the dull ache of an omnipresent worry. Although I'm well-aware I'm not the first person to feel this way, it's deeply embarrassing to admit quite how much I've thought about my body over the course of my life. While boyfriends and jobs have come and gone and I've moved across continents and scaled career ladders, worries about my BMI have remained a steadfast theme, consuming my thoughts whenever I'm at a low ebb.

Growing up, health wasn't just a distant concern to be dealt with in middle age; it was directly correlated to how I looked. As a teenage smoker and obsessive calorie counter, exercise was what you did to fit into jeans, not to feel strong. Higher education offered few chances for reform, and during this period I ate one single, specific meal every night – a "Salmon Cottage Pie" ready meal with 348 calories per serving. Ironically, I also regularly consumed entire bars of chocolate and bottles of white wine, so to say my diet logic was faulty is somewhat the understatement.

Post-university, my supermarket shopping became a little more varied. Instead of just one meal, I bought all the meals. My weight fluctuated dramatically, which unsurprisingly made me feel appalling. I can remember when my mum got married we had to lop the bottom of my bridesmaid's dress off and stitch the fabric up the sides as I'd gone from a size eight to twelve in the three months between fittings – I'd gained more than 15lb (6.8kg) and couldn't fit into a single pair of my jeans. I'd then skip meals, smoke a lot and lose a stone (6kg) just as quickly. The whole sorry yo-yo thing consumed my every waking hour; my looks oscillated from bloated to sickly, and I suffered from near-constant stomach gripes. While my weight was never a medical concern, and I'm aware that, at 5ft 3in (160cm), a UK size 12 (US 8) is close to the average size of a 22-year-old woman, it was my whole attitude and the anxiety that came with it that was truly unhealthy. I could wake up at 2.30am and spend the hours until my alarm went off devising ways to get thinner. Or else just use the time to hate myself. Thinking about it now makes me feel incredibly depressed.

While I managed to quit the daily pack of cigarettes, as for exercise, that went out the window completely as soon as I left high school. Any vigorous movement was absent from my life until I was around 29. It was at this point that I realized that a part of my bottom no longer fitted into my knickers; in fact both cheeks had begun to slide inexorably down towards the backs of my knees. My calves were totally lacking elasticity and I couldn't do a single sit- or push-up. Combined with grey, congested skin and a pain in my hips that nothing, not even four G&Ts, could cure, I finally made the decision that it was time to seriously do something about my lifestyle.

This story might be hard to believe if you look at my Instagram page. People have often commented in the past that my body looks great on social media and said how envious they are, which makes me feel both validated and uncomfortable. Because, while it's true I'm happier with my body than when I was in my twenties – though see below for caveats – it hasn't been a straightforward road to get to where I am now, either psychologically or physically. I started small and over the past few years have significantly changed my attitude to my wellbeing. While my nutrition obviously needed an overhaul, it was exercise that really started the whole ball rolling. Sometimes I've loved it, sometimes it's felt like a drag, but overall fitness has provided a positive anchor in my life and helped me weather all sorts of emotional storms. Due to exercise, I've had periods when I no longer thought or talked about food all day long and, for about three years before my pregnancy, my weight stayed within a 5lb (2.3kg) range – something which helped exorcize a lot of demons (no pun intended). During those times, I've felt proud of parts of my body and how far I've come and have been able to let more things go. I haven't obsessed about exactly how thin my legs looked in a picture or worried as deeply about my cellulite. But I've never stopped being critical – no matter if I weighed under 7st (44.5kg) or over 9st (57.1kg), there have always been flaws I've perceived with my body.

The things I fixate on now have become increasingly bizarre, and without a doubt that's down to the fact that I've started taking so many pictures of myself for Instagram. For example, I'm obsessed with my knees – specifically the pocket of fat that sits at the thigh and knee join. It is the only thing I look at in pictures and I'm continually conscious of the strange "knee vaginas" or "knee baby faces" I can see in them (both terms coined on social media). Back in the day when I was a calorie counter, I had no specific problem with any part of my legs – but now I'm in better shape than I ever was in my youth, I'm endlessly googling "knee liposuction". I also want a brace for my "Nanny McPhee" teeth (which I used to see as British and charming), I've just got my eyebrows microbladed (I certainly hadn't considered this in the pre-selfie era as I have a fringe) and I can imagine a world in which I might have a different nose – all because I turn the camera on my face more than once a day.

Objectively speaking, I know that there is nothing wrong with the way I look. But this isn't about objectivity. I'm talking about the impact that a barrage of images of "perfection" can have on your subjective standards of beauty and the result these standards can have on your self-perception. Social media has changed our notions of beauty and created a culture in which we are blitzed with this ideal. "There is an onslaught of beauty pressures that bombard girls' daily lives," says Laura Choate, author of "Swimming Upstream: Parenting Girls for Resilience in a Toxic Culture", in *Psychology Today*. "If they listen to these messages, they come to believe two things: (a) I should look like this and if I did, I would be happier, and (b) practically anyone can look like this if they work hard enough and buy the right products and merchandise. So not only do many girls start to believe that they should be focused on attaining the 'perfect physique', they also believe something is wrong with them if they are somehow unable to reach this goal. And they develop a negative body image as a result." Who can't relate to that thought process?

And it's not just comparing your body against other people's bodies that can cause issues. Before, we only had our "thin jeans" to taunt us and perhaps holiday snaps to remind us of when we were in good shape. Now our iPhones and iCloud accounts are packed with photo diaries of our own looks captured on a near-daily, if not weekly, basis. I got my first iPhone five years before I had grey hairs or wrinkles. Aside from being able to see myself age 27, I also have a record of what my body looked like, offering ample not-so-flattering compare-and-contrast opportunities. This digital record of thousands of pictures, as opposed to the 26 or so we printed at a time from our disposable cameras, means we are locked into a battle with reality and construction, which would have been unthinkable in the pre-digital, pre-social media age.

Girl on Girl

An interesting departure here is that in many ways the male gaze has been moderated by the advent of social media sites like Instagram, which have a female-heavy demographic. While there's no doubt that social media still acts as a platform for us to showcase our attributes to potential partners (not forgetting the identities we create through images selected for online dating profiles), it's often female-to-female validation that women are looking for with their posts. My personal profile has an 85 per cent female demographic, and I've found that the "sexier" images create less engagement. Of course, that doesn't mean that you can't find pornographic or hyper-sexualized images of women on Instagram – it's just that the main audience is less concerned with cleavage. While there are, of course, pockets of communities across all social media platforms in which more curvy, Kardashian-esque (usually equally unobtainable) figures are increasingly aspired to, there is one body type that continues to be ubiquitous: fit, thin and rigorously gym-toned.

Some of this can be blamed on the advent of #fitspo. We've all seen the #FitNotThin hashtag so beloved by fitspiration and wellness bloggers, and it's clear that social media has helped up the level of muscle tone now considered to be necessary for an ideal physique. However, while this development has been applauded, the influence of "fitspo" bodies has been more complicated. In a 2016 study, researchers coded a set of six hundred "fitspiration images" taken from Instagram for body type, activity and objectification. The results showed that the majority of images of women contained only one body type: thin and toned; the 2.0 body may be masquerading as something new, but it's still the extremely limited version of beauty we've been consuming for decades – just with a 21st-century tweak. In a 2015 study, researchers found that viewing images of this new beauty standard of athleticism is just as bad from a self-worth perspective as exposure to simply thin women if the athletic women pictured are "*both* muscular and slim". The mantra "strong is the new skinny" is a misnomer. What we really mean is "strong but *still skinny* is the new skinny".

The truth is that these images don't make most women feel empowered and motivated; instead they just make them feel depressed. A survey of 276 Australian and American women aged 18–25 found that the more often participants looked at "fitspo" images, the more likely they were to be unhappy with their own bodies, and a 2017 research article showed a clear link between orthorexia nervosa (an obsession with "clean" or healthy eating) and fitspiration image consumption.

"Of course, social media has played a massive part in the shift in recent attitudes to fitness – and health," says Pip Black, co-founder of London-based Frame gyms. "There are a lot of beautiful, slim girls on social media who are naturally toned and lean. Yes, they work out regularly, but the truth is that they'd look great either way. And they are followed by thousands and thousands of other women – many of them young, impressionable girls who see that body shape as the norm. It's not like back in the 2000s when everyone wanted to be super skinny – now we all have to have a six-pack. But this time around, a lot of disordered eating and excessive exercise passes as acceptable under the banner of 'fitspo'."

Pip explains how a focus on matching up to the bodies we see on social media can totally transform a woman's life. "Exercise today is always, always about getting 'the body'. For us that's something that's really discouraging. Often you will find that people in their peak 'super slim' shape are working out like that and not eating enough because they're not happy. They're putting all of their efforts into being totally internalized and thinking they can control at least this one area of their life. It's not anorexia, but it's disordered eating to varying degrees. That's just not something anyone should aspire to, no matter what it looks like on social media."

There are other dangers to this new body type for women's health which go beyond self-worth. Joan Murphy, Pip's co-founder at Frame, highlights an issue which we are definitely not talking about enough, and one which I can definitely relate to: "When it comes to striving for a six-pack, people are often only considering the now and what they see in the mirror in front of them. They're not thinking about fertility, bone density or gut health. The sorts of things that go along with cutting out major food groups and stripping things out of your diet. And, even more worryingly, women are taking their cues from people in the world of social media who don't have either the experience or training to advise others."

Last year I experienced a knock to my battle to conquer my body issues because of a struggle to conceive. The first advice from my fertility doctor was to ease off the exercise routine because – something that we don't think of when we're rabidly consuming Instagram bikini shots – too much exercise can harm your fertility. And, for some people, too much exercise doesn't mean doing an Ironman. Achieving the "fitspo" look of a flat tummy with defined abs, long, lean arms and legs, a gravity-defying bum and a photographic clavicle – basically all the things that look good on Instagram – can come at a cost to your monthly cycle. While every woman is different and will be affected differently by exercise, for me personally, whenever I've got closest to achieving all those things at once, my periods stop. While some super-toned, slim women, including models, dancers, athletes, gymnasts and #fitspo girls who look great on the beach, may not find their fertility is impacted by their workouts, others – like me – will. Just because a body can look fit and aspirational on social media doesn't mean it is actually functioning in a healthy way.

If I do a lot of cardio, I don't ovulate. It makes sense in the context of fight or flight – if you've got all that cortisol and adrenaline running through your body, it doesn't exactly suggest, "Time to get up the duff," to your highly sensitive reproductive organs. My low fat-to-muscle ratio and exercise routine may also have contributed to a condition called luteal phase defect, which often combines late ovulation with a shortened second half of your cycle. Without treatment for this, I wouldn't have been able to ever conceive. It's hard not to blame myself, and my relationship with health and food, for the fact that I struggled to get pregnant. Of course, there's nothing wrong with trying to get fit and feel great about yourself, and of course, some people naturally have a body type which will easily build muscle. But that is not everyone – and striving to achieve a look beyond your natural body shape can be deeply unhealthy.

We need to learn to see our bodies for what they do as much as what they look like. Exercise in a social media context can be one big competitive sham. Wellness should be about feeling "well". Which means not being totally exhausted or killing yourself. As fashion and health blogger, Niomi Smart, explains, "Real health is about the feeling of wellbeing rather than the way you look. It's so easy to be deceived by looks – you can have the fittest looking body but not actually be particularly healthy. I personally don't have a defined six-pack or bulging biceps, but I feel the best version of myself and I know that I'm healthy."

What *does* make you feel good is exercise that is fun *and* manageable. While you might think that isn't possible, it's really a case of trial and error. If you hate something (beyond the moderate burn) don't do it again – but focus on what it is you hate. Was it the pace? Was it the intensity? What would have made it better for you? The first few tries at exercise after a break will inevitably make you feel exhausted – but when you leave, do you feel uplifted?

While I haven't entirely got it figured out, I do believe it is possible to feel a sense of insecurity and reasonably realign your thoughts to a more positive place. If seeing a beautiful girl in a bikini or lingerie makes me feel envious, I try to think about something that I *do* like about my body. If I look through a set of pictures where I see something about my figure that I hate, I try to take a breath and put it into context with the rest of myself and my achievements. Sometimes I fail and go into a spiral. Other times I manage to keep it in check.

It's easy to forget that your own thoughts construct your own reality. If you keep focusing and thinking negatively about something, in the end it will eat away at your esteem and confidence. Exerting discipline over your mind's wanderings is an exhausting task, but it's one of the only ways to recast your frame of reference when it comes to body perception.

#BodyPositivity Rules?

One area of hope for change has been in the body positivity movement led by legions of women disillusioned with the one-size-fits-all standards that social media (as well as other media and society at large) perpetuates. In an attempt to unlearn social stigmas, the body positivity movement is about recasting every body type, shape and size as equally valuable. While the roots of body positivity can be found in the fat acceptance movement, focused on the prejudice that overweight people experience, it's come to encompass all body types. Social media has been integral to the spread of the message, simply because visual platforms like Instagram and Facebook have allowed women to see other women posting confident images of what they really look like, "flaws" and all. From scars to stretchmarks to cellulite, alongside less conventional body shapes, the movement has helped undermine the idea that only slim, toned bodies have a place in public life. Take body activist Kenzie Brenna's #CelluliteSaturday to plus-size blogger Simone Mariposa's Twitter campaign #WeWearWhatWeWant – social media has also encouraged women who struggle with their imperfections to stop endlessly beating themselves up about their bodies.

Callie Thorpe, a successful plus-size blogger, describes how body positivity and digital media completely changed her attitude to her body and dramatically enhanced her self-esteem. "Weight was always an issue for me," she explains. "At the age of nine I was put on steroids and my nan, who raised me, was always a comfort feeder. After she died when I was 13, my problems developed further, because I turned to food to deal with my grief. I was on a diet from around the age of ten and over the years I've punished myself in every way you can imagine. At university things escalated and I was using laxatives and going on ever more extreme diets: cayenne pepper, cabbage soup, just plain starvation – you name it, I tried it. The level of self-hatred and anxiety I felt over those years was just crazy. After trying to lose weight unsuccessfully for a holiday, I finally decided to google 'Plus-Size Swimwear' as I'd never bought a swimsuit before. A plus-size blog called *GabiFresh* popped up and it's not an exaggeration to say that finding it completely changed my life. For the first time in years it felt like I could breathe a bit and I realized that it was time to stop punishing myself."

The body positivity movement has been accused by some of "promoting" obesity, however, as Callie explains, it's more about a sense of pragmatism and a realistic approach which fosters a belief in your right to happiness, no matter what the body you inhabit: "I'm just saying that if you are the size you are, you don't have to kill yourself every day or hate everything about yourself. You can wear a nice dress to your wedding, go to the gym and feel confident in your fashion choices no matter what you look like – and social media has given me the platform to challenge those assumptions. People often accuse me of promoting obesity just because I'm putting myself online. But that just isn't the case. It's also worth saying that my life isn't all buzzy, buzzy self-love, body positivity, bloody perfect every day. Some days I feel shit and worry that an outfit is too tight. Or I'll go to an event and I'll feel out of place as I'm the only woman of my size there and end up leaving. I just have to keep coming back to the truth that I'm trying to be the best version of myself both mentally and physically. If someone doesn't like me because I'm a size 24 [US size 20], I can only feel sorry for them."

Rather than just being confined to the blogosphere and social media, there are signs that the body positivity movement is starting to make inroads into wider attitudes. In 2016, Ashley Graham, a US size 16 (UK 20) model, was featured on one of three *Sports Illustrated* covers in celebration of their annual swimsuit edition, and the insanely unrealistic proportions of the Barbie doll (36-in/91-cm chest, 18-in/46-cm waist, 33-in/84-cm hips) were finally, after nearly 60 years, addressed. As 92 per cent of American girls aged three to twelve have owned one of the iconic dolls, the release of petite, tall and curvy body variations (alongside diverse skin tones and hair types) has been heralded as a win for the body positivity movement. However, it's not all been good news – what the digital world giveth with one hand, it taketh back with the other.

"While social media has changed so many things for me for the better – I've modelled for plus brands, I was the first plus-size columnist for *Marie Claire* and I've managed to build a career around my journey – I've also dealt with a lot of negativity," explains Callie. "Recently I've had a shit ton of abuse because I was featured in *Vogue* and someone wrote an article about it which was shared in a fat-hating forum, leading to more than nine hundred abusive comments. People said I should be tied to a car and dragged along the road. They told me to kill myself, to die. That I'm disgusting, that I don't deserve to be a model or in *Vogue*. That I make them sick. That I'm going to die of diabetes and my husband is going to bury me... Anything you can think of was said. While it's definitely brought me opportunities, social media has also brought me a lot of pain."

The rise of fat-shaming has been the flipside of the "body positivity movement" coin and highlights the issue of cyberbullying, one of the very worst ravages of the digital world, which will be dealt with at length in the next chapter. Needless to say, the negative experiences that women like Callie and other plus-size women go through can have a serious impact on their mental and physical health (it's been proven that stress around excess weight actually encourages over-eating). While communities have increased the visibility of multiple body shapes on social media and can provide a solid support network, we're a long way from liberating women from either social stigma or the beliefs that we've all internalized over years of prejudice.

However, that is not something reserved for just plus-size women or indeed those whose body shape falls outside the accepted standards. It's also worth pointing out that there's a vocal and equally vile "skinny-shaming" mob out there, adding to the truism that no matter what your body, there will be people who reduce you to a set of measurements, which are apparently up for criticism. As Callie articulates, "The truth is the majority of women struggle with their weight no matter what size they are because we are never told that what we are is acceptable. There's always something new that we need to change. When women are slim, but not quite there in terms of the images that are presented by social media – maybe they're a curvy size 10 or 12 [US 6 or 8] – then they can have even worse problems with body image than I do with mine. It's crazy to acknowledge that, because there's obviously a disparity in terms of privilege, and the way people are treated in the world as a thin woman in comparison to being a fat woman. But I can completely see that thinner women can go through equally distressing experiences as I have. For me, I know I will never look like those stick-thin images and I guess there's a sense of liberation in that."

✗ ✗ ✗

The sad reality is that social media puts pressure on every woman, even if you are the one that others are #BodyGoals-ing over, because social media is a hyperspeed reflection of our *prejudiced society*. Fat, thin, toned, soft, pregnant, tall, short, narrow, wide, flat butt, bubble butt, whatever. No-one is immune. Feeling empowered and proud of your body isn't something that is found by fitting into your "thin jeans". A single digit dress size doesn't protect you from the sticks that we use to beat ourselves with – and dealing with issues around body image isn't something that is reserved for tall, short, curvy, over- or underweight body shapes. So, next time you start hating on yourself or let an image of a "beautiful" body torture you, just think: that girl is quite possibly lying awake in bed thinking about her baby face knees at 4.30am. You are *definitely* not the only one struggling.

Takeaways

1. Pause the screens

If you are starting to feel the pervasive effects of social media on your body image and self-esteem, take some time away from your devices. Will social media disappear if you don't look at it for 24 hours? No.

As hard as it might feel to be severed from your social lifeline, regular breaks are good practice in order to regain some perspective and balance. Delete the apps from your phones, tablets and laptops (rather than actually deleting your accounts) and re-download them when you're ready to come back. Nothing will have changed, I promise you.

2. Admit your feelings

Another theme that has cropped up time and time again during my interviews with women working across social media is envy. Jealousy and envy are dirty words in female culture, and to admit you covet what someone else has is tantamount to admitting that you're a bitch. But envy is only an issue when you let it fester and morph into something negative, whereas the pang you might feel when confronted with someone else's achievements or beauty is entirely natural and certainly no indication of meanness. It is completely possible to be happy for someone's fortune while envious of it at the same time. And it's not unusual for another woman's beauty to make you feel inadequate.

"I'm only human and of course when I see an image of Alexis Ren or other models prancing along a beach in skimpy bikinis with the most incredible bodies, I obviously then feel like a potato," says Niomi Smart.

"But then you have to remind yourself that everyone's body is different and comparing yourself to someone with a totally different body shape is such a waste of energy. I'd rather aspire to have the work ethic and ambition of other women rather than their physical appearance."

It's not bitchy to want a different or better life, and ambition can also be an incredible force for good. The issue is when you try and pretend you don't have those feelings and when you replace them with resentment or rejection.

3. Know you are not alone

If you only take away one thing from this chapter – or indeed from this entire book, I would hope it's the fact that *we are all in the same boat*. Or at least in the same fleet of slightly different boats. The pressure that you feel when it comes to body image isn't exclusive to you – it's a broad societal burden that we all have to bear.

This isn't just an issue for one generation – it's for all social media users across extensive age, economic and regional demographics. No-one is immune. Those who have grown up after the social media and mobile phone revolutions won't have experienced a world in which body images *weren't* shoved down their throat, all day, every day. Yet those who were exposed to this new world after they reached adulthood can still be affected in just as powerful ways. If, as we see from the testimonies above, influencers themselves are under the influence, what hope have we all got?

"I'll find that I put up a picture on Instagram looking like I'm really confident, but a day or the week or even an hour before that I might have been crying my eyes out, thinking, 'Oh my God I'm so fat; I'm so disgusting; I want to rip my skin off. I hate myself...' influencer Roxie Nafousi explains. "But then you post a picture and maybe it gets likes and comments and then you get to feel good for a moment. But it's a vicious cycle, because then someone else is obviously going to look at your image and think, 'Oh, she feels great about herself, she loves herself – Why don't *I* love myself?'"

While it's true there has never been a halcyon time when all women loved their bodies, it was inarguably easier to find some context before the onslaught of social media imagery. But this is where we are now, and all you can do is arm yourself with tools to protect yourself from both the new and old body anxieties and strive to find acceptance. Grab a true girlfriend, open a bottle of rosé and share how you're feeling. You're not weird, you're not a loser, you're not a narcissist. You're just a woman living in the 21st century.

However thin, curvy, toned, tight, bodacious or booty-ful you may become, you will never be able to measure up to a body blueprint that often doesn't even exist in real life.

The magic solution isn't some newfangled starvation dirt or food-group elimination method. It's boringly and predictably only an acceptance of what you have that can set you free.

4. Feed your confidence, not your demons

One of the first steps of this practice is to identify the things that you are proud of or else feel a sense of acceptance about. If you can't think of anything, ask a good friend to help you highlight your assets. Write them down and keep them somewhere you can access them – I have mine on my iPhone Notes. Every time you feel those body anxieties creeping in, refer back to the list and say the words to yourself either out loud or in your head. It's all about stopping the thoughts in their tracks and rebalancing the assessment of yourself. Dwell on those things and swirl the positive words around until you feel the "hate-me"s subsiding. It sounds pretty esoteric, and I'm the first to raise a red flag for scepticism, but this one does actually work.

It's also worth remembering that everyone has a completely different lens and vastly varied standards when it comes to ideal bodies and faces. For example, I am relatively flat-chested – something some people feel insecure about. For me personally, however, the opposite is true. I love having small boobs and would never trade them for a larger cup size, even if it were safe, painless and free to do so. A plastic surgeon

I met last year said that in her game you're immediately taught to rid yourself of presumptions about other people's insecurities – a woman might come in with a huge mole on her face, but start talking about unnoticeable stretchmarks. What you see isn't what I see, and vice versa. That's another thing you have to hold on to – in the vast majority of cases, no-one else thinks your hideous flaws are hideous. In fact, they probably don't even notice them at all.

The one thing that is guaranteed to drive you cray cray is endlessly denying yourself pleasure (and that actually applies to everything in life). Managing your diet in a bid to change your body is sensible if you are unhealthily overweight and perhaps understandable if you've been on an indulgent trip, gone through an injury or just fallen off the wagon of your normal routine. But if you live on a *never-ending* diet, spend your life obsessing over going up or down a few pounds and this state of affairs is making you desperately unhappy, you have fallen into the self-esteem danger zone.

The inevitable truth is that there's no one catch-all "secret". You are not going to suddenly discover a diet that lets you enjoy all the food you want but somehow magically also makes you slim down a dress size. Over the years I've done: Slimming World; SlimFast; Weight Watchers; Atkins; the high-fat, low-carb diet; the low-fat, high-carb diet and the 5:2. I spent nine months entirely sugar-free (not even an apple crossed my lips) and I've been Clean & Lean and under control. And not one of them changed my figure substantially or for long. No matter what the diet industry tries to sell you, there is no regime that will change your bones, melt your fundamental proportions or insert an overnight thigh gap. And that reality is the same for every individual you follow on Instagram – Facetune or no Facetune.

Chapter 3:
Why Social Media is
Ruining Your **Health**

Of the many accusations made against social media, it's the impact on our health – or more specifically, our mental health – that's really making us sit up and smell the matcha latte. It's certainly the issue which inspires the most hand-wringing among parents, psychologists and educators. And little wonder: the research is starting to make Facebook, Instagram, Pinterest et al. look like the next generation of Big Tobacco.

Certainly, when it comes to our wellbeing, there's an argument that social is the new smoking. Sounds laughable? Well, just consider that Justin Rosenstein, the engineer who created Facebook's "like" button, has equated Snapchat to heroin; Shirley Cramer, the chief executive of the UK Royal Society for Public Health, said in a statement that "social media has been described as more addictive than cigarettes and alcohol"; Instagram has been accused of manipulating exactly when users receive likes on posts in order to keep them hooked; industry kingpins have admitted that certain features have been explicitly designed to take advantage of our neurological vulnerabilities; and that the vast, vast profits from this culture of addiction are lining the pockets of Silicon Valley's very few. Sounding more familiar?

On a cultural level, we are beginning to contend with the darker side of social media. A number of recent feature films have addressed the new pressures on our mental health; check out Elizabeth Olsen in *Ingrid Goes West* and Ben Stiller's *Brad's Status* – two standouts among a glut of Instagram-inspired titles (the majority of which are teen horrors with spooky titles like *Friend Request*). Alongside the Hollywood treatment, journalists around the globe have taken up the issues, casting light on the once untouchable world of tech. Elsewhere, governments and schools are increasingly attempting to regulate the apparently un-regulatable, demanding safeguards, fines and contractual assurances that improvements in the social media environment will be made. The big worry is: are we too late?

Digitally Depressed?

No matter where you come from, how much money you have or whatever your age, you or someone close to you has experienced mental health issues, whether you realize it or not. It is a universal experience and part of the fabric of all our lives. In the UK half of all cases of mental illness start before the age of 15 and 1 in 4 girls is now clinically depressed by the time she turns 14. In the US as a whole, approximately 44 million adults will experience mental illness in any given year. Just imagine if we were talking about a physical disorder here: if 25 per cent of British teenage girls and 20 per cent of Americans adults had bird flu, we'd be in full end-of-the-world-is-nigh panic. Instead, because it's an "interior" health issue, something that can be kept "secret", it's been allowed to spiral out of control in plain sight. While there are other factors at play, it's widely accepted that social media has been a major reason for this epidemic. As the *Harvard Business Review* succinctly states: "The more you use Facebook, the worse you feel." And yet we still log on and allow our kids to do so too.

Yes, it's unquestionable that social media has acted as a platform to enact change for the cause of mental health. It has brought people who are suffering together and provided a space for them to share their experiences and connect with others who can empathize and offer considerate advice. Social media can prove invaluable to people going through health crises by introducing them to people who have overcome issues and moved on to thrive even when illnesses are chronic. There are certainly silver linings. But in this area what we're all trying to figure out is the weight of the cons vs the pros. How can we use social media to connect, articulate and come to terms with the issues that we're experiencing but avoid the near and present danger to our mental health that every social media platform has on an *architectural* level? And who can we trust to make the changes needed to improve a space which clearly has never had our best interests at heart? That answer, quite obviously, can't be the very firms who are making a mint off our misery.

For the over three hundred million worldwide sufferers of depression, social media has provided support but also led to desperation. While there's been plenty of research to link increased levels of depression with higher levels of social media use, there's also the argument that the more depressed you are the more you choose to use social media, skewing the stats. Reaching out to your friends and followers online for a hit of validation to try to improve your mood is an obvious motivation, and really who hasn't been there?

From a depression perspective, I've generally been pretty resilient when it comes to feeling low. Even in the midst of challenging times I have always kept a sense that, no matter how much I may be going through a level of hormonal despair, I'll always be able to pull myself back from the brink, seek help or rationalize my experience into something manageable. However, I have had first-hand experience of being with someone who didn't have that ability and know how destructive these issues can be, not just for the individual who is suffering, but also for every other person around them. Depression can blight lives and lead to desperate experiences which can be so far away from what you would ever want to publicly share. When I was a lot younger, I was in an abusive relationship with a partner who suffered from anger-management issues and depression. To be clear, my ex-partner never hit me. He threw plates of food at me, smashed up furniture, punched holes in walls next to my head and once in a rage ricocheted his fist into my cheek, but it wasn't like you see on a soap opera. It was generally everything but physical contact. I'd be called a whore, a cunt, a piece of shit; I'd come home to him sitting in a darkened room just waiting to explode. While I didn't go through the pain of physical violence that so many women suffer, and in no way do I seek to equate my experience with theirs, I do understand what it feels like to hide the truth of living with a mental health crisis from the rest of the world.

How the hell did I get there? It's a question I've asked myself endlessly over the years and I still don't really have an answer. I was very young, I'd fallen in love and equated having a "short fuse" with being male. This was something I had, for one reason or another, come to accept as the norm. Every time there was an outburst, there would also be a heartfelt apology, an assurance that he would see a counsellor and that it wouldn't happen again. Because alcohol was often involved in the early days I wrote it off as a "boy blowing off steam" kind of thing, as if that made it OK. Back then, these flare-ups would happen rarely, and in between we had what felt like the most adoring relationship. I felt secure, that I was in something special and no-one else really mattered. He completely and utterly spoiled me with affection and constantly complimented me. Looking back, that level of intensity and co-dependency obviously wasn't healthy and I was certainly addicted to the affection and validation. Our lives revolved around each other and, from the outside, it seemed like soulmate love: deep and emotionally connected – like two pieces of a jigsaw puzzle. When he downloaded an app on my phone which would "always let him know where I was", I was sanguine about being traceable at all times. When he'd leave 27 missed calls and aggressive voicemails on my phone, I'd rationalize it and felt guilty for being in an underground venue without checking my messages. When he told me I was only "allowed" to go out twice a week, I reasoned that it was reasonable. I walked into a web of control and recriminations blindly and willingly because I was, like so many of us, needy for love and scared of being alone.

Of course, it wasn't all one-sided when it came to the arguments. I could be extremely cutting and often undermined him – a product of a total loss of respect and patience for his problems – and I pretty much always stood up for myself (mostly because the accusations were so completely ridiculous). That was perhaps what fanned the flames of the outbursts. Over time, the fact that he couldn't control his aggression and was constantly losing his shit then grovelling meant I became extremely contemptuous of him. Because I argued back, I convinced myself that I wasn't a victim. However, the truth was that I'd often cower in the cataclysmic rows. It's impossible not to be wholly intimidated by a full-size man in the midst of red-eye rage, and I'd often run out the house or lock myself in the bathroom to try to escape.

From a treatment perspective, we researched anger-management courses and he went through a few bouts of CBT and other therapies, but generally nothing seemed to help – that was just the way our life had become: unpredictable, aggressive and full of trauma. Over time I became so used to the eruptions, which by then were rearing their heads on a weekly basis, that I became numb to it. It's far easier than you can imagine to pretend that things aren't happening, to close in on yourself and armour against them. I normalized the situation and told myself that everyone had issues. By ignoring the destructiveness and persuading myself that it wasn't unusual, I facilitated the continuation and escalation of the behaviour 100 per cent, and from the outside, I was entirely complicit in the charm offensive. I remember a girlfriend once telling me, "never say anything bad about your boyfriend to your friends, as that's all they'll remember," and I followed her guidance to a T, keeping schtum and never confiding in anyone. After it was all over, I confided in a few close friends about what had really been going on and they were totally stunned and appalled. They would never have forgiven him, so the stakes really are high when you share this kind of experience.

It wasn't me that ended the relationship but when it broke down, though I was crushed, there was definitely a sense of relief. In lots of ways I emerged seemingly unscathed and was lucky in the fact that I never actually thought I was a slut or a whore. I was also, thankfully, young enough to move on and learn from my mistakes. Basically, I always thought I was going out with someone with problems and it was my job to help him through it. He was the broken bird, I was the one to fix him. In hindsight, of course I know you can't repair anyone else; they have to heal themselves. And you are *never* in love with someone who scares you. Although I do bear some scars, the relationship taught me a huge amount. Today I'm also much warier about compromising my independence, in a good way. I make much more time for my friends and, as much as I love him, my boyfriend isn't the only person I need in my life, which is obviously far healthier. I'm not looking for drama or that full-on desperate-yet-destructive love because I know it's nothing but two people dragging each other through hell. I also know that your sense of validation should come from within, otherwise it's not real. Esteem and security aren't things that can be conferred on you by other people, they're things you have to work on building and maintaining from inside. What people think of you will never be as good at providing support as what you think of yourself.

I feel this is worth sharing because we tend to have a distorted image of what a woman who has been through these kinds of problem looks like. But that just isn't right. One in three women in the US and Australia experience domestic violence in their lifetime. In the UK the police receive a hundred calls an hour relating to domestic abuse. And in Italy, 40 per cent of women report suffering psychological abuse from a partner or ex-partner. As shocking as that is, it's the reality of being a woman living in the 21st century for so many. Of the hundreds of women you're following on social media, a third of them will be in a violent relationship at some point in their lives. Women who look like me. They could have everything that you think you want, at least on the surface. Their lives could look entirely aspirational from the outside. Living with mental health issues is so often hidden from view and our screens and isn't always all about the person that is suffering with the problem. While social media didn't exist when I had my experiences, I know there is absolutely zero chance I would have ever let anyone know what I was going through on that kind of platform – instead I would have been using it as just another tool, a particularly effective one to publicly paper over the cracks.

"Social media is still rife with seemingly 'perfect' lifestyles, but I feel it's becoming a collective responsibility to be more honest," says Charly Cox, a poet and writer who has been vocal on her blog and social media about mental health issues and her Bipolar II diagnosis. "Sharing the banalities and extremes of mental illness can be liberating, community-building and powerful – all things far beyond a perfect aesthetic. For me, it's become about giving a sense of reality to what's going on outside of the parameters of the square in a digestible, honest and approachable medium." While she praises the platforms for offering an opportunity to articulate her issues and campaign for de-stigmatization, Charly also blames the environment for encouraging unhealthy attitudes. "As a 22 year old, I think most of my insecurities have been bred from bad online behaviour. Once you're online, you're out there, aren't you? Reading comments made me quite unwell for a while. I've done some mad things off the back of a stranger's opinion. I genuinely once put extra strong Veet [a chemical hair removal cream] on my face because someone said I looked like Bradley Wiggins. It was the aftermath of having scratchy little carpets grow back on my face that [stirred me to] develop healthier mechanisms to attack how I looked at social media. The biggest and most positive change was being more honest. I unfollowed all the accounts I looked at in a midnight slump, clawing at my love handles wondering why I couldn't look like them, and suddenly found it became a more positive meditation. I found myself scrolling for information, inspiration and decent well-meaning conversation, instead of a warped reality and ideas that I didn't need."

As for the response to her social media honesty, in the main, Charly says, her experience has been positive: "People, generally, are less cruel and judgemental than you believe they might be. I hold a lot of reassurance in knowing that those who are following or engaging in mental health content have been so subjected to their own levels of judgement, that they're unlikely to want to offer it back at you. There was a time when I was inundated with comments that perhaps I was an alcoholic because I'd had a particularly heavy week of events/parties and that stung. In a wave of people uniting in community and forum sometimes you do find yourself in a space where others feel they're equipped (or worse, doing you a favour) to give you an unsolicited diagnosis, but it's best to shrug that off and see it as a way of people caring. I've come to accept that what I'm going through, whilst difficult and hard and frequently excruciating, is actually quite normal. I'm sharing stories and thoughts and feelings that have been felt and experienced hundreds of times before, that now, whilst they have my own personal spin on them, don't leave me feeling naked but united. I struggle with the word brave, but I know it's said with kindness; hopefully one day we won't see people being honest as a brave act, but one we all partake in daily as part of normal life."

The real point here is that more people than you can know live with secrets that they edit out of their life projections to the world. Mental health struggles have long been part of this "interior" and often domestic experience. However, today we have the power to share our experiences and use honesty on social media to shine a light on even the darkest days, and hopefully, by doing so, we can start to change the story for everyone. If we could tell the truth rather than curate what we wished to be true, it would serve us all. There is no shame in struggle, but if there's no mention of it in our perfected digital lifestyles, we only feel all the more shamed. Life is messy and complicated, and sometimes really ugly, and if we want social media to be a healthier environment, it needs to reflect that too.

Marketing Your Mental Health

Social media firms have transformed how we relate to each other, and they spend a huge amount of time, energy and money on understanding how each of us tick, so they can extract maximum engagement – read profits – from us. Their very business model is based on our behaviour and they have been quietly gathering information on our habits for over a decade. Will regulators ever be able to catch up with the body of knowledge that has been gathered as a result of billions of dollars of investment in order to curtail – or even understand – the extent of these firms' power? Unlikely.

It's disheartening, but hardly surprising that social media platforms seem reluctant to change anything which could dent their share values. Facebook's revenues of $40.6 billion in 2017, and the sheer economic force that these firms wield, seem to make them impenetrable and exempt from any outside scrutiny. Even in the light of the recent data scandals, the world's biggest social media site continues to churn out advertising profits. These tech giants may pay lip service to making incremental improvements, but by operating under the guise of "making the world a better place", and preaching social utopia while making profits off the back of our unhappiness, they've effectively gaslighted billions of us. Why would they limit the impact their products have on our feelings of insecurity, envy, anxiety and inadequacy when all these things are apparently marketable?

So how does it work? An internal Facebook document obtained by *The Australian* in 2017 sheds some light on the level of manipulation. It explains to a lucrative advertiser that the Silicon Valley-based social platform can monitor posts and photos in real time to determine when young people feel "stressed", "defeated", "overwhelmed", "anxious", "nervous", "stupid", "silly", "useless" and a "failure". They can provide information on young people's more rudimentary behaviour: their relationship status, number of friends, location and rate of social media use on smartphones and desktop. Disturbingly, they have also mined data on users who have discussed "body confidence", "working out" and "losing weight" and can serve that up to advertisers too. If you've ever felt like social media kicks you when you're down, that may very well be because it has been programmed to do so. As former Google ethicist Tristan Harris says, this level of detailed emotional information offers "a perfect model of what buttons you can push in a particular person". By targeting people at a low ebb – say with weight-loss products, cosmetic services, loans or holiday offers – conversion will undoubtedly be increased. Ultimately, Facebook is selling the emotional levers of its users to the highest bidder.

Everyone's looking for a pick-me-up sometimes and social media provides you with the instant opportunity for retail therapy to cure your deflated feelings – it's just hard to swallow that these platforms can strategically collect information on when exactly you appear at your most vulnerable then peddle it on to companies unscrupulous enough to take advantage of your weakness to make the sale. While Facebook was highly critical of the information obtained by the newspaper and has pledged to "do better" at prioritizing its users' mental health, we know from countless behavioural studies that people often compensate for low mood, feelings of failure and insecurity by consuming more. Keeping us feeling down about ourselves is good for business, no matter what any CEO might say. Ever wondered why social media sites are free? It's certainly not for any altruistic purpose. Instead it's because you – or your data – *are the product* and advertisers are the customers. If all this time you thought Facebook et al. were programmed to serve you, it's time for a rude awakening.

The kind of insights that social media platforms have on you are generally kept under wraps – very few people ever get to work with the algorithms which learn to read your mind then feed you what advertisers know you want to see – but occasionally there's a slip-up. Like in 2014, when a study was released showing that Facebook had used a newsfeed experiment to see how they could control our emotions. By manipulating the feeds of 689,003 unsuspecting users, the site assessed the impact of surfacing more negative or positive stories and hiding certain emotional words. The study showed that "emotional states can be transferred to others via emotional contagion, leading people to experience the same emotions without their awareness." Basically, your friends can depress you without you even having to interact with them, and Facebook at any point can engineer what you see to mess with your mind. A representative released a statement defending the ethically dubious experiment (which they hadn't felt the need to notify those nearly seven hundred thousand users it was carrying out, by the way), saying they had undertaken the test "because we care about the emotional impact of Facebook and the people that use our product," and "felt that it was important to investigate the common worry that seeing friends post positive content leads to people feeling negative or left out." Perhaps the intentions were good, but make no mistake: social media platforms are entirely aware of where you are at emotionally and that knowledge gives them the power to persuade you to click on that designer dress which, yes, might blow your bank balance but will probably make you feel – at least momentarily – better. Trying to save for an apartment? You'd be wise to swerve social media and keep your emotions to yourself.

The Millennial Malaise: Anxiety Strikes

Growing up I'd never really heard of the word anxiety. I knew what teenage angst was, but I didn't realize it was part of anything wider than wearing a Nirvana T-shirt and being fractious with your parents. I was aware that I had problems dealing with stress, that exam season would trigger a bout of IBS or skin rashes (little mini blisters across my cheeks and cold sores), and that I'd often feel a deep sense of panic and feel I couldn't catch my breath. But there was never a sense that it was anything psychological, or even treatable. Being so driven at such a young age had made me obsessive about being "top" at everything at school. When I was six years old I suffered from glandular fever and spent nearly a month out of school in and out of hospital. My biggest concern was that I didn't miss any work. By 16, I was organizing three after-school academic clubs, taking extra GCSE lessons in free periods, working 20 hours a week at a supermarket, running 3 miles every morning, competing on sports teams and had dropped about a stone in weight from meticulous dieting. Another bout in hospital, this time for pneumonia, didn't stop me in my tracks. There was absolutely nothing my parents or teachers could do to stop me – I had to be perfect at everything. Looking back, I was, quite obviously, a classically anxious child, who often pushed herself to both mental and physical exhaustion. But when I was a young, there just wasn't the same cultural understanding that "nerves", "worry" and relentless unease were a particular mental health issue: I was just a precocious and stressed kid.

Today things are very different. Anxiety has been identified as *the* biggest mental health threat facing young people. Around 17.5 per cent of female college students in the US have been diagnosed with or treated for anxiety, and the blame for this drastic uptick has been laid squarely at the door of perfectionism – the layers and layers of pressure that is the millennial generation's undoing. A recent study of over forty thousand Canadian, British and American college students found that "multidimensional perfectionism" (which includes the pressures of social media ideals) is the main driver behind the surge in anxiety issues. These encompass generalized anxiety disorder, panic disorder, phobias, social anxiety disorder, obsessive-compulsive disorder and post-traumatic stress disorder. During my school days, of course there was a certain level of competition. But it totally pales in comparison to the overwhelming levels of perfection that can be consumed on social media today.

Aside from how they look and who they're friends with, millennials are struggling with the demands to achieve perfect grades, secure perfect jobs and nail down their life partner at an increasingly earlier age. Not to have achieved all these goals by certain stages of their life is often treated as a catastrophe. Through consuming information about each other digitally, the pressure to conform to increasingly normative and restrictive targets – the idea that there is only one very narrow path to success: great job, nice home, six-pack, hot partner – is creating a collective sense of inadequacy.

Fashion blogger Lindsey Holland, better known as @RopesOfHolland, who runs a YouTube series tackling mental health, explains how benchmark anxiety got the better of her. "My feeling of anxiousness started in a relationship I was in during my early twenties. I'd never felt secure, because I wanted to pin him down for all those expectations I had at the time – the perfect wedding, kids – and he just wanted to run 10,000 miles away from me. Social media can make you feel like there are deadlines passing you by, and there was a time that I'd be pretty upset if someone around me got engaged – I'd find myself obsessively looking at their pictures on Facebook and thinking about what kind of ring I'd have. I was only 25, but I really felt that I needed to achieve those life goals. For me, anxiety is like going into fight-or-flight mode with massive surges of adrenaline which you just can't stop from coming, and looking at Instagram or Facebook used to really fuel my anxiety. It always made me feel that I was less than someone else – you can literally drive yourself mad with comparison. I'm not in the same rush to achieve all those goals as when I was younger, but it's taken me to get to 30 to become more relaxed about what other people are doing – I still want to be married and to have babies, but I now know it's not a race."

Anxiety is an issue which can be treatable, and many, many people recover from its worst ravages, either with or without the help of medication. While my pregnancy brought my anxiety back into sharp focus (more on this in a later chapter), I've spent most of my recent life without any anxiety at all – helped mostly by going through lots and lots of failure. Not getting a place at Oxbridge was the first step to dealing with anxiety. Perfect grades and a perfect UCAS application didn't equate to a perfect university acceptance for me, and while it was the first major botch-up of my life, it definitely helped to take the pressure off. When I received my rejection letter, I also had my first moment of teenage rebellion, cut my afternoon classes, took a train into London and went straight to Tiffany's on Bond Street to spend my supermarket earnings on lots of jewellery... If only Facebook had been there to facilitate that emotional transaction... More failure followed: the seven job interviews I got rejected from to get my first full-time job, my inability to ingratiate myself with my first boss, getting divorced before I was 30, failing my driving test, the long list of other men that have broken up with me... While at the time these things felt insanely stressful, overcoming failure can make you fearless, and mine, over time, certainly cured me of my relentless perfectionism. However hard you work to be perfect, life has a habit of getting in the way.

I don't need to be "top" any more and I'm definitely not so fixated with being a good schoolgirl in every circumstance. Sure, some old habits die hard (I'm anally tidy and won't let anyone visit my apartment unless it's in showroom state, I can feel a deep sense of worry vis-à-vis my body image and I struggle with confrontational social situations), but one of the reasons that social media doesn't – in the main – make me feel anxious is that I've become comfortable with my heavily flawed, imperfect self. I would also say that the defective version of me is far, far more likeable than the one that was straining to be an A* student in all aspects of her life.

One of society's biggest problems at the moment is that modern parents have become so risk-averse that they're no longer allowing their offspring to fail – at anything. As "enmeshment" parenting (a highly involved parenting style in which the parent literally lives for a child's success) grows ever more intense, young people aren't being given the opportunity to deal with their own screw-ups, which fuels an even deeper anxiety that they must not deviate from their prescribed script. But the truth is that we all need to fail sometimes, in order to learn that perfection isn't the be all and end all and that the sky doesn't fall in if you don't ace every element of your life. Also failure doesn't necessarily lead to failure. It can, in fact, enhance your success and make you able to enjoy that success to the full – it is a blessing that we shouldn't all be trying so hard to disguise. So many things have gone "wrong" for me and my life has not met the benchmarks I had once hoped it would. But being able to release the standards that I had set for myself I've dodged a life of anxiety and ultimately found my own individual version of success.

The anxiety of failing #LifeGoals can cripple a student's ability to perform in exams, interact socially, impede their ability to graduate and then hamper their attempts to enter the job market. It's long been thought that perfectionism is a motivator and there's no doubt that it can spur you on to push your limits. But it's also an affliction which can lead to serious health consequences. Perfectionism got me to the top of my class, helped me run 1,500m (1 mile) in under five minutes and definitely spurred me on to achieve top grades throughout my education. It also drove me to starve myself until I was a stone underweight and found no enjoyment in any of my accomplishments, led me on to the path of insomnia and caused stomach issues that took years of acupuncture and alternative therapies to deal with. It did not make me happy in any way.

Over social media's lifetime in the UK there's been a rise of self-poisoning by girls of 50 per cent, an increase in hospital admissions for self-harm among girls by 68 per cent, and a 400 per cent increase in girls being treated in hospital for cutting themselves. Over the same period there hasn't been the same spike in difficulties with boys. In the US suicide rates have been back on the rise since 2010, after two decades of decline and, while rates for girls remain significantly below that of boys, they've doubled between 2009 and 2015 to hit a forty-year high. A San Diego State University study shows the increase of young people taking their own lives directly mirrors the surge in social media use, pointing to a correlation. Another study has shown that teens "overusing" social media with five hours or more of daily engagement were 70 per cent more likely to have suicidal thoughts or actions than those who reported one hour of daily use. *All* of these issues have been linked to the dramatic increase in the amount of young people suffering from anxiety.

This barrage of statistics may feel overwhelming. But for some reason we're not overwhelmed enough to do much about it. It's easy to think that we don't have any agency to change things, but we need to keep reminding ourselves that these sites didn't exist a generation ago. For starters, it seems a no-brainer that every social media site should have parental controls and effective age regulation and that each user should have to prove his or her date of birth to enable them to a) log on in the first place, and b) have their access level determined. You can't smoke, drink, drive or have sex until you reach a lawful age, simply because these activities are potentially harmful for young people. Social media has proven over and over again to have destructive effects on the malleable minds of early adolescents, so the same legislation and safeguards should apply in the digital world too. Every social media site should have easily accessible support systems for those who are having depressive, anxious or suicidal thoughts, and it should be each platform's responsibility to make sure that these services are effective. There should also be very clear warnings that images can be distorted, edited and curated to suggest a level of faultlessness that doesn't exist.

Elsewhere, the perils of perfectionism both on and offline should be taught as a mandatory part of every school syllabus, and we all should be conscious of our own social media use and actually set a good example. Every single person should be aware that in 2018 a shocking 25 per cent of teenage girls in the UK have been diagnosed with mental health issues. But instead, we're touching our phones on average 2,617 times a day and letting the money-making social media machines operate with impunity. WTF are we doing here?

Relationship with Ourselves: Popular, But All Alone

Think about the last time you sat with nothing but your thoughts. Shunning all distractions, confronting what was going on in your head with nothing else except for your own mind to bounce off. Personally, the only time I really am totally "alone" in that way is when I wake up in the night. Although I always start these wakeful periods with mindfulness exercises, I often end up having some of my clearest thoughts in the dead of night. But while my musings may be razor-sharp in the wee hours, they are also punishing and sometimes overwhelming, and the relief which comes with dawn break is palpable. Why? Because I can pick up my phone, relax and stop spinning around whichever crisis – practical or existential – was filling my mind. Scrolling through my phone makes me feel entertained, distracted and safe; on days when I'm feeling particularly low, exhausted or overwhelmed it calms me and allows me to switch off the stream of consciousness snaking around my brain. It also eases my passage to actually getting up, something which, as a person who struggles with sleep, is no mean feat.

There is zero doubt in my mind that I'd prefer to be with my phone than just my self. Aside from the fact that I find it easy, familiar and less stressful, it also stems the intense boredom of self-exploration and alleviates the intensity of my thoughts, dialling things down to a manageable level.

An often-cited 2014 experiment led by Timothy Wilson of the University of Virginia examined how able we are to sit with and entertain ourselves over a short period – six to fifteen minutes – of time. Aside from the majority reporting that they hadn't enjoyed the experience (and several hiccups as subjects found literally *anything* they could do to distract themselves – from stealing a pen to writing a to-do list to using the instruction paper to practise origami), it was the participants' response to the "shock experiment" which most dumbfounded the researchers. Each of the subjects was wired up and given the opportunity to shock themselves whenever they wanted over 15 minutes. Despite the fact they'd already had the opportunity to test the level of shock, and despite the fact that many of them said they would *pay money* to never feel the shock again, a quarter of the women and two-thirds of the men did indeed opt to shock themselves again when left in solitude. One subject pressed the button 190 times in 15 minutes – they felt *that* uncomfortable with their own thoughts, that anything, even physical pain, was better than a quarter of an hour's reverie. Interestingly, the study found that the results were not dependent on age or smartphone/social media use – it isn't just millennial tech addicts who have problems sitting with just their own thoughts.

"Solitude is where you find yourself... If we're not able to be alone, we're going to be lonelier," says Sherry Turkle in her TED Talk, and in many ways, I can relate. Working on my own at home every day has definitely changed my perception of solitude, and for a time I became pretty much incapable of escaping some kind of screen or device. If I was a little more than a hand's reach away from one of them, I got twitchy. Aside from being in the shower (with my phone perched on the sink, just in case), my day ended up being a catalogue of screen segues – from my laptop to tablet to phone to TV. It takes proper discipline to unplug.

Whether or not avoiding time with myself in the day is having an impact on the intensity of my insomnia episodes at night is something I've definitely considered. While there's a solid body of research proving the link between high levels of social media use and disturbed sleep, it's usually blamed on the "wake up" signals created by blue screens, or not switching off early enough. But what if it's because our brains haven't had a moment to reconnect to the self, or sufficient time to come back to our centres? Solitude allows our bodies to catch up with our minds, allows the brain to rest and side-step burnout, and triggers the parasympathetic nervous system, which slows the heart rate, reduces blood pressure and relaxes our muscles. It also allows space for creativity and aids concentration. Without solitude, we are naturally wired, and that's even before we put stimulating screens in front of our faces. Today Americans average only 6.8 hours of sleep a night (less than the health recommendation of 7–9 hours a night), with 40 per cent logging less than 6 hours, according to a Gallup poll. How much is that to do with the collective aversion to solitude? When you consider that a lack of sleep is associated with – take a breath – higher levels of diabetes, heart disease, obesity and depression, as well as a reduced life expectancy, it's easy to see why turning our backs on ourselves threatens not just our mental but also our physical health prognosis.

Zero Escape:
"Screenager" Cyberbullying and Harassment

One danger to mental health that parents *are* more conscious about than ever, is the menace of cyberbullying. This school-gate scourge has commanded so much media attention that parents and teachers alike are hyperaware. However, the threat of online intimidation and victimization is certainly not just reserved for kids: cyberstalking and harassment has become part of the tapestry of digital life. One in every twenty-five Americans online (about ten million people) have either had explicit images of themselves shared against their will or have been threatened with that exposure. For women younger than 30, it was 1 in 10. Another survey found that 47 per cent of Americans who used the internet had been victims of online harassment. Online persecution of black internet users and people that openly identify as lesbian, gay and bisexual was significantly higher. Hate, harassment and hounding aren't just niche www.com experiences – instead they've become worryingly normalized.

The 2.0 bully has distinctive features, especially because social media never sleeps. Our 24/7 connection means that there are no safe spaces – not even locked in our houses or bedrooms. Just think of all those hours we spend plugged into the matrix and imagine that every minute links you to your tormentor, or at least to the threat of torment. There's also the potential for a much greater degree of anonymity for bullies and the difficulties that come with trying to remove bullying digital content – whether it's statements, images or video footage from social media platforms. Once the information is out in the digital ether, stopping it circulating can be near impossible. One of the most horrifying aspects is that you may not even know who these trolls and bullies are – it can just be the bad luck of the draw that you've inspired someone to unleash a personal hell through their keyboard.

Reports suggest that up to 50 per cent of school-age girls go through some level of digital harassment (though for extreme cases it's under the 10 per cent mark) and up to 40 per cent don't tell their parents. While the vast majority of cyberbullying of young people occurs in tandem with the traditional schoolyard tactics of ostracizing, name-calling and physical intimidation, even a short period of digital aggression can, it has been proven, have severe effects on mental health, including rates of depression, anxiety and self-harming behaviours. A study of 2,215 students concluded that cyberbullying can lead to problems processing emotions, disruptions in socially appropriate behaviour, an impaired ability to interact successfully with others and a significant decline in normal levels of concentration. Although there is a level of healthy scepticism about the true impact of cyberbullying – as a hot, zeitgeisty topic among already over-cautious and fearful parents, some teachers and psychologists say that it's been used to mask other issues – the UK's National Society for the Prevention of Cruelty to Children has said it recorded an 88 per cent increase in calls about the issue in the five years between 2011 and 2016.

It's also not just traditional social media platforms providing the theatre for this new upsurge; a host of new "honesty sites", including the much-maligned Sarahah app, have been embroiled in stories of intense digital harassment. Sarahah allows users to send anonymous messages and describes itself as a tool to "Improve your friendship by discovering your strengths and areas for improvement; Let your friends be honest with you." While honesty may be the best policy in some instances, it seems not so great when you don't know where the feedback is coming from. Instead of a two-way street, Sarahah doesn't allow you to know who has so thoughtfully revealed their candid appraisal of your character and you maddeningly can't respond to messages – though you can thankfully block anyone who sends offensive or unwanted posts. Initially programmed for workplace feedback, the app has proven a hit with teens desperate for validation. The goal is to receive positive messages, which they can then share via screenshots on Snapchat. While it sounds convoluted, it's yet another example of the ways in which social media can compound our feelings that we are not worthwhile unless someone else says so and we can share that with our community. Last year Sarahah reached the top of Apple's App Store in 30 countries, including the UK, Ireland, the US and Australia. Already banned in several schools, due to its use in anonymized digital bullying, the site echoes the fears around other anonymous platforms like Ask.fm and Sayat.me, which have both been implicated in teen suicides. While Ask.fm is now under new ownership and has developed a more rigorous response to abuse, Sayat.me, which once had 30 million users, many believed to be teenagers, was taken offline after a British 15-year-old boy took his life. Investigations continue but it has been reported that abusive messages it is believed he had received through the app may have contributed to his death. It can be hard to understand this burning desire to know what people "really think about you", but it's the crucial question at the heart of all insecurity and certainly related to a drive for perfectionism in friendships. Sadly, it also welcomes trolls with open arms.

Cyberbullying of teens is one area where social media sites have responded to concerns. Notably, Facebook has a transparent process for removal of content, which is aided by a support dashboard. However, the social platforms have had constant criticisms of slow response rates and a lack of staffing and investment, which is needed to make the facilities function effectively. Yet again it seems that these sites are failing to put their money where their mouths are. Equally, when digital abuse moves beyond simple user-to-user attacks (with fake accounts being set up and rerouted IP addresses being employed), victims – both young and old – have found that getting social platforms and lawmakers to take them seriously is an uphill battle.

The impact on mental health that this often long-running abuse can have is significant, and it's not just for vulnerable teens or children. A recent Australian study showed that over three-quarters of women under thirty had experienced digital harassment and one in five of them felt depressed, with 5 per cent feeling suicidal because of it.

And these women seem just as reluctant as the schoolkids to report their experiences, most probably because the police have such little sympathy or power to support them. In the UK, in all digital harassment case files reviewed, care for the victim was deemed to be inadequate. *Every single case*. As our law enforcement agencies struggle to contend with the issue, the number of tracked offences has, concurrently, been rising sharply. To give an idea of the extent of the problem, a terrifying 20 per cent of women aged 15–29 have been digitally stalked in some way in the US.

There can be no discussion of cyberbullying without mentioning the exploitation of sexual imagery of women and girls which they have either shared of their own volition or felt pressured into doing so through sexting. Half of all millennials in a 2015 survey said they'd uploaded a nude shot via social media, with Snapchat leading the charge. The problem is that once the picture has been sent, you have to trust that the recipient isn't going to pass it on without your permission. If things turn sour in a relationship, "revenge porn", or the digital dissemination of sexually explicit images or videos, is rife. The charity Childnet International found that more than half of UK teenagers have friends who have shared intimate images of someone they know and 14 per cent of girls say they have been pressured into sharing nude images. To say things can get nasty is an understatement – whether the images are sent to your family members in a direct message, streamed on YouTube alongside commentary about your figure, or shared among your work colleagues with a supporting hashtag, the result is the same: a deep feeling of inescapable shame. Little wonder that US campaign End Revenge Porn found that 51 per cent of US victims have contemplated suicide.

Social networks don't allow the sharing of naked images of people under 18 – it's one of few red lines that they won't allow to be crossed and is seen as strictly a legal matter. But if you're over 18, it can be soul-destroyingly difficult to get such images taken down, especially as they will often be linked from vile revenge porn site to site in an apparent digital quagmire. From a judicial perspective, while it remains illegal in principle to share an explicit image of another person without their consent, in practice, it's painfully difficult to prosecute. Data obtained from the Crown Prosecution Services between July and December 2017 showed that 61 per cent of reported cases in England and Wales resulted in no action being taken – and the same data showed that some victims were as young as 11.

Around the globe, governments have tried, often in vain, to respond to the phenomenon. In Israel, the offence is punishable by five years in jail and those found guilty are prosecuted as sexual offenders, while the targets are recognized as victims of sexual assault. The Japanese Revenge Porn Prevention Act imposes a potential ¥500,000 fine or three years in prison. But no matter where the initial sharing of imagery happened, all legislation is beset with complex difficulties in successfully prosecuting or removing the content from the internationally disparate digital addresses. With the advent of "deepfakes" – AI computer-generated pornography whereby people use artificial intelligence to very convincingly swap the faces of actors in pornographic films with people they know – the need for strident measures from social media sites has never been more necessary. But once again, they will take no responsibility for the damage wreaked through their platforms.

One of the big issues is the sheer amount of personal information we are all sharing – material which can be manipulated by both unscrupulous criminals and digital trolls to take harassment beyond a crappy comment here or there. Ask yourself, how often are you geo-tagging your images on social media? Do you openly celebrate your birthday and disclose your age every year? What about that risqué snap you sent to that guy on Tinder after a couple of rosés? Perhaps you congratulate your mum or your friends on their birthdays? What about your place of birth? Is that accessible in your basic info? Even if you trust that your private details will be kept private, how much could be gleaned if someone really wanted to take advantage of you? Have you ever posted an image with your road name or house number visible?

Do you post your holiday journey to the airport on Stories or Snapchat? The exact address of your hotel? Social media can be a hunting ground for thieves, trolls and stalkers – and while you're flaunting the very best sides of your life to your legitimate friends and followers, you're also opening yourself up to people who can exploit you. Conscious social media is about being aware of how all our projections of perfection can come with a price tag – in the very worst cases an empty bank account, an invaded and ransacked home or a relentless tormentor who has the power to publicly disseminate your private information, including the most intimate of imagery.

In the UK last year, five hundred people a day were impersonated by a criminal trying to steal their money, buy items or take out a loan in their name. Home alarm specialists ADT say up to 78 per cent of burglars use social media to target properties, and according to research at Bedford University, cyberstalking is now more common than physical harassment. This isn't hyperbole, instead it's a moment to check ourselves and consider just how much information we've leaked along our digital footprint – and how much of it might hurt us mentally, both in the long and short term. Don't get paranoid, instead get protected.

Sharing Ill Health: A Blessing or a Curse?

Sickness is bleak, depressing and colossally sad. In the ceaselessly upbeat world of social media, anything that's a downer can feel out of place and, for those dealing with chronic illness or physical health episodes, navigating the unwritten rules about how to share their experiences is still tricky territory. Not every internet user is compassionate: some will see sharing about sickness as attention-seeking, and continual updates with bad news may end up being ignored by those who are unable to cope with the realities of ill-health. This, understandably, can be incredibly hurtful to those who are suffering.

How or why people decide to go public about their medical conditions has always been a matter of deep personal choice, though as with all elements of our lives, social media is rewriting the relationship between privacy and disclosure. These days it's almost impossible to evade exposure of obvious ailments, from losing your hair to broken bones, unless you stay clear of all digital documentation – no birthday group shots for you. There are also clear risks in sharing sensitive health information online, especially when there are stigmas around particular illnesses, not least the impact it might have on your insurance premiums due to woeful gaps in the law. Professionally it may also be problematic, leaving a traceable record of your illness and setting off alarm bells for an employer that you might be unfit for a position. Discrimination is very difficult to prove when you've served up the information in the first place, and the fact that people can access elements of your medical records without even talking to you can have widespread implications for your digital reputation.

For a generation of oversharers, there are other hazards to take into consideration. When you're so used to airing your laundry online, it can become habitual to do so, even when the stakes are higher and the potential for "sharing regret" increases. While you're in the midst of illness you may feel compelled to reveal intimate details of your experience, but on the road to recovery you might feel less happy to have that information and those images of yourself available to the public at large. The problem is, of course, that online they are practically indelible.

What's more, sometimes in the world of digital health, not all is quite as it seems. High-profile cases of sickness fraud – including the now-notorious story of Belle Gibson, a wellness blogger who falsely claimed to have cured her brain cancer with only natural remedies and nutrition – have proven that these communities are vulnerable to fake-news violations and misinformation by immoral charlatans. Building a social media empire off the back of the sympathy she found online for her phony diagnosis, and raising money for charities which she failed to donate, Gibson is an extreme example of how, even in the sensitive realm of sickness, there are con-artists at work.

However, these concerns don't seem to be stemming the tide, and a significant proportion of people *are* sharing their medical issues, with up to 40 per cent of people saying they have posted online about a health-related issue. One of the biggest reasons is that there is a wealth of information, advice and support out there, just waiting to be harnessed. Collective experience of health, and information around specific conditions, is so much more diverse and broad than one person's journey, meaning that for those struggling, there's a wealth of intelligence, treatment plans and specialist recommendations ready to be accessed through peer-to-peer support.

In 1983, a study of people with epilepsy found that only 6 per cent had ever spoken to anyone who shared the same illness. Today 4.5 million people a week use apps like HealthUnlocked, a social network which matches you with other people dealing with the same health issues. Patient empowerment has changed the terms of the medical game, and advocacy around specific illnesses has helped develop what has been termed "sickness subcultures", with some of the most highly engaged communities anywhere online. These support groups can be a lifeline to those who have been housebound by their illness, especially if there is functionality for digital social interaction, so it's little wonder there's been such a boom in health-related social applications – there are currently thousands of apps available on Apple's App Store, covering everything from haemophilia to asthma.

Lauren Mahon, a blogger and social media manager, was diagnosed with breast cancer at 31 and used her platforms to both document her experience and campaign for greater awareness. Her journey highlights the unbelievable power as well as the challenges of sharing a health account online. "Cancer is such an unknown," Lauren explains, "so when I was being sent off for scans, bloods and egg-freezing, I remember wishing I'd known what to expect, just a little bit. That was one of the reasons I knew I wanted to do something to raise awareness online in the hope it might help another woman like me. It wasn't until the week before my treatment started that I actually found the confidence to say what was happening and go "public" on social media. I know it sent a shockwave through my following, especially as I was a young, healthy, happy woman – it just wasn't the serious news that anyone was used to hearing. When I made the decision to be honest and open about my experience, I knew I had to do it the whole way. Warts and all – or, in my case, pooping in the bath. It's a grim reality, but by normalizing the conversation we make the world a slightly less scary place for all those facing or who will face this disease. For me, the very hardest part is definitely dealing with your own mortality on a daily basis. Being in the cancer community is incredibly powerful, and the experience binds you and means you're never alone. However, it also means that you make friends with people who may not make it and see spread and recurrence coming from every corner, and that can make it a difficult space to exist in sometimes."

Social media communities who have followed an individual's illness can also, she explains, add a level of complexity to moving on once into recovery. "I lost a fair few followers when I went on holiday to Sri Lanka this year, and I wondered if it was because people were only interested in the gritty, sad side of cancer and now that I feel as though I'm on the up, it's boring? My good friend Laura, who has also just kicked cancer's butt, posted something recently that said, 'They want to see you do well but never better than them,' and that does ring true." Other worries have included the reaction from others in a professional capacity. "I have worried that I'm not desirable for potential employers because I'm perceived as this 'cancer girl'," she says. "But I also know I'm so much more than that, and any person or business that wouldn't want me around because of it isn't worth my precious time anyway. Honestly, I truly have no regrets because launching my campaign, GIRLvsCANCER, gave me a space to curate and show my own experience, my way, rather than the clinical, scary way shoved down our throats in the media. I'm also so proud that my coping mechanism is helping others cope too."

Another subject for debate centres on how much you share about someone else's health issues – however much they might impact the reality of your life. Traversing this complicated line, Claire Marshall, the content creator behind the beauty and lifestyle blog and YouTube channel *Hey Claire*, has tussled with what to reveal and what to conceal about her mother's declining health to her audience of nearly a million subscribers. "My mom was diagnosed with early-stage dementia in 2011, but we didn't know how quickly she would deteriorate," Claire explains. "I've always tried to be very open and honest with my followers and I'm so appreciative of them. When I first started out and everything was happening with my mom, I didn't really have many friends or a solid support network to lean on, so my audience really became my family. Those few hundred followers were the closest I had to a network, and I shared a lot of what was happening in my life. For example, the first time my mom forgot my birthday. Nowadays, I think there are times when some of my followers feel I'm holding back, but it's really just out of respect for the other people who are now in my life, including my mom."

✗ ✗ ✗

Social media has revolutionized our experience of health and fundamentally changed the way society treats both mental and physical conditions. There is no going back: what was once incredibly personal has become incredibly public. In so many ways this can be liberating and life-affirming. But while social media has facilitated changes in cultural attitudes, fostered communities and undermined the stigma around both mental and physical health, it also has been a significant trigger for the contemporary mental health crisis.

Not everything or everyone online are there to help you, least of all the social media firms themselves. There can be long-lasting consequences to what you share about your wellbeing, as with all aspects of your life, and if you've been sleep-walking into spending untold hours on social media, it's time to wake up to the damage it may be doing to you. Consciously consume, know your rights and stay awake to the information that you are sharing, because the truth is: your very health depends on it.

Takeaways

1. Learn your triggers

One of the first steps to dealing with anxiety can be to accept that it's an element of your makeup. "As soon as you acknowledge that anxiety is part of your reaction to certain triggers, you can start to learn to manage it," explains Lindsey Holland. "There will be some situations that you go into that will cause a strange build-up of feelings and emotions, but the key is to recognize them because you can then begin to talk yourself down. After a while you realize that everything comes from pressure that you're putting on yourself, and that means that only you are capable of reducing that burden."

There is no catch-all cure for feelings of anxiety, but more than anything it is vital that you work out what sets you off personally. For lots of people that will be something that they consume on social media, so the way you use these digital tools is fundamental to managing issues.

Start by adopting best-practice tactics:

* Unfollow anyone that makes you feel inadequate.
* Limit the amount of time you spend on your phone.
* Push yourself to engage with social things outside your online life.
* Try to work out why certain triggers are setting you off – what are you actually worried or nervous about?
* Begin to identify things that are actually dangerous (say, a risk of injury or death) rather than just scary.
* Remember that there is a difference between those two things – and that difference is your perception. (Something that might seem scary, like starting a new job, is definitely not a risk to your life, whereas something that might not seem frightening at all – like deciding not to use sunscreen on the beach – may actually be dangerous.) This is a technique I use a lot to try to really drill down to how I'm actually feeling and stop my automatic anxiety response. For example, writing this book is scary but not dangerous, so it shouldn't fuel my angst.

To use myself as an example for the last point, I have an active, worry-prone mind and I've taken a lot of gambles in my life: leaving jobs without another one to go to, moving country with no real plan, deciding to set up my own business in a new and unproven market... These leaps of faith have been terrifying and have certainly caused me turmoil. But understanding worse-case scenarios and acknowledging that they are generally not *dangerous* has enabled me to take them while relatively keeping a lid on the anxiety.

2. Let go of the milestones

If seeing other people hit milestones makes you feel inadequate, ask yourself why. Why do you need to be on a timeline? Who says so? Life is generally not compliant with your plans: that's life, and it's just the way it is.

I'm 34, unmarried with a baby and still can't drive. I didn't get to edit a magazine, I don't have a garden or stairs in my house – my deadlines have come and gone years ago. Seeing that other people do have those things could get me down, but knowing I run my own business instead – something I never thought would be part of my life – and have a solid, healthy relationship that doesn't require a ring or a bouquet to make it complete makes me realize that there are better things out there than what I thought I wanted and needed. Happiness and success aren't one straight line or a ladder of equally spaced rungs. It's a topsy-turvy, unpredictable journey of highs and lows. Feeling anxiety about going off course is entirely misplaced because there is no course. I'm still happy and successful in my own way, even though most of the things I had on my life plan didn't work out.

3. App yourself happy

One of the issues with social media is that we can feel out of control of our consumption of it. We know our constant scrolling is making us feel bad, but we're not sure how to police ourselves. One solution is to use technology to help you get to where you want to be. Today there are a host of new tools out there to help you break bad habits and can help you develop a healthier – and happier – relationship with social media. Here are a few examples:

* The iOS app Moment tots up every minute you spend on your phone and allows you to see exactly which apps are draining your time.
* AppDetox (for Android) allows you to create specific rules for access to certain apps with time-based limitations, as well as an option which requires you to walk to get access to more screen time. By literally locking your apps it forces you off social media and back into real life.
* The Freedom app can block distracting apps and websites across your computers and any Apple devices at once, allowing you to schedule in specific times of the day when you just can't access them. You can also block the whole of the internet if you really need to focus on a task at hand.
* Need something a little more extreme? Check out Off the Grid, an app for Android phones that completely jams your phone for however long you ask it to. Whether you're heading out for dinner with friends or are adamant that you want to put your phone down at 9pm every night, you can entirely check out. You can also be safe in the knowledge that people attempting to contact you will be informed that you're currently "off-grid", that loved ones can be added to a "whitelist" to ensure important calls can still get through, and that you can still access your camera, because, well, you know why.
* If you'd rather not rely on apps, you could even connect your router at home to an outlet timer to cut off access to the internet for your whole abode at a set time every day.

These aids may sound dramatic, but they are definitely effective. Self-control can be an issue for everyone, but there is a whole host of technology at your fingertips to help you protect yourself.

4. Schedule some solitude

Just thinking that you want to spend less time on your phone is not enough. When there's something that's as attractive as social media on offer, your habits don't just change – you actually have to make a concerted effort. One of the ways that you can help yourself is to timetable daily, or even weekly, moments of quiet. As we know from the electric shock experiment above, a lot of us struggle with alone time and sitting with our own thoughts. Guided meditations are one way of learning to be relaxed in our own company, but it's not for everyone. Start by taking just five minutes every day to sit up in bed before you run to the shower – and make sure your phone isn't reachable. You might like to make a cup of hot water and lemon, or else just take a moment to scan how you're feeling. Mindfulness exercises can help if your thoughts become overwhelming, and knowing that there are only five minutes to get through can help make it more manageable. Over time, try extending the length of time you spend with yourself. Remember the aim is not to run away from your thoughts but confront them. It's not meant to be easy, but over time you are more aware of how you feel about things, and as a bonus, it might even help you fall and *stay* asleep.

I'm definitely working on this one as we speak.

5. Get real about digital security

Using the same password for everything? Have no idea what two-step verification means? Time to start getting serious about your security. Aside from giving cyberbullies and trolls potential access to your information and identity, slack digital security can open you up to all kinds of fraud. I have two girlfriends who have had their social media accounts hacked and all the images deleted, and of course, the perpetrators gained access to all their personal details too.

These days profiles can be used for all sorts of services and site logins way beyond just social media, so keeping control of yours should be a major priority.

Sounds boring? It is, but it's also so worth it. I've spent untold hours sweeping through my profiles removing any images which might point to my address or personal information. However, it can be tricky to encourage others to be as mindful as you are – if someone posts a birthday ode to you on their profile, for example, it can be difficult to ask them to take it down. But think of it this way – would you tell any stranger on the street your date of birth? It can be hard to scrub information from the internet, so the best practice is to never reveal it in the first place. And just remember, however much effort it might take to protect yourself, it's just a fraction of the headache you'll have if you let someone else get their hands on your info.

It's also crucial to think carefully before you send any images to anyone. The rule is: don't trust anybody with imagery which you wouldn't be happy posting on your own Instagram. If you don't want to be sorry, be safe.

6. Know the risks as well as the rewards

Community, acceptance and support are just some of the benefits of sharing both mental and physical health issues online, but it's important not to be blind to the realities of the risks too. Your digital footprint is crucial to the professional recruitment process and, sadly, no matter how much attitudes *are* changing, discrimination against those battling health issues remains rampant. Indeed, half of people with diagnosed mental health illnesses say that they had not been hired because of it. You should consider that if you disclose your problem to the internet, you are disclosing it to any potential employer too. This is not a reason not to share, but it is a reason to be conscious about the way you do it.

Charly Cox explains her rationale: "This issue used to be a constant struggle for me, but now ultimately it boils down to the truth that if a future employer has seen me talk openly about my mental health and found issue with it, it's not going to work out anyway. But there's definitely a way to go about it. Keeping things conversational is a good rule of thumb; anything too self-confessional or worrying which has potential to spark concern suggests it's not something you're dealing with well. By no means should you feel the need to make it light or limited, but try to find an overarching message or point through sharing your own experiences, as it makes it look less like a plea for help. Always think: why do I want to share this particular story? Will someone find solace within it? Will it make someone feel less alone? Stigma is still there, and it will take a while for those with judgement to see it for what it is. Ultimately though, pushing through a fear of judgement has been much more rewarding and boosting for me than sitting silent and knowing nothing's changing. Strangely, it's also made me feel more in control of my own mental health."

Chapter 4:
Why Social Media is
Ruining Your **Relationships**

*Man is by nature a social animal; an individual who is unsocial
naturally and not accidentally is either beneath our notice or
more than human.*
— ARISTOTLE, *POLITICS*

How would you define a friend? Is it someone you could turn to no matter what? Just call my name and I'll be there? Or is it someone who you're in near-constant contact with, speaking to all day, every day? Is it the person you've got the longest "Snapstreak" (chatted on Snapchat for over three days straight) with? How much one-on-one time do you have together? And what are your conversations like – deeply engaged and empathetic, or more interrupted and punctuated into bite-size snippets?

The impact that social media is having on all of our relationships, spanning our families, friends and romantic couplings to our very relationships with ourselves, has been fundamentally altered by the way we use our devices to communicate with each other. What we now need from our networks is in flux, and the very nature of friendship and the foundations on which we believe they should be based have changed almost beyond recognition. The question is: *is social media enhancing our social lives, or is it doing the exact opposite?*

Humans are by definition social beings. From a genetic perspective, we have evolved to live in social groups for both protection and reproduction. Being social makes us buoyant: connection to a group makes us happier; social exchanges reduce the stress hormone cortisol, while simultaneously raising feel-good oxytocin and serotonin. Being social is basically like biological crack – so is it any wonder that we've become so very quickly, so very deeply infatuated with *social* media?

"As humans, we thrive by building relationships. It's very primordial. Social media plays right into what really makes us tick as human beings," explains Dr James A Roberts, a professor in marketing and an expert on digital consumer behaviour. And who can argue? Logging on to read thoughtful comments and messages from friends, seeing what loved ones are busy getting up to and reading insightful stories which make us feel connected to our digital tribe can create an instant sense of belonging.

It can also relieve any feelings of loneliness and reduce the geographical differences between us that are part of modern lifestyles. But it's no panacea and the very reasons that it's so seductive have also become causes for concern. "As relationships are so important to us, there's an argument that the more we use social media, the better. But that's only if we're *actively* interacting with other people – sending messages and pictures and connecting," Dr Roberts continues. "But really what we're finding is that much of social media use is *passive*, characterized by 'lurking' or 'creeping'. We're spending hours not actually socializing, but merely viewing other people, consuming sanitized, best-case scenarios of each other's lives. Instead of the feel-good hormones we might expect to be pumping through our veins instead, we're torn between feelings of FOMO and inadequacy."

The tech companies have jumped upon this distinction between active and passive social media consumption as the new paradigm for determining "good" vs "bad" social media relationships. The argument is that if you're actually using platforms to meaningfully connect, then you'll reap the positive rewards that digital socialization can offer. On the other hand, if you stay schtum and just lurk, stalk and creep, your mental health and happiness will be at risk. As an admission that social media can be bad for us, it's a start, but there are many, many other factors at play when it comes to the ways in which social media has changed our relationships. The distinction between active and passive use is too simplistic to nail it. Essentially, our phones and social apps haven't just changed how we make relationships, they've also changed what we believe relationships to be.

Quantity Over Quality:
Friendships in the Digital Scape

With our phones by our sides we are never alone. Even though I work from home on my own I speak to lots of different people via social media, email and messaging services. In fact, I'd say I have some kind of exchange with at least 50 people a day, about half of whom are people I know and half are those I don't know at all. In the olden days, speaking to 50 people would be an über-social day, but now, in our mediated world, it's pretty unremarkable. Being alone with technology feels markedly less alone. In 2008, Clive Thompson coined the term "ambient intimacy", a description of the cumulative impact of comforting pieces of micro-information which we're all consuming daily about each other. Instead of having to make an effort to meet with friends in person, we can skim "weak ties" to get those little hits of connection which we crave. By plugging into our phones we can escape ourselves and the strain of solitude and swim in a simulated sea of social interaction.

This state of affairs has an interesting impact on widely accepted psychological theories. For example, "Dunbar's Number", named after anthropologist Robin Dunbar, suggests that there's an upper limit on how many people we can know before connections start to fray. In 1998, he published his beliefs that the human brain can only manage a finite number of relationships, somewhere around the 150 mark. Other psychological studies have supported the reasoning by showing that social human groupings generally taper off around that number. I currently follow 838 people on Instagram, I've got 848 friends on Facebook and 303 on Twitter. And that's before we even get into the responses I give to comments from the approximately fifty thousand followers across all my platforms. And I'm not unique in this; most of us are now connected to a veritable ton of people. So how are we doing it when our human brains can only apparently cope with 150 contacts?

The answer is simple: *most of these people are not your friends.* They can't give you the connection you seek, and the apparent intimacy they offer is all an illusion. This is harsh but true, and what's more, the research proves it: teens who visit social-networking sites daily yet meet up with their friends less frequently are the most likely to agree that "A lot of times I feel lonely," "I often feel left out of things," and "I often wish I had more good friends." A 2014 study showed that a quarter of people didn't feel they had *one person* they could confide their personal troubles and triumphs to. Loneliness has been shown to be as damaging to our health as smoking 15 cigarettes a day, and it's become worryingly normalized across all ages and social backgrounds. The UK government even just appointed a "Loneliness Minister" in an effort to tackle the issue.

Spending my days alone but constantly connected doesn't stop me from feeling isolated. It doesn't stop me from jumping on my boyfriend the moment he walks in the door, desperate for some kind of human contact. It really just makes me feel alienated in my little silo, working as a one-woman band. And the people I'm connected to? Apart from those I'm genuinely intimate with, most of them are what has been termed "parasocial friends" – remote connections similar to those we can form with celebrities or even fictional characters. Keeping up with their movements can use up some of the emotional space in our Dunbar number, pushing out the people with whom we have authentic connections. Spreading myself thinly over hundreds, if not thousands, of people means that I have less time for my real-life mates. One of my new year's resolutions was to devote some of the four and a half hours per day I'd been filling with screen time to face-to-face meetings instead. Yes, it takes a chunk out of your day, but only a chunk you'd be wasting on your phone. More connection doesn't mean less isolation. It just means we're using our social time on shallow and non-meaningful snippets of friendships – or ambient intimacy – rather than the real thing.

Filtering Our Communications

I wasn't a popular kid in school. By the time I got to secondary school, this time a selective, private girls', I'd developed a loner status and being left out was just what I expected. To be honest, it made me feel a bit miserable, but not inconsolable – I had my hobbies and my books and I was nerdy enough to enjoy going to school for the learning. I always looked forward to exams and got on very well with my teachers. Need I say any more? Not really having any friends was part of my young life until I was 14, when ditching my glasses, getting a "Rachel from *Friends*" haircut and picking up a new smoking habit somehow gained me entry into the popular group at school. It was an extraordinary teen film-esque moment and the feeling of being accepted by a *clique* changed the rest of my school experience. Even though I was never really properly "in" (I still had a roster of deeply uncool after-school activities, including clarinet lessons and greenhouse monitoring), it was also when the troubles started. Girls can be mean and running with a crowd of high-achieving, pretty adolescents led to the start of a life-long anxiety around female friendships.

One of my biggest problems used to be that I often put my foot in it. "Saying what you see" is a good skill for a writer and journalist, less so a teenage girl trying to navigate a complex and highly strung set of social rules. I regularly made blunders which could come off as tactless and the result would often be an ejection from the social circle for an unbearable period of weeks, sometimes months. Each and every time it happened, it was like my world fell apart. Even today I'm highly aware of how my words could be construed by friends and I deliberate over ways of approaching issues, avoiding conflict at all costs. I still find it nearly impossible to contend with any difficult conversation in person and, while I'm good at hiding it, the amount of hand-wringing, tears and nausea that confrontation both in the workplace and in my social life causes me is off the charts. Social conflict has the power to paralyze me and completely take over my life: I can't think, I can't eat, I can't sleep. And

I definitely cannot just "let it go". If a friend is upset with me, it hollows me out, and while I've got much better at accepting that not everyone *in general* is going to like me, issues still emotionally floor me.

Over the ensuing 20 years, I've learned to be more diplomatic, but those youthful experiences have certainly impacted the way I prefer to communicate with friends today. One of the big attractions of conversing via mediated technology – whether it's text, email or social media – is that you have the power to review and edit your words until you get them "just so", something I find hugely comforting. I'm actually also massively telephobic (talking-on-the-phone-averse). However, like most millennials, I'm entirely at ease emailing anyone to ask for anything and feel both articulate and confident communicating via the written word. WhatsApp is an entirely stress-free environment for me. In fact, everything about communicating via technology appeals, whereas a lot of face-to-face interaction – especially anything awkward or potentially aggressive – brings me out in a cold sweat.

In this, according to Sherry Turkle, professor of social studies of science and technology at MIT, I am not alone. In her 2012 TED talk, which has been viewed more than four million times, she explains how technology has eased our path to connection while undermining our ability to have face-to-face conversations. As she says, "Texting, email, posting, all of these things let us present the self as we want to be. We get to edit, and that means we get to delete, and that means we get to retouch. Human relationships are messy and demanding, and we clean them with technology." When I look back at the social struggles I experienced in my adolescence, I know 100 per cent that had I had the option to use my phone to communicate with my teenage circle, to present myself through a filter, I would have used it as exclusively as possible. I was so scared of saying blunt things and what people might think of me that the ability to perfect my conversations would have been far too alluring.

A survey of American millennials by OnePoll found 65 per cent don't feel comfortable engaging with someone face-to-face, and 80 per cent prefer conversing digitally. As today's schoolkids increasingly prefer to connect remotely, there's little reason to leave the house. The number of teens who get together with their friends nearly every day dropped by more than 40 per cent from 2000 to 2015. We want access to each other – but crucially we want it in a controlled environment. Of course, there are potential drawbacks to digital communication – the fact that everything you say is "on record" adds a sense of pressure and the threat of cyberbullying is rife. But in general, digital communication allows us to sterilize our relationships and avoid the challenge of looking someone in the eye when having to say things which feel tricky. Avoidance is part and parcel of the way we connect today.

"In the past I've got into heated discussions with a friend and I've said something in the moment because I was so emotional. Whereas I find if I message my friend saying, 'I feel upset about what happened,' it gives them time to digest that message and think about what they want to say back, which often helps to calm the situation," explains Lily Pebbles, a blogger, YouTuber and author of The F Word, a book on modern female friendship. "I know I sometimes hide behind a screen – I've definitely decided to go to WhatsApp before calling a friend in person. It's almost like a pre-warning, so I'm not just coming from out of the blue and having a go about something. The idea of just calling someone or turning up at their doorstep to have an argument – I'd be terrified!"

At this stage of my life, the majority of my significant relationships (aside from that with my partner) happen through technology. My immediate family all live abroad. While my mum was living in Cape Town it was typical for us to only see each other at Christmas. My brother lives in Germany so it's easy to go year to year without having any physical contact. However, the three of us message each other approximately 467 times a day on our WhatsApp group chat. I know pretty much everything about their lives. Sometimes it can feel like a burden to keep up with the thread, but it's completely transformed our family dynamic. My brother and I didn't get on when we lived together as kids and we grated each other's gears during a two-year stint sharing a flat in my early thirties. Online, however, we are perfect, respectful siblings. Equally, my best girlfriend Beth lives in New York but we maintain a daily connection via technology. We have discovered each other through our screens, and while face-to-face conversations established and solidified our early friendship, now as our lives keep us closer to home, technology serves as a more than capable conduit. For me, on a personal level, social media and advances in communication technology have offered me an incredible opportunity to keep in touch with the people I most care about. I have become the perfect long-distance friend and feel authentically invested in my digital relationships.

However, and this is a *big* however, I'm aware that by reducing how often I do something I don't like to do (any type of tricky face-to-face conversation), my skills have become further depleted and my anxieties around them have heightened, and then some. The types of conversations I now rate as tricky have become more and more extensive. I also find it extremely difficult to be spontaneous and would rarely just pick up the phone to catch up with a friend or ask them over to my flat on a whim. There's a feeling that I can't interrupt them by asking for their time at too late notice, or that it's intrusive to call at the weekend, or during their evenings. Far better to text so they can get back to me in their own time.

It's not that I actually lack social confidence in terms of face-to-face meetings – my job is so sociable that it would be impossible to do if I didn't like meeting and talking to people, and I make acquaintances very easily. It's more I've become very used to the social media age pre-agreed boundaries for developing and maintaining those relationships, even among close friends. One thing that I've noticed is these confines often keep things shallow in real life – sharing is not quite the same as actually caring. Gone are the days when I'd have DMCs (deep and meaningful conversations) into the wee hours, listening intently to my girlfriend's struggles. The intensity of those friendships has simply worn off, and communication via technology has certainly had its part to play. It's definitely hard to type out heavy feelings among the emojis; far easier to gloss over it all and keep things light and message-digestible.

If I'm feeling these issues in my thirties, is it any wonder that there are reports of young people entering the workplace entirely lacking in basic interpersonal skills? Making eye contact, small talk, picking up the phone and performing in meetings are all areas that young millennials are said to be failing in. Michaela Launerts, author of *#GirlCode,* explains that young office recruits are "so used to being able to filter themselves before they post something online that they get stuck in a kind of real life stage fright."

From personal experience, I'd also say that favouring digital communication in all cases is something that is catching – you don't have to have been born after 1990 to have altered the way you get in contact with people. The first magazine office I worked in at the *Sunday Times* was a loud, boisterous cacophony of phone calls, with colleagues interviewing, cajoling and sometimes outright screaming down their handsets at poor, unsuspecting PRs. At my last office job, a fashion-tech company, I didn't even have my own phone. In fact, there was only one landline on the whole floor. Work progressed in monastic silence, or else punctuated with intense music, and it was easy to avoid face time for days on end. Of course, we did chat, but it wasn't a prerequisite to functioning in the workplace – you could use the social and work-related Slack channels to connect to your colleagues, and for everything else there was email. While there were plenty of millennials on staff, the screen communication culture was common to everyone, no matter what their age. It's just how offices are these days. It's easy to say, "So what?" – as long as we're still chatting and able to work and build relationships, even if it is only through our screens, really how much has changed? Isn't this just evolution in progress? However, it's worth considering: a) why we've been so keen to adopt this new way of communication, and b) what we miss in the process. The first answer is simple: it's easier and quicker to communicate with a screen than with a person who might stammer and stutter their response, and we love convenience more than anything. The second answer is thornier, but also more profound.

In the 1960s and 1970s Alfred Mehrabian, currently professor emeritus of psychology at UCLA, put forward research on the relative importance of verbal and non-verbal messages in the context of communication of emotions. He suggested that only 7 per cent of successful communication is in the words we use, 38 per cent in our tone of voice and 55 per cent in our body language. Although this research is clearly focused on face-to-face interactions and has been widely critiqued over the ensuing decades, it points to how important non-verbal cues can be for the delivery of our emotions. This will not be news to anyone who has been *seriously* misunderstood through digital communication. How many times have you made a joke via text only to get a "?" back from your friend? Or suggested something by email which has been received as being aggressive or thoughtless when that was the last thing you meant? How much less likely would the confusion have happened if you'd been there in person to add a wink, a nudge and maybe a sardonic smile at the end of your memo?

It's not rocket science to understand why we might feel more bonded to our friends in person rather than via text, but it's depressing how often we're happy to substitute the ersatz communication for the real thing. In *Reclaiming Conversation: The Power of Talk in a Digital Age*, Sherry Turkle makes a striking case for the need to preserve conversation. Aside from surveying the worrying lack of social development among school-age children, she makes the ultimate point: "Face-to-face conversation is the most human – and humanizing – thing we do. Fully present to one another, we learn to listen. It's where we develop the capacity for empathy."

Without empathy, we can't tell when we hurt each other; we lose the ability to read our colleagues', parents' or children's subtle cues; we forget each other's emotional ticks and nuances. Hiding behind a screen makes us regress in our levels of emotional and social intelligence. And over time we become more and more a mystery to each other, degrading the quality of our human connections until we feel deeply alone.

And when it comes to romantic relationships, the behaviour of those who've grown up in the anti-social social age is especially poignant. Dr Jean M Twenge, a professor of psychology at San Diego State University and author of *iGen* (defined as the generation born between 1995 and 2012 who can't remember a time before the internet), notes that in her 25 years of research there has never been such an abrupt shift in behaviour between generations. Let's take dating as an example. In 2015, only about 56 per cent of US high-school seniors went out on dates, whereas for baby boomers and Generation X, that percentage was around 85 per cent. Why go out on dates to get to know each other when you can just send each other snaps and lurk on each other's stories from the comfort and physical and emotional safety of your own bed? Aside from not dating, teens also aren't having sex – the number of sexually active teens in the US has declined by almost 40 per cent since 1991 and the teen birth rate in the UK has halved since 1998. This generation doesn't drink or take drugs in the same way either – in the UK levels of alcohol consumption have plummeted to their lowest levels in over a decade and teens in the US are less likely to be taking illicit drugs than their predecessors. So, what are they doing instead of sex, drugs and rock 'n' roll? I'll give you two guesses and they both start with the smartphone.

Romance is Dead: Break-Ups in the Digital Era

Romantic Instagram relationships are perhaps the easiest to fall for. However cynical you might be, and even if you manage to avoid every Katherine Heigl romcom, the dream of "happily ever after" stares back at you, seemingly from every screen. And this is especially true when it comes to social media. When I got married eight years ago, I was pretty culpable when it came to projecting only the good side of my relationship online. That wasn't because I was trying to manipulate what the outside world thought of me (at least consciously) – it was more that I only took and shared pictures when we were happy. But still, no-one could ever have guessed that it wasn't a fairy tale, and I was more than happy to perpetuate that myth.

Even though I view them with a heavy dose of cynicism, gushingly romantic gestures on social media can still make me slightly bereft because they play to our deeply internalized ideals of happy ever after. Nearly half of a Pew Research study group of teenagers (47 per cent) agreed that social media offers a place for them to show how much they care about their significant other, with 12 per cent feeling this way "a lot". I think we all know someone who falls into that 12 per cent – somebody who spends most of their time posting dreamy love scenes, or writing heartfelt messages to their partner on social media (check out @TheCoupleGoals on Instagram, currently boasting over four million followers. Warning: not for the faint- or broken-hearted). Their love seems to be the core of their social media existence and identity, with "I" morphing into "we" progressively with every "Relfie" (yes, that's a relationship selfie). Of course, in the same way that we've learned that individuals present a hyper-idealized view of themselves and their bodies on social media, the same thing happens with the way we present our partnerships. Just think, when did you last see a shot of an argument in progress or one of the not quite so thoughtful things (underwear left on the floor, loo seat up, every cup in the kitchen used and unwashed...) that all our partners on occasion annoy us with? But contrary to expectations, research has proven that those who post the most about their other half are in fact the least secure in their relationship status. A 2014 study showed that when people felt more insecure about their partner's feelings they tended to make their relationships visible on Facebook on a daily basis. The truth is you never know what is actually going on behind the screens or those closed doors.

To use my own marriage as an example, having presented happy images of wedded bliss on social media, I was just as shocked as anyone when my husband left me a couple of weeks shy of my thirtieth birthday. With just the shirt on his back he was gone overnight, and aside from one brief meeting later when I said goodbye to our terrier, I've never seen him again. It is to this day the most shocking thing that's ever happened to me and marked a definite juncture between being a person who believed in a world of controlled rites of passage and someone who understands that life is often messy. After eight years of sharing the same bed as someone, a shock break-up is always going to send you a bit bonkers. When you've been married in front of all your friends and family, and implicitly in front of today's broader social media network, it's a whole lot worse. I was – how can I put this – stark, raving, off-the-charts deranged. Googling "Divorce before 30" (obviously my first step at day zero), served up countless news stories replete with stats proving the high likelihood that youthful "I dos" will end in Splitsville. You can find pieces that explain, "You still have a chance" (thanks, *Elite Daily*), advice blogs telling you that your divorce will be "one of the best experiences of your life" (spoiler alert: not until well down the line) and a few nicely written anecdotal accounts (*HuffPost* has a heartfelt series if you find yourself in a similar position). But there's no guide to surviving the bat-shit period, no conversation about how to keep it together and very little mention of the deep, gnawing shame that comes with a failed marriage so young, in a world demanding perfection.

After a few days of trying to work out how I could change myself so he would want me again, everything became a haze. I was immediately adamant that I had to keep it together and only took one day off work. I stopped sleeping almost entirely. A few moments from that time are clear: my miserable birthday dinner where everything tasted of cardboard; the first Christmas on my own with my family distraught to see me in such a state; and the well-meaning private messages sent to me via Facebook and Instagram, from married friends who "couldn't believe" that it had happened but who very soon I would never hear from ever again.

From the social media perspective, I had approximately one thousand images on my Facebook profile of my ex-husband and they tortured me for months. Whenever I was travelling, or up awake at night, I would look through them all in a manic, masochistic binge. The wedding shots obviously cut deep, but the most painful were the early-day unglamorous shots – the pictures of us falling in love. As Ira Hyman, professor of psychology at Western Washington University, explains in *Psychology Today*, "Facebook holds everything in an unchanging past. All those happy pictures. All that togetherness. The version Facebook retains is the idealized version of that old relationship and the glorified, impossible version of your previous partner. Only the good times reside in the network's memory." Social media kept my rose-tinted specs well and firmly on, and plugged into a past which was, to every intent and purpose, completely over.

After a couple of months of mooning, I nipped it in the bud and deleted every image of him – and yes, it took hours. Also, when I packed up his stuff, I sent off every photograph of us, every keepsake, every love note. I donated my white dress and its associated veil to charity and wiped the flat clear of anything that would set me off. When you're trying to keep your dignity (which really means being able to leave the house and not end up in hysterics), it's important to be totally ruthless. I fully deleted him from both my online and offline lives, which was a massive wrench at the time but definitely helped the grieving process.

When your audience, be that three hundred Facebook friends or thousands of YouTube followers, has consumed your relationship online, it can feel like a huge pressure to explain where the hell this other person has gone from your life. I kept quiet about it, but then at the time I didn't have the kind of following I do now. Lizzy Hadfield, a YouTuber who regularly shared posts featuring her ex, had a lot more pressure to deal with the public fallout. "I was really, really nervous about telling my followers about my break-up last year," she explains. "So much so that I put a proper plan together because I was so worried about how it would be received. I did feel responsible for protecting my ex, and it was definitely frustrating to feel I had to justify things, because breaking up is hard enough to do behind closed doors. But I knew I had to do it in a respectful way. There ended up being a lot of negativity towards him, which is horrible because *I* put myself out there online, and while I've weighed up the repercussions of that, other people – your friends and family – shouldn't have to deal with it. But I guess that's just the way it is and part of your privacy that you sacrifice when you live your life on screen."

My break-up rock bottom was spent in The Bowery Hotel during New York Fashion Week, February 2014. I was lonely, in terrible debt, terrified of the logistics of my divorce and had burned my face with hair straighteners, creating five shiny blisters on the side of my face. During *fashion week*. I still wasn't sleeping and had a huge workload ahead of 12-hour days, 2am deadlines and 5am wake-up calls. I still had to get up every morning, put my face on and pull together a chic outfit. I had a photographer shooting my looks for a social project I was working on for my magazine's channels and, of course, felt the pressure to post on my own social platforms too. When I look back at those images I can see the pain in my eyes, but no-one really would have ever guessed what was going on and I certainly wasn't telling. Instead, from a social media perspective, it just looked like I was having a glamorous time at New York Fashion Week wearing lovely clothes and staying in a five-star hotel... Yet another example of how entirely inaccurate social media perceptions can be.

The biggest thing with any break-up is that you have to keep somewhere in your muddled mind that you will come out the other side. My "other side" moment happened on my first ever trip to Los Angeles, one of the reasons that the city will always be dear to me. It was a mere seven weeks after my break-up and things were pretty bleak. I was in town to interview two towering female names in international fashion – Diane von Furstenberg and Tory Burch – and both of them were incredibly inspiring. Halfway through my interview with Diane, she stopped me and asked, "Is there something going on with you?" While I thought I'd been hiding the black hole that had taken residence within my heart, it seems the subterfuge wasn't enough to fool DVF. I ended up giving her a précis of my situation, and in turn she gave me two pieces of advice which have stuck with me ever since.

Firstly, she told me that, "the body has no memory for pain", something which seems impossible to believe when you're in the depths of despair, but is one of the most useful and accurate pieces of counsel I've ever been given. Even now, as I'm writing about that time, it's as if it happened to some other person. I can't completely connect to that pain – my body bears no physical scar of that emotional sucker punch and, while I'm not saying I don't have some psychological echoes from that time, in the main I've just moved on. However hard things get, you have to hold on to the fact that the pain will pass and you *will* come back to yourself. Secondly, Diane said to me, "It's time to change the lenses in your glasses. You think he left you, but the truth is he set you free."

She was right: my ex actually did set me free, but I felt entirely unequipped to deal with the new world of romance. Dating after you go through any kind of break-up isn't straightforward, but the lie of the land had completely changed since I'd last been single. And that was because of one thing – Tinder.

Digital Dating: The Stats

The technosexual revolution has been developing for decades (I actually found my mum's husband for her on Match.com nearly 20 years ago when I was 16), but it wasn't until Tinder hit in 2012 that *everyone* got swiping. Racking up 1.4 billion swipes a day, the fact that the app is loosely connected to your Facebook account (drawing profile images and making connections apparently based on people you already know) and now also Instagram-integrated makes it feel more like a social media platform crossed with a game than the more dorky dating sites (requiring endless personal statements and multiple-choice surveys).

My personal experience of app dating is similar to those of lots of my cohorts: terrifying at first, a few LOLs in between, but ultimately really only a place to get your head back in the dating arena. When your confidence is way down and someone has made you believe you're unfanciable and unlovable, even having a single "match" on a dating app can boost your self-esteem. Reintroducing the idea that someone, somewhere, might want you (even if only for a moment), the apps can definitely help you start to find a way back to your mojo. Sure, I was stood up on dates, had an odd encounter with a chap who excused himself after the starter and didn't return until the dessert course (Like, seriously, where did he go? And why did he come back?) and got ghosted by guys who I'd kissed on the street in drunken clinches. None of those things were fun, but they were fundamental steps in my romantic rehabilitation. What can be harder to deal with is months of app-exclusive dating, something which has been shown to lead to a decline in self-worth, esteem and body-image security, according to a recent study. "Tinder users report having lower levels of satisfaction with their faces and bodies and having lower levels of self-worth than men and women who do not use Tinder," explained Jessica Strübel, co-author of the research.

The truth is that digital dating can be an excruciatingly slow process. Aside from the fact that most people you meet sadly will not be Mr or Mrs Right, keeping up conversations long enough to meet up with someone when you have the rest of your life going on can feel an impossible challenge and lead to "dating burnout" – where all the conversations and dates become a blur. When you have Bumble, Hinge, Tinder and Happn notifications buzzing on your phone all day and all night, there's not much room for anything else – like, say, a normal social life or, you know, work. In the 2017 Match.com "Singles in America" survey, 15 per cent of singles said they felt addicted to the process of dating and 54 per cent of women felt exhausted by the whole process.

Dating apps are now even more closely linked to social platforms, and there's even been a recent shift to moving proceedings directly onto social sites themselves. Instagram is now a dating app, if you choose to use it so. Views of Stories are often seen as the first preamble to a romantic connection, and I have scores of girlfriends who are attuned to *exactly* who has been viewing the snapshots of their day, even if that means scrolling through thousands of followers to find that hot-guy handle in the haystack. Someone interested might then take the next step of the "casual like", which could actually be casual, progressing on to multiple likings of posts, culminating in the attention-seeking "back-stalk like" (liking an image more than three weeks old). At this point you would be assured that you have an admirer, and could feasibly expect a DM (direct message) to come through. Moving off Instagram to texting or WhatsApp would be the next logical step, before potentially, maybe, hopefully arranging a date. If this all seems like an insane social media dance with weird and unintelligible rules, that's because it is. If it takes this long to get a guy to meet you, is it any wonder we're constantly glued to our phones?

"It's definitely disconcerting to see a guy watching your stories when you thought they were out of the picture. You start thinking, 'Is he into me again? Does he miss me?'" explains Kelly Agnew, a New York-based senior fashion and beauty editor at Refinery29. "If you let it, the search for a romantic partner online can take over your entire life, because in a big city, it's really the only way to meet a guy. Over the years I've definitely had to take some time off from the apps, because I couldn't fathom spending another night in bed swiping left and right – who has the time, let alone the finger strength, for that? Plus, my workload is pretty full-on, I have a Thursday night dance cardio class I hate to skip and I value my time with my girlfriends and self-care way more than drinks with some random guy. Sometimes you just have to get back to the rest of your life. That said, I definitely have got the whole first-date thing down, perhaps *too* pat. I vet most guys before I right-swipe with a deep internet background check, order the same tequila cocktail [on a date], hell, I even wear the same outfit nine times out of ten. When I'm really focused on dating, I might see two guys a week. Not that it doesn't have its fun moments, but in general the word I'd use to describe it is gruelling. But of course, you keep going back to it, because one day one of those guys is going to be 'the One'. Or at least that's what you tell yourself."

In the end, I did meet someone new, but not on a dating app. In fact, even though we were both Tindering hard, we'd never have met digitally as he was four years too young for my age filter. One of the biggest problems with digital dating is that most of us have no idea what we actually want. In my mind, I was looking for an "adult" 30–45, someone who had made their way in life and was at least 6ft (183cm) tall. Instead I fell in love with a 5ft 9in (175cm) 26 year old who lived in a shared rental without a sitting room, worked weekends and definitely didn't have it all figured out. Our lifestyles were not instantly compatible and it took some serious work to iron out the kinks between my relationship expectations and his relationship experience. But he did – and still does – give me a run for my money, and that's really the only thing that matters.

While wild horses couldn't keep me away from him, I'm not sharing daily pictures of him on social media or making endless status updates about my levels of adoration (and hell would have to literally freeze over before he did either). We've been dating for four years, own an apartment together and are about to have our first child – yet we're both still "single" on Facebook. This reticence to share isn't only because I know what it feels like to read the gushy stuff when you're heartbroken (and I wouldn't want to be the cause of pain for someone else), but also because I just don't feel the inclination to do so. I don't care what anyone thinks about my relationship or my sweetheart; he doesn't need to be "visible" to be important, and on the odd occasion that I do post something public, it's really just for him. I'm still a hopeless romantic, but the prism through which I view couplehood has changed completely.

Green-Eyed Detectives

We've discussed the power of envy to turn our social media experiences into compare-a-thons, but the related feelings of jealousy really crank things up a notch when it comes to the realm of relationships. Have you ever kept tabs on someone through social media? Maybe it was a crush or a new romance and you were trying to scope out their single status or your relative attractiveness to their previous flames? What about a proper partner? Perhaps you've had a quick look at who they're following and liking on Instagram? Or the slightly less acceptable sneaky read of their private messages when they forgot to log out of your iPad? How about your exes? In truth, could the secret service actually do with hiring someone as expert at digital reconnaissance as you? If so, you are part of the new *social surveillance* culture, a world in which every step we take and every move we make is being monitored by people we know and love.

Over a quarter of young people – 27 per cent – say social media makes them feel jealous or unsure about their romantic relationship. As soon as you connect with, or indeed pre-stalk, a new lover on social media, you are served with a huge amount of information on his or her interactions with their community, which may or may not include a lot of people they've hooked up with. Aside from being able to scroll through a decade's worth of photos and associated comments, you're constantly updated with their "current activities", broadcasted for all to see. If they so happen to innocuously like a picture of their ex, their gym instructor or work colleague, you know about it immediately. And you can start to stew. The very fact that you are consuming information about your partner outside his or her physical presence totally upends the normal context of romantic relationships. If you'd been there when your other half complimented someone, you'd more than likely brush it off immediately. Reading it in comment form can somehow make it feel like a betrayal, or perhaps the beginning of a secret conversation chain that *may* one day lead to you being dumped by text. Again, it's the lack of non-verbal cues which can really mess with your perspective and your mind. Innocent engagement can be easily construed as suggestive, and even the very fact that your new partner is connected to his past paramours can feel like a dagger to the heart. If a picture of him at a drinks party you didn't know about suddenly pops up on your newsfeed, it's easy to think, "Why wasn't I invited?" Then, "Who was he there with?" when, in fact, it could have been a spur-of-the-moment post-office quick pint which just so happened to get uploaded to social media. It's our public and constant access to things which were once private that can set the green-eyed monster into overdrive.

However, it's not just in the emerald eye of the beholder. Social media has definitely increased the opportunities for flirtation as well as emotional and physical adultery. The fact that the screen is there, acting as a filter, can mean appropriate relationship lines are easily blurred; it's easy to think it's just messages online and not really anything to do with real life, right? Actually, not so right. As many as a third of all divorce cases in the UK now report the words "Facebook" in the proceedings, and more than 80 per cent of US divorce lawyers say the role of social networking in irretrievable marital breakdown is on the rise. If we add in the stats on social dating sites, it starts to become difficult to believe that anyone's keeping it in their pants. A report last year showed that 64 per cent of people had "seen somebody on Tinder who they knew to be in an exclusive relationship", and 56 per cent reported that they had female friends who used Tinder while in relationships. What we know is that social media is very good at making us feel that our lives are inadequate and that the grass is greener pretty much everywhere else. No relationship is perfect, and rocky patches are par for the course. During those moments, it's almost too easy to lose sight of your ethical compass and turn for comfort to the seemingly endless supply of alternative, idealized partners available at the swipe of your iPhone screen 24/7... Is it really any wonder that so many of us have come to the conclusion that tweeting must mean cheating?

It's Either Me or The Phone

Even if you're not playing away from home, social media can cause strife in your relationships. "Phubbing" or "phone snubbing" is the term which best describes what we're doing when we use our phones excessively instead of engaging with our romantic partners, and it's been shown to have a huge impact on the success of a relationship. "What we found was the more often your partner uses his or her phone in your presence, the higher the level of conflict in your relationship," explains Dr Roberts. "This conflict isn't always voiced – sometimes you might say, 'Put down your phone and talk to me,' but other times it's a silent feeling of rejection. Either way, being 'phubbed' leads to conflict and lower relationship satisfaction, and if you extend that out it can be connected to divorce and certainly to one's happiness."

It's hardly rare to feel that your partner is ignoring you in favour of a glowing screen. Of course, usually it's entirely hypocritical. Reviewing my Moment app, which tracks my iPhone use throughout the day (my average is four hours and twenty-six minutes per day, with about one hour fifty minutes on social media as part of that colossal use of 26 per cent of my waking life), I can see that a significant part of my screen time is during the evenings when I'm sitting next to my boyfriend. It's exceedingly easy to point the finger when you feel that you're being neglected in favour of something more interesting on your loved one's phone, but there are few saints left when it comes to digital distraction. It's easy to say, "Let's talk more," but unless the pair of you can commit to phone-free time, that next article or social media picture or email is far too alluring. I get phubbed, but I'm also a phubber. Some evenings we just phub all night, which is sadly not a euphemism.

x x x

These are just some of the ways that social media has transformed my personal relationships. It's not a stellar list. If you too are dealing with any – or all – of the issues highlighted above, try not to entirely despair, because a lot of them can be dramatically improved by making changes to your behaviour. I'm not going to lie: it's definitely easier said than done. But making a conscious and informed decision about how you deal with some of these feelings really is the first step. As for me, I'm logging off to go and meet a real friend, no offence intended.

Takeaways

1. Connect emotionally offline

I get it; we all have busy lives. But there are few more important things to our happiness than our relationships, and they are *definitely* worth the investment. If time is of the essence, you need to get really brutal and honest with yourself about which of your relationships are priorities and which you're just going through the motions with. Making a cull, however heartless it sounds, will give you the quality time you need to connect deeply with the few instead of superficially with the many. Just remember Dunbar's rule – the more time we give to pseudo relationships, the more thinly spread we are where it matters.

It's true our friends may have got used to the more hands-off approach that you've both probably been following of late. To ensure your more assertive behaviour isn't seen as intrusive or overly needy, it's worth initiating a conversation, which could happen via technology, about how you feel. Tell them that you want to spend more quality time with them both in person and on the phone and that you're missing the real-life connection. If they don't respond well to your suggestion of more offline interaction, they probably deserve a one-way ticket to your cull list.

2. Stop hiding behind your screens

"Do something that scares you every day," is one of those hackneyed Instagram quotes that catches in your gullet. While I believe in the power of taking risks, doing something scary every day is no-one's idea of fun. However, when it comes to face-to-face clashes, the only way any of us are going to get any better at dealing with intimidating in-person situations is, sadly, practice. Conflict-avoiders like me are most often worried about people liking them and the risk of losing favour. In these situations, I often spend hours, if not days and weeks, mentally preparing exactly what I'm going to say, going over and over my words – which is one of the reasons it's so much easier to do it virtually, because you can edit it down to convey the perfect message.

However, what happens when you stop focusing on the things you say and instead concentrate on listening to the person at the other end of the conversation? It's so easy to obsess about the way that our words *might* be received that you can forget that conversations are two-way streets. Try showing vulnerability, coming at the issue honestly and sensitively, but also truly hearing what the person says – this is a sure-fire way to ease the stress. Basically, it takes two to tango, so share the pressure.

3. Forget the pre-nup, it's all about the phone-free agreement

"With relationships, we know excessive phone use is a bad thing because it divides our attention," says Dr Roberts. "To help improve the situation, I always suggest smartphone-free zones and time periods. Try marking out places in your home where smartphone use is forbidden. Some of the obvious ones are not using it in the bedroom – both something that helps with your sleep and sex life – and limiting your use when you're with your children, with your partner on a date, or at dinner. With these little victories, you can prove that it can be done. You don't have to go cold turkey, but if you want to make your partner feel valued and properly protect your relationship, you have to try and balance the time you spend without your phone."

4. Try to meet people IRL

When did you last make a new friend offline? In the past year, have you asked someone (or graciously accepted an invitation) on a date *in person*? It doesn't take long to lose confidence in making real-life connections, and once you're out of practice, it can seem like an insurmountable struggle to approach people you don't know well or at all. While the digital hacks for meeting people can be incredibly convenient, they can also conversely make you feel more apprehensive about making new offline relationships. After all, why should you have to go through that discomfort when you could do it all behind the safety of a screen? The real answer is that, however much technology can give fate a helping hand, by avoiding opportunities to meet people organically in your environment you are only going to reduce your chances of meeting people that truly mean something to you. The combination of on- and offline networking is a powerful strategy when you want to meet new people. Feeling unable to chat to a fun-looking girl at the end of your Pilates class or feeling so overwhelmed at the idea of speaking to a person you'd like to date who is already – even peripherally – in your life is something really worth working at.

While I am no expert on friend- or courtships, I have over the years met thousands of people through my job. And I can safely say that everyone gets those tingly butterflies when introducing themselves to people they don't know, but quite like the look of. But you have to keep saying to yourself: what is the very worst that can happen? OK, they could look at you blankly and say they are not interested in conversing with you, but that would be highly unlikely and pretty rude. Sure, they might not jump at your attempt to get to know them...but they quite possibly will. Isn't it worth the roll of the dice?

Although I don't have a formula, finding common ground is obviously a great starting point. One of the nicest things about meeting people IRL is that you can often skip weeks of intermittent messaging and progress a relationship far quicker. And you can tell far more speedily if you're both wasting your time on a fantasized version of each other. There's no right way to meet people, but stubbornly deciding *not* to consider the people walking in and out of your life every day is certainly not going to lead to a richer pool of potential relationship candidates.

Chapter 5:
Why Social Media is
Ruining **Motherhood**

Of all the sticks women beat themselves with, perhaps the thorniest of all is that of needing to be a "good" mother. While new narratives around choices of childlessness are breaking through, it's still a truism that the vast majority of women will, at some point, become mothers. Indeed, at the last count of British women turning 45 in 2016, 82 per cent had at least 1 child. While parenting manuals may fall in and out of fashion, discussions around IVF might trend and debates around the pros and cons of different types of birth will rage on, motherhood remains fetishized, scrutinized and pressurized across the globe. Invariably reflecting the issues of society at large, social media has an unsurprisingly complicated track record when it comes to the challenges women go through along the many stages of parenthood.

Polished, pretty and relentlessly positive, the aspirational cult of social media "mama-hood" isn't fundamentally much more than an updated version of her Stepford sister. OK, she may have ditched the Betty Draper nipped-in waists for head-to-toe Isabel Marant bohemia, and her home might be stacked with tasteful Californian casual décor rather than chintz. She might even go on a Women's March. But the sanitized, yet oh-so-stylish, version of what a mother could look like, projected apparently effortlessly across Pinterest, Instagram and Facebook, can be enough to crush the morale of even the most adept of new mums. Organic weaning, matching alpaca sweaters (for your brood of five, no less), tousled beachy hair, "snapped-back" bodies and prolific outdoorsy activities combine to make Gwyneth Paltrow look like a runner-up in the perfection stakes. This is motherhood as a beauty advertising campaign, a staged glorification, both impenetrable and immaculate. And it's a standard which entirely masks the messy, weary and at times monotonous reality which every mother trudges through. It also elevates a sense of complete maternal sacrifice – and idea that with your baby's birth you too have been reborn as a different person without the interests, passions and achievements which once made you the person you were. What you are is a mother; it's your only definition. When we talk about being sold a fantasy on social media, the mama "glow" really takes the proverbial biscuit.

Motherhood, especially the first time around and in its earliest days, can be a time of intense vulnerability for many women. It's also a period which has been highlighted by researchers and psychologists as being particularly treacherous for dealing with some of social media's most pernicious pressures. When we're already sleep deprived and disassociated from our bodies, social comparison and feelings of inadequacy have the potential to rupture self-esteem and identity, and threaten our mental state.

More than a third of British mothers will experience mental health issues related to parenthood, and while social media can provide support in the form of community groups related to pretty much anything you can imagine across the motherhood gamut, it can also put women under even more stress to compete with each other. Watching other mums bake their kids vegan treats, with their pristine homes in the background and handsome husbands just out of eyeshot, can understandably make another mother who hasn't showered in three days and has only eaten take-out noodles for the past two weeks feel somewhat incompetent. How can other women appear so capable? Is it because they can afford help? Or is it just because they're better mothers? If so, how am I getting this so wrong? Did I birth a monster baby? Am I already a...*bad mother*?

As Kat Farmer, a mother and the blogger behind *Does My Bum Look 40 in This*, says, the reality for most women is not characterized by clear countertops and cupcakes. "I had three children under four – and the entire experience was a blur. I do look back and think about how incredibly vulnerable you are at that point from so many different aspects. You're attacked by so many different emotions. Your work is at that point probably in the toilet. Career? What career? You're up to your knees in nappies and you are most definitely not looking at your finest. Your house looks literally like a squat and you're bone-knackered. You also have no money. Really, you couldn't be at a lower ebb. At that point, social media can be pretty tough. It's a very exposed spot."

The "mamas" who present coffee-table versions of the motherhood experience may not be doing anything new: we've seen these interpretations of child-rearing before in magazines and advertising. But in the social media age they're that much more potent as these are *actual mothers,* not models who've been cast alongside photogenic cherubs. You've possibly watched their bellies swell over nine months and probably heard the ins and outs of their (natural, non-medicated, obviously) birth stories. You know how they came up with their baby's name and how they decided to decorate their nursery. You can't deny that they are "real", so you start to believe a little at least of what you see.

Happily, there's also been a sustained and vocal reaction to the sugar-coated version of child rearing, inspired by feminist thought and the strong voices of women who, to put it bluntly, are fed up with being made to feel like shit by the perfect social media mother. The average age of a mum in England and Wales hit 30.3 in 2015, and the number of women over 40 having babies overtook those 20 and under. The US picture is broadly similar, with the typical age for first-time motherhood around the 28 mark and more women giving birth between ages 30 and 34 than 25 and 29. This means that it's increasingly more mature women who are going through the experience, often with established careers, financial independence and a full case of life experience in tow. They have more of an inkling when they're being duped. The "warts-and-all" honest motherhood movement has begun to chip away at the glow approach, with women sharing images of their less-than-perfect postpartum bellies, accounts of their disillusionment and depression, and a raw version of motherhood which exhibits its hardships. True, there are criticisms (seriously there are criticisms about *everything* related to motherhood on social media, so buckle up for judgement) that some of this has gone too far to the point of martyrdom and that honest motherhood is creating an excessively bleak picture for what to expect when you're expecting. But it's definitely a welcome rejoinder to the airbrushed version of motherhood that has dominated the space.

Many women – even those who may present glossy and glamorous lifestyles on social media – are also deciding to join the conversation, as Laura Fantacci, the Italian co-founder of influential digital magazine *Wardrobe Icons*, explains. "Aesthetically, for what I'm doing professionally, showcasing the chaos of real home life on social media wouldn't feel right, but whenever I have a voice, I'm not shy about saying that life isn't always picture-perfect. I don't want to hide behind the 'this is the best moment of your life' message because, for me, initially the experience was overwhelming and definitely not entirely positive. At times, I felt scared to be alone with my baby. Life suddenly stopped having a rhythm designated by day and night and had just become an existence on a loop. I was so sleep-deprived and deeply drained – I found out later that I was coeliac, so that compounded the exhaustion. I remember my husband leaving in the morning and I was just counting the seconds until he came home. Everything was magnified because of my expectation of what it would be like. I had pictured the whole thing to be this glowy, serene, happy time. So, there was a huge element of disillusionment. It was disappointment in myself, in how I handled it and how poorly I'd coped. It was also a disappointment in the reality of motherhood."

While it's encouraging to see these more nuanced depictions, they don't relieve the weight of our ideals. A 2015 University of Northern Colorado study showed that even women who do not subscribe to "motherhood ideologies" are at risk of experiencing increased stress and anxiety, and decreased self-esteem in the face of the pressure to be perfect. Even if we are woke to the fact that all mums deal with explosive nappies, tantrums in public places and the soul-destroying exhaustion of two-hour feeding rotations, there is evidence that we continue to internalize guilt and self-doubt. And that's something that's not good for our kids.

Sarah Schoppe-Sullivan, professor of human sciences and psychology at Ohio State University, has shown in her research that striving to be the perfect mother can actually backfire and make you a worse one. "The quest to be a 'perfect' mother may actually harm a mother's parenting," she explains. "In my lab's research on new parents, we found that mothers showed less confidence in their parenting abilities when they were more worried about what other people thought about their parenting." So much of looking after a baby is about confidence – the countless daily decisions you make all hinge on feeling secure about your ability to make the best choice for your child. Without confidence, you endlessly question yourself, creating a tense, highly stressed environment for the whole family. Feeling calm and sure of yourself has been proven to benefit your child's development, whereas when parents are significantly stressed during their child's early years, one study showed that some of their genes (involved in insulin production and brain development) were affected into adolescence. Social media has not invented the perfect mother. But it has certainly strengthened the façade and turned the screws on what that perfect mother should look like. More than 80 per cent of women in a UK survey in 2017 said that Instagram and Facebook "added pressure to be the perfect mum". Even those who embrace elements of imperfection and project a confidence in their own shortcomings are not immune to the pressures. No-one it seems is impervious to the glow.

Getting Pregnant, Staying Pregnant, Being Pregnant

You might have heard that we're in the midst of a fertility crisis. Everywhere we turn – whether it's our parents, our newspapers or our

GPs – we're made aware that our eggs are passing their sell-by date, slowly, yet inexorably, going bad inside us. As soon as I hit 28, it seemed to be all everyone I knew talked about, and it's still a major topic of conversation among both my followers and friends. The truth is it's no joke: sperm counts among Western men have halved over the past 40 years, and as women have delayed trying to conceive, their chances of having a family have markedly declined. There's evidence that the memo has been received and that women are aware that starting their journey to motherhood at a younger age improves their chances of success, however, there are also plenty of impediments to this trend reversal – many of which I can relate to personally.

At the time of writing, I'm about to give birth in less than two weeks – if our son decides to come on time. I'll be 34 years old and a few months shy of geriatric motherhood. I first started trying to conceive when I was 32, and the monthly feelings of failure were one of the hardest things that I've ever had to deal with. My story is entirely ordinary in many ways. While I required medical assistance and drugs to conceive, I didn't go through IVF and, in comparison to what many, many other couples go through with multiple losses, hardships and the huge expenses incurred by fertility procedures, I know I've been fortunate. However, there's no doubt that social media made a massive impact on my experiences with both my fertility and my pregnancy, and at every step of the way it's had a bearing on my mental state.

I decided to post an "announcement" bump image on social media when I was 16 weeks pregnant, simply because there was no hiding it any more (my belly has tracked at the 98th percentile the whole way through – this hasn't been a subtle pregnancy...and, yes, I'm nervous for my vagina). While my boyfriend and I couldn't have been happier to share the news, it was definitely a bittersweet moment. Because over those months of trying, I had found it increasingly hard to stay upbeat as every woman I seemed to know or follow on Instagram effortlessly produced one bundle of joy after another. I was adamant that my bump wasn't going to add to that tally or compete in the ever more creative "reveals" that we're becoming accustomed to on social media. I just really wanted to be entirely honest and let any woman who was in the same position as I'd been know that she was not the only one going through it. In fact, as around one in seven couples in the UK and one in eight couples in the US are said to have trouble conceiving – whatever social media might suggest – they're part of a significant minority and very far from being alone.

I'm not used to feeling a really deep stab of social media envy. We all get FOMO, but that crushing covetousness has never been my digital Achilles heel, and since my divorce, I've managed to keep a sense of perspective when consuming other people's lives. But the baby thing was different because it wasn't about "happiness" or "success" – it was about a biological process. Motherhood is so tied up with identity and can penetrate to the core of who you are, not just what you have. Unlike other life achievements, there are no halfway houses. You can't ever be nearly pregnant – you either are or you're not, and feeling let down by your body is a different kind of sense of failure than, say, feeling inadequate about your work ethic and career success. Trying to conceive while you're consuming endless images of beautiful babies in fresh cashmere bonnets can feel lonely, bewildering and horribly, horribly self-centred. No-one wants to feel anything but elation for other couples having babies, but while I'm ashamed to say it, I didn't always feel entirely happy for other people. Actually, seeing other women getting pregnant, especially on social media, where I had little idea of their backstory, often caused me pain as well as biting jealousy.

It's no-one's fault. Lots of the posts I can remember feeling hard to swallow weren't at all boastful or smug, just simply poignant snapshots of love. But the experience has definitely moderated the way I feel about sharing my journey to motherhood, as I know that there will be women registering images of my burgeoning bump who feel just like I did. I'm not saying that it's stopped me posting pictures of myself – at the end of the day I don't have a body double that could have filled in for me as I grew outwards. But I am very conscious of the way, if all goes well, that I'll be posting about my baby, as I know from experience that my happiness might strike some other not-so-happy chords elsewhere.

Not being able to get pregnant when you desperately want to is one of the most wretched experiences a couple can go through. The monthly cycle of dashed hopes, the constant questioning (If I had to pay for every time I googled "causes of infertility", I'd be bankrupt. And let's not talk about what I've googled since...) and the insidious feeling of self-doubt can have an impact on all areas of your life. I know I'm by no means alone going through nearly a year of "TTC" (trying to conceive) – but that time has armed me with some really strong opinions on how the medical profession and we as a community deal with it. If I hadn't sought specialist help, I wouldn't be pregnant now – because I've been advised that, due to a cycle condition, I'll probably never be able to get pregnant without the help of drugs. And had I listened to pretty much everyone around me impatiently telling me to be *patient*, I'd most likely still be at square one.

Women trying to conceive are bombarded with two entirely contradictory directives both from the media and healthcare professionals. The first has been endlessly discussed – and involves the ticking clock. Approaching 35 – colloquially known as the fertility cliff-face – we're told that our egg quantity and quality is reducing at a clip every six months or so. When I was 27, a GP told me to start trying as soon as possible as I couldn't "expect" to have children after I was 30. Unfortunately, there was a slight spanner in the works as my husband left me right around that deadline, so baby-making plans were stalled. It took me another couple of years to meet a new, willing partner and if we decide to/are able to get pregnant again, I'll be on the wrong side of that cliff face.

Even if we discount the financial imperative to delaying child-bearing – it's a fact that the older you are when you have a child, the higher your wage-earning potential in the long-run – these guidelines seem to forget that life has a habit of getting in the way. Failed relationships, redundancies, insecure living situations, huge student debt or just not finding the right person in our increasingly solipsistic culture are just some of the endless bumps in the fertility road. But that doesn't mean that the biology can be ignored – by age 40 only 40 per cent of women will be able to have a baby naturally, with that decline in outcome having dwindled swiftly from around the critical age 35 marker.

The other message, which flies entirely in the face of *the deadline*, is that of serene perseverance. GPs in the UK repeatedly told me that I needed to try for 18 consecutive calendar months before we could even have a discussion about my fertility. When I brought up specific concerns from my cycle history – like the fact that sustained exercise often stopped my periods coming or that my ovulation pattern didn't seem to match up to what all the "how to get pregnant" guides advised, I was treated as if I was an entitled brat, impatient for her Starbucks order. I get why the message of forbearance is followed: it takes some time to get your cycle back on track after coming off contraception, then maybe a month or two more to get your dates right. But a year or 18 months of patience, when you're also being counselled that the end of the runway is approaching daily ever nearer, is deeply stressful and makes you feel constantly like you're either a) not doing enough and it's going to be too late before you know it or b) being too demanding and need to lighten up.

One thing that a lot of women who fell pregnant immediately have said to me is that they almost didn't have time to register what they were doing before the magnitude of what was going to happen to their lives hit them. When you've been trying for months, that issue is certainly reduced – the huge life change was everything I longed for – however there is, instead, an additional pressure on the pregnancy, because if it doesn't work out, you know it might take just as long again to get pregnant. Like a lot of women, I had huge pre-12-week anxiety – the stakes are so high and you are so out of control it's almost impossible not to feel that way. Add in the hormones (both natural and the drugs) and the level of research I couldn't help myself doing on my phone during nights of restlessness, I became full of doom.

I was very, very negative and entirely unprepared for the way that pregnancy would affect me mentally. The very idea of me feeling anything but joy sounds bonkers, right? I'd just spent all that time desperate to be pregnant, then all I did was sit around crying about *maybe* losing my baby and spend my nights awake spinning, thinking about all the things that could go wrong. Night times, in fact, have been the worst throughout my pregnancy, but at the beginning especially, I had endless harrowing dreams, filled with dead babies specifically from literature – Tess of the d'Urbervilles' Sorrow, Fanny Robin's unborn child from *Far From the Madding Crowd*. Every time I woke up from one of them, I felt so ashamed. Why couldn't I just be happy like all the other pregnant women we see out there? Why was I letting my mind take me down these terrible paths of subconscious fear and despair?

After my 20-week scan, the low moods and tears did give way and I had a couple of months of feeling pretty positive, until birth anxieties started to kick in as I hit my third trimester. Again, the amount of information that was available to me through my phone meant I could probably write a Ph.D thesis on the risks of childbirth. Being informed is one thing; losing yourself in obsessive googling for days on end is quite another. It wasn't that I didn't know the dangers of excessive search engine use...but I just couldn't stop myself. We all have ways of coping with stress. For some people it's making a spreadsheet, for others it's all about distraction techniques. For me it's always been about preparation, but sadly childbirth isn't an experience you can revise for – though I've definitely given it a good punt. There is zero doubt that having 24/7 access to a limitless amount of information in the form of scholarly articles, magazine and newspaper features, as well as blogs and social forums through my phone, completely and utterly exacerbated my anxieties. My researching was compulsive and it took finally bursting into tears at my 34-week hospital appointment for me to really tell anyone what I was doing and start working on stopping myself. When you're hooked in all day, every day, it's so easy just to stumble across one more article or one more Facebook group with opinions on what you should or shouldn't be doing to prepare for such an intimidating experience – the temptation to look just in case I found out that one vital, elusive piece of information just proved too great.

Although I've been practising mindfulness, listening to hypnobirthing tapes and generally keeping myself busy, it's not like I've suddenly been able to relax and "trust my body". The truth is that there are no guarantees and childbirth is a lottery. I've been incredibly lucky with support from women's counsellors and my midwives as well as friends and family who suspected that something wasn't quite right – and I realize that if I hadn't found the courage to acknowledge that I was struggling, I'd still be on that social media-fuelled self-destructive path. I've found it incredibly hard to be open about any of these feelings, both the downs and the anxieties, even on my own platforms, simply because there is a huge amount of guilt that goes alongside it. How dare I feel overwhelmed, teary or have panic attacks when there are so many women who would do anything to have a baby growing inside them? I also think when you're expecting to feel so happy and you don't, you can't help but implicitly worry that you're losing your mind, which is also not something I'd ever want to advertise – it still takes a lot to admit that we're grappling with anything that could be construed as mental instability.

But we need to be more open about this both personally and publicly, because the truth is not everyone has a great pregnancy and every woman's experience is entirely unique to her own body and complex balance of hormones. If your pregnancy isn't going quite as you dreamed it would be, and you feel both mentally and physically out of kilter (I haven't even mentioned the "morning" sickness – needless to say, my hormones were not kind to my stomach either), social media can present a massive issue, especially over these early months. The fact that you are advised not to tell anyone that you're with child means you can't be yourself in any way and, if you're someone who uses the real-time tools like Stories or Snapchat, you can feel under immense scrutiny. Can they see the bump from this angle? Has everyone already guessed? Does your client or boss know already? I didn't reveal to people that I was being sick, having anxiety episodes or dealing with narcolepsy because it was meant to be a secret. Over the really bad weeks, I stopped uploading content entirely, which in the grand scheme of everything was clearly not an issue, but at the time made me feel stressed. Even if you don't use social media for work, you can feel that constant pressure to share regularly – there's a reason that it's called a feed: it's always hungry for content.

The changes that your body goes through during pregnancy are not only sometimes overwhelming (as well as incredibly impressive), but they can create some issues in the social media environment. By week ten, I was in maternity jeans and my boobs had gone from a 32B to a 34E. Several followers asked me if I'd had a boob job – which while funny also underlines how hyperaware social media audiences are about body shape. But until you have your 12-week, or even your 20-week, scan, culturally it's expected that you keep your pregnancy under wraps. It's an understandable practice: when around 20 per cent of pregnancies end before the 12-week mark, there's the sense that you want to be sure before you share, or else if something goes wrong, you'll be dealing with both the personal and public fallout. During the early stage, every picture I took either used a handbag to obscure my belly or involved me sucking in and angling forward so my dress didn't hug the bump. It's not a new issue that women struggle with hiding early pregnancy, but social media definitely brings a whole new layer to that subterfuge.

After revealing that I was expecting, some of the comments I've received about my body have made my eyes pop out of my head. Unsolicited observations are part and parcel of the pregnancy package, but there's something even more unbelievable when people feel they can put them in writing for everyone to read. Followers have said that I looked like I was ready to give birth at five months, that I must be having twins because I'm *so* big, that I've got a "BIG BABY" in there. Once, when I posted a Story snap of a pizza I was eating, someone took the time to direct message me that I really needed to watch my diet as I was getting so big. I really do wonder if people think these things are funny, or if it's that they've become so conditioned to expect women to look like Victoria's Secret models that a real pregnant woman boggles their mind. Gaining weight during pregnancy is not an *optional* thing. To make sure your baby is healthy, you need to add 28–35lb (12.7–15.9kg), and if you were slim before, it might be more. Sometimes that isn't glamorous and that weight goes to your chin, your bingos, your saddlebags. Often, you'll find your legs and ass covered in cellulite and, alongside the other pregnancy benefits (for me so far: varicose veins, skin tags on my neck, hormonal breakouts, thinning eyelashes, swollen sebaceous glands under my arms…), you might not exactly feel like Beyoncé.

The advent of the #fitspo pregnancy and the images we see on social media of women lifting heavy weights up to their due dates or keeping their six-packs intact into their third trimester may be the genetic reality for some women, but it's definitely not the norm. I had a seriously fit and flexible body before my pregnancy and managed to keep up with exercise during my second trimester. But between the early months of sickness and later months of pelvic pain, the burpees have been well and truly out of the picture. Again, these were not *options*. With the "helpful" comments, muscular "motivation" bodies and svelte celebrity pregnancy shots, social media can be a tricky space for all pregnant women, let alone those who have suffered from body and eating-related issues in the past.

Another thing I've had a lot of is people asking me how I can *still* be pregnant. I've seen it written on other pregnant women's walls too, and it's something that speaks volumes about the nature of social media: people get bored with the same story – they know you're pregnant, but they're impatient to see the update. But guess what? Pregnancy takes 40 weeks (or, for some heroes, up to 43). That's more than three-quarters of a year. It's not a new campaign or a hairstyle you're trying out, and it doesn't give a shit about social media attention spans. For so, so many women pregnancy is not like falling off a log. Not everyone has a wonderful nine months or has some romantic conception story primed for their YouTube birth video. Getting pregnant can feel like a monthly fading dream. Staying pregnant can feel like a marathon you haven't even started to train for. Being pregnant can feel terrifying and lonely and create a complex web of emotions. Some of us, even if we exercise and eat as well as we can, will have a "massive" belly. Some of us can't exercise because we'll puke if we bend over and can only keep bread and cheese down. You don't get a say in that. Where some feel depressed, others will feel anxious. Of course, there will also be women who breeze through the whole thing, not really even noticing that they've got a bun in the oven. But that can't be the only experience that we feel comfortable sharing on social media, because it is just so thoroughly misleading.

When I did reveal some of the things that I'd gone through, the response was phenomenal. I received thousands of messages from women who said they had felt the same things, or were struggling through the same processes, and all of them thanked me for acknowledging them on social media. While it's every woman's prerogative to share exactly what she wants, if things aren't so rosy you don't have to beat yourself up about it. Yes, pregnancy is a gift, but that shouldn't have to mean that a perfect nine months is the only acceptable experience you're allowed to have.

The Big Taboo: Pregnancy Loss and Social Media

Of course, it's not just struggling to fall pregnant that has implications for our social media use. Even more heartbreaking is going through a loss, especially when the bump is "out" on social media. Up to a million miscarriages happen every year in the US and an estimated one in five of all pregnancies don't make it.

However, what was once a silent and dreadful thing, spoken only about in hushed tones, is now slowly being shared across blogs, forums and, yes, social media. Mark Zuckerberg himself has been part of breaking the taboo. When in 2015 he announced on Facebook that he and his wife, Dr Priscilla Chan, were expecting a baby girl, he revealed that they had previously experienced three miscarriages. He explained: "You feel so hopeful when you learn you're going to have a child... You start making plans, and then they are gone. It's a lonely experience. Most people don't discuss miscarriages because you worry your problems will distance you or reflect upon you – as if you're defective or did something to cause this. So you struggle on your own... When we started talking to our friends, we realized how frequently this happened – that many people we knew had similar issues and that nearly all had healthy children after all. We hope that sharing our experience will give more people the same hope we felt and will help people feel comfortable sharing their stories as well."

While the courage to share is spreading, there are limitations too. Clinical psychologist Dr Jessica Zucker specializes in women's reproductive and maternal health and is also the woman behind the #IHadaMiscarriage hashtag and @IHadaMiscarriage Instagram account – a space for women to tell their stories of loss. As she explains, in many ways, social media can be seen to offer a community of support: "When you share a loss on social media, most often you will find an outpouring of love and you may find everyone's comments are hugely supportive. But the question is: do they follow up a week later, a month later, a year later? Typically, people are so inept about talking about pregnancy loss just generally, and especially stillbirth, which is obviously much rarer. And while there is this initial declaration on social media of wanting to be there, in terms of actual substantive support, women often find themselves feeling very alone. A loss is not something you just get over, it's a process. Social media often appears to provide support, and yet, are these real friendships? It can give a sense of connection, but there's just not the same level of responsibility to each other."

That support can, however, be a comfort at the bleakest of times. Pippa Vosper, a British influencer and boutique owner, lost her son

Axel when she was five months pregnant last year, and she describes the sense of community she found as "a blanket of love". Her story illustrates some of the challenges, but also positives that can be found when dealing with tragedy in the connected world. "My husband and I had been trying to conceive for three years and I couldn't wait to post a picture on social media after three months to tell everyone that I was pregnant. I was so excited! All the congratulations and comments came in and you feel like, 'I can do it; I'm not broken.' There was such a sense of relief. When, after five months, we lost our son, I decided the sooner the better to share the news, because a lot of the pain comes from well-meaning friends who continue to ask about the baby. Strangely, posting the news to Instagram was the moment that it became real to me. It was a week after Axel had died and I took the picture and wrote what I felt was right. I'd been at home with my husband and it had been very surreal: your belly is still pregnant looking and your mind plays lots of tricks with you when you're dealing with that level of grief. But when the messages started coming in it felt like confirmation that baby was really gone."

Pippa says the level of community that she found online was "Truly incredible. There are still a few ladies – that I've never met – who continue to check up on me every few weeks, just to see if I'm OK. Of course, you also feel exposed, but knowing there are people out there that care about me has meant so much. At the time, lots of people shared their stories with me, which was very difficult to hear at the beginning, but also very much appreciated, because I thought I was literally the only person I knew who this had happened to. I felt very alone and I was embarrassed. I thought people were going to judge me, that they would think it was because of my spinning classes or because I'd been working in my shop. But knowing that other people had dealt with similar experiences was a definite comfort." As for the long-term impact on her social media attitude, Pippa explains that it's made her much more fearless and honest. "The experience has definitely made me a lot more 'real' on social media. Beforehand, my Instagram had been very party, party, travel, travel. No-one knew who I was. When Axel died, I had no choice but to expose my real self. Telling tens of thousands of people that your baby has died was extremely difficult to do, because it was so very private. But since I'd been public with the pregnancy, I had to be public with the loss and pain too."

Anna Saccone Joly, an Irish-American YouTuber with an audience of over a million subscribers, lost a baby in a missed miscarriage in 2016. She also says that sharing the experience, which she did in both a personal and a family vlog with her husband, helped her to appreciate how widespread her experience was. "We knew that we were going to have to tell people eventually and it was definitely really difficult. But, at the same time, it was really rewarding because we had so many people reach out to us to say they had been through the same thing," she explains. "When you address something that's generally unspoken and make it OK to talk about it, you realize that you're not alone at all. That's probably the nicest thing about social media. It might feel like a shameful thing when you're going through it, but it's not: it's just very, very common."

By helping to normalize one of the worst things a woman can experience and providing the vehicle to share honest accounts, which can guide expectations, social media has been instrumental in facilitating a true shift in the cultural understanding of miscarriage. When talking about the many positives that these platforms have brought to our lives, this has to be a shining light.

Gaming Pregnancy: The Apps

Another element of the pregnancy journey that's been altered in the digital dimension has been the unprecedented level of documentation that accompanies the gestation period. Technology is changing the experience of pregnancy, specifically through the birth of the pregnancy app, which has popularized the week-by-week collection – and sharing – of data on your impending arrival. Whether it's in the form of belly photographs, which can be stored on not just your phone but also posted to social media in weekly updates for your friends and family to scrutinize, or information about your due date, we are compiling vast pools of records on what it means to be pregnant. These apps' game-like approach also allows you to track your unborn foetus's development in real-time, inch by inch, pound by pound, and usually compare them in size to a piece of fruit week by week. Giving a daily countdown to "B-day" as well as information about symptoms and encouraging words about how close you're getting to the end of the marathon, they offer motivation, reassurance and a feeling of achievement as you tick off the weeks. In addition, they're a rich resource of information about pregnancy, with features like "Is it Safe?", and they allow you to keep a check on your activities as well as providing access to social forums populated by millions of other women from across the globe. A 2015 research paper by Gareth Thomas and Deborah Lupton describes pregnancy apps as covering "threats and thrills", as they both "portray the pregnant body as a site of risk requiring careful self-surveillance using apps to reduce potential harm," and "use ludification [gamification] strategies and encourage the social sharing of pregnancy-related details as part of emphasizing the enjoyable aspects of pregnancy."

Whether you go for a "belly bump" time-lapse video, a more traditional still-shot collection of images via apps like "The Bump", which also has interactive 3D visualizations of what your baby looks like inside you, or the classic BabyCenter "Pregnancy Tracker & Baby Today" app which is downloaded *millions* of times a month, the sheer amount of information at your fingertips on not just your own pregnancy, but countless other women's, is unparalleled. Pregnancy apps are among the most engaged with across the entire app market and can create a powerful sense of wellbeing for expectant mothers. However, at a closer glance, you start to realize how very specific are the assumptions around pregnancy that these apps endorse. Firstly, the information provided is typically heavily gendered – these are apps entirely geared to women, and generally heterosexual women at that, because apparently there's only one person accountable for a baby and that's the mother.

As Thomas and Lupton continue, "pregnant women are portrayed as ideally self-responsible, enthused about their pregnancy and foetus to the point that they are counting the days until the birth and enthusiastic about collecting and sharing details about themselves and their unborn (often via social media)."

There's also a constant drive to consumption, with daily highlights of things you need to buy to make sure your pregnancy progresses without a hitch. But as you provide these apps with your due date, sometimes the sex of your baby and even the knowledge that you are still pregnant, behind the adorable short features and blueberry to pumpkin size guides, many of these companies are selling your data to as many global retailers as possible. According to research carried out by Janet Vertesi, an assistant professor of sociology at Princeton, a pregnant woman's data is worth 15 times the amount of a regular internet punter. And there's seemingly little escape. As soon as you Google "Pregnancy Test", share your conception news on Facebook or download a pregnancy app, you are hounded night and day by brands looking to capitalize on both your new retail needs and insecurities. Vouchers arrive in the post, offers are emailed to your personal account. There is no privacy in pregnancy: you're just too valuable a digital consumer.

Elsewhere in the app world there is a host of actual games, often geared to young girls, which offer new – and sometimes highly worrying – representations of what pregnancy is all about. Take the truly terrifying Barbara Pregnant Shopping app, which introduces the game's Barbie doll-lookalike heroine thus: "I've got wonderful news for you girls: our darling Barbara is expecting a baby! But still Barbara is feeling a bit unconfident. Don't you think she needs something to cheer her up? And every girl knows that there is no better way to raise a girl's spirits than a nice shopping spree! You are Barbara's closest friend, so why don't you take her out for some quality shopping in her favourite mall? Now Barbara is in her fashionable self again and she feels prepared to welcome her baby!" In the Newborn Baby & Mommy Care app we find yet another svelte, blonde Barbie clone and you can "dress the newborn in adorable clothes, accessories and toys!" From Pregnant Mommy's Salon Spa Fun to My New Baby Princess, which enables little girls to "care for a mother during her pregnancy in the pink castle", it seems that all skinny, young, white, blonde women apparently need to be fashionable and well-groomed even as they hit the 40-week mark.

While we may be hearing dissenting voices about the realities of the journey to motherhood from some corners, when it comes to our smartphone apps, pregnant women are reduced to burgeoning bodies and lucrative commercial opportunities, conditioned by patronizing stereotypes and prejudiced one-size-fits-all identities. As long as she keeps off the unpasteurized cheese and gets her manicure down, she'll be well on her way to maternal success. This week I've scanned an article on my pregnancy app about how to get "Glam for the Delivery Room", and read about a woman who made sure she finished icing a cake even though she was in labour. Maybe the Stepford wife hasn't had a 2018 makeover after all.

The Act of Becoming a Mother: Crowd Birthing and Bounce-Back Bodies

Once upon a time, women gave birth either at home or in hospital in female-only environments, with the father pacing outside with cigars on hand, ready for the "mother and baby doing well" exhale. Fast-forward to the social media age and the tableau looks remarkably different. Detailing your child's birth in ever more cinematic formats has, increasingly, become the norm and, in the blink of an eye, there's been a mainstream acceptance that something which was once one of life's most private, behind-closed-door moments is now appropriate to air to your friends, family and extended public audience. A 2013 survey conducted by a baby photo agency found that, on average, a newborn baby has his or her image uploaded to social media within 57.9 minutes – just shy of an hour – showing just how dramatically the etiquette around birth has evolved.

As parents seek out sharable content to mark the birth of their baby, birth videos have become a booming business. The presence of professional photographers or videographers in the delivery room is no longer a rarity, and parents even work with specialized video editors to put together their birth story film. Anyone expecting will be inundated across social media with studio photographers and birth filmmakers offering deals on "full birth documentary coverage". Taking cues from celebrities and influencers, who have often brought their followers along with them in their pregnancy journeys and want to share the ins and outs of the climax, culturally what counts as TMI has drastically shifted. Images of full-frontal disclosure – we're talking shots of the placenta and babies crowning here – have been popping up across my Instagram and Facebook for months now. Type in "birth stories" to YouTube and you'll find over 3 million clips covering everything from C-sections to water births, the graphic to the art house, the most traumatic to the almost casual. Alongside the video footage are the blogs and social media posts, which are sometimes thousands-of-words-long accounts of individual women's journeys. There's even the real-time Twitter and Facebook birth status updates, which, though rarer, aren't entirely shocking any more. In some ways, this is all totally understandable. Childbirth is one of the most dramatic things that happens to women in their lifetimes and we're all fascinated by it, because, you know, it's an insane miracle. For social media users seeking connection and validation, the birth story offers a huge opportunity to engage with their audience and share something that other people can't help themselves to watch or read.

However, no matter what your personal opinions on the birth story phenomenon, there's little doubt that these labour vlogs, blogs and images are piling even more pressure on to the already heightened atmosphere of modern delivery. In a 2015 study of two thousand UK mums by video blogging site Channel Mum, 60 per cent felt that, as birth becomes more social, it's also becoming more competitive. Few births are predictable and a good proportion don't go exactly the way we might have hoped. A recent survey found that half of all new mothers experience regret, shame, guilt or anger after birth, mostly due to unexpected complications and lack of support. More than 70 per cent say they felt pressured to do things a certain way.

The opposing camps of medicalized vs natural childbirthers have created a social media stand-off comparable to modern political polarization, with each slinging judgements and criticisms at each other. If you post about an emergency C-section or, heaven forbid, an *elective* C-section, you can expect someone to pipe up with a judgey comment about how you've let your baby down by not pushing. While it's true that, even in our recent history, women were deprived of a lot of agency around childbirth, and over-medicalization – often for professional profit – is still a reality in lots of developed counties, the new tyranny of natural birthing is influencing women to believe that, unless they shun interventions and rely on nature to run its course, they've somehow failed their baby. In *TIME* magazine's 2017 cover story entitled "The Goddess Myth", most of the women surveyed said a natural birth was extremely or very important, yet 43 per cent ended up needing drugs or an epidural, and 22 per cent had unplanned C-sections. Is it any wonder they might feel as if they'd failed?

The pressure of living up to a birth story that you can be proud to share is certainly adding yet another layer of stress to a beautiful, but, yes, often traumatic experience. If you've been vocal pre-birth about your "normal" birth plans, of course you're going to feel inadequate if you "succumb" to the drugs. If you've talked about the cons of C-sections for your baby's gut microbiome, you might not be so thrilled to share that you were wheeled into surgery. Until every woman can hold her head up high and say her baby came into the world just as he or she should have, oversharing will come with pitfalls and pressures – many of which will contribute to how a woman views herself postnatally.

Of course, she's not the only one appraising herself after she leaves the labour ward, because the cultural fascination with pregnancy is now about to enter into the "how long until she snaps back" chapter. The scrutiny of the postpartum body is perhaps the most malicious of all issues surrounding motherhood in the digital age, and while celebrities have long dealt with the spotlight when it comes to regaining their pre-pregnancy figure, now, due to social media, we're all under the microscope. In a recent survey, 52 per cent of women said that getting their figure back was their biggest post-birth concern ahead of their relationship and career. And for some inexplicable reason, there seems to be a public ownership of how and at what speed that weight-loss should progress. The thing is that you're damned if you do and you're damned if you don't. If a woman appears to drop her baby weight too quickly, returning within weeks, if not days, to close to her pre-pregnancy shape, she'll be crucified by an audience who make assumptions about eating disorders and diets that she might have embarked on. If she's still carrying an extra 25lb (11.3kg) six months later, she'll feel conversely that she's come up short in comparison to the images posted by other women on social media. Just take a cursory glance at the #PostPartumFitness – it's enough to make any woman staring down at her jelly belly feel that she's not good enough.

As Dr Jessica Zucker explains, "You don't even have to be following these women to see the super-fast return to perfect bodies. Your [Instagram] Explore page, or adverts for this or that weight-loss method, will do that for you. There are a bunch of images out there of women doing side-by-side photos of, say, 39 weeks vs 9 days postpartum. I have both personal and professional feelings about those kinds of message. I can't help wondering why they are sharing this and why they have decided to share it in that way. Do they think it's health promoting, are they looking for praise or is it to make other mothers envious?"

If you google "The postpartum body" one of the hits that comes up is a problem/solution guide to offer tips on getting back into shape. Sadly, the language is full of all the judgements which seem par for the course in this realm. Take this tip, for example: "Many moms-to-be don't stick to a regular upper body workout during pregnancy, leading to flabbiness and weakness." Just what every new mum needs to hear. We know that postnatal depression (PND) isn't a rarity – in the US it's estimated that 15 per cent of all women experience symptoms – and these body politics are definitely part of the PND picture. A 2017 study showed that exposure to images of "snapped-back" new mums fostered a host of negative feelings in women, including body self-consciousness, depression, frustration and hopelessness that they're unable to lose weight as rapidly after childbirth as celebrities. Social platforms were perceived "as having a unique influence because [these messages were] viewed as coming from 'real people', including friends and family."

Troublingly there is also almost no conversation about the dangers of returning to exercise too quickly and most online advice suggests that after six weeks a woman can/should be back on the gym circuit. Whereas the truth is, new mothers can cause serious and sometimes irrevocable damage to their bodies if they hit it too hard too soon. Whether you've given birth naturally or not, the pelvic floor is the only muscle any new mum should be focusing on. Running, any weight work, sit-ups and most core work can further damage the pelvic floor leading to incontinence and prolapse. Seriously sexy stuff, I'm sure you'll agree. If your abs have split in pregnancy – known as diastitus recti, and something which is hugely common – any type of core work before you've slowly knitted the muscles back together can have long-lasting physiological and aesthetic consequences. Equally, if you've had a C-section you need to give the 7 layers of tissue that have been cut through time to heal. For 3 months, that's going to be aggressive, but it will continue to 6–12 months. There's a reason why women who give birth by C-section are counselled to wait a year before trying to conceive again – it's a major operation. Snapping back in this context doesn't just seem like a huge pressure, it's actually massively foolish and certainly not something to be applauded. The idea of a celeb with abs of steel, pounding a treadmill three months post-partum doesn't seem so aspirational when you consider that she might have lost control of her pelvic floor. Obviously that is not everyone's story, but if you speak to any physiotherapist or personal trainer specializing in post-birth fitness, they will tell you: take your time, or else.

Anna Saccone Joly believes that the pressure women are under immediately after giving birth has been intensified by the new media revolution, and she is passionate about covering the postpartum body in a realistic way. "Social media has definitely made me feel a lack of confidence about my body, even now I'm into my fourth pregnancy," she explains. "I think you have to be really careful, especially if you have been through a history of eating disorders or disordered eating. So many women go through pregnancy and post-pregnancy having problems with their body image or maybe food to some extent. It's just not spoken about. It's like you're meant to go through those months and not notice that your body is changing; it's meant to not affect you. But you're still the same person, and the same things and thoughts are going to still go through your mind. Body image in post-pregnancy is so important and you can definitely get lost on social media looking at people that don't look remotely like you, with body types that are not remotely like yours. And when they seem to just bounce back, you can't help but compare yourself. But that is not anything to do with you or your body. Post-birth is such a fragile, precious time. If anything, people need to be rallying around you and trying to build you up, not putting posts on social media making you feel bad about not losing baby weight. That is the least of your concerns at that time. You need to stay focused on really, really looking after yourself mentally as well as physically. The body is amazing and it will do what it needs to do naturally, but you need to give it time."

Whenever there is this level of unrealistic pressure, there will always be dissenters who have the courage to speak out against it – that is one of social media's most positive attributes, and it's certainly the case with the postpartum body. Real, undoctored images of stretchmarked tummies, C-section scars and protruding "pooches" are increasingly being shared by new mothers as an antidote to the "snap-back" narrative. Instead of racing to your body starting line, the #TakeBackPostpartum message is to embrace the way that your skin and figure looks, no matter what the impact of childbirth. While we all love babies, no-one seems to want to look at what it can take to make them. From Demi Moore onwards, we've become accustomed to seeing pregnant women on magazine covers – sometimes completely naked. The question is: why wouldn't we celebrate the post-birth body in the same way? Why is it so shameful that it has to be hidden until it more or less resumes its former shape?

All post-pregnancy bodies should be praised, whether they naturally spring back, prefer to take their sweet time or maybe only go forwards into a new shape. While it's a great thing that mums can now be seen as sexy, it's unrealistic for the vast majority to look like a "yummy mummy" instantly. The real truth is that there are far worse things that can happen while giving birth than stretchmarks, and the focus on the superficial side of reconstructing your body after it's been another human being's house for nine months is so limited it's almost laughable. It's time to tell the crowd to go home and heal at our own pace.

Mama Mafia:
The Pros and Cons of Online Support

Remember the natural vs medicalized childbirth stand-off? That, my friends, is just a penny in a pocketful of change. Before I go on, it's worth taking a moment to highlight how incredibly supportive some women find the community spirit that they find online among other mothers. If you're geographically isolated or struggling to leave the house, the comfort of knowing that there is a sisterhood going through the same experience at the click of a laptop button can provide a support system where one is lacking. These communities, especially on Facebook, have seen a huge uptake among mothers with children at all stages, from newborn to teenage. In the US, 81 per cent of mothers use Facebook to connect with friends, family and motherhood communities. Parents in general are particularly active on the platform: 75 per cent log on daily, including 51 per cent who do so several times a day, and 74 per cent say they receive support from social media. As a tool for parenting and resource for information, these platforms have become indispensable for many mothers, and that's only to be lauded. Nothing is more reassuring than having a lifeline you can reach out to at 3am in the morning to get advice on what's going on with your screaming baby.

And yet. What social media gives, it takes away. While communities can support, they can also almost immediately descend into catfights. Without going into the *rights and wrongs* about the way you've chosen to raise your child, because woe betide you fancy a glass of wine while breastfeeding, move your baby into his own room before six months, hold them back a year from school or – inhale deeply – decide not to vaccinate, it's worth discussing the dawn of the digital school gate. Outside traditional social media platforms, specific forums for discussion of topics related to motherhood have developed to supplement the groups you'll find on Facebook and the like. Generally launched with the best intentions, many of these spaces have become battlegrounds between keyboard warriors, places where misinformation, prejudice and searing judgements abound. The depth of that scrutiny has been so internalized that 68 per cent of mums using social media admit they feel their parenting decisions have been judged at least sometimes by other mums. A healthy debate is one thing, but these forums can also get mean – often verging on hateful.

One woman who has experienced the darker side of mothers-only forums is Laura Fantacci. "I've definitely felt the judgement of other women in a pretty full-on way. I basically decided to close my blog, *Wearing it Today,* because I just couldn't handle the criticism any more. It had got to a point where I felt I was constantly doing or saying something wrong and I was just sick and tired of all the negativity – I just didn't want it in my life any more. A friend had sent me a Mumsnet [British-based forum for mothers] thread about me – which started innocently enough and then very quickly got vile. So vile I couldn't finish reading it. I just had to block it out of my mind and not think about it at all for a few days. Whenever I have to google my own name the thread comes up and it literally repels me. For me, it was just too much to bear."

Especially for first-time mothers, insecurity and a lack of confidence in parenting abilities can surface in many different ways. For example, a 2018 study found that the mothers who post the most on social media are actually the ones who are most likely to be seeking validation or are depressed. Much of the vitriol of the "mummy wars", where battle lines have been drawn across parenting philosophies, styles, sleep-training regimes and educational attitudes are down to misunderstandings and assumptions – as well as those niggling doubts that perhaps the way you've chosen to raise your child isn't actually the "right" one. Catherine Monk, a psychologist and professor at Columbia University Medical Center, explains in *TIME* magazine, "There's a crescendo of voices saying, 'If you don't do X or Y, you're doing it wrong,'" The result is "a kind of over-preciousness about motherhood. It's obsessive, and it's amplified by the internet and social media."

"With my first baby the judgements and comments that people posted really affected me," Anna Saccone Joly recalls. "I remember receiving messages saying that I was so lazy because I wasn't getting out of bed, or that I was using pregnancy as an excuse not to do anything. Then when the baby was born it got even worse because everyone has an opinion about how you're doing everything wrong. It's definitely easy to get sucked into reading the comments and the forums, because the truth is that you *don't* know what you're doing. But with all these criticisms and judgements, you have to remember that you don't know where they're coming from or who is writing them. You just have to take everything with a grain of salt."

When and if you return to work is another area of deep disagreement, with the guilt that many mothers feel about leaving their child or, conversely, staying at home compounded by the social judgements. In the US 88 per cent of workers don't receive paid family leave and in the UK 70 per cent of all women work, but there's still a sense that it's a *choice* whether or not to return to the jobs market. That if only women were happy to sacrifice their Jimmy Choo habit or flagrantly expensive city lifestyles, they could make the decision to be a "proper" mother and stay home to raise their family... Why have children if you're just going to let someone else take care of them? Etcetera, etcetera. The decision to go back to work six or eight weeks after birth isn't something that most mums relish, but it's a reality for many women that, however much they scrimp and save, or move out to the suburbs, they still need to work. And, hell, maybe they want to too.

On the flip side, by choosing to stay at home many women are made to feel like they are happy to live off their partner as a kept woman, rather than the truth of the matter: they are performing an economic service. If it costs between £12–18/hr for another woman to mind your child, your time is obviously equally valuable. Childcare is a job. And not just any job. It's relentless, intense, sometimes mind-numbingly boring. It requires confidence, experience and a cool head. There is no lunch break, there are no union rules. And often you do it entirely alone. So, when you're made to feel that you're setting feminism back, or that you're throwing your career down the pan, it takes a better woman than me to hold her sleep-deprived tongue. From a financial perspective it often makes sense to go back to work asap if you have one child. But two or three in full-time childcare? The maths just stops working in your favour.

With the shift to freelance lifestyles, there's also been an under-reported impact on maternity leave too. As more of us than ever work for ourselves and work from home, the traditional post-birth leave, whether covered by your employer or not, is evolving. Take Korean fashion designer Rejina Pyo, who runs her own label from her home in London. "I went back to work almost immediately after I gave birth to my son, because there was no-one else to run things and I had responsibilities to my factories and retailers," she explains. "I also had a new collection to design. As I hadn't put my email 'out of office' on, work was always present – I was back on email the day after I delivered, though it took about two and a half weeks to get back on my feet again. As the days pass, you become a new person. Because you don't have the luxury of time, you work out how you can fit things in differently and approach your workload in a different way – having a young child is an incredible procrastination killer. Of course, I envy women who have a clearly defined maternity leave that allows them to disconnect from their email for months and months. Of course, I would have liked to spend my time with my baby just holding him while I was feeding instead of multitasking. Of course, it made me feel guilty that I still had to go to a meeting or answer an email. But when I left the hospital, the midwife said to me, 'Firstly you give birth to a baby, then you give birth to your placenta and then you give birth to guilt,' and over the past months I've realized that all women carry that feeling of guilt and inadequacy inside them to some extent, no matter what they do." Stay at home, go back to work, send your baby to a nursery, get a part-time nanny…whatever you choose to do you're going to lose. Which, in a strange way, is liberating. When it comes to work and motherhood, there is no way to gain society's acceptance, so ultimately you should just do you.

***

Social media has provided a 24/7 community for mothers and dramatically impacted the sense of isolation that many women once felt. It's been a vehicle for changing cultural attitudes and has begun to break down taboos around miscarriage and the postpartum body. But it's also polarized attitudes on what kind of mother you are, leading to an increased feeling of judgement and anxieties around parenting decisions. Highly charged spaces, social media groups and forums can often undermine confidence in the difficult compromises that every woman has to make as she raises her child and possibly returns to her career. Hanging in a see-saw balance, both the very good and very bad of social media can be seen through its relationship with modern motherhood – but only we can filter the experience to capitalize on the positives while leaving the judgements and venom behind. Ultimately, only you know how you want to raise your child and that is absolutely no-one else's business.

Takeaways

1. Get real about the fantasy

If something looks too good to be true, it's because it is. Pinterest perfect motherhood is something which doesn't exist, simply because all babies scream, puke, smear their food over their faces and dirty their nappies, and if you're involved in caring for your kids at all, you'll be dealing with these great levellers day in, day out. If you really wanted to, you could tidy a space in your kitchen, add some muffin mix to a pan and put your child in a cute outfit. It would probably take about 20 minutes of your day to curate this kind of content, snap it and share it. For the next 23 hours and 40 minutes, you could be stuck to your sofa in sweatpants with baby sick in your hair and no-one outside your four walls would know. You could be feeding your baby McDonald's and no-one would know. The thing is that *anyone* can edit the reality, so there's exactly zero point using those images against which to judge yourself or what you're doing.

But perhaps it's worth stopping and considering if these "perfect" mamas are making you feel inadequate because they seem to be better at taking care of their baby or if you are just envious that they're rich and have a nice island in their kitchen? All children cry, all children wake up in the night and need feeding, all children are a challenge. So, if it doesn't look like that on social media, then you know it can only be fantasy – never forget that. Unfollow at will.

2. Take your emotional temperature

Consuming social media at any point when your emotions – and potentially hormones – are running wild is something we all need to keep a check on. When you're in a balanced frame of mind, seeing shots of your friend's families or an influencer's cute birth story is totally manageable. When you've just got your period after months of peeing on sticks and perfunctory ovulation sex, it's less so. Dr Jessica Zucker explains, "If a woman comes to me and keeps saying that everybody else around her seems to be pregnant, I always ask how much social media she is consuming. I tell her to really check in with herself: is this triggering? Is it helpful? Is it depressing, or making you angrier? Is it inciting more feelings of shame? Taking holidays from scrolling is key on social media, particularly for people who are so overwhelmed emotionally that they can't get a sense of perspective. Yes, there are plenty of pregnant women and mothers on social media, yet we don't know how hard it was for them to get pregnant. It's so easy to think, 'she's glowing', or 'she obviously got pregnant on her first try'. We can very quickly persuade ourselves that she never struggled. Women on Instagram that you don't know aren't any different from a stranger on the street. She may have had a stillbirth. She may have spent $100,000 on fertility treatment to get her child. She may have had an egg donor. *We don't know anything.* When we see these images on social media, it tends to stir feelings that everybody else's life is perfect and ours is fraught and distraught. That can create an abject sense of loneliness when you might think that social media would instead foster a sense of connection. I really hope that people take breaks and listen to themselves when it comes to struggling with that."

3. Give yourself some grace
While you may be lucky enough to slip back into your skinnies after a few weeks, statistically it's unlikely. Equally even if you do fit into your old clothes, you'll doubtless be looking down at a belly, ass and thighs which aren't quite the same firmness or texture as they were before. This isn't some weird aberration, or a genetic quirk your mum hasn't told you about. This is just normal. Atrophied muscles, bad backs, weak pelvic floors and a significantly weakened core are just to be expected, as is loose skin, visible coloured stretchmarks and, if you had a C-section, an obvious scar. If you don't have a chef to cook your meals or a personal trainer to build you back up, again that's OK. Only celebrities and the mega-rich do. Instead, buy a couple of pairs of new jeans to bridge the gap between the elastic band maternity styles you've dreamt of

burning and your pre-pregnancy denim collection. You don't have to go mad with building a whole new wardrobe, but don't punish yourself trying to squeeze back into your old size in the first weeks and months. Also, you can thank the Lord that the one-piece is back en vogue, although if you want to wear a bikini or crop top, no matter what your new belly looks like, you go, mama.

4. Social media mums aren't the parenting police

In the vast, nebulous world of parenting, the most notable thing is utter lack of objectivity – in that nearly everything we know about motherhood is an evolving moveable feast of conjecture, fashion and opinion. There are very few set-in-stone standards, like don't drink and take drugs when you're pregnant, and in general, child-rearing advice is in a constant state of flux with no rules that fit all. All you have to do is ask your mum, who was probably told to put her baby to sleep on its tummy, to turf the wee mite into its own room after two months and that she could sleep however she liked when pregnant (whereas research now dictates that babies are put to sleep on their backs and in your room for six months minimum and that pregnant women should only sleep on their side – preferably the left). Of course, anything that improves a baby's chances of good health is amazing – but we have to keep a sense of perspective and know that what we may be so sure of today may be judged in a completely different light in the space of just a few years.

Which brings us to the social media "mummy wars". If you find yourself pitched in a parenting battle online, it's worth keeping in mind that however convinced you are of your chosen philosophy's rightness and however certain you are in your own certainty, you could potentially be wrong. In the 1920s, parenting experts counselled to never hug or kiss your children, and in the 1950s pregnant women were encouraged to smoke. So, you know, there's a precedence for at least a margin of error. Think about it: Amazon returns over a hundred thousand results under the search term "parenting books", which means there are apparently more than a hundred thousand ways to raise your child. It's understandable that we might feel overwhelmed by this lack of clarity, and it's hardly a surprise that a recent study found that women who read the most baby manuals have the most symptoms of depression. But the scary truth is that there isn't a *right way* to be a mother, there's just what we believe. So, the next time you read in a forum that sleep training is "abusive" or see a Facebook post claiming attachment parenting is "anti-feminist", just keep in mind that as long as you feed, clothe and love your child, the rest really is just your choice, just as it is any other mother's. Advice is all well and good, but it's time to leave the judgements behind.

Chapter 6:
Why Social Media is Ruining
Your **Career & Money**

Social media is a world of leisure and pleasure.

Every day we scroll through a fantasyland where life is a mix of holidays, spa trips and home-made acai bowls. It's a place where £2,000 ($2,600) handbags seem inexplicably within reach – even if they cost more than your monthly take-home pay. A rolling conveyor belt of not just goods but also experiences continuously passes before your eyes until you start to believe that *this* is what the meaning of life looks like. Status these days isn't just about the car you drive or the watch you wear. What you do says as much about your success in life as your financial portfolio. Shots of yourself, front row at a Beyoncé concert; reportage of your bucket-list trip to see the Northern Lights; plate pics at a ritzy restaurant – these are the new symbols of success.

Although Australian real-estate mogul Tim Gurner got an international drubbing in 2017 for suggesting that millennials should spend less on avocado toast and save their dollars for a house deposit, there's an element of truth to the fact that living for the 'gram costs cold hard cash – which we're spending on impressing instead of investing in things that other people can't see. A 2017 Direct Line survey of 18–34 year olds revealed that a third of millennials had bragged about their expensive branded goods on social media and 20 per cent said there is no point owning nice things if other people don't know about them. When a presence on social media seems to be a prerequisite for a modern social life, consumerism for content's sake begins to look less like frivolous spending and more like a basic necessity, which everyone "deserves".

It's true that there have always been ladies who lunch and gentlemen of leisure, but on social media *everyone* lives a jet-set life. However, just like a game or a simulation, not everything is quite as it seems. Let's call a spade a spade: something doesn't add up. Unless everyone we know has won the lottery recently, how could they all possibly be paying for it? We know that the average salary does not support a billionaire lifestyle and that people generally have to go to work from nine to five. So how come most mentions of the way we earn our keep are vague and concentrated on office promotions or holiday parties? Where are the 10pm nights on a deadline or meetings which make drying paint look dynamic? Where are the nightmare bosses, computer system failures or terrible canteen food? I don't know about you, but work has sometimes felt like it was my *entire* life. So why don't we see any evidence of it? Reducing our careers to sidenotes, inflating our finances beyond our wildest dreams and airbrushing out anything which requires actual grit, sacrifice, pain or determination, social media is a fairy tale in which the mundane doesn't figure. And that can make us feel alone in the sometimes-soul-crushing experiences that most of us have to deal with in order to pay our own way in life.

The inspiration for launching my site and the reason it's called Work Work Work are down to this very issue. In 2016, I went on a group holiday with a collection of professionally impressive women. Among us were two business owners, a global PR director for one of the biggest fashion businesses in the world, a senior VP at one of the world's biggest television production companies and a well-known celebrity makeup artist and beauty blogger. The holiday – dreamy in so many ways – was often punctuated by calls from our respective offices and no-one was entirely "off". But the only pictures any of us shared from the trip were the cocktails, designer bikinis and sunset views. Sitting back on my sunlounger in paradise, multitasking between a tricky office email and filtering a picture of my lunch for Instagram, I realised how complicit I was in the mass glamorization of our lives; it started to make me feel really culpable. I was suddenly painfully aware that what I was doing – what a lot of us are doing – was telling the next generation of working women coming up behind us that life is all a beach, career success is straightforward and money isn't an object. Which is complete and utter *bullshit*. Every single one of the women on my trip had worked for well over a decade to get to a position where they could afford the cocktails, designer bikinis and sunset views. We had all paid our dues, and then some, and none of us had been born with a silver spoon or handed our success on a plate.

Fashion agent Gabriela Moussaieff represents some of the world's highest-paid set designers and makeup artists, and her work life takes her around the globe on what, she agrees, could look like one long luxurious holiday. While she might be posting shots from her hotel suite, she explains that the reality of life in the fashion fast lane is an optical illusion: "It's easy to forget that, when I'm travelling, I basically have double the amount of work to do. I'm constantly catching up on what I'm missing in the office in between back-to-back meetings, plus I'm working full-on on two different time zones, so there's not really any time to sleep. It is punishing. That glamorous, jet-set life you see on social media? That's just one second that I stopped to take a picture – the rest of the time I'm struggling to keep my head above water."

I'm in no way saying that women shouldn't be proud and share their achievements. But by only presenting half of the story – the rewards without the strife – something which social media explicitly and implicitly encourages, we are all misrepresenting the expectations for both our peers and younger women looking at our lives. There's no doubt that these images shape how others believe life should, or at least could, look like. Is it any wonder that millennials have been labelled the most entitled generation of all time? If all they're seeing is a jolly good time, why wouldn't they think that success comes for free? How can we be surprised that 40 per cent of them believe they should get a promotion every two years, regardless of their performance? Of course they're going to think they'll be a CEO by the time they're 25. It's exactly what the motivational memes on social media have taught them to expect.

The far bleaker reality is that everyone sometimes feels like their life is a version of *Groundhog Day* – a relentless stream of toil in the office, toil through their commute and even the odd toil during the evenings, weekends and holidays too. Even if you love your job, everyone has tough times in the workplace. And, while it might all look like roses online, the vast majority of those young women travelling the world with brands on social media also have dodgy work–life moments too. However much you dress it up on Instagram, when it comes to work, there's always a catch – no matter what you do.

Who Got the Money?

Talking about money in pretty much all situations is considered unacceptable, right? While disclosing your salary has become *slightly* more tolerable in the fight against gender and racial discrimination, blurting out how much you spent on this or that is still definitely seen as déclassé. It's still true that most of us would prefer to share graphic details about our sex life than reveal our monthly bank balance, and it can sometimes be hard to even gauge what you should or shouldn't be paying for basic life requirements like rent, because everyone is too evasive to reveal what they're shelling out. How much cash you really have and what you really earn are perhaps the ultimate taboos – and while that's nothing new, there's no doubt that adding social media into the mix has distorted the perception of how many disposable pounds/dollars/euros/yen/pesos/florins/krone/rupee we're all apparently sitting on.

In my opinion, having a frank discussion about money is one of the most important conversations that we should be having in the social media age. I come from a resolutely modest background. However if you look at my social media account you could easily believe that I'm very wealthy as I definitely have a lot of the trappings of privilege. The shots of me on yachts or images featuring my multiple designer handbags could easily lead viewers to that conclusion. Although I do now earn a good salary and have been able to buy an apartment in London, I'm certainly not rolling in it and I definitely didn't always have the financial stability that I do now. Both of my parents grew up in social housing and were working class to the core. Insecurity around money was a huge part of my upbringing and we often struggled. Like many baby boomers, my parents managed to climb a rung and buy their own home, but when they split there was a lot of hustling. We got by – but money always ran out and that was something I was acutely aware of from a young age.

What really changed my perception of the value of money was enrolling in a selective private girls' school when I was 11. Dad had found a job back in Germany, where my brother and I were both born, but even with child maintenance payments and Mum's secretarial salary, we were far from well-off. However, dad's company offered financial aid for education and he stretched his means to cover the shortfall to send me to a school which my parents believed would give me the best chance in life. It was there that I first really realized that we didn't have much in comparison to some other people. At my primary school, everyone had been in the same boat, give or take, but now girls in my class lived in huge detached homes with acres of land; they wore designer shoes and talked about labels like Burberry and Moschino; their parents drove huge cars and they went skiing and to the Caribbean on holiday. It was like looking on Instagram, but for real – everyone else had so much material stuff, whereas I just didn't. And they knew it too. I can still feel the embarrassment of hearing 12-year-old girls talking about the shabby carpets and small rooms of our two-up, two-down semi on the wrong side of the tracks. Being poorer when everyone else is richer is crappy, no matter how you dress it up, but it's particularly hard when you're young and you haven't yet got a perspective on what happiness is really all about.

These days, when you're a teenager living a normal life, viewing the world through the lives of people flaunting their exaggerated financial position, *everyone* feels like I did at secondary school. Social media doesn't just skew expectations and inspire avarice, it also makes you feel like you're relatively on the breadline, and that can deeply undermine your confidence when you're still trying to work out your place in life. It wasn't like we were worse off growing up than the majority of people – no matter what it looks like on social media, the barefaced truth is that financial struggle is a huge part of most people's lives. But it's the context of what you see all around you that defines how you view yourself, and in the social media age nearly all of us are comparatively poverty-stricken.

When everything seems to come so easy to other people all around you, it can be hugely demoralizing and demotivating. The only way I managed to build the life I have today was by working *really, really* hard. I've legitimately had more jobs than I can remember. Paper rounds, stacking shelves, waitressing, cleaning, retail, temping, secretarial work, cringe promo-girl work, extras (as in on films) work. That is how I got my money, and it was draining, unglamorous and often boring. I also *really, really* studied in school, which is how I got a lot of opportunities afterward. How often do we hear on social media about the power of education to transform your life? Far less than we hear about how teeth whitening can apparently do the same.

Those are the realities behind the achievement of your aspirations. A strong work ethic is far more likely to get you the fantasy life than losing weight to look like a wellness blogger. Social media projects a bankrupt values system in which material goods aren't related to work, and that is such a dangerous message. Millennial and Generation Z kids will grow up to be poorer than their parents, but in an environment where everyone seems to have more than ever before. No wonder these generations are the most anxious, disenchanted and depressed of recent times.

A Rude Awakening:
The Devil Definitely Wears Prada

However hard I'd slogged before I started my career, nothing prepared me for trying to get a job working in fashion. Back when I started out, there was no legal imperative to pay interns anything and consequently most of my fellow slaves were extremely wealthy and privileged. I interned for *free* for two entire years, 9am–7pm, every single day of the week at various fashion magazines and newspaper supplements. The "expenses" didn't even cover my train fare. I managed financially by getting a place on a master's degree and using the subsidy from my dad's company (which continued to support my education until I was 26) for my rent. So that I had some money to live on, I got a job on the shop floor and did other side gigs to top it up. It was a whirlwind time – interning during the week, simultaneously studying for my master's, plus the retail grind. I also moved out to the countryside so I could afford my rent – which meant a four-hour round commute. Physically and mentally it was entirely unsustainable, but I got through it – like many others before me and since.

When I met university friends I had plenty of glamorous stories to tell them and could post pictures to Facebook of champagne events and celebrity shoots. But what I didn't mention was the reality of what the early days of my career looked like. A lot of it happened exclusively in a cupboard – and I don't mean a chic, architect-designed office: it was a 3-sq-metre (32-sq-foot) broom cupboard with rotting brown flooring and 72 rails shoved mercilessly inside. During the first seven months of interning, all I did was return clothing samples. Literally just packing and writing dockets on little pink sheets. After a while I was given the responsibility to *request* samples as well. Over the two years I did get to work in all sorts of studios and ran still-life shoots on my own, but in general the job was: request clothes, pack clothes, book courier, unpack clothes, return clothes. When I finally got my first "proper" job on a magazine, I thought that there might be a change-up in tasks. Sadly not. I didn't escape the cupboard. For another two years I had to sit at a desk inside a fashion cupboard since part of the "role" was to guard the clothes at all times for insurance purposes. As in, I was a clothing bodyguard – a bit like a scarecrow, but for Manolos. But obviously that wasn't the way I was selling it to anyone who asked, and I proudly advertised my job titles on every social platform.

I've had some incredible bosses and mentors in my career, but I've also had editors who have left screaming voicemails on my phone, who have harangued me at high-decibel level in front of all my co-workers, who have thrown clothes and shoes at me, and who have made me suck back the tears. One editor made me wash and dry her socks in a public bathroom. Another one would often call me before 6am to talk about her marriage issues but then, behind my back, tell everyone else in the office that I should be fired. Often it got weird and a lot of power play and mind control went on. I was scared to go on holiday in case someone logged into my emails and somehow used something I'd said against me to get me sacked. The stress was constant. My underling status was constantly reiterated and opportunities were often in short supply. However hard I worked, the most important thing was that I understood my place in the office hierarchy – at the bottom. The relationships with a couple of my bosses were probably abusive. I don't think these issues are exclusive to fashion offices – every industry has people who think that they need to crush you to make you earn your spurs. There's a word for them: bullies. However, there do seem to be an oversupply of this personality type in the fashion business in particular – thus the Devil sports Prada. Unsurprisingly I didn't communicate any of this via social media.

When you come from a background in which traditional, blue-collar jobs are the norm, you don't really have anyone to help you work out what is and what isn't OK. The jobs my family had experience in were either factory-based or clerical. Understandably my family *really* didn't understand my career choices. With all that money invested into my education, why the hell was I working for free? For two years? Why was I putting up with a boss who called me at all hours and seemed to despise me?

Then there was the financial side. I got my first paid job in London at 24, which came with a salary of £15,500 ($20,500). After tax, I had just under £1,000 ($1,300) to live on a month. My rent was cheap in the countryside (£350/$460 per month), but the train in was expensive (over £200/$260). After bills, debts and everything else, I had about £80 ($100) to play with a week. Whenever people who work in fashion talk about "investment buys" and how a £300 ($400) dress is accessible (hands up, I have definitely done this), I always try to remember back to my mid-twenties and how much of a fucking struggle it was. It's so important to remember that the reality behind a job title is often just as much of a fantasy as a Facetuned waistline. In your twenties it may seem that everyone around you is doing *so* well, but how much do you really know about the tasks they do day in and day out? Those trainee-lawyer friends, record-company execs or junior publishers – how do their colleagues treat them? Social media lets us exaggerate the positive sides of our jobs until they are almost unrecognizable from what we actually experience between nine and five.

My next job increased my salary to £19,000 ($25,000) but then I didn't get a raise for the next three years. By this point I was on a national magazine, working 60-hour weeks. While it was dodgy re paying rent, it was also when the free clothes thing started. The glamorous lives of women working in fashion and social media that you see on Instagram and Facebook are all created around this booty. The holidays, the flights, the shoes, the bags, the makeup, you name it – they probably got it for free, or at least at a hefty discount. The perks for editors, YouTube influencers and fashion PRs can be fantastic. At the beginning, I just got a posh breakfast here and there and a dress from River Island. Over the course of my career it's become designer bags, business-class flights and hotel suites in Tokyo, São Paolo and New York. But the key thing is that this lifestyle isn't paid for via *my own bank account*. Most women working in fashion would never be able to pay for all these amazing goods and experiences themselves.

Slowly over my twenties my salaries crept up – not because I got raises but because I changed jobs fairly regularly and negotiated as hard as I could. By 27 I was earning £30,000 ($40,000) and when I left my last staffer role on a magazine, aged 31, I was up to £36,000 ($48,000), which is close to the average London salary. On that amount, I lived a more secure life, but I was by this point in my thirties, single again and really wanting to buy a home for myself. The crunch point (excuse the pun) came when I had to call my dad to ask to borrow some money to get a filling for a cavity. Not being able to afford to go to the dentist when you're living a five-star lifestyle just suddenly seemed too pathetic – the numbers of my life just didn't make sense. I ultimately decided to leave a job that I really did love, pretty much exclusively because of money. Living on accessories is fine when you're young, but to be a fully independent woman who isn't waiting for Prince Charming to sweep her into an open-plan warehouse apartment means making financially responsible decisions. And living a life for the perks had become entirely irresponsible.

I decided to set up my own business – a minefield I stumbled my way through, making mistakes at every corner. But within a year I was earning more than double my magazine salary. After that year, I moved on to an in-house editorial role in fashion tech (which I think was probably my last "job") with a salary of £80,000 ($100,000), and 18 months of hardcore saving later, I bought a flat. While my dad helped and my boyfriend chipped in (we have a joint mortgage), the majority of the deposit was mine and the mortgage was based mainly on my earnings. Now I'm back working for myself again, life isn't straightforward; I feel a huge amount of angst about money, which a secure salary would mitigate. The first few months of waiting for invoices to be paid are particularly brutal. Some months are amazing and I feel on top of the world. Other months I earn *way* less than I did when I had a day job. Falling pregnant has been a challenge too – I worry about maintaining clients and get scared the projects will dry up as I navigate a new life with a newborn. But that's the trade-off – I'd prefer to earn less, be my own boss and have control over my time.

While it might not look like it, most people on social media are living lives just like yours. I'm certain that if Instagram had existed when I'd started out I'd have decided that everyone in fashion was so rich and privileged that it would have been unthinkable for me to even begin to try to break into such a glamorous industry. It would have just seemed like too far a jump from the reality of my life. When you work in an office, you see women wearing nice clothes and handbags. But you can recognize their clothes and handbags. When you look on Instagram, people who work in sexy industries seem to have new clothes and handbags every single day. Or even *twice* a day. Their homes are stacked with designer pieces which are on sale on 1stdibs for £6,756 ($8,946). When you google the hotel they geo-located, Booking.com lets you know rooms *start* at £600 ($800) a night. They are not just wealthy; they are seemingly gazillionaires.

I try to keep things as real as possible on my platforms. If I buy a pair of shoes, I'll wear them in circa 50 Instagrams before they get a rest, and I've posted about how much I love old clothes. I would never, ever work with a brand and not disclose a financial transaction. Not everything in my life or on Instagram is a free dinner, but I'm fortunate enough that a lot of it is, and that so exponentially misrepresents the true picture of my financial situation. Until I bought my flat, I was still sharing a rickety two-bed with my brother and boyfriend well into my thirties and I had no savings, as in not a penny, before I was 31. I feel incredibly thankful that I've been able to buy my current place, but the truth is that it's a 52-sq-metre (560-sq-foot) shoebox on the first floor with no outside space and scant storage. I've made it look really nice (hopefully in real life as much as on social media) and I do share pictures of my décor as interiors, as it's a huge passion. But again, creating a beautiful space takes money, which when you don't have tons of it, means time. It took over a year to buy our dining chairs, because we could only afford them one by one. Without abundant wealth, you can't just click your fingers and have a Pinterest-ready home, stacked with timeless design classics and eccentric, unique trinkets.

So why go into such exhaustive detail about my finances? Basically, because, like me, so many of the people that you follow on social media are in a far more modest position than they may seem to be. What we *all* need to do is kick our assumptions to the kerb, because again, the more we build up expectations, the harder it is for us all to deal with the fact that a lot of this stuff is going to be out of our financial reach, potentially forever.

Spend, Spend, Spend

One of the gravest problems these expectations create is an inability to moderate our materialistic desires. There's zero doubt: social media can drive really dangerous and irresponsible financial behaviour. Why not put that Zara haul on the credit card when everyone else seems to have a new Chloé bag every week? Don't you deserve to book that all-inclusive holiday to Ibiza, even though you know the monthly payments are going to cripple you with debt? #YOLO after all, and since x, y and z seem to manage, you should be able to too, right?

Well, probably not. Consumer debt in the US rose to $12.7 trillion in 2017 and, on the other side of the Atlantic, unsecured personal debt is predicted to hit £15,000 per household in the UK in 2018. A recent study suggests that, while debts are increasing, what we're spending money on is changing: it's experiences rather than things that we're now racking up on our plastic. And the reason the debts are mounting? "A short-term focus on not missing out on that opportunity" – aka FOMO. Take travel, for example. A 2017 report showed that 49 per cent of millennials will go into debt to pay for a trip and, according to a survey by financial planning company LearnVest, Americans take an average of six months to recover financially from a vacation. It's not that I can't understand the motivation: going on holiday is lovely, everyone else seems to be doing it and it also offers great Instagram fodder. But are seven days really worth bankrupting yourself for? For a lot of people, the answer is, very obviously: yes.

Remember when you went to the mall because that was the only place you could buy things? Since the internet explosion, retailers have a whole new arsenal of ways to lure us into spending our cash. Aside from the many, many online stores and countless traps like banner ads and content marketing, we also have social media apps as "inspiration" channels, advertising endless services, products and experiences. There's a reason that social media is big business: peer-to-peer endorsement is incredibly effective at persuading you to part with your money. Almost 40 per cent of adults with social media accounts say that seeing other people's purchases and vacations on social media have prompted them to look into similar purchases or vacations, and more than 11 per cent spent money after seeing someone else's post, according to a recent poll by the American Institute of Certified Public Accountants.

Nene Granville, a fashion and lifestyle PR, explains the mentality: "I'd just been made redundant and I was working on my next steps to launching my own business. Money was obviously a worry. But then I saw this lamp on my Insta-feed and just had this feeling that I had to buy it right away or I'd miss the opportunity. After I'd made the purchase, I realized how crazy it was – you definitely have to catch yourself in those moments. We all need to realize there is more to life than what you think you need to buy on Instagram."

In summary: social media is making us spend money we don't have, buy things we don't need, to impress people we don't know. However, so much of it – at least from the fashion/influencer perspective – isn't real, and I hope my story helps to convey that.

I wasn't raised with money; I didn't have enough for most of my twenties and I made a career in fashion without a single industry contact. A lot of my friends and colleagues are in the same position and are making ends meet in crazily pricey cities and most usually living in the red. While they might have brand new dresses and shoes to keep them up with the Instagram Joneses, they are struggling just as hard as the rest of us to get on the property ladder, to pay their bills and all those other "real life" things that social media obscures. "Two thousand-dollar bag with no cash in your purse," may be Kanye's most eloquent depiction of contemporary materialism, and it certainly applies here.

Of course, there are thousands of young bloggers making bank and the new social media economy has definitely broadened the ability for women from all backgrounds to earn a more than respectable living from lifestyle media. But plenty of them aren't anywhere near as wealthy as you might think. As Anna Newton, of The Anna Edit blog and YouTube channel, explains: "I don't come from money or have a hugely extravagant lifestyle. Yes, I will buy a nice bag now and again, but I'm a real homebody and love spending my time in watching Netflix. The truth is that a lot about the way I live my life isn't unobtainable. I think it's so important to remember that you can't measure your happiness by going on luxurious holidays and posting about them."

Ultimately the message is to take everything on social media with a pinch of salt and remember that you have no idea if all that Instagram swag is "real" or not. From the scores of connections I've made in the industry, only very few are seriously rolling in it. Some do come from privilege, some earn a ton and whittle it away, but the vast majority are "normal" and certainly don't have salaries that could cover the actual receipts of their digital life. There are fashion designers, PRs, influencers, editors and a host of other chic-looking women with fancy job titles who have all come from resolutely ordinary backgrounds. And, while social media might make it look like they have always had everything, they haven't. They had to work for it.

Wait, what? A Deficit of Attention

Does social media make you better or worse at your job? Apparently it's a contested question, but I think we all know the answer.

Let's create the scenario:

You get into work on Monday morning all fired up and ready to go with a mental to-do list playing through your mind. You nail the "must-respond" emails, and as a "reward" have a quick check on your phone to see if anyone has messaged you. You see your family WhatsApp group has accrued 31 messages, so you decide you'd better catch-up or else you'll be lost in the thread. While you're doing that a push notification comes up from Instagram telling you an old school friend has commented on that gym pic you posted from class this morning. You immediately respond. You also see you've had seven new emails and two texts. Mentally adding them to your to-do list, as they're much more interesting than that work you've got to do, you approach them first – after all, you did nail those emails already this morning. Approximately 22 minutes later, you return to your work, which just doesn't feel quite so satisfying any more, but you exert some discipline and focus. You realize you have 19 windows open on your desktop. Seven minutes later you hear your phone ping and, somehow, it's back in your hand again. You put it down and try to recapture your train of thought; what was it you were writing again? Maybe it's on one of these tabs... No, that's not it, but you can now tell your friend Holly that, yes, she should definitely buy that dress. Ugh, back to work. The cycle continues torturously until lunchtime, when, thank the Lord, you can scroll without the guilt as you walk and text to the closest lunch spot. You reach the end of the day and, while you've managed to tick off most of your original list you've also: watched three YouTube videos; spent 47 minutes on Instagram; looked at 12 pictures you could add to Instagram and googled lots of synonyms to help you write a seriously witty caption; didn't post any of the 12 pictures; replied to six WhatsApp conversations with a total of 54 messages; pretended you were researching a new marketing objective while actually updating your Snapstreaks; checked your Tinder inbox seven times; and also inadvertently bought a pair of Miu Miu-alike shoes from Topshop as you saw they were on sale on Facebook. Oh, and there's a DM from LinkedIn... Maybe it's a new job you need, because this one really seems exhausting? The sun sets, you're the last one in the office and your scattergun brain is frazzled. All you can think of doing is tumbling on to your sofa and ordering takeaway...while sitting all evening long watching Netflix with your laptop open and your phone twitching in your palm. Sound familiar?

The description above is a reality shared by far too many of us. Four out of five employees access their private accounts during work time and spend up to 2.35 hours a day on social media, depleting their productivity by an estimated 13 per cent. In a recent blog post, the Bank of England reported that it takes office workers an average of 25 minutes to get back on task after an interruption, while workers who are habitually interrupted by email become likelier to "self-interrupt" with little procrastination breaks. The more we indulge in goldfish brain activity, the more we need these interruptions to function – indeed 34 per cent of people say they use social media at work to take a "mental break". These micro pauses, which come complete with a dopamine hit, are reported to be rewiring the way our brains actually work.

Pre-internet, I can remember being able to work solidly with no respite for two or even three hours at a time. I was a smoker back then, so I'd schedule myself some nicotine time every couple of hours. But aside from that, I was laser-focused on the task at hand and very efficient. Now I'm lucky if I can manage 15 minutes without needing to divert, or more euphemistically "rest", my brain. I am much less productive and it means my work day bleeds over into my free time. It's not so much "work hard, play hard", it's more a blended day of constant work and play (internet/social media) in which I'm incessantly being pulled between what I should be doing (writing this book) and what I'd prefer to be doing (watching Kylie Jenner's pregnancy announcement).

What we know is that our brains prefer novelty over the mundane same-same, which is why distractions are so damn attractive. We also know that multitasking can make us feel superficially more fulfilled with the way we work – even though, in terms of productivity, we actually achieve less. Psychologists now refer to two types of attention: spotlight and floodlight. When we are focused on a single task, we use our spotlight brain to centre all of our efforts on its completion. But when we split our concentration between several tasks, we employ a floodlight approach, where we work on more than one thing at a time. The bad news is that our brains are terrible at this. Indeed, researchers at the Institute of Psychiatry at the University of London concluded that multitasking with electronic media caused a greater decrease in IQ than smoking marijuana or losing a night's sleep. Worse news is the level of multimedia multitasking, as described above, is potentially leading to a reframing of our cognitive paths to favour the less productive, less aware mental juggle.

The brain is a remarkably flexible organ, subject to dramatic shifts in the way it responds to what we feed it. This ability to alter to new experiences is known as neuroplasticity. Many things can change the brain, from learning a musical instrument, taking up a daily crossword to moving to a new city, so it's hardly a surprise that our smartphone use is having an impact. A Microsoft study showed that human attention spans have reduced from 12 to 8 seconds since 2000, and it's worth noting that a goldfish can actually hold a thought for 9 seconds, so I guess we owe them an apology. Heavy multitaskers tend to develop a smaller grey matter area, which is the area of your brain that governs your attention control. If you've become too dependent on your devices and all their many entertainments, chances are you'll find it increasingly hard to be attentive, no matter what the situation.

Other studies have shown evidence that smartphones are changing the way we remember, navigate and even find happiness. Being "present" is something which meditative practices such as mindfulness and yoga teach us is fundamental to our wellbeing, but a 2010 analysis of nearly a quarter of a million responses using the iPhone app trackyourhappiness showed that our minds are wandering elsewhere about 47 per cent of the time, and the more our minds digress, the less happy we are. Whatever we are doing, from shopping to exercising to lovemaking, we're happier when we don't divide our thoughts – even if those contemplations are entirely neutral. Multitasking may seem to be great, but we find our greatest happiness from being present and doing just the *one* thing at a time.

The fact that we're brain-training ourselves to multitask may, as several academics have suggested, mean we're on the road to a new "superhuman" brain. Others are less convinced, including Mark Bauerlein, a professor of English at Emory University in Atlanta. His 2009 attention-span-testing title, *The Dumbest Generation: How the Digital Age Stupefies Young Americans and Jeopardizes Our Future (Or, Don't Trust Anyone Under 30)*, was pretty clear on his opinions nearly a decade ago. As with a lot of social media research, the jury is officially out. In the workplace, 71 per cent of people say that social media helps them keep in touch with their contacts and 46 per cent use it to find information they need to do their job, which sounds awesome. But how can we know whether or not it's making us smarter, better workers? Perhaps consider a 2015 study of pedestrians in Midtown Manhattan: 42 per cent of those who walked into traffic during a "Don't Walk" signal were wearing headphones, talking on their mobile or looking down at an electronic device. Which doesn't exactly scream "brainiac", does it?

I'm no neuroscientist, but I know my own brain and I know it can now take in huge swathes of information across multiple platforms but has an inability to focus for long periods (I'm talking 20 minutes plus) of time. Whether I'm less intelligent or capable in the workplace now than I was at 18 is up for debate (though those 4 years working in a cupboard can't have helped), but I definitely struggle with tasks which I'd have found very easy before I had a phone to lure me in with its tantalizing array of diversions. We can say swings and roundabouts, but I'd lean personally to saying that social media reduces my ability to think, write and concentrate, which, for a writer, is pretty fundamental. I feel like I'm permanently dealing with information overload and have deep guilt about the amount of time I waste when I could be working. Even though I need the internet for my work, I dream of how much I could get done if the Wi-Fi cut out.

Younger millennials can't even remember a time when their brains weren't like a pinball machine, but the good news is that mindfulness and digital detox have been proven to help us rebuild our attention span and nothing we're doing to our grey matter with the constant multitasking appears to be irreversible – the adaptability works both ways. The brain is an amazing organ, but it needs the right diet of behaviour in order to do what you need it to. Periods of phone-free work and not multitasking across multiple media are essential to retraining our minds to be able to spotlight focus. Think of it as the fruit and vegetables of your day. In this analogy, scanning your attention across multiple platforms is like a diet of hamburgers and eclairs – instantly satisfying, but in the long term not so great for you. (I've just switched my phone to airplane mode – if you want to get any work done today, I'd suggest you do too.)

Work Outside of Work: Everybody Hurts Sometimes

When it comes to work–life balance, careers and finances obviously fit on the former side of the scales. However, there's plenty of work that goes on outside the office: namely the work that we put into ourselves. While the concept may sound very self-help, becoming a better version of yourself – be it through trying to improve your confidence, motivation or self-acceptance – has become part and parcel of 21st-century womanhood. Personal development is often hidden work, however it's something which social media addresses, though only on the most shallow and superficial terms. The Insta-quotes "Be the Best Version of You!", "Life Improvement Begins with Self-Improvement", or, my favourite, "Dear You, Make Peace with Mirror & Watch Your Reflection Change", are just some examples of the limitless number of saccharine "inspirational" quotes which allude to the efforts that go on behind the filters. But one thing that's been obscured in the social media deceit is the truth that we can't gauge other people's sense of inner contentment through a picture. No matter what your background or life experience, none of us know what it's like to be inside each other's heads. Self-esteem isn't hereditary, and the stark reality is that some of those women you follow who look like they have the world at their feet are more lost than you could ever imagine.

Leandra Medine, founder of ManRepeller.com, expands. "I know that a lot of my experience is wrapped up in the position of privilege I am coming from, both broadly as a white Western woman and more specifically as one who is lucky enough to live in New York and who was raised in a comfortable environment. So often I find myself thinking twice before sharing some version of a lament because I know how tone-deaf that can come across. The thing of it is, though, personal experience is...personal, right? And we all experience the range of emotions – despair, grief, sadness – for various reasons. These reasons might be profoundly different, but the grief of a woman (not myself) dressed entirely in pearls and diamonds and expensive fabrics is no different from that of someone else's? Maybe she is less grateful (it's not for me to say), but she is still feeling a bleak sense of nothingness."

All of us go through times of bland sadness and deep heartbreak, no matter whether we have one hundred or one million followers. Of course, wealth can ameliorate some of the worst effects of life's barrage of challenges, but we all have to work to weather the rough times and a healthy bank balance is certainly no cure-all charm. We are also all complex beings, with both baggage from our past and psychological quirks and ticks created by our specific brain chemistry. You just can't buy contentment, no matter what it might look like when you scroll through your feeds. Working on ourselves is perhaps the biggest task that most of us will face in the pursuit of happiness and no number of trips or designer shopping splurges can make a dent in a process which can be both painful and relentless.

From my experience interviewing, working and travelling with women from all walks, I can, hand on heart, say that the ones who look like they've got it all figured out from the outside are often the ones who are struggling on the "journey" to self-improvement. Influencer Camille Charrière explains why the jet-set life – at least in her particular case – isn't always all it's cracked up to be. "I know how incredibly fortunate I am and that I've got an incredible job, which I'm certainly not complaining about," she says. "But if I'm being really truthful, the lifestyle that goes alongside it can play havoc with my mind. I often lack a solid structure to my life, and it's so easy to get sucked into the Instagram lifestyle. This hotel review here, that party there. A stop-off with a friend, another three-day trip on the other side of the world. Suddenly you've been on ten trips without a reality-check. Your washing is piled high to the ceiling and none of your bills have been paid. No boyfriend, no family time; everything that's important to you is in a total shambles and you're constantly exhausted. But it's so difficult to get off that bus, and practise self-care – far easier to escape all those kinds of thoughts by just jumping to another trip or agreeing to another event. When you're someone that can get really down, it can be a slippery slope. It's taken me until my thirties to be really aware of what I need to do to take care of myself – and it's the kind of boring things like staying in, trying to centre myself and being alone. The kinds of things that you're not going to ever see on social media." Of course, it can be hard to believe that other people are going through relatable issues with personal development when all you see is the best sides of their days showcased, but there are very few fully formed 21 years olds out there with unshakable confidence, self-esteem and direction – no matter what it might seem like from their social profiles. Mostly they're just trying to figure it all out too.

x x x

The advent of the digital age has been the architect of a distinct emergency in self-worth among women. Everything looks so rosy through a social media lens, and when young women enter the workplace they often feel cheated and demoralized that the reality of their burgeoning career doesn't match the image they've been conditioned to expect. The years of graft and grit, which were once seen as inevitable when starting out at work, have been so filtered out of the story that new generations are entirely unprepared for the slog ahead – thus the millennials' reputation for entitlement. Young women can also feel alone with issues of personal development and can easily come to the conclusion that they're the only ones who tussle with self-belief. But the truth is, if we really want to break through those glass ceilings, we've all got to come together to start shattering these illusions and be honest with both each other and ourselves.

Takeaways

1. Stop making presumptions about other people's finances
You are categorically not the only one struggling to make ends meet. As we don't live in a Communist society, inequality is a fact of life. But social media can make everything seem even more unequal than it actually is. Yes, the *Rich Kids of Instagram* are probably spending your annual salary in an evening, but there are also those who attempt to imitate a wealthy lifestyle just for the 'gram. Ask any hotel concierge or boutique owner and they will tell you how many people come in just to take an image in the lobby or dressing room and upload the image to social media as if they were staying at the property or actually buying the things they've tried on. Even IKEA has its share of fantasists, who use the merchandized sets as if they were their own homes for social media shots (especially for Tinder apparently...). Products can be purchased, photographed and returned; just because someone posts a picture from an expensive restaurant doesn't mean they ordered more than a coffee.

Of course, these are all pretty deliberate levels of *Instasham*, and most people will not be going to such lengths to inflate the material aspects of their lives. But the guiding principle of sharing the very best sides of our existence means many people consume in a conspicuous way – "it didn't happen unless it's on Facebook". But again, you have no idea how much it all goes on to plastic or, in the case of influencers, how much of this stuff has been gifted. Just as most people look more attractive on social media, so do their bank balances. Don't let yourself be fooled – you're under no pressure to keep up with anyone's online presence, especially because it's not even their real life.

2. Once-in-a-lifetime experiences don't happen every week

Knowing what "once in a lifetime" actually means to you is the first step to gaining back some control. Make time to consider and write an entirely personalized bucket list of things that you *really* want to do – things that actually *mean* something to you. It could be places that you've dreamed of travelling, physical challenges you've hoped to overcome or simply a quiet retreat somewhere (perhaps one with a no-phone policy!). Then, when other opportunities come up, you'll be in a good place to know whether they are worth the investment or not. And keep in mind that people who seem to flit from one amazing experience to another cannot logically be passionate about all of them. Living for content is just no way to exist – especially if you want a financially secure future.

3. Nothing worth having comes for free

Again, depressing, but sadly true. While you may not see the work in action, every successful person will tell you that their success is built off the back of graft. You're not getting promoted unless you prove yourself. Ultimately anyone can fail if they don't put the legwork in.

While you might roll your eyes at hearing social media stars talk about their workload, it's worth remembering that if it were so easy to build a successful social media business, everyone would have quit their jobs and be running successful YouTube channels by now. Most social media mavens are workaholics, who don't really understand the meaning of downtime, and the competition is *fierce*. As Victoria Magrath, the face behind the *Inthefrow* blog and YouTube channel, explains, "You could look at my social platforms and think I live my life in paradise. And, yes, I can physically be there. But wherever I travel will include hours of time spent inside my hotel room working. I remember one work trip my boyfriend Alex and I did to Mykonos, and it was absolutely beautiful. But we did maybe three or four photoshoots per day and when we weren't shooting we were sat in a shaded area until the sun set, just editing, editing, writing, writing, shooting, shooting. Literally we arrived home and we'd just worked solid. When your business is content, everything is a picture opportunity." There are cons to the pros, just like any other job, and the pictures only tell one part of the story.

Keep in mind that behind every social media post there is some element of work. For every staycation I post about, I've also had days and days sitting at my desk working on copywriting or marketing text – some of which is not sexy or exciting at all. But that's how I pay my bills, and you have to respect the work as much as the rewards. Also, people's lives are much more ordinary than they look on social media – their parents probably don't drive Porsches, they most likely didn't grow up in a mansion. Keep your expectations grounded in reality and make decisions based on your long-term financial priorities rather than short-term FOMO issues. God, it sounds like a slog, doesn't it? That's because it is.

Final note: remember, if you marry only for money, you'll be paying for the rest of your life. Just in case you were considering that option...

4. Be a uni-tasker

Focusing on just one thing at a time may sound like an anathema to the digital generation, but for the sake of experiment, at least give it a try in the workplace, because I will guarantee that you'll get more done and feel happier with yourself.

Step one: put your phone on charge, out of reach (but still in earshot, just in case there is an emergency and someone has to call. I put mine in the bedroom, but an out-of-immediate-reach drawer is a good option too).

Step two: remove any notifications from your desktop or laptop for a defined amount of time per day.

It might look like you're busy and important as you flip between devices, but the reality is that you're not. You're inattentive, less productive, and driving yourself round the bend trying to split your focus in too many directions. We know you can train your brain and that it will respond to the stimuli you give it, so flex the single-thought message and see how quickly you can improve your concentration. Be less floodlight, more spotlight.

I now try to keep 11am–1pm as a distraction-free zone – which enables me to respond to the morning's urgent emails first thing, and then gives me the opportunity to engage with my "phone business" (basically WhatsApp) afterwards, over lunch. Knowing that there's only a finite time I have to be without my phone helps me stick to it, and my productivity has definitely improved over those two hours. Now I'm in the swing, I try to do the same in the afternoon, so at least four hours of my day are focused. Although I'm still on and off my phone for the rest of the day, I feel much happier with my productivity, and it's a real sense of achievement to complete something fully rather than half-doing 97 things at once.

Chapter 7: Why Social Media is Ruining Your **Politics**

The straw that broke the camel's back? Or just the inevitable fallout from an industry which grew too big, too fast?

The recent political and privacy scandals concerning social media sites, particularly Facebook, reveal a lot about the human nature of both users and creators. While the exposés about the extent that Facebook manipulated or allowed the manipulation of our personal information continue to trickle into the press at the time of writing (to date we have learned that Cambridge Analytica, a data company employed by Donald Trump's 2016 election team, harvested personal information from around 87 million Facebook accounts without their permission in order to target US voters with political messages based on their psychological profiles; that Facebook knew of the breach back in 2015 but did nothing to stop it; that Facebook scrapes information about users who aren't even logged on to their accounts via a tracking pixel embedded on other internet pages; that the platform has created so called 'shadow profiles' to collect data on people who *don't even have a Facebook account*), the most significant point is the fact that we all so willingly and trustingly gave up so much of our personal information to social media platforms and third parties in the first place. The point that they've been so unscrupulous in their exploitation of those details really is par for the corporate course. But the real question is: why have we all been so careless? The answer says a great deal about the potency of the addictive, almost unthinking, behaviour that social media encourages, and it underlines how oblivious we've all been, casually entrusting the new media platforms with our own – and our friends' – information.

As the old adage goes, if something looks too good to be true, it usually is. Have you ever wondered why most social media sites are free? Sure, back in the day, you could have believed that the founders of Facebook and the like were altruists, aiming to change the landscape of society. Initially all these platforms failed to come close to breaking even. In 2012 Facebook posted $157 million in losses and the very future of the platform seemed untenable as it struggled to work out how to monetize its reach. Understandably, we all felt more relaxed about our privacy settings when we thought we were dealing with student idealists who just wanted to make the world a better place. Obviously, we were more comfortable sharing information about ourselves with these new-era visionaries than with, say, governments. But now we know we were suckers. They weren't utopians at all; they were just like any other businessmen, only dressed up in sweatpants and logo tees.

In nearly every instance I can think of, there's zero chance I'd ever reveal my political leanings on- or offline, no matter who was asking. I'd definitely think, "This must be a scam," or even, "Mind your own business." However, when I first signed up to Facebook, I marked my political affiliation on my "About" page. I also gave information on where I went to school, which university I went to and where I worked. I updated the platform on where I lived and who I was related to; what I liked and disliked; my age, sexual orientation and relationship status. And even if I hadn't explicitly told the platform all of this, we now know that Facebook would have been able to draw data from my posts and likes to psychologically profile me – and go on to help political parties and companies target me on the basis of that information. I, like millions, trusted the platform not to abuse my transparency and thought very little about the dossier of documentation I eagerly shared with them. It's only since working on this book that the true complexion of the social media business model has been laid bare and I've really given it a second thought.

Time and time again these platforms have proven that they're not worth our faith. Social media sites have been unable to address the issues of cyberbullying and unable to fundamentally curb extremism, terrorism, and sexual and racial hate. They've allowed politically motivated lies and fake news to run rampant and facilitated nefarious electoral influence and interference. Their response to concerns about the dangers created by their businesses have always been that free speech, the construction of the internet and the makeup of the human character make it impossible for them to police each and every user. Yet these same sites have invested millions in learning about how we all individually tick – psychologically, politically and economically – in order to sell that data to the highest bidder. Mining our demographics on a granular level has been possible, so it seems inconceivable that more can't be done to root out the menaces. As with any business, if you want to know the true intentions, follow the money – consumer data makes cash; patrolling subversive elements, not so much.

The only explanation for our foolishness is that we were all so distracted by totting up likes, consuming each other's edited existence and desperately curating content to nourish our own digital feeds that we gave the dodgy stuff a free pass. Our own insatiable voyeurism, craving for validation and drive to keep up appearances allowed these businesses to legally (and potentially illegally) reap reward from our identities and alter our perceptions of the world at large. We were all so caught up with where our ex-boyfriends were going on holiday that we nonchalantly allowed these platforms to use us for financial gain, ignoring the silent death knell of privacy as we knew it, spinning ever deeper down into the social media spiral.

All these platforms have done is what they were programmed to do. They've been designed to keep us obsessed for as many seconds, minutes and hours as possible and extract the maximum amount deemed valuable from our lives. Knowledge is powerful and we made them almost omnipotent. The reality is that the habit-forming and seductive makeup of social media platforms caused us to turn a blind eye to our own vulnerabilities, ultimately because we just didn't care enough. Even though we suspected it wasn't really very good for us and that we'd given up far too much of our personal information in exchange, we couldn't pull ourselves away. What's more, we were all happy to pay the price for "free" social media. It's only now, 12 years after Facebook was made public to everyone over the age of 13, that we're finally opening our eyes to the true cost.

Confidence and Cowardice: Political Polarity Online

In the 2000s being politically engaged as a teenager certainly didn't win you any cool points. Back then I was a fierce debater with very rigid ideas about my political philosophy – which, aside from my teachers, no-one was interested in hearing about. I read voraciously, thought meaningfully and formed many of my adult views, including a belief in progressive social politics and modern liberal economics. I've voted in every election, stayed engaged with manifestos and read both left- and right-leaning papers pretty much every day of my life.

However, I've never really talked about politics on social media and have rarely used my voice or platform for party-political or even broader socio-political and civic issues. Which is strange, even to me. The reasons behind my reticence are many and varied. Firstly, I built my social media presence most significantly on Instagram as an offshoot of my professional work on a fashion magazine and my thoughts on domestic policy didn't feel like a sage or appropriate addition in between the shots of shoes and fashion shows, regardless of whether *all views were my own* or not. It's worth noting that it wasn't so long ago that politics came under the same umbrella as religion and sex – something you didn't mention in the pub and kept to yourself in the office. Having a political opinion even five years ago was something you probably didn't advertise, unless you worked in political circles or wanted people to know that you were *a serious person*. Neutrality and a lack of bias have always been the aims of good journalism, and while, of course, there is no such thing as total objectivity, touting your politics wasn't seen as a boon, let alone something necessary to enrich your personal brand values. Your vote is still between you and the ballot box after all, and as my grandad often reminds me, people died for our right to political privacy.

Obviously, the dial has shifted. While social media has brought political discourse to vast numbers of new participants – always a dream of democracy – it has also fundamentally altered the environment of political debate, making it an often intimidating, polarizing and threatening space. I've always had major anxiety issues with Twitter, which almost from its inception became an ungovernable platform for outrage and aggression. One of the things I always loved about collegiate debating was the Voltairian level of mutual respect afforded to both teams. You could vehemently oppose what someone was saying, but you never lowered your rebuttal to a personal attack. You'd never dream of low blows mentioning a rival's race, background or gender. Nor would you respond to their arguments with rape or death threats, or suggest that you "knew where their children lived". Political discussion and social media have, as we have seen, walked hand in hand with hate. Without even having to mention the sexual harassers, terrorists, neo-Nazis and Russian bots that are rife on platforms like Twitter, the levelling of political theatre has had the unintended consequence of degrading the level of common courtesy. Over half of respondents to a 2016 Pew Research study said they found social media uniquely disrespectful, and 84 per cent said that social media is a space where people say things when discussing politics that they'd never say in person.

Social media has also created a climate in which there's little room for rumination or reflection. Every little thing you say can be pounced on and either wilfully or unwittingly misconstrued. There's little to no opportunity to process your thoughts or listen to reasoned argument – you're now apparently meant to know your opinion instinctively and arrive at your final view of any world event in an instant. And woe betide you make an honest mistake or slip up in your language as you punch out your 280 characters on-the-go. The fallout can be savage.

While there's obviously a place for reasoned critique, what social media has created is a polarized, correct vs incorrect eco-system. However, which of us are without fault? In order to stay the right side of the crowd and protect ourselves from trial by public jury, self-censorship and bowdlerization (removing any potentially offensive material) appear to be the only games in town – unless you fancy facing an army of pious righteousness.

Pandora Sykes, a fashion and social commentary journalist and pop-culture podcast host who regularly uses social media to discuss hot-button issues, agrees that the digital space can be highly charged. "We're living in the age of taking offence, and there's not much that you can say on a public platform without getting a comeback from somewhere. Everyone has become very binary – there isn't much scope for nuance or grey areas. The digital world is so polarized that it's almost impossible to find a centrist identity, which is really scary, because the vast majority of people fall into the middle of opinion. There's also this level of sanctimony which says you *must* be engaged with everything, and that scares off a lot of people who would like to learn and need to learn but don't feel like they have the confidence or knowledge to even enter these conversations. We're at this really tricky juncture, where any time you try and express a sense of conflict you have in trying to figure something out, there's a public takedown."

And that takedown can be blistering, forever associating your name in the digital realm with whatever you were deemed to have said or done wrong. In terms of digital reputation, it really does seem best to keep your thoughts to yourself. Pandora offers an example of the kind of issues that can incite the digital masses: "Take the recent discussion around transgender access to female-only spaces – say, opening Hampstead Ladies' Pond to trans women. If anyone expresses any sense of reservation online, they are point-blank referred to as a TERF [Trans-Exclusionary Radical Feminist]. There is no room for manoeuvre or discussion; no chance to debate anything really at all. As a white, cisgender woman, I would avoid talking about the subject publicly, because I'd be so terrified of being told I'm trans-exclusionary, when actually all I'd ever want to do is discuss the process of how we protect women, but *of course* opening up that definition to include all those who identify as women too. The truth is things are complicated. Shifts in attitude and policy don't happen overnight. But today there is an expectation that it should and that anyone who doesn't instantly agree is standing in the way. Everything has become so immediate online that there is very little understanding that change in real life takes time."

Social media platforms, like the internet, were developed to be open and free systems above all else. The inability to regulate them is, we are constantly told, hard-wired into their original code. Free speech has always taken precedence over our safety, and from their very beginnings, nearly all of the platforms decided to ignore the ticking time bomb of digital hate. From a legal perspective, the only areas of corporate accountability are focused on hosting child pornography and copyright infringement, and the laws established in the social media salad days are woefully limited. These sites don't have to fear being sued for nearly anything their consumers use their services for – even if they were to, say, share footage of mass murder or rape. As far as criminal law against an *individual* is concerned, a social media comment must contain a credible threat of violence, breach of court order or constitute stalking or harassment in order to be deemed unlawful and subject to prosecution. Which leaves a *vast* latitude for the worst of human behaviour to thrive, multiply and disseminate without any liability. Permanently attuned to potential offence, some social media users seem poised at all times to pounce and unleash vitriol. Personally, the pros of sharing my political and civic commentary rarely outweigh the threat of the roused rabble. I have to be really passionate about something to talk openly about it, and generally it will be related to my personal experiences rather than a matter of principle.

There have been rare instances when I've spoken out about the politics of the day. Brexit, as an event, marked a huge watershed for me in terms of my political identity. As I was born in Munich and every other member of my immediate family lives on the continent, I've always seen myself as European first, British second. Even though I went to university in Scotland, I've travelled very little around the UK, have no connection with the countryside and have far, far more knowledge and experience of life in other European cities like Copenhagen, Amsterdam and Paris than anywhere in Britain outside London. As a child of the EU with mixed heritage and a seriously limited sense of patriotic fervour, I was stunned at how out of step my vision of the world was in comparison to my fellow countrymen and women. I'm the only person in my family who doesn't have a claim on European nationality and, as my boyfriend is Irish, even my son will be an EU citizen. To have your identity – and more than likely freedom of movement – stripped from you without your consent is always going to be a bitter pill to swallow, and the nature of the Brexit campaign and social media's involvement in the spread of misinformation (which, like in the US election, has been alleged to include Russian influence) only made the result harder to take. When I posted about my dismay on Instagram, I got a lot of positive response but was also called out as a "snowflake" – the hysterically non-offensive catch-all, which apparently describes someone who thinks they are unique and is unable to handle the grit of real life.

While you'll often be encouraged to use any platform you might be present on to promote causes, that presupposes we all have the capacity to deal with largely unpredictable reactions. Of course, the response can be hugely supportive, help you build a voice and enact change, but the opposite can also be the case. Not everyone wants to spend their days sifting through troll-like comments, so it's understandable that so many prefer political engagement-lite options, such as "clicktivism" (simply clicking a button to support a petition or cause) or sharing an innocuous picture. "Often when people are too intimidated to enter into the debate, they opt for a removal of words instead," says Pandora Sykes. "So, they just put up a picture of Paris or Grenfell Tower with a broken heart emoji to show they're engaged or empathetic. The dangerous thing about that is, instead of going online to read and listen, people have realized they can just put a picture out there, get some likes and feel like they've done their bit. But what's often needed is a damn good conversation, which you rarely find on visual platforms."

Sometimes I definitely feel cowardly when I don't participate in debates about things I care about, and I'd love to be in a position where I didn't worry that sharing my opinion would open the door to aggression and grief. In the current environment, you either need really tough skin and an un-rattleable sense of confidence and conviction to share your opinion, or else you need to be entirely ignorant of the potential consequences. My relative political silence on social media has also bled into my real life. I feel much less comfortable talking about charged issues among friends, as my digital self-censorship has changed the way I express my opinions and made me much more careful about what I say in all contexts. In some ways that's a good thing – being aware of sensitivities and how my privilege spins my outlook is a positive development. But as I lean out of the conversation, many more are leaning in, and the new, more polarized and uncompromising environment has totally shifted the rules of engagement.

A Divided Front: The F-word in the Millennial Age

One area of the public sphere for which social media sites have come under sustained fire is their apparently retrograde attitudes to the female body. While anyone can access pornographic imagery in a nanosecond across any and every social media site, when it comes to female nudity – especially breasts in non-sexual contexts – the new platforms have applied a holier-than-thou attitude. The charges of gender discrimination date back to 2013, when Facebook removed footage of filmmaker Lina Esco running through the streets of New York topless as part of her #FreeTheNipple campaign. Aiming to decriminalize public nudity and establish equality between the male and female chest, the project received a huge amount of attention from celebrities and the general public when the social media platform argued that the films contravened its guidelines. Soon Facebook and Instagram were removing images of women breastfeeding. In 2015, Liverpool-based mother of two Kaya Wright posted a selfie nursing her son in a closed breastfeeding-support Facebook group. After she received a message from moderators saying they were reviewing the images, she spread her story and the site was soon inundated with other women posting similar selfies in solidarity. While Facebook clarified that nursing images were fine "in principle", they reiterated that the nipple must not be visible. The hypocrisy is stunning – all sorts of sexually charged images of girls in bikinis revealing their derrieres and hoicked-up cleavages are fine, but a woman feeding her child in the most non-sexual setting possible is somehow unacceptable.

LA-based fashion editor and publisher of *Voyage d'Etudes* magazine Paula Goldstein has had plenty of experience with the Instagram body police. "There's a lot of nudity on my social media profile, simply because I'm a naked person," she explains. "I love clothes and style, but I don't obsess over them at all. I feel very happy in my own skin and my own body, and I think that's also what drove me towards the West Coast – a level of feminine nudity is much more accepted here. My friends do hang out naked and it's not a strange sexual expression or about showing off or anything like that. I've always seen my own nudity as a human expression, and I think most people that know me wouldn't say I'm overly sexual. Of course, I'm not stupid: I know provocation on social media attracts some weird attention and creepy men. And that bothers some people, but it doesn't really bother me. What I do have an issue with is how these sites choose to censor the female body. My 'nudity' is definitely not pictures of me in perfect bikinis on perfect beaches, like you can see on countless other accounts. There's a rawness to my nakedness – with nothing filtered nor polished. And I think that's why it jars with some people. It's a strange thing – a sliver of skin can somehow be more provocative on social media than a G-string bikini. Photographer Petra Collins got banned from Instagram for wearing swimwear which showed her pubic hair – apparently that was considered over-sexualized. But girls who are shaved and wear bikinis are allowed all over the platform. You have to ask: who is making these rules?"

Expressing a feminist point of view on social media can be problematic, and opinions vary deeply on how the female body fits into the picture. "There's definitely an argument that being sexual – especially when it's influenced so heavily by the male gaze – means you can't be feminist, but I actually think that most young women go through a period when they are trying to understand who they are sexually," Paula continues. "Sometimes that involves a form of expression which might make you feel uncomfortable when you come out the other side. But what it means to be empowered is that you have the freedom to go through that journey and work out what it means to *you* personally to be a sexual individual. And I definitely went through that online."

In the post-#MeToo environment, and in the midst of the burgeoning "fourth-wave feminism" movement, the plot has thickened exponentially. What is and what isn't feminist, or "feminist enough", is now subject to judgement online – a realm which has become the increasingly contentious front line of gender politics. "We're now in a situation where lifetime feminist Germaine Greer is being banned from student unions because of her apparent insufficient commitment to the feminist cause," notes Pandora Sykes. "Her contribution to feminist thought cannot be denied. She may not be a millennial feminist or a 'fourth-wave' feminist. But to dismiss her and other women like Margaret Atwood, who was jumped on for daring to criticize the nature of the #MeToo campaign, is completely nonsensical. As a feminist, not everything you do has to be a feminist act. For example, the Instagram account @MotherofDaughters [operated by author, midwife and mum of four Clemmie Hooper] recently did a sponsored post about Venus razorblades and two of her little girls were watching her as she shaved her legs. She'd written in her caption that she hadn't talked to her daughters about hair-removal options yet, but they enjoyed watching her shave her legs – something like that. Comments rolled in saying, 'Call yourself a feminist? How can you be teaching your girls to shave their legs?' As if you can't do both. I'm a feminist and I shave my legs. And my armpits. So what? It's ridiculous to suggest you can't be a feminist and wear a tight black dress, or an outfit that shows your cleavage. As with so many issues which get dissected to the nth degree on social media, it feels like we career from one extreme to the other, in a way which ends up being exhausting and unproductive in terms of actually facilitating dialogue and enacting change."

I was raised to believe fiercely in equality between the sexes – be that financial, social or in terms of opportunity. However, I often find myself disagreeing with the ways in which the f-word has been re-defined in the millennial age. For example, I deeply believe, like Canadian author Margaret Atwood, that a man deserves a fair trial when accused of sexual assault, rather than public lynching through social media. I'm highly sceptical of Hollywood's hijack of the #MeToo movement, and while the principles of the #TimesUp campaign are obviously laudable, IMHO wearing an LBD on the red carpet doesn't really cut it as an agent for change. While I agree that Germaine Greer's use of the verb "whingeing" to describe women recalling their abuse is unfortunate, ultimately I also believe that consent is consent – and by conflating rape with incidents where women have had a choice whether or not to engage in sexual conduct is counter-productive and can trivialize the seriousness of women's experiences of sexual violence. These and other – pretty moderate and essentially non-radical – views I will continue to keep to myself on social media because, like many other women of judicious opinion, I feel the space has become too hostile for me to express myself in.

While it's amazing that feminists are no longer cast as man-hating, strident bitches, the new media platforms have encouraged a sense of one-upmanship and competition in terms of how complete your feminist credentials *really* are. The result has pushed the conversation to the margins, alienating even those of us who have always championed gender equality. Exactly as Germaine Greer predicted, women have found themselves pitted against other women. Instead of uniting in a single attempt to fight rape and a culture of sexual violence, factions of feminists, each of different strands, battle online to take each other down in pithy Twitter one-liners. And just as Margaret Atwood recently argued in the *Globe and Mail*, "In times of extremes, extremists win. Their ideology becomes a religion; anyone who doesn't puppet their views is seen as an apostate, a heretic or a traitor, and moderates in the middle are annihilated."

As far as truly enacting change in gender inequality and sexual abuse, division in the ranks will only ever hinder the sisterhood. And rifts, polarity and extremism are exactly what social media breeds. As we all become more outspoken and insults are volleyed to and fro, digital aggression serves only to increase discord and undermine the people power which might have led to decisive action. It might look like things are changing, but it's mostly smoke and mirrors.

The Badge of Honour: Wokeness

Being "woke" (aware of injustice) or active politically in the social media age has serious cachet, upturning decades of civic apathy. Teenagers now wear their politics on their sleeve, announce their stripes in their social bios and are as likely to travel to a rally or march as a music festival. After generations in the doldrums, student protest is cool again. As Kenyan-born lifestyle influencer and animal-rights campaigner Kelly Eastwood explains, today we're living in an era where engagement is the new norm. "Social media has changed everything about the way we live and what we accept as standard. Ten years ago, if you'd been sitting at brunch and the whole table started to take pictures of their food, you'd be appalled – but now it's become a totally acceptable thing to do. The same is true when it comes to voicing your opinions. The more we see other people expressing their political or social beliefs and thoughts on social media, the more we feel comfortable, and even a sense of pressure, to do so ourselves too. It's a case of, 'If their opinion is valuable enough to be shared, so is mine.' Now everyone has a platform and has a right to use it as they see fit; what might have once been an internal or private thought process has become highly public."

For all the criticisms of vapidity and ubiquity among social media users, the power of the digital soapbox – from a political perspective – cannot be ignored. Helping those with a cause to find their people, engage with others and magnify their message, social platforms have proven incredibly formidable when it comes to effecting change in both attitudes and political policy. Anna Whitehouse, the journalist behind the @mother_pukka Instagram account and the Flex Appeal campaign – which aims to eradicate maternity discrimination in the workforce and encourage flexible working for both mothers and fathers – explains how social media transformed her personal crusade. "Everything started for me from a very human place when I just couldn't make work work for me," she begins. "I posted on Instagram to say, 'I've quit my job and these are the reasons why', and the response was overwhelming. That's when I realized that I wasn't alone and that maybe I could use the platform to fix the situation that so many women are dealing with. The word 'influence' has taken on some quite sinister connotations over the past couple of years, and the idea of people quietly swaying our behaviour and making people buy stuff doesn't feel positive at all. But I just thought, why can't I use the platform to influence change – not just for me, but also for my daughters? What I know is that this unicorn, rainbow emoji-fuelled, hyper-positive world we often see on social media isn't reflective of what is going on in the streets. Life isn't all positive. So, my drive was to link the pixels with what's actually going on in real life."

Similarly, Kelly Eastwood explains how she has exhibited some of the not so easily digestible sides of human nature on her social media channels: "All you can do is shine a light on what matters to you... I've always gone to protests and social media has been a great way for me to take my audience along. Even if there are only a few of us actually there in person, thousands of others can be there outside the embassies, campaigning virtually alongside me. I recently protested at the Japanese embassy against dolphin slaughter on the coast of Taiji and the sheer number of messages I received afterwards was awe-inspiring. It happened during London Fashion Week and, in terms of connecting with my audience, the protest posts were by far the most engaged with over the week. It wasn't the catwalks that people cared about, it was an authentic expression of political action. There's no doubt in my mind that social media can be an incredible way to reach people and get more people on board. As an influencer, you have to make a choice. Do you want your influence to stop at where people eat or how people shop? Or do you also want to use that position to influence the decisions that people make? Something more fundamental that will make a difference? I want to influence people's buying mentality and awareness of the cost of their purchases on the environment. If you're telling people what to buy, you can also tell people what they should be mindful of."

However, on social media "tall poppy syndrome" (our cultural tendency to cut people down once they've risen above the parapet) is rife. "While it's never been easier to express your opinion, often people don't want to hear what you have to say," says Kelly. "For example, I'm vocally anti-fur in all walks of my life, including on social media. But when you start that conversation in the digital realm, instead of people saying, 'That's interesting, why?', you frequently get hugely defensive and aggressive messages from people criticizing you for being sanctimonious. If you touch a nerve with your opinion, you have to realize that there will be some kind of fallout. On social media it can become, 'This is my opinion, fuck you,' vs 'This is my opinion, fuck you back.' I'm an adult and I can take it, but look at the kids from the latest high-school shooting in Florida. If you've ever wondered how social media has changed the state of play, seeing grown-ass politicians tweeting horrendous things about children gives you a good clue. However, from my experience, young people do seem to be developing that hard shell at a very fast pace because they are exposed to the intensity and severity of that kind of language every day and from a much younger age. To them it's what's to be expected, but I don't know if that's a good thing for the way we communicate with each other or for society at large."

Even something which might seem less contentious, like flexible working arrangements for women, has been met with defiance. When Anna Whitehouse launched her campaign, not all the response was positive. "We've definitely experienced some resistance over the course of the project, and usually it comes from a place of cynicism. I have to be constantly transparent about the fact that we don't make a penny from the work we do for the campaign. There's also a lot of 'Does she think she's the first person to come up with the idea of flexible working?', which obviously I don't. But before Instagram I'd have literally just been shouting to the contacts on my phone; now I can shout to anyone and everyone who will listen, and that is incredibly useful when you want to spread a message."

For better or worse, the rules of digital political engagement are shifting and we all have to plot our position on a new battlefield. Of course, that position could be conscientious objection. "I don't think you necessarily need to have something political to say on social media – there will always be a market for fluffy cats, incredible shoes and someone who can edit in a way that *Vogue* magazine can," argues Anna. "I still think there is a huge space for that brief respite from the intensity of the everyday world and I don't believe that everyone needs to be shouting a message."

One thing is for sure, we're collectively becoming more discerning and savvy to the ways in which people are using their influence. Many social media users are craving deeper connections which go beyond the #ootd (outfit of the day). As Kelly Eastwood says, "Although Instagram may be a place to get away from the real world to have a switch-off scroll, it's also a place where you can engage with people on a much more important level." However, when businesses – and individuals – are using political causes as engagement bait, getting behind a movement for a mere moment or to increase their following, there's no doubt that the potency of people power becomes diluted. There's no point saying something for the sake of saying something; wokeness as a posture does nothing to enact change. We've all seen how social media outcries have been followed with inaction and inertia – to really alter our realities, whether politically, socially or culturally, opinion needs to be galvanized into action, and that's something that can't be achieved through social media alone.

The Echo Chamber

While the digital slanging matches continue apace, elsewhere an equally worrying feature of social media works in the exact opposite direction – to insulate you entirely from what people outside your social circle think and believe. One of the most notable aspects of consuming algorithmic-based media is the fact that you are only served content that the platform "knows" you will like. News, features, events and commercial products which surface on your feeds are curated to suit your tastes and socio-political flavour; new suggested connections are nearly guaranteed to share your belief system and point of view. It's a space where, day to day, you could imagine that all reasonable people agree with you, or at least understand where you're coming from. Which is why it can be quite a surprise to find your perspective on the planet isn't actually shared by the majority of people.

Platforms like Facebook have further contributed to the polarity of opinion and partisan animosity through news bias – for example, feeding liberal news articles to people who have either identified as left-leaning or clicked enough likes on left-leaning pages. Considering that two-thirds (67 per cent) of Americans get a portion of their news from social media, this can have a powerful influence. As we can go weeks without hearing the "other side" of the argument, when these views do break through – as a heated offshoot in a comments stream, for example – it can be profoundly shocking. It can also become almost instinctual to conclude that the other side must just be ill-educated and ill-informed. After weeks, months and years of being fed a diet of media that reflects your internal compass, instead of being well-practised at considering the other side of the coin, it's all too easy to dismiss detractors as idiots – after all, have they not read the news? The reality is that they have – it's just different news to the version tailored for you.

For the first time since 1992, majorities in both parties voting in the US 2016 election expressed not just unfavourable but *very* unfavourable views of the other party. In a 2016 Pew Research study, 70 per cent of Democrats surveyed by Pew Research said that Republicans were "closed minded", while 47 per cent of Republican believed Democrats to be "immoral", and social media has been cited as an agent for this development. Basically, the new platforms have increased our inability to empathize and the level of contempt which we have for those who disagree with us. What's more, over a third of social media users say they are "worn out" by the amount of political content they encounter and more than half describe their online interactions with people they disagree with politically as stressful and frustrating. It doesn't sound fun, does it?

While partiality is hardly a new thing, and people have read or watched media supporting their political persuasion since time immemorial, the holistic, always-on nature of social media has sent it into hyperdrive, simply because it exposes us not just to one publication's view on world events, but also all of our friends' collective perspectives too. When everyone you know thinks the same way, it's extremely easy to convince yourself of your own righteousness. Early on in my career I was taught about the importance of subjectivity. The "truth", if it is ever out there, can only be found by consuming both what you do and *don't* like. Social media sites have been consistently spoiling us, feeding us with content that pleases us in an attempt to curate an environment that is uniquely attuned to our personal preferences. When that is shattered by reality it can feel like a betrayal. Whether it was the US election or the Brexit vote, we have slowly realized that we are all existing in different bubbles and, politically, social media is driving us further and further apart.

Change is afoot at the biggest social media companies, prompted not by worries regarding how they are impacting our bodies, health, or identity but by how they are affecting our votes. The Russian influence in 2016's US election through a drive to manipulate voters' beliefs caused an international uproar. When compounded by the impact of the data scandals, Facebook saw more than $60 million wiped off its value; the number of US respondents who viewed the company unfavourably jumped from 28 per cent in October 2017 to 43 per cent in March 2018; and advertisers including Mozilla and Sonos cancelled their ads while Tesla pulled their page completely. The alleged election interference scandal was a huge catalyst for change – so much so that there are shifts in legislation on both sides of the Atlantic. And in response to the mounting #DeleteFacebook campaign, a slew of new policies has been implemented on the platform to protect our privacy – third-party apps are now restricted from accessing certain kinds of information, including our religious or political views, and there's a new feature to be added to everyone's newsfeed to instantly show users what information apps have collected on them.

But will it truly make any difference? Notably Mark Zuckerberg has declared that Facebook hasn't registered a noticeable change in user behaviour since the personal data scandal ("I don't think there has been any meaningful impact we've observed"), and it's hard to believe that with so many people using the site to maintain their business, family and social connections that a mass exodus will actually happen. Anyhow, most people had an inkling that their data was being mined: we've all been followed around the internet by ads originating from a Facebook status update and, while the sheer extent of the privacy breaches are alarming, it's not a total shock that there was a catch – all those ad profits had to be coming from somewhere. Of course, aside from the convenience of keeping up with our networks, if we deleted Facebook en masse, we'd also all have to give up snooping on each other's lives and those little dopamine hits of validation too. Which, dispiritingly, seems unlikely.

× × ×

From a political perspective, social media has made it easier for us to engage, but at the cost of the erosion of empathy. It's made the differences between us greater and undermined our ability to debate, discuss and deliberate. There are no "safe" spaces to be political on social media, and while it may be fashionable to be active, it's often deeply unpleasant, frustrating and intimidating. It may even have changed the way you see and experience the world, influencing your beliefs, attitudes and even your vote. If we are all going to continue to use social media (as it seems that no outrage is too great to keep us from logging on), there must be ways that we can protect ourselves from data grabs and animosity while using the platforms to enact change, convey our opinions in a respectful manner and listen to those whose point of view differs from our own. These goals should all be at the top of Zuckerberg and friends' to-do list, because if they're truly looking to create a social media utopia, it has to respect and support its users rather than trade them off to the highest bidder.

Takeaways

1. Be aware that your data is a commodity

There is now no excuse – we all know that our own and our friends' data is a valuable commodity and subject to manipulation. We understand that social media sites sell our personal details and that businesses and political bodies can use that information to decide who to target in their campaigns. Whether they want you to buy something or believe something, they all have something to sell. The adverts you see, the news that you're fed, all of it is based on what you share about yourself. So, what can you do? The first step is to take an hour to thoroughly understand all the privacy settings for every platform that you use. Of course, privacy policies are dry and lengthy, and while they are available on every platform, who has the time to do more than scan pages of text? However, what you can do instead is simply assume the worst and go through the privacy settings for each, reducing the reach of your posts and information to either just yourself or you and your friends. Close the circle slightly and your information will not be so widely accessible. Yes, it's an extra step and, yes, the platforms will still have some of your information available for sale, but you will have done your very best to protect yourself in the digital space – something which in today's context seems eminently sensible.

2. Consider the format

Not all platforms are created equal and different social media environments call for different ways of conversing with your audience.

"I think you have to think about the format in which you're engaging in a political conversation," explains Pandora Sykes. "I got into Instagram Stories because I read *a lot* of newspaper and magazine features and it's one of the things that people always comment about on our podcast. I wanted to share what I was reading, but in a way that if you were interested you could look at it, but if you weren't you could just ignore it. So that's why I decided to put it on Instagram Stories rather than my permanent IG [Instagram] account, where it might be flanked by pictures of my friends or images of me working with fashion brands. Not that there would be anything intrinsically wrong with that, but it just feels right that it has its own outlet. I guess it's a little bit less in your face – no-one wants political opinion pushed down their throat."

Twitter is a more natural space to share a short comment on a news story; bringing the same URL into a family discussion on a Facebook stream is far less appropriate. Facebook will always be a great place for events, whether you're organizing them or publicizing them. Due to its high level of inter-generational use, it's also a great place to keep in touch with family and distant friends. However, that is also one of the reasons that political discussions become so problematic: when things get heated, it's not just someone from a random Midwestern town that you're debating with – it's your Uncle Bob. Political discussions on Facebook are like all your worst family Christmases rolled into one, with the arguments both indelible and open for all your "friends" to see.

Think about what you want to achieve from your political post – is it simply to show solidarity, or to educate others on a cause which hasn't had much airtime? Do you want to shine a light on a great piece of journalism or is it really that someone has said something that's riled you and you feel the need to retaliate? Aggression, both direct and passive, rarely results in a positive outcome when you're trying to communicate your thoughts, especially to a hostile audience. When you've decided what you want to achieve, consider where it is best to share meaningfully and tailor your message to the platform.

3. Listen more than you tweet

Seeking out opinions which diverge from your own can be a chore, and it can certainly be both alarming and depressing to hear beliefs which differ fundamentally from what you passionately feel is right and just. But by cutting opposing voices from the conversation, your echo chamber will remain hermetically sealed and your understanding of reality will continue to be worryingly skewed. Debate has always been central to a healthy political system, and that doesn't mean a digital altercation. Practise listening and asking questions – making sure that they're neither patronizing nor sanctimonious. Engaging doesn't mean just expressing yourself, it means participating. Work on how you speak to other people on social media and employ a code of values which you can be proud of; as a rule of thumb, if you wouldn't say something in real life, don't say it online either. If other people are disrespectful or abusive – block them. However, if they just have a different opinion to you and convey it in a civil way, make time to respond – remain engaged in the world around you.

4. Do your research

"Before you make any grand statement on social media, you have to be very aware of what you are saying and what you truly believe in. In such a fast-paced environment, it's easy to make snap assessments, but it's definitely worth taking your time when it comes to conveying your opinions," explains Kelly Eastwood.

Thoroughly researching an issue you care about involves hearing thoughts from all angles and only then coming to your conclusion. If you only pay cursory attention to a story or make a decision based on soundbites and headlines, you're likely to come a cropper. To avoid egg on your face and supporting something you actually don't entirely understand or believe in, do your homework.

5. Focus on tangible change

Opinion has become amorphous on social media, but to actually enact change you need laser focus. "The ability to amplify your voice across social media offers individuals an unprecedented opportunity," Anna Whitehouse explains. "You can make a difference, but there has to be a simple drive to what you're trying to change and there needs to be real emotion behind it. Mine is so clear: I don't want my girls to have an oak door slammed in their face the minute they have children. I don't want to build them up to work hard in school and university and to tell them, 'You can do what you want,' only to have employers say, 'Actually you can't because you've had a baby.'"

As soon as you've settled on your goal, the next step is to anchor your efforts on a single, definable objective. "What's really important is to find something tangible to focus your campaign on," Anna continues. "The call to action for the Flex Appeal is to get companies to sign up to the Equality and Human Rights Commission Working Forward pledge. Simple. Businesses and governmental bodies continue to struggle to connect with people on a one-to-one level. The EHRC had all the stats, all the research, all the information to why companies should be working flexibly, but they couldn't get their message across on a personal level. Whereas I had a voice on social media, which could make a more intimate connection. Since I've been pushing the campaign (alongside the EHRC, of course) 380 big companies have signed up to the pledge, including businesses like BP, BT, John Lewis and Virgin Money. If you're asking about the positives of social media, it's pretty bonkers that nearly four hundred companies have endorsed change on a contractual level basically because I set up an Instagram account. There's no doubt that social media can create powerful voices, it's just understanding how to harness your reach to spread your message."

6. You don't have to have an opinion on everything

Another point to consider is that not every issue requires your voice. In the era of political social media activity, it can be only too easy to believe that your opinion on the daily news is necessary – especially if you want to continue the conversation across your account. But just because something happened, it doesn't need your assessment. Ask yourself, is the issue actually something I'm really interested in? Is it something I'm going to post about on social media again? Is it something that I'm donating money to or going to rallies and talks about?

As Pandora asks, "Are you invested? If so, post confidently and unashamedly. But definitely consider why you are posting. You don't have to put something out there for the sake of it because, actually, that's more insulting than not, and we mustn't presume to be experts on everything. It doesn't make you unintelligent if you don't comment. In fact it's the very opposite."

Epilogue:
How Social Media is
Changing Your Future

Like a moving target, the sheer pace of social media's evolution means that you can never quite put your finger on how it has already reshaped and will next alter your life.

Remember when social media sites were only static images on a grid? Before Snapchat and Stories made every second of your life upload-able, complete with half-decent filters and funny GIFs? Or when there was no such thing as a Tinder Super Like, tweets were limited to 140 characters and "click to shop" was all but a dream?

For anyone trying to rationalize or downsize their social media use, the constant pace of change proves another obstacle: if you don't keep up, there's always that feeling that you're going to be left behind. However, as ever, knowledge is power, and looking just a few junctions ahead on the map can both prepare you for the next phase in the social media story as well as help you question exactly how you want to integrate these new developments into your already heavily laden social media schedule. Having an idea where the world of social media may be taking us will help you futureproof your relationship with your favourite platforms as well as enable you to be conscious of the way you interact and engage with its new developments. Equally, there's a value in considering exactly how important it is to stay "up-to-date". Not entirely understanding an update or being familiar with a new filter feature won't harm your happiness, but feeling an obsessive pressure to use every new digital toy thrown your way very well might.

It's worth remembering that, unless you're a social media professional and are being paid to keep up with digital novelties, interactions with in-app innovations aren't mandatory. As they are made expressly to increase eyeballs and suck you further and further into the world inside your screen, you're well within your rights to ignore them completely. The future of social media may seem dizzying, but the underlying premise will stay the same. It might appear that the platforms themselves are the product that these businesses are selling, but that's not the case. *YOU* are the product. Social media sites sell audiences to advertisers, something which will become more and more evident as trust and transparency – or at least paying lip service to transparency – become the next buzzwords.

Influence, But Not As We Know It

Becoming an "influencer" once meant amassing thousands or hundreds of thousands of followers, building a personal brand and contacts at designer labels, then living your best life for all to see. But the super-blogger era is about to face some stiff competition – simply because "influence" as a currency is evolving. We've established that not everything we see on social media is "real", or at least how it is experienced offline, and confirmed that there's a level of curation and simulation involved to varying degrees (depending on one's Photoshop skills). So, it's perhaps little surprise that the next social media step involves influencers that are *entirely* unreal.

The computer-generated influencer, or avatar, lives a fantasy aspirational life. She wears Balenciaga trainers, attends Prada catwalk shows and takes selfies with celebrities...but she's just a figment of a digital designer's imagination. The gamification of social media is about to move up a notch as accounts like @LilMiquela, a Spanish-Brazilian American computer-generated model and music artist based in California, merge elements of fan and science fiction with social media marketing and advertising. With over a million followers – many of whom don't care that she's basically Lara Croft for the Instagram generation – what Lil Miquela wears and where she goes in her Insta-It-girl lifestyle can be just as influential as if she were flesh and blood. With a Spotify single release last year and new narratives for followers to engage with, Miquela is the highest profile of a new wave of tastemakers for whom IRL simply doesn't exist. Of course, you can see the appeal for brands – no potential for off-message rants or chance of a meltdown on Stories. The pseudo influencer is nearly human, but not human enough to undermine a marketing directive.

Elsewhere, the power of the micro-influencer is slowly being harnessed. Even if you have five hundred followers, what you recommend can be valuable to brands, especially if they had a way of incentivizing you to promote their products at scale. Step in a host of new platforms which allow nearly *anyone* to profit from their ability to affect other people's buying decisions. Don't think you've got enough followers to be an influencer? It's time to get savvy. Rina Hansen, co-founder of micro-influencer platform Brandheroes, explains: "Currently our platform has over five thousand micro-influencers working in more than forty countries, each with between five hundred and ten thousand followers. Heavyweight brands, especially in the beauty market, are starting to seriously invest in smaller influencers because they know how effective they can be. Whereas macro-influencers [30k-plus followers] have an average engagement rate of 1.8 per cent, micro-influencers can have over 8 per cent engagement. And when you think you can get around a hundred micro-influencers for the price of one macro-influencer, you can see the appeal. I'd also say micro-influencer content is seen as more relatable and authentic and really more like a digitized version of word of mouth. Our vision is that in the future there will be a true democracy on social media, because we believe that every person is their own media platform, whether they have five hundred or three hundred thousand followers. Everyone should be rewarded for sharing the brands and the services that they love."

So, how does it all work? You might have heard about cryptocurrencies like Bitcoin and the blockchain technology which powers them. The premise is simple: an international, independent banking system which exchanges "coins" for services and goods. This digital banking system has plenty of applications for social media, offering nearly *anyone* the opportunity, no matter how small their audience, to get paid as a micro-influencer. As Rina explains, "with our platform, as soon as content is approved by a brand then uploaded with the correct hashtags, the influencer gets paid in a points system. These points, which we call Brandcoins, are then redeemable against products in our webshop. We realized almost immediately that with so many global influencers we needed a global currency, and the architecture of the platform has been built like a cryptocurrency."

The technology is in place and the brands are already on board, so it's only a matter of time before micro-influence goes mega. When your audience is mini in size, it's also likely that you'll know most of your followers personally, so the question is: are you ready to start profiting from influencing your friends and family? And, perhaps even more profound, is the question of what it means for our collective mental state and relationships when we are *all* curating worlds to appeal to brands and influence our personal networks to buy things. The dawn of the mass monetization of both our lives and our address books is here; will you be joining in?

As for the established influencers, especially those who have already been blogging and 'gramming for a decade or more, things are also changing. Shini Park, a polymathic content creator who started her blog in 2008, explains, "The innocence there once was in blogging and social media – the true desire to share creativity just because? That's basically over. It's pretty much a business through and through." Sandra Hagelstam, the Finnish bombshell behind @5InchandUp goes on to explain that these days "just" blogging isn't enough: "today there's a sense that it's not enough *just* to be an influencer. As we all become known as characters, people are looking for more than just self-promotion. I get it – I'm 30 now and I don't want to be known only for my outfits forever, which is why I decided to diversify into acting, something I've always wanted to do. Two years ago, I started studying and my first film is coming out this summer. Having a strong following is really useful for any other career path you want to explore and I've seen a lot of influencers have started to move into music, consulting or writing." Shini agrees: "Influencers who have been blogging for a long time are starting to see their social accounts as a showcase for their other talents. It's like a portal into your portfolio career." And where the old-school influencers lead, the rest of us shall follow: forget about taking the perfect picture of poached eggs; now you need to be filming a music video for YouTube, brushing up on your life-drawing skills and penning a book to stay interesting.

So, what are the implications? If you can create an avatar to project the social media lifestyle you'd like to be leading, does it matter any more if you gain a few pounds, have a bad hair day or breakout? Might we be released from the pressure of being the face of our own personal brand and no longer chained to the limitations of the genetic lottery? If I made a computer-generated version of myself, I'm not sure I'd replicate the snaggletooth, open pores or knee fat, and perhaps I'd care less about them in real life if I knew I didn't have to worry about what they looked like in a picture. Or perhaps instead I'd prefer to go blonde. And tall. And *really* leggy. Think of the savings in air miles if you didn't actually have to go to Paris/Santorini/Marrakech, but could just super-impose yourself into hotels for social glory. I can definitely see the appeal of being able to live my "real life" away from the pressure to publish, but would people still be as eager to invest in experiences if they could manufacture them digitally? If something doesn't happen unless you Instagram it, where will we be when you can Instagram things that don't even happen? Not just a swipe of Facetune, but an entire Second Life virtual version of yourself; your complete existence fabricated?

Elsewhere, when it comes to micro-influence, if everyone can be a player in the social media economy and we all have the power to make money from each other, does the social world become fully transactional? No longer a place to connect, but to collect? As new media platforms become ever more commercialized and co-opted by advertisers, it's understandable that people will seek spaces to recreate the original atmosphere and environment that social media used to stand for – but that doesn't mean they'll shut their accounts. On the contrary, if social continues to become monetized and professionalized, it will retain its user base, but entirely lose the intimacy and authenticity it once represented. No wonder the people that first made social cool are so keen to showcase other career opportunities.

The Move to Dark Social

If social becomes a purely buy-and-sell space, where might we all go to express ourselves socially? The trend towards off-social communication isn't some newfangled concept – since 2015 there have been more messages sent via private services like Messenger and WhatsApp than on public platforms like Facebook and Twitter, and it's been years since anyone considered public walls a place for private discussions. These days it seems inconceivable that you'd post your Saturday night plans for all to see or have tête-à-tête chats across public feeds. Of course, the recent privacy scandals have served to underline this shift: fewer and fewer of us see the new media platforms as primarily a place to chat with close friends; instead they've become spaces for personal branding, recommendation and content sharing. In 2016, Facebook noted a 21 per cent drop in original, personal updates as users around the globe have increasingly learnt to commune through memes, articles and video clips. By reposting content viewed elsewhere, the platforms have become more like information loops, with viral news and entertainment trumping shared personal content. If the trend isn't reversed, soon Facebook will become faceless – a glorified news filter with annoying ads on the side. Though, as the biggest social network in the world also owns WhatsApp and Messenger, it's unlikely to be running short of personal information to sell any time soon.

The idea of social media interaction happening outside the social environment has led to what tech insiders are calling the rise of "dark social", or social sharing which can't be tracked by analytics. But don't think these "off social" spaces are closed to advertisers and social media professionals: they will be coming for your messages sooner than you can type "CUL8TR". By using chatbots, artificial intelligence and voice assistants, brands are looking to offer personalized shopping experiences on messaging apps. Paid social advertising spend was up to $41 billion in 2017, but an estimated 75 per cent of sharing occurred off social – meaning there's a huge amount of communication for brands yet to exploit. Before you know it, your messages may also come with a sidebar of exclusive instore offers and that link your friend sent you to those Topshop shoes might soon be followed up by a message from an instore customer service team. Seriously creepy stuff.

One solution to the endless incursion into our communication platforms is a fee-based model in which users exchange data anonymity and ad blocking for a subscription. Apple co-founder Steve Wozniak told *USA Today* that he'd quit Facebook in early 2018 due to concerns regarding the use of his personal data, but that he would consider rejoining – even for a fee – if he could opt out of data-based advertising, and there are plenty more of us out there who would be prepared to pay for anonymity. In order to recoup lost profits from tougher restrictions and regain the trust of users turned off by the data grab, it's only a matter of time before the concept of free social media begins to erode.

So, what would a subscription-based social media service look like, and what would it mean for your digital diet? Imagine if you could screen all the advertising noise and keep all of your personal information personal. How much would that be worth to you? A hundred a year? Or perhaps more? You'd still be able to communicate with your friends and upload your personal branding updates, but shield yourself from the incessant efforts to make you buy things. One such service is the platform Vero, which launched quietly in 2015 and has been dubbed "the anti-Facebook". The platform's manifesto states, "People naturally seek connection... As time passed an imbalance began to form between the interests of the [social] platforms and the best interests of the users. And a false sense of connection left us lonelier than ever... So we decided to create something more authentic. We created a social network that lets you be yourself... We made our business model subscription-based. Making our users our customers, not advertisers. The greatest social network is the one that already exists between people. Vero's mission is to make it available online." Operating under the tagline "true social", Vero (meaning truth) allows you to choose the audience for your posts from "close friend" to "follower" to reduce the pressure you feel when posting and publishes updates chronologically rather than via an algorithm (something which has attracted the creative community). Vero's CEO Ayman Hariri explained to US technology site The Verge that on other social media sites "you're performing for the crowd. Research shows that people are becoming more and more negatively affected by having to do that all the time. We wanted to create an online social network...that allows you to just be yourself."

With over three million downloads and counting, and having enjoyed a brief stint at the top of Apple's App chart in early 2018, Vero has shown that the appetite for a lower stakes, ad-free, more *humane* social is clearly there. But will a subscription service inevitably lead to a two-tier, class-based experience? One where those that have the money to protect themselves enjoy an ad-free environment, while others are forced to endure incessant prompts from spurious companies trying to sell us weight-loss shakes? With all the debate and dismantling of regulations around net neutrality (the principle that internet service providers treat all data equally and no-one has access to a preferential service – so providers cannot slow, block or charge money for specific websites), a hierarchy of access to the web appears just around the corner. Without a doubt, the egalitarian ideals of the digital world are under serious threat.

Social Media Concierge

We've discussed what a time-sap social media can be on your life. Who couldn't think of a better use for those two hours plus on average of scrolling every day? Step in the new industry of social media management. Whether you employ a living, breathing individual to clear your DM inbox, respond to comments and post encouraging messages to your followers (and yes, this is actually a job in 2018), *or* look forward to the new developments in robotics and AI to help you run your on-platform life, the chance to reclaim some of your precious time is now within reach. It's just a question of how happy you are to pass over your digital personality to someone, or indeed something, else.

Whether you'd prefer to hire someone to capture a special day – to live-tweet your wedding for example, because these days a photographer just isn't enough – or to maintain your social accounts updates from a professional perspective, there are plenty of services available to you. W Hotels offers a $3,000 (£2,300) package for your *big day*, ensuring that your hashtag is on point, and your guests are "encouraged" to participate digitally. And CEOs are adding social maintenance to the list of roles required of their PAs. For the rest of us, there's software just around the corner. Google's experimental lab Area 120 is currently working on a new system simply called Reply, an AI-based autoreply system that will work across platforms such as WhatsApp, Messenger, Skype, Twitter DMs and Slack. In an email to testers, the lab says, "You probably get a lot of chat messages. And you want to be there for people, but also for people in the real world. What if replying were literally one tap away?" The age of assistance will offer us all a digital secretary. By using information in our calendars, tracking our commute through Google maps and using chatbot technology, soon Reply and similar services will be able to offer passable responses to simple messages, freeing us from the weight of the constant stream of communication.

Aside from the convenience, the end of the line of this thinking has pretty dramatic implications for human interaction, because the more we get used to and accept robots standing in for us, the more the power of conversation and connection gets undermined. "We're lonely but we're afraid of intimacy. So, from social networks to social robots, we're designing technologies which will give us the illusion of companionship without the demands of friendship," foresees Sherry Turkle in her TED Talk. While it might seem to be alleviating the pressure cooker of always-on messaging, AI and chatbot technology will ultimately only serve to drive us further apart.

Imagine you need to have a really complicated conversation with a friend or family member and you just can't face the confrontation. Or to take it down a notch, you've got a really *boring* conversation to have with a friend or family member, say a grandparent or an old school friend who goes on and on endlessly. Don't tell me you wouldn't be tempted to palm the conversation off to a passable robot. I have one family member that I often just let speak away from my ear on the phone. Seriously, aside from the occasional "um" and "ah" from me, they're happy to continue on with their soliloquy. I would definitely be tempted to use a robot to deal with them on WhatsApp or Facebook if I could, which sounds dreadful.

But really who has the time to listen? We have to ask ourselves though, what do we lose when we stop practising the art of conversation? And when did we all get so incredibly rude?

Another related development in technology involves providing elderly people with robotic social company. In the UK, 17 per cent of seniors are in contact with their friends, family and neighbours less than once a week and two-fifths of older people say that their television is their main companion. So obviously it makes sense that social robots could provide what society currently can't. But the trend for delegating our interactions to machines can only lead in one direction, and how desperately depressing that the only connection you might be getting is through a *Blade Runner*-esque replicant. As ethics and what is culturally acceptable shifts in line with the technology, it's everyone's job to preserve true human contact both on and offline, or else – like many of the other skills that innovation has rendered obsolete – the very thing that defines us, makes us happy and fulfils us may be degraded and eventually lost.

Augmented Reality Bites

Think social media has become as all-encompassing as it could ever be? Think again, because virtual reality is about to add yet another level to the totality of your experience. The fourth dimension is already here, and now Facebook, Google and Snapchat are all on the cusp of launching mainstream applications – through a variety of affordable virtual reality (VR) headsets. Ever since Facebook purchased virtual-reality company Oculus VR, there's been a social arms race on. If you've not experienced VR, in a nutshell: when you put on a headset you become blind to the real world and immersed in a completely alternative reality, say on a safari or swimming with sharks. *Augmented* reality conversely superimposes computer-generated graphics on to your real-world environment, so instead of looking out your window and seeing a rainy street below, you'll see a sunny pavement – think the technology behind Pokémon GO and Snapchat filters. Both VR and augmented reality have broad applications for the future of social media.

Wearable technology may have hit stumbling blocks along the way (remember Google Glasses?) but the next step is still undoubtedly the device which eliminates the division between us and the screen. In 2017, Facebook launched a beta version of Spaces, a multi-user virtual reality platform that lets Oculus Rift and HTC Vive headsets customize avatars based on their profile pictures and interact with friends in a virtual online environment. The tagline of Facebook's virtual dimension is, "Spend quality time together wherever you are", and it's certainly mind boggling that you could virtually occupy the same space as your friend in Tokyo or Cape Town. Another platform, AltSpaceVR ("be there, together"), allows users to attend concerts, business meetings and house parties virtually. Until now, these platforms have been just about limited to gamers and early adopters, but with the launch of Oculus Go in 2018, a headset priced under £200/$200 (joining Samsung's Gear VR headset priced at around the price of under

£100/$150), the technology is set to go mainstream. Currently about 6 per cent of the British population currently own a VR headset and new, more accessible headsets are already being developed.

In many ways, the VR focus on actual social interaction serves as a rejoinder to the passive personal-brand consumption that we now see on social media platforms. And while avatars remain cartoon-like, there's a sense of naivety to the digital connection. But of course, it's only a matter of time before the technology evolves and 4D Miquelas start to populate virtual spaces, bringing all the swag of social media aspiration with them. Just imagine the stab of envy if you could actually experience to a fully immersive level all the blogger holidays, shopping trips and ritzy dinners. The level of voyeurism if you could actually *be there* for their birth stories and mountaintop engagements... If you think you're obsessed or addicted now, just imagine how much deeper down the rabbit hole you could go.

Tech Humanism: Believe It When You See It

As the studies revealing the harm social media is inflicting on our youth and the scandals around the use of our personal information pour forth quicker than the news cycle can cover them, there's a new, vocal movement of tech insiders, arguing for a more nuanced, considered approach to our social consumption. Snapchat CEO Evan Spiegel has blamed social media for inspiring "mindless scrambles for friends or unworthy distractions"; Jack Dorsey, CEO of Twitter, has highlighted "conversational health" as a priority; and Mark Zuckerberg has repeatedly mentioned the phrase "time well spent" alongside concerns for Facebook users' wellbeing. Structurally, social platforms are being altered in an attempt to lessen the worst of the media's negative effects – a development being labelled *humane tech*. "Compassionate design" may be trending in Silicon Valley circles, but you'd be forgiven for raising a serious eyebrow in scepticism. Until lawmakers embark on a concerted attempt to police social sites on a global scale, operating profits will continue to guide any attempts at self-governance. While Facebook and friends may publicly address the concerns highlighted in this book, how could we possibly trust those so deeply enmeshed in the system – both culturally and financially – to supervise the necessary corrections? It's akin to asking Big Tobacco to ditch the nicotine.

Now my eyes are open it's much harder to pull the wool back over them. However, that's not to say that there aren't individuals working to create healthier social products, and there's little doubt that we're going to see all sorts of new functions and warnings for our mental health along the way. But I, for one, will be taking matters into my own hands.

When you stop to think about how far social media has come in such a short lapse of time: of avatars and chatbots, of lives voluntarily lived in an all-seeing Panoptican, of addiction to aspiration, and expectations so completely moulded, it begs the questions, where will it all end?

Can we even begin to understand how social media will stretch out and contort itself in order to fit further into our daily lives? Will generations ahead look back at our pre-digital social existence and feel the same way as we do about the advent of electricity? Will old-fashioned conversation be somehow a lower form of civilized communication? Technology has already stopped being an add-on to our lives – so intrinsic and fundamental as it now is to our existence. The fact that social media is a human code created entirely by other humans who understand our instincts, primal desires and emotional responses, marks another stage in the evolution of our society, and one that's not likely to reverse any time soon. As with all progress, there will be laments for the good old days, but ultimately the thing of most importance is that we collectively use our agency to consume *consciously*, no matter how alluring the new technology might be. Forget about the new Atkins, Paleo or 5:2 – in the digital age it's your social media diet that really matters, and in this case, you really are what you eat.

Indeed, the biggest change for the future may come from disenchanted users desperately seeking a reprieve. As we all start to talk more openly about the way social media makes us feel, as we begin to realize that we are not alone in our addictive, often masochistic, behaviour, as the shine slowly wears off the fantasy, the bubble will struggle to stay intact. And maybe, just maybe, we'll be able to leave our destructive habits behind and enjoy social media for what it is: the best 1 per cent of our lives, with the real stuff, the other 99 per cent, hidden for only our real friends to discover.

Endnotes

All websites accessed 17 July 2018.

Introduction

7   *2.77 billion of us* http://www.statista.com/
    statistics/278414/number-of-worldwide-
    social-network-users/

7   **95 per cent of Americans** http://www.
    pewinternet.org/fact-sheet/mobile/

9   **"brain hacking"** Tristan Harris coined
    the term: https://www.youtube.com/
    watch?feature=share&v=JgkvTRz_
    Alo&app=desktop

9   **women use social media** http://www.
    pewinternet.org/fact-sheet/social-media/

10 **just one hour a day** McDool, Emily,
    Powell, Philip, Roberts, Jennifer and Taylor,
    Karl, "Social Media Use and Children's
    Wellbeing", IZA Discussion Paper No. 10412,
    December 2016, p.22.

11 **children admitted to hospital** Data
    obtained under the Freedom of Information
    Act by the National Society for the
    Prevention of Cruelty to Children (NSPCC)
    found that 18,778 children aged 11 to 18
    were admitted to hospital for self-harm in
    2015/16 in England and Wales. This is up on
    the 16,416 in 2013/14 and represents a 14 per
    cent rise. Peter Wanless, chief executive of
    the NSPCC: "It is clear from the thousands
    of calls Childline receives that we have a
    nation of deeply unhappy children. We
    know this unhappiness is partly due to the
    constant pressure they feel, particularly
    from social media, to have the perfect
    life or attain a certain image which is
    often unrealistic."

11 **"pressure to be the perfect mum"**
    "Data from London-based mothers'
    meet-up app Mush found the image-
    based social network was making many
    women feel more isolated. More than
    80 per cent of respondents said Instagram
    and Facebook 'added pressure to be
    the perfect mum'"; cited in the *Evening
    Standard*, https://www.standard.co.uk/
    lifestyle/london-life/perfect-lives-of-
    instamums-are-making-london-mothers-
    feel-inadaquate-a3468426.html

11 **"social media representations of
    ideal families"** http://www.abc.net.
    au/news/2017-11-14/how-social-
    media-is-fuelling-anxiety,-perinatal-
    depression/9143318

11 **frequently compared themselves** Coyne,
    Sarah, McDaniel, Brandon and Stockdale,
    Laura A, "'Do you dare to compare?':
    Associations between maternal social
    comparisons on social networking sites and
    parenting, mental health, and romantic
    relationship outcomes", *Computers in
    Human Behavior*, vol. 70, issue C, May 2017,
    pp.335–340.

11 **"detract from face-to-face relationships"**
    https://hbr.org/2017/04/a-new-more-
    rigorous-study-confirms-the-more-you-
    use-facebook-the-worse-you-feel

12 **"passively consuming information"**
    https://newsroom.fb.com/news/2017/12/
    hard-questions-is-spending-time-on-
    social-media-bad-for-us/

12 **eight social media accounts**
    GlobalWebIndex, "GWI Social Summary,
    Q3 2016"; http://insight.globalwebindex.
    net/hubfs/GWI-Social-Q3-2016-
    Summary.pdf

13 **the typical mobile phone user** https://
    blog.dscout.com/mobile-touches

13 **unlocks their phone** ABC News report
    confirmed by Apple; https://abcnews.
    go.com/Technology/guess-average-
    iphone-user-unlocks-device-day/
    story?id=38510812

13 *seven years* **of our lives** More than 50 per
    cent of millennials use their phones for up
    to three hours a day. If we multiply three
    hours a day by 365 days then by 60 years
    (worldwide life expectancy of 70 minus the
    first 10 years) then you get 65,700 hours,
    which equates to approximately seven
    years; The Smartphone and IoT Consumer
    Trends 2017 study, published by B2X in
    cooperation with Professor Dr Anton Meyer
    and Professor Dr Thomas Hess from the
    Institutes of Marketing and New Media
    at the Ludwig-Maximilians University
    of Munich; https://resources.b2x.com/
    registration-study-smartphone-and-iot-
    consumer-trends

13 using their phones on the toilet From a 2013 poll of 2,000 people conducted by Sony & O2; cited in the *Telegraph*, https://www.telegraph.co.uk/technology/mobile-phones/9914594/Quarter-of-men-admit-to-sitting-down-on-the-loo-so-they-can-keep-using-mobile-phone.html

14 lose their sense of *smell* https://www.scribd.com/doc/56263899/McCann-Worldgroup-Truth-About-Youth

14 by or in their bed Accel and Qualtrics, "The Millennial Study", October 2016; https://www.qualtrics.com/millennials/

14 within 15 minutes of waking "Mobile Consumer 2015: The UK Cut: Game of Phones", Deloitte, 2015; http://www.deloitte.co.uk/mobileuk2015/assets/pdf/Deloitte-Mobile-Consumer-2015.pdf

14 the longer your screen time Levenson, Jessica C, Shensa, Ariel, Sidani, Jaime E, Colditz, Jason B, Primack, Brian A, "Social Media Use Before Bed and Sleep Disturbance Among Young Adults in the United States: A Nationally Representative Study", *Sleep*, vol. 40, issue 9, 1 September 2017.

14 "empathy gap" Turkle, Sherry, *Reclaiming Conversation: The Power of Talk in a Digital Age* (Penguin, 2015).

15 at their last social encounter http://www.pewinternet.org/2015/08/26/americans-views-on-mobile-etiquette/

15 inhibits conversation Przybyliski, Andrew and Weinstein, Netta, "Can you connect with me now? How the presence of mobile communication technology influences face-to-face conversation quality", *Journal of Social and Personal Relationships*, vol 30. issue 3, 2013, pp. 237–246.

21 compare their appearance Fardouly, J, Pinkus, R T and Vartanian, L R, "The impact of appearance comparisons made through social media, traditional media, and in person in women's everyday lives", *Body Image*, vol. 20, March 2017, pp.31–39.

23 social comparison theory Festinger, Leon, "A Theory of Social Comparison Processes", *Human Relations*, vol. 7, issue 2, May 1954, pp.117–140.

23 improvement in self-appraisal Wills, T A, "Downward comparison principles in social psychology", *Psychological Bulletin*, vol. 90, issue 2, September 1981, pp.245–271.

24 biggest worry online https://www.girlguiding.org.uk/what-we-do/our-stories-and-news/news/over-a-third-of-girls-say-the-pressure-to-live-the-perfect-life-online-is-affecting-their-wellbeing/

24 feelings of jealousy From a poll of around 1,500 social media users by the charity Scope; cited in the *Telegraph*, https://www.telegraph.co.uk/technology/social-media/10990297/Social-media-users-feel-ugly-inadequate-and-jealous.html

26 "social-validation feedback loop" https://www.axios.com/sean-parker-unloads-on-facebook-god-only-knows-what-its-doing-to-our-childrens-brains-1513306792-f855e7b4-4e99-4d60-8d51-2775559c2671.html

27 "affect their thoughts" https://www.bangkokpost.com/news/local/394102/youngsters-warned-over-elfie-addiction

27 examine the brains of teenagers Sherman, L E, Payton, A A, Hernandez, L M, Greenfield, P M and Dapretto, M, "The Power of the 'Like' in Adolescence, Effects of Peer Influence on Neural and Behavioral Responses to Social Media", *Psychological Science*, vol. 27, issue 7, July 2016, pp.1027–1035.

27 viewing likes underneath a picture *ibid.* and http://newsroom.ucla.edu/releases/the-teenage-brain-on-social-media;

28 high level of likes https://www.newstatesman.com/science-tech/social-media/2017/01/both-hugely-uplifting-and-depressing-how-do-social-media-likes

29 "exploits this craving" https://www.theglobeandmail.com/technology/your-smartphone-is-making-you-stupid/article37511900/

29 increase your life satisfaction The Facebook Experiment, Copenhagen Happiness Institute, 2015; https://docs.wixstatic.com/ugd/928487_680fc12644c8428eb728cde7d61b13e7.pdf

30 lied or misrepresented themselves Toma, Catalina L, Hancock, Jeffrey T, Ellison, Nicole B, "Separating Fact from Fiction: An Examination of Deceptive Self-Presentation in Online Dating Profiles", *Personality and Social Psychology Bulletin*, vol. 34, issue 8, May 2018, pp.1023–1036.

31 screen candidates before hiring https://www.careerbuilder.com/advice/social-media-survey-2017

32 "erosion of authenticity online" https://www.newstatesman.com/science-tech/social-media/2018/03/inside-story-one-instagrammer-s-fake-trip-disneyland

Chapter 1: Why Social Media is Ruining Your **Identity**

38 **mobile phone than a toothbrush** According to the Mobile Marketing Association Asia, there are 6.8 billion people on the planet and 5.1 billion of them own a mobile phone, but only 4.2 billion own a toothbrush; https://60secondmarketer. com/blog/2011/10/18/more-mobile-phones-than-toothbrushes/)

39 **the self-promotion–envy spiral** Krasnova, Hanna, Wenninger, Helena, Widjaja, Thomas and Buxmann, Peter, "Envy on Facebook: A Hidden Threat to Users' Life Satisfaction?", *Wirtschaftsinformatik*, 2013, p.12.

39 **"Of the seven deadly sins"** Epstein, Joseph, *Envy* (The Seven Deadly Sins series), (Oxford University Press, 2003).

39 **the power that envy has** Mujcic, Redzo and Oswald, Andrew J, "Is envy harmful to a society's psychological health and wellbeing? A longitudinal study of 18,000 adults", *Social Science & Medicine*, vol. 198, February 2018, pp.103–111.

41 **most damaging platforms** https:// www.rsph.org.uk/about-us/news/ instagram-ranked-worst-for-young-people-s-mental-health.html

41 **"dual coding theory"** Paivio, Allan, *Imagery and Verbal Processes* (Holt, Rinehart and Winston, 1971) and Paivio, Allan, "Mental Imagery in Associative Learning and Memory", *Psychological Review*, vol. 76, issue 3, May 1969, pp.241–263.

41 **that image-based advertisements** Childers, Terry L and Houston, Michael J, "Conditions for a Picture-Superiority Effect on Consumer Memory", *Journal of Consumer Research*, vol. 11, issue 2, September 1984, pp.643–654.

42 **"Instagrammability" of a destination** A survey by home insurance company Schofields Insurance asked over 1,000 UK adults aged between 18 and 33 what was most important when choosing a holiday destination; cited in the *Independent*, https://www.independent.co.uk/travel/ instagrammability-holiday-factor-millenials-holiday-destination-choosing-travel-social-media-photos-a7648706. html#r3z-addoor

43 **"memeification of human experience"** https://www.theguardian.com/ commentisfree/2018/jan/17/ instagrammers-travel-sri-lanka-tourists-peachy-backsides-social-media-obsessed

44 **caption didn't match what they felt** From the *Women's Health*-National Alliance on Mental Illness, 2017; https:// www.womenshealthmag.com/health/ a19973575/true-emotion-behind-smiling-instagram-pictures/

46 **"breadcrumbs of the same persona"** https://www.theguardian.com/media-network/2015/sep/24/online-offline-personality-digital-identity

48 **impostor syndrome** Sakulku, Jaruwan, Alexander, James, "The Impostor Phenomenon", *The International Journal of Behavioral Science*, vol. 6, issue 1, 2011, 75–97.

48 **inadequate about their own lives** A poll of around 1,500 social media users by the charity Scope; cited in the *Telegraph*, https://www.telegraph.co.uk/technology/ social-media/10990297/Social-media-users-feel-ugly-inadequate-and-jealous. html

50 **"familiar strangers"** Milgram, Stanley, "The Familiar Stranger: An Aspect of Urban Anonymity", *The Division 8 Newsletter, Division of Personality and Social Psychology*. Washington: American Psychological Association.

50 **"strange familiarity"** Senft, Theresa, "Micro Celebrity and the Branded Self" in *A Companion to New Media Dynamics*, Eds Hartley, John, Burgess, Jean and Bruns, Axel (Wiley-Blackwell, January 2013), pp.346–354.

52 **"works in progress"** Gilbert, Dan. "The Psychology of Your Future Self" TED. June 2014. Lecture.

Chapter 2: Why Social Media is Ruining Your **Body Image**

60 **uploaded approximately 24 billion selfies** https://blog.google/products/photos/google-photos-one-year-200-million/

60 **preparing for selfies** From the Dove Self Esteem Project 2015; https://www.dove.com/uk/stories/campaigns/nolikesneeded-campaign.html

60 **turn their phone camera on themselves** From a Now Sourcing and Frames Direct survey, 2016; cited in *Teen Vogue*, https://www.teenvogue.com/story/millennials-instagram-selfies-study

62 **act of snapping a selfie** Shin, Youngsoo, Kim, Minji, Im, Chaerin, and Chong, Sang Chui, "Selfie and self: The effect of selfies on self-esteem and social sensitivity", *Personality and Individual Differences*, vol. 111, June 2017, pp.139–145.

62 **"a craving for reassurance"** https://www.telegraph.co.uk/women/life/we-take-1-million-selfies-every-day---but-what-are-they-doing-to/

62 **crop, filter or doctor** https://www.beautyheaven.com.au/makeup/concealer/beauty-tips-for-selfies-14200; http://www.dailymail.co.uk/news/article-2948410/More-half-women-admit-editing-social-media-photos-posting-despite-two-thirds-thinking-s-wrong-magazines-it.html

63 **nine out of ten teenage girls** https://www.telegraph.co.uk/news/health/news/11875084/Nine-out-of-10-teenage-girls-digitally-enhance-their-own-Facebook-pictures-claim.html

65 **negative thoughts about their body** https://www.glamour.com/story/body-image-how-do-you-feel-about-your-body

67 **report eating and body-image concerns** Sidani, Jaime E, Shensa, Ariel, Hoffman, Beth, Hanmer, Janel and Primack, Brian A, "The Association between Social Media Use and Eating Concerns among US Young Adults", *Journal of the Academy of Nutrition and Dietetics*, vol. 116, issue 9, September 2016, pp.1465–1472.

67 ***20 minutes* of scrolling on Facebook** Mabe, Annalise G, Forney, K Jean and Keel, Pamela K, "Do you 'like' my photo? Facebook use maintains eating disorder risk", *International Journal of Eating Disorders*, vol. 47, issue 5, July 2014, pp.516–523.

67 **"eating disorders thrive"** https://eu.usatoday.com/story/news/nation/2014/06/01/social-media-helps-fuel-eating-disorders/9817513/

67 **eating disorders had nearly doubled** https://www.telegraph.co.uk/news/health/news/11647713/Number-of-teenagers-admitted-to-hospital-with-eating-disorders-doubles.html

68 **one in five anorexics** https://www.telegraph.co.uk/women/womens-health/11649411/How-social-media-is-fuelling-the-worrying-rise-in-eating-disorders.html

68 **every 62 minutes someone dies** http://www.anad.org/education-and-awareness/about-eating-disorders/eating-disorders-statistics/

71 **"onslaught of beauty pressures"** https://www.psychologytoday.com/intl/blog/girls-women-and-wellness/201511/why-are-media-beauty-ideals-toxic-our-daughters?amp

73 **images of this new beauty standard** Benton, Catherine and Karazsia, Bryan T, "The effect of thin and muscular images on women's body satisfaction", *Body Image*, vol. 13, March 2015, pp.22–27.

73 **looked at "fitspo" images** Fardouly, Jasmine, Willburger, Brydie K and Vartanian, Lenny R, "Instagram use and young women's body image concerns and self-objectification: Testing mediational pathways", *New Media & Society*, vol. 20, issue 4, April 2018, pp.1380–1395.

73 **clear link between orthorexia nervosa** Turner, Pixie G, and Lefevre, Carmen E, "Instagram use is linked to increased symptoms of orthorexia nervosa", *Eating and Weight Disorders*, vol. 22, issue 2, June 2017, pp.277–284.

73 **"fitspiration image"** Tiggemann, Marika and Zaccardo, Mia, "'Strong is the new skinny': A content analysis of #fitspiration images on Instagram", *Journal of Health Psychology*, vol. 23, issue 8, March 2016, pp.1003–1011.

Chapter 3: Why Social Media is Ruining Your **Health**

84 **equated Snapchat to heroin** https://www.theguardian.com/technology/2017/oct/05/smartphone-addiction-silicon-valley-dystopia

84 **"more addictive than cigarettes"** https://www.rsph.org.uk/about-us/news/instagram-ranked-worst-for-young-people-s-mental-health.html

84 **manipulating exactly when users receive likes** https://www.theglobeandmail.com/technology/your-smartphone-is-making-you-stupid/article37511900/

84 **neurological vulnerabilities** https://www.theguardian.com/technology/2017/oct/05/smartphone-addiction-silicon-valley-dystopia

85 **half of all cases of mental illness** Kessler, R C, Berglund, P, Demler, O, Jin, R, Merikangas, K R and Walters, E E, "Lifetime Prevalence and Age-of-Onset Distributions of DSM-IV Disorders in the National Comorbidity Survey Replication", *Archives of General Psychiatry*, vol. 62, issue 6, June 2005, pp.593–602.

85 **1 in 4 girls** https://www.theguardian.com/society/2017/sep/20/one-in-four-girls-have-depression-by-the-time-they-hit-14-study-reveals

85 **44 million adults** https://www.nimh.nih.gov/health/statistics/mental-illness.shtml

85 **"The more you use Facebook"** https://hbr.org/2017/04/a-new-more-rigorous-study-confirms-the-more-you-use-facebook-the-worse-you-feel

86 **worldwide sufferers** http://www.who.int/news-room/fact-sheets/detail/depression

89 **One in three women** Australia: Cox, P/Australia's National Research Organisation for Women's Safety (ANROWS), "Violence against women: Additional analysis of the Australian Bureau of Statistics' Personal Safety Survey 2012", *Horizons Research Report*, Issue 1, October 2015, p.2; Worldwide: https://edition.cnn.com/2013/06/20/health/global-violence-women/index.html. US: National Coalition Against Domestic Violence, https://www.speakcdn.com/assets/2497/domestic_violence2.pdf

89 **a hundred calls an hour** HMIC, "Increasingly everyone's business: A progress report on the police response to domestic abuse", December 2015, p.28; https://www.justiceinspectorates.gov.uk/hmicfrs/wp-content/uploads/increasingly-everyones-business-domestic-abuse-progress-report.pdf

89 **40 per cent of women** https://www.thelocal.it/20170328/over-8-million-women-suffer-psychological-abuse-in-italy

92 **internal Facebook document** https://www.theguardian.com/technology/2017/may/01/facebook-advertising-data-insecure-teens

92 **"what buttons you can push"** https://www.theguardian.com/technology/2017/oct/05/smartphone-addiction-silicon-valley-dystopia

93 **newsfeed experiment** https://www.nytimes.com/2014/06/30/technology/facebook-tinkers-with-users-emotions-in-news-feed-experiment-stirring-outcry.html

93 **released a statement** *ibid.*

95 **17.5 per cent of female college students** American College Health Association, National College Health Assessment Spring 2014 Reference Group Executive Summary; http://www.acha-ncha.org/docs/ACHA-NCHA-II_ReferenceGroup_ExecutiveSummary_Spring2014.pdf

95 **"multidimensional perfectionism"** Curran, Thomas and Hill, Andrew P, "Perfectionism is increasing over time: A meta-analysis of birth cohort differences from 1989 to 2016", *Psychological Bulletin*, December 2017, advance online publication.

98 **rise of self-poisoning** https://www.theguardian.com/society/2016/may/16/teenagers-girls-self-poisoning-uk-alcohol-mental-health-self-harm

98 **increase in hospital admissions** https://www.theguardian.com/society/2017/oct/18/self-harm-girls-aged-13-to-16-rose-68pc-three-years

98 **cutting themselves** https://www.theguardian.com/society/2017/sep/23/stress-anxiety-fuel-mental-health-crisis-girls-young-women

98 **difficulties with boys** "https://www.theguardian.com/society/2017/sep/23/stress-anxiety-fuel-mental-health-crisis-girls-young-women

98 US suicide rates https://nypost.com/2017/11/14/rise-in-teen-suicide-connected-to-social-media-popularity-study/

98 forty-year high https://www.huffingtonpost.co.uk/entry/suicide-rates-teen-girls_us_59848b64e4b0cb15b1be13f4

98 taking their own lives Twenge, Jean M, Joiner, Thomas E, Rogers, Megan L and Martin, Gabrielle N, "Increases in Depressive Symptoms, Suicide-Related Outcomes, and Suicide Rates Among U.S. Adolescents After 2010 and Links to Increased New Media Screen Time", *Clinical Psychological Science*, vol. 6, issue 1, November 2017, pp.3–17.

98 "overusing" social media *ibid*.

99 25 per cent of teenage girls https://www.theguardian.com/society/2017/sep/20/one-in-four-girls-have-depression-by-the-time-they-hit-14-study-reveals

99 touching our phones http://uk.businessinsider.com/dscout-research-people-touch-cell-phones-2617-times-a-day-2016-7

100 sit with and entertain ourselves Wilson, Timothy D, Reinhard, David A, Westgate, Erin C, Gilbert, Daniel T, Ellerbeck, Nicole, Hahn, Cheryl, Brown, Casey L, Shaked, Adi, "Just think: The challenges of the disengaged mind", *Science*, vol. 345, issue 6192, July 2014, pp.75–77.

101 "Solitude is where you find yourself" Turkle, Sherry, "Connected, but alone?" TED. February 2012. Lecture.

101 6.8 hours of sleep a night https://news.gallup.com/poll/166553/less-recommended-amount-sleep.aspx

102 explicit images of themselves shared Lenhart, Amanda, Ybarra, Michele and Price-Feeney, Myeshia, "Nonconsensual Image Sharing: One in 25 Americans Has Been a Victim of 'Revenge Porn'", Data & Society Research Institute and the Center for Innovative Public Health Research data memo, December 2016; https://datasociety.net/pubs/oh/Nonconsensual_Image_Sharing_2016.pdf

102 47 per cent of Americans *ibid*.

102 up to 50 per cent of school-age girls https://www.theguardian.com/uk-news/2017/aug/14/half-uk-girls-bullied-social-media-survey

103 up to 40 per cent don't tell their parents https://www.theguardian.com/society/2015/sep/22/cyberbullying-teenagers-worse-than-drug-abuse-says-report

103 study of 2,215 students https://jamanetwork.com/journals/jamapsychiatry/fullarticle/210833

103 88 per cent increase in calls https://www.theguardian.com/society/2016/nov/14/nspcc-records-88-rise-in-children-seeking-help-for-online-abuse

104 three-quarters of women under thirty https://www.theguardian.com/lifeandstyle/2016/mar/08/online-harassment-of-women-at-risk-of-becoming-established-norm-study

105 deemed to be inadequate https://www.theguardian.com/uk-news/2017/jul/05/stalking-and-harassment-crimes-routinely-badly-handled-uk-report-says

105 digitally stalked https://datasociety.net/blog/2016/11/21/online-harassment/

105 Half of all millennials http://www.dailymail.co.uk/femail/article-3225666/HALF-millennials-admit-sent-naked-pictures-text-quarter-say-rely-online-dating-sites-love.html

105 shared intimate images https://www.childnet.com/blog/press-release-uk-youth-targeted-with-sexual-harassment-on-the-internet

105 contemplated suicide Figures from the End Revenge Porn campaign; http://www.wired.co.uk/article/revenge-porn-facebook-social-media

106 no action being taken http://www.bbc.co.uk/news/uk-37278264

107 impersonated by a criminal https://www.theguardian.com/money/2017/aug/23/identity-fraud-figures-cifas-theft

107 burglars use social media https://www.adt.co.uk/protecting-you/adts-top-tips-for-online-security

107 cyberstalking is now more common https://www.telegraph.co.uk/news/uknews/crime/8439833/Computer-stalking-outstrips-face-to-face-harassment.html

109 people with epilepsy Conrad, Peter, Bandini, Julia and Vasquez, Alexandria, "Illness and the Internet: From Private to Public Experience", *Health*, vol. 20, issue 1, January 2016 pp.22–32.

Chapter 4: Why Social Media is Ruining Your **Relationships**

120 **"ambient intimacy"** https://www.nytimes.com/2008/09/07/magazine/07awareness-t.html

120 **finite number of relationships** Dunbar, Robin I M, "The social brain hypothesis", *Evolutionary Anthropology*, vol. 6, issue 5, December 1998, pp.178–190.

121 **"A lot of times I feel lonely,"** https://www.theatlantic.com/magazine/archive/2017/09/has-the-smartphone-destroyed-a-generation/534198/

121 **confide their personal troubles and triumphs to** https://spectator.org/59230_loneliness-american-society/

121 **as damaging to our health as smoking** Holt-Lunstad, Julianne, Smith, Timothy B, Baker, Mark, Harris, Tyler and Stephenson, David, "Loneliness and Social Isolation as Risk Factors for Mortality: A Meta-Analytic Review", *Perspectives on Psychological Science*, vol. 10, issue 2, March 2015, pp.227–237.

124 **prefer conversing digitally** https://www.news.com.au/finance/business/weve-raised-generation-hopeless-millennials-who-lack-basic-life-and-workplace-skills-and-its-a-big-issue/news-story/f3256c05c19c356002103eb50e50cee1

124 **get together with their friends** https://www.theatlantic.com/magazine/archive/2017/09/has-the-smartphone-destroyed-a-generation/534198/

126 **"real life stage fright"** https://www.news.com.au/finance/business/weve-raised-generation-hopeless-millennials-who-lack-basic-life-and-workplace-skills-and-its-a-big-issue/news-story/f3256c05c19c356002103eb50e50cee1

127 **verbal and non-verbal messages** Mehrabian, Albert, *Silent Messages* (1st ed.), (Wadsworth, 1971).

128 **56 per cent of US high-school seniors** https://www.theatlantic.com/magazine/archive/2017/09/has-the-smartphone-destroyed-a-generation/534198/

128 **the number of sexually active teens** https://www.theatlantic.com/magazine/archive/2017/09/has-the-smartphone-destroyed-a-generation/534198/

128 **teen birth rate in the UK** https://www.theguardian.com/society/2016/jul/18/how-uk-halved-teenage-pregnancy-rate-public-health-strategy

128 **UK levels of alcohol consumption** https://www.independent.co.uk/news/health/alcohol-drinking-britain-habits-booze-consumption-ons-data-a7716186.html

128 **less likely to be taking illicit drugs** https://edition.cnn.com/2016/12/13/health/drug-use-teens/index.html

129 **show how much they care** Lenhart, Amanda, Smith, Aaron and Anderson, Monica, "Teens, Technology and Romantic Relationships", Pew Research Center, October 2015; http://www.pewinternet.org/files/2015/10/PI_2015-10-01_teens-technology-romance_FINAL.pdf

129 **make their relationships visible** Emery, Lydia F, Muise, Amy, Dix, Emily L, and Le, Benjamin, "Can You Tell That I'm in a Relationship? Attachment and Relationship Visibility on Facebook", *Personality and Social Psychology Bulletin*, vol. 40, issue 11, September 2014, pp.1466–1479.

131 **"holds everything in an unchanging past"** https://www.psychologytoday.com/intl/blog/mental-mishaps/201406/how-social-networks-can-inflame-jealousy?amp

134 **"lower levels of satisfaction"** Strübel, Jessica and Petrie, Trent, "Love me Tinder: Body image and psychosocial functioning among men and women", *Body Image*, vol. 21, June 2017, pp.34–38.

134 **addicted to the process** https://www.bustle.com/p/new-app-ona-wants-to-make-your-dating-life-better-but-its-not-a-dating-app-36054

137 **social media makes them feel jealous** Lenhart, Amanda, Smith, Aaron and Anderson, Monica, "Teens, Technology and Romantic Relationships", Pew Research Center, October 2015; http://www.pewinternet.org/files/2015/10/PI_2015-10-01_teens-technology-romance_FINAL.pdf

138 **a third of all divorce cases** https://www.mirror.co.uk/news/technology-science/technology/facebook-now-crops-up-third-5011205

138 **80 per cent of US divorce lawyers** http://aaml.org/about-the-academy/press/press-releases/e-discovery/big-surge-social-networking-evidence-says-survey-

138 **"seen somebody on Tinder"** Weiser, Dana A, Niehuis, Sylvia, Flora, Jeanne, Punyanunt-Carter, Narissra M, Arias, Vladimir S, Hannah Baird, R, "Swiping right: Sociosexuality, intentions to engage in infidelity, and infidelity experiences on Tinder", *Personality and Individual Differences*, vol. 133, October 2018, pp.29–33.

Chapter 5: Why Social Media is Ruining **Motherhood**

143 at least 1 child https://www.telegraph. co.uk/news/2017/11/24/proportion-women-never-have-children-has-doubled-generation/; http://www. pewsocialtrends.org/2018/01/18/theyre-waiting-longer-but-u-s-women-today-more-likely-to-have-children-than-a-decade-ago/

144 a third of British mothers According to a 2017 online survey of 1,800 British parents by the BBC Radio 5 live and YouGov; https://www.bbc.co.uk/news/health-42140028

145 The average age of a mum https://www.ons.gov.uk/peoplepopulationandcommunity/birthsdeathsandmarriages/livebirths/bulletins/birthsummarytablesengland andwales/2015

145 US picture is broadly similar https://www.bloomberg.com/news/articles/2017-05-17/women-in-30s-now-having-more-babies-than-younger-moms-in-us

146 "motherhood ideologies" Henderson, Angie, Harmon, Sandra & Newman, Harmony D, "The Price Mothers Pay, Even When They Are Not Buying It: Mental Health Consequences of Idealized Motherhood", Sex Roles, vol. 74, issues 11–12, September 2015, pp.512–526.

146 experiencing increased stress and anxiety ibid.

147 "The quest to be a 'perfect' mother" https://www.theguardian.com/commentisfree/2016/may/10/perfect-mother-good-parenting-child-behaviour

147 "pressure to be the perfect mum" https://www.standard.co.uk/lifestyle/london-life/perfect-lives-of-instamums-are-making-london-mothers-feel-inadaquate-a3468426.html

148 sperm counts among Western men https://www.theguardian.com/lifeandstyle/2017/jul/25/sperm-counts-among-western-men-have-halved-in-last-40-years-study

149 one in seven couples in the UK https://www.nice.org.uk/guidance/cg156/chapter/context

149 one in eight couples in the US https://news.aetna.com/2016/09/1-8-couples-fertility-issues/

156 a million miscarriages happen http://time.com/3849280/pregnancy-miscarriage/

156 one in five of all pregnancies https://www.independent.co.uk/life-style/health-and-families/features/new-research-could-help-to-predict-which-women-are-at-risk-of-miscarriage-a6910141.html

160 "the pregnant body as a site of risk" Thomas, Gareth M, and Lupton, Deborah, "Threats and thrills: pregnancy apps, risk and consumption", Health, Risk & Society, vol. 17, issues 7–8, November 2015, pp.495–509.

161 pregnant woman's data https://thinkprogress.org/meet-the-woman-who-did-everything-in-her-power-to-hide-her-pregnancy-from-big-data-80070cf6edd2/

162 uploaded to social media https://www.telegraph.co.uk/technology/10268615/Babies-appear-on-social-media-within-an-hour-of-birth.html

163 becoming more competitive https://www.daynurseries.co.uk/news/article.cfm/id/1570243/An-audience-at-birth

164 regret, shame, guilt or anger http://time.com/4989068/motherhood-is-hard-to-get-wrong/

164 "The Goddess Myth" http://time.com/4989068/motherhood-is-hard-to-get-wrong/?xid=tcoshare

165 getting their figure back http://www.dailymail.co.uk/femail/article-3586743/New-mums-worried-snapping-shape-relationship.html

166 15 per cent of all women https://www.nimh.nih.gov/health/publications/postpartum-depression-facts/index.shtml

166 "snapped-back" new mums Coyne, Sarah M, Liechty, Toni, Collier, Kevin M, Sharp, Aubrey D, Davis, Emilie J and Kroff, Savannah L, "The Effect of Media on Body Image in Pregnant and Postpartum Women", Health Communication, May 2017, vol. 33, issue 7, pp.793–799.

168 active on the platform http://www.pewinternet.org/2015/07/16/parents-and-social-media/

169 parenting decisions have been judged http://www.dailymail.co.uk/femail/article-2676671/70-parents-feel-judged-decisions-make-child-three-quarters-given-advice-without-asking-it.html

170 seeking validation or are depressed
Schoppe-Sullivan, S J, Yavorsky, J E,
Bartholomew, M K, Sullivan, J M, Lee,
M A, Kamp Dush, C M, Glassman, M,
"Doing Gender Online: New Mothers'
Psychological Characteristics, Facebook
Use, and Depressive Symptoms", *Sex Roles*,
vol. 76, issue 5, March 2017, pp.276–289.

170 "over-preciousness about motherhood"
http://time.com/4989068/motherhood-
is-hard-to-get-wrong/?xid=tcoshare

170 don't receive paid family leave https://
www.nytimes.com/2015/06/22/upshot/a-
federal-policy-on-paid-leave-suddenly-
seems-plausible.html

170 70 per cent of all women work
https://www.ons.gov.uk/
employmentandlabourmarket/
peopleinwork/employmentandemployee
types/bulletins/uklabourmarket/
march2018

176 read the most baby manuals Harries, V
and Brown, A, "The association between
use of infant parenting books that promote
strict routines, and maternal depression,
self-efficacy, and parenting confidence",
Early Child Development and Care,
September 2017.

Chapter 6: Why Social Media is Ruining Your **Career & Money**

177 expensive branded goods https://
www.directlinegroup.com/media/news/
brand/2017/26072017.aspx

188 Consumer debt in the US rose
Federal Reserve Bank of New York,
"Quarterly Report on Household
Debt and Credit", May 2017; https://
www.newyorkfed.com/medialibrary/
interactives/householdcredit/data/pdf/
HHDC_2017Q1.pdf

188 predicted to hit £15,000 https://www.
bbc.com/news/uk-42498343

188 experiences rather than things https://
www.home.barclaycard/media-centre/
press-releases/consumer-spending-grew-
5-point-5-per-cent-in-april.html

188 "A short-term focus" Tully, Stephanie M
and Sharma, Eesha, "Context Dependent
Drivers of Discretionary Debt Decisions:
Explaining Willingness to Borrow for
Experiential Purchases", *Journal of
Consumer Research*, vol. 44, issue 5,
June 2017, pp.960–973.

188 go into debt to pay for a trip https://
nypost.com/2017/06/21/most-americans-
will-go-into-debt-to-pay-for-a-vacation/

188 six months to recover financially https://
www.reuters.com/article/us-money-
travel-vacation-idUSKBN19B1SY

**189 spent money after seeing someone
else's post** https://www.aicpa.org/press/
pressreleases/2016/keeping-up-with-the-
joneses-goes-online.html

192 Four out of five employees Garrett, R
Kelly and Danziger, James N, "Disaffection
or expected outcomes: Understanding
personal Internet use during work", *Journal
of Computer-Mediated Communication*,
vol. 13, issue 4, July 2008, pp.937–958.

192 depleting their productivity http://www.
teamleasegroup.com/blog/social-media-
affecting-workplace-productivity

192 25 minutes to get back on task https://
www.theglobeandmail.com/technology/
your-smartphone-is-making-you-stupid/
article37511900/

192 to take a "mental break" http://www.
pewinternet.org/2016/06/22/social-
media-and-the-workplace/

**192 rewiring the way our brains actually
work** https://www.theguardian.com/
technology/2018/mar/04/has-dopamine-
got-us-hooked-on-tech-facebook-apps-
addiction

193 greater decrease in IQ https://
www.forbes.com/sites/
vanessaloder/2014/06/11/why-multi-
tasking-is-worse-than-marijuana-for-
your-iq/#316ae27d7c11

193 attention spans have reduced https://
www.bbc.co.uk/news/health-38896790

193 our minds digress Killingsworth, Matthew
A and Gilbert, Daniel T, "A Wandering Mind
Is an Unhappy Mind", *Science*, vol. 180, issue
6006, November 2010, p.932.

194 new "superhuman" brain Brogaard, Berit:
"The Superhuman Mind: Free the Genius in
Your Brain" (Hudson Street Press, 2015)

194 keep in touch with their contacts http://
www.pewinternet.org/2016/06/22/social-
media-and-the-workplace/

194 walked into traffic Basch, Corey H,
Ethan, Danna, Zybert, P and Basch, C E,
"Pedestrian Behavior at Five Dangerous
and Busy Manhattan Intersections",
Journal of Community Health, vol. 40,
issue 4, August 2015, pp.789–792.

Chapter 7: Why Social Media is Ruining Your **Politics**

206 uniquely disrespectful Duggan, Maeve and Smith, Aaron, "The Political Environment on Social Media", Pew Research Center, October 2016; http://assets.pewresearch.org/wp-content/uploads/sites/14/2016/10/24160747/PI_2016.10.25_Politics-and-Social-Media_FINAL.pdf

214 "In times of extremes" https://www.theglobeandmail.com/opinion/am-i-a-bad-feminist/article37591823/

218 news from social media Shearer, Elisa and Gottfried, Jeffrey, "News Use Across Social Media Platforms 2017", Pew Research Center, October 2017; http://assets.pewresearch.org/wp-content/uploads/sites/13/2017/09/13163032/PJ_17.08.23_socialMediaUpdate_FINAL.pdf

219 Republicans were "closed minded" Pew Research Center, "Partisanship and Political Animosity in 2016", June 2016, https://assets.pewresearch.org/wp-content/uploads/sites/5/2016/06/06-22-16-Partisanship-and-animosity-release.pdf

219 "worn out" Duggan, Maeve and Smith, Aaron, "The Political Environment on Social Media", Pew Research Center, October 2016; http://assets.pewresearch.org/wp-content/uploads/sites/14/2016/10/24160747/PI_2016.10.25_Politics-and-Social-Media_FINAL.pdf

Epilogue: How Social Media is Changing Your Future

231 messages sent via private services http://uk.businessinsider.com/the-messaging-app-report-2015-11

231 21 per cent drop https://www.bloomberg.com/news/articles/2016-04-07/facebook-said-to-face-decline-in-people-posting-personal-content

232 opt out of data-based advertising https://eu.usatoday.com/story/tech/2018/04/08/apple-co-founder-steve-wozniak-says-hes-leaving-facebook/497392002/

233 "allows you to just be yourself" https://www.theverge.com/2018/3/2/17067610/vero-social-media-ayman-hariri-downloads

234 "We're lonely but we're afraid of intimacy" Turkle, Sherry, "Connected, but alone?" TED. February 2012. Lecture.

235 17 per cent of seniors https://www.campaigntoendloneliness.org/loneliness-research/

235 television is their main companion *ibid*.

237 own a VR headset https://yougov.co.uk/news/2017/05/19/vr-headsets-more-popular-tablets-and-wearables-wer/

237 vocal movement of tech insiders https://www.theguardian.com/news/2018/may/03/why-silicon-valley-cant-fix-itself-tech-humanism

Contributors

Kelly Agnew @kellyagnew

Lauren Alexander @laurenalexander

Pip Black @moveyourframe

Camille Charrière @camillecharrière

Charly Cox @charlycox1

Kelly Eastwood @thelondonchatter

Laura Fantacci @laura.fantacci

Kat Farmer @doesmybumlook40

Paula Goldstein @paulasanexplorer

Nene Granville @industrymenu

Lizzy Hadfield @shotfromthestreet

Sandra Hagelstam @5inchandup

Freddie Harrel @freddieharrel

Lindsey Holland @ropesofholland

Victoria Magrath @inthefrow

Lauren Mahon @girlstolelondon

Claire Marshall @heyclaire

Leandra Medine @leandramcohen

Sara Melotti @saramelotti_

Gabriela Moussaieff
   @gabrielamoussaieff

Joan Murphy @moveyourframe

Roxie Nafousi @roxienafousi

Anna Newton @theannaedit

Shini Park @parkncube

Lily Pebbles @lilypebbles

Rejina Pyo @rejinapyo

Anna Saccone Joly @annasaccone

Niomi Smart @niomismart

Pandora Sykes @pandorasykes

Callie Thorpe @calliethorpe

Courtney Trop @alwaysjudging

Pippa Vosper @pippavosper

Anna Whitehouse @mother_pukka

Lucy Williams @lucywilliams02

Dr Jessica Zucker @ihadamiscarriage

Index

Acknowledgements

Without the support and candour of the many women who are featured in its pages, this book would be nothing. I'm so grateful to my digital network for trusting me with the not-so-perfect sides of their lives. I hope I've done you proud.

Offline, there's another bunch of exceptional ladies to thank: my literary agent Abigail who first persuaded me to start this project and has put up with months of my hormones. Also, my editors Romilly, Leanne and Louise at Octopus for believing in me and bringing their razor-sharp eyes to every sentence.

And, while it's a woman's world, I also need to thank my brother Sam for his feedback and skilful research, and my other half, Haden, for holding the baby and keeping me going through the dark days of sleep deprivation. I quite literally wouldn't have been able to do it without you.

Finally, the biggest thank you to my mum, Bev, who taught me that life is a patchwork of love and that oversharing is caring.

Introduction to British Politics

Joanna Tuck
10, Essex House.

Introduction to
British Politics

Analysing a Capitalist Democracy

JOHN DEARLOVE and PETER SAUNDERS

Polity Press

First published 1984 by
Polity Press, Cambridge and Basil Blackwell, Oxford.
Reprinted in 1985, 1986, 1987

Editorial Office
Polity Press
Dales Brewery, Gwydir Street, Cambridge CB1 2LJ, UK

Basil Blackwell Ltd
108 Cowley Road, Oxford OX4 1JF, UK

Basil Blackwell Inc.
432 Park Avenue South, Suite 1503, New York, NY 10016, USA

British Library Cataloguing in Publication Data

Dearlove, John
  British Politics.
  1. Great Britain—Politics and government
  —1979—
  I. Title   II. Saunders, Peter
  320.941   JN231

ISBN   0-7456-0010-7
ISBN   0-7456-0011-5 pbk.

Library of Congress Cataloging in Publication Data

Dearlove, John.
  Introduction to British politics.
  Bibliography: p.
  Includes index.
  1. Great Britain—Politics and government—1979—
2. Great Britain—Economic policy—1945—
I. Saunders, Peter R.   II. Title.
JN231.D4   1985   320.941
ISBN 0-7456-0010-7
ISBN 0-7456-0011-5 (pbk.)

Typeset by Banbury Typesetters Ltd.
Printed and bound in Great Britain

Contents

Introduction

British politics have been undergoing some quite dramatic and fundamental changes and upheavals over the last few years. As the country's economy has lurched into recession, and as different sections of the population have posed different and often irreconcilable demands across a variety of issues ranging from the deployment of nuclear weapons to the future of the welfare state, so long-established political arrangements have begun to crack under the strain. New patterns of political alignment, new types of political organisation, and new sources of political conflict have emerged.

One manifestation of these changes has been the erosion of the two-party system. In 1981, the Social Democratic Party was formed, and just over 2 years later, in alliance with the Liberals, secured over 25 per cent of the popular vote at a general election. This result was not reflected in Parliament, however, where the Alliance won just 23 seats (the Labour Party, with 2 per cent more of the vote, won 209 seats!). The Alliance complained about the inequities in the electoral system and called for a new, written, British constitution to include proportional representation.

The 1983 general election was no less traumatic for the Labour Party which recorded the worst defeat in its history. Almost as many working-class people voted Conservative as voted Labour and the party (together with many political analysts) was at last forced to recognise that it had no automatic support base among manual workers, many of whom were now avowedly anti-socialist in their views and sentiments.

Labour's defeat also nailed once and for all the fallacy, so common on the Left, that when capitalism gets into a mess, the masses will fall in behind a radical socialist alternative. Throughout the 1970s and early 1980s, Labour's rank and file activists had pushed the party away from the 'middle ground' to embrace the explicitly socialist programme of state intervention which proved electorally disastrous. Meanwhile, during this same period, the Conservatives had been moving off in the opposite (free market, anti-state) direction under the zealous Right-wing leadership of Margaret Thatcher with the result that party politics had become polarised to an extent unprecedented in the post-war years.

By the early 1980s, both major parties had, in their different ways, come to reject most of the basic principles by which governments had attempted to run the country since the Second World War. Neither Labour nor the Conservatives were any longer content to support the so-called 'mixed economy', for while the former urged a massive extension of public ownership, the latter set about privatising many of the major nationalised industries. Both parties similarly rejected the economic policies which had been adopted following the end of the war as the means for ensuring continued growth and relatively full employment. Labour came to place its faith in greater economic planning by the state while the Conservatives embraced a monetarist, anti-state strategy which brought inflation under some kind of control but at the cost of driving unemployment to new record levels. Finally, while Labour increasingly criticised the inadequacies of the welfare state, the Conservatives busied themselves with dismantling it.

As unemployment rose, social services deteriorated, and the plight of large sections of the population grew steadily worse, so the Conservative Government became increasingly concerned about the possibility of social unrest. The police and the army were strengthened and legislation limiting civil liberties was pushed through Parliament. In the summer of 1981, riots broke out and spread through many English cities resulting in damage estimated at £45 million. The Home Secretary immediately announced increased expenditure on more effective riot-control equipment and police pay was again increased as unemployment continued to rise.

While some groups took to the streets in direct and angry confrontation with the police, others developed alternative modes of airing their grievances. The peace movement re-emerged from hibernation and women mounted a long and weary vigil outside the Greenham Common airforce base in protest at the deployment of Cruise missiles under the control of the American Government. This protest in turn reflected the growing vitality of the women's movement, and throughout the 1970s and 1980s, this and many other movements – ranging from tenants' associations to the gay-rights campaign – sprang up to give voice and expression to interests and concerns which could no longer be contained within the straitjacket of conventional party politics, interest-group politics, or class-based movements.

The development which more than any other struck at the very heart of the established system of state power was the growth of nationalist movements in Scotland, Wales and Northern Ireland. While the threat posed by Scottish and Welsh nationalism was (temporarily) overcome at the end of the 1970s, the question of Northern Ireland has proved intractable. British troops were deployed in the province in 1969 and have remained there ever since, while the minority nationalist population has continued to demonstrate its resolute hostility to continued British rule by, among other things, electing Sinn Fein candidates, one of whom starved himself to death in a British military prison in Belfast.

The sovereignty of the United Kingdom state was also under threat during this period. In 1973, the UK joined the European community and ceded certain crucial powers to the European bureaucracy in Brussels. This, together with the growing dependence of the British Government on an American-dominated military alliance and the weakness of the British Government in the face of pressure from the International Monetary Fund, led many commentators to doubt whether Britain was any more in control of its own destiny.

All of these tendencies help to explain why, from the 1970s onwards, democracy itself came to be questioned from a number of different quarters. For those on the Right, 'mass' democracy began to look like a luxury which the country could no longer afford. Politicians, political scientists, military personnel, and police chiefs began to complain about 'elective dictatorship' and 'adversary politics'. They wondered whether government was not becoming 'overloaded' by democratic demands, whether trade unions could any longer be allowed to disrupt the pursuit of profitability, and whether it was necessary to curtail established rights in order to defend the established social and economic power structure. Those on the Left by contrast, came to see aspects of liberal democracy as little more than a sham. They saw the potential in participatory democracy and contrasted this with the reality of the non-responsive power of multinational corporations, the machinations of the banks and finance companies, and the secrecy of the various state agencies over which ordinary people had virtually no control. On both Right and Left, therefore, democracy came to be seen as a problem: there was too much for the Right, and not enough for the Left.

This brief review of contemporary developments indicates the extent to which British politics have been in turmoil over the past few years. We attempt to make sense of these changes in this book for we believe that the turmoil in British politics has caught existing accounts wrong footed. What then do we see as the limitations of the existing text books on British politics?

THE LIMITATIONS OF THE ESTABLISHED LITERATURE

It is not possible to generalise about texts on British politics as there is no single tradition of writing on the subject. Having said that, the dominant, mainstream, political science texts have tended to focus almost exclusively on the democratic aspects of British politics. For most of this century, the emphasis has been on the liberal-democratic constitution and the formal institutions of Parliament, Cabinet, and Prime Minister. More recently, political scientists have come to deal with the process of policy-making taking into account the significance of parties and interest groups. Yet despite this development a narrow view of politics and power has continued to prevail. Too much has been taken for granted. Too much has been ignored because it does not fit within a democratic perspective. British politics have been defined either as being about describing the institutions of the state (with the presumption that power is somehow *in* those institutions), or as involving an explanation of the process of public policy-making through an emphasis upon the role of parties and interest groups.

In this mainstream literature, therefore, no real attention was paid to the non-democratic aspects of British politics; no attention was paid to the substance of public policy so as to deal with just who benefited from government action (and inaction); no attention was devoted to the implications which flowed from the fact that Britain possessed a capitalist economy that was operating in a world market; and there was no recognition that power was caught up in 'private' matters, dull routines, and inaction as much as in the more public arena of governmental institutions and formal political participation.

Texts of this kind tended to be complacent, and they are characterised less by their explanatory rigour than by their unthinking praise for, and commitment to, the system of democracy in Britain.

In the 1970s, teaching texts articulating the conventional and orthodox wisdom about representative and responsible government continued to emerge, but at the same time they were becoming increasingly out of step with informed opinion as to the 'reality' of our politics and problems. Established political scientists could be heard expressing their unease about the drift of democratic politics in Britain. Instead of praising the British constitution as a sweet success it was increasingly seen as a sour problem that was the root cause of our economic ills and in need of change. Part and parcel of this critique was the recognition that the conventional wisdom was at odds with reality and so could no longer explain it. Political scientists were telling us that we had to break out of the conventional wisdom in order to make any kind of sense of the sorts of changes in British politics which we discussed above. Instead of talking about responsible party government, these critics came to talk of adversary politics, and instead of seeing interest groups as contributing to a cosy pluralist democracy they saw them as leading to a dangerous overload of demands and to a crisis of governability itself. Leading political scientists slowly dumped the conventional wisdom and took on a New Right perspective that was critical of big government and mass democracy because of the damage they were apparently causing to Britain's economic performance.

In fact, all the ballyhoo about the need to break out of the conventional wisdom conceals the essential continuity between that wisdom and the New Right accounts of British politics that have assumed a key place in the political science of British politics *and* in British politics itself. Although there is a change in the assessment of British politics, the system is still characterised as democratic above all else. In effect, political scientists have chosen to look at our political economy with an eye fixed only on politics, and on democratic politics at that. They have failed to focus on capitalism and take it seriously because the mere mention of capitalism has been dismissed as a coarse ideological irrelevance. In consequence, political scientists have continued to overlook the political significance of economic power. Where they have considered economic interests, their analyses have been limited to simple studies of the 'links' between government and industry which go no further than tracing the 'backgrounds' of those involved in politics and the interest-group organisations of business and labour.

Of course, texts defining British politics as democratic politics are not the be all and end all of the literature. A smaller, rival, tradition of critical writing, inspired by a Marxist perspective, is particularly attentive to capitalism and class. This perspective tries to place the institutions of the British state within the larger social and economic context, stressing the functions they perform in the defence of a class-based and divided society. There are considerable merits in this body of work, but there is often the presumption that British politics can be explained and simply 'read off' from a knowledge of Marxist theory backed up by a cursory glance at the underlying realities of economic power in Britain without the need for any concrete research into the messy stuff of politics itself. Moreover, if mainstream political scientists have failed to take capitalism seriously, then Marxist analysts have failed to take democracy seriously. From the Marxist perspective, democracy in Britain has been seen, all too easily, as mere 'bourgeois democracy' – as democracy for the capitalist class and the denial of democracy for the working class. Democracy, and even politics itself, is regarded as so snugly contained by, and fitted to, the essentials of capitalism that it offers no real prospects for change. Democracy simply buttresses (often by concealing) the power of the economically dominant class. It then follows from this that democracy can safely be ignored by the 'serious' student of British politics since *real* power lies not in parliaments or local councils but in company board rooms and (when the time is ripe) on the streets.

In many ways the Marxist accounts are the opposite side of the coin to the mainstream and New Right political science accounts. Marxist accounts are attentive to capitalism and economics to the detriment of a sustained concern with democracy, whereas mainstream and New Right accounts are attentive to democracy and to a narrow conception of politics to the detriment of a serious concern with the political implications of capitalism. Each tradition has its blind spots. Each tradition tends to operate in dismissive ignorance of the rival tradition: many political scientists have seen Marxist accounts of British politics as 'biased', value-loaded, and inattentive to the 'facts', and most Marxists have seen 'bourgeois' political science as offering accounts that simply mystify reality, legitimise the status quo, and deal only with unimportant facts and the surface froth of democratic politics.

So, the texts on British politics have been polarised in a way that has reflected the increasing polarisation within British politics itself. More than this, authors have rarely been self-critical of the ideas they have been putting forward, and many have not been clear as to the theory guiding their work and the selection of the facts which they present. By and large *both* traditions of scholarship are over-confident, static, partial, and ahistorical, and too eager to presume that politics today can be explained through a reliance on either liberal-democratic theories or Marxist theories, both of which have their roots in the experience of the nineteenth century.

In fact contemporary developments in the world of British politics and the turmoil and change which abound have rocked *both* traditions of scholarship and their advocates know it. In consequence the rival perspectives on British politics are increasingly uncertain of their explanatory grip on a political reality that seems to defy any simple appreciation and which mocks the attempt to apply nineteenth-century nostrums to late twentieth-century issues. Some say we are witnessing a crisis of capitalism, others that we are experiencing a crisis of democracy, but in an intellectual world in which theories compete, few are prepared to suggest that the situation is a complex mix of problems to do with capitalism *and* democracy – and much else besides.

It is here that we see the distinctive contribution of this book. We are not exclusively committed to any one theory or perspective; we do not feel a need to take simple sides with respect to the different traditions of scholarship; and we consider that the rival traditions are as much complementary as competing. To be a good political scientist you must be keenly alive to the marxist tradition, and to be a good Marxist you must know 'bourgeois' social science. British politics are complicated and it makes no sense to see all wisdom as residing within one perspective.

THEORIES AND METHODS

Our concern is to liberate the student of British politics from the blinkers of the conventional textbook wisdoms *and* the increasingly conventional radical alternatives to those wisdoms. The first and crucial step towards such a liberation lies in the recognition that the study of politics entails the analysis of power in all its aspects. To achieve this, it is necessary to consider critically the insights which derive from a number of rival traditions including mainstream political science, the New Right, Marxism and neo-Marxism, and political sociology.

No one perspective enjoys a monopoly over explanatory wisdom; nor can understanding be advanced if we are constrained by the limits of any single discipline. There is no single simple key which can unlock the complex reality that is British politics, and no single theory can provide all the answers. This is because theories, perspectives and even disciplines often differ in what it is that they are trying to explain.

There are different views as to the *essentials* of politics and power which means that the focus of attention is different in various traditions of work. These traditions also differ in the *levels* at which they attempt to generalise about political power which means that some approaches are more specific in terms of time and place than others.

For example, if you consider that politics are essentially to do with the business of government and the elected part of the state machine, then theories pertaining to elections and democratic procedures will clearly be central to your approach. If, however, your view of politics is broadened somewhat to include, say, the wider process of *public* policy-making by government and state, then your theoretical focus will also need to be wider since you will wish to consider the activities of interest groups as well as many other parts of the state system. And if your concern is with *private* power as it operates not just in and on the state but throughout the economy and society, and if you see this as the very essence of politics, then you will not wish to devote much attention to the analysis of elections, or Parliament or even the civil service, but will rather seek to focus on the significance of 'private' organisations and interests which may never be seen in the Palace of Westminster and which thus rarely feature in other kinds of theories.

None of these approaches is necessarily 'wrong'. Nor can we say that one approach is 'better' than another because it embraces a broader focus, for such judgements will depend on what it is we are interested in explaining at the time. Certainly there is no reason to assume that, if we draw on one of these perspectives this rules out the possibility of drawing on any other. Although academic debate and argument among those who are committed to different theories often proceed as if their approaches were mutually incompatible, it is clearly the case that different theories which focus on *different* questions posed at *different* levels of generality may in fact turn out to be *to some extent* complementary.

We should, however, be wary of simply cobbling together different theories in an attempt to develop a fully rounded picture. Just as we cannot develop a comprehensive understanding of Western art by focusing exclusively on Picassos or on Constables, so too our political analysis cannot be limited to any one tradition. Moreover, if it is the case that our understanding of the art world is likely to become very confused if we simply stitch together fragments from 'Guernica' and 'The Haywain', then so it is with our theoretical understanding of political power. Some theories are, to a greater or lesser extent, incompatible with each other, and if this is the case we cannot expect to achieve analytical clarity by sticking them together.

It is therefore one thing to say, as we do, that few theories are ever entirely wrong (or for that matter entirely right), but it is quite another to suggest that the truth of the matter can, therefore, somehow be attained by mixing them all together. Some theories *are* more valid than others in respect of specific questions which they address, and *the task is to sort out which sorts of issues are best explained by which sorts of theories.*

This, however, is easier said than done! Any social scientist will tell you that theory-testing is an extremely hazardous business, mainly because there is invariably a dispute over what is to constitute a 'fact'. Not all facts are problematic – it is a 'fact', for example, that the Conservatives achieved a parliamentary majority at the 1979 and 1983 general elections – but most of the 'facts' which we need to draw upon in order to start explaining things can be and are disputed by people who are committed to different theories. This is because we tend to see the world through our existing theories.

It is our theories which tell us what we are looking for and, in many cases, what we are looking at, and this means that different people wedded to different theories all too often end up disputing each other's interpretations of the evidence or simply talking past one another.

If 'facts' are to a large extent dependent upon our existing theories then there are obviously real problems involved in trying to evaluate competing theories against them. Nevertheless, it remains the case that some theories do seem able to explain certain problems more plausibly or more comprehensively than others and so the critical and self-aware observer does not have to accept that any theory is as good as any other at explaining a given problem. We can offer no simple acid test of theoretical validity, but it is possible to go some way to evaluate different perspectives in terms of their logical consistency and their explanatory power with respect to specific aspects of politics at particular moments of history.

In the chapters that follow, we set down some of the major perspectives which have been advanced to account for developments in British politics, and we attempt to evaluate them against each other *and* against historical evidence of what the British state has done, how it has done it, and with what consequences for different groups in the population. In particular, we shall be evaluating the various theories we encounter in terms of what they tell us about the organisation and use of power in and on the contemporary British state.

We begin the book with a critical assessment of those constitutional theories which see political power as lying within particular democratic state institutions. As we proceed through the book, however, we gradually expand out from the institutions of the state and formal constitutional, or institutional, approaches to power. We recognise that the non-elected institutions of the state exercise substantial power. We argue that political power is also caught up in the behaviour and activity of political parties and interest groups in particular issues and policy areas. However, we also recognise that this 'obvious' behavioural, action-oriented perspective on power does not go far enough since it is also vital to attend to the power that is caught up in inaction and non-decision-making in society and economy as well as just in government and politics. In effect, as you read through the book you will be moving away from simple statements about *where* power lies (be it in the institutions of the state, in parties, pressure groups, or particular social classes) in order to consider more complex and abstract themes bearing on *how* power is used (and not used) and to *whose* particular advantage given the actual substance of state activity and the balance of public and private provision for social needs in Britain.

THE PLAN OF THE BOOK

In Chapter 1 we look at the historical development of the British constitution and of constitutional theory in terms of the interests caught up in trying to change and defend the formal rules of the British political game. The Constitution and constitutional theory are important because the former is *in* politics and the latter is *about* explaining politics.

In Chapter 2 we explore three perspectives on party politics in Britain. First we explore the mainstream model of responsible party government; second, we consider the New Right argument about adversary politics; and finally we deal with the Left perspective which is critical of the Labour Party and sees party politics itself as irrelevant of major consideration.

This is then followed in Chapter 3 with a discussion of the world of interests and groups from three points of view. First, we set down the essentials of pluralist democratic theory; second we deal with the New Right assessment about an overload of interest-group demands leading to ungovernability; and finally we look at the Left perspective on interests in British politics which sees pluralism as wrong and which talks instead about the dominance of business groups in the system. As well as dealing with these three perspectives we also explore community action at the local level and the alleged trend to corporatism at the central level of the state.

Chapter 4 examines the argument that the established constitution is in crisis because it no longer explains things and secures support for the system. We go on to explore three packages of proposals for a new constitution: that of the (essentially Conservative) constitutional authorities; that of the Liberal/SDP alliance; and that of the Left of the Labour Party.

In Chapter 5 we attend to the power and significance of the non-elected parts of the state machine, much of which is uncontrolled by the elected government of the day, and all of which is poorly considered from within the mainstream and New Right perspectives. We pay particular attention to the civil service, and the nationalised industries, the judiciary, the police, the security services, and the military.

Our focus is expanded still wider in Chapter 6 where we turn from an analysis of the organisation of state power to consider a sociological perspective on power in British society as a whole. In this chapter we discuss the domination which groups can achieve in our society through ownership of capital, through professionalism, and through closing off opportunities to others on the basis of gender and race. All of this leads us to consider whether or not there is some elite group which effectively controls our society from behind the scenes.

In Chapter 7 we are concerned to deal centrally with Marxist perspectives on British politics, paying critical attention to two of the most influential marxist theories of recent years – those of Ralph Miliband and Nicos Poulantzas. In this chapter we not only evaluate this debate in theoretical terms, but we also consider its significance for the British Labour Party in the contemporary period.

The next three chapters focus on particular aspects of state activity in order to bring earlier theoretical themes and arguments to bear upon empirical and historical examples of what the state has actually done.

In Chapter 8 we concentrate on the attempts by successive British Governments to arrest the decline of the country's economy over the last 100 years or so. We show how economic policy has come full circle back to a kind of *laissez faire* in an ever-more desperate search for remedies following the failures of Keynesian demand-management and the limitations of half-hearted attempts at 'socialist' planning.

This is followed in Chapter 9 with an examination of the history of social policy, and we consider the different explanations which have been offered to account for the growth (and more recently, the erosion) of the welfare state.

In Chapter 10, we discuss the role of the state in securing social order, and trace the shift of emphasis which has occurred in recent years between 'soft' control agencies such as schools and the media, and 'hard' control agencies such as the police and the military.

We move in Chapter 11 from a focus on what the state does and why, to an analysis of the levels at which the state apparatus is organised on a geographical or territorial basis. First we consider the local level; second, we attend to the almost hidden regional agencies; third, we consider the national question and the particular problem of Northern Ireland; and finally, we look at the International Monetary Fund, the North Atlantic Treaty Organisation, and the European Community – international organisations that do so much to control and constrain British politics and policy-making.

The book ends with a conclusion in which we draw together the theoretical arguments and historical evidence reviewed in earlier chapters in an attempt to clarify the nature of the changes which are currently affecting British political life. The particular focus of this concluding chapter is on the emerging tension between capitalism and democracy in Britain — a tension that has been exacerbated by the long-term decline in the country's economic performance.

In his bleak novel *The Grapes of Wrath* set in the American mid-west during the depression years of the 1930s, John Steinbeck reports a conversation between a poverty-stricken tenant farmer and the driver of a bulldozer who has been sent to clear the tenant off the land. The driver, staring down the barrel of the tenant's rifle, claims that he is not responsible for the tenant's plight:

'It's not me. There's nothing I can do... You're not killing the right guy.'
'That's so,' the tenant said. 'Who gave you orders? I'll go after him. He's the one to kill.'
'You're wrong. He got his orders from the bank. The bank told him: "Clear those people out or it's your job".'
'Well, there's a president of the bank. There's a board of directors. I'll fill up the magazine of the rifle and go into the bank.'
The driver said: 'Fellow was telling me the bank gets orders from the east. The orders were: "Make the land show profit or we'll close you up".'
'But where does it stop? Who can we shoot? I don't aim to starve to death before I kill the man that's starving me.'
'I don't know. Maybe there's nobody to shoot...'

Fifty years on, with the economy again in crisis, many of us are just as bewildered as Steinbeck's farmer about who, if anybody, is culpable. Indeed, our economy and society have become even more complex in the intervening period such that it is now more difficult than ever before to pin down the source of the power which reaches out to touch all our lives. In such a situation, it is the task of political analysts to try to unravel the tangled web of power and domination in our society. The chapters which follow are an attempt to explore precisely this puzzle.

CHAPTER 1

Power, Politics and the British Constitution

Everyone knows that the British constitution provides for a system of representative and responsible government.

A. H. Birch (1964) Representative and Responsible Government, *London, George Allen and Unwin, p13.*

How is the country governed? By the government is the first answer that you will be likely to give, and in a way the answer is right. But who governs the government? The answer is that Parliament does. But last of all, who governs Parliament? And the answer to that is that the People of this Country *govern Parliament. And so you will see that the real answer to the question 'Who governs the country' is that 'The Country Governs itself'.*

H. O. Arnold-Forster (1900) The Citizen Reader, *London, Cassell, p. 35.*

WHY STUDY THE CONSTITUTION?

What is the British Constitution; what is constitutional theory; and why should a book about the location and exercise of power in Britain spend time dealing with these matters? There are three main reasons for our interest in the constitution.

1   The established constitution and the rules that are part of it are an aspect of the constraining context that operates *on* everyday politics. The constitution helps to shape politics and also regulates public access to, and the behaviour of, the various institutions of the state (such as the Cabinet, the House of Commons, the civil service, the military, the judiciary, and the police) that in their different ways have the right to exercise public power, if necessary through the use of physical force, within the United Kingdom. For example, a general election for the House of Commons must be held at least every 5 years but only certain people have access to the vote and not all votes for different parties are of equal power in the absence of proportional representation making for a close correspondence between votes cast and seats won; the House of Lords (once a very powerful state institution) can now only delay bills passed by the House of Commons; the Prime Minister 'must' come from the Commons; and it is 'expected' that a government will resign and call a

general election if it is defeated in a vote of confidence on the floor of the House of Commons.

2   The constitution is actually *in* politics. No constitution is ever safe above the rough and tumble of political life. It is often the focal point for fundamental conflicts. It is, therefore, subject to change at moments of political crisis as particular interests scramble to shape the constitution and the rules of the political game to their own advantage. In this chapter we shall identify two periods of decisive constitutional change since the eighteenth century, and in Chapter 4 we will deal with the substantial pressures for change with respect to the contemporary constitution.

3   Constitutional theory is *about* politics and aims to identify the location of state power. Moreover, the established theory always sits in a position of political and intellectual prominence as *the* mainstream perspective supposedly making sense of British politics as a whole. In setting down and discussing that theory we are, therefore, dealing with the 'official' view of British politics – with the view that dominates public discussion and the accounts in the media. Constitutional theory, in explaining how the various institutions of the state work together and in offering a particular theory of representation connecting state to society, seeks to provide us with answers to large and profound questions about who governs and how; about who should govern and how; and about the respective rights of people and the privileges of property in British politics.

So, let no one tell you that the study of the British constitution and constitutional theory is a boring irrelevance. The issue is not *whether* we should study the constitution, but the problem is one of deciding just what *is* the constitution and determining *how* best to study it.

WHAT IS THE CONSTITUTION?

The British constitution is not written down in a single legal document which enjoys a special political status above ordinary law. This does not mean that the constitution does not exist. Moreover, there are laws of constitutional significance, such as the various acts regulating the franchise and granting the vote, and the Parliament Act, 1949 which limits the capacity of the House of Lords to delay bills passed by the Commons to just 1 year. But much is vague and outside of the law. In this state of affairs, to answer the question, 'What is the British constitution?' is to say a number of rather different things.

1   In the most basic sense, we can simply say that the British Constitution is the 'set-up' *as it is*. It embraces the various institutions that make up that state – the House of Commons, the Cabinet, the civil service and so on – as well as the fundamental practices and rules that

identify which institutions have power and how they relate to each other and to the larger political community. The trouble with this formulation is that it does not suggest *how* we can be sure as to just what is the constitutional set-up, and this is a particular problem once we recognise that the power of particular institutions is subject to change and that there are disputes as to what are (and should be) the fundamental practices and rules. In some ways, however, these disputes have been contained because certain scholars have written books on the constitution that have endured to be widely regarded as so authoritative that they define the parameters of acceptable constitutional debate and almost the very constitution itself.

2   So, we can suggest that the British constitution is what the experts *say it is*. In a country without a written constitution, the work of Bagehot, Dicey, and Jennings, has actually been the written codification of the customs, conventions, precedents, and traditions that have never been simply set down in single, legal document.

3   But it also makes sense to say that the British constitution is what the authorities *say it should be* because their views on these matters help to police everyday political practice, pulling it into line with the constitutional theory which they themselves advance as the proper way to conduct politics. Britain does not have a supreme constitutional court to pass judgement on what is 'unconstitutional' and it is left to the constitutional authorities to do their best to enforce particular patterns of constitutional political behaviour.

Now, the constitution as it 'really' is, as it is said to be, and as it is said it should be, only really line up in times of political (and therefore constitutional) stability when there is agreement on clear and simple constitutional fundamentals. In times of political crisis and upheaval, political and governmental practice (what 'really' happens) and established constitutional theory (what the authorities say should happen) are likely to be out of step and there are severe limits as to what the constitutional theorists can do to shape behaviour. With political change, the established constitutional authorities find themselves in a situation where they are forced to come to terms with new and emerging patterns of political power and practice that are *outside* (but pressing in on) the established constitution that is supposedly made sense of through their theories. Politics is fluid. It is ill-contained within established structures and processes. Rude *power* is out of mesh with the prevailing patterns of legitimate constitutional *authority*. Established constitutional theory is tired. There will be disputes as to what should be the constitution. There is even likely to be doubt as to just what is the constitution. If the established set-up survives the pressures for change then the established constitutional theory will be of use as a rough guide to political and governmental practice, but if that set-up 'breaks' then the established theories will be left beached. New constitutional theories will rapidly come to assume centre stage. In these moments of fundamental change political practice makes all the constitutional running. Established theory is swept aside: it is of little importance in shaping governmental behaviour, still less in enabling us to understand it.

The fact of change ('flexibility'), uncertainty, and complexity, means that there is no simple answer as to what is the British Constitution. We have to attend to the dynamic tension between constitutional theory and political practice, and to change over time. This has a direct bearing on how we should study the constitution.

HOW TO STUDY THE CONSTITUTION

We have highlighted the importance of recognising that the Constitution is subject to change in response to political conflicts, and so we have pointed to the need to study the Constitution (and constitutional theory) historically, politically and critically, with an eye to the tensions between things as they are and things as it is thought they are and should be.

We are, therefore, critical of the constitutional approach that has tended to dominate the field of constitutional study *and* the textbook accounts of British politics. This approach places a heavy emphasis on the institutions of the state alone; it describes institutions and institutional relationships in suffocating detail; and because it focuses on constitutional 'law' quite uncritically it tends to see the connections between state and society formally, simply, and legalistically in a way that ignores informal patterns of power in society and economy. Institutions, such as the Cabinet, are sucked out of the larger political and societal context that gives them meaning, and they are regarded as having a life and importance all of their own. Describing minute aspects of the state apparatus, such as Commons Committees, in some kind of vacuum becomes an end in itself. There is little grip on the system as a whole. Exploring, explaining, and analysing the actual working of the overall set-up in a self-conscious, critical, and systematic way tends to slip from concern. Most of those who have studied the twentieth-century constitution have ceased to see it as a living, moving thing that has to be studied historically, that has to be studied in relation to interests and political forces, and that has to be understood within the context of larger developments within society and economy. There has been a failure to see constitutional theory and political practice as in dynamic interaction each with the other; there has been a failure to recognise that interpretations of the constitution are always relative to time, place, and our position as observers; and so there has been the simple view that the constitutional set-up as it is, as it is said to be, and as it is said it should be, have all been as of one. In effect, those who operated from within the comfy confines of the constitutional approach, froze the constitution when the set-up is never fixed. In consequence, there has been the pretence that a single perspective grounded in the nineteenth century can capture the essentials of things today, and so constitutional theory has itself been frozen in a way that has confined the parameters of constitutional debate.

There is no good intellectual reason why the study of the British constitution should have slipped into the static sterility of the constitutional approach. In our discussion of the constitution we shall break out into a critical, historical, and political approach. We shall begin where most constitutional accounts begin with the development of the nineteenth-century constitution, but we shall look at in the context of the balanced constitution that it replaced.

THE BALANCED CONSTITUTION

The orthodox theory of the eighteenth-century constitution was provided by the influential jurist and lawyer Sir William Blackstone in his lectures at Oxford in 1765. In Blackstone's view:

the true excellence of the English constitution [is] that all the parts of it form a mutual check upon each other. In the legislature, the people are a check upon the nobility, and the nobility a check upon the people; by the mutual privilege of rejecting what the other has resolved: while the King is a check upon both, which preserves the executive power from any encroachments. And this very executive power is again checked and kept within bounds by the two houses, through the privilege they have of enquiring into, impeaching, and punishing the conduct (not indeed of the King, which would destroy his constitutional independence; but, which is more beneficial to the public), of his evil and pernicious counsellors. Thus every branch of our civil policy supports and is supported, regulates and is regulated, by the rest.

Now, although the mixed constitution of checks and balances between King, Lords, and Commons may have been the *theory* of the constitution, the precise *practice* of eighteenth-century politics was recognised as very much more basic. Executive power – the power to set down the broad policies to be followed by the state and the ability to carry out or execute the laws — was in the hands of the King, but the means for carrying it out had to be provided by parliament. If it were left to itself the House of Commons could produce independent members in a way that would make the King's Government impossible since it could refuse to grant the money needed to carry out his will. So, if clashes, deadlock, and instability were to be avoided, ways had to be found to ensure harmony between the three 'checking' institutions of the state. What this meant in practice was that the House of Commons had to be 'managed' by the King and the Lords.

Through their power of patronage, the King and the Lords were able to exert 'influence' over the composition of the lower chamber so oiling the relations between the King and the representatives of the people and cementing the elements of the constitution into some kind of working whole. Crudely expressed, corruption was of the political essence and was the practical counterpoint to the constitutional theory of balance. The King exerted his influence, not just because forty or fifty Members of Parliament held government posts, but because others in the House of Commons looked to him for financial help in fighting elections, or they looked to him for contracts, pensions, and favours for friends. For its part, the House of Lords was able to exert an influence in the context of a restricted franchise and a distribution of parliamentary seats that bore less and less relation to the actual distribution of the population at large. In 1830, 70 English boroughs had 100 or less voters; Old Sarum and Dunwich were uninhabited constituencies; and in 1793 it was estimated that 400 Members of Parliament out of a total of around 530 were nominated or dependent on noblemen in such a way that they were likely to lack the chance to display any real independence of mind in their parliamentary behaviour.

Constitutional authorities defended this general state of affairs and the restricted franchise and the unreformed House of Commons. No one in authority seriously considered that the labouring masses had any political rights. Moreover, there was the fear that if they secured the vote then they would destroy the delicate balance of the Constitution and much else besides. The conception of the political community which underlay this exclusive franchise, and the idea that corporate bodies (rather than individuals) should be represented, meant that the supporters of the theory and practice of the eighteenth-century constitution held the view that every major legitimate political interest *was* represented in Parliament – if not directly then at least 'virtually' through the broad mix of members from different places and of varying backgrounds.

The ideology surrounding the constitution was one thing, but, in hard-power terms, the balanced constitution was essentially aristocratic. At its worst it may have been a parasitic racket representing only itself to the detriment of all, but on the larger canvas of society it gave political power to a narrow group of substantial landowners in loose alliance with merchant princes and the small towns which returned members to Parliament. In stable times the constitution 'worked'. The trouble was that by the end of the eighteenth century times were unstable. New interests came into being which were outside of the established set-up. The middle classes, based on manufacture in the emerging industrial towns, and a working class made out of these self-same developments, gained a consciousness of the fact that they were unrepresented and politically disadvantaged within the eighteenth-century constitution. Manchester, Birmingham, and Leeds returned no members to Parliament. Long before the century closed, pressures were building up for constitutional change *and* for more profound changes in the social and economic system itself. The writing was on the wall for the old system: it was doubtful whether the established constitution could hold.

On the immediate constitutional front, corruption was attacked; virtual representation was no longer seen as enough; and whilst some attacked the rights of landed property in politics urging the principle that every man of means should be directly represented, some went further to attack the political privilege of all property arguing for the 'rights of man', complete equality, and a democratic republic based on the true sovereignity of all the people. One thing is very clear, the limited eighteenth-century political contest between Court and Country – between the ins and outs to government *within* Parliament – was transcended by a more fundamental division within society between those who wished to change the political and social order and those who were determined to defend the status quo, the eighteenth-century Constitution, and the established basis of representation. At the time there was the recognition that 'society was on the brink of a great struggle between property and population'. Not surprisingly, the nature of political argument shifted. New issues and a new vocabulary bubbled to the surface of public debate, and different answers came to be given to enduring questions about who should govern and how. More concretely, attention focused on Parliament. The corruption and reform of the House of Commons became *the* central issue dividing the supporters from the opponents of the existing political system.

As the excluded social forces grew in political strength, so they pressed in on the established constitution in ways which eventually caused it to buckle so that it came to be more in line with their views as to how things should be. In all of this, the Great Reform Act, 1832 stands as some kind of landmark development in the history of constitutional theory and political practice since it broke the essentials of the eighteenth-century constitution and also entrenched a new principle of governmental organisation. The passing of the act was associated with massive political unrest, and a campaign of civil disobedience hovered over the proceedings in Parliament. The act itself grew out of uneasy tensions and alliances between middle-class and working-class reformers and the entrenched aristocratic interest, in a situation in which the tie-up between class interests and politics was anything but neat, simple and easy to unravel.

The middle classes faced both ways and walked a tightrope. On the one hand they resented the entrenched power of the landed aristocracy. On the other hand they feared the working class who were also pushing for constitutional change against the aristocratic interest. They wanted the House of Commons to represent the opinion of the middle orders of Britain for (as one reforming MP put in 1830) 'there has arisen in the minds of the wealthy and enlightened middle classes of the country a conviction that there did not exist between them and the legislature a sufficient link'. But they did not want change and the link to be forged if it were to lead on to wild and radical measures for democracy, equality, and a social revolution that would threaten their larger position of power within the developing economy. For the middle classes Britain meant business and they wanted constitutional change to prevent revolution not promote it. This being the case it was seen as essential to set a financial qualification for the franchise that would give the vote to 'decent' farmers and shopkeepers whilst excluding the lower social orders who might use their votes to plunder the public purse for their own advantage.

For their part, although the die-hard aristocratic opponents of change were desperately anxious about opening the floodgates, they nevertheless came to see that the price of resistance was becoming too high and might even bring disaster and revolution. As they were forced to respond to the pressure for constitutional change the established interests saw a glint of light at the end of the political tunnel and came to entertain the hope that if the middle classes were allowed a subordinate share of power then they just might turn from being poachers to gamekeepers of the system and so side with the aristocracy in helping to keep the working classes in order. In other words, if it were possible to remove the grievances of the middle classes against those above them, then it might also be possible to nip off the danger of an alliance between the middle classes and the working classes below them. There was the hope that modest constitutional change might attach the middle classes to the established institutions of the country by making them consider the House of Commons as an ultimate tribunal where their grievances could be discussed and remedied.

Naturally enough, all of this placed the working-class organisations in a cruel dilemma. They were forced to ponder on whether the Reform Bill would end the old system, or, in aiding the middle classes, merely add to the strength and number of working-class oppressors. In fact, the act was a necessary, but not sufficient, condition for wider social upheaval, and it is impossible to pass a pat judgement on its political implications. In the longer run, a measure which drew the line between voters and voteless was bound to increase the consciousness of the latter in ways that would encourage an upsurge of working-class political aspirations. The act may have been intended as a 'final measure' by those who wished to steady things, but the flow of politics is rarely so easily contained by the comma of a constitutional concession. In the shorter run, however, the property qualifications for the franchise set down in the act did effectively exclude the working class from political participation through the ballot box, although the franchise itself was only increased by some 220 000 in England and Wales. At the time, what was of greater political significance was the redistribution of seats in the House of Commons. Small boroughs lost 141 members, and the newly developed industrial areas of the North and Midlands secured representation through the creation of 65 new seats. The British constitution was adjusting to the changed realities of economic power in the country at large.

The act affected the working of the political system in a number of significant ways so that it makes sense for us to see the constitution in very different terms from those which focused on the balance between King, Lords and Commons.

1 Although the politics of patronage lingered on, it was no longer possible for a small number of landowners to control the composition of the House of Commons, and the new independence this gave the Commons also reduced the controlling power of the King.

2 The personal will of the King was no longer decisive in government, and the effective choice of the Prime Minister and his leading Cabinet colleagues passed out of his hands and became a major role for a powerful House of Commons.

3 The act not only created a situation in which the House of Lords had to give way to the House of Commons, but in providing for the 'representation of the people' it admitted a new principle of linkage between the state and society. The House of Commons would no longer reflect the ancient idea and be representative of 'whole' boroughs, county communities, or corporate interests but would be representative of unorganised masses of individual men since at this time no women had the vote. The House of Commons was to become a representative assembly of independent members chosen by individual electors who had the right to vote and direct representation and, through this, the opportunity to enjoy government based on their consent and *indirect* choice.

Simply expressed, the 1832 act opened up a new political space. Members of the House of Commons came to enjoy power. They were at the centre of things. They also enjoyed a distinct autonomy from the Lords, the King, and the Ministers of the Crown. Moreover, although their constitutional and political position depended on their new relationship to 'the people' they were not instructed delegates of their constituents any more than they were at the mercy of the party whips in the Commons. So, the House of Commons *as a body* was independent of Lords and King, and Members *within* the Commons enjoyed an independence of action inside that chamber. The cumulative effect of all these developments quite simply destroyed the balanced constitution.

The dynamic between politics and the constitution – between practice and theory – had resulted in constitutional change. Social, economic and political developments crushed the eighteenth-century constitution and hence the credibilty of the established constitutional theory. This was noted by all manner of commentators in the middle years of the nineteenth century, but it was the banker, journalist, and cautious liberal, Walter Bagehot who provided the authoritative account of the new set-up in his study of *The English Constitution* published in 1867.

In observing the 'contrast' between 'the living reality' and 'the paper description' of the British constitution (in observing the gap between practice and theory) Bagehot did two things of significance.

1 He shot down once and for all the established accounts of British politics; they were 'quite wrong' as descriptions and explanations of how things worked.

2 He provided us with a new theory as to the essential reality of governing, in the period of classical parliamentary government, in the period when members of the Commons enjoyed a golden age of independence between the fall of patronage and the rise of highly organised political parties.

How, then, did Bagehot describe and explain the essence of the British Constitution: who governed and how?

Bagehot distinguished the 'dignified' from the 'efficient' parts of the Constitution. The dignified parts 'impressed the many' and secured public support so that the system was legitimised, but they did not actually govern or wield any real power. The efficient parts were not perceived as significant and powerful by the public but they nevertheless had power and 'governed the many'. Identify the efficient parts and you identify who governs; identify the dignified parts and you identify how they are enabled to do so.

Bagehot argued that the King and the House of Lords had ceased to exercise power and had become simply dignified parts of the constitution. The House of Lords could only delay and revise legislation, and in our 'disguised republic' the constitutional monarch always had to act on the advice of ministers responsible to the Commons. It was the House of Commons, and the Cabinet and the Prime Minister that came from the Commons, that Bagehot saw as the efficient working parts of the Constitution as these got on with the job of actually running the show. Bagehot argued that 'the relation of Parliament, and especially of the House of Commons, to the executive government is the specific peculiarity of our Constitution', and he made the point that 'the efficient secret of the English constitution may be described as the close union, the nearly complete fusion, of the executive and legislative powers'. In practice it is impossible to maintain any rigorous separation between executive power and legislative power – between the power to set down the broad direction of the state and to carry out the laws, and the power to make laws and general rules – and, in Britain, Bagehot saw the fusion as taking place in the Cabinet which he said was a committee of the legislative body chosen by the Commons to be the executive body and rule the nation. The House of Commons had a number of functions, but the elective function of choosing the Cabinet was the 'most important'. It was precisely this opportunity to make and unmake Cabinets which led Bagehot to argue that 'the ultimate authority in the English constitution is a newly elected House of Commons': 'we are ruled by the House of Commons'. This was putting the matter very tartly, and Bagehot recognised that things were not quite this simple. For sure Cabinets were made and unmade on the floor of the House, but the Cabinet for its part could unmake the House of Commons because it enjoyed the right to ask for a dissolution and after the election it could look for support from amongst members in a new House of Commons. It was precisely the subtlety of the checking relationship between Cabinet and Commons that led Bagehot to make the point that 'the English system...is not an absorption of the executive power by the legislative power; it is a fusion of the two'.

So, around the middle years of the nineteenth century, Britain was seen to have acquired a new liberal constitution – that is a constitution of limited public participation where there was an executive which was responsible to a directly elected parliamentary assembly and which had taken few powers to intervene in economy and society.

In the accounts of British politics which were published at the time, ministerial responsibility was seen as the key and essential principle of the whole system. Two kinds of responsibility were usually singled out.

1 In law and in theory, the individual minister was, in effect, the same as the Department: he was responsible for everything that went on in his office (whether he knew about it or not) and might be hauled over the coals and forced to resign if Parliament disapproved of his personal acts, the general conduct of his Department, or acts done (or left undone) in the name of his departmental officials.
2 There was the notion of the collective responsibility of the Cabinet or Government. Two things were involved here. On the one hand, an individual minister should resign if he could not publicly agree with the policy of the Cabinet as a whole. On the other hand, if the Cabinet as a whole was defeated on a major issue in the House of Commons then it should either resign (as happened five times between 1852 and 1859), or else ask for a dissolution of Parliament in the hope of being able to secure the support of a new House of Commons.

Informed commentators, then, came to describe and explain the working of the British constitution in the following way. A limited, but informed, middle-class electorate (composed of less than one in six adult males) enjoyed the right to elect persons of calibre and substance to represent their opinions and serve the national interest in the House of Commons. Constitutionally, and in theory, Parliament as a whole was sovereign since the House of Commons was but a part of Parliament and for a bill to become law the assent of Lords, Crown, and Commons were all needed. Politically, and in practice, however, the House of Commons was the working guts of Parliament, and, in addition, it alone had the job of selecting (and checking) the Cabinet as the executive to govern the country. The Cabinet, for its part, had to put policy before Parliament, and had to supervise the implementation of legislation through the control and coordination of the civil servants working in the departments of state. The civil service itself was obscured from view – it was simply composed of *servants* with no independent power. They were charged with administration and implementation (but no policy-making) and were controlled by, and responsible to, their elected political masters.

In effect, everything flowed to and from the House of Commons: the civil servants were held responsible to the Commons through their ministers; the Cabinet was collectively responsible to the Commons; the monarch only acted on the advice of ministers responsible to the Commons; and the Lords were always to defer to the legislative views of the Commons. For its part, the Commons itself was representative of a limited electorate although there was no expectation that the electorate, should, or would, seek to impinge on the independence of members' judgements. Britain was said to enjoy a system of responsible parliamentary government: power was in the Commons, and the Commons was responsible to the small electorate. There was little that was truly democratic about this constitutional set-up since it was a system that was only representative of those with property. Moreover, there was nothing egalitarian about the set-up and there was no expectation that the state would do much and interfere extensively in the 'private' sphere of power and economic arrangements: these were seen as best left to the unseen hand of 'impersonal' market forces. (See Chapters 8 and 9 for a discussion of the growth of state intervention since the nineteenth century).

Most authoritative commentators on British politics in the period between the Reform Acts, 1832 and 1867 did not just describe and explain our politics. They also applauded the constitution, and the pattern of political participation, class rule, and limited legislative activity that it embodied. The 1832 act aimed to give the 'middle orders' in society political influence and it also provided for a framework within which landed wealth and industrial wealth could adjust their conflicts of interest without resort to force. Bagehot exaggerated when he described the middle classes as 'the despotic power in England' but there is no doubt that the balance of power tilted away from the large landowners that dominated the House of Lords and towards the industrialists who were represented in the House of Commons. Having said that, industrialists never 'took over' the state. They were partly absorbed into the ethos of the aristocracy. They also worked towards and in alliance with the landed interest in the context of a low-profile, informal, state where there was a shared unease about the pressures for change that were coming from the lower social orders.

Would the balance of power tilt further; would the liberal constitution of limited participation and limited intervention be forced to expand outwards and assume a liberal-democratic form in which *all* adults had the vote? A liberal constitution of limited government based on the self-reliant individualism of a middle-class electorate, an 'independent' House of Commons, and government by consent, was one thing. A liberal-democratic constitution, with the danger of 'class legislation' (the phrase

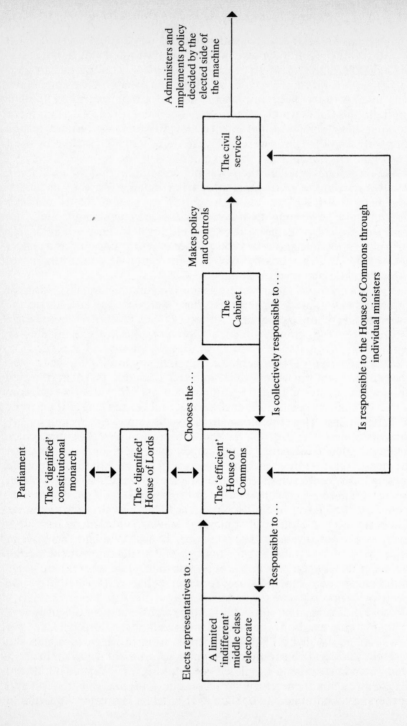

Fig. 1   THE LIBERAL CONSTITUTION OF PARLIAMENTARY GOVERNMENT

used to voice the fear of a working-class takeover through the ballot box) and an intrusion into the rights of property through the more direct, participatory, and collective democracy of a mandated House of Commons of delegates close to working-class constituencies, seemed to be quite another. Commentators were forced to ponder on the implications of allowing, or not allowing, the enfranchisement of the working class in a context in which either course of action seemed fraught with danger.

THE LIBERAL-DEMOCRATIC CONSTITUTION

Defending the 1832 settlement involved justifications which talked about the rights of those who had a propertied 'stake' in society with the related gloss that education was a prerequisite for the 'responsible' exercise of the franchise. Intellectuals of the age believed in parliamentary government, not a democratic system; in liberty, not popular government; and the spectre of social and economic equality itself was seen as the dark side of the claim for adult suffrage. All thoughtful Victorians were alive to the implications of industrialism. They knew that their society was riding a tiger. They were conscious of the ups and downs of working-class agitation for political rights, the vote – and more.

In theory (and in the long run) liberals, such as J. S. Mill, were prepared to recognise that representative government based on the whole people was the best form of government since political participation would promote the virtue, intelligence and 'development' of the people. In practice (and in the short run), however, they wanted to see government by the 'fittest'. Although they were keen to protect the governed from governmental oppression they were also anxious about the legislative implications of majority rule, fearing that popular participation would tumble into the chaos of working-class domination. Some were keen to shunt popular participation into the civic training ground of local government. However, the fear remained that excluding the working man from an involvement in the national political system could make for problems. Maybe the 'honest' working man would entrench himself in his own institutions and, in isolation, be a danger to the unity and strength of the whole nation; and maybe prolonged intransigence, accompanied by inevitable police control, would break down the divide between the labouring classes and the 'dangerous classes' so causing the popular forces to unite and assume a truly menacing character that would be beyond concessionary control. Perhaps it was even safe to yield. Maybe the working class was loyal and could be trusted to display 'goodwill' and deference to their 'betters'; and maybe there was even party advantage to be gained from seizing the initiative on reform.

Like it or not, democracy (which at the time meant votes for male workers) gradually came to be seen as inevitable. It became a question of making the best of a bad job. In the end a strange combination of working-class agitation and pressure from outside of the state system together with an increasingly confident upper-class establishment inside the system anticipating the pressures for change and trying to contain them both served to encourage the Conservatives to pass the Reform Act, 1867. This act made working-class males a majority of the electorate in the country at large. The act has been seen as one of the decisive events in modern English history because it transformed the country into something called, and approximating, a democracy. By 1886, two in three adult males – almost 4.5 million people – had the vote in England and Wales, whereas some 50 years earlier the electorate stood at little more than 650 000.

So, after a protracted struggle the liberal state – the state of limited participation and limited state activity – was grudgingly democratised. This is always noted. What is usually glossed over is the fact that, in the process, democracy came to be 'liberalised' in that its radical and egalitarian ideals were softened so that, in practice, democratic politics worked *within* the prevailing system of power in economy and society. Democracy ceased to embody the cry from below for the overthrow of the limited liberal state and the competitive market society to which it was connected. Instead democracy came to embody the more limited claim that the working class had the right to compete *within* the established state institutions and *within* the established society, with the clear expectation that they would not use the state to intervene in society to effect fundamental change. No working-class party immediately burst on to the scene to dance on the floor of Parliament. The politics of deference – the rich man in his castle the poor man at his gate – held change in check. Politically, the democratic aspirations of the popular-radical tradition were effectively contained within a Liberal movement dominated nationally by middle class and aristocratic elites, and the Conservatives mobilised many working-class Tories into their camp. In other words, democracy did not immediately deprive the upper classes, and the Liberal and Conservative Parties, of political leadership. They still carried the ball, but the electors moved from being spectators to doubling as occasional umpires as well. Contrary to the hopes and fears of those who had taken sides on the issue of democracy, political practice rather seemed to suggest that liberal (that is limited) democratic government and a class-divided society could fit nicely together without disaster and the overthrow of that society by democratic excesses. Here was cause for surprise and celebration. Here was cause for a new constitutional theory that would ease the liberal orthodoxy aside as at odds with the facts in order to describe, explain, and laud, the essentials of the new liberal-*democratic* constitution – a constitution in which there was an uneasy, and ultimately unstable, mix of the limited government of liberalism with the popular participation and equality of democracy.

Of course, there were important continuities between the liberal constitution and the liberal-democratic constitution. Notions of responsibility were still seen as of the essense, and the permanent, civil service, side of the state machine was still kept from focus. However, the injection of democracy into the prevailing set-up pulled 'the people' and political parties into view and there was a change of emphasis as to what was the constitution.

If the accounts of British politics between 1832 and 1867 pointed to the sovereignty of Parliament, then the accounts that came to the fore after that period made the additional point that the sovereignty of the *people* was behind this and was now of the constitutional and political essence. If the liberal accounts saw the House of Commons as at the centre of things, then the liberal-democratic accounts saw the Commons as a dignified part of the constitution that lacked real power. If Bagehot's text can be regarded as authoritative for the golden age of parliamentary government, then Albert Venn Dicey's *Law of the Constitution*, published in 1885, came to be regarded as authoritative for the period of parliamentary democracy since then.

Dicey was concerned to deal with the 'guiding principles' which he considered pervaded the modern constitution of England. He centred his attention on the sovereignty of Parliament, the conventions of the constitution, and the rule of law.

The sovereignty of Parliament meant that Parliament could make and unmake any law whatsoever; there was no higher legislative authority; and no court was in a position to declare Acts of Parliament invalid. However, Dicey went on to note that there were both 'internal' and 'external' limits to the actual exercise of this sovereignty. The internal limits derived from the 'nature' and 'character' of the sovereign, but it was the external limits that were seen as of especial significance in the context of a democratic polity. To this end Dicey distinguished legal sovereignty (which was with Parliament) from political sovereignty (which was with the electorate). Put another way, Dicey welded the established *theory* of parliamentary sovereignty onto the new *practice* of liberal-democratic government so creating the new constitutional theory.

The conventions, or unwritten rules, of the constitution were seen as of crucial significance since they secured 'in a roundabout way what is called abroad the "sovereignty of the people"' thus making for a governmental system in which 'the will of the electors shall by regular and consitutional means always in the end assert itself as the predominant influence in the country'. Simply expressed, the conventions of the constitution, in ensuring the supremacy of the House of Commons, have 'one ultimate objective. Their end is to secure that Parliament, or the cabinet which is indirectly appointed by Parliament, shall in the long run give effect to the will of that power which in England is the true political sovereign of the state – the majority of the electors.' Dicey felt able to boil the British constitution down to 'one essential principle': 'obedience by all persons to the deliberately expressed will of the House of Commons in the first instance and ultimately to the will of the nation as expressed through Parliament.' In his book on *Law and Public Opinion in England,* Dicey made the point that 'the English constitution had been transformed into something like democracy' going on to argue that 'in a democratic country the laws which will be passed, or at any rate will be put into effect, must be the laws which the people like'.

Since Dicey, most constitutional authorities for most of this century have seen liberal-democratic constitutional theory and British political practice as of one. Established constitutional theory has made sense of the British constitution and British politics in the following way. This, then, is the 'official' view of British politics.

All adults enjoy the right to vote in free general elections that must be held at least every 5 years. The extension of the franchise to all adults created a situation in which political parties had to compete for the mass vote and so had to organise the electorate to support their candidates at the polls. The electorate, for its part, no longer votes on the basis of the calibre of the candidates, but rather votes for a programme of policies and for the party which they wish to see form a government over the next 5 years. The party which commands a majority of seats in the House of Commons wins a general election. By convention, the monarch sends for the leader of the majority party in the Commons. The leader becomes the Prime Minister and forms a government by choosing the Cabinet from amongst party colleagues in the Commons and in the Lords. In theory, the Cabinet is still collectively responsible to the Commons, and so it is possible for a government to be defeated on a motion of no confidence in the Commons so that it would be forced resign, call for another general election, and face judgement at the polls. In practice, however, this is not the case because the party organises the Commons as well as the electorate and the leadership of the majority party forms the government and Cabinet. Rigorous party discipline ensures the party government of the day nearly always has the support of its parliamentary majority in the Commons. In this state of affairs, the liberal-democratic account of the constitution completely reverses the liberal account of the relationship between Commons and Cabinet. Instead of the Commons controlling and checking the cabinet, the cabinet and prime minister are seen as very much in control of the Commons. In consequence, the convention of collective responsibility (so central to the liberal constitution) becomes drained of much of its significance and Parliament as a whole is reduced to a dignified rubber stamp of the 'efficient' Cabinet and Prime Minister. The liberal accounts saw the cabinet as chosen by the Commons, but the liberal-democractic accounts see the cabinet as chosen by, and directly responsible to, the electorate itself. The Commons assume no mediating role of any significance in the process of cabinet formation: it is simply there to register the popular will in terms of the number of seats held by particular parties. Within liberal-democratic constitutional theory, the people have the ultimate political power and exercise it through general elections – elections that assume a place of quite massive constitutional significance. Liberal theories centre their attention on the almost free-floating power of the Commons, whereas liberal-democratic accounts by-pass the significance of the Commons in order to place a twin emphasis on the government (the Cabinet and the Prime Minister) and the people in special relationship each to the other. The constitutional authorities see a transmission of orders from the many to the controlling few in the government whereby votes inserted at one end of the system become popular public policies and laws at the other. An electoral chain of command pushes orders up so that the people control things at the same time as those in authority are responsible down to the people or to the government of the people. The people choose the government and the government carries out the policies on which it fought the election and controls the Commons and civil service. In a downward direction, the government is responsible to the people through a general election, and the civil service is responsible to the Commons – the representatives of the people – because the convention of individual ministerial responsibility is still in force (as 'proved' by the resignation of Foreign Office ministers in 1982 over the failure of the Foreign Office to anticipate the Argentinian invasion of the Falkland Islands). From the liberal democratic perspective on British politics everything flows to and from the Cabinet and the Prime Minister. It is they who govern, but in the last analysis it is the people who rule themselves. The leading authority on the constitution in the twentieth century, Sir Ivor Jennings, had no doubt that Britain was an outstanding example of a democratic system at its best because the rulers governed according to the will of the people in the sense that there was a 'close relation between the policies followed by the Government and the general ideas of the majority of the electorate'. He saw the whole machinery of government as keenly attuned to public opinion because the character of the government depended on the results of the last general election; because there must be an election at least every 5 years; and because the electors had a genuinely free choice between candidates putting forward different policies.

So the people are free, they choose their rulers, and the rulers govern according to the wishes of the people.

Chapter 4 will make it clear that there is today a crisis of credibility with respect to this particular theory of the constitution, but, even so, it is still actively promulgated as an account of the reality of British politics. In 1979, J. A. G. Griffith, Professor of Public Law at the London School of Economics, made the point that

'it is still quite common to hear the constitution described – even lovingly described – as a piece of machinery cleverly and subtly constructed to enable the will of the people to be transmitted through its elected representatives who make laws instructing its principal committee, the Cabinet, how to administer the affairs of the state, with the help of an impartial civil service and under the benevolent wisdom of a neutral judiciary. Not only is this the explantion given to thousands

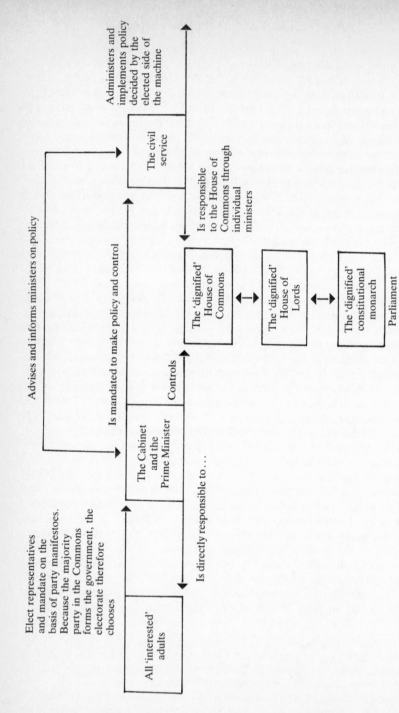

Fig. 2 THE LIBERAL-DEMOCRATIC CONSTITUTION OF CABINET, OR PRIME MINSTERIAL GOVERNMENT WITHIN A PARLIAMENTARY DEMOCRACY

of schoolchildren but I have to tell you that it also finds its way – in a more sophisticated form – into the curricula of some institutions of further and higher education.

Now, this sketch of the established liberal-democratic constitutional theory has been painted with a broad brush. It captures the fundamental agreement that has given a unity to the perspectives of leading constitutional authorities, but it does not reveal the disputes that have existed *within* liberal-democratic constitutional theory. Two disputes are of central significance with respect to the location of power in the state. First, there is the dispute as to the role of the civil service and the relationship between permanent civil servants and elected ministers. We will attend to this dispute in Chapter 5. Second, there is the dispute as to the respective powers of Cabinet and Prime Minister and we will deal with this now.

In the liberal constitution in the period of classical parliamentary government between 1832 and 1867, a variety of factors served to mean that there was a delicate balance between the Commons and the Cabinet (between the legislature and the executive) so that each could be said to enjoy a measure of power. With the coming of the liberal-democratic constitution after 1867, the rise of a mass electorate and the force of party organisation and loyalty inside the Commons changed the relation between the Commons and the cabinet. The cabinet moved into a position of greater power and control unchecked by the legislature, and the Commons was seen as having lost most of its powers because of the informal reality of party in government. In this system of Cabinet government, the Prime Minister was regarded as *primus inter pares,* as first among equals, and as just the leading member of the Cabinet team. In recent years, it has been argued that the position and powers of the Prime Minister have altered so considerably that it makes sense to talk about the rise of prime ministerial government and the transformation of the Cabinet into yet another 'dignified' part of the constutition. From this perspective, the Prime Minister is increasingly regarded as the keystone to the system enjoying unchecked and autocratic powers equivalent to an elected monarch and in excess of those enjoyed by presidents who have to contend with the legislature 'checking and balancing' their powers. What, then is the essence of the thesis about prime ministerial government and how adequate is that perspective on the location of executive power within the British constitution? What powers does the Prime Minister enjoy?

Power over the party. The Prime Minister is leader of the majority party in the Commons. The majority party want their leader to be successful and party loyalty is an important force within the British system.

Power over Parliament. In a situation in which the Crown can only act on the advice of her ministers and where the Lords have been stripped of powers, the Commons is the pre-eminent part of Parliament. Moreover, in a situation in which party organises the Commons, power over the party is also power over Parliament. Since a Prime Minister without a majority in the Commons is an impossibility, he or she is seen as in a position to make any law he or she sees as fit.

Power over the people. The mass media, and the television in particular, places the Prime Minister in the public eye as *the* government, and general elections have increasingly become personalised contests between rival party leaders. All this enhances the position of the Prime Minister and the Prime Minister is also in a unique position to control the flow of information about the work of government and can manage public information, publicity, and the media itself, to personal political advantage.

Power over the Civil Service. As government has expanded so has there been an increasing need to coordinate the administrative side of the state machine. The Prime Minister has the power to instruct the civil service on the conduct of its business and is aided in this task by a variety of formal and informal groupings at 10 Downing Street. The key civil servants look to the Prime Minister, and the Prime Minister is able to decide which civil servants will hold the most important positions in the departments.

Power over the Cabinet. The Prime Minister appoints ministers, reshuffles Cabinets, dismisses ministers, and promotes ministers. The fact of around 100 or so ministerial appointments in the context of the demise of the independent members and the rise of the career politician gives the prime minister a 'hold' over party colleagues because of his or her capacity to advance political careers. A minister who wants to climb the hierarchy is dependent on the Prime Minister, and the easiest way to earn prime ministerial gratitude is through loyal and obedient service. The Prime Minister has control over the machinery of the Cabinet, determining the agenda, setting up Cabinet committees, circulating (or not circulating!) papers written by Cabinet ministers for the Cabinet, and announcing the decision reached without taking a vote. The large size of the Cabinet; the increased activity of the state; and the limited time for 'efficient' Cabinet debate, all serve to encourage the Prime Minister to by-pass the Cabinet in favour of informal talks with individual ministers and a keen reliance upon an inner Cabinet of particularly trusted and sympathetic colleagues.

Power over ministerial conduct. In addition to the power to appoint, dismiss and promote ministers, all new Prime Ministers issue a personal minute of procedure for ministers which lays down a whole range of requirements for behaviour. The Prime Minister has the capacity to determine the scope of the various offices, or to take-over a department either in practice or by actually adding to his or her own responsibilities.

Other powers of patronage. In addition to prime ministerial patronage with respect to ministers and civil servants, the Prime Minister has the right to advise the Crown on the creation of peers; expects to be consulted with respect to the appointment of chairmen of nationalised industries; and can appoint ambassadors, chiefs of staff, and the heads of the security services (MI5 and MI6).

Power to decide how and when the government shall be terminated. Since the First World War, it has been recognised that the Prime Minister has the undisputed right to choose the date of a general election by asking the Crown for a dissolution of Parliament. Some commentators suggest that the power deters supporters from rebellion since they would be reluctant to create a situation in which they could be faced with an arduous election campaign that could jeopardise their seats. The threat of prime ministerial resignation may also serve to whip the Cabinet into line when less subtle forms of persuasion have failed.

The powers attaching to a Prime Minister are considerable, but what can we make of the thesis about prime ministerial government? Critics, whilst accepting that the powers of Prime Ministers *have* increased, suggest that the thesis as a whole exaggerates. It fails to consider the operation of informal, and often invisible, restraints on office and so lifts the Prime Minister out of the complex constraining context of action. For example, the Prime Minister does have the constitutional right (or 'prerogative') to choose the other ministers to form a government and administration, but no Prime Minister is ever politically 'free' in the exercise of this choice. It is a well-established convention that a minister should be an MP or a peer; the Ministers of the Crown Act, 1964 (in limiting the number of ministers and parliamentary secretaries that can sit in the Commons) forces the Prime Minister to select a nucleus of ministers from the Lords; leading figures in the majority party practically demand a Cabinet place – and a ministry of their choice; new young members need to be nurtured; and even leaders of factions within the party might have to be given office if only in the hope of softening their opposition to the broad drift of government policy. In a similar way, the fact that the Prime Minister is leader of the party and the fact that the majority party in Parliament invariably supports the Prime Minister's lead and the legislation set before them, does not 'prove' that the party itself is without influence over the Prime Minister. Leaders are only leaders because they have followers; no leader can for long ignore the views of followers; and the absence of overt party constraints on leaders should not blind us to the fact that leaders need to *anticipate* the reactions of their followers if they are to retain a measure of needed support and loyalty. Few things come for free, not even party support for a Prime Minister. Of course it is difficult to generalise over time and between parties with respect to the relations between party and Prime Minister, but in the recent past it has become clear that the Labour Party *outside* Parliament has been concerned to exert a greater measure of effective control over Labour Prime Ministers.

In fact, the whole prime ministerial government thesis presents us with a singularly 'flat' view of power that is only attentive to action on the surface. It fails to see the complex (and often hidden) *relational* aspects of power which effectively make a nonsense of simple statements about who has power. We need to explore the tricky fields of constraints, the power significance of inaction and no conflicts, and the extent to which the structure of executive power may be different with respect to different issues at different times. Simply expressed, it is next to impossible to generalise about the reality of prime ministerial government. When a government is weak and under pressure and when policies are seen to be failing, little authority may attach to a Prime Minister and the advantages of office are rapidly turned to personal disadvantage. Moreover, the secrecy that bedevils British government is of such a kind that it is hard to discover the truth on matters of state power. Cabinet memoranda are not published and the Official Secrets Act effectively prohibits anything but titbits of information coming onto the public agenda for consideration.

As in so many debates on the nature and location of power in Britain it is not possible to come to a firm and lasting conclusion as to the nature of prime ministerial power relative to the position of the cabinet since Prime Ministers have always differed in their degree of command of the cabinet. However, it is important to remind ourselves that the debate itself is a very narrow one once we are sensitive to the larger canvas of power in Britain. The debate only attends to *executive* power *within* the state and on the *democratic* (or elected) side of the state machine at that. In Chapters 5, 6 and 7, we will be attending to a world of power that is left unconsidered within the debate about prime ministerial government. This debate easily tumbles into a narrow institutional and constitutional approach to power and politics. The liberal-democratic constitution is seen as the only context and as the be-all-and-end-all of things so that the economic and societal context of power and the constraints which this imposes on Cabinet *and* Prime Minister alike are outside of the framework of serious consideration.

CONCLUSION

In this chapter we have pointed to the importance of coming to terms with the British constitution and constitutional theory since they are both in and about British politics. Both need to be studied, and studied historically, politically, and critically, and that rules out any reliance upon the constitutional approach. In substantive terms we have dealt with the development of things since the eighteenth century. The major theme has been to note the tension between constitutional theory and political practice, and the frequent limitations of established theory as an adequate explanation of the actual practice of British politics. The chapter has come to rest with a description of the currently established, liberal-democratic, constitutional theory – a theory which argues that the constitution provides for a system of Cabinet or prime ministerial government within a larger parliamentary democracy in which Parliament is legally sovereign and the people are politically sovereign.

So far we have not dealt critically with liberal-democratic constitutional theory, but in the chapters that follow we will begin to explore the cogency of this perspective as an explanation for British politics. We will start by attending to the part played by political parties and interest groups. At one time both were seen as sustaining of democracy in Britain. More recently, however, party and interest group practice has been seen as at odds with liberal-democratic theory. This tension between political practice and the established constitutional theory suggests that the constitution may once again be in crisis and liable to change, but we will not be dealing with those questions until Chapter 4.

WORKS CITED AND GUIDE TO FURTHER READING

Bagehot W. (1963) *The English Constitution,* edited and with an introduction by R. H. S. Crossman, London, Fontana.
The classic account of the liberal constitution in the period 1832 to 1867. The distinction between the 'dignified' and the 'efficient' parts of the constitution continues to be of importance, and Bagehot's anxieties about democratic government find an echo in writings on the constitution over 100 years later.

Benn, T. (1982) The case for a constitutional premiership, in *Arguments for Democracy* (ed. C. Mullin), Harmondsworth, Penguin.
A statement as to the immense powers of contemporary Prime Ministers and a powerful case for their being limited.

Blackstone, Sir W. (1809) *Commentaries Upon the Laws of England* 15th edn, 4 vols, London. T. Cadell & W. Davies.
Included is the classic account of the balanced constitution of the eighteenth century.

Brock, M. (1973) *The Great Reform Act,* London, Hutchinson.
Useful account of the factors leading up to the passage of the Reform Act, 1832 which enlarged the franchise and redistributed parliamentary seats.

Crossman, R. H. S., Introduction in Bagehot, *The English Constitution.*
Lively discussion of Bagehot and his ideas. Crossman himself makes the case that 'the post war epoch has seen the final transformation of Cabinet Government into Prime Ministerial Government'.

Dicey, A. V. (1950) *Introduction to the Study of the Law of the Constitution* 10th edn, London, Macmillan.

The classic account of the liberal-democratic constitution from 1867 onwards. Still in print; still widely used in courses on constitutional law; and still seen by many as a realistic and accurate account of British politics today.

Dicey, A. V. (1914) *Law and Public Opinion in England During the Nineteenth Century* 2nd edn, London, Macmillan.
Deals with the close connection between the laws passed by Parliament and public opinion in the context of a democratic polity. By the time the second edition was published, Dicey's commitment to individualism and 'freedom' had led him to regard democracy and socialism together as a grave threat to the country.

Griffith, J. A. G. (1979) The political constitution, *Modern Law Review*, **42,** 1–21.
Uncomplicated perspective on the contemporary constitution which is seen simply as the overall set-up, shaped by the shifting fortunes of real power.

Hanham, H. J. (ed.) (1969) *The Nineteenth Century Constitution 1815–1914,* Cambridge, Cambridge University Press.
Full and very thorough account of the nineteenth-century constitution, but rather long and dry and not very political or critical.

Himmelfarb, G. (1966) The politics of democracy: the English Reform Act of 1867, *Journal of British Studies,* **6,** 97–138.
Discusses the background leading up to the enfranchisement of the male working class and the implications of that development. Sees the act as of decisive significance in British politics.

Jennings, Sir I. (1941) *The British Constitution,* 4th edn, Cambridge, Cambridge University Press.
Schoolkids book on the constitution. All the liberal-democratic myths are there, lovingly laid out for the uncritical reader.

Jones, G. W. (1965) The prime minister's powers, *Parliamentary Affairs,* **18,** 167–185.
Puts the case against the prime ministerial government thesis.

Mackintosh, J. P. (1977) *The British Cabinet,* 3rd edn, London, Stevens and Sons.
Full historical account of the development of the Cabinet. Mackintosh argues that a fairly definite type of Cabinet government existed from the 1830s to the 1870s; there followed a period of transition leading to a form of prime ministerial government which he sees as assuming a fairly definite pattern from the late 1930s.

Mill, J. S. (1964) *Representative Government,* London, Everyman's Libarary.
The classic liberal case for representative government, but tinged by Mill's fear of popular participation and a working class franchise.

Rees, J. C. (1977) Interpreting the constitution, in *The Study of Politics* (ed. P. King), London, Cass.
A delightful essay critically assessing the interpretations of Sir Ivor Jennings, Sir Ernest Barker, L. S. Amery, and Harold Laski. Hard to get hold of but well worth the effort.

CHAPTER 2

Power, Parties and Pressures
Part I Political Parties

Democratic government is now established on two columns, parties and interest groups.

J. Blondel (1974) Voters, Parties and Leaders, *Harmondsworth, Penguin, p. 158*

Many familiar assumptions about the British party system are under challenge.

D. Kavanagh, Party politics in question, in D. Kavanagh and R. Rose (eds), New Trends in British Politics *London, Sage, 1977, p. 191.*

In the period after the Second World War, British political science came into its own. Political scientists who were in the intellectual vanguard chose to pay less attention to the constitution and to constitutional theory, and there was a growing consensus that the constitutional approach was a hindrance to understanding British politics. There was the call for a 'scientific' approach that would dig beneath the formalities of the constitution into the harder practice of informal politics, political behaviour, and the process of public policy-making itself.

Central to much of this new wave of work was the increased attention that was paid to political parties and interest groups. In this and the next chapter we want to critically explore three broad perspectives on the significance of parties and pressures in British politics.

1   For much of the period since the Second World War, *mainstream political science* praised parties and interest groups as enhancing of democracy in Britain and talked in terms of responsible party government and pluralist democratic theory.
2   From the mid seventies, the *New Right* came into intellectual and political prominence. Their perspective was anti state intervention and the practice of democratic politics, and pro the virtues of individualism and the freedoms associated with a free-market capitalist economy. Instead of seeing parties and pressures as enhancing of things they talked in terms of adversary party politics and an overload of interest group demands having harmful effects both politically and economically.
3   *Left, and Marxist, perspectives* on British politics are sharply critical of the political and economic status quo. They tend to focus attention on the state and the implications that flow from the capitalist economic base.

They are not particularly attentive to party politics (but they are critical of the Labour Party), although they are attentive to interests in British politics and are sharply critical of the pluralist perspective seeing the interest group world in terms of imperfect competition.

In this chapter we will deal with perspectives on political parties. In the next chapter we will deal with perspectives on interest groups, where we will also offer a concluding assessment of the ideas and theories discussed in both Chapters 2 and 3.

RESPONSIBLE PARTY GOVERNMENT?

Political parties have often been attacked as bad things in the body politic. In the 1950s, however, a particular *kind* of party system came to be regarded as utterly indispensable for the democratic control of government and that kind of party system was seen as well-established within British political practice. What, then, were seen as the essential elements of the British party model, and how do these elements add up so as to make for responsible party government and the popular control of public policy?

1 A *two-party system* with free regular general elections.
2 *One party forms the government.* The other party forms the opposition; criticises the government; keeps its ear to the ground of public opinion; and stands ready to form a government should it win the next election.
3 *The parties are in close competition* each with the other. Neither party can expect to be in permanent government or permanent opposition: each party 'swings' in and out of office. The competitive situation keeps the governing party on its toes and sensitive to the public's view of policy. The hope and prospect of office means that the opposition party will play by the established, conventional, rules of the game. This serves to ensure moderation and contain political conflict to manageable proportions, and it also sustains the legitimacy of the system of rule so enabling law to be enforced with only limited policing.
4 Parties aim to win office and they compete for the support of the electorate at the polls on the basis of *programmes of policies,* or manifestoes, that are set before the electorate for their judgement. In effect, the parties organise and simplify the alternatives into policy packages that give the voters a meaningful and effective choice, so ensuring that the electorate is 'consulted' at general elections with regard to fundamental legislative changes.
5 The fact of electoral competition, and the role of party programmes in that competition, means that parties try to draw up *popular programmes* of policies that will appeal to, and secure the electoral support of, the populace at large.
6 *Individual voters* are rational and informed; they have an appreciation of their own best interests; and so they *give the parties programatic*

support and vote according to the parties' past or prospective action in office in the light of their own knowledge and interests.

7 The party which wins a majority of seats in the House of Commons forms the government and has a *mandate* to put its programme of policies into legislative effect.

8 Each party is 'disciplined' and possesses sufficient *internal cohesion,* so as to ensure that once in office it is able to carry its programme through the House of Commons and into law. Members of parliament are not, therefore, individually responsible to the electorate since they are members of a party team that is collectively and directly responsible to the electorate as a whole.

In effect, parties are regarded as the midwives between the people and popular policies. If there are two parties each putting forward programmes which they are pledged to carry out if elected to government, and which they are able to carry out because they possess sufficient internal cohesion, then the electorate in choosing a programme (and a programme at that which has been drawn up to appeal to their interests) mandates a party to carry out its programme and holds the party accountable for its adequate fulfillment at the next election. If the electorate then considers that the governing party has broken its promises, or that the opposition party has since worked out more acceptable policies, it will vote out the established governing party and give the opposition party a chance. If this cycle obtains, then it is argued that government is controlled, and public policy is congruent with the wishes of the majority of the electorate for most of the time.

How adequate is this perspective on party politics in Britain? We have to attend to the evidence in four broad areas. First, do we have a two-party system? Second, do we have single-party government? Third, do parties put forward programmes of policies that are 'different' and offer a real choice, and is it the case that the winning party carries out its programme if elected to office? Fourth, do the electorate vote for a party on the basis of the programmes that are put forward, or is there a better explanation to make sense of voting behaviour and the nature of public support for parties?

Is Britain a two-party system?

We need to be careful in answering this question. First, we have to attend to the facts with respect to different periods of our politics. Second, we should recognise that a two-party dominance in the House of Commons may not reflect the pattern of electoral support in the country at large since our first-past-the-post electoral system makes it difficult for third parties to break through into parliament in proportion to their support in the country. For example, in the election of February 1974, the Liberals with over half of the votes of the Conservative and Labour Parties only secured 14 seats instead of the 122 to which they were proportionately 'entitled', and in the 1983 election the Liberal-SDP Alliance secured 26 per cent of the vote but only 23 seats whereas the Labour Party with only 2.2 per cent more of the vote won 209 seats. If the 1983 election had been fought under a system of proportional representation instead of a Conservative landslide in the Commons, the Conservatives would have had roughly 285 seats (and not 397), Labour 180 and the Alliance 160, resulting in a hung, three-party, parliament and a scramble to form a coalition.

Two-party dominance was at its greatest in the period between 1945 and 1970 when the Conservative and Labour Parties won all but 8 per cent of the vote and 2 per cent of the seats. The model of responsible party government was born of this experience and it tended to elevate the politics of the moment into a law of nature that has distracted attention from the more fluid aspects of Britain's political experience. The political turbulence of the 1970s and 1980s disturbed this cosy conceptualisation of things. In the election of October 1974, 25 per cent of the vote went to third-party candidates and they secured thirty-nine seats in the Commons. The election of 1979 seemed to mark something of a return to 'normal' in that third parties had their vote cut back to less than 20 per cent and they were only able to secure twenty-seven seats. In the election of 1983, however, third parties polled some 28 per cent of the vote and secured forty-four seats.

We now have a multi-party Britain, but we have yet to experience a fundamental departure from a two-party House of Commons. In the period after the First World War Labour replaced the Liberals as one of the two major parties in the Commons without the aid of proportional representation, but we will have to wait and see whether the Liberal–SDP Alliance can fight back into Parliament under the established first-past-the-post electoral system.

What are the facts about single-party government in Britain?

We can be brief in dealing with this question. Since 1900, Britain has been governed by outright, formal coalitions of two or more parties for 7 years between 1915 and 1922, for 1 year from 1931 to 1932, and for 5 years from 1940 to 1945. Between 1910 and 1914, 1930 and 1931, and 1977 and 1979 (the period of the 'Lib-Lab Pact'), the party in office lacked a majority in the House of Commons but was maintained in office by a tacit agreement with one or more smaller parties. From 1932 to 1940, Britain was governed by National Government which, although predominantly Conservative, was by no means wholly so. For a total of 3 years – in 1924, from 1929 to 1930, and from 1976 until the Lib-Lab Pact of 1977 – a minority government held office without even a tacit agreement with other parties. In other words, Britain has been ruled by a government of what is generally regarded as the normal British kind – a single-party government with a majority in the House of Commons, capable of getting its measures on to the statute book without open or tacit agreements with any other party – for only 54 of the 84 years of this century.

Party programmes

Three questions are before us when we attend to the evidence on party programmes. (a) Do the parties put forward programmes of policies? (b) Do the programmes offer a meaningful choice? (c) Do the winning parties actually implement their programmes and deliver of their mandate once in office? It is on these points in particular that the left perspective on party politics advances a critique against the 'reality' of responsible party government in Britain.

Do the parties put forward programmes of policies? In 1834, Peel was appointed prime minister. He issued the famous Tamworth Manifesto, nominally addressed to his constitutents, but actually communicated to the London daily press so as to operate as a programme submitted to the whole electorate. Since that time, and first fully developed by the Radical wing of the Liberal Party, it has been normal for parties to fight elections on the basis of a manifesto of policy promises. Moreover, over time, the manifestoes have tended to become longer and more specific. Of course, many policy statements are little more than vaguely embodied aspirations as to how parties would like to see Britain develop.

Blondel in his study *Political Parties: A Genuine Case for Discontent?* claims that 'in the great majority of cases programmes are unclear, often limited in scope, and not closely connected to the goals which the party proclaims' and he goes so far as to assert that 'on balance parties do not really have programmes'. This certainly overstates the situation, but there is no doubt that party leaders in Parliament like to keep a free (and vague) policy hand, and in their speeches and campaigning around election time they are more likely to attack opponents and invoke positive symbols than to get down to the specifics of their own party programmes. This tendency has been noted by left activists and left academics. The Labour Party has been consistently criticised for failing to put forward a clear radical and socialist programme. When it is pointed out that a number of Labour programmes *have* been markedly radical, as in 1945 and 1983, then it is claimed that the leaders have failed to be behind them and give them their solid backing and support.

Do the programmes offer a meaningful choice? One problem in analysing party programmes derives from the fact that there is no unambiguous index by which one can assess the extent of 'real' choice between them. Whether one thinks that the differences between the programmes are big or small, or too big or too small, depends on value judgements and political perspectives. Left academics have consistently held the view that there is no 'real' choice on offer to the electorate at the polls. They argue that a socialist alternative is not offered because the Labour Party is not so much concerned to *abolish* capitalism as to *manage* it better than the other parties. Having said that, however, most left academics and activists when it comes to the electoral crunch *do* vote Labour, excusing their commitment by saying that they do so 'without illusions' but perhaps signalling by their actions that they do see some kind of meaningful choice at the polls.

In fact, most commentators (and many left academics) would feel able to divide the post-war period into three distinct phases in terms of the kind of choice offered to the electorate by the parties in their programmes. First, the 1945 election would be regarded as some kind of high point in terms of the programme choice offered to the electorate by the Labour and Conservative Parties: Labour was out to create a new socialist Britain whilst the Conservatives were still rooted in the Old Toryism of empire and unregulated capitalism. Second, the 20 years from the mid-fifties provided a period of only marginal differences in programmes both from election to election *and* between the parties. This was the period of 'consensus politics'. Both the major parties were agreed as to the need for a welfare state and a mixed, but managed, economy that would soften the rough edges of capitalism as they cut into the needy. Under the leadership of Hugh Gaitskell, the Labour Party was dominated by a 'revisionism' that edged away from socialism and dropped a commitment to the nationalisation of private industry. For its part, the Conservative Party, under the intellectual leadership of R. A. Butler, came to terms with the changes wrought by Labour from 1945–51 and adjusted to the new mood in the country so that it grudged towards state intervention in support of some kind of equality. This, then, was the age of 'Butskellism' – the age of consensus and social stability. Third, the political turbulence of the seventies born of economic failure and increasing unemployment, destroyed consensus and brought 'conviction politics' and real choice back to the fore with a vengeance: the Conservatives rediscovered old roots in their opposition to state intervention and their commitment to the free market; the Labour Party rediscovered socialism and attacked the free market of capitalism at the same time as they were eager to fashion an interventionist state; the specifics of nationalist sentiment ebbed and flowed in unpredictable ways; and only the Liberal–SDP Alliance seemed eager to try and recreate the moderate consensus politics and policies of the fifties, and they did this despite growing signs that the social and economic conditions that made those policies viable had ceased to exist.

Do the winning parties actually implement their programmes and deliver of their mandate once in office? Now, it is one thing for parties to produce programmes which offer a choice, but it is quite another matter as to whether the parties actually implement their programmes once in office.

In fact, a great many of the most important decisions by British Governments have been introduced without any prior leave by the electorate as has been the case with respect to the repeal of the Corn Laws, 1846, the passing of the Trades Disputes Act, 1927, the departure from the Gold Standard in 1931, the decision by the post-war Labour Government to opt for a nuclear-defence policy, the decision to apply for membership of the European Economic Community in 1961, the passage of the Commonwealth Immigration Act, 1968, as well as a host of foreign-policy matters over the years. Moreover, the very stuff of electoral competition and the media coverage of our politics revolves around the issue of 'U turns' and 'broken promises' with politicians confessing (but excusing and explaining) the gap between promise and performance – programme and policy – with talk about being 'blown off course' by circumstances, accidents, and the pressure of unanticipated world events beyond their effective grasp or control. Naturally enough this kind of discourse is not unrelated to the facts of the situation. The 1970 Conservative manifesto, *A Better Tomorrow* stated: 'we will stop further nationalisation' but this did not stop a Conservative Government nationalising Rolls Royce just 8 months into office. The manifesto also stated 'we utterly reject the philosophy of a compulsory wage control' but in 1972 such a policy was implemented before collapsing into failure. (For a fuller discussion of this see Chapter 8.) For its part, the Labour Government of 1964–70 did a 'U turn' on a number of pledges (most notably by restoring charges for the health service), and although the party entered office in 1974 with a series of clear policy commitments more radical in tone and in aspiration than any that the party had endorsed since 1945 the promise of industrial regeneration and social justice was in the end renegued. The contrast between the aspirations of opposition and the actual development of policy in government could hardly have been starker. Given these kind of records, it is perhaps not too surprising that Blondel can claim that the implementation of party programmes is 'spasmodic and half-hearted' and that the influence of programmes on policy-making is 'rather weak'. In fact, the evidence is more complex than this simple assertion suggests.

Rose, in his book *Do Parties Make a Difference?*, argues that 'the 1970–74 Heath Government fulfilled at least 80% of its manifesto pledges...[and] the 1974–9 Labour Government...acted unambiguously upon 54% of its manifesto commitments and gave some evidence of action upon another 19%'. However, and rather more fundamentally, Rose goes on to make the point that 'the gap between what governments can do and what the public (and for that matter, the government) wants to achieve is greatest in the management of the economy'. In effect, governments implement the 'small scale "do-able" policies' and so 'fulfill most of their pledges', but the production of promised 'economic benefits...appear to lie beyond the reach of either party'. So, 'parties do make a difference in the way Britain is governed...[but] the differences in office between one party and another are less likely to arise from contrasting intentions than from the exigencies of government'. Rose goes on to make the point that 'parties are only part of the political system' and 'much of the party's record in office will be stamped upon it by forces outside its control'.

Interestingly, this is exactly the kind of argument developed and elaborated by left academics in their critique of 'Labourism' and the 'Parliamentary Socialism' of the British Labour Party. They argue that to rely exclusively on the electoral or parliamentary road to the goal of socialism is to shut-off the possibility of attaining that goal precisely because it *overestimates* the power of party and the democratic state; underestimates rival centres of power; and minimises the moderating implications of parliamentary democracy and much else besides. In other words, Labour, through control of the House of Commons, may form a government but it will not be fully in *power* because there is power in the secret state, in the private centres of economy and society, and in the international market itself, and all of these things lie beyond the easy grasp of a parliamentary majority. We will be discussing these matters in later chapters. For the moment, however, we should recognise that the concern to strengthen intra-party democracy through constitutional reforms designed to hold the Parliamentary Labour Party accountable to the rank and file. may do little to ensure that any future Labour Government delivers of its manifesto (and possibly socialist) promises since these reforms do not come to terms with power, the state, and the market. Simply expressed, good intentions and intra-party democracy can only carry socialism so far.

Does the electorate vote for parties on the basis of their programmes or policies?

Our final 'test' of the responsible party model involves attending to the nature of public support for parties. It is easy to berate parties and governments for their failures and shortcomings with respect to programmes and implementation, but the conception of government by responsible parties requires certain things of the general public. How informed are the electorate about policies and programmes, and do they vote for parties on the basis of their programmes?

If we look back to the middle years of the nineteenth century and to the debates about the extension of the franchise to the working class then hopes were expressed as to how voters *should* behave at the same time as there was anxiety and fear as to how they *would* actually behave. On the hopeful front, there was the view that voters should be either rational and informed, or deferential. On the darker side, there was the fear that ignorance would rule and that deference would fail to hold things in check. Bagehot was anxious that the established parties might bid for the support of the working man, and he was even more anxious that a working-class party might arise that would then press for the interests of that class through the ballot box and through Parliament. So, on the one hand, hope that reason and deference should prevail; on the other hand, fear that ignorance and the politics of class and class conflict would actually prevail.

In the years since those debates we have witnessed the rise of the Labour Party and the specific concern to secure independent working-class representation in the House of Commons. Moreover, on the academic front, the detailed empirical study of electoral behaviour through sample surveys has come into its own so that we now have a great deal more information on which to explore the hopes and fears of those who took sides on the issue of democracy at the same time as we are provided with information to check out the reality of key elements of the responsible party model in Britain.

At the most general level, we can say that the electorate has not lived up to the hopes of those who looked to an active and informed public involvement in policies and elections. More specifically, the model of responsible party government carried within itself the view that the electorate would not just be informed about politics but would vote for the party which has a programme of policies in accord with their own view as to how things should be. Moreover, the 'floating' voters – those who were not in total agreement with any party – would stand above the party battle and would carefully assess the rival policy packages on offer before casting an informed vote, affecting the swing, and determining which party would form the next government. Early electoral studies have revealed just how far these pictures are removed from the realities of electoral choice. Voters had limited information about the policy positions of the parties and often supported a party in spite of its policies instead of because of them. Moreover, some studies suggested that the crucial floating voters were not characterised by a high degree of interest, involvement, and knowledge, but by ignorance and indifference, and they were less involved in following the election campaign than were those who were keenly attached to a party.

In 1963, Butler and Stokes began a series of surveys which set a new pattern, and a new standard, for the study of voting behaviour in Britain: their sample was large, nation-wide, and was interviewed several times between 1963 and 1970; and the authors were concerned to apply a rigour that had been absent from most of the earlier single constituency studies of electoral choice. Quite simply, *Political Change in Britain* is the landmark text in the field of voting behaviour research. What light does it throw on the extent of public information about parties and programmes, and on the nature of public support for parties?

Butler and Stokes 'challenge any image of the elector as an informed spectator', noting how 'understanding of policy issues falls away very sharply indeed as we move outwards from those at the heart of political decision-making to the public at large', and how attitudes are formed towards even the best-known policy issues to only a 'limited degree'. Having said that and confirmed the conventional wisdom, however, Butler and Stokes went further. They were concerned to push beyond the simple and trite observation that issues do not matter in electoral politics in order to ask a more detailed question as to the 'terms' on which they are likely to matter. They point out that three conditions must be met if an issue is to affect the relative standing of the parties at the polls. First, the issue must be one on which attitudes are widely formed (and the vast majority of issues fail such a test); second, opinion on the issue must be skewed rather than evenly balanced; and third, the public must see the parties differently in relation to the issue. During the early sixties Butler and Stokes argue that social services was an issue that satisfied the three conditions; its effect was 'substantial'; and it 'worked strongly to Labour's advantage' – although their evidence for all of this was weak. By and large, however, they argued that the behaviour of the electorate was shaped less by their stance to particular policy issues and more by generalised attitudes and beliefs about the party's 'image', and they specifically pointed out 'how little the mass of voters could be said to respond to the policy alternatives at Westminster in judging the claims of the rival parties'. So, there is little in this study to sustain the hopes of nineteenth-century liberal-democrats or to confirm the adequacy of the responsible party model as a realistic characterisation of the behaviour of voters in our politics. Indeed, the conventional wisdom on these matters over the whole of the post-war period has held that a majority of people are either ignorant of, or disagree with, the specific policies of the party they support.

When we are dealing with the literature on voting behaviour, we are dealing with a literature that has come to display turbulence in the face of electoral behaviour that has become increasingly volatile and unpredictable. Put another way much of the conventional wisdom looks rather tired in the face of emerging realities. Alt and associates, in their study of the electorate at the time of the February 1974 election, argue that it is easy to exaggerate the extent to which voters are politically illiterate, unfamiliar with issues, and unable to identify the policy stands of the parties. They suggest that the weakening of party identification may mean that voters' preference on issues will be determined less by established patterns of party identification and more by their own positions and their perceptions of party policy. Simply expressed, in a situation in which voters detach themselves from a close identification with parties then issues come to assume a greater significance in voting behaviour and electoral choice. It is difficult to come to a firm view on these matters, but the nature of support for third parties is clearly of particular significance and affords a crude test of the Alt view – especially in the case of new parties where there can be no established sense of partisan identification. What sense can we make of support for these parties at the polls? Is it based on the positive pull of their policies, or is it more of a protest vote reflecting a generalised sense of disenchantment with the workings of the two-party politics? Information on the nature of public support for the SDP throws a certain amount of light on these kind of questions because the party was not formed until 1981.

At the very outset, the party leadership took the view that manifestoes and policy promises were part of the 'old' politics that was responsible for Britain's troubles. In taking this view they clearly struck a chord with their potential supporters since there was a developing sense of unease about the established parties failing to deliver the promised policy goods. A poll carried out into the reasons why people voted for the SDP candidate in the Warrington by-election of 1981 revealed that only 9 per cent did so because they supported SDP policy; 8 per cent did so because they admired the well-known candidate; and nearly 70 per cent voted for 'negative' reasons – the most frequently cited being their opposition to the extremism of the two established parties. In the general election of 1983, 63 per cent of the vote for the Liberal–SDP Alliance was motivated by dislike for the other parties rather than by a positive liking for their own party of choice – still less for their policies. This kind of evidence does little to suggest that support for new parties is 'rational' and based on an informed judgement as to party policy. Indeed, we might even be inclined to suggest that third parties that are buoyant in the opinion polls, and have a diffuse appeal beyond specific regions, are only able to sustain their support on the basis of an attractive ambiguity about their main policy objectives that precludes the presentation of crisp programmes and, therefore, the possibility of programmatic support.

Breaking the mould of British politics may mean breaking the legitimacy of programmes, manifestoes, and the ideology of responsible party government itself. Of course, the electorate may not be fools, and they may pass 'rough judgements' at the polls about which party may govern 'better' in the future in the light of past performance and potential promise, but there is little point in our pretending that we can 'explain' voting behaviour on the basis of the electoral appeal of party programmes even though this is the way politicians and the media often tend to present the essence of electoral politics and party choice. In Chapter 6, we shall see that, in order to make sense of voting behaviour and party choice, it is vitally important to attend to the significance of sociological factors rather than to the more obvious political factors that bear on issues, parties, candidates, and leaders.

Taken together, the evidence assembled under the four points of assessment rather suggests that the conventional model of responsible party government is at odds with the facts and so does not provide an adequate explanation for party politics and the making of public policy. It has been true in *parts* for a *period* of British politics but it is not the theoretical key to unlock the essence of things as was once thought to be the case. We are not alone in taking this view.

ADVERSARY PARTY POLITICS?

For much of the period since the Second World War the responsible party model was at one with the informed consensus and 'common-sense' as to the working of our system. The conditions of the fifties meant that it was 'natural' for praise to be heaped on to democratic politics since it seemed to be doing the job very nicely. Capricious economic forces were managed by democracy so that slump and unemployment were things of the past, and a welfare state had been created by democracy so ensuring that wealth and poverty (and hence any material basis for class conflict) were also cast into the dustbin of history. In the sixties, the mood of buoyant self-satisfaction gave way to a mood of self-doubt and angry introspection. On the welfare front poverty was rediscovered, and on the all-important economic front there was a growing awareness that we just could not get adequate growth out of our stagnant economy. The concern to solve the problem of our economic decline in the context of a competitive world situation encouraged the search for explanations for that decline. There was increasing discussion of the relationship between the poor performance of the British economy and certain features of the political system.

By the seventies, and part-and-parcel of the demise of consensus and the rise of conviction politics, the New Right had grown and was in a position of political and intellectual prominence. From this perspective democratic politics, and the two-party system in particular, was *the* problem and the cause of our economic ills. Nowadays, most political scientists no longer praise the responsibility of our party system but instead talk of, and condemn, our system of 'adversary politics', where an 'electoral auction' is said to lead to an irresponsible 'elective dictatorship', which then manages the economy in such a way as to create an injurious 'political-business cycle' that hinders our long-term economic growth. So, at one and the same time, we have been provided with a new characterisation of the British party system that challenges the cogency of the responsible party government model, *and* we have also been provided with an explanation for economic policy-making and for the decline of Britain's economy. What, then, is the precise nature of the adversary politics thesis? How adequately does it make sense of party politics? How adequately does it account for the development of economic policy and the poor performance of the British economy?

The adversary system, based on a party duopoly of seats in the House of Commons and party monopoly (or an elective dictatorship) of the government, has come to be seen as our national style of politics. Within the Commons it is said to lead to constant petty squabbles; the mindless negation of government through excessive (and purely partisan and irresponsible) opposition; the oversimplification of complex issues into two (and only two) contrasting alternatives; and the grand clash and confrontation of the cult of debate. All of this is said to crush consensus and cooperation, and to destroy any basis for stable, moderate, and pragmatic policies that survive over the lifetime of one government. Left of centre policies alternate with right of centre policies violently, rapidly, and on the basis of ideological considerations alone unrelated to the 'real' needs of the situation. A Committee sponsored by the Hansard Society for Parliamentary Government to 'look at problems arising out of the apparent failure...of government and industry to work together effectively' argued that 'industrialists have been justified in recent years in criticising the government for failing to provide a stable economic framework within which they can plan and invest in the long-term'. The committee pointed out that 'industry cannot grow steadily in a situation where industrial policy three years from now could be in the hands of politicians of utterly opposed political views'. Evidence from leading industrial companies to the Trade and Industry Sub Committee of the Expenditure Committee of the House of Commons in 1973 made it clear that too frequent changes in government policy and in the nature of controls and incentives covering the location of industry had led firms gradually to discount government policy when considering new investment in a way that was injurious to growth and the creation of new employment.

Not too surprisingly, this kind of perspective on Britain's economic and political troubles has been best expressed by third parties outside of the established adversarial two-party system. In *Twelve Tasks for Social Democrats,* issued on the day of its launch in 1981, the Social Democratic Party made the point that in order 'to secure Britain's livelihood in the nineties we need a consistent economic strategy in the eighties, one that is not disrupted every few years by a political upheaval' and by 'pointless conflict, the dogma, the violent lurches of policy and class antagonisms that the two old parties have fostered'. In *Towards a New Political Agenda,* published in 1977, the Liberal Party had no doubt that

Britain's political structure obstructs economic and social reform. The stylised confrontations of adversary politics produce heated debate and a flood of legislation but rarely encourage reassessment of the conventional wisdom or result in agreed and constructive change. The cycle of government proposals and opposition promises of repeal, repeated with each change of government, has disrupted economic and industrial relations, disturbed the housing market and the education system and reshuffled the pattern of Whitehall, without achieving any new consensus or reversing Britain's decline.

Those who criticise adversary politics because of its alleged tendency to lead to frequent reversals in economic policy see the problem compounded by the fact that government within this system is unduly influenced by the extremists in the party ranks. Moreover, and to add insult to injury, these off-centre policies are never supported by a clear majority of the electorate. The electorate's views are seen as stable, centrist and moderate, but, in the context of an electoral system that bolsters the two-party system and blocks the easy rise of third parties of moderation, the House of Commons is 'unrepresentative' and the party activists unchecked. So (it is argued), a party comes to power claiming a mandate to implement its manifesto of seaside promises, and in the process established policies are mindlessly repealed in the struggle to deliver election commitments and please the party faithful. However, as the reality of the economic situation presses in on the government so it is inevitable that more sensible and pragmatic policies are adopted 2 or 3 years into office. Unfortunately, just as these newer policies begin to bear fruit, the country is hurled into the turmoil of another general election and the cycle of misguided mandate and policy change starts all over again. These bouts of manifesto madness, U-turns, and broken promises, not only frustrate business confidence but also lead to public disillusion so that authority dribbles out of government and the legitimacy of the overall system is called into question. In other words, the adversary system is said to have both economic costs *and* political costs.

Now, the economic costs attributable to the adversary system are not just seen as a function of the frequent reversals of *ideologically* motivated policies. Critics of our two-party system also point to the injurious implications that flow from the 'vote motive' and the *practical* effects of electoral competition within the political market place. Simply expressed, the fact that party politicians are operating within an 'unfair' electoral system in which the name of the game is to secure votes in order to win governmental power means that elections are turned into policy auctions in which the parties, through their manifestoes, bid for popular support and the highest (and most irresponsible) bidder wins all. On the 'supply' side the parties will always be tempted to bribe the electorate and promise more than they can safely deliver after the votes are in the bag. Moreover, this pattern will be reinforced on the 'demand' side of the electoral equation. First party competition will generate 'excessive' expectations in the electorate. Second, the electorate will have every incentive to vote for more government services because they do not pay for them directly and individual tax payments may bear little (if any) relationship to the benefits which they may derive from such services. In other words, the system of competitive vote bidding acts like a ratchet encouraging ever more government services at the same time as it penalises a government prepared to take 'tough' decisions that may hit particular interests in the short run even though these decisions may work to the advantage of all in the longer run. Moreover, the higher taxes that are an inevitable counterpart of more government services not only act as a disincentive to saving and investment, but also 'overload' the economy and crowd out opportunities for economic growth at the same time as the opening up of export markets and the defence of the home market is made ever more difficult by the inevitable inflation.

Although the government has to operate within the context of the economic realities of the day and 'should' have regard to the long-term interests of the economy as a whole, critics of adversary politics point out that a short-term concern for vote maximisation at the next general election is never far from the government's mind and this conditions the way in which it manages the economy and makes economic policy. Finer, in his study of *The Changing Party System,* is not alone in taking the view that it is a 'matter of proven fact that governments try to manipulate the economy to improve material conditions in time for the next election'. Now, observations of this kind are not new. They have been the commonplace stuff of the party political debate that is adversary politics. What is new is that this phenomenon of the political management of the economy is being more systematically and seriously explored within the burgeoning New Right literature on the 'political-business cycle'.

This literature, whilst being mindful of the ordinary business cycle of boom and slump, growth and recession, is especially mindful and critical of what is seen as the increasing coincidence between the five-yearly election cycle and the rhythm of the economy. It is suggested that governments, in managing the economy, have to work out a trade-off between inflation and the level of employment. They have to do this because it is seen as impossible to have both low inflation *and* a high level of employment since the former requires a low level of demand whereas the latter requires a high level of demand to keep people in jobs making things for sale. The trouble is that governments are said to manage demand and work out the inflation-employment trade-off with party political electoral considerations uppermost in their minds. As an election approaches, the government of the day will pump money into the economy and so engineer a boom, lower unemployment, and win popular support at the polls in the hope of securing another term in government. Immediately after the election, however, the party in government will find it necessary and politically safe to raise unemployment in order to combat the inflation that was itself set in train by the politically engineered pre-election boom. It is argued that this politically motivated business cycle is bad because it shifts the economy away from 'natural' long-run optimal levels of steady growth. Simply expressed, it is claimed that state intervention in the management of the economy, and a commitment to maintaining full employment, has actually caused a high level of inflation. This has made it difficult for Britain to compete on the world market, and this in turn has eventually led to a worse slump and level of unemployment than would otherwise have been the case had there been no political intervention in the working of the naturally self-regulating free economy of the market.

The party political implications of all this in the context of the language of everyday politics are clear enough. Those who are critical of governments creating political-business cycles are critical of state intervention in the economy at the same time as they are full of praise for the beneficial effects of free-market progress. This is the language of the

New Right. It is also the language of Thatcherism. At its hard edge it is critical of the threat of socialism itself, but it is also critical of Keynesianism – that theory of economic management which dominated the political consensus from the Second World War to the mid-seventies and which sought to maintain full(ish) levels of employment on the basis of governments managing the economy by manipulating the level of demand by putting money into, or taking it out of, the economy. We will be discussing Keynesianism more fully in Chapter 8, but for the moment we must attend to the adequacy of the adversary politics thesis. Is party politics like that, and does the thesis explain policy-making and Britain's economic 'failure'?

At one level we can suggest that the adversary politics perspective is more at one with the reality of party politics than is the thesis about responsible party government in Britain, but we really need to attend to the facts with respect to two broad areas of concern. First, there may be the rhetoric of party political conflict and policy change, but what is the reality with respect to the continuity and stability of economic policy? Second, what is the evidence on the nature of political-business cycles in Britain?

Andrew Gamble, in an article on 'Continuity and discontinuity in economic policy', has explored the first question with great care over the period 1960–81. He is sensitive to the problem of testing the thesis since it is difficult to separate out the influence of parties and politicians from that of other institutions, groups, interests, and the whole context of economic policy-making. Moreover, he highlights the necessity of clarifying the meaning of continuity and of economic policy, pointing out that economic policy can be divided into three principal areas. First, there is foreign economic policy-making involving the external relations of the national economy to the world economy; second, there is stabilisation policy and the whole field of macroeconomic policy and the 'management' of the economy; and finally, there is industrial policy covering all those aspects of governmental responsibility over the economy aimed at improving long-run efficiency, output and productivity. So, how many policies were reversed by the incoming government, and which policies and areas of policy were left untouched? Gamble argues that the adversary politics thesis over-generalises from a few instances to the whole of economic policy. The thesis comes into its own with respect to industrial policy where significant discontinuities in policy *can* be attributed to the government changing hands. But with respect to foreign economic policy (excluding the issues of our membership of the European Economic Community) and stabilisation policy the evidence for continuity is rather more plain than the evidence for discontinuity. Many of the major issues have rarely entered the adversary debate; changes often turn out on examination not to be related to parties at all; and in the all-important field of foreign economic policy-making (which sets the limits which shape the rest of economic policy) the continuity of policy and its generally non-controversial character is what is striking. It is hardly surprising that Gamble concludes that 'there is only limited evidence that there have been significant discontinuities in economic policy-making caused by the adversary positions adopted by the parties'.

What of the facts with respect to political business cycles in Britain? Nordhaus has looked at the evidence in nine countries over the period 1947–72. He found that although the coincidence of business and political cycles was 'very marked' with respect to the United States, New Zealand and Germany, this was *not* the case with respect to Britain because pressing action on the balance of payments swamped the cycle of economic policy-making revolving around elections. Alt's book on *The Politics of Economic Decline* has explored the nature of political business cycles in Britain alone and has dealt with the possibility that governments might run the economy to their own electoral advantage through manipulating the rate of inflation, disposable incomes, and unemployment in such a way as to rally short-run popular support at election time. He finds no real evidence of any government attempting to hold down the rate of inflation in the short run in order to promote its own popularity at election time. Before the elections of 1964, 1966, and 1970, real personal disposable income *was* rising at more than double its normal rate of growth – so supporting the political business cycle thesis, but Alt suggests that these 'short pre-election spurts may not do the government of the day all that much good, and there is no evidence that they do (at least if short-term enough) the economy any particular harm'. He suggests that there is little evidence that any British Government ever managed the unemployment rate simply with a view only to winning the next election. Alt is wisely tentative in his conclusions given the nature of the available data but he is prepared to argue that there is 'no evidence that any British Government in the period [since 1964]...believed it could "steal" an election by mortgaging the future in the interest of an economically better present'. The problem with the political-business cycle literature lies in the fact that it attempts to deal with the popularity of governments and the nature of public policy-making *solely* on the basis of a consideration of economic variables alone and so isolates the economic dimension out of the larger political context and ignores the vital part played by non-economic factors in contributing to electoral success. The argument that governments (foolishly and shortsightedly) attempt to win electoral support through the creation of mini-booms and full-employment at the cost of inflation just before an election approaches *does* accord with the common-sense of the fifties and sixties but the evidence is by no means entirely supportive of this perspective. Moreover, the Conservatives won the election of 1979 with a specific commitment *not* to manage the economy on the basis of short-run considerations alone, and they won again in 1983 *without* creating a mini boom and with over 3 million unemployed which surely confounds a thesis which suggests that economic good times are the major route to electoral success.

All things considered, then, we should be cautious in taking on board the view that economic policy-making and economic decline are explained by the adversarial nature of the two-party system. We say this, not simply because of the weight of evidence we have just set down, but because of two additional factors of significance. First, we should remember that the British economy has been in relative decline compared to the rest of the world for a hundred or more years – long before there was ever any concern expressed about adversary politics. Second, we should not forget that political parties are only a *part* of the political system and they are not in sole control of Britain's economic destiny. As this book unfolds we will be considering the impact and significance of other centres of power within polity, economy and society, but first we will be exploring the part played by interest groups within British politics. Theories of party politics may not be able to unlock the essential reality of British politics and public policy-making, but what of interest groups?

WORKS CITED AND GUIDE TO FURTHER READING

Alt, J.E. (1979) *The Politics of Economic Decline,* London, Cambridge University Press.
Detailed consideration of a mass of survey data on the public response to the economic decline of the sixties and seventies. Chapter 7 deals with 'Political business cycles in Britain'.

Alt. J.E., Sarlvik, B. and Crewe, I. (1976) Partisanship and policy choice: Issue preferences in the British electorate, February 1974, *British Journal of Political Science* **6,** 273–90.
Suggests that the weakening of party identification may mean that issues assume a greater importance in determining electoral choice.

American Political Science Association, Committee on Political Parties (1950) Toward a more responsible two-party system, *American Political Science Review* **44,** Supplement.
Classic presentation of Britain as the happy home of responsible party government.

Blondel, J. (1978) *Political Parties: A Genuine Case for Discontent?* London Wildwood House.
Not a particularly powerful study, but concludes that 'parties will die on their feet in the West'.

Butler, D., and Stokes, D. (1969) *Political Change in Britain,* London, Macmillan.
Landmark text in the field of voting behaviour research. Their expectation that there would be 'the progressive conversion of the working class to the Labour Party' and the decay of working class Conservatism, shows us that survey research and a 'scientific' method do not always get things right.

Epstein, L.D . (1980) What happened to the British party system?, *American Political Science Review,* **74,** 1–22.
Discusses the changing assessment of the 'British party model' by American political scientists. Could usefully be subtitled, 'From responsible party government to adversary politics'.

Finer, S.E. (1980) *The Changing British Party System, 1945–79,* Washington, D.C., American Enterprise Institute.
Argues that the party system he 'had been accustomed to applaud had become positively dysfunctional to the British system of government'. Attack on British parties and a plea for reform.

Finer, S.E. (ed.) (1975) *Adversary Politics and Electoral Reform,* London, Anthony Wigram.
First in the field with the adversary politics thesis and a powerful case for electoral reform.

Gamble, A. (1982) Continuity and discontinuity in British economic policy, 1960–81. (Paper presented to the annual conference of the Political Studies Association, University of Kent, 1982.)
Coldly and carefully tears apart an aspect of the adversary politics thesis.

Hansard Society for Parliamentay Government (Committee chaired by Sir Richard Marsh) (1979) *Politics and Industry: the Great Mismatch,* London, Hansard Society.
Set up to look at problems arising out of the failure of government and industry to work together. Blames politicians for only attending to short-run electoral considerations.

Liberal Party (1977) *Towards a New Political Agenda: Reform of Government,* London, Liberal Party.
The Liberal Party case for constitutional, and especially electoral reform.

Nordhaus, W.D. (1975) The political business cycle, *Review of Economic Studies,* **42,** 169–90.
Looks at evidence with respect to political-business cycles in nine countries over the period 1947–72.

Rose, R. (1980) *Do Parties Make a Difference?* Chatham, N.J., Chatham House Publishers.
Concentrates on what parties do in office. Argues that they do not matter as much as is often thought because they are only part of government and are hemmed in by constraints.

CHAPTER 3

Power, Parties and Pressures

Part II Interest Groups

in these years [1964–1970]... the pressures generated within the post-war system substantially and visibly escaped from control.

S. H. Beer (1980) *British pressure groups revisited: pluralistic stagnation from the fifties to the seventies*, P.A. Bulletin, **32**, 8.

In the early years of the 1950s, the growing entrenchment of the theory of responsible party government, and a lingering attachment to the traditional liberal-democratic theory of the constitution, blocked the easy rise of an emphasis upon interest groups affecting the overall thrust of public policy in Britain. By the early 1960s, however, no political scientist who was worth his or her salt doubted the fact that interest groups provided *the* key to unlock the workings of British politics. In effect, the intellectual centre of gravity slowly moved from parties to pressure groups and a new theory emerged that quickly gained wide acceptance. Why, then, did interest groups come into focus; what was this new theory; how adequately does this theory make sense of British politics; are there alternative perspectives on the part played by interests and groups in British politics; and how adequate are those perspectives?

A number of factors pulled interest groups into view.

1   At the most obvious level interest group activity increased in the post-war period in response to more state involvement in managing the economy and in welfare provision. Interest groups not only prompted state intervention, but that intervention in disturbing the established equilibrium did much to draw-out still more activity as interests fought to defend their patch in the face of other interests jockeying for advantage.
2   Of itself, however, the reality of group activity was probably of less significance than was the fact that the established theories of British politics suddenly came to appear as 'wrong', so prompting the search for new ways to make sense of things. By the mid-fifties, party programmes and party politics no longer seemed to matter because nothing major was at issue, and so the theory of responsible party government appeared to be increasingly irrelevant. On the more formal, constitutional, front, survey research on voters revealed a reality utterly at odds with the conception of the active and informed citizen that was built into the

traditional liberal-democratic theory of the British constitution so confounding the credibility of *that* perspective on British politics as well. So, established perspectives were tattered and there was 'room' for a new theory of British politics that would be at one with the facts and celebrate the achievements of the post-war consensus.

3   As political science developed in the fifties, leading British political scientists came to display a keen sensitivity to intellectual developments in America at the same time as American political scientists were eager to come over to study British politics. The 1950s was the golden age of interest-group theory in America and if it could 'explain' American politics then there was the tempting presumption that it could do the job of making sense of British politics as well.

So, a tangled combination of factors led to a spate of work on interest groups in Britain. What was the nature of this work, and what was the explanatory theory at its gut?

PLURALISM

Students of the 'new group politics' often studied a single (usually successful!) group in great detail – such as the Confederation of British Industry, the National Farmers Union, or the British Medical Association, or else they studied group activity in a particular issue – such as capital punishment, commercial television, rent control, or race-relations legislation. However, they invariably began their work by defining interest groups and distinguishing them from political parties. Parties were regarded as governing coalitions that 'aggregated' interests and policies before putting up candidates at elections with a view to winning and actually undertaking the *direct* government of the country. For their part, interest groups assumed a rather more modest role in that they were content to 'articulate' a single interest and policy. Because of this narrowness of interest they could not (and did not seek to) form a government but exerted pressure on the government of the day in order, *indirectly,* to shape the particular direction of a facet of public policy to their own advantage. Having defined interest groups in this way, it was customary for early students of the interest group world to sort it out into those groups that were promoting a 'cause' or an issue, and those groups that were active in trying to advance the immediate material and 'sectional' interests of their own members. Moreover, research rather suggested that the former groups mounted one-off campaigns targeted at parliament or public opinion, whereas the latter groups (and especially the trade unions and employers associations) were of greater power and were likely to be in regular day-to-day contact with ministers, government, and the permanent administrative side of the state machine.

Theory to explain just why and how particular groups were influential in shaping public policy to their advantage was not well developed, and easy talk about the exertion of 'pressure' – as if that said anything – only sidestepped the explanatory problem. Having said that, however, we can tease out from the textbooks of the sixties an implicit theoretical perspective that bore on groups and was designed to make sense of British politics as a whole. 'Pluralism' was the new theory of British politics that burst through both the party and the constitutional perspectives on things. Baldly expressed, those who subscribe to that theory see it as important to explain the process of public policy-making since that is regarded as the essential stuff of British politics itself; they see interest groups as of central and determining influence in that process; and they see the group process as enhancing of democracy in Britain. These, then, are the three bare defining elements of pluralism, but in fuller form a pluralist perspective embraces the following elements.

1   The chief characteristic of society is that it is 'open' and made up of many interests that freely and automatically form themselves into a whole variety of groups. Morever, because individuals are likely to be members of more than one interest ('cross-cutting ties') and more than one group ('overlapping membership') this will soften or moderate a commitment to any single interest. This view quite clearly rejects a left perspective: the idea that society is made up of just two classes; that economic class is the only major, or 'real', line of cleavage; and that conflict is deep, bitter and unrelenting.
2   Individuals on their own are not particularly significant in politics. They do not participate directly in the policy-making process and they are not well-informed. Put another way, this perspective rejects the ideal of participatory democracy as a utopian dream, and regards the expectations for citizens integral to liberal-democratic constitutional theory as unrealistic.
3   Elections and party politics are rather less significant in securing democracy and representative and responsible government than was once thought to be the case. After all, elections only occur once every 5 years, and the parties can only attend to the broad lines of policy and so do not represent particular interests in any meaningful way.
4   Interest groups, then, and not individuals, parties, or classes, are the crucial building blocks of the British polity. Individuals (who know where their own best interests lie) participate in politics through groups and are effectively represented by groups.
5   No interests are left outside the group world. Even those interests that are unorganised have the 'potential' to organise should the need arise, and even inactive and apathetic citizens enjoy an 'indirect' influence if only because elected politicians have to 'anticipate' their wishes in order to win elections so that they can get back into office to bargain with the more active interests.
6   No one interest group is dominant in the policy process: there is

balance and equilibrium. This view contradicts two rival perspectives on the world of interest-group politics. First, and contrary to the Marxist perspective (to be discussed more fully in Chapter 7), business groups do not dominate the political process, in part because they are divided amongst themselves, in part because they face the 'countervailing power' of organised labour, and in part because they face general competition from other groups as well. Second, and contrary to the New Right perspective (to be discussed later in this chapter) organised labour is not the dominant interest in British politics.

7   Political power is 'fragmented' because the resources that are the basis of power and influence are widely dispersed and 'non-cumulative'. For example, an interest group may be rich but it may be ill-organised, just as a poor group may enjoy power because it is active and well-organised. Pluralists, in fact, attach much significance and power to action, involvement, and skill in the political market place. None of this means that they see perfect political competition in the interest group world, and influence as equally distributed among all groups and interests in society. However, they do challenge the view of those left-inclined social scientists who see money and wealth – 'economic power' – as the only solid basis for political power. Pluralists tend to see politics as analogous to an idealised economic market place of free and fair competition.

8   There are many issues actually in politics and an infinite range of potential issues. However, the political system is 'open' and there is nothing to prevent any issue coming onto the governmental agenda for action and decision if an interest group seeks to put it there.

9   Although a group may be active and especially influential within a limited range of issues that are of pressing concern to it, such a group will take no part in a whole host of other issues where different groups will be active and influential.

10   Because there are many groups and interests in society; because groups can come and go as they wish; and because they all enjoy some measure of influence in particular issues, politics is fluid and everchanging and the policy process is best characterised as one involving bidding, bargaining, negotiation, accommodation, compromise, and checks and balances.

11   So, competition, and not polarised conflict, is the name of the political game, and that competition is kept moderate and restrained because of the implications that flow from cross-cutting ties between groups; from the existence of potential groups on the sidelines of activity; from the rules of the political game; from the role of the state; and from the whole context of pluralist politics. We need to elaborate on some of these latter points.

12   All political activity within a democracy takes place within the context of 'public opinion'. In Britain, the political system is grounded in a fundamental consensus as to the desired ends of public policy and the means to attain them, and so the rules of the interest group game are set

by society to ensure 'fair play' and free access for all legitimate interests that want the ear of government.

13   The state is open, neutral and fragmented. Put another way, the state is seen as divorced from any one class and is not regarded as the cohesive instrument of the economically powerful (there is no ruling class); the state is not a biased 'establishment' serving only itself; and the very fragmentation of the state provides for multiple access points for all interest groups. Government provides the 'arena' where all major group disputes are debated and resolved. It also acts as a 'referee' of the group struggle: it holds the ring and secures the public interest by restoring the balance and moving in when one group goes too far, and it also protects the interests of the inactive and inarticulate. All of this is at odds with a left perspective on the 'capitalist state'.

14   The outcome of interest-group activity is roughly equitable. Every legitimate group secures its fair share and the equilibrium of interest-group interaction provides for public policy that is a reasonable approximation of society's preferences so securing the general interest at the same time as the overall system is rendered stable and legitimate. Of course, Britain is not a democracy of the kind envisaged by those nineteenth-century theorists who focused on the active and informed citizen, and so it is not a democracy that is in accord with the 'old-fashioned' liberal-democratic theory of the constitution, but interest-group competition provides for a good *working* democratic system. So, from the pluralist point of view traditional liberal-democratic theory is 'wrong' because it is unrealistic. They argue that democratic theory needs to be adjusted to the realities of governing Britain in the twentieth century. Once this is done they argue that interest groups can be seen as good for democracy and the very essence of what democracy in Britain is all about.

The recognition of interests and groups in society, and a concern to see them in relation to government and the development of public policy represented an important breakthrough in the study of British politics. There was a developing awareness that politics went beyond the institutions of government, and that the connections between state and society involved more than attending to the formal implications of regular general elections and the play of party politics. Politics came to be seen as a social and collective activity which rose above the individual but which somehow fell short of the ideal of the nation or the whole community.

At first blush, the pluralist perspective on British politics seems to be at one with a common-sense appreciation of the facts. There *are* many groups (4000 in Birmingham alone) and it *is* difficult to boil all interests down to something called 'class'; on a number of issues (and at certain levels of the state) we *can* discover a pattern of competitive interest-group politics in which no one group appears to be overwhelmingly dominant; and on occasions the state *does* simply referee the group struggle and is content to ratify the outcome of the balance of competing forces. Having said that, however, we need critically to explore the pluralist perspective. How adequately does it make sense of British politics and the part played by interests and groups?

There are three bodies of writing that bear on this question and we will consider each in turn.

1   In recent years, as the New Right has come to prominence, a considerable number of political scientists have changed their assessment of the part played by interest groups in British politics. Like pluralists, they continue to see groups as of fundamental importance. However, unlike pluralists, they no longer praise their activity as enhancing of democracy and stable government, but instead condemn the whole interest-group system as being out of control. Not only do they see organised labour as overwhelmingly dominant within the world of interests, but the absence of any checks on the system has led to what they call an *'overload of demands'* on government. This, they say, has contributed to the *'ungovernability'* of Britain and to a whole host of economic problems as opportunities for investment and long-run growth are 'crowded out' by the reality of evermore taxation raised to finance the public services demanded by interest groups.

2   The Left and Marxist perspective on British politics argues that pluralism is a theory at odds with the facts and ignores important phenomena in relation to interests and power. *Pluralism is regarded as an ideology* which masks the reality of power and so helps to legitimise a system which is grounded in inequality and an absence of fair play. Not surprisingly, left-inclined social scientists go on to take the view that good sense can only be made of British politics if the pluralist ideology is set aside and a start to understanding is made elsewhere than in the world of interest-group activity. We will set down the bones of the left critique of pluralism in this chapter, but will attend to the more positive aspects of the left perspective on British politics in later chapters.

3   Social scientists in the mainstream of debate and those on the Left have become increasingly alive to the fact that competition is not always the reality of interest-group politics and that the relation of some groups to the state is different from that set-down in pluralist theory. In the field of economic policy in particular, business and labour have come to work so closely with the interventionist state that they are seen as governing institutions in their own right. In this situation it is argued that *corporatism,* or tripartism, better captures the reality of crucial state–interest–group relations.

OVERLOAD AND UNGOVERNABILITY

In February 1974, the Conservative Government called an early general election: their incomes policy was in tatters and their attempt to legislate on industrial relations had been beaten back by action on the factory floor and the streets. The country was on a 3-day working week and the mineworkers were solidly in favour of strike action in support of their pay claim. The election was fought on the issue, 'Who runs the country, the government or the trade unions?', and the Conservative Government lost. Labour scraped into office; the miners secured a 30 per cent pay rise; and the Industrial Relations Act was repealed. The press was horrified and questioned whether Britain was still governable under a democratically elected administration. It was clearly time for political scientists to reassess their pluralist perspective on interest groups: groups were real enough but were they still a 'good' thing?

Most political scientists quickly came to argue that things had gone badly wrong: some groups were too powerful and the system as a whole was seen as out of control so that there was an overload of demands on government. Four reasons were advanced for this state of affairs.

1   *The public as a whole* had fallen victim to the revolution of rising expectations and they displayed a lack of 'realism' as to the constraints that bore on the capacity of governments to provide ever more. These expectations were nurtured by the adversarial nature of electoral competition and they pressed hard onto government. As the state had come to intervene more and more in the field of welfare provision it fed the ethic of equality and broke down the constraining check of deference (of poor people in their place), so *itself* contributing to a growing lobby for 'more' and 'better' public provision.

2   Within the system of government, the increased numbers of *bureaucrats and officials* involved in welfare and public-service provision were themselves a powerful lobby for more state activity. They had a personal stake in improving their own incomes (and they were aided in this by the growth of white-collar and public-sector trade unions), and they had a professional commitment to improve the lot of the clients of their services. Both factors meant that bureaucrats had every incentive to try to maximise the budgets of their own service without any regard to the larger implications of this for the scale of state activity and public expenditure.

3   *Local authorities* were faced with demands for improvements in service from local community groups. They often found it difficult to resist these demands. At the same time, however, their 'own' capacity to supply new and improved services was restricted by their dependence on the limited income from rates. Increasingly they looked to the central government for more grants and financial help. In so far as they secured a satisfactory response then they succeeded in lifting their own fiscal crisis up to the central level of the state.

4   The *trade unions* in particular were too powerful. They were pre-eminent within the interest-group world and were unchecked. Two world

wars had drawn them into close and cooperative contact with government. The post-war commitment to full-employment increased their bargaining power; the strike weapon in the context of a complex and interdependent economy meant that they could exert considerable 'pressure' through their capacity to disrupt and delay; and as inflation came to be seen as *the* problem (and as a problem caused by 'excessive' wages demands backed by strikes) so trade unions found themselves in a new position of strategic importance and power. To try to preserve industrial peace and control wage inflation governments were forced to adopt a carrot-and-stick approach to the trade unions. However, the limitations of the stick forced governments to try and win voluntary cooperation through concessions and 'social contracts'. The experience of the sixties and seventies suggested that the trade unions were a political force to be reckoned with.

Taken together, these four factors were said to have made for an expansion of participants in pressure politics and for an expansion of demands on government. In effect, the New Right wisdom was telling us that we have had too much of a good thing. The moderate pluralism of bargains, balance, and compromise within rules of the game designed to ensure fair play and fair shares for all had somehow been transformed into the perverted and self-defeating hyperpluralism of strong groups and weak government operating on the basis of a free-for-all where might was right. Too many groups all refusing to take 'no' for an answer had made for problems precisely because a democratically based government needing popular support was reluctant to refuse demands and was weak in the face of them. In consequence state intervention increased and public expenditure rocketed.

The problem of demand overload was seen as further compounded by two related factors. First, the increased weight of demands came at a time when the actual problems thrust before government were not only more complex and intractable, but were also more interdependent – solve one (say, inflation) and you only caused another (rising unemployment). Second, demand overload and intractable and complicated problems came at a time of decreased government capacity, effectiveness, and authority. A series of conspicuous policy failures and U-turn retreats served to reduce public support for government, and willing consent to the law. Moreover, the absence of economic growth limited the government's effectiveness to supply and fund the expanding demand for services.

Now, observers sensitive to the problem of overload (and quietly concerned with the survival of the free market and the profitability of private enterprise), detected a vicious downward spiral at work between economic and political factors. A stagnant economy heaps increased demands on government as more people are in need. This, however, occurs at a time when the government has limited financial slack to be able to respond. Inevitably, therefore, the government fails to deliver the goods as demanded, as expected, and sometimes even as promised. This failure undermines governmental authority and weakens the legitimacy of the whole political system so that the governability of the nation is called into question. There is no easy way back up out of the spiral because if a government attempts to buy back public support in order to alleviate the 'political' problem of governability then this not only overtaxes the economy but stimulates inflation so further exacerbating the 'economic' problem and making sustained and balanced growth all the more difficult.

What can we make of this perspective on British politics? It cannot be simply dismissed, still less ignored, because it deals with phenomena of real significance that are in the public eye. The trade unions *are* a problematic force both in and on the uneasy edges of the system of power; a variety of factors *have* conspired to produce an upsurge of competing participants and conflicting demands; elected governments *have* frequently shown themselves to be weak and vacillating in the face of pressures and problems; and certain democratic aspects of the British polity *have* heaped problems on to the capitalist economy in a way that has 'crowded out' opportunities for growth. Put another way, the overload, or hyperpluralist, perspective is more keenly attuned to the realities of aspects of politics in the seventies than is the pluralist perspective which was very much a product of the cosy consensus politics of the fifties and sixties. However, this comparative assessment of the respective merits of two bodies of work does not mean that we can regard the hyperpluralist perspective as an adequate explanation of British politics.

The New Right emphasis on adversary politics and an overload of demands has been more of a *critique* of democracy in Britain than it has ever been a rigorous description of, and explanation for, British politics. It has been self-consciously policy-oriented and has fed directly into the political debate with a series of *prescriptions* which involve cutting back the activities of the state and changing the nature of democracy in Britain. At best it provides us with a partial and intensely partisan perspective because it is keenly committed to the view from the top – to the view of those who are more in control than controlled, and who are, therefore, centrally concerned to secure political stability and sustain a particular pattern of economic relations based on the economic order of capitalism and the free market. The New Right in choosing to focus on, and criticise, pressure groups, parties, and elected governments as the very stuff of British politics, chooses to *ignore* other phenomena that are of political significance, such as the power of the secret state that we will be considering in Chapter 5. Moreover, although it is a perspective which is critical of things, criticism is *restricted* to politics, and to democratic politics at that, and there is no attempt to direct critical attention to the functioning of the economic system and to the power which lurks hidden within it. We will be exploring these matters in later chapters. The hyperpluralist perspective may have sought to distance itself from the pluralist perspective on British politics, but there is much in common between the two orientations. The emphasis is still on interests overtly organised in political action, and this occurs to the detriment of a sustained consideration of the implications of inaction, the problem of interests forming themselves into groups, and the whole context of politics and power. These points are discussed in the Left critique of pluralism.

PLURALISM AS IDEOLOGY

Left-inclined social scientists argue that the pluralist perspective on British politics is grossly inadequate because it adopts a restricted frame of reference; takes too much for granted; and fails to deal with the whole problem of political inaction. In consequence, it actually masks the true reality of power in Britain and so serves as an ideology legitimising and stabilising the system as one worthy of public support. Let us elaborate on these points.

The pluralist conception of politics is overly restricted. Pluralists actually *define* British politics as public policy-making, and so they see politics as somehow 'explained' once they tell us how those policies are made as a result of the activities of the various interested groups. This means that the public-policy process is treated as an end-in-itself.

   Left-inclined critics see two main things as wrong with this conception of politics. First, the fact that pluralists are only interested in explaining what they choose to call *public* policy-making means that they confine their attention to those issues that involve government and the state in a very direct way. They accept all too easily the public/private distinction and so rule out a consideration of those 'privately' made decisions in the economic sphere that have profound implications for the life chances of millions of people. Left-inclined critics of pluralism reject the utility of the public/private distinction as ideological; they reject the idea of a self-contained autonomous politics distinct from the economy and economic power; and they argue that decisions made by businessmen in 'private' enterprise have a massive public aspect that needs to be explored because those decisions involve the exercise of very real power.

   Second, the concern of pluralists to explain the *making* of public policies means that they emphasise inputs into the political system to the detriment of a serious consideration of public-policy outputs. Pluralists are centrally interested in identifying who participates in public policy-making. They tend not to explore what difference it makes who takes part in the public-policy process, or else they assume that the beneficiaries of public policy can simply be 'read-off' from information about group participation because of uncomplicated assumptions about all groups being able to participate in order to advance their own interest. Left-inclined critics argue that pluralists ignore the more fundamental question of who actually benefits from public-policy outcomes and wrongly assume that participation is power.

Simply expressed, and taking these two points together, pluralists are charged with asking the wrong question (who participates instead of who benefits) about just the public aspect of policy-making so that they ignore the 'private' aspect of power and policy-making altogether.

Pluralists ignore the problem of group formation. They operate on the assumption that every individual is the best judge of his or her real interest and they define interest groups in terms of 'shared attitudes'. In consequence, they tend to see a simple one-to-one relation between attitudes, interests, and group organisation, and so they take the interest group world as a given that arises 'naturally' in a way that calls for no complicated explanation.

Left-inclined critics of pluralism reject this as inadequate. They recognise that not all interests in society are organised into groups and in order to explain this state of affairs they see it as important to consider two phenomena that tend to be ignored by pluralists.

First, there is the problem of information. For example, all of us have a stake, or an objective interest, in a healthy environment but we may not be aware of the ways in which the environment is being polluted to the detriment of our health. If we lack the information that is vital in enabling us to gain a subjective awareness of our real interest then we are hardly likely to be a position to get together to organise.

Second, the issue of group formation goes beyond the simple matter of information, because not all interests are 'allowed' to develop a sense of their own collective identity. For example, the poor and the unemployed are largely outside of the interest group world. This is best explained, not by suggesting that they do not have interests in common or that they are satisfied with things as they are, but by attending to the crushing significance of those ideas in society which preach that to be poor is an individual's *own* fault and reflects his or her lack of preparedness to study and train, to work hard, to postpone having a family, or what have you. In a similar way, for homosexuals to organise as a group involves their coming to terms with themselves in the context of a society which has certain views as to what is 'normal' and proper with respect to sexual behaviour. These views do not make it easy for individuals to come out, still less for the interest to come together in public political activity. Before women could form into groups to press for change they too had to challenge ruling ideas – ideas which suggested that their proper place was at home with the family.

We will discuss the nature of interests more fully in Chapter 6, and will be discussing the nature of social control more fully in Chapter 10. For the moment, however, it is sufficient to note that the formation of interest groups is a problem of the highest order; the group world cannot be taken as a given but needs to be explained; and we have to attend to the determinants of individual consciousness and awareness, and the part they play in the development of groups and political conflict. The pluralist perspective will not help us deal with these problems because it is more interested in political behaviour than in the role of ideas in society. Pluralists provide only a partial perspective on the inactivity of certain interests and groups. They assume that people know where their own best interests lie; they assume that people will automatically participate in politics if their interests are threatened; and they assume that all interests possess the 'potential' to organise and be influential in politics. Because of the assumption that people will always squeal politically if their toes are trodden on, pluralists tend to interpret political inactivity as a sign of a rough satisfaction with the prevailing state of things.

Left-inclined critics, whilst recognising that political inactivity *can* be construed as a measure of satisfaction and power for certain interests, nevertheless argue that this is *not* the case for all interests and in many cases they regard inactivity as symptomatic of a powerlessness and fatalism which renders any activity pointless. So, from the left perspective, political inactivity *can* be a sign of satisfaction and strength, but it can also be a sign of disaffection and weakness. In concrete terms, Miliband has argued that in a capitalist society, the interests of private capital will invariably and necessarily be taken into account in the development of public policy and so we should not expect to see business leaders standing on a soap box anymore than we should expect to see those who enjoy the ear of government organising on the streets. However, there are groups outside of the mainstream who do not press their views on the state even though the individuals concerned may be keenly alive to the possibility of their lot being improved as a result of state action. This inactivity is best interpreted as indicative of a powerlessness, but is perfectly 'rational' once we recognise that the group is making certain calculations as to the likely *response* to their views and demands. If a group anticipates no response at all, a blunt refusal, or even an attack upon its very integrity, then it makes good sense to keep its political head down below the level of activity. Simply expressed, there is no point in talking politics to the powerful if you are powerless and cannot force them to listen *and* act on what you have to say. For groups in this position the right to take part in politics represents little more than the right to whistle in the wind.

Pluralists exaggerate the extent to which all groups enjoy some influence. Left-inclined critics of pluralism argue that the interest-group world is one where there is imperfect competition and business dominance. Of course, there is the recognition that there are certain issues of no moment to business (such as abortion, or capital punishment), but within their particular sphere of concern the Left regards the business interest as overwhelmingly influential, and trade unions (in particular) are seen as in an inferior position. Government cannot be indifferent to the long-term success of business. If it does not facilitate economic growth and expansion then it limits its capacity to raise taxes and so cuts into the public revenue on which its own power depends. Moreover, because depression, inflation, or other economic distress can bring down a government, and because jobs, prices, production, the standard of living, and the economic security of everyone, all tend to rest on the performance of business, politicians and administrators alike have to regard business as *more* than just another interest group. The persistence of inequalities with respect to the distribution of income and wealth, and the survival of capitalism itself, are seen by the Left as attesting to the privileged position of business within economy, society, and polity.

Pluralists only study an aspect of power. For pluralists, power is only really seen as existing in action, participation, and decision-making within the public arena of politics and government.

Left-inclined critics reject the idea that power is only embodied in action and decision, and is specific to particular issues and concrete policy situations. They see power as 'structured' beyond and behind public participation in particular issues, and they point to another 'face' of political power caught up in the fact that certain issues do not even get onto the public policy-making agenda for action and decision at all. In effect, they argue that the governmental agenda cannot be taken as a given. We are challenged to recognise, first, that power is involved in non-decision-making, in inaction, and in non-participation, and, second, that interests are advantaged and disadvantaged by the fact that certain issues are not on the governmental agenda for complicated reasons that take us behind the scenes of the public face of policy-making and into the murky waters of the constraining role of ideas in society.

Pluralists fail to see the inherent 'bias' of the state. Although left critics do not agree among themselves as to how to explain this bias towards the interests of the propertied class, they are unanimous in rejecting the pluralist assumption that the British state is 'neutral' as between different classes. We will discuss Marxist perspectives on the state in Chapter 7.

The pluralist perspective on British politics was built up by political scientists who were predisposed to provide an account of interest-group politics which presented it in a good, democratic light. The facts were not approached cold. The research dice were loaded in favour of pluralist conclusions. First, pluralists tended to study successful groups. The early emphasis upon the powerful house-trained group going about things the proper way built up a picture of group influence and success within the context of the play of a moderate and restrained politics. Second, when pluralists studied issues in British politics then they tended to latch onto issues that generated controversy and a highly visible politics of action and interaction. Issues such as the abolition of capital punishment or the legislation on abortion inevitably revealed a picture of an open, competitive pattern of politics where the state was often content to sit back and referee the group struggle. These studies were not 'wrong', but it would be wrong to conclude that this pattern of interest-group politics holds for all issues. Third, the emphasis on groups, issues, policy-making, and action sucked attention away from the more unchanging aspects of British politics, from non-issues and non-groups, and from the winners and losers of the outcomes of public policy, and all of this suggests a picture rather at odds with the fair and equal pluralist heaven. Fourth, pluralists try to have it both ways when interpreting the power significance of inactive interests and groups: they minimise the influence of the rich when they are inactive, but choose to exaggerate the influence of the poor unless they are inactive. So, pluralists argue that if those of economic wealth are not directly involved in public policy-making then this is some kind of proof that they lack political power, but if poorer people are not directly involved then it is suggested that they are satisfied and enjoy power because politicians will 'anticipate' their concerns and they themselves possess the 'potential' to organise for their own advantage.

All things considered, then, the left claims that pluralism tends to provide a top-down view of British politics. In dealing with the surface politics of the moment and with the politics of participation and satisfaction it tends to reproduce the bias of the system under scrutiny because it provides a description couched in terms set by the system itself. The pluralist perspective makes no attempt to criticise British politics, and it chooses to bend democratic theory in a conservative direction so that it justifies and defends the established order. Pluralism is insensitive, and inattentive, to the view from the bottom; to the politics of the powerless; to the ill-organised and unincorporated politics of movement, protest and riot; and to the power of government and the state to rebuff demands for change and to destroy certain groups.

Now, those of a pluralist persuasion may be tempted to suggest that the left-inclined critique of their perspective is itself ideological and simply the product of bigoted minds disaffected from the established order and inattentive to the facts. Such a view would be wrong because many of the points of critique that we have just set down have been backed up by solid research into the concrete world of interests and groups. Research on interests in local politics, and research on the 'third world' of groups at the national level with only limited and sporadic access to government, has revealed a picture of the interest-group world starkly at odds with the rosy optimism of the pluralist perspective .

In the 1960s, in response to changes in social structure and expectations, and in the context of a party and interest-group world that would not embrace new interests and demands, large numbers of inner-city residents formed themselves into loose groups to press for changes in public policy and in the balance of the public-private provision of the basics for a decent life. Research has revealed that these community action groups were invariably regarded with hostility by Conservative *and* Labour councils. Moreover, these groups found themselves to be in a catch 22 – no win – situation so far as their own political action was concerned. If they were relatively inactive and presented their demands through what the councillors defined as the 'proper' (private) channels then their demands rarely secured a favourable response. However, as soon as they moved on to a more public and active presentation of their demands then councillors condemned this activity, the demands themselves were ignored, and the groups were held up to public ridicule as a threat to democracy and the general interest. We have ourselves observed and documented many such cases in our studies of local politics in Kensington and Chelsea, and Croydon, where relatively powerless groups of underprivileged people were frequently ignored by councillors when they played by the rules of the game, and were vilified when they did not. For many groups, public-pressure group activity was no sign of their power, but it was a testament to the frustrated powerlessness of those who could not get the ear of government, still less their positive action – no matter what they did or did not do. The rules of the game, then, far from being set by society so as to ensure fair play for all, seemed to be set by the local authorities. Moreover, these rules served to protect established policies *and* the easy access of those groups and interests advantaged by them, at the same time as groups urging change were ruled out of court by a whole series of exclusion devices.

On the one hand, interests in line with the prevailing policy and ideology of a local authority tend to secure effective access and substantive policies that advance their interest without any need for activity and organisation. In Croydon, big-business interests were influential in local politics but their involvement was personal and informal and their influence was rarely in evidence in action on policy-making as the local authority was keenly sensitive to their concerns without any need for pressure-group prompting from outside.

On the other hand, poorer residents, *in spite* of their organisation and activity, could often do very little to press their demands through to a successful policy outcome. They were frequently left out in the cold and were fobbed off with symbolic concessions – such as a tatty play space instead of a decent nursery. If these groups persisted in their protest then they were drawn into sham 'participation' exercises with the local authority that experience shows did more to neuter their dissent than to advance their real interests. In either case, the basic fundamentals of substantive council policy were left quite untouched.

Research rather suggested that there often seemed to be a dual political system of interests, action, and demands at the local level. One was inactive, close to the council, and powerful. The other was active and noisy, far-removed from the council, and powerless. Neither of these patterns of politics was really pulled into view by pluralism, because that perspective could not cope with too much raucous political activity – still less with too little or none at all.

CORPORATISM

During the 1970s, some political observers, recognising the unequal participation and influence of certain interests in public policy making, began to argue that British politics could better be described as 'corporatist' rather than pluralist. The very phrase corporatism is a problem since it continues to evoke the spectre of Italian fascism and authoritarian rule. Moreover, there is a profound lack of agreement on what the concept actually refers to. Some see corporatism grandly as a total *economic system* distinct from capitalism and socialism; some see corporatism as a particular kind of *'state form'* distinct from, say, parliamentarianism, where citizens participate in the determination of policies through the exercise of voting rights in relation to a parliament; and still others see corporatism rather more modestly and fruitfully as connoting a particular system of *interest-group politics* and representation distinct from the pluralist system that we have just discussed.

Different authors may define corporatism differently, but we should not worry too much about this since corporatism is a highly complex phenomenon and different dimensions, or aspects, of it are covered by these diverse conceptualisations. Put another way, certain elements are common to the corporatist perspective on politics in the West, and so, although there are different schools of theory, it is possible to fuse some of these together in order to recognise that we are looking at a perspective that bears on interests and the state within the contemporary period of economic development. Much of this work will be discussed in Chapter 8 when we will be dealing with the way in which the British state has handled the economy. In the context of this chapter, however, it is particularly important to deal with the corporatist perspective on the politics of organised interests since it provides some kind of challenge to the pluralist perspective (even though pluralism and corporatism share a number of basic assumptions), and it fleshes out elements of the left critique of pluralism (even though much corporatist theory is hostile to a Marxist theory of the capitalist state).

Corporatists share with pluralists a belief that the basic building blocks of the polity and the political process are groups formed around interests and that these have somehow taken over from the significance of representation through elections, parties and parliaments. However, corporatists are sharply critical of the pluralist perspective in so far as that perspective sees the interest-groups system as competitive, 'democratic', equal, and open to all, so that it leads to policy outcomes that give fair shares to everyone. In this sense, then, corporatists see pluralism as basically 'wrong' – as a theory at odds with the facts. But, like left critics, they recognise that the pluralist perspective serves as a powerful ideology legitimising (by mystifying) the established political order.

In one of the classic articles on corporatism Schmitter (1979) clarifies the distinction between pluralism and corporatism in the following way.

Pluralism can be defined as a system of interest representation in which the constituent units are organised into an unspecified number of multiple, voluntary, competitive, nonhierarchically ordered and self-determined (as to type or scope of interest) categories which are not specially licensed, recognised, subsidised, created or otherwise controlled in leadership selection or interest articulation by the state and which do not exercise a monopoly of representational activity within their respective categories.

whereas:

Corporatism can be defined as a system of interest representation in which the constituent units are organised into a limited number of singular, compulsory, noncompetitive, hierarchically ordered and functionally differentiated categories, recognised or licensed (if not created) by the state and granted a deliberate representational monopoly within their respective categories in exchange for observing certain controls on their selection of leaders and articulation of demands and supports.

Now, we should not quibble about Schmitter's definition of pluralism (which is somewhat different and rather more wordy than is our own perspective on this theory) since Schmitter is intent on making the point that the system of interest politics as it currently exists is at odds with the pluralist viewpoint in crucial ways that bear on the nature of interest groups and the access of particular interests to the state.

In fact, other writers within the corporatist tradition seek to go beyond this emphasis upon the *structure* of interests in order to suggest that this new pattern of interest-group politics has itself served to contribute to more extensive *state intervention* in economy and society. In Cawson's words, 'corporatism in its broadest meaning is a pattern of articulation between the state and functional interests in civil society which fuses representation and intervention in an interdependent relationship'. Powerful interest groups prompt state intervention; state intervention has implications for the nature of the interest-group world; and each reinforces the other leading to an increasingly closed and tight pattern of interest group/state relations.

More than this, there are those within the corporatist tradition who go even further. They recognise that the development of both state intervention and a corporatist system of interest representation go together, but they go on to suggest that this is tied into a particular *period of capitalist development*. They note that in the early days of capitalism, the role of the state was limited to the enforcement of a legal structure necessary for the market to function. This was the era of competitive capitalism and the *laisser-faire* state which simply sought to guarantee freedom of contract and trade at the same time as it dismantled the restrictive apparatus of the feudal economy and secured public order at home and defence from abroad. This era was not to last for long. War, international competition, industrial concentration (and the demise of competitive capitalism), technological developments, declining profitability, and the political implications of the great depression of the 1930s (and the related decline in any faith in the self-regulating virtues of unfettered capitalism) all heightened tensions, increased the need for order and stability, and prompted the search for a 'better' way of handling economic and political affairs. Large and powerful interest groups came together co-ordinating the activities of whole economic sectors and enforcing membership on those they saw as 'their' people. State intervention increased, in managing the economy ('Keynesianism'), and in areas of social policy (the 'welfare state'). In the course of these developments, corporatists argue that the competitive and open pattern of pluralist politics passed into comparative insignificance. Certain interests were able to secure exclusive access and an inside track to the ear of government as well as a permanent relationship to the administrative side of the state machine. The peak associations of business and labour were important in the economic sphere as they controlled resources that were needed by government if public policy was to be effective and capable of implementation and enforcement. In this state of affairs, these major interests were no longer in a position of having to simply press in on government from the outside. The fact that they were *needed* by the state, because there was a 'public' dimension to their activity, meant that they were actually co-opted into governmental decision-making: they were *asked* to give advice, and, more than this, they came to act as agents through which state policy was actually implemented. So, certain interests, but *only* certain interests, came to enjoy a quasi-legal status so that they almost became a part of the state and governing institutions in their own right. Other lesser interests and associations continued to exist but they were excluded from influence in crucial areas of public policy and were left out in the political cold.

Simply expressed, there is the suggestion within the literature on corporatism that it is possible to link the growth of corporate, closed, forms of interest representation to developments with respect to the interventionist state in the context of needs of the capitalist economy at a particular, advanced (or late), stage of development. It is these three points about interests, state, and economy, that serve as the cutting edge, and the defining elements of corporatist theory.

The insights into politics derived from a corporatist perspective have been applied to Britain by Keith Middlemas in an important book on *Politics in Industrial Society* which carefully explores the experience of the British system since 1911. Middlemas recognises that 'the accepted version of the constitution...has become inadequate'; he asks 'is it possible to discover a hidden code which explains more fully the behaviour of political parties, other institutions and government?'; and he argues that it *is* possible to 'establish a theory...of British "governance" in the first half of the twentieth century'. In bald form, Middlemas argues that around the time of the First World War the nineteenth-century British political system had broken down under the weight of the antagonism and conflicts in industrial society. A deep change took place in the nature of government. Parliament and party became increasingly irrelevant, and trade unions and employers' associations came into positions of political prominence. Indeed, 'the main theme' of the book is the argument that the triangular pattern of cooperation between government and the two sides of industry built up a new form of harmony which lasted until the mid-sixties and led to the trade unions and employers' associations being elevated to a new sort of status so that they became 'governing institutions' sharing some of the political power and attributes of the state itself. In this 'process of corporate bias', what had once been merely interest groups crossed the political threshold and became part of the extended state. The control which state and interests together could exert over society and economy contributed to a uniquely low level of class conflict for much of the twentieth century so ensuring a political stability that reached a head over the period 1945–65. Middlemas concludes by arguing that 'the nineteenth century concept of the state is wholly outdated, even when the modifications of early pluralist theory are taken into account'.

What can we make of the corporatist perspective on British politics, and just how stable is the pattern of politics which is suggested by those who point to close collaborative arrangements between particular interests and the state in pursuit of ever more state intervention?

There is no doubt that the corporatist literature is important: it is ambitious; it is sensitive to the tie-up between politics and economics (in a way which pluralism never was); it deals not just with the process of public policy-making but with the substantive outcomes of that process as well; and it is keenly alive both to the clashes of interests and to the forces which have tended to hold those clashes in some kind of check. Having said that, however, we should not exaggerate the stability of corporatist arrangements since this particular method of representing and accommodating interests is threatened by a number of factors.

1   There is the threat of rank-and-file revolts from within those groups that are tied in closely to the state. Trade union leaders may well enter into 'social contracts' with governments and pledge themselves and their members to wage restraint and productivity improvements in return for social benefits and an extension of trade union powers, but their control

over their own members is limited and unofficial strikes can, and have, destroyed deals worked out at the top.

2   Marxists, convinced as to the eventual overthrow of capitalism, argue that corporatism is at best a short-run institutional solution to the deep-seated conflicts between capitalists and workers. It may paper over things and succeed in buying time, but it cannot overcome the class-based conflicts that will eventually bubble up to the surface. Indeed, as workers come to recognise that the corporatist game is rigged against them – wage restraint in return for the 'benefits' of a social contract, whilst everything is done to foster profits for the capitalists – they will rebel against it. In fact, this perspective on the demise of corporatism exaggerates the likelihood of a renewed revolutionary impulse and ignores the implication of the new mood of 'realism' born of recession.

Indeed, it is the fact of recession which rather suggests that the greatest threat to the persistence of corporatist arrangements may come, not from the Left and labour, but from the Right and from the industrial capitalists themselves – those interests, that is, that the Left have seen as having benefited most from corporatism. Recession, in making people unemployed, weakens worker organisations and limits the utility of the strike weapon (the *only* real weapon of labour) because labour is reluctant to come out in a situation in which the hold on a job is precarious. In this state of affairs, there is no *need* to buy-off union potential for disruption and dissent through collaborative arrangements with the state and with promises of state benefits born of more intervention. Corporatism, then, may be a fair-weather flower. It may have bloomed with the post-war boom, but it may wither with recession as it is no longer needed to secure stability. Moreover, the increased state intervention that was part of the trend to corporatism imposed costs and taxes that capitalists are showing themselves eager and able to shrug off given the support of the politics of Thatcherism.

3   A corporate tie-up between privileged interests and state may be threatened by the emergence onto the political agenda of new groups and new 'citizen' concerns that fall outside of the incorporation that bears on groups caught up in *economic* issues and the division of labour. Those at the receiving end of policies made as a result of corporate arrangements – the policy-*takers* rather than the policy-*makers* – have often been forced to bear the costs of those arrangements. Moreover, as some kind of consciousness of this has filtered through, so we have witnessed the rise of an unincorporated politics of protest as a challenge to the incorporated politics of order and control. Inner-city riots, the politics of nationalism, peace protests, community action, and the emergence of single-issue movements around the felt concerns of blacks, women, the youthful, and the disenchanted, may not prove to be permanent features on the

political scene but whilst they are around they are likely to defy easy incorporation into the snugness of the state.

A corporatist perspective on the politics of interests in Britain contains powerful insights that draw our attention to major developments with respect to interest politics, state intervention, and the development of the economy. Having said that, you would miss a lot in British politics if you were to put all your interpretative eggs into the basket of corporatist theory. We have already suggested that corporatist arrangements may lack stability and staying power, especially in the context of recession, and that the other side of the coin to those arrangements is the unincorporated politics of protest. The reach of corporatist theory is over ambitious: it makes sense of things but only with respect to *some* groups; *some* issues; *some* periods; and at *some* levels of the state. Corporatism tends to 'fit' the facts best with respect to the major functional economic groupings of capital and labour; with respect to issues of economic policy (especially in so far as they concern incomes) in periods of boom when labour cannot be easily disciplined by market forces; and at the level of the central state. Take any one of these four ingredients away and you will be much less likely to find a close corporatist tie up between particular interests and the state in pursuit of increased state intervention. Many groups, and even more interests, are outside the corporatist system (clients and consumers in particular); many issues continue to reveal a pattern of competitive politics (especially moral issues like abortion) or protest politics (especially on environmental issues); and at the level of the local state the absence of any real concern with economic policies and the central concern with consumption issues suggest that the soil may not be so warm for the development of corporatist arrangements.

CONCLUSION TO CHAPTERS 2 AND 3

In the last two chapters we have looked at the part played by parties and interest groups in British politics. More particularly, we have looked at different perspectives, or theories, on these phenomena. We have set down, and assessed, the theories of responsible party government, pluralism, adversary politics, overload and ungovernability, and corporatism. We have also explored the left-inclined critique of responsible party government and pluralism, so highlighting the extent to which theory is up against theory as much as any theory is assessed up against facts. Where, then, have we got in our understanding of British politics as a result of focusing on perspectives on parties and pressures?

It is not possible to come to a clean and simple judgement. No one of the theories we have set down is all wrong, any more than any one perspective is all right so providing us with a single key to 'explain' British politics. Like the parson's egg, each theory is good in parts: they provide insights into *aspects* of British politics at particular *periods* of our history. Having said that, some theories are better than others. In the concluding part of this chapter we want to pass rough, but clear, judgement on these matters so that you know where we stand.

The theory of responsible party government and pluralist democratic theory together provided the mainstream interpretation of British politics for most of the period since the Second World War. They eased their way into becoming the established constitutional theory and they praised British politics during the good times of economic boom. By the mid-seventies, however, these theories were subjected to challenge. Most political scientists became keenly alive to their limited explanatory worth, and the New Right condemned British democracy pointing to the adversarial nature of party politics and to the dangerous overload of interest-group demands.

Responsible party government and pluralism fitted some of the facts of British politics for some of the time, but they were always overoptimistic and crucially flawed in ways we have pointed to in the body of this chapter.

On the party front, programmes are often vague, do not always offer much choice, and in crucial policy areas are not adequately implemented. Moreover, the electorate often seems to vote for a candidate and a party in ignorance of, and in spite of (rather than because of), the party programme that is on offer.

For its part, pluralism adopts a restricted frame of reference and takes too much for granted so that it skates on the surface of political life and only deals with the politics of participation and the politics of satisfaction to the detriment of any consideration of other less 'obvious' things: there is little that is deep and illuminating about the pluralist perspective and crucial concerns are ignored as irrelevant to politics: pluralism is less wrong than limited.

We regard the left critique of pluralism as cogent, but it goes over the top in seeing everything about pluralism as completely wrong since it is the case that an open competitive model of interest-group politics does fit the facts on certain issues. Moreover, the left perspective on interests is not without its own problems. It hangs too much on the concept of class and fails to explore the changes and complexities that bear on this; it tends to be gross in its handling of the power of business; and it is unsure in its handling of the power of organised labour, seeing it both as lacking in any real power, but as somehow having the potential to become a ferocious force capable of transforming the capitalist system totally. In this chapter we have only really attended to the *negative,* critical, edge of left theory in so far as it challenges rival perspectives on parties and pressures. We will however, be critically assessing the more *positive* aspects of left theory in later chapters.

The theses about adversary politics and overload came to the fore as the fact of economic recession bit into public consciousness: these were the pessimistic theories for the bad times. In fact, the adversary politics thesis overgeneralises about the extent of policy instability; the evidence affords only limited support for the existence of political business cycles; and given the long-term trend of Britain's economic decline it is absurd to blame this on the nature of party politics in the sixties and seventies.

For its part, the thesis about overload struck a chord since it fed off the common-sense of the media. It was, however, always hotter as a critique of British democracy and working-class participation, than it was in providing a careful analysis of interests and power in British politics.

Proponents of adversary politics and overload present themselves as providing new hard-edged perspectives at one with the facts and at odds with the model of responsible party government and pluralism. In fact, they share assumptions and limitations in common with the theories they reject, and differ only in the way in which they *assess* the worth of British democracy in the context of changed economic circumstances. In all four theories attention rests on the 'public' and accessible features of democratic political life to the detriment of any substantive and critical concern with the economy and with the non-democratic secret state that we will be exploring in Chapter 5.

The strength of the corporatist perspective lies precisely in the extent to which it does deal with the substance of state intervention and with the implications of the particular stage of capitalist development. However, we see the thesis as overambitious since it only holds for certain groups and issues and for a particular period of British politics – and that period, may have passed at least for the moment.

Parties and pressure groups *are* important parts of the British political system, and they do assume a position of power and some prominence in linking economy and society to the polity and the state. But for all that, they are only *parts* of the political system, and in the chapters that follow we will be attending to the significance of other things. First, however, we will attend to the crisis of the contemporary constitution – a crisis that is partly revealed in the literature about adversary politics and overload since these perspectives challenge accepted constitutional theory, condemn British politics, and point to the need for constitutional reconstruction.

WORKS CITED AND GUIDE TO FURTHER READING

Beer, S.H. (1982) *Modern British Politics,* 2nd edn, London, Faber.
Edges into a corporatist perspective, but the classic study of British politics from a pluralist point of view.

Cawson, A. 1(1982) *Corporatism and Welfare,* London, Heinemann.
Sparkling essay within the corporatist tradition arguing that corporatism fits the facts with respect to public policy-making in the sphere of social policy.

Dearlove, J. (1973) *The Politics of Policy in Local Government,* London, Cambridge University Press.
Based on the London Borough of Kensington and Chelsea. Chapter 8 in particular, challenges the pluralist perspective on interest groups in local politics.

Douglas, J.E. (1976) Review article: the overloaded crown, *British Journal of Political Science,* **6,** 483–505.
A discussion of the 'ungovernability' thesis. Accepts the overload argument and so of limited critical worth.

Eckstein, H. (1960) *Pressure Group Politics,* London, George Allen and Unwin.
One of the pioneering studies of pressure politics in Britain. Looks at the British Medical Association and tries to explain the reasons for its 'effectiveness'.

Grant, W., and Marsh, D. (1977) *The CBI,* London, Hodder and Stoughton.
The first major study of the role of the Confederation of British Industry in the British political system. A bit of a disappointment. The authors argue that their evidence 'seems to fit happily with a pluralist analysis'.

King, A. (1975) Overload: Problems of governing in the 1970s, *Political Studies,* **23.** 284–96.
Feeds into the politics of Thatcherism with the argument that 'political scientists...should be concerned with how the number of tasks that government has come to be expected to perform can be reduced'. Never says *why* political scientists should have this as their concern.

King, A. (ed.) (1976) *Why is Britain Becoming Harder to Govern?* London, BBC.
Published to accompany three television programmes on the subject. The article by David Coates is a good critique of the whole overload/ungovernability thesis.

Middlemas, K. (1979) *Politics in Industrial Society,* London, Deutsch.
Sees 'corporate bias' as the hidden code to explain the experience of the British system of government since 1911.

Miliband, R. (1979) *The State in Capitalist Society,* London, Weidenfeld and Nicolson.
Still the classic account of British politics from a marxist perspective. Chapter 6 on 'Imperfect Competition' provides a critique of pluralism.

Rose, R. (1979) Ungovernability: Is there fire behind the smoke? *Political Studies,* **27,** 351–70.
Defines ungovernability 'as the prospect of a fully legitimate government losing its effectiveness, losing popular consent, or both'. See signs of fire behind the smoke.

Saunders, P. (1979) *Urban Politics,* London, Hutchinson.
Based on the London Borough of Croydon. Chapter 1 contains a critique of pluralist theory and a discussion of the concept of 'interests'.

Schmitter, P. (1979) Still the century of corporatism?, in P. C. Schmitter and G. Lehmbruch (eds), *Trends Towards Corporatist Intermediation,* London, Sage.
Classic article on corporatism looked at from the point of view of a particular system of interest group representation within capitalism.

CHAPTER 4

The Constitution in Crisis

I have reached the conclusion that our constitution is wearing out.
Lord Hailsham, The Listener, *21 October 1976*

The introduction of proportional representation is the linchpin of our entire programme of radical reform.
SDP/Liberal Alliance, Working Together for Britain *(1983)*

Labour will take action to...abolish the undemocratic House of Lords as quickly as possible.
Labour Party, The New Hope for Britain *(1983)*

For much of this century things have seemed pretty clear on the constitutional front. There was a flurry of constitutional activity between 1906 and 1914, and the House of Lords had its powers cut back by the Parliament Act, 1911, so formally putting the 'balanced' constitution to rest. Since then, however, in spite of a hiccup of concern during the depression of the 1930s, the British constitution has been seen as settled and so constitutional debate could itself settle down. By and large, constitutional authorities, parties and public alike were pleased with the set up. In the period since the Second World War, political stability, economic growth, and a broad societal consensus, meant that the constitution as it was, as it was said to be, and as it was said it should be, were all seen as of one, pulling together in mutual support in a way that called for 'no change'.

In the 1960s, there were minor (and seemingly unconnected) grumbles about many of the *parts* of the constitution. Local government was inefficient and lacked leaders of calibre; the civil service was too amateurish; the House of Commons needed a strong committee system; policy coordination and planning were poor; and many felt that there was scope for reform with respect to the redress of individual grievances against the state. However, these grumbles, and the piecemeal reforms and constitutional pseudo-changes which they inspired, did not spill over into a generalised sense of unease about the *essence* of the liberal-democratic constitution itself. There was almost a concern to avoid the problem of the British state. There was the hope that entry into the

European Community would offer the solution of a magic external escape route, and the drive for institutional efficiency embraced the pretence that the old system could be made to work 'better' whilst it was still left pretty much intact. It was all desperate, delaying stuff.

Developments since the late 1960s changed things. Constitutional fundamentals have been opened up with a vengeance. Entry into the EC challenged parliamentary sovereignty; the growth of direct action and extra-parliamentary politics in Northern Ireland and on the mainland challenged the rule of law and the stability of the liberal-democratic state; the ups-and-downs of nationalism in Wales and Scotland challenged the unitary state and threatened the break-up of Britain; the use of referenda [popular and direct votes on *issues*] revealed the crumbling legitimacy attaching to the indirect democracy of voting for *people* to parliament; the conventions underpinning cabinet government were buffeted by a trend to 'open government' that weakened collective responsibility and Cabinet solidarity; and developments within the Labour Party have had constitutional implications at the self-same time as the Liberals and SDP have sought to imprint themselves directly onto the British constitution with proposals for radical constitutional change including proportional representation.

All these developments have made for confusion. Experts were increasingly unclear as to what *was* the British constitution. However, they were very clear that a 'gap' had somehow opened up between the favourable tone of established constitutional *theory* and the horrors of day-to-day political *practice*. Instead of limited liberal-democracy they saw unrestrained mass democracy pushing the state into ever more intervention; instead of responsible party government they saw adversary politics; and instead of the harmony of pluralist group competition they saw only overload and hyperpluralism with the trade unions as the new lads on the top. There was agreement that British politics had slipped beyond the explanatory grasp, *and* the control, of the established constitutional theory. More than this, the Royal Commission on the Constitution detected 'discontent', 'mistrust' and 'disenchantment' with the prevailing set-up, pointing out that 'the people of Great Britain have less attachment to their system of government than in the past'. In this kind of *political* situation, and in the context of an *economic* decline that was 'blamed' on the excesses of democratic politics, instead of praising the British constitution as the best in the world, the constitutional authorities agreed that things were very badly wrong. Fundamental constitutional reconstruction was called for as a matter of urgency.

In little over a decade, constitutional clarity was replaced by confusion; praise was replaced by piercing critique; and support for the system was replaced by the demand for a new constitutional settlement to reshape politics. Simply expressed, the set-up as it was, as it was said to be, and as it was said it should be, had all pulled apart in a way that called for change. By the mid-seventies, then, the constitution was clearly in crisis.

Instead of just being part of the context *within* which politics occurred and was constrained, it has become an issue *in* politics on which interests and parties were keenly divided.

On the surface, the Conservative victory of 1979 seemed to blunt the case for change and in a 1981 Commons debate on the British constitution the minister of state at the Home Office boldly put the case for no change, arguing that 'this is a time when we should stand up for our great tradition of parliamentary democracy...I think that it is a great and positive system, a marvellous system...There is nothing more important than that we should stick up for the system that we have inherited down the ages, and that still has so much to offer the people of our country.' In fact, even as he spoke, the forces for change were there and rallying: the critique of the established constitutional authorities was eating into things below the froth of party politics; the Liberal–SDP Alliance considered that the 'key to...change lies in electoral and constitutional reform'; and Tony Benn, generally recognised as leader of the radical left in the Labour Party, was telling large and enthusiastic audiences up and down the country that 'constitutional questions are the key to power in a parliamentary democracy' and that 'socialists need to give at least as much attention to the institutions of the state as to the power structure of the economy'. Of course, the Conservatives won again in 1983, but the fact that they secured two-thirds of the seats in the Commons with less than half of the popular vote encouraged the centre parties to cry still louder for electoral reform at the same time as the Left were forced to ponder on the fact that had there been proportional representation then the Conservatives would not have been able to form a government without the moderating support of another party in the coalition.

So, the play of party politics at the ballot box may give us interludes of constitutional peace, but we cannot escape the fact that the British constitution is still up for grabs, in politics, and on the agenda for change. We are in a period of decisive constitutional significance. The writing may be on the wall for the established system. It has presided over our economic decline for decades and even now is failing to reverse it. Moreover, public support for the system has become problematic in a way that poses some kind of challenge to the legitimacy and authority of the state itself. Economic decline is tangled up with political turmoil in a way that has made for a crisis of the constitution. Politicians of all persuasions entertain the hope that their brand of constitutional reconstruction can set things aright so enabling the state to recover, square the circle, and create the conditions for both economic growth *and* social cohesion.

Although it is doubtful whether the established set-up will hold, the future form of any new constitution is uncertain. There is now no consensus on the British constitution. The rest of this chapter will set down three broad and differing perspectives on what should be the form of a new constitution for Britain. First, we will set down the

Establishment perspective of the constitutional authorities – the perspective, that is, of those who do so much to say what *is* the constitution in the absence of a written legal document. The Conservative Party itself has tended to lend its weight to the prevailing set-up (perhaps because it can win within it), but the constitutional authorities are, by definition, Establishment figures and they are often identified with Toryism. Moreover, if the forces for constitutional change do grow, then the Conservative Party itself could well be forced to contemplate constitutional change in order to hold things. Were this to be the case then the party would almost certainly adopt the essentials of the Establishment perspective – the more so since this perspective is keenly attentive to many of the contemporary concerns of the New Right. Second, we will set-down the perspective of the Liberals and SDP – the parties that have been most active in pressing the case for a new constitution precisely because they do not think they can win within the rules of the old one. Third, we will set down the perspective of the Left within the Labour Party – the party that has very belatedly come to an awareness of the significance of constitutional politics and of the need for change.

THE ESTABLISHED CONSTITUTIONAL AUTHORITIES

In 1976, Lord Hailsham, an elder statesman of the Conservative Party who had been (and was to become again) the Lord Chancellor – the most powerful position in the British legal system – was invited by the BBC to give the Richard Dimbleby lecture: he called it 'Elective Dictatorship'. Lord Hailsham carefully unpicked the shreds of legitimacy attaching to the established constitution and called for 'nothing less than a written constitution for the United Kingdom, and by that I mean one which limits the powers of Parliament and provides a means of enforcing those limitations both by political and by legal means'.

In 1980, Lord Denning, the then Master of the Rolls – perhaps the second most powerful judicial position – delivered the Richard Dimbleby lecture. His lecture, entitled 'Misuse of Power', ran through eight instances of possible misuse of power by sovereigns, politicians, ministers, and the media. Lord Denning recognised that 'in our constitutional theory Parliament is supreme but he saw the judges as the real 'guardians of our constitution' and he felt that they ought to be able to pronounce on the validity of the conventions and 'ought to have a power of judicial review of legislation similar to that in the United States: whereby the judges can set aside statutes which are contrary to our unwritten constitution – in that they are repugnant to reason or to fundamentals'. Lord Denning raised the obvious question as to whether the judges might misuse their power – power which he wished to see dramatically increased – but he argued that we 'need have no fear...Someone must be trusted. Let it be the judges'.

Lord Hailsham and Lord Denning have not been alone in their views as to what is wrong with the established constitution and what kind of new constitutional settlement is needed.

What is wrong with the established constitution?

The sovereignty of Parliament has been the linchpin of our unwritten and flexible constitution; it can be traced back in our political practice and constitutional theory for almost three centuries; and yet the constitutional authorities have come to see it as *the* fundamental constitutional problem needing challenge and change. These authorities, be they judges, constitutional lawyers or senior political scientists, have come to this view as they have been forced to ponder on two things.

1 They have become crushingly alive to the *presence* of external political checks on the power of Parliament. Elections are said to limit Parliament because they give power to electors who ignorantly demand ever more state intervention. The need to secure obedience to the laws passed by Parliament is said to limit what Parliament can do in a situation in which there are those who are prepared to openly defy the law on the streets, with strikes, and with the gun.

2 As they have pondered on the growth of state intervention (which they largely regard as undesirable) so they have come to bemoan the *absence* of legal limitations on parliamentary sovereignty and competence which could hold that intervention in check.

This concern about the sovereignty of Parliament has to be seen in the context of political realities as seen by the constitutional authorities. In theory, Parliament consists of Crown, Lords, and Commons, and the assent of all three parts is needed for a bill to become law. In practice, however, the sovereignty of Parliament has increasingly become the sovereignty of the Commons, and the sovereignty of the Commons has increasingly become the sovereignty of the government and the majority party. More than this, many constitutional authorities have become uneasy about the behaviour of governments in the light of the doctrines of mandate and the manifesto which are said to give effective power to party activists and extremists outside of parliament. In hard reality, therefore, many authorities consider that the sovereignty of parliament really means the sovereignty of an unrepresentative party boss who is then given a free constitutional rein to wreak unlimited havoc. Constitutional authorities are critical of the established constitution precisely because it has somehow allowed, and not limited, the emergence of the pattern of party politics and state intervention which they regard as so disastrous for Britain and her economy.

Now, there is something new and strange about all this. Since the coming of manhood suffrage in the last century, constitutional authorities have tended to applaud the demise of parliamentary government, the decline of parliament, and the rise of the strong one-party executive. They painted a picture of responsible party government and saw the electorate as an adequate check upon cabinet (or prime ministerial) government within our praiseworthy system of parliamentary democracy. Nowadays, however, the constitutional authorities are unhappy about the electoral check; they are very unhappy about the demise of the undemocratic checks of Crown and Lords; they are profoundly uneasy about the power of party in government; and so they are critical of the reality of what Parliamentary sovereignty has become. In bald terms, many of today's most prominent constitutional authorities have grown anxious about the working of unfettered representative democracy and majority rule. What do they think should be done? What kind of constitution would they like to see established?

Proposals for a new constitution

First, the constitutional authorities want to limit the sovereignty of Parliament by law; second, they want to reinvigorate the various checks on the power of a democratically elected government through changes designed to bolster a more 'balanced' constitution; and third, they look to the checks implicit in a genuine revival of Parliament and parliamentary government.

Proposals *to limit the sovereignty of parliament* tend to centre on the introduction of a written constitution with judicial review and the entrenchment of a Bill of Rights as some kind of 'higher' law beyond easy parliamentary repeal. The function of a written constitution would be to set down the laws and conventions relating to the main institutions of the state, the relations among them, and between them and private citizens. There would be a concern to clarify the confusion which exists as to the 'right' and 'proper' principles for the British constitution today and then there would be an attempt to secure them against repeal or amendment except by some specially prescribed procedure that would involve more than a simple majority in the House of Commons. For its part, a Bill of Rights insists that certain rights, privileges, and liberties are basic and must be afforded to all individuals notwithstanding what transient governments might wish to do.

Expressed in these general terms it is easy to see how such a code of rights could be regarded as a 'good thing'. The problems start, however, once we move on to consider just what rights should be included in any Bill; once we consider the difficulties of implementation; and once we assess the implications of any such legally enforced code and written constitution for the functioning of our system especially as these things involve the position of the elected government and the judges. Let us deal with each of these problems in turn.

Most of the constitutional authorities who have lent their weight to a

Bill of Rights for Britain, envisage our incorporating the European Convention for the Protection of Human Rights and Fundamental Freedoms into our domestic law. We ratified the treaty in 1951 but under our constitution this gives no right of action in our domestic courts. Now, there would be a certain logic in this incorporation, for, if we were to have a Bill of Rights enforced in Britain, then in a situation in which we have ratified the European Convention it would be difficult for us to bypass these rights and draw up a completely new set. Moreover, if we were to attempt this, then getting an agreed set of principles approved by Parliament would open up conflicts as to the rights to be included, and if a new code was eventually passed then their existence alongside the European Convention would create confusion and cause additional difficulties for the courts.

The problem is that the European convention only really gives expression to traditional liberal and democratic freedoms bearing on such things as freedom of association, speech, belief, the press, and so on. These freedoms are clearly of importance in the face of the *public* power of the state, but they give small comfort to those who would like to see the position of individuals strengthened in relation to the exercise of *private* power in the economy. In fact, those who support the introduction of a Bill of Rights tend to see the state in essentially 'negative' terms: it is regarded as the only real threat to individual freedom and liberty (apart from that posed by the collective activity of trade unions) because freedom itself is defined negatively as simply involving an absence of *public* and legal restraint on individual action. There is a lack of any sympathy for a more 'positive' view of the state as a collective and democratic instrument. From this point of view the state is not seen as a threat to freedom, but is rather regarded as a vehicle for securing broad community and individual rights against the power of vested 'private' interests within economy and society. Such a view inevitably embraces a rather more positive perspective on freedom itself, requiring the provision of real opportunities for all individuals to do worthwhile, life-enhancing, things. From this point of view there is room for the state to assume an interventionist role for the many in a way that may well eat into the freedoms of the few who exercise private, economic power – power that many constitutional authorities are actually concerned to protect and defend through their stress on the importance of liberty, and constitutional limitations on taxation, state intervention, parliamentary sovereignty, and the play of democratic politics itself. Many constitutional authorities, like the New Right, seem to be keener on securing economic freedoms for particular individuals than they are to secure broad social freedoms for the mass of the population *against* the freedoms of the few.

In fact, behind the bland constitutional concern to protect human rights through a Bill of Rights, there often lurks a partisan and intensely political concern to restrict the role of the state because of an attachment to a theory of limited government, born of a desire to use the law to defend the private sphere and capitalism, so hitting at the possibility of socialism and the democratic road to its attainment. Be this as it may, the constitutional authorities who support the introduction of a Bill of Rights to limit Parliament, government, and the state, nevertheless recognise that it calls for a fundamental constitutional change if it is to be more than just a pious declaration of good intent. Simply expressed, they see a need to mount a successful two-pronged attack on the established doctrine of parliamentary sovereignty.

1　If a Bill of Rights is to limit the exercise of political power through the state then it really has to be 'entrenched' beyond the repeal of future parliaments. This hits at the doctrine that Parliament cannot bind, or curtail, the powers of future parliaments.
2　If a Bill of Rights is somehow entrenched as a higher law, then all ordinary legislation will need to be checked against that law. This will involve judicial review through some kind of supreme court of the United Kingdom. Judges would be charged with the duty of interpreting and protecting the constitution so keeping the legislative sovereignty of Parliament within written, legal, limits. This hits at the established doctrine that the courts recognise no legal limits to Parliament's legislative power.

The constitutional difficulty of this attack is clear enough. The proposals to limit parliamentary sovereignty stumble against the sovereignty of parliament itself. The problem to be solved seems to block the solution! Not surprisingly, therefore, constitutional authorities eager for change have pondered long and hard, not so much on how to introduce a Bill of Rights or a restraining written constitution (that, after all, could be effected by a simple Commons majority backed by the usual formality of assent by Crown and Lords) but on how to ensure that such a new settlement sticks and lies safe beyond the repealing vote of yet another simple Commons majority. There are a number of tortured perspectives on how to get round this problem, but they are themselves fraught with problems.

The idea of using a Constitutional Commission and a referendum to endow any new constitution with a special prestige does not alter the fact that within our constitution referenda are of an advisory character only and have not served to limit Parliament's ultimate discretion. Moreover, constitutional lawyers may write about 'old' Parliaments being able to bind and limit a 'new' Parliament, and may suggest that a 'new judicial attitude' (whereby judges no longer accept that they are subordinate to Parliament) would make for a fresh start so that 'the doctrine that no Parliament can bind its successors becomes ancient history', but these tricky *legal* formulations do not alter the fact that constitution-making occurs in the context of a *political* reality which limits what is feasible, acceptable, and enforceable.

Interestingly, however, the fact that the British constitution is in part what the constitutional authorities say it is means that an insidious kind of constitutional change is *already* occurring simply as a result of authoritative attacks on the sovereignty of Parliament as a 'dogma' and a 'myth' that needs to be challenged. Although any 'alternative doctrine must be highly speculative', the influential *Halsbury's Laws of England* goes on to recognise that

for many constitutional theorists the question of whether parliamentary sovereignty presupposes that Parliament must always remain sovereign and cannot be bound by the legislation of its predecessors, or whether Parliament's sovereignty entitles it to restrict its power to legislate, or deprive itself of the power to legislate, remains open.

One thing is very clear: the road to constitutional change via a Bill of Rights, a written constitution, and an attack on parliamentary sovereignty is likely to be a long and bitter haul.

A number of things are part of the concern *to secure a more 'balanced' constitution* – the second essential of the new constitution envisaged by the established constitutional authorities.

1   There is a concern to strengthen the position and power of the House of Lords. There is the grudging recognition that, as it stands today, the House of Lords is an indefensible anachronism and that only limited legitimacy (and therefore power) can attach to a second chamber whose membership is largely based on heredity and which has an overwhelming and permanent majority for the Conservative Party. In order to give the House of Lords a more effective role in the governmental process (and in order to buttress its position against the threat of abolition) there is the recognition that it needs to secure increased public support, and in order to secure that there has been the dawning realisation that changes are needed in the composition of the second chamber. There is no consensus on this, but in broad terms there is a concern to water down, or phase out, the hereditary element in favour of elected members representing 'interests' or regions and possibly chosen by proportional representation.

2   There is now a much greater preparedness to see the Crown shift from a limp constitutional role into a much more active and independent role in matters of decisive constitutional significance. For example, Lord Crowther-Hunt considers that the Queen would be perfectly 'justified' in withholding her consent from a bill which sought to abolish the House of Lords even if the government proposing this had secured a mandate through the manifesto set before the people at a general election. Moreover, if the centre parties succeed in breaking through into parliament in large numbers then the prospect of coalition government would be increased and this would give the Crown a role in the making of governments since it would no longer be a simple and automatic matter of sending for the leader of the majority party in the Commons.

3   A written constitution with judicial review clearly involves staking out a position of greater political power for the judges. In fact, independently of current concern about the constitution, there has been a trend to 'judicial activism' that has resulted in a situation in which the courts have shown a much greater willingness to become involved in challenging the use of ministerial discretion and prerogative powers. As the constitutional authorities gradually detach themselves from wholehearted support for our system of democracy so they envisage the judges assuming a role of extended significance in defending liberty and in checking what they regard as the misuse of political power. Politically, the judicial conception of the public interest tends to embrace the promotion of certain views normally associated with the Conservative Party and there is a greater likelihood that Labour Governments will encounter challenges through the courts if only because they tend to be more interventionist and to challenge the status quo.

The final major aspect of the new constitutional settlement seen as desirable by the constitutional authorities embodies a concern *to revive parliamentary government and the power of an independent House of Commons* unchecked by outside interest and direct democratic pressures. The current situation in which the government, through party discipline, is able to control the House of Commons and absorb its powers unto itself is regarded as undesirable. There is a concern to increase the independence of members and to devise institutional relationships to facilitate a balance of powers that would give the Commons a more effective checking, choosing, and legislating role of the kind it enjoyed prior to the extension of the franchise and the organising implications of political parties in the nineteenth century. The weakening of party and the creation of a strong committee system are seen as of especial importance in this regard. There is the hope that their ability to delve deeply and acquire information would enable them to hold ministers and government to proper account.

This catalogue of proposals for constitutional change does not exhaust the perspective of the constitutional authorities, but the emphasis is on limiting Parliament, asserting the power of the judiciary, balancing the constitution, and reviving parliamentary government. Caught up in the concern to balance the power of the Commons is an attempt to recapture elements of the eighteenth-century constitution in a way that waters down the democratic side of the state machine; caught up in the concern to secure a more independent House of Commons is an attempt to revive the pre-democratic nineteenth-century liberal constitution; and caught up in the concern to limit parliamentary sovereignty is an attempt to limit democracy itself. At the present point in time there are those who are of the opinion that no sacrifice is too great for our democracy, least of all the sacrifice of democracy itself to the power of the judges and enslaving legal limitations. Central to all of this is a concern to limit state intervention and the play of politics itself because of a preference for the freedoms and liberties available to some in the context of the 'naturally' self-regulating and ordered free market of capitalism. Lord Hailsham may be critical of the British constitution, but he is clear that 'whatever else has been the cause of our failure, it is not capitalism, or free enterprise in any form'.

THE SDP–LIBERAL ALLIANCE

In 1979, Roy Jenkins, ex-Labour minister, President of the European Commission, and soon to be a born-again British politician, was invited by the BBC to give the Richard Dimbleby lecture. In his 'Home Thoughts from Abroad' he chose to talk about the state of British politics and how the 'system' had gone wrong and ought to be changed and improved. He considered that the established two-party system had become a rigid tyranny that lacked public support and was injurious to our economic performance – the adversary politics thesis. He argued that the established system made 'the moderates too much the prisoners of the extremists'; he made an 'unashamed plea for the strengthening of the political centre'; and he considered that 'the case of proportional representation is overwhelming'.

Liberal interest in electoral reform goes back over 100 years. The emergence of the Labour Party in 1922 as the second largest political party and the fact of alternating Labour and Conservative Governments in the period since the Second World War heightened Liberal interest in proportional representation – the more so from the 1960s onwards when their increasing vote in the country was not matched by seats in the House of Commons.

The election of February 1974 was some kind of turning point in the case for electoral reform and constitutional change. It did not simply result in a situation in which the Liberals won 2.2 per cent of the Commons seats in return for 19.3 per cent of the national vote since Labour also sneaked into office with only 37.1 per cent of the votes cast – less than the Conservative total. An election that had been fought by the Conservatives on the issue of, 'Who runs the country – government or trade unions?', was won by a party that was seen by many as in the pay of the unions and there was the spectre of socialism via the ballot box. There was now the more general view that the established electoral system was too generous to the two major parties. Moreover, it was seen as too generous at a time when those parties had become more extreme. In effect, it was claimed that the unpopular and disastrous system of adversary politics and the threat of democratic socialism was in existence *because* of the working of the established electoral system. Criticism of that system and interest in proportional representation surged.

In 1974, Anthony Wigram founded Conservative Action for Electoral

Reform and urged the adoption of proportional representation because 'the present electoral system could easily give power to a Socialist Party controlled by an extreme left wing group.'. In March 1981 the SDP was launched and immediately announced that 'the present "winner takes all" system of electing MPs is unfair to the voters and opens the door to extremism, whether left or right. We need a sensible system of proportional representation in which every vote really counts.' As sure as night follows day the Social Democrats moved into uneasy alliance with the Liberals. In the First Report of the Joint Liberal/SDP Commission for Constitutional Reform they announced that 'electoral reform is an absolute priority for Britain, since we believe it to be a precondition both of national unity and of social and political progress' and (they failed to add) for their own sure breakthrough into Parliament itself. The Liberals and the SDP as outsiders to the established system have emerged as the champions of constitutional change with a whole package of proposals for a new constitutional settlement.

To a great extent their analysis of the problematic nature of the established set-up tends to parallel that advanced by the constitutional authorities in that they are attentive to the political and economic problems of adversary party politics, elective dictatorship, and the overload of conflicting demands. Not surprisingly, then, their package of proposals for constitutional change has much in common with the perspective set down in the last section. They see a place for a Bill of Rights, a written constitution and constitutional court; they want to increase the checks on government through a more balanced constitution consequent upon the establishment of a reformed, elected, second chamber with increased powers of delay; and they look to a revival of the position of Parliament and parliamentary government.

They depart from the perspective of the constitutional authorities, however, in their advocacy of proposals for devolved and decentralised government, and for more open government. Moreover, the constitutional authorities tend to adopt a 'legalistic' approach to constitutional change and are pessimistic as to the prospects for democratic politics. In consequence, they seek to prevent democratic damage and state intervention by choosing to emphasise the desirability of setting legal limits to the powers of a democratically elected parliament. By way of contrast, the Liberals and Social Democrats adopt a more 'political' approach to constitutional change and they are rather more optimistic as to the prospects for democratic politics in Britain. In consequence, they are less concerned to fashion a constitution that would limit democratic politics than they are to introduce a constitution that would facilitate a new *type* of democratic politics that would then make more likely coalition government and the kind of moderate, stable, policies which they regard as at one with the broad mass of public opinion and in the national interest itself. It is in this connection that, notwithstanding their commitment to a whole new constitutional settlement, they are primarily concerned to effect electoral reform. They see this as the 'linchpin' of their 'entire programme of radical reform' and as the key to a 'new' politics and a 'precondition' for further constitutional change.

Let us, then, explore the arguments surrounding the issue of electoral reform. What is the case for the established system; what is the case against this system and for proportional representation; what are the prospects for implementing change; and what are the implications of proportional representation for representative and responsible government in Britain?

The case for the established electoral system

Under the established system for electing members to the House of Commons, each elector has only one vote in a general election; each constituency returns only one Member of Parliament; and Members of the House of Commons are elected on a first-past-the-post (winner takes all) system whereby the candidate with the most votes wins the seat whether or not he or she has an overall majority of all the votes cast in the constituency. The established system has been defended on a number of grounds.

1   It is simple, well-established and well-understood, and requires only a short ballot paper on which the voter needs to put a single 'X' against the name of the preferred candidate. Compact, single-member, constituencies (as opposed to large, multi-member, constituencies) provide for one representative in a way that is said to facilitate constituent–member contact and the redress of individual grievances.
2   More fundamentally, however, defence of the established electoral system is caught up with a belief in the virtues of the Responsible Party Government model that we discussed in the Chapter 2. From this perspective a two-party system and one-party government is of the essence. It is recognised that the established electoral system *does* discriminate against third parties securing seats in proportion to votes, but this is defended because of the virtues that are seen as flowing from the fact that the system helps to ensure that just one party has a secure majority in the Commons and is therefore able to form a government without the need for coalition. In this state of affairs, the electorate is presented with a clear choice between alternative programmes and parties for government in a way that enables the *electorate* to choose the government *and* the broad drift of public policy for the next 5 years. In effect, under the present system a voter is doing *more* than simply choosing a parliamentary representative. The electorate is able to choose a candidate, a party, a programme, and a government; the electorate knows roughly what the government will do once in office; and so the electorate knows who to blame and which party to vote out of office at the next election.

3   In addition to providing for strong and responsible government it has been claimed that the system provides for moderate government because the two parties in a two-party system must strive to occupy the middle ground where the votes lie thickest and this obliges them to control their extremists who might dissuade the middling voters from giving their support.

The case against the established electoral system and the case for proportional representation

Liberal and Social Democratic critics of the established electoral system reject this defence as a caricature of the real situation.

1   They claim that the stability of government is more apparent than real. They argue that the post-war period is best characterised as one involving policy change and instability, and that, since the crack-up of the consensus in the 1960s, one doctrinaire and mandated government has been replaced by another with scant regard to appeals to the middle ground of public opinion. They point out that under the first-past-the-post system a small swing in votes tends to produce a major change in parliamentary strength so 'exaggerating' a party's lead in parliament in a way that leads to sharp swings in policy when there are only small shifts in voting and still more limited changes in public opinion.
2   They recognise that the system has tended to provide for 'strong' government in that most post-war governments *have* been able to count on an absolute majority of seats in the House of Commons, but they regard this strength as a bad thing. They take this view because they are alive to the fact that since 1935 no government has been elected by a majority of the electorate and secured 50 per cent of the popular vote. In reality, therefore, strong government has simply enabled a series of 'minority' governments to push their policies through the Commons. Moreover, this has taken place against the policies of the previous party government so entrenching the instability of adversary politics as the price to be paid for a strength that really works against the moderate majority in the population at large.
3   They question the extent to which the system provides for representative governments noting not just the underrepresentation of third parties, but the fact that, in the elections of 1929, 1951, and February 1974, the party which returned the largest number of MPs actually had a smaller share of the vote than the runner-up party in the Commons so that the electoral 'winner' was, in fact, the governmental 'loser'.

Now, all of this is seen as bad enough, but in our developing multi-party system they see less prospect of single parties having absolute majorities in the House of Commons. Put another way, even without a change in the electoral system there is the prospect of more 'pacts' of the kind which existed between Liberals and Labour between 1977 and 1978. Of course, on occasions, single parties may still be able to gain absolute parliamentary majorities but they will be likely to do so on the basis of much smaller percentages of the popular vote. For example, in October 1974 the Labour Government secured the support of 39.2 per cent of those who voted and just over a quarter of the electorate; in 1979 the Conservatives gained 43.9 per cent of the vote and the support of around a third of the electorate; and in 1983, the Conservative landslide of seats (their parliamentary majority trebled) was based on just 42.4 per cent of the vote – less than they got when they lost in 1964, less than they got in 1979, the fifth-lowest Conservative vote since the war, and the lowest vote-count by a government with a secure majority since 1922.

Although Liberals and Social Democrats claim that the established electoral system does not work as its defenders say it should, they are at their most forceful when they point out that the established system is 'unfair' and unrepresentative. There are two broad aspects to this and both bear on the relation of seats in the Commons to votes in the country. First, it is pointed out that the Labour and Conservative Parties secure seats in the Commons in numbers far larger than warranted by their voting strength in the country. In 1983, for example, the Conservatives won almost two-thirds of the seats in the House of Commons with less than half the nation's backing and a modest 30.8 per cent of the total electorate, while the Labour Party won almost a third of the seats with only 27.6 per cent of the votes. Second, and obviously related, there is the position of 'third' parties. A third party whose candidates may obtain many thousands of votes in each of the constituencies that it contests without ever coming top of the poll in any, can amass a national vote in the millions without winning a seat. This problem does not affect all third parties to the same extent since the problem of 'wasted votes' bears heavily on those parties whose support is spread across the country as opposed to those whose support is regionally concentrated. In February 1974, for example, the Liberals, with 19.3 per cent of the vote, secured only fourteen seats, while the Ulster Unionists with only 1.3 per cent of the total UK vote won eleven seats. In October 1974 the Liberals with 18.3 per cent of the vote won thirteen seats, while the Scottish National Party with only 2.9 per cent of the total UK vote secured eleven seats. In 1982, the Joint Liberal/SDP Commission for Constitutional Reform calculated that if in England there was, as compared to the 1979 general election, an even switch of votes from the Labour and Conservative Parties to the Alliance such that each of the three groupings secured 33 per cent of the vote, then the Alliance would still only gain 56 seats as compared to 207 for the Conservatives and 253 for Labour. Not until the Alliance secured about 37 per cent of the vote would it become the largest single grouping in the Commons. We can see in these figures how crucial is the issue of electoral reform to the success of the Liberals and Social Democrats.

Both points about unfairness are revealed once we note that in the election of 1983 the Conservatives secured one Commons seat for every 33 000 votes; Labour one for every 40 000; and the Liberals and Social Democrats one for every 340 000. The ratio of seats won was 17 : 9 : 1, yet the spread of votes was much closer producing a rough ratio of 3 : 2 : 2. We may have a system of 'one person one vote', but Liberals and Social Democrats point out that we do not yet have a system of 'one person one vote *one value'* since some votes are more equal than others. Not surprisingly, they argue that if we persist with the established electoral system then we will continue with the problems of government which they identify. Moreover, as the public themselves come to recognise that many more votes are being 'wasted' and that their votes bear little relation to the final result in the constituency or the country, so declining turnout and public disaffection will increase in a way which will really threaten the legitimacy of the whole system.

The problem of implementing proportional representation

The remedy for pretty much all of the above, and for much else besides, is seen to lie in the introduction of proportional representation for all national and local elections. The immediate problem, however, lies in implementing such a system. The Labour and Conservative Parties who benefit from the present system have set their teeth against a change which would undermine their prospect of regularly forming a government on their own. The likelihood of change lies in one of a number of possibilities – all in the long term, and all problematic.

1   If the centre parties gain a clear majority in a future Parliament then they claim that they would immediately introduce a bill to effect proportional representation. The problem is that the prospect is unlikely given the way that the established system works. Moreover, if they were to break through within the established system then they just might be a little less enthusiastic about introducing proportional representation as 'a first priority' since it could let one of the parties they would have displaced back into the game.

2   If a future Parliament is 'hung' with the centre parties holding the balance of power between Conservative and Labour then the Liberals and Social Democrats have made it clear that the price of their giving support to any minority government would be a binding agreement to introduce proportional representation. However, it is by no means certain that either of the established parties *would* agree to change since they would be bidding away long-term electoral advantage in return for a

short-term in office in a coalition government in which they might have only limited power. Moreover, it is not clear that either party *could* agree to a change and still hold itself intact. What kind of deal could the SDP possibly do with the Labour Party when they split with Labour because of the developing strength of the Left in the party? Equally, what kind of bargain could be struck with the Conservatives if the dominant tendency in the party remained Thatcherite Right wing? In the event of a hung parliament there is the probability of constitutional deadlock, and the possibility of political breakdown and a realignment of parliamentary support for particular parties. In either case an early general election is likely to be called to resolve things. If the centre parties were seen to be self-interested in blocking the formation of a government through their insistence on a deal to introduce electoral reform then this could reflect badly on them in the election so cutting back their seats – and the prospect for proportional representation.

3   There is the particular position of the Conservative Party. In 1978, over one-third of Conservative MPs voted for a form of proportional representation for the proposed Welsh Assembly. Moreover, the party as a whole is clearly opposed to the election of a Labour Government. The established system may let the Conservatives into office with less than half the popular vote, but it also invites the prospect of a future Labour Government elected to office on perhaps 32 per cent of the vote and with the support of less than a quarter of the electorate as a whole. While the Conservatives are secure in Parliament and on the offensive then they can see no need for electoral reform as they struggle to recover a Tory England. However, they are put into a more defensive position if they suffer a crushing defeat in any future election and if the two-party system continues to weaken. In this kind of situation they might be concerned to hold on to what they have by accepting a change in the electoral system that would block the prospect of a Socialist Government committed to extensive state intervention and a more 'extreme' kind of constitutional reconstruction. The moderate Conservative, Sir Ian Gilmour, favours electoral reform precisely because he is alive to the fact that: 'after electoral reform, no Labour party led by Mr Wedgwood Benn, say, would ever win a majority in the country. If the Labour Party wished to participate in government it would have to shed its Marxist–Trotskyist wing or make it impotent.' Put another way, thoughtful Conservatives recognise that electoral reform would probably secure the right of middle ground in the face of socialist challenge but at the cost of blocking the returning prospect of the chance to implement the hard-right vision. It is an issue that could split the Conservative Party.

4   Finally, there is the position of the Labour Party. Earlier this century they broke through the Liberal–Conservative two-party system without the help of proportional representation, and under the established electoral system they have been able to form governments on their own with less than 40 per cent of the popular vote. Their crushing electoral

defeat of 1983 in conjunction with the realisation that their share of the popular vote has been in steady decline since 1951 has, however, forced a reassessment. First, had proportional representation been in force in 1983, then the Conservatives would not have been able to form a government on their own and coalition would have forced a moderation of policies. Second, if the Liberals and Social Democrats had been able to squeeze a few more votes from Labour supporters, then it could well have been the Labour Party that finished up with just a few seats in parliament out of all proportion to votes cast. Third, there is the growing recognition that Labour could not carry through a radical programme of change without mass support. In other words, they may win within the established system but it does not get them very far if they are not carrying the people with them in a popular crusade for change. Simply expressed, from both a defensive *and* offensive point of view there are good reasons why Labour needs to think hard about electoral reform.

The implications of proportional representation for
representative and responsible government

Leaving aside the prospects for proportional representation, what would be the implications of such a system for the functioning of the British political system? Are there problems caught up in the case for change? We need to pay particular attention to two things. First, there is the issue of 'fairness'. Second, we need to consider the role of the electorate and the accountability, or responsibility, of government to the people.

1   On the surface a system of proportional representation is self-evidently fair to parties and people, since parties favoured by the people at the polls would secure seats in the Commons in direct proportion to their votes in the country. The argument cannot be stopped at this simple point, however. Elections are not just about electing representatives to Parliament. Elections are also about government and governmental power. It may be fair to give third parties seats in Parliament in proportion to their votes in the country, but it is quite a different matter when the implications of this situation are considered in terms of the follow through to governmental power. It is far harder to argue that it is fair to create an electoral system that will put the centre parties into a governmental position where they will be likely to hold an almost permanent balance of power between Labour and Conservative. Simply expressed, a relatively poorly supported centre party with well under 20 per cent of the vote, but with some eighty or so seats, would invariably be in government; would be in a position to determine whether Conservative or Labour were drawn into government with it; and would, therefore, be able to exert an influence over the direction of public policy out of all proportion to their votes and support in the country at large. Proportional representation in Parliament might translate into disproportionate power

in government in a way that would make the established first-past-the-post inequalities look rather more fair than is often seen to be the case. Of course, there may be those who would argue that the entrenchment of the middle ground in power would be a good thing that would lead to moderate government and stable policies, but let them not argue that it would also be fair or would give the majority of people what they wanted of government.

2 What are the implications of proportional representation for responsible government? Since the Second World War, with the exception of the quasi-minority Labour Government of 1974–9, Britain has experienced single-party government backed by an overall majority in the Commons. Proportional representation would not make majority government of this kind impossible (we would have it if more than 50 per cent of the electorate wanted it) but it would make it very much less likely. Put another way, proportional representation would make minority or coalition government very much more likely. For example, after the election of 1983 the Conservatives had an overall majority in the House of Commons of 144 seats and the Liberals and Social Democrats had only 23 seats. However, if that election had been fought under some system of proportional representation then the Conservatives would have had a majority over Labour but would have been in a very substantial overall minority since the Liberals and Social Democrats would have held 160 or so seats. The Conservatives may have tried to go it alone and form a minority government, but some kind of party-splitting coalition government could well have been more likely.

Coalitions are not alien to British political experience but it is as well to consider the implications of this form of government. In a situation in which no one party is likely to be in an overall majority in the Commons then the electorate is just not in a position where it can realistically choose between alternative programmes and alternative teams of leaders sure in the knowledge that the winning team will be available to form a government and eager to try and implement its electoral programme. The electorate cannot do this because proportional representation makes it less likely that there will be a single winning governmental team. Of course, two parties may announce before an election that they are prepared to go into coalition with each other but they cannot guarantee the election result that would make that coalition possible. So, the electorate can choose representatives for Parliament but it is less able to choose a government and a programme that will be implemented. There may be deadlock and paralysis, but the government that will eventually take office will emerge *after* protracted bargaining between the parties in Parliament *after* a general election and without any reference to the electors and their wishes. The result will be a governing coalition for which no one voted, and with policies (born of the necessity for compromise to effect the coalition) which were never set before the electorate for their approval and support. Moreover, the coalition government so formed will not have to (or even be *able* to) face the electorate at the next election since the parties to the coalition will be free to fight again as independent entities. Each will probably claim credit for the popular policies, and each will probably blame the other coalition partner for the unpopular policies. Simply expressed, the accountability, or responsibility, of single-party government to the people – a responsibility that has been of the very *essence* of our system of parliamentary democracy – would be rendered less likely with proportional representation. Having said that, governments would be more responsible to Parliament; Parliament would be stronger relative to the executive; and party leaders could be 'weaker', but we should remember that there is nothing essentially democratic about reviving the parliamentary government of the nineteenth-century liberal constitution. Indeed, increasing the power of an independent and autonomous parliament could further weaken the connection between government and the people and could institutionalise our passivity as spectators to a game over which we have no real control and only limited influence.

If the Liberal–SDP Alliance were ever in a position to implement electoral reform, a reformed and strengthened second chamber, and legal limits on the sovereignty of Parliament, then we could find ourselves with a constitution which entrenched the middle ground and which offered a democracy of dazzling choice but no decision, and a less-accountable government than that which we currently enjoy within the established constitution.

THE LABOUR PARTY

Models for Transformation

In the past, the Left in British politics has not displayed a keen interest in the subtleties of the British constitution because two strategic models for socialist transformation, the parliamentary and the insurrectionary, have dominated thinking, debate, and action. More recently, however, a variety of factors have rather changed this state of affairs and encouraged the search for a third road to socialism. What, then, are these models, and how have they shaped the Left perspective on the British constitution, and on the need for change in the rules and the institutions of the political game in Britain?

The parliamentary road. The parliamentary road to socialism has been the major tradition within Britain where the Labour Party has long been the dominant organisational force on the Left and amongst the working class. Revolutionary violence (and even extra-parliamentary politics) is rejected as undemocratic, undesirable, and unnecessary. There is the view that socialism will come gradually (but inevitably) through a democratic Parliament as a result of the cumulative effect of piecemeal reforms pushed through Parliament consequent upon regular electoral victories enabling the Labour Party to form a government, organise Parliament, and determine law-making. Parliament is seen as at the controlling centre of the state. The state machine as a whole is regarded as neutral and autonomous from economic power, and so is available to be driven to the left if Labour is in the majority in the Commons.

From this point of view, the liberal-democratic British constitution is applauded as pretty much the best in the world and so no case is made for constitutional reconstruction.

The insurrectionary road. The insurrectionary road to socialism is associated with Lenin and the experience of the October Revolution in Russia. It is not a strategy that is organisationally entrenched with British political experience, but it is intellectually entrenched as a challenge to the viability of the parliamentary road to socialism. Parliamentary socialism is regarded as elevating the parliamentary means above the socialist end, so precluding socialism and sacrificing it to the struggle for office and government. Elections are not seen as providing a pathway to power. They simply 'incorporate' the working class into the established system and so legitimise that system in a way that stops any real change. Parliament controls nothing. It merely conceals the true reality of power that resides untouched by democracy in the rest of the state apparatus and above all in the market economy itself. Meaningful change cannot come through the existing political system. A liberal-democratic polity and a capitalist economy fit so snugly together in mutual support that democracy is regarded as the best possible political shell for capitalism. Reform and reformism are out. The gradualism of concession merely shores up the essentials of the established system by creating an illusion as to the possibilities of change. Moreover, by curbing the worst excesses of capitalism, concessions cut into the grievances of the working class so turning them away from action for fundamental transformation. The Labour Party has much to answer for from this perspective. In 'managing' the system at crucial moments; in neutering the discontent of the working class; and in holding out the prospect of socialism via Parliament, the Labour Party is seen as part of the problem blocking transformation and so has no part to play in securing socialism. Revolution is necessary. The system as a whole has to be 'smashed' and set aside by a vanguard party of intellectuals which leads the working class in extra- and anti-parliamentary action towards socialism (see also Chapter 7).

From this point of view, the liberal-democratic British constitution is not taken seriously. It is dismissed as an irrelevant façade that conceals the reality of class rule behind the smokescreen of a democracy that exists only in form but not in substance. The British constitution is simply an unimportant part of the 'superstructure' of society and economy that is explained by, and cemented to, the all-important and all-determining economic 'base'. From this kind of perspective on the road to socialism, to even consider reconstructing or reforming the British constitution is regarded as a trifling nonsense that borders on the evil of a naïve reformism itself.

So, from the dominant parliamentary perspective the Left takes the British constitution for granted as a good thing, and from the insurrectionary perspective the Left sees the British constitution (if it sees it at all) as beyond the pale of reasoned consideration and change. From both points of view there has been no tradition of serious, sustained, and critical debate on the limits and potentialities of the British constitution and liberal-democracy.

Third road to socialism. Over the past few years, part of the Left in Britain has moved into a more considered view as to the limits of elements of the British constitution, at the same time as it has become increasingly alive to the merits of elements of that same constitution – especially in so far as they bear on the issues of democracy, the sovereignty of Parliament and the people, and civil liberties. Moreover, the Left has tended to turn away from applause for insurrection – at least in so far as prospects for change in Britain are concerned. These two developments have prompted a concern to transform the constitution of the Labour Party and the British constitution in the struggle to fashion a third road to socialism. Let us elaborate on these developments.

1   The fact that those on the right and in the Establishment have become increasingly critical of the British constitution (critical that is of party politics, pressure-group politics, parliamentary sovereignty and unlimited democracy itself) at the same time as they defend the integrity of capitalism and attack socialism, has rather disturbed the orthodoxy as to the close fit and supporting connection between liberal-democracy and capitalism. The Right has prompted the Left to ponder that perhaps capitalism and democracy have come to the parting of ways; perhaps there is more life in the democratic road to socialism than many have chosen to suppose; and so perhaps there are things that need to be defended and advanced from *within* the British constitution itself.

2   Most socialists have become increasingly critical of the monopolistic and authoritarian role of Communist parties in one-party systems in a way that has made them cast doubt on the desirability of insurrection. History rather suggests that the discipline needed for insurrection lingers on as an authoritative force *after* the revolution in a way that blocks the larger end of a socialism that advances opportunities for freedom and self-development through a true democracy of equals. Moreover, in the British context, the fact that Leninist and Trotskyist groupings are hopelessly divided and have never been able to move beyond a fringe rôle

and secure any kind of solid base in the working class has, as a matter of practical politics, forced them to reconsider their own position *and* that of the Labour Party.

3   It is one thing to recognise the limited possibilities of insurrection in Britain, but it is another thing to move from this into support for the Labour Party. The Labour Party has remained a problem for socialists, as the experience of Labour in government after 1966 and over the period 1974–79 rather confirmed. (This will be more fully discussed in Chapter 7). At a time when many socialists were moving away from a naïve faith in the prospects for revolutionary change and towards uneasy respect for democracy, Labour in office was doing little to justify belief in the viability of *their* vision of the road to socialism. The Left seemed to be caught on the horns of a dilemma: insurrection was regarded with increased scepticism and democracy with increased respect, but parliamentary socialism continued to reveal its all too familiar limitations. The realisation that it was important to defend democracy, and that it was difficult to dodge the Labour Party, forced many to consider *transforming* the constitution of the party so that the leadership in Parliament was more accountable to the party outside.

These constitutional concerns within the Labour Party have profound implications for the British constitution itself. First, senior members of the Labour Party broke with the party over the issue of these constitutional changes in order to form the SDP, and we have already seen that the SDP wishes to fashion a new constitution for the country. Second, part and parcel of the internal debates about the constitution of the Labour Party are larger debates about the limits and problems of the British constitution and these spill over into a case for reconstructing the British constitution itself in order to fashion a different kind of democracy and a third road to socialism.

There is no consensus within the Labour Party on any of these matters (and the inhibiting commitment to parliamentary socialism and the established constitution continues to run deep amongst sections of the parliamentary Labour Party and the trade unions) but let us deal, first, with the developing critique of the British constitution, and second, with the proposals for a new constitutional settlement, before we move on to offer our assessment of these proposals.

What is wrong with the established constitution?

A dominant tradition of thought within the Labour Party 'sees' the British constitution in terms rather different from those which we have so far set down. Simply expressed, more cautious judgements are made as to the democracy on offer within the system. The constitution is not seen in the rosy terms set down in Chapter 1, but neither is democracy seen in the new gloomy terms set down in Chapters 2 and 3.

Because the Left has not been sensitive to the established debates on the British constitution it has not been attentive to the potentialities for change which have flowed from the absence of legal and constitutional limits on Parliament. Instead, the Left has chosen to attend to the presence of other limits and constraints that are seen as blocking the prospects for socialism via parliament. The constitutional authorities were mindful of the constraints imposed by elections and trade unions, but the Left sees democracy in Britain as constrained, not by these things, but by the presence of unaccountable economic power and by the independent power of those closed and secret parts of the state machine that are not popularly elected and that are not even truly accountable to, or effectively controlled by, that part of Parliament that is subject to regular election by the people. The civil service, the House of Lords, the Monarch, the judges, the police, the military, the security services, the Bank of England, a host of Quangos, and even the cabinet and the absolute premiership, are all seen as enjoying varying degrees of political power without any balancing responsibility to hold them in check – as we ourselves will suggest in Chapter 5.

In addition to stressing these 'internal' limits on parliamentary democracy in Britain, stress is also placed on 'external' factors that have contributed to a loss of powers and to a significant reduction in the scope of our capacity to govern ourselves. Attention centres on the position of multi-national companies and the role of the USA and the implications of our NATO membership, but special attention centres on the implications of our entry into the European Community and the position of the International Monetary Fund. We will be discussing these matters more fully in Chapter 11, but let us elaborate a little now on the Left perspective on the European Community and the International Monetary Fund.

The United Kingdom became a member of the European Community in January 1973. Parliamentary sovereignty is still intact in so far as Parliament can still repeal the act committing us to entry. However, so long as we remain in the Community, Parliament has effectively handed over a number of functions that it has traditionally fulfilled. On entry, the British Parliament had to take over lock, stock and barrel forty-two volumes of legislation passed by Community institutions. It also entered into an open-ended commitment to incorporate into British law all future community legislation in those areas where the Community has competence, and to make such a law virtually unamendable by our domestic Parliament. Britain is seen as having surrendered power to the Common Market in a way that has limited our freedom of manoeuvre and turned us into a colony of an embryonic West European federal state.

As we shall show in Chapter 8, the Labour Party entered office in 1974 with a radical programme but in severe economic conditions that restricted the freedom of manoeuvre enjoyed by the Chancellor of the Exchequer and his cabinet colleagues. The severity of the world recession and the weakness of the pound combined to lead the government to borrow foreign currency from the International Monetary Fund in December 1975. When the government went back again in 1976, the second loan brought with it a Fund investigation into Britain's economic policy and the requirement of more cuts in public expenditure as a condition of the loan. The fact that the Fund was only too willing to lend in return for a written undertaking that domestic economic policy would follow the lines agreed in negotiations between Treasury officials and the Fund investigators in the autumn of 1976, involved what many Labour activists saw as a loss of governing powers to an external force that was anti-socialist.

Proposals for a new constitution

What are the implications of the above assessments for the issue of constitutional reconstruction in Britain?

We can pull out of the Common Market and out of NATO, but there are practical limits as to what can be done from within British politics to overcome the external constraints on the development of public policy in Britain since we are part of the world economy.

The 'internal' limits on democracy in Britain are a rather different matter, however, and part and parcel of the Left description and critique of the established British constitution is the call for a new constitution for Britain that would somehow lift those limits. Two broad concerns give a certain coherence to their package of proposals for change. First, there is the concern to strengthen the democratic element of the state machine and a related concern to weaken the independent power of the other, more secret, parts of the state. Second, and part of the power battle over the constitution of the Labour Party, there is a concern to secure a democracy in Britain different from that entrenched within the established liberal-democratic constitution and different from that envisaged by the Liberals and Social Democrats.

Strengthening democracy. The concern to strengthen the democratic element within the British constitution poses a direct challenge to the authorities who seek to reinvigorate the 'balanced' constitution of Crown, Lords, and Commons, and finds its most obvious expression in the commitment to abolish the House of Lords.

1   The present House of Lords is seen as a wrecking chamber with a built-in Conservative majority and a crippling power of delay that only exists to put a brake on a reforming Socialist government. The case for abolition was made more urgent as a result of the experience of Labour in government after 1974. In the 1974–5 session the government was defeated in 100 Lords divisions, and in the 1975–6 session it was defeated in 120 divisions. A membership based on the hereditary principle and the

patronage that is needed to create life peers is seen as deeply offensive in the context of a democracy. Moreover, reform is ruled out because either the new second chamber would be less democratic than the Commons in which case it should not be able to delay legislation, or if it was just as democratic then there is no point in having two chambers, the more so since there is the potential problem of constitutional deadlock between them.

2   Republicanism is not strongly expressed within the Labour Party. There is little sentiment in the population at large for attacks upon the position of the monarchy, and the 'fact' that we have a constitutional monarchy contains within itself the idea that the Crown has no personal political power but exercises prerogatives solely on the advice of ministers responsible to Parliament. For the most part this is true, but the Crown does have the direct and personal power to refuse to dissolve Parliament before the expiry of its full term and does have the power to invite a person to form a government. Although the Labour Party as a whole has not taken a stand on the political position of the monarchy, Tony Benn has expressed the view that these two powers of the Crown should be transferred to the Speaker of the House of Commons because he stands apart from the political parties and is directly answerable to the Commons for the conduct of the chair in a way that does not apply to the position of the Crown. In the event that no single party enjoys an overall majority in the Commons then the issue of sending for the Prime Minister and refusing a dissolution become matters so charged with political manoeuvring that the Crown would be drawn into politics in a public way that would be bound to invite a keener scrutiny as to what should be her proper rôle within the British constitution. Tony Benn is clearly not able to resolve the position of the monarchy within our system but he highlights a problem that may need to be confronted at some point in the future. Other aspects of the concern to strengthen the democratic side of the state machine bear especially on the position of the civil service, the Prime Minister, and the House of Commons.

3   A number of changes are advocated to secure a civil service that is more accountable to Parliament and more amenable to the control of ministers. A Freedom of Information Act (also supported by the Liberals and the Social Democrats) is advocated to open up to public scrutiny the workings of government departments. In addition, it is argued that ministers should have a larger say in the appointment and transfer of senior departmental officials with whom they would be working; that ministers should have their own private political office of specialist and political advisers; that junior ministers should be involved in the work of departmental and interdepartmental committees which are at the moment the preserve of departmental officials; and that backbenchers should be more closely involved in the decision-making process through bringing them into government departments.

4   In Chapter 1 we discussed the thesis about prime ministerial

government. Sections of the Left agree with that thesis and are of the opinion that the powers of the Prime Minister are too great. In order to secure a 'constitutional premiership' that is less powerful and more accountable to the party and parliament, there are those within the Labour Party who would wish to change the British constitution so as to restrict the powers of a Prime Minister. Two proposals stand out. First, there is a concern to limit prime ministerial patronage in a number of areas (and the concern to abolish the House of Lords is in part born of a desire to deny the Prime Minister the constitutional right to create peers). Second, instead of continuing with the constitutional convention whereby the Prime Minister has the right to choose a government and a Cabinet, there is a concern to transfer this to Members of Parliament when Labour is in office, giving them the right to elect Cabinet ministers.

5. The proposed abolition of the House of Lords, and the concern to limit the powers of the Prime Minister, the government, and the civil service, would place a greater burden on the House of Commons. In order to enable that chamber to adequately fulfil its main function of scrutinising legislation, over-seeing the executive, and representing the electorate in the national forum of debate, a number of changes in the procedure of the House of Commons are part of the Labour Party package for constitutional reconstruction. They propose an improved procedure for the handling of bills; making legislation easier to follow; and, of course, the cry for improvements in the present Select Committee system. All of this is familiar uncontroversial stuff, and the Labour Party proposals for increasing the power of the House of Commons are not at odds with the perspective of the constitutional authorities or the Liberals and Social Democrats. However, although the Labour Party may want to see a stronger House of Commons, there is no wish to revive parliamentary government. The Labour Party is in favour of that element of the 'Westminster Model' that has to do with single-party government grounded in secure majorities in the House of Commons and it is, in consequence, opposed to proportional representation. However, the concern to increase *intra*-party democracy and change the balance of power within the Labour Party bespeaks of a profound commitment to create a *kind* of democracy in Britain very different from that entrenched in the established constitutional set-up and different from that desired by the constitutional authorities and the Alliance who both wish to see legal limits on Parliament as well as a revival of the autonomy of parliamentary government itself. Let us, then, deal with this second aspect of the Labour Party's proposals for constitutional change.

Changing democracy

Any consideration of the Labour Party concern to change the kind of democracy on offer to the people within a new British constitution has to begin by attending to the battles within the Labour Party and to the resulting changes that have occurred in the constitution of the party.

The Left in the party at large, anxious about the failure of the party in Parliament to press for socialism when in government, have been concerned to change the relationship between the parliamentary party and the party outside Parliament through the implementation of three changes in the party constitution. First, there is the issue of the mandatory reselection of MPs – the idea that all sitting Labour Members should submit themselves for reselection by the local party at least once during the lifetime of each Parliament. Second, there is the issue of the method for appointing the leader of the Labour Party and the idea that this should no longer be in the gift of the parliamentary party alone. Third, there is the issue of the party manifesto for a general election and the idea that this should no longer be drawn up just by the leader on the basis of informal consultations. Mandatory reselection was won in 1979, and a new method for electing the leader of the party was adopted in 1981 which gave trade unions and constituency parties a major say, but there has still to be a change in the way in which the party manifesto is drawn up.

The intent behind these changes within the Labour Party constitution spills over to pose a challenge to the kind of democracy that has been seen as the essential hallmark of the liberal-democratic British constitution.

If we look back to Chapter 1, we can see that the constitutional authorities regarded the British constitution as properly providing for representative government of a liberal-democratic kind. Within our system of parliamentary democracy, only *inter*-party competition was seen as crucial and desirable. In keeping with the emphasis on liberalism, there was the idea that party competition should be restrained and moderate so that it would involve gradual change and only limited state intervention. In keeping with the emphasis on parliamentarianism there was the idea that party power should reside within the parliamentary leadership alone. Party leaders should be free to devise programmes designed to appeal to the electorate as a whole, and they should only have to hold themselves vaguely accountable to the people through the direct mechanism of regular general elections. It was always an elitist kind of limited democracy that was applauded – a democracy of powerful, autonomous, but cautious, leaders, in limp relation to passive and uncommitted followers who had nothing to give but their votes and unquestioning support. Political practice was condemned when it went beyond this constitutional state of affairs.

There was little room for popular participation except through the ballot box, and the public was given no real right to press demands onto governments or parties. As soon as political parties rediscovered their roots, dropped their concern to maintain a consensus, and regained a conviction, they were condemned because they were adversarial and offered a real choice. The bursts of intra-party democracy within the Labour Party, reflected in the cry that 'Conference should decide', were

invariably condemned as at odds with the essentials of the British constitution and as offensive to the magic, unmediated link between parliamentary leaders and 'their' supporters (not controllers) in the electorate at large. Interest-group activity could just about be tolerated as long as it was moderate and operated within the suffocating rules of the political game. ('Ask nicely and quietly, and if we say "No" don't press us, just give up and drop your demands.') But if that activity became more strident and refused to take no for an answer; if it became more popular, participatory, and direct, taking to the streets and becoming something called 'extra-parliamentary politics'; and if it threatened to overload the capacity of the state, then it was condemned – and condemned as at odds with the
liberal-democracy of the British constitution.

Now, the changes of power in the Labour Party, and the changes in the constitution of the party, challenge the legitimacy and limitations of exactly this kind of limited, liberal, democracy. *Intra*-party democracy is seen as vital to supplement the reality of interparty competition at the polls. There is the view that the party leadership in parliament *should* lack autonomy and should be held accountable to the party rank and file outside of parliament. Popular participation is applauded. The direct democracy of extra-parliamentary politics, be it in the form of trade union strikes or campaigns of civil disobedience by peace protesters, is defended. Simply expressed, parliamentary democracy and the representation of individual electors by unfettered parliamentary leaders is challenged in favour of party democracy and the representation of collective (class) interests where the majority wishes of the party activists outside Parliament in the constituencies are interposed between the parliamentary leaders and the electorate to limit the former and to provide the party programme for choice by the latter. Manifesto is the cement, and a mandated democracy (whereby MPs are delegates to be instructed by activist supporters outside Parliament) is the building. Established elements of parliamentary democracy in Britain are challenged. Prime ministerial power, and therefore prime ministerial government is challenged; Cabinet government and collective responsibility are challenged because of the claim that the first allegiance of a Labour minister is not to the Cabinet but to the mandate given by the party conference; parliamentary government and the autonomy of MPs to deliberate as representatives is challenged through the notion of mandate reducing them to delegates; and liberal-democracy itself is challenged because of a refusal to accept limits to participation and to the rôle of the state in the struggle to attain socialism through democracy. These plans for a fundamental reshaping of democracy in Britain find little support outside the party, but there are those who consider that the interaction between parliamentary and extra-parliamentary action constitutes a dual strategy that provides a viable third road to socialism.

Assessing the proposals for a new constitution

What can we make of this package of proposals for a change in the British constitution? In what follows we list some of the obstacles that lie in the way of these changes, and we also point to some of the contradictions that we see as bedevilling and limiting the Left perspective on a new constitution for Britain.

1   The party itself is not united in its support for a new constitutional settlement, and the bulk of the parliamentary party is unsympathetic to the attempts to recover a more radical kind of democracy in Britain. The Left in the party came into a position of some power in the late seventies in the wake of the limitations of Labour in office over the period 1974–9, but the resurgence of the Right and soft Left in the eighties, and following the election disaster of 1983, rather suggests that a brake will be put on radicalism in the name of 'realism' and 'necessity'.

2   Party support amongst the electorate has been in lumpy decline since 1951 and the Labour share of the vote in 1983 was the lowest since 1918. Labour will have to struggle to get back into office and it is doubtful whether a frontal attack on the established constitution will win back support – and popular support is vital in the context of the other obstacles which their proposals face.

3   All the other parties are fundamentally opposed to Labour's plans for constitutional change precisely because they are alive to the policy implications caught up within the proposals. Labour may hope that socialism can come through Parliament, others fear that this may well be so.

4   Abolition of the House of Lords is not a simple matter, and the idea of creating 1000 peers to swamp the Lords to effect its abolition could be blocked. Moreover, if Labour were to be successful in abolishing the Lords then this could well backfire because of the position of the courts. The judiciary (with increasing reluctance) limit their rôle in politics because they accept the notion of parliamentary sovereignty and enforce Acts of Parliament recognising that they have no right to declare them unconstitutional. If the House of Lords was abolished then the courts might jump at the chance to take the view that 'Parliament' – Crown, Lords, and Commons – had ceased to exist. If Parliament were no more then this would jeopardise the concept of parliamentary sovereignty and could invite a more active judiciary to intervene in limiting the powers of the House of Commons in the name of defending the constitution. Politically, the position of the courts would be problematic but if Labour did not enjoy mass support for their plans then other parties could rally support to the courts in order to secure a written constitution limiting Parliament so entrenching *their* view of how the constitution should be

and checking the prospect of socialism coming through Parliament and democracy.

5   The experience of the 1974-9 Labour Government rather suggests that the civil service can effectively ignore or work around political advisers, and a number of Labour ministers proved to be none too keen to have such advisers since they can limit them as much as they can limit and counter the civil service.

6   Past reforms with respect to the use of committees in the House of Commons to check government, cabinet, and executive, failed to achieve as much as reformers had hoped in part because MPs invariably want to become a part of the executive themselves. Moreover, the concern to strengthen the position of the Commons not only looks slightly odd in the light of the concern to strengthen the party *outside* of Parliament but also runs the risk of detracting from the power of a Labour Government.

7   The concern to extend intra-party democracy within the Labour Party looks hollow in the light of the entrenched position of power of the (often undemocratic) trade unions whose block votes effectively determine the outcome of Conference deliberations. In addition, the level of activity required to stay the race within a party concerned to increase political participation effectively excludes from power all but the most intensely committed in a way that can defeat the object of securing extensive participation as a vehicle for advancing the aspirations of ordinary men and women.

8   The concern to extend democracy in Britain looks odd in the light of the party's consistent opposition to the introduction of proportional representation. It smacks of pragmatism over any kind of principle, and a pragmatism at that which could be counterproductive for the position of the Labour Party in Parliament since it could be pushed into a third-party status and allow the Conservatives to form a government without the support of 50 per cent of the voters. It is true that a new electoral system brings with it the heightened prospect of a coalition government in a way that challenges the kind of accountability sought by sections of the Labour Party: it would no longer be easily possible to remove a government – still less to control it from outside Parliament. However, the commitment to the democratic element of democratic socialism looks somewhat thin in the light of the eager preparedness to stay with an electoral system that could enable the party to scramble into office in the face of the fact that well over 60 per cent of the electorate did not want them there and would not support their plans for radical change.

9   Although the party is right to be wary about the constitutional implications of the Bill of Rights, is the kind of democracy they envisage an adequate safeguard for the rights of individuals in the face of what is likely to be a rather more powerful state? If it is important to safeguard individual rights in the face of private power should not this concern be extended to cover rights in relation to public power as well?

All things considered, the Labour Party still has to do a lot of thinking on the issue of restructuring the British constitution, but Tony Benn is right to make the point that 'constitutional questions are the key to power in a parliamentary democracy' and that 'socialists need to give at least as much attention to the institutions of the state as to the power structure of the economy'.

CONCLUSION

In the last two chapters we set down the mainstream and the New Right perspectives on British politics that were critical of the workings of democracy in Britain: parties had become too adversarial, and interest groups were overloading the system with demands for increased state intervention. In addition, we also set down aspects of the Left's critique of the workings of parties and pressures.

In this chapter we have followed these *academic* critiques into the real world of political *action* in Britain. We have highlighted the extent to which constitutional experts, political parties, and sections of the public are also discontented with aspects of British politics and with the established constitution. Moreover, we have set down three bundles of conflicting proposals for a new constitutional settlement that are seen as offering a 'better' system.

In fact, there are no objective criteria as to what would be a 'better' constitution for Britain. Conflict revolves around the form of a new settlement precisely because the rules of the political game and the power of particular state institutions are not matters that are neutral in their implication for the power of particular interests over the state and for the nature of public policy and for the likely role and direction of the state itself.

1 The proposal of the constitutional authorities to limit parliamentary sovereignty by law increases the political power of the (highly conservative) judges and would block the prospect of Britain having a democratically controlled interventionist state geared to the attainment of socialism.
2 The proposal of the Liberals and the Social Democrats to introduce proportional representation would give them greater power over the democratic side of the state machine. In consequence it would probably heighten the prospects for the kind of 'moderate', stable, policies which they see as the key to a better Britain.
3 The proposals of the Labour Party to check and control the power of the secret state (when combined with proposals to limit the autonomy of parliamentary leaders, and to defy the introduction of proportional representation and legal limits on Parliament) have as their object a concern to fashion a constitution that would facilitate change, overcome obstacles to socialism, and block the prospect of moderation and compromise in office.

As we have entered a period of constitutional crisis, so a number of things that have been integral to the British constitution since the late nineteenth century have tended to pull apart in the call for change. The uneasy mixture of liberty and equality, capitalism and democracy, institutionalised in the messy and self-destructive compromise of liberal-democracy itself no longer holds together. There are those who emphasise the importance of the limited state of liberty and the rule of law over the significance of democracy and parliamentary sovereignty, just as there are those who emphasise the importance of recovering a tradition of democracy and popular participation that brooks no limits in the drive for equality and societal transformation. Different conceptions of democracy war with each other, and those who have lost their faith in the democratic method (in the name of the end of liberty) retreat into wanting to limit it by law.

We may be in a period of decisive constitutional significance, but the absence of any consensus blocks the prospects for easy constitutional change. Maybe the established set-up will hold; maybe the old British science of muddling through will prevail; but maybe a break will be made – although the form of any new settlement will depend upon the power of particular interests in society.

WORKS CITED AND GUIDE TO FURTHER READING

Benn, T. (1982) *Arguments for democracy,* Harmondsworth, Penguin.
Leading figure on Labour Left attacks 'the power of the establishment' and sets out 'the way ahead'.

Crowther-Hunt, Lord, Abolishing the House of Lords, *The Listener,* 4 December 1980.

Crowther-Hunt, Lord, How the Queen might finally save the Lords, *The Guardian* 11 January 1982.
Robust case from a constitutional authority on how the Crown should assume a key role in defending the House of Lords against the abolitionists.

Denning, Lord, Misuse of Power, *The Listener* 27 November 1980, and reprinted in his (1982) *What Next in the Law,* London, Butterworth, 1982, Part 8.
Senior judge and constitutional authority attacking the misuse of power by just about everyone within the established set-up – except the judges – and making a case for the judges having more power within a new written constitution.

Gilmour, Sir I. (1978) *Inside Right,* London, Quartet.
A wide-ranging study of conservatism by a leading Conservative on the left of the party. Part Three, Chapter Five, 'The Constitution', sees things as wrong with the established constitution and wants to see (among other things) electoral reform and a stronger House of Lords.

Hailsham, Lord, 'Elective Dictatorship', *The Listener* 21 October, 1976, and elaborated in his (1978) *The Dilemma of Democracy,* London, Collins.

Senior Conservative, leading lawyer, and a constitutional authority, who attacks the established constitution and calls for a new written constitution limiting Parliament and therefore giving more power to the judges.

Halsbury's Laws of England, Vol. 8, *Constitutional Law,* 4th edn, London, Butterworth, 1980.
The book on the laws of England. Paragraph 811 on the sovereignty of parliament repays a very close read because it challenges the 'orthodox doctrine' and eases its way towards recognising the case for limiting Parliament.

Hodgson, G. (1981) *Labour at the Crossroads,* Oxford, Martin Robertson.
Left Labour perspective analysing the failures of parliamentary socialism/ Labourism and making a case for a 'third road to socialism' : 'an interaction between parliamentary and extra-parliamentary action'.

Jenkins, R., Home thoughts from abroad, *The Listener,* 29 November 1979.
The lecture that set the ball rolling for the formation of the Social Democratic Party. Critique of adversary party politics; concern to strengthen the political centre; and a case for electoral reform.

Johnson, N. (1980) *In Search of the Constitution,* London, Methuen.
Excellent (high-Tory) account of the limitations of the established constitution and a plea to 'refashion the rules of the political order' with a written constitution, electoral reform, a revival of Parliament, and so on.

Joint Liberal/SDP Commission for Constitutional Reform (1982) First Report: *Electoral Reform,* London.
Carefully argued case for proportional representation in 'natural communities'.

Joint Working Party of Liberals and Social Democrats (1981) *A Fresh Start for Britain,* London.
Two-part paper setting up the need for more joint ventures. Argues for 'fundamental change in our adversarial party system' and sees electoral and constitutional change as the 'key'.

Labour Party (1983) *The New Hope for Britain.*
The election manifesto. Contains a section on the need for constitutional reform.

Liberal Party, Reform of Government Panel (1980) *A New Constitutional Settlement,* London.
Criticises the established constitution; argues that 'change is necessary'; and concerned to see a new written constitution with proportional representation, devolution, a Bill of Rights, a reformed House of Lords, and so on.

Maude, Sir A. and Szemery, J. (1982) *Why Electoral Change?* London, Conservative Political Centre.
Conservative case against proportional representation.

Norton, P. (1982) *The Constitution in Flux*, Oxford, Martin Robertson.
Full, academic coverage of areas of current constitutional dispute. Best available.

Phillips, O. Hood (1970) *Reform of the Constitution,* London, Chatto and Windus.
Leading constitutional authority makes an early case for a written constitution.

Royal Commission on the Constitution (1973) *Report,* Cmnd 5460, London, HMSO.

Set up in response to the nationalist pressures for assemblies in Wales and Scotland. Emphasised the need to preserve the essential unity of the UK but alive to problem of maintaining consent for system.

Social Democratic Party (1981) *Twelve Tasks for Social Democrats,* London.
Issued on the day of the party's launch. The first task was 'Breaking the Mould', but the second task was 'Fair Elections'.

Social Democratic Party/Liberal Alliance (1983) *Working Together for Britain.*
The election manifesto. Very short, but refers to the need for constitutional reform.

Wigram, A. *Constitutional Reform Now* (No date) London, Conservative Action for Electoral Reform.
A brief pamphlet by a Conservative making a case for proportional representation as it would put 'an end to socialist extremism.'

CHAPTER 5

The Power of the Secret State

The first state secret is this: who is actually in charge?

D. Leigh (1980) The Frontiers of Secrecy, *London, Junction Books, p.1.*

Democracy is . . . a principle that is unacceptable to the establishment in our society. That establishment, by which I mean leading men in the City, captains of industry, press barons, those at the top of the church hierarchy and the professions, is determined that the government in Britain should remain elitist, oligarchic, bureaucratic and secretive. Indeed, government in Britain today is so secretive that even the true nature of our constitution is hidden from the people.

B. Sedgemore (1980) The Secret Constitution, *London, Hodder and Stoughton, p.11.*

Take any parliamentary country, from America to Switzerland, from France to England and so forth – in those countries the real business of 'state' is performed behind the scenes and is carried on by departments, chancelleries and general staffs.

V. I. Lenin (1976) The State and Revolution, *Peking, Foreign Languages Press, p. 57.*

The constitutional, mainstream and New Right accounts that have been at the very centre of our discussions in the first four chapters of this book have dominated both the academic *and* the public discourse about British politics. It is time for us to break out because it is our contention that these accounts provide us with only a partial and restricted explanation because democracy and democratic theory are seen as the be all and end all of the matter. On occasions, accounts of this kind actually mystify the essential reality of crucial aspects of the British political system. Things are left out of account; things are written out as irrelevant of consideration because a narrow view of what is political prevails; and, when certain things are explored, then the use of a democratic perspective alone means that their true role can be misrepresented in a way that blocks understanding. It is our claim that there is more to British politics than meets the eye; there is more than the public and democratic face of governmental power and the huff and puff of parliamentary debate; and there is more to the state and state power than government and Parliament. It is time to dive beneath the democratic froth and go a little deeper. It is time to push behind the *public* face of *popular* politics in order to consider state, society, and economy, and this will be the focal point of our discussion in the next three chapters.

In this chapter we will deal with what we call the secret state – we will deal, that is, with those state institutions which are *non-elected,* which enjoy subtantial *autonomy* from the control of government and Parliament (no matter what constitutional theory might assert), and which tend to be *closed and secretive* as to the ways in which they exercise their very *substantial powers.* In concrete terms we will be discussing the civil service; the nationalised industries (including the Bank of England); the judiciary; the police; the security services; and the military.

It is one thing for us to assert that the institutions that make up the secret state are of importance in British politics, but it is another thing for us to study these institutions and actually demonstrate their power and significance. There are two major problems caught up in trying to explore the political significance of the various institutions that make up the non-elected side of the state machine.

First, the dominance of democratic perspectives on British politics has obscured some parts of the state. There is the idea that when a party wins a general election and forms a government it also wins unto itself *all* state power. Government is seen as in control of the secret, non-elected, state. Government is regarded as the powerful motor at the heart of the state machine, and the secret state is seen as neutral, disinterested, anonymous, impartial, unbiased, objective, and devoid of any independent political significance and power because it is just regarded as available to be *used* as an implementing, administrative, tool for policies determined in the democratic and public arena of government and Parliament. Bluntly put, the secret state is seen as obedient and responsible to the government of the day and it is seen as accountable to the people through Parliament. Harold Wilson put the orthodox position very nicely shortly before he won 'power' at the 1964 general election:

The state machine is neutral. It is like a car waiting to be driven. Whichever way it is steered, the machine will go. What matters, therefore, is the driver. If the man behind the machine is a Labour man, the machine will move towards Labour. Not only Parliament, but the vast machinery of the state which it controls — the police force, the army, the judiciary, the educational institutions, the BBC etc. are politically neutral and loyal to their political masters.

From this perspective there is *not* the idea that power may flow downwards from the secret state; there is *not* the idea that the secret state may control democratic government and the people themselves; and there is *not* the idea that the secret state may be an unaccountable power that needs to be studied in its own right independently of democratic theories and assumptions as to its insignificance and lack of independent power.

Second, there is the problem of secrecy itself. The cabinet is at the pinnacle of the elected side of the central state and yet even the organisation of that institution is a deep secret. The secrecy of the non-elected side of the state machine is even more of a problem. Civil servants rarely appear on radio or television to explain themselves; judges consider that their deliberations in court must remain secret; the police regard an interest in their work as hostile and political; and the security services scarcely even exist officially. Secrecy is entrenched in law. The catch-all provision of section 2 of the Official Secrets Act, 1911, makes it a crime for any crown servant or contractor to disclose any information learned in the course of his or her job, just as it is also an offence even to receive such unauthorised disclosures. Although the Public Records Act, 1977, releases dead and outdated files to the public and researchers thirty or more years after they were written (so reducing the 50-year rule established in 1968) the system still has so many constraints and loopholes that it would be more accurate to describe it as a 30-year 'if no official weeder has any serious objection and we can manage to sort them for you' rule. Students eager to uncover facts about present-day politics are faced with problems of secret information. The Defence, Press and Broadcasting Committee (commonly known as the 'D Notice' Committee) 'advises' the press not to publish supposedly sensitive matters of state, and behind this formal system is a more pervasive and informal system of 'private and confidential' letters and 'personal' chats with 'responsible' political journalists that will dribble out facts and misinformation to those deemed to be safe and reliable in their defence of the power of the state.

Notwithstanding these two problems of studying the various institutions that make up the secret state, what are we trying to do in this chapter and why? There is a negative and a positive aspect to our concerns.

The following two points embrace the *negative,* critical side of what this chapter is about:

1 The dominance of democratic perspectives has contributed to a series of well-entrenched orthodoxies as to the position of the various parts of the secret state. These need to be recognised and clearly set down since they occupy a position of political importance.
2 Because we regard the democratic perspective as flawed in crucial ways, we will challenge the adequacy of these orthodoxies as providing any kind of realistic account of the power and position of the various institutions that make up the secret state. In other words, after we have set down the orthodoxies, we will unpick them and set them aside as wrong.

At a more *positive* level we need to realise that there is no ready-made theory into which we can simply plug the facts. We will discuss the limitations of Marxist theories of the state in Chapter 7, but in this chapter we are not aiming to provide our own theory of the secret state.

Our concern is to modestly open suggestive chinks of light into the workings of state institutions that are out of the public eye but which nevertheless enjoy power at the same time as they are surrounded by ideas which only serve to block understanding. To this end we are of the opinion that information on the following points will help us to start to make good sense of the part played by the secret state in British politics.

1　What is the social and educational *background* of those in positions of power in the secret state, and how 'open' or 'closed' is the process of recruitment to those positions? We are not justified in making simple and direct inferences from the background of elite groups to the ways in which they employ whatever power they possess. Equally, it would be wrong to assume that an institutional elite recruited from a narrow and specific class background will only develop policies that promote the interests of the class corresponding to that background to the detriment of society at large. Having said that, information about recruitment and background *does* matter because it provides an indication of the complex of social forces which impinge on the upbringing of an individual and which help to fashion and maintain values and assumptions. Moreover, a *common* background of experience amongst those who enjoy political power in the state encourages the formation of common values and a certain kind of unity. All of this conditions the way in which the world is viewed and discretion exercised. Simply put, the ethos that tends to come from a particular background is of significance for political action *and* if that background is shared by those in power *and* if they enjoy a certain autonomy then it will have a decisive influence on public policy and the direction of the state.

2　What is the nature of the *socialisation* process within the various institutions making up the secret state? People may be recruited into these institutions from particular backgrounds but once in an institution they are subjected to the impact of the culture and ideology of the institution itself in ways which will have still keener implications for behaviour and action.

3　What is the *organisational structure* of the institutions of the secret state? What is the nature and location of power in an institution; to what extent is power concentrated in the hands of a few people; and to what extent is an institution bureaucratic or authoritarian in its mode of operation so that members are obliged to follow rules and procedures in a way which limits the exercise of individual discretion?

4　At the largest level, what can we say about the function or *role* which a particular institution fulfills within the context of the larger society within which it operates and takes its significance? How far do the various institutions of the secret state secure the established order or change it, and how are they significant for the working of democracy in Britain?

Let us begin our discussion of the power and significance of the institutions that make up the secret state by dealing with the civil service.

Orthodoxies assessed

The orthodox position with respect to the power and position of the civil service is clear enough. Civil servants are politically neutral, serving with equal loyalty governments of any political persuasion. They do not enjoy political power because they do not make policy (that is for ministers and the elected side of the state machine alone), and so they do not control the direction of the state. The civil service has the job of administering and implementing the policies determined by government and passed by Parliament, but it is also available to advise a government on how best to achieve governmental objectives. *The Times* put it all very nicely in a leader in 1977: 'The constitutional position is both crystal clear and entirely sufficient. Officials propose, ministers dispose and officials execute.'

The former Conservative Prime Minister, Edward Heath, said of his time in office: 'I would say quite clearly and definitely that the civil servants were under ministerial control. I have absolutely no doubt about it. In my ministerial life this has always been the case. What is more, I believe that civil servants like to be under ministerial control.' Sir Brian Hayes, the permanent secretary at the Ministry of Agriculture would not dissent from this view:

Civil servants ought not to have power because we're not elected. Power stems from the people and flows through Parliament to the minister responsible to Parliament. The civil servant has no power of his own, he is there to help a minister and to be the minister's agent... I think the job of the civil servant is to make sure that his minister is informed; that he has all the facts; that he's made aware of all the options and that he is shown all the considerations bearing on those options. It is then for the minister to take the decision. That is how the system ought to operate and that is how I think, in the vast majority of cases, it does operate.

Ministers and civil servants who have been intimately involved in the process of policy-making are sometimes prepared to paint a picture at odds with the 'official' view, however. Tony Benn, who has held six ministerial posts in five Labour Governments argues that civil service power has grown in such a way that it 'contains' proposals for change caught up in the manifestoes of parties winning a general election. He notes that 'the bold challenge of the 1964 Labour government's "New Britain" manifesto was gradually absorbed and finally defused by 20 July 1966, when the Treasury persuaded the then Chancellor to insist upon a package of economic measures that killed the national plan and instituted a statutory pay policy'. Lord Armstrong, who as Sir William Armstrong was head of the civil service, candidly recognised that he 'had a great deal of influence' as a civil servant and that 'the biggest and most pervasive influence is in setting the framework within which the questions of policy are raised'.

This picture of civil-service power, extending far beyond the confines set by liberal-democratic constitutional theory, is supported by the Labour MP, Brian Sedgemore, in his book on *The Secret Constitution* –and he has seen the relationship from both sides since he was once a senior civil servant in the Ministry of Housing and Local Government. Confirming Armstrong's perspective, Sedgemore notes how it is difficult for ministers to 'break out' of the 'atmosphere' or 'value system' that exists within departments, and he gives countless examples of civil servants 'frustrating' ministerial power over the issues of nuclear power and Labour Government policy on industry. In a major study of the crucially important expenditure process that allocates money to the various spending departments, two American academics 'dispel the simplistic view' that the process turns on Cabinet discussion and on ministers putting their cases to the Chancellor of the Exchequer for detailed consideration. Heclo and Wildavsky 'show how a vast amount of the expenditure business is conducted between Treasury and department officials' alone. Although ministers are expected to fight for their corner, 'ministers' limited involvement in the expenditure process is an inevitable fact of life given restrictions on their time, interests and tenure in office...Ministers also fail to become more involved because civil servants prefer it that way' *and* can keep them out.

Minister and civil servants

It is one thing to set down statements which challenge the orthodox perspective as to the relationship between ministers and civil servants, but it is another thing to put flesh onto these bones. In more substantial terms, what is it that leads us to suppose that the balance of power is tilting in favour of civil servants? Put more polemically, what are the limitations of ministers, and what are the factors which advantage the position of civil servants in their dealings with their elected masters.

Ministers face a number of disadvantages in their dealings with their civil servants.

1   The average ministerial tenure in a particular department is unlikely to be more than 3 years. For example, between 1944 and 1976 there were nineteen Ministers of Education. It is clearly difficult for a temporary intruder to come to terms with, and get on top of, the established 'departmental view' that he or she is likely to face and may seek to confront and change.

2   When government changes hands, no incoming minister is given access to the papers and files of his or her predecessor. This means that

whatever losing battles civil servants may have been fighting are lost to history. They are able to start afresh with a clean sheet but armed with knowledge which enables them to anticipate and counter the arguments of new ministers.

3 Ministers are caught up in a Whitehall and parliamentary timetable that is not of their making; that is beyond their control; but within which they are constrained to operate. Because of this, ministers find it difficult to give an informed 'no' to a cogently argued civil-service case – especially when it requires urgent ministerial decision and action.

4 Ministers are not just ministers, they are also senior party politicians with responsibilities in the Commons and in the country. This limits the amount of time and energy which they can devote to running and controlling their ministry. The sheer burden of work, and the weariness which it must engender, inevitably plays into the hands of the permanent and professional civil servants.

5 The emergence of 'super ministries' and giant departments has probably posed increased problems for ministerial control, because the sheer scale and range of problems considered cannot be matched by 'super ministers'.

6 Entry into the European Community has had quite crucial implications. It has increased the burden on ministers. It has also resulted in a situation in which British civil servants have had to develop close working contact with their European colleagues in order to 'prepare the ground' and this has inevitably circumscribed ministerial freedom of action both in Europe and at home.

Civil servants possess a number of resources which give them considerable advantages in their dealings with ministers.

1 Ministers are almost exclusively dependent on their civil servants for information and for expert advice. Civil servants control the flow of information 'passed up' and they process the information that comes through from various outside pressures.

2 No minister can possibly deal with all the policy work that is undertaken for them by their senior civil servants. Information, analysis, and policy options must be carefully selected and sifted by civil servants so that ministers are presented with manageable briefs. Inevitably, however, this concern to 'protect' ministers from an overload of work means that only a limited range of options are presented for ministerial consideration and action — and it is the civil servants who do the limiting on the basis of what they define as feasible.

3 Civil servants do a great deal to set-up the policy framework within which debates occur and decisions are taken. They define what is sensible, realistic, responsible, and practical, and so come close to defining political reality itself.

4 Civil servants have more time to devote to policy matters than

ministers, and they have more information and expertise to help them in their deliberations. They are less likely than ministers to have to perform juggling acts with their time since they are full-time, permanent, career officials, with less busy agendas and a background of expertise in 'the system'.

5   The sheer pressure of demands on ministerial time inevitably means that 'less important' policy decisions *are* taken by civil servants. It is a nonsense to suppose that there is a simple distinction between matters of policy and matters of administration, and it is even more nonsensical to suppose that certain people can do just one thing whilst others do just the other. Whilst it might be the case that civil servants 'only' take less important policy decisions, it is they who are largely responsible for defining what is, and is not, important, and so they come close to defining what is the appropriate field for ministerial decision.

6   Ministers and civil servants identify closely together as part of the executive when they face the legislature (Parliament) with its potential for embarassing critique. However, the fact that ministers are keenly dependent on their civil servants in order to get a bill through Parliament gives those servants a role of power and importance in determining the shape of the legislation.

7   Civil servants enjoy a virtual monopoly of the written words that float around the state machine. Indeed, at Cabinet meetings, civil servants not only provide practically all the papers for discussion, but it is a civil servant who provides the authoritative minute of the meetings. So, the Cabinet decides what the civil service says it has decided on the basis of policy papers which civil servants themselves have drafted!

8   The civil service actually controls all the internal affairs of the state administrative apparatus. This control was given as the price to be paid for formal civil-service servitude to ministers. It has, however, given the civil service an immense power, enabling it to resist critique, and block and neutralise changes in the way in which it conducts the business of the state. The criticisms of the civil service that were made in the early sixties – about its amateurism, unaccountability, and lack of experience in industry and technology – remain almost as valid as ever. Moreover, when the Labour Government of 1974–9 attempted to get round the 'problem' of the civil service through the use of specialist political advisers, the civil service froze them out so neutralising their effectiveness, keeping them away from crucial documents, and shunting them into the role of office boys running between ministers, Transport House, and Labour Members of Parliament.

Of course, we can never come to a firm and settled view as to the relationship between ministers and civil servants. Much *does* depend on personalities, issues, and the will of government. Having said that, it should be clear that we see the civil service as more than just administrators giving advice to ministers. They are a power in the land,

and in order to make sense of the way in which they exercise that power it is important to attend to the recruitment and socialisation of top civil servants, and to the structure and role of the service as a whole.

Recruitment and socialisation

Over the years the civil service has grown. In 1854, there were just 16 000 civil servants including the Post Office employees, but by 1979 there were 730 000 civil servants excluding Post Office employees. In fact, behind this figure of growth lurks the more profound reality of two civil services: one is small and helps to make state policy, and the other is large and only really helps to carry out that policy. Only 2000 or so people really count in Whitehall.

The civil service is a career service: once in, people tend to stay in and move up the ladder to positions of power and responsibility, and people are rarely recruited into those positions from outside the service. This reality makes the recruitment of university leavers for administrative posts of particular importance since in 25 or so years time these are the people who will be the influential civil servants dealing on a day-to-day basis with both ministers and major policy. What, then, can we say about the social origins and educational backgrounds of the 100–200 people who are recruited as administration trainees each year?

The civil service tends to recruit in its own image. Each generation of civil servants favours people much like themselves. The Sixth Report from the Estimates Committee on Recruitment to the Civil Service, compared recruitment into the administrative class over the periods 1948–56 and 1957–63. They found that

the proportion of successful candidates from Oxford and Cambridge went up from 78% to 85%. The proportion from boarding schools went up from 31% to 37%, while those from LEA maintained and aided schools went down from 42% to 30%. The proportion with fathers in the Registrar Generals occupational class I went up from 38% to 46%, and those in manual occupations went down from 22% to 15%. The proportion who took degrees in classics went up from 21% to 24%, while social science fell from 24% to 17%, and mathematicians, scientists and technologists remained almost negligible dropping from 4% to 3%.

The Expenditure Committee of the House of Commons produced a report on the Civil Service in 1977 and they set down evidence with respect to bias in recruitment for the period 1971–75. The familiar pattern of biases was confirmed. There was a preference for applicants from private schools; whilst 21.6 per cent of applicants were from Oxbridge, they made up 50 per cent of recruits; and whilst 42.5 per cent of applicants had degrees in arts and humanities, they nevertheless accounted for 56.7 per cent of recruits into the service.

Social background is not everything and it is vitally important to attend to the way in which recruited individuals move up the civil-service hierarchy into what is recognised as a small, closed, secretive, solidaristic community of mandarins with their own language, norms and particular patterns of clubbability.

For the administrative trainee, the transition from a powerless apprenticeship spent learning the ropes under a senior civil servant to actually helping to run the machine is a slow and gradual one in which progress is monitored all along the way. After 2 years in the service, the best administrative trainees are 'fast streamed' and promoted to Higher Executive Officers, but it is not until they are appointed to the level of Principal at around 30 years of age that they involve themselves in policy matters, although even then they work within the framework laid down at more senior level. The 'high-flyers' can expect promotion to Assistant Secretary by 35, but all the time reports and assessments by senior civil servants are crucial to advancement. In order to move into the highest ranks of the service one insider pointed out that: 'You must be clubbable. It's a team game. I worked for a while with X... Very able...one of the very best people in the Service. But he's a loner, he gets up the nose of his colleagues, so he won't become Permanent Secretary.' He was right.

This pattern of recruitment is the image of the service and promotion according to seniority if in conformity with the norms of the service does not simply result in a service which is keenly alive to the need to protect its own interest, but also serves to favour the maintenance of established patterns of policy commitments in the face of demands for change. These tendencies are reinforced by the bureaucratic nature of the civil service structure.

Structure and role

The civil service is a bureaucratic organisation. Administration is in the hands of appointed officials who possess the requisite expertise and knowledge, and business is conducted on a continuous basis, in accordance with rules where an hierarchy of authority prevails. Such a system is indispensable given the range and complexity of the tasks performed by the British state. However, its superior rationality over other forms of organisation means that it possesses a permanence and an indestructability that gives it a power transforming it from an implementing tool at the service of others to a decision-making body in its own right. As the German sociologist, Max Weber, observed 70 years ago, any attempt to run a complex society *without* a bureaucracy would result in chaos, and yet running a society *with* a bureaucracy inevitably involves a loss of control to the bureaucrats themselves. It is easy to see why some can argue that it is the bureaucrats that control the state, and that the state controls the masses, and this is a complete reversal of democratic theory. The problem of the civil service taking over the state is only one of the dangers inherent in bureaucratic organisation. There is also the danger of bureaucracies becoming 'rule-bound', with bureaucrats defending themselves from criticism by slavishly following the rules even though this may occur to the detriment of the ends to be secured and at great cost to individuals caught in the rules.

The end result of all this is that the civil service tends to serve as a powerful conservative force within the state machine. It is sceptical of the case for change; committed to continuity and ordered, steady, progress, and so is eager to contain the wilder excesses of party politicians keen to implement their manifestoes with practical talk of the need to attend to 'reality' and 'the facts'. The civil service is organised in such a way that it is best able to exert a negative power which blocks the cry for innovation. It is keenly attuned to the maintenance of established policy (after all, it did much to establish that policy over the years), and the recruitment and socialisation of senior civil servants suggests that the service is likely to be concerned to maintain the essentials of the established society and economy. Indeed, the commitment of senior civil servants to the preservation of the established economic order is perhaps revealed in their spectacular migration to jobs in private industry which has gathered pace over two decades. In the early sixties there was only a trickle. But the trickle soon turned into a stream and after the head of the civil service himself, Sir William Armstrong, became chairman of the Midland Bank the floodgates were open. Most Senior Permanent Secretaries now expect a clutch of new jobs after they retire at 60 and this may well have implications for the way in which they choose to conduct official business. Moreover, none of those who have retired have opted to work for trade unions, and although some have moved into public bodies, such as the Arts Council or Nature Conservancy, the rush is to the boardrooms of industry. Civil servants on boards is a symbol of the extent to which private industry is increasingly dependent on government favours (see Chapter 8). Moreover, when we attend to the similar background and education of those on the boards of private industry (discussed in Chapter 6) then we can see that there is the basis for a collusion betweeen state and economy which has some of the ingredients for the makings of a power elite or a ruling class.

THE NATIONALISED INDUSTRIES

It would be nice and easy for the student if the formal world of British Government and administration were as simple as Chapter 1 suggested with central departments responsible to Parliament through government ministers. This is not so. Even if we leave aside the informal politics of parties and pressures and the world of local government, we still need to consider the place and power of a variety of statutory authorities for special purposes that enjoy varying degrees of autonomy from the elected side of the state machine and whole or partial exemption from the normal processes of accountability to Parliament and effective control by ministers and government.

In the last section on the civil service, we pointed out that it enjoyed a position of power *beyond* that specified in constitutional theory. In this section we are dealing with bodies that constitutional theory actually *allows* to have a distinct measure of autonomy from democratic accountability and control, even though the constitutional position of non-departmental public bodies is unclear and unsettled. There is nothing that can be described as 'system' and no one is quite clear just how many *ad hoc* bodies there are, although some estimate around 3000. A variety of terms, such as public enterprise, nationalised industry, public corporation, and Quango (quasi-autonomous national government organisation), are used almost interchangeably. The sheer number of such bodies makes it difficult to reduce them to any kind of classificatory order although some are clearly commercial, others promotional, and still others are predominantly regulatory or simply advisory. We cannot cover all of this, and in this section we are concerned to deal with the nationalised industries where the public corporation is the dominant organisational form, and with the Bank of England. We are dealing with the problem of striking a balance between the conflicts inherent in giving public undertakings of an industrial or commercial character a large measure of independence and autonomy in their day-to-day activities whilst reserving for the government the kind of political control that is needed in matters of major policy so as to secure an overall economic and social strategy. Put another way, there is the problem of permitting the management to operate in the market and follow commercial principles, whilst ensuring that larger social, political, and economic goals are pursued in the public interest.

Nationalised industries can be defined as those bodies whose assets are predominantly in public ownership and which are engaged in trading activities so that they derive the greater part of their revenue directly from customers. There is little need to justify our giving these bodies attention since in 1977 they had about 1.75 million workers and were responsible for over 16 per cent of total fixed investment, and they cover such vital fields as fuel and power, transport and communications, and manufacturing itself, including cars, steel, shipbuilding, and aerospace.

Most of us are accustomed to think of nationalisation as a left-wing thing that happened in the period of the Labour Government of 1945-51 so as to abolish the private ownership and control of industries in order to secure common ownership, public control, and socialism itself. Such a view is mistaken, or at least exaggerated. As we shall see in Chapter 8 many of the industries which Labour decided to nationalise in 1945 were already partially under some form of public ownership and control or subject to a high degree of government regulation, and the form of nationalisation adopted, the public corporation, dates from the inter-war period when Conservative Governments set up the BBC, the Central Electricity Board, and British Imperial Airways. Moreover, such a view minimises the significance of that phase of nationalisation which took place in the 1970s when whole industries would have collapsed but for the massive injection of public funds. These nationalisations were far from being inspired by socialist goals: Rolls Royce Aero Engines, for example, was nationalised by the Conservative Government in 1971.

From the outset of nationalisation, there was an overriding concern to secure business efficiency. This was seen as necessitating the very minimum of political interference, and political control was regarded as a bad thing to be avoided. Two things were of significance in this regard, the public corporation form, and the composition of the boards that were put in day-to-day control of the industries.

The public corporation form of organisation institutionalises the hostility to effective political control and parliamentary accountability. It is a body outside the ordinary machinery of ministerial government and is not headed by a minister but by a board; ministerial responsibility extends only to those matters specified by the relevant statute and in all other respects the board of the corporation is free to pursue its activities in the way it considers best; the employees are not regarded as civil servants; and it is exempt from the forms of parliamentary control applicable to government departments so does not need parliamentary approval before spending money and is not directly answerable to Parliament except through the minister in ways limited by convention and statute.

When the London Passenger Transport Board was created before the Second World War, the Labour politician Herbert Morrison (who was Minister of Transport at the time) expressed the keen desire to see 'the best business brains we can secure' because he regarded it as 'obvious that the people in charge . . . must have great industrial and managerial ability, and we must be prepared to pay what is necessary in order to secure that ability, if the undertaking is to be efficient'. This pattern of recruitment to the boards of nationalised industries has continued. There has been no concern to secure the representation of workers and consumers; there has been no element of industrial democracy, still less of workers control; and top private businessmen and (more recently) managers and technical specialists whose main careers have been within the corporations have continued to fill the vast majority of board positions. The continuing ties between the nationalised industries and the 'private' ones are reflected in the interlocking of the public boards with those of private companies: part-time members of the public boards frequently hold many directorships in private companies as well.

Because nationalised industries are half-way houses – both business enterprises and government institutions, in some ways independent of the government and in others not – it is difficult to be precise as to who 'really' runs them – the more so because it is difficult to generalise as between different industries and over time.

The minister appoints the board of the corporation (the most vital of the minister's powers); approves the capital-investment programme;

sanctions the raising of capital finance from external sources; has the right to information as required; and is empowered to give the board directions of a 'general character' in relation to matters appearing to the minister to affect the public interest. For its part, Parliament can concern itself with the nationalised industries through general debates, through questions to the relevant minister, and (before it was abolished in 1979) through the Select Committee on Nationalised Industries. In fact, all of these devices have proved to be of limited worth in securing any kind of effective accountability because questions cannot go into detail (and ministers are not required to answer) and the staffing of the Select Committee was never really adequate to the massive tasks at hand.

It is important to realise that a formal statement as to the respective powers of ministers, Parliament, and boards, does not help us to get to the reality of things because the constitutional position of public corporations is confused, unsettled, and unclear. Having said that, there *is* a problem as to the division of labour between boards and ministers, appointed experts and elected politicians. Attempts to resolve it through giving the boards responsibility for 'day-to-day administration' and the ministers responsibility for 'general policy', or through giving the boards authority over 'purely commercial' matters whilst the ministers attended to the 'public interest' and 'social' considerations, have never been very successful.

What matters, however, is less the formal division of labour and the niceties of constitutional theorising, and more the actual practice and *principles* on which the industries are run regardless of who is really in control. The fact that the boards have always been dominated by business people provides a clue on this score. Since the 1960s, however, commercial considerations have assumed a position of operating pre-eminence and the nationalised industries have, in effect, been required to pursue a profit to the detriment of social service considerations such as keeping uneconomic railway lines open to serve needy rural customers or working pits to secure jobs in the depressed areas in which many coal mines are located. What happened was that the Treasury became worried in the late 1950s that public expenditure was getting out of control and starting to rise in relation to national income. Governments had to attend to this because of the inevitable implications for taxation. Regardless of party, therefore, governments sought to ensure that the nationalised industries financed a greater proportion of their capital expenditure out of their operating profits. This trend towards the nationalised industries behaving like normal commercial undertakings was reinforced by the shift in balance of the nationalised industries away from the old public utilities with captive British markets towards 'newer' industries such as steel, cars, aerospace, oil, and shipbuilding, all of which had to operate in highly competitive international markets with prices set by international trading conditions. Having said that the nationalised industries have been increasingly required to operate according to the logic and requirements of impersonal market forces, they have been forced to do so with one hand tied behind their backs as this has not occurred to the point where state-owned industries have been allowed to borrow, spend, or expand their sphere of activities like any privately owned enterprise. Quite the reverse, since after 1979 a trend to 'privatisation' involved the nationalised industries being divested of whatever profitable assets and activities the private sector was willing to buy.

A number of things are clear and are of significance for politics, power, and democracy in Britain. First, the nationalised industries are not, and never have been, effectively accountable to parliament and people. Second, workers and consumers have had little say in the conduct of affairs and have never assumed any kind of controlling position. Third, in so far as the elected government has been able to exert a measure of control then it has been increasingly forced to do so by allowing market considerations to hold sway over operations. With the long post-war boom of the 1950s there was space for social considerations to come into play. As the reality of recession and Britain's weak trading position has hit home, however, so the nationalised industries and all those who run them and work in them have been increasingly dominated by profit and loss, and market considerations, to the detriment of any substantive attention to social considerations. In this sense to try and identify *who* runs the nationalised industries – boards or ministers – is a mistake. The industries operate in an impersonal competitive context that sharply constrains the room for choice and decision by anyone who is nominally in charge. We will be returning to the nationalised industries again in Chapter 8.

The Bank of England was nationalised as a publicly-owned corporation in 1946, but the Bank had effectively ceased operating as a purely 'private' institution long before this and was already subject to regulation through Acts of Parliament. The Bank assumes functions of staggering importance because it is at the very centre of the financial system. It is responsible for the execution of monetary policy; it manages the national debt and note circulation; it acts as a banker both to the banking sector and to government; it provides advice on economic policy; and it supervises the banking sector and is responsible for the good order of the financial system as a whole.

Books on British politics tend to ignore the Bank of England. If noticed, the official view of its position is taken on board quite uncritically. The Bank is seen as a simple 'agent' of government: it gives advice on monetary and other economic policy, but at the end of the day the Chancellor of the Exchequer and other government ministers decide, and MPs on the floor of the Commons and in commitees are free to question closely the decisions of government. This is the theory, but the reality is somewhat different.

First, the Bank, although nationalised in 1946, was nationalised in close consultation with the Bank itself and although the government wanted control it wished to minimise 'political aspects' and to emphasise to the world of international finance the integrity *and* independence of the Governors and Directors of the Bank. The Bank was established as an organisation separate from government, with an independence larger than that enjoyed by other nationalised industries, and it continues to enjoy a life of its own today.

Second, *formally,* the Bank may be just an agent of the government, but in *practice* the Bank is in a position of such authority that it can almost determine policy. In 1964, for example, Labour won the general election, but in the context of a sterling crisis that pulled the Governor of the Bank into a position of policy prominence. The Prime Minister, Harold Wilson, has described the daily reality of handling these repeated financial crises: 'The Governor of the Bank of England became a frequent visitor...we had to listen night after night to demands that there should be immediate cuts in Government expenditure. ... It was not long before we were being asked, almost at pistol point, to cut-back on expenditure.' It was not long, either, before the Governor's advice was formed into government policy. Interestingly, what 'advice' the Bank actually gives is not known outside of government, so limiting the possibility of effective public and parliamentary scrutiny.

Third, in recent years a number of factors have tended to increase the influence of the Bank. There is now much greater importance attached in economic management to monetary policy and so policy-makers have to pay more attention to the views of the financial markets. In addition, the Bank's statistical and economic expertise has been strengthened. These developments increase the importance of ensuring the adequacy of the arrangements for securing the accountability of the Bank, but there is scope for unease on this score.

Until 1971, the Bank did not even publish the accounts and its annual report was so 'meagre' that the Select Committee on Nationalised Industries was led to argue that the Bank was effectively 'accountable to nobody'. For its part, the Bank would claim that the Court of Directors was responsible for the proper running of the bank, but two things need to be said about this.

First, this responsibility hardly goes far enough since, apart from the Court, no one is in a position to know about things so as to judge whether the Bank has been properly conducted. Secrecy surrounds the operations of the Bank, and although this is defended in terms of the need for 'confidentiality' and 'independence' and the desirability of 'doing good by stealth', it does mean that much has to be taken on trust. The Treasury are not (nor do they want to be) in a position to be responsible in great detail for the way in which the Bank manages its affairs; governments have not welcomed enquiries into the relations between the Bank and themselves; and Parliament lacks expertise and information.

Second, the Court itself consists of a Governor, Deputy Governor, and sixteen Directors of whom no more than four can be employed to give their exclusive services to the Bank. Governors, Deputy Governors, and executive directors have all been appointed from within the Bank or from the world of merchant banking. The presence of the twelve non-executive Directors on the Court could be seen as a form of accountability. However, the Wilson committee to review the functioning of financial institutions pointed out that the usual pattern was one of eight directors from industry, three from the merchant banks, and one trade unionist and 'the circle from which such individuals are drawn has become too limited with the passage of time and unrepresentative in a looser sense'. The close relationship between the world of finance in the City and the Bank makes it inevitable that some see the Bank as a lobby and a voice for the interests of the City itself in a way which places a very particular practical gloss on its formal independence.

Under pressure from Parliament and public opinion the Bank has become more open in recent years. Since 1971, the Bank has published annual accounts; its annual report has become more informative; and it has availed itself of opportunities to explain itself through its *Quarterly Bulletin*. For all this, however, secrecy continues to surround crucial aspects of the Bank in spite of the fact that it is a power of significance in public policy-making in a country regarded as enjoying democratic government.

THE JUDICIARY

Orthodoxies assessed

A certain mystery needs to attach to the nature of law and to the role of judges in order for the legal judicial system to secure the kind of public support and legitimacy that will make for obedience to law with the minimum of force and coercion. Put another way, an image is needed to put the law and the judiciary beyond the reach of the kind of critique that would damage its credibility. In Britain, the orthodox view sees law in a technical, mechanistic way, as sovereign; as readily understood; as fair and rational; and as way above the hurly-burly of political and class conflict. From this kind of perspective, Parliament alone makes the law, and the judges are simply there to declare and apply the law to particular cases and disputes relying on precedent and a literal reading of the statutes. Judges are regarded as arbiters in disputes who operate in accord with a process – the Rule of Law – that secures justice and fair play for all regardless of the class, age, sex, or race of those before them. Judges are independent from the government of the day, and are outside of politics itself. They are impartial, neutral, unbiased, and disinterested in their application of the law to particular cases.

It follows from all of this that judges are *not* regarded as powerful in their own right (because they are presented as lacking the opportunity for discretion and are themselves bound by the sovereign law that is not of their own making); judges are *not* regarded as in any way in politics (because the theory of the separation of powers and a variety of conventional and statutory provisions are seen as securing their independence); and judges are *not* regarded as law-makers (because that is regarded as the proper and exclusive function of Parliament alone).

In fact, all of these orthodox views are pretty much wrong. Judges are powerful figures within our society who can legitimately deprive people of their freedom; they are in politics; and they are active in actually making law.

As a variety of developments have served to demystify the position of judges, so the orthodoxies that surround and defend them are being opened up. Lawyers are forced to recognise this even though their position means that they have an interest in upholding the myths. For example, Lord Reid, who was Lord of Appeal from 1948 to 1974, recognised that 'there was a time when it was thought almost indecent to suggest that judges make law – they only declare it.... But we do not believe in fairy tales any more. So we must accept the fact that for better or worse judges do make law.'

In Britain, laws are of two kinds. There is statute law and common law, but the former predominates over the latter wherever there is conflict between the two, and much statute law is made to change and replace parts of the common law. Statute law is made by Parliament – or rather it is put through Parliament by the government acting on the 'advice' of its civil servants. Common law is made by the judges. As they decide cases and state the principles on which they are basing their decisions so the accumulation of principles builds into a body of law because of the power of precedent as a guide to future judgements in similar cases. It has never really been in doubt that judges 'make law' through the development of common law (even though the full significance of the power and discretion involved in this has been downplayed because of the emphasis upon the limiting implications of simply following precedent), but there has been a reluctance to recognise that the interpretation of statute law is also a 'creative' function that involves making law. In fact, there are still disputes as to how far judges should go in this field of creative, or 'activist', law making. Now, in interpreting statute law, judges are faced with a number of choices and courses of action. They can engage in a literal interpretation, having regard to the 'natural' and 'ordinary' meaning of the words in the statute; they can engage in a purposive interpretation, having regard to the intention of the framers of the statute through a scrutiny of the relevant debates in Parliament; or they can have a keen regard for the ways in which acts have been interpreted in the past so placing a heavy reliance on precedent, and the close reading of previous cases and judgements.

Judges, then, are always involved in politics and law-making. They enjoy power because they always have room to exercise choice and discretion. Having said that, the precise *extent* of their involvement in law-making and politics is not a settled matter. In recent times a number of factors have served to increase their political involvement.

First, increased political controversy has led to governments pulling the judiciary directly into politics outside of their courts in order that they can preside over a variety of commissions, committees, and administrative tribunals. Extrajudicial activity of this kind has been important in the control of restrictive practices, in industrial relations, in Northern Ireland, and in response to the inner city riots of the early eighties. In effect, the image of the judiciary as impartial, fair, and disinterested has been used to cool-out disputes and render acceptable subsequent political decisions that may bear harshly on particular interests. In the process of this, however, the image of the judiciary can easily become tarnished in ways that injure its role in the courts.

Second, and as we saw in Chapter 4, senior figures from within the judicial establishment have become increasingly critical of the established political and constitutional set-up. They have called for a new written constitution with a Bill of Rights and judicial review that would give the judges a massive increase in political power enabling them to frustrate the democratic will and declare certain Acts of Parliament 'unconstitutional' and, therefore, illegal and unenforceable in the courts.

Third, on the more narrow judicial front, over the last 20 or so years there has been a change of judicial 'style' amounting almost to a change in the nature of the judicial process itself. This has occurred because the Law Lords slowly came to regard themselves, not so much as passive restaters of accepted doctrines, but rather as the activist and incremental developer of new doctrines. The Law Lords 1966 practice statement on precedent was a crucial landmark in the extension of the creative role and in the assertion of a more activist and interventionist stance in law-making:

Their Lordships regard the use of precedent as an indispensable foundation upon which to decide what is the law and its application to individual cases.... Their Lordships nevertheless recognise that too rigid adherence to precedent may lead to injustice in a particular case and also unduly restrict the proper development of the law. They propose, therefore, to modify their present practice and, while treating former decisions of this House as normally binding, to depart from a previous decision when it appears right to do so.

In effect, the Law Lords were shifting from a formalistic concern to 'be consistent', logical and certain in their application of the law, into a more flexible concern to 'be fair'. This lifted some of the self-imposed constraints which they had set upon their creative, law-making role, and led to their emphasising the importance of applying 'principles' over precedent.

Discretion, recruitment and socialisation

To say that judges are involved in politics and law-making is to deny a widely shared view as to the function and position of the judiciary. However, it does not tell us *what* laws they make; it does not tell us *how* they go about their task and exercise discretion; and it does not indicate the kind of *factors* that serve to influence (and bias) the nature of their law-making.

Judges may be formally independent of the legislature and the executive (this is what the separation of powers is all about) and they may try to be fair and impartial, but they are human with human prejudices. They cannot stand outside of society because they live and operate within it. They cannot discard their politics and prejudices when they put on their wigs and their gowns and they inevitably take their attitudes into court and pass judgements on the basis of their beliefs and biases. Moreover, they perform their function in the context of a divided society where they themselves are manifestly unrepresentative of the population at large in terms of age, sex, education, and social background.

In an influential and provocative book on *The Politics of the Judiciary,* John Griffith has looked at the ways in which judges of the High Court, the Court of Appeal, and the House of Lords have made law, and dealt with the cases before them. In effect, he was concerned to tease out the bases on which their decisions were made and the themes in their judgements in order to try to see whether they displayed a wide spectrum of judicial opinion or a consistency of approach that was located in a fairly narrow part of the spread of political opinion in Britain. Griffith argues that judges undertake their tasks with an eye to securing the 'public interest'. He recognises, however, that what is, or is not, seen as in the public interest is a political question which admits of a great variety of answers. He goes on to argue that

the judicial conception of the public interest, seen in the cases discussed in this book, is threefold. It concerns first, the interests of the state (including its moral welfare) and the preservation of law and order, broadly interpreted; secondly, the protection of property rights; and thirdly the promotion of certain political views normally associated with the Conservative Party.

In the case of private property, and especially large property owners and the holders of land, Griffith shows that the courts have continually intervened to limit and curtail the powers of governmental interference. As evidence of judicial sympathy for the political views of the Conservative Party, Griffith points to the implications of court judgements with respect to trade union cases and race relations cases, and highlights the extent to which judges come down heavily on those expressing minority opinions and those who seek to change society through squatting, picketing, or engaging in demonstrations and protest. The judicial stance to black people is specifically discussed in a book on *Whitelaw* by Paul Gordon. With respect to the interpretation of immigration law (discussed in Chapter 6) Gordon argues that judges, far from standing as a bulwark of freedom between the individual citizen and the excesses of the Home Office, have chosen (with few exceptions) to side with the Home Office so confirming the view that the black presence in Britain is unwanted. Moreover, in interpreting the Race Relations Acts that were designed to outlaw discrimination in a number of areas, Gordon suggests that the judges have adopted a restricted view that has done little to protect the position of the black British against entrenched patterns of racism that the law was supposedly designed to uproot. Steven Box recognises that it is in the final stage of sentencing that a judicial bias in a particularly blatant form is revealed. Judges, like laymen, have in their minds a number of cultural stereotypes which can be applied to particular situations so as to neutralise the criminality of a person whose behaviour is technically criminal. In this way, individuals guilty of similar offences may finish up with sentences that are very different simply because of who they are and how they are assessed by the judge. Box's research is by no means systematic but from the examples he gives it could be inferred that judges 'are less inclined to send to prison such persons as barristers, ex-public schoolboys, doctors' sons, privately educated females, accountants, civil servants and corporation executives'.

It is one thing to suggest that judges display a consistent bias in judicial law-making, but it is another thing to explain just why and how this consistent pattern of judicial behaviour comes about. In our view, it is important to have regard to the nature of the judicial world and to the background and socialisation of those who are part of it.

In 1976, there were some 3700 barristers in practice, there were 11 Lords of Appeal, 15 Lords Justices, and 73 High Court judges. The higher judiciary, then, comprises some 100 persons, but the truly effective number of policy-makers in the Divisional Court, the Court of Appeal, and the House of Lords is fewer than 30. The world of the higher judiciary is a small, tight, inward-looking one. Paterson, in his study of the *Law Lords*, found that they paid little attention to the views of academic lawyers and steered clear of politicians, preferring to lunch together and discuss cases amongst themselves.

What of social background of the more senior judiciary? In broad terms four out of five full-time professional judges are products of public schools (and exclusive ones at that), and of Oxford and Cambridge Universities. Over the whole period 1820–1968 the higher judiciary has been dominated by those of an upper and upper-middle class background. Although the social background of lay magistrates who deal with minor offences and committal hearings is by no means as exalted as that of the senior judiciary, a survey for the period 1966–67 revealed that 77 per cent of magistrates were from professional or managerial backgrounds whereas only 18.3 per cent of the population at large was from that background. At the other end of the scale no magistrates were from a semi-skilled or an unskilled manual background, in spite of the fact that 28.5 per cent of the population at large were in these social groupings.

How do people become senior judges and what are the implications of their recruitment and socialisation for the pattern of judicial behaviour? The appointment of judges is in the hands of politicians (and especially the Lord Chancellor) but convention limits the choice. At one time it was accepted that a political career in Parliament was an advantage for a barrister aspiring to a judgeship. Since the First World War, however, legal and professional qualifications have assumed a greater prominence. Nowadays, the scope for party political considerations having much sway is restricted by the convention that judges should be appointed from the ranks of barristers of at least 10 or 15 years standing with around 20 years of practice at the bar. So, when Lord Chancellors are making their appointments to the High Court they are choosing from a group of experienced barristers between the ages of 45 and 60, and the number of genuine possibilities may be as small as half-a-dozen. People whose personal habits were unconventional or uncertain would not be picked, and a candidate's political convictions would not be expected to fall outside a spectrum from right-wing Labour to traditional Tory opinion.

So, judges come from a particular class: stay in that class (in 1981, High Court judges were paid £32 000); and by and large have the social and political views characteristic of that class. Inevitably a body of elderly upper-middle-class men who have lived unadventurous lives tend to be old-fashioned and conservative in their views and out of step with social, cultural and ethical change, for they have no first-hand knowledge of how the great majority of people live their lives.

Although knowledge as to the background of senior judges goes some way in explaining the way in which discretion is exercised, it would be a mistake to make too much of this since it is doubtful whether drawing judges from a 'lower' social and educational background would change things very much. The distinguished judge Lord Devlin does

not believe that measures of this sort would make a pennyworth of difference. Let the practice of law be opened up by all means and let the judiciary be composed of the best that the practice of law can produce. You will find, I am sure that judges will still be of the same type whether they come from major or minor public schools, grammar schools, or comprehensives, whether they like to spend their leisure in a library or a club. They will all be the type of men [sic]...who do not seriously question the status quo....You can see this already at the university where students in the law faculties all over the world are nearly always on the right.

Lord Devlin's candid observations about the 'type of men' attracted to the profession of the law needs to be buttressed by an assessment as to the implications of judicial socialisation. Before a lawyer becomes a judge, the years of affluence as a successful barrister, and the social life that is part of that world, tend to produce a conformity to the norms of the legal profession that transcends the implications that might flow from a long-lost working-class upbringing. If a working-class hero did become a successful barrister and did continue to hang on to a political viewpoint beyond the pale, then he or she could not expect to secure a judgeship so as to be able to put those views into some sort of effect that would push the law into new and more radical directions.

The judiciary and democracy

We have argued that the judges wield political power; make law; and cannot be politically neutral since their position as part of established authority constrains them to behave in conservative and illiberal ways that preserve the essentials of the status quo.

The problem is that Britain is a kind of democracy and yet the judges who make law are unaccountable and effectively beyond removal from office. Judicial law-making is manifestly undemocratic. Can this powerful activity continue to be regarded as acceptable and legitimate in a country that is supposed to enjoy a liberal-democratic constitution in which all power flows up from people through elected representatives? Moreover, potential problems of legitimacy and acceptability are compounded once we recognise that judges are in no sense 'ordinary' people representative of the population at large. Simply expressed, should we continue to trust the judges as defenders of our rights and give them *carte blanche* to behave as they will, or should we devise democratic mechanisms to render them accountable and restrain their independence and power?

THE POLICE

In 1908 there were just 30 376 police in England and Wales in over 250 separate forces, but by 1982 there were 118 451 police backed up by 43 496 civilians and organised into just 43 forces with close links between them. Spending on law and order has been spared the axe on public expenditure that has been wielded since 1979. Expenditure on police in England, Wales and Scotland in the financial year till March 1982, amounted to £2430 million, and police pay was increased by 55.8 per cent between May 1979 and September 1981 so ensuring that practically all the forces were at, or above, their authorised strengths. Nor do these figures reveal all. The Special Branch was formed in 1883 to protect the security of the state against 'subversive' organisations. In the 1960s there were only about 200 special branch officers but by 1978 the Home Secretary was able to tell the House that there were 1259 Special Branch officers in

England and Wales although their activities were practically never referred to in the annual reports of chief constables. In addition, we need to weigh into account the 'private police' – those employed in the security and private detective industries – who perform functions similar to the 'public' police but who are controlled by private enterprise. In 1971, it was estimated that there were approximately 105 000 private police in the whole of the United Kingdom. The legal controls on these organisations amount to very little and they are supervised by toothless watchdogs.

What do the police do; what is their function and role in society; and how do they go about their tasks?

Orthodoxies assessed

From the orthodox point of view the police have two major tasks. They have the job of maintaining the Queen's peace and preserving public order, and they also have the job of trying to prevent crime and are faced with the urgent task of catching those who break the criminal law. It is asserted that the police are not a body of people distinct from the general public, and as they go about their tasks they are mindful of the need to secure widespread public support and acceptance and so they adopt a low and non-violent profile, choosing to police 'by consent'. From this perspective the police are regarded as outside of politics and as lacking in any real power because they are regarded as totally bound by, and accountable to, the law of the land.

Analysing the role and function of the police is not easy, but against this picture it is our contention that the police *are* a distinct body isolated from the communities they serve; they do *not* simply rely on policing by consent; and that they *do* assume a political role. There is a political aspect to policing because the police do have very real powers and are in a position to exercise discretion in the use of these powers; they are *not* simply bound by the law; and in many ways they are an unaccountable power unto themselves. They are part of the state because they exercise crucial public functions involving the use of legitimate force; but they are part of the secret state because they operate in a closed world that lies way beyond the reach of effective democratic and popular control.

We will attend to the public order aspects of policing in Chapter 10 on social control. For the moment we will deal with the police role with respect to crime and criminals. First, we will demonstrate that the police exercise discretion and are not simply bound by the law. Second, we will attempt to explain the way in which that discretion is exercised by attending to the social background and socialisation of the police into particular values.

Police discretion

No rule is ever entirely self-evident. No matter how carefully a rule is drawn up and how meticulously it is elaborated, those who have to enforce it will always enjoy some discretion in determining how it should apply (or even whether it should apply) in any given instance. Rules, in other words, are not self-explanatory; they have to be interpreted before they can be applied.

In British society, law-breaking is very common among all social classes, all age groups, and both genders. An obvious case in point is motoring offences, for most of us who drive probably exceed the speed limit or engage in some manoeuvre which could conceivably be construed as 'dangerous driving' or 'driving without due care and attention' almost every time we get out onto the road. Our deviancy does not end there, however, for a number of 'self-report' studies have shown that large proportions of the population have, from time to time, engaged in quite serious crimes involving theft (e.g. shoplifting or stealing from the place of work), violence and other offences against property and people. These studies also show, however, that few of us are ever caught, charged and sentenced.

Now it is clear that in many cases the very definition of our behaviour as 'legitimate' or 'illegitimate' will be open to negotiation. Whether or not executing a U-turn in the High Street constitutes 'dangerous driving' will depend largely on how the police officer who observes the incident decides to interpret it. Similarly, the elderly woman who is stopped outside Woolworths carrying a jumper which she has not paid for may be defined either as 'old and confused' or as a 'thief' caught in the act. Is the umbrella carried by the football fan on the way to match a harmless precaution against the weather or is it an 'offensive weapon'? And does that noisy West Indian house party that resonates on towards dawn constitute a 'breach of the peace', or even behaviour liable to excite such a breach?

These are the sorts of judgements which police officers are called upon to make in their everyday work. When called upon to make them, they do not look to the law, for the law does not tell them how reckless a U-turn has to be before it is dangerous, how senile old ladies have to be before they cease to be responsible for their actions, what an offensive weapon actually looks like, or how many decibels of reggae music are permissible at 3 a.m. on a Sunday. Instead, they use their 'common sense'. Or, to put it another way, they use their discretion.

We all rely a great deal on 'common sense' to get us through the day, and the police are no exception. Every time we meet somebody, we draw on the common-sense knowledge which we have accumulated over the years to tell us what sort of person it is, how we should treat them, what we should expect of them, and so on. We 'know' that middle-aged men wearing pin-stripe suits and carrying a pink newspaper are businessmen, and we 'know' that businessmen disapprove of gum-chewing, drink shorts rather than pints, support the Tory Party, live in suburbia etc., all of which enables us to select the appropriate mode of behaving towards them. Sometimes, of course, our common sense wisdom leads us astray – the pin-striped, bowler-hatted gentleman turns out to be a jewel-thief, or the bearded youth in the faded denims turns out to be the owner of a computer software firm, but more often than not our 'first impressions' are more or less accurate and enable us to fill in the gaps as the interaction proceeds.

The police operate in exactly the same way. They do not (and given the extent of deviant behaviour in our society probably cannot) proceed in their work except on the basis of certain shared wisdoms regarding the sort of people who engage in specific kinds of behaviour in specific kinds of situations. What is involved here is a process of typification – if you 'fit' the type then the police are likely to show an interest in you, and if you do not then they will not.

Middle-aged women do not get stopped and searched as they enter a football ground on a Saturday afternoon because the police 'know' that potential troublemakers are young, male and festooned in their club's colours. Middle-aged men wearing pin-stripe suits and driving a Rover are stopped much less often than young people driving Minis because the police 'know' that young people are more likely to have stolen the car, that there is likely to be something defective on the car, that the driver is likely to have been drinking, and so on. Young blacks standing on a street corner are constantly questioned by the police while white adults may go about their (lawful or unlawful) business for years without ever speaking to a police officer, for again the police 'know' that young blacks are likely to be in possession of drugs or stolen goods, or are likely to be plotting a mugging or a burglary.

Once stopped by the police, a suspect may still be able to convince an officer that she or he is not the 'type' that she or he appeared on first sight to be. Careful manipulation of language, facial expression, humour and demeanour may result in say, an informal caution ('Make sure you get that tyre seen to') rather than an arrest, for any incongruity in the impression made is likely to sow a doubt in the officer's mind. However, the subsequent interaction may confirm the officer's first impressions, in which case the suspect is likely to be escorted to the police station and charged notwithstanding his or her pleas of innocence. Indeed, the police have been known to have been so sure of the guilt of suspects that they have forcibly extracted confessions from them in order to make their charges stand up in court.

All of this, of course, raises the important question of where the police get their common-sense knowledge from in the first place. The answer is that they rely partly on a shared stock of knowledge, which is passed on within the force to new recruits by the 'old hands', and partly on images which they receive through the newspapers they read and the television programmes they watch. From their colleagues and from the media they learn how to recognise typical criminals, and for as long as these common-sense cues pay off, they will be reinforced and passed on in their turn to later generations to work with.

Now it is important to emphasise that common-sense policing is problematic. Some drunken drivers are young males driving Minis; some muggers are black youths who hang around street corners; but not only does the exercise of discretion mean that police develop tunnel vision such that they do not and cannot see other offenders who do not fit the stereotype, but it also becomes a self-fulfilling prophecy. This is because only those people who fit the type are apprehended, and this then shows up in the official statistics and in media reports where people of that type will figure prominently: where ye shall seek, so shall ye find! So it is that the common-sense knowledge of the police creates a pattern of officially recognised crime which then reinforces the original stereotyping. It is in this sense that sociologists have referred to the process whereby crime is 'socially constructed', for whether or not someone ends up in court is likely to depend as much on the social interaction with the police as with the nature of that person's actual behaviour.

Recruitment and socialisation

Unlike judges, unlike senior civil servants, unlike the military, and unlike most Members of Parliament, most police officers (even senior ones) do not come from backgrounds privileged by wealth or private education, and promotion is through the ranks, so that few university graduates are to be counted amongst the elite few at the top. The police are an interesting exception to the general pattern of recruitment to the institutions of the secret state.

First, the parents of police recruits are mainly upper-working class or lower-middle class. A survey carried out in 1962–63 (the most recent available) revealed that just over 60 per cent of police officers interviewed were the children of skilled manual or low-grade non-manual workers, although city police were generally of a somewhat higher social-class background. Second, the police force is an almost exclusively white organisation. In 1981, black officers made up only 0.5 per cent of the Metropolitan Police and just 0.3 per cent of the total strength in the rest of England and Wales. The riots in Britain's cities in the summer of 1981 encouraged the police to try and recruit more black officers in order to make policing more acceptable to black youth. This attempt has been a failure and it is doubtful if the recruitment of people of West Indian origin will increase whilst they continue to see the police as instruments of oppression. In the year ending October 1982, the Metropolitan Police recruited forty-six black officers but the proportion of black applicants who actually joined the police declined from 12 per cent in 1981 to just 8.6 per cent in 1982. Third, the police force is very much a male organisation. In London, only 9 per cent of the uniformed force are women and just 4 per cent of the CID are women because of the pervasiveness of a 'cult of masculinity' which sees women as inferior. The Metropolitan Police discriminates unlawfully against the entry of women into the force because it operates on the basis of an unofficial 10 per cent quota. Only 7 per cent of women applicants are accepted into the Metropolitan Police compared with 17 per cent of men. Fourth, police officers appear to have been slightly better educated than is typical of working-class children, but have failed to attain a standard of educational achievement normally reached by middle-class children. The Policy Studies Institute inquiry into the Metropolitan Police, published in 1983, suggested that entry standards into the force were too low by international standards. Fifth, the values, and especially the political values of the police are right of centre. A careful survey of police recruits and probationer constables carried out in 1982 produced evidence which suggested that the police force attracts conservative and authoritarian personalities, and other studies have shown the police to be more conservative than the general public. Police training does little to counter this. It produces a temporary liberalising effect. Continued police service tends to result in increasingly illiberal and intolerant attitudes because of the nature and pervasiveness of the informal police subculture. The Policy Studies Institute survey found that 'certain themes tend to be emphasised in conversation in an exaggerated way: the prime examples are male dominance (combined with denigration of women), the glamour (but not the reality) of violence, and racial prejudice'. Women police officers are commonly described as 'plonks' and were not in general highly regarded; racialist language between officers was 'on the whole expected, accepted, and even fashionable'; and because much police work was dull and routine there was a zeal for action and a certain appetite for aggravation reflected in the fact that the 'immediate response units certainly look forward to disturbances and, in fact, tend to find anything else boring by comparison' and in the researchers noting that excessive force was used in almost 10 per cent of observed arrests.

The background and education of police recruits means that they tend to be marginal people with status anxieties. They have accepted the typical ways of thinking, acting, and feeling of the traditional middle class, but they have not really acquired a job that quite matches up. They can hope to allay their anxieties by policing in a way that reniforces the expectations of middle-class opinion so giving themselves more of a foothold in 'respectable' society. This is difficult, however, given the nature of the job and the social distance between the police and the rest of the community. The police world is a closed one and the police officer is isolated from 'normal' society. The 1962 Royal Commission on the Police revealed that nearly two-thirds of police officers said that they encountered severe difficulties in making friends outside the force, and 58 per cent said that the public were reserved, suspicious, and constrained in conversation. Inevitably, therefore, the police perspective on society and crime derives from the perspectives of other police officers and is institutionalised in the values that make up the informal subculture. In addition to this the average police officer is likely to take a cue from the mass media, and (given the political values of most officers) is likely to look to the conservative, slightly puritanical and self-righteous daily tabloids since they reinforce what is 'known' to be true by most police. In this kind of situation, stereotypes quickly build up as to just who are criminal types, and these stereotypes reveal particular biases and presuppositions. Nor is this just a matter of individual police attitudes or of the informal subculture since many of these perspectives are formally institutionalised within the force.

In 1977, David Powis, Deputy Assistant Commissioner to the Metropolitan Police, produced a book called *The Signs of Crime: A Field Manual for Police*. The book consists of detailed information on how to spot crime, criminals, and suspicious characters. The picture that emerges is clear enough: respectable, unsuspicious people conform to extremely conventional middle-aged, middle class and respectable working class modes of appearance, life style and political belief. Anything else is suspicious, and the further it deviates from the respectable model then the more suspicious it becomes. In addition to how to spot criminals, new recruits are also advised to watch out for people who 'although not dishonest in the ordinary sense, may, owing to extreme political views, intend to harm the community you have sworn to protect', with Powis continuing that 'while there are subtle differences between these types of extremists and thieves, it is difficult to put one's finger on the material distinction'.

Police stereotypes and police theories as to the groups and areas most likely to be involved in crime effectively ignore the white-collar crime that tends to occur in 'private' but because stereotypes and theories guide action they tend to become self-fulfilling. The police, then, are powerful because they have the scope to be able to exercise discretion. Moreover, they tend to exercise that discretion in particular ways conditioned by background and socialisation within the force. Does all this mean that the police are an unaccountable law unto themselves?

Police Accountability

In theory, the police are accountable in two ways. First, they are accountable to the law in the sense that police officers are as responsible to the criminal law for their actions as any other citizen. Second, the police are also accountable under Acts of Parliament to local Police Authorities (sometimes called Police Committees) consisting of two-thirds elected county councillors and one-third local magistrates; to central government through Her Majesty's Inspectors of Constabulary; and, in some instances, to the Home Secretary and the Secretary of State for Scotland.

In practice, however, accountability to law is of limited worth because the judiciary are unable and unwilling to monitor the ordinary activities of the police. This is hardly surprising since one would not expect to find the judges anti-police, and critical in their stance towards the police as a whole. So, the 'myth' of accountability to law is increasingly becoming a mere verbal formula that in practice gives greater and greater discretion to police officers about how to exercise their wide powers.

For their part, local Police Authorities enjoy very limited powers of control. They are charged with ensuring 'the maintenance of an adequate and efficient police force'. They can determine the size of the force and the level of provision of equipment and buildings (*but* this budgetary control is subject to the approval of the Home Secretary); they can appoint the chief constable and other senior ranks (*but* the approval of the Home Secretary is needed); and they can discuss policing policy for their areas (*but* 'direction and control' and 'operational' decisions are left in the hands of the chief constables alone who fiercely defend their unfettered control in these matters). In fact, most police authorities do not even choose to use the limited powers that are available to them. They tend to defer to their chief constable's professional expertise and judgement; they see their role as supportive of that person's policing policy; and they rarely exercise their right to call for reports on matters of local concern so they lack the basic information to enable them to assume a more interventionist role in controlling the police. By the mid-1970s local police authorities had come to be little more than providers for, and admirers of, the police.

Interestingly, the accountability-to-law argument (which as we have seen means very little in practice) has been used to block moves for an effective controlling role for Police Authorities. There is the idea that the major responsibility for law enforcement is reserved to the chief officers of the police and, in the exercise of this function, it is seen as best that they are answerable to the law alone and not to any 'political' police authority. In this state of affairs, chief constables enjoy a position of immense political independence quite unlike that enjoyed by the officers responsible for other locally provided services. In local government there is clear accountability to locally elected councillors and an expectation that the broad lines of policy will be set by the elected representatives of the people and not by the non-elected officials who are expected to assume more of an administrative and implementing role, yet the local Police Committees are a clear exception to this.

All things considered, then, the police are virtually impervious to any control by elected politicians other than the Home Secretary, and that is the way they want to keep it. Most senior officers do not want to see the party political 'contamination' of the machinery of justice and they distrust the competence of, and abhor the idea of accountability to, politicians and community representatives whether elected or appointed.

Over the past few years, however, there have been calls for increased democratic accountability, and particular controversy has arisen over the Metropolitan Police where there is not even a police authority (the force is controlled directly from the Home Office). The pressures for a change in the relations between the police and the policed communities, and the pressures for democratic control, are considerable and show no sign of abating. The Home Office has been forced to respond whilst defending the position opposed to democratic control. In a 1982 circular to the clerks of Police Authorities and to the chief officers of police, the Home Office pointed to the need for 'regular consultation' with 'consultative groups'. However, the Home Office makes it very clear that those involved should be alive to 'the limits of consultation' and there is no sense in which they are making any plans for the community control of police – rather the opposite, since they are being forced to respond to pressure by giving a little in the hope of being able to block the lot.

The public may have but limited control over the police, but if they feel they have been wronged by the actions of the police what are the procedures for complaints?

Police complaints

In 1965 there were 9301 recorded complaints against the police in England and Wales; in 1972 there were 15 543; and in 1976 the number had risen to 22 738. Since 1978, the major category of complaints has been of assaults by police.

The Police Act, 1964 placed on a statutory basis the procedures for investigation that had been followed for several decades. The chief officer of each force was responsible for ensuring that any complaint from a member of the public was recorded and investigated. Where the complaint involved an allegation of a criminal offence by a police officer, then the investigator's report was to be referred to the Director of Public Prosecutions unless the deputy chief officer had satisfied himself that no criminal offence had in fact been committed.

Throughout the sixties and seventies there were grumbles about the absence of any independent element in the complaints procedures. It was seen as wrong that police officers alone were responsible for investigating *and* judging the conduct of other police officers – the more so given the seriousness of some of the complaints and the extent to which the procedures violated notions of natural justice. The Police Act, 1976 established the independent Police Complaints Board for England and Wales, but the Board was only able to intervene at an extremely late stage. It was not caught up in the actual investigation of complaints and it has rarely given the appearance of using its powers to the full. In the 5 years 1977–81, the Board disagreed with the deputy chief officer's decision not to bring disciplinary proceedings on only seventy-seven occasions and in almost every case the deputy chief officer accepted the Board's recommendation or succeeded in persuading the Board to change its mind: in only one case did the Board find it necessary to direct that disciplinary proceedings be brought. Of course, all of this might be construed as attesting to the rigours of the police investigating themselves, but to some it smacked of a kind of collusion between police and the Board where there was a need for more public light. To some extent, the Board itself was mindful of the problems of the situation and in their 1980 Triennial Review Report they recommended that there should be an independent element in the *investigation* of complaints arising from serious injury. The Police Federation (the police trade union) expressed 'total opposition' to this idea, and a government working party reported in 1981 that such a procedure was 'impracticable and unnecessary'. The clamour of concern about police investigating police was fuelled by some grisly tales. The Home Secretary was forced to set up another working party, and by 1982 the government was able to propose a 'three-tier approach' for handling complaints against the police whereby 'the most serious complaints would be subject to investigation by a senior police officer, normally, but not exclusively, from an outside force under the supervision of an independent assessor', who would be the chairman of the Complaints Board.

Those who continue to push the case for a fully independent system feel that this limited proposal adds almost nothing to the present system. At the same time, however, there is a strong police and 'law and order' lobby opposed to any independent element at all. It is clear that the handling of public complaints against the police is likely to continue to be an issue in British politics itself.

The role of policing

There is discretion, power, and politics caught up in the police's selective enforcement of the criminal law. Indeed, crimes such as 'mugging' have a quasi-political character to them, with the term itself being used as a kind of code word to describe the larger social conflict which exists between blacks and the police in urban trouble spots where policing by consent has been replaced by 'fire-brigade' tactics using mobile squads. Moreover, it is inevitable that the content and administration of criminal law in a class-divided society will in part reflect the interests of those who are economically dominant – how else could it be? Having said all that, it is nevertheless true that the police officer's primary function is to preserve peace and maintain social order. It is here that the political aspects of police work are most significant because the police are at the hard end of social control in a way which involves them in the preservation of a particular kind of economic and political order. We will be discussing the social control aspects of the police work in Chapter 10. For the moment, it is sufficient to note that the police are a powerful force that is practically accountable to no one.

THE SECURITY SERVICES

There is deep within the British state an ensemble of agencies concerned with security and subversion in the defence of 'our' national and public interest. This most secret arm of the secret state consists of a number of large organisations. There is MI5 (also known as the Security Service), founded in 1909, geared to the threat of domestic subversion, and with an estimated staff of between 4000 and 5000; there is the rapidly expanding Special Branch, a political police who serve as the running boys and arresting arm for MI5; there is MI6 (also known as the Secret Service) geared to collecting intelligence and organising spying outside Britain; there is the Government Communications Headquarters at Cheltenham, geared to radio eavesdropping around the world at a cost of £100 million per annum, and with a staff of around 4000 at Cheltenham but some 20 000 world-wide; the three armed services each have their own intelligence bodies coordinated by the Defence Intelligence Staff; each Ministry has its own security force responsible for the security of personnel and documents; and there is the massive private security industry geared to policing at work and with links into various state agencies. The cost of all this is an official secret.

In this section we are entering a twilight world of turned-up collars and defensive organisations that operate beneath the threshold of public consciousness and behind walls of silence where little is even visible until a crisis exposes things onto the surface of political life. Officially, MI6 does not even exist; the Prime Minister alone is shown the proper MI5 budget (as opposed to the doctored documents which go to Parliament); and when a Labour MP asked the Home Secretary, in March 1970, to make a statement on the extent and nature of the Special Branch's political records he was told: 'the security of the state necessarily requires that I should be in possession of certain information about political affiliations, which it would not be in the public interest to disclose'.

We are not simply dealing with organisations about which little is known; we are also dealing with organisations that hover on the very edges of legality in terms of their existence and actions. MI5 is not established by statute, nor is it recognised by common law. Even the Official Secrets Acts do not acknowledge its existence. Political surveillance is the central function of the Special Branch and MI5, but they operate almost entirely outside the law in this work. This is not to say that they break the law: quite simply there are hardly any laws for them to break. Having said that, there is no clear legal basis for phone-tapping and the interception and opening of letters, and the casual approach of practice in these matters is probably in breach of the European Convention on Human Rights. Statements to Parliament have given the impression that no person's phone can be tapped without the written authority of the Home Secretary. In practice, however, the Home Secretary is but rarely involved and certain 'official' tapping does not even require a warrant. Sensitivity about the whole subject has meant that only twice have official figures ever been published on the extent of phone tapping: in 1955, 231 warrants were said to have been issued, but by 1979, the figure had increased to 411. Not surprisingly, unofficial estimates have set the figure far higher at between 2000 and 4000 a year. Home and office numbers of union leaders and others involved in major industrial disputes are frequently, even routinely, tapped. The practice of opening the mail of those opposed to the prevailing social order is as old as the postal service itself, and today, every major post office has a set of cards listing the groups, individuals, and companies whose mail is specially sorted for attention before delivery. The Post Office Investigation Branch employs several hundred people.

Orthodoxies assessed

It is one thing to say that Special Branch and MI5 engage in surveillance, but what is the larger function of the security services within British politics?

Orthodox views sympathetic to the security services scarcely exist since polite society chooses to ignore the reality of the state within the state. Having said that, D Notice number 10, marked 'Private and Confidential', tells us (or rather those allowed to see D notices!) that 'the Security Service is responsible for countering threats to the realm arising from espionage, subversion, and sabotage'. Moreover, the *Daily Mail*, in August 1955, (mis)informed its readers that 'the job of the Special Branch is to see that the people of Great Britain can sleep safely in their beds'. From this kind of perspective, the security services are supportive of democracy, and liberty. They protect our freedoms from foreign enemies and from subversion and terrorism at home. Enemy spies, terrorists, and violent revolutionaries may have cause to fear the role of the security services, but the ordinary citizen will be left untouched by their activities and should be thankful that they enable us to enjoy our liberties undisturbed.

In fact, these kind of comfy perspectives on the work of the security services are inadequate. They fail to bring out the increasing extent of state intrusion into civil liberties, and they also fail to attend to the implications of security-service activity for what has traditionally been seen as the normal rough and tumble of ordinary politics within a democracy. Unfortunately, the kind of secrecy which surrounds the security services in Britain precludes the kind of analysis that has been possible with respect to other parts of the state machine. Even so, it is possible to look at their role in British politics from a perspective more realistic than that contained within the framework of status quo supporting orthodoxies.

The role of the security services

Over the years, the interpretation of 'national security' and the 'common enemy' has changed its ground. During the Second World War, the Germans and their allies were the threat. After the war and with the onset of the Cold War between East and West, the countries of the Communist bloc were cast in this light. More recently, however, the common enemy is no longer seen as operating quite so far from these shores. Of course, there has long been an anxiety about the threat of domestic subversion, but nowadays the enemy is seen as right here – in the factories, on the streets, in the media, and in the organisation of any protest for change. All this has inevitably meant that the activities of the Special Branch (increased in size six fold since the 1960s) and MI5 have been pulled into positions of relevance for British democracy.

Alongside the changing focus of security concern has gone an expanding perspective on just what constitutes subversion. In a book recounting his experiences of being tried under the Official Secrets Act, Crispin Aubrey puts it this way:

Eighteen years ago, a subversive was described by Lord Denning as someone 'who would contemplate the overthrow of government by unlawful means'. By 1975, a Home Office minister, Lord Harris, announced that subversive activities now included those which are intended to 'undermine or overthrow parliamentary democracy by political, industrial, or violent means' – no mention this time of breaking the law. Three years later, Home Secretary Merlyn Rees said in Parliament that the Special Branch used its powers to 'collect information on people I think are causing a problem for the state'.

Aubrey goes on to make the point that 'the shift from revolutionaries to someone who creates discomfort in high places could hardly have been more clearly spelled out'. Who are the targets of the security-service surveillance? And how do the security services go about their task of keeping tabs on those *they* choose to call 'subversive'?

There is no easy answer to the first question because the security services enjoy a great deal of autonomy in their work, and they are confronting what they see as a moving target in their unending duty of saving Britain from herself. During the 1950s references were commonly made to the monitoring of 'communists'. By the 1960s, however, the fading fortunes of the Communist Party and the rise of new 'extreme' left groups and extra-parliamentary action were creating problems for the security services, forcing them to expand their interest into new territory. In broad terms we can say that for 'subversive' read 'all those actively opposed to the prevailing order' for the security services are involved in clearing up political nuisances that challenge the status quo. In dramatic terms they are in the game of counter-revolution, but their everyday work-a-day world involves them in the surveillance of political activists.

Naturally enough, the security services have to be selective as they go about their mission, but their attention is restricted by the fact that threats are seen as coming from the left and from those opposed to the private enterprise system of capitalism rather than from the right and those aggressive in securing profits. For the security services, securing Britain can come to mean holding back the tide of social change and trying to reverse it so as to recover their image of what Britain *should* be like for all decent British folk. In a quite literal sense, the security services are a reactionary element in British politics.

We are painting a hard picture. It might comfort 'ordinary' members of the public were it to be the case that the security services were only interested in 'leading' activists on the left. This can hardly be given the scale of security operations. For example, the Special Branch's files record the names of around 3 million people, and a card will be opened on an individual for little more than writing to a newspaper or signing a petition to Parliament. Regular approaches are made to employers, doctors, government officials (and university teachers) for snippets of information; protest marches are photographed and regular meeting places of organisations watched; and behind all this is the network of informers and *agents provocateurs* providing information on strikes, factory occupations, political life in universities and colleges, and daily life on the streets of such places as Brixton and St Paul's in Bristol. The Police National Computer at Hendon is not without its significance for the political surveillance of ordinary people. The computer fulfils a number of functions but the largest involves maintaining a file of registered keepers and owners of vehicles covering 23.25 million adults. In 1977 it was revealed that the Police National Computer record on a particular vehicle included the fact that its owner 'was a prominent member of the Anti-Blood Sports League', and the following year a member of the Gay Activists Alliance found that details of his association were recorded on his vehicle file. All of this involves the surveillance and monitoring of many, many ordinary people, but the security services are, naturally enough, especially interested in political leaders and so cover the activities of their elected 'masters' with a keen interest.

Every new Member of Parliament is placed on file at the Registry of MI5, but there is a particular interest in left-wing Labour MPs – sometimes at the behest of the Labour leaders themselves. After losing the three general elections of the 1950s, and convinced that a return to power was only possible if the party was purged of its 'extremists', the Labour leader, Hugh Gaitskell, established a committee of three MPs in 1961 specifically to investigate those MPs thought to be communist supporters. A meeting was arranged between the Committee and MI5, and the names of fifteen Labour MPs were handed over for investigation. The investigation involved telephone tapping, shadowing, the opening of mail, examination of bank accounts, and other 'routine' methods used by intelligence services. The inquiries proved negative, but it is probable that the security surveillance of certain Labour MPs goes back long before the initiative of Hugh Gaitskell just as it certainly extends forward beyond the 1960s. Chapman Pincher, the *Daily Express* journalist and expert on security matters, admitted to having an 'Intelligence report' from 1978 in his possession which states that 'at least 59 serving Labour MPs...have current or recent connections with Communists, Trotskyists, or other Marxist organisations'.

Security-service interest in the Labour Party moves beyond a simple interest in the activities of individual MPs to a larger interest in Labour Governments themselves. Both MI5 and MI6 were involved in the distribution of the notorious Zinoviev letter, a classic Red scare forgery which contributed to the downfall of the 1924 Labour Government. In 1977, Sir Harold Wilson accused certain officers of MI5 of having tried to undermine him and his government. In the nature of these things we will never know the whole truth on this, but Pincher advises us that

the undermining activities which Wilson complained of were not only genuine but far more menacing than he revealed. Certain officers inside MI5, assisted by others who had retired from the service, were actually trying to bring the Labour Government down and, in my opinion, they could at one point have succeeded.

This sort of information is staggering. It is nothing short of a body blow to those who choose to believe that the security services are simply involved in securing British democracy against threat.

The security services are not just interested in the ideas and activities of elected politicians since they are also concerned with the views of the permanent officials and civil servants, and so screen those who work, or apply to work, in government departments. There is nothing new about this, but in 1952 a process of 'positive vetting' was introduced which involved a much greater in-depth investigation into a person's life and background. Of course 'mistakes' have been made, but this has had the useful function of legitimating a tightening of the whole procedure. Positive vetting is now applied further down the hierarchies in the civil service and the military; the emphasis is on seeking to exclude from entry those with 'subversive connections' so necessitating the investigation of *all* applicants; and 'sensitive' work no longer just covers classified information of use to the enemy but any information politically embarrassing to government and state. In bald and general terms all of this serves to mean that anyone with the remotest connection to a left-wing organisation is liable to be weeded out, not appointed, quietly sacked, or moved to another job.

The Security Services and Democracy

What is the significance of all this for politics in a democracy, and what issues thrust themselves forward for concerned consideration given the scale of the security services and the increasingly sophisticated technological back-up which they have available for surveillance?

First, there is the threat to civil liberties and the threat to the political freedoms of ordinary individuals. We are supposed to be living in a polity in which we enjoy the right to do more than simply vote governments in and out once every five years. We can criticise the powerful; protest at the injustices caught up within the established system; and dissent from the prevailing orthodoxies in the struggle for a better tomorrow. However, it is precisely the practice of these kinds of rights that is increasingly under scrutiny in the name of national security. If we cannot make a phone call, attend a public meeting, or be active in a trade union without fear of surveillance and possible harrassing action by the security services, then just how free are we? Simply expressed, there seems to be a contradiction between the democratic right to support political ideas and pursue actions contrary to those of the prevailing order, and the consistent surveillance and possible harrassment of those engaged in these activities.

Second, there is the problem of the autonomy of the security services. They enjoy a staggering freedom of operation and are self-perpetuating oligarchies operating outside the law on the basis of their own political judgements. The elected side of the state knows precious little about what they get up to. They are outside the system of democratic accountability to Parliament and people.

THE MILITARY

Few things matter more than defence from foreign attack and security at home, and the military are at the sharp end of these things. First, they are charged with the task of defending the state's territorial integrity; second, they may be involved in activity overseas such as the acquisition, subjection and maintenance of new territories; and third they are available to suppress internal dissent so assisting in the maintenance of the existing social order when it is under challenge. We need not look back to the Second World War to be reminded of the centrality of these matters in British politics: the Falklands War took place in 1982, and the military have been active in the 'troubles' in Northern Ireland since 1969.

When we deal with the military we are dealing with a number of momentous things. We are dealing with death and killing: during the 1960s, studies concluded that a tactical nuclear war in Europe would result in between 2 and 20 million deaths even on favourable assumptions. We are dealing with jobs: well over a million jobs in Britain are dependent on British military spending. We are dealing with massive sums of public money: in the financial year 1979–80 the British military budget was £8558 million representing about 4.7 per cent of the gross domestic product and it was planned to increase this by 3 per cent in real terms annually until 1985–86 – and this at a time when it was seen as 'impossible' to pay for various urgent social needs where public expenditure was being cut. We are dealing with institutions that are centrally involved with one of the most basic defining activities of the state itself. We are dealing with matters which arouse public emotions and which stimulate protests against public policies. We are, then, dealing with something that is always of central significance in British politics. The existence of a body of armed men and women with power to coerce inevitably raises potential problems of civil–military relations and civilian control and we want to attend to these problems in this section. Who controls the military, and who determines the nature of defence policy?

Orthodoxies assessed

From the formal, constitutional, point of view, the supreme command of all air, sea, and land forces is vested in the Crown. The Crown, however, has to act on the advice of ministers, and the Secretary of State for Defence (always a leading member of the Cabinet) is specifically responsible to Parliament for giving such advice, aided and assisted by two ministers of state and two parliamentary under-secretaries of state. The power to conduct foreign and external affairs is similarly vested in the Crown by royal 'prerogative' right through common law and by statute which means that what ministers do in this area does not require parliamentary consent. Having said that, however, it is part of the orthodox perspective on these matters to again suggest that the convention of the responsibility of ministers to Parliament for their actions always permits the Commons to question the Foreign and Commonwealth Secretary or any of his or her team of ministers.

From the conventional constitutional point of view, collective ministerial decisions are the name of the political game. Decisions of state are taken by the Cabinet and Cabinet committees and it would be pointed out that the Defence and Overseas Policy Committee of the Cabinet (chaired by the Prime Minister) is the key decisional structure for the matters under consideration in this section. Moreover, it is part of the conventional wisdom to suggest that parliamentary control over the three armed services is effectively guaranteed by two devices. The first is financial. The money required to maintain the services is requested by ministers, and then debated and granted by Parliament on an annual basis. The second device concerns the discipline of each force. The disciplinary codes of the services, without which neither mutiny nor desertion would be illegal, are made lawful only through statutes that require regular parliamentary approval if they are not to expire.

From this orthodox point of view, Britain is regarded as possessing a long history of stable civil–military relations in which the civil power and the elected side of the state has continually prevailed over the non-elected military establishment. The military can exert *influence* over defence and security policy through officially approved channels, but it is seen as lacking in any real political *power*. It has gradually become apoliticised, and in accepting a non-political role for itself it has limited its purpose to the loyal service of the policies and objectives set by the elected government of the day. Simply expressed, the government is said to run foreign and defence affairs (checked by Parliament) and the military willingly accepts their own position of political subordination.

The pre-eminence of civilian authority and the apoliticisation of the military is usually explained in terms of 'political culture' and the 'professionalisation' of the military. According to Finer in *The Man on Horseback* (his study of the role of the military in politics) Britain has a 'high' or 'mature' political culture because public attachment to civilian institutions is strong and widespread. In this state of affairs there are few opportunities for military intervention and the military can expect little public support should they choose to intervene. For his part, Huntingdon sees the stability of civil–military relations and the supremacy of civilian governments as hinging upon the degree of professionalisation demonstrated by the officers corps. As the British military became fully professionalised at the turn of this century, so they accepted the nation state as the highest form of political organisation; held that war was the instrument of politics; and saw themselves as the obedient servants of statesmen. Civilian control was essential to military professionalism and it gave the military the greatest amount of autonomy and job satisfaction. These two explanations for civilian control are at a high level of generality. Other writers have explained the pattern of civil–military relations in Britain somewhat differently, pointing, for example, to the absence of both 'opportunity' and 'disposition' for military intervention in the context of a situation in which there has existed a close class relationship between the officer corps and the political governing class.

What can we make of this traditional, or orthodox, perspective on the political power and position of the military in British politics? As with the orthodox perspectives on the position of judges, the civil service, the police, and so on, there is the familiar concern to deny that non-elected parts of the state machine enjoy political power. But is this the reality of the position of the military and are they under effective civilian control? In fact, the position is not as simple and stable as the traditional picture suggests, and the established explanations for civilian control tend to be vague, over-general, and complacent.

Throughout this chapter we have made it clear that the state is more than just the government of the day. In the case of defence, decisions are not the sole prerogative of the Defence Secretary, nor of the Cabinet, still less of Parliament, and if they were then the policies would hardly be workable. The military, in the form of the Chief of the Defence Staff and the Service Chiefs of Staff organised into the Chief of Staff Committee, have a right of direct access to the Prime Minister and they come to Whitehall and Westminster with expertise, information, and emotion on their side which gives them a role beyond that of simply offering advice. For their part, most politicians are reluctant to become involved in what they believe to be a specialised and technical area outside their competence. David Owen (who as a Labour minister was responsible for the navy for 2 years) has made it clear in his book on *The Politics of Defence* that

working within a defence ministry one becomes increasingly aware that the military are reluctant to accept guidance in the detailed process of policy-making.... The insidious process of military indoctrination, a heady mixture of pomp and secrecy to which most politicians involved in defence are susceptible, tend to blunt ones' normal sensitivity. One can easily become a part of the very military machine that one is supposed to control.

Decisions on defence emerge out of a complex of secret relations between the elected government, permanent civil servants, the military *and* the pressure from the arms industry, but the actual numbers involved are small. Moreover, the NATO states, and especially the USA, not only help to shape the international environment within which decisions are taken, but also intervene more or less directly over specific issues and the general direction of policy. Put another way, civilians are not as in control of defence and the military as the traditional picture suggests: their room for manoeuvre is limited by the constraints imposed by other centres of power; by the effects of decisions taken by previous governments and ministers; and by the implications of membership of international alliances.

In the rest of this section we will deal in more detail with crucial aspects of the making of defence policy; with the background of military leaders; and with the prospect for increased military involvement in British politics. We will touch on the position of the military in the field of internal security (a position which is rather more extensive than the traditional picture suggests) but will deal with this more fully in Chapter 10 on social control.

Decision-making on defence

In this section we want to deal with four things: the secrecy that surrounds defence policy; the impact of the arms industry on that policy; the implications of NATO membership for British policy-making on defence; and the self-generating momentum of military expenditure.

Secrecy. In 1940 two physicists working in Birmingham wrote a memorandum which described how a 'super bomb' based on a chain reaction in uranium might be made. In March 1940, the memorandum was shown to the senior government scientific adviser. The memorandum was kept secret, but led to the establishment of a committee which guided

British research on atomic energy in 1940 and 1941. The wartime Prime Minister, Winston Churchill, excluded most members of his Cabinet from discussion about atomic weapons during the war, and this practice has continued ever since.

The Labour Government, elected in 1945, launched Britain's independent atomic-research programme, but it did so without the knowledge of the general public, without any parliamentary debate, and without the knowledge of most of the Cabinet and much of the Ministry of Defence. The decision to make a British Bomb was taken by an *ad hoc* Cabinet sub-committee called 'GEN 163' to disguise its real purpose, but the 'decision' came after numerous small preliminary steps had virtually ensured that development would be approved. Those who were in the know deliberately encouraged ignorance of the decision, and expenditure on nuclear weapons technology was hidden from public and parliamentary scrutiny. In January 1947, the Cabinet formally 'decided' to give the go-ahead to a military nuclear programme, but by then it was already well under way. Even so, the production of the bomb still remained a secret and in 1951 *The Economist* was discussing 'rumours' that a nuclear programme existed.

Under a 1962 agreement with the USA, Britain was able to construct a force of five nuclear-powered submarines equipped with Polaris ballistic nuclear missiles. The 1964–66 Labour defence review cut the number of submarines to four – the first was launched in 1966, the last in 1970. From 1974 the Labour Government ran a Polaris improvement programme to modernise the warheads of the missiles. This decision to modernise was to cost in the region of £1000 million, and was taken by the Prime Minister and just three members of his Cabinet. The expenditure itself was not mentioned in the defence estimates, and the decision was simply presented in Parliament as a *fait accompli* about which they could do nothing.

In a similar manner, the decision to acquire the Trident submarine system at a cost in excess of £5000 million, as well as the decision to base Cruise missiles in Britain, were both taken by Prime Minister Thatcher and just a few of her closest Conservative colleagues, on the basis of 'advice' from NATO allies and especially the USA.

Simply expressed, in defence decisions of quite crucial moment there has apparently not been any frank and detailed discussion by the full Cabinet, simply because most important decisions have just not been taken by the Cabinet. This makes a nonsense of the suggestion that we enjoy Cabinet government. The nonsense is further compounded by the obvious absence of parliamentary accountability. Parliament has utterly failed to act as any kind of check on the executive in this area. An executive-inspired secrecy has ensured that parliamentarians are deprived on the most basic information needed to probe, and, if questions are asked in the Commons, then they may not be answered because of the convenient claim that it would 'not be in the national interest to go into details'.

The Arms Industry. Britain has a major arms industry, among the largest, if not the largest, in Western Europe. A handful of companies are involved in the design, development, and production of weapons systems, but they are backed up by thousands of subcontractors. It is estimated that some 733 000 civilians have jobs in arms manufacture.

The industry suffers from the chronic problem of excess capacity in that demand for military equipment provided by the British defence budget is insufficient to absorb its potential output. This problem has been compounded by two developments. First, through the 1970s, the costs of military equipment continued to increase far more quickly than inflation in the rest of the economy so that more money was needed just to cover the same output. Second, as an awareness of Britain's grinding economic decline bit into the consciousness of governmental budget-makers so they have sought to restrict the scale of public expenditure – and this at a time when the arms industry 'needed' more money to keep ticking over at the same level.

In this state of affairs, the arms industry cannot simply sit and wait for government orders. Nor do the government expect this. In the context of huge development costs and lengthy lead times before any new weapons are produced for 'sale' to the government, production needs to be guaranteed. This, and the demands of strategic planning for new weapons, place defence contractors in a strong bargaining position. The government purchases 70 per cent of the output of the British arms industry. Contracts simply cannot be allowed to fail and fold, in consequence clauses are often included which make it impossible for defence contractors to lose money.

In order simply to survive, let alone expand to absorb the surplus capacity, the arms industry has to place continuous pressure on the state to increase military spending *and* to extend contracts for major new weapons programmes despite massive cost increases from one generation of weapons to the next. The 'success' of this pressure is reflected in the scale of the defence budget and in the balance of that budget as between manpower and equipment. The defence budget for 1981–82 was up 8 per cent in real terms over 1978–79 spending levels, and whereas equipment counted for 34 per cent of military expenditure in 1975–76 it was up to 44 per cent in 1981–82. The industry does not just have an interest in pressuring government for a larger defence budget since it has a larger interest in the escalation of the arms race between countries since this enables it to offer 'improvements' (which eventually find their expression in runaway costs) to counter the 'improvements' in the weapons produced by the other side.

The military are, of course, not outside of these pressures for public

spending on defence, since their survival and reputation similarly
depends on a capacity to secure more. Not surprisingly, the weapons-
production system is tightly linked by personal contact and overlapping
interests to the military users of weapons, a linking that has led many to
speak of the existence of a 'military–industrial complex'. In reply to a
question in Parliament in 1976, the Defence Minister, Roy Mason,
revealed that in the 6 years 1971–76, no less than ninety-seven serving
officers and eighty-six Ministry of Defence civil servants joined firms
which had contracts to supply arms to the Ministry of Defence. Arms
manufacturers and arms users sink or swim together and they know it.
Together they exert a quite massive pressure on the defence budget and
the elected government of the day since they monopolise the sources of
information about military and weapons matters and so they can play a
part in generating self-serving scares about external threats, 'missile
gaps', and so on.

NATO membership. The North Atlantic Treaty which Britain signed on 4
April 1949 took effect on 24 August of that year, the date of the
formation of NATO itself. NATO was to be an instrument of collective
defence against a perceived threat from the USSR, but it was also an
American vehicle for influencing, reconstructing, and stabilising politics
in post-war Western Europe. More than 90 per cent of Britain's annual
military budget is devoted to commitments to NATO.

The USA's obvious authority and power within NATO has been
reinforced by its monopoly within the Alliance of nuclear weapons, and
its eager preparedness to supply a 'nuclear umbrella' to cover Western
Europe. True, Britain has had its nuclear-powered submarines equipped
with Polaris missiles. However, these are targeted according to NATO
plans, and although it is said that they could be used independently if
Britain's 'supreme national interest' were jeopardised this is effectively
nullified because targeting information for the force comes from US
satellites and the force is probably included in the US Single Integrated
Operation Plan for nuclear weapons. Given all this, it is hardly surprising
that Smith can claim that 'NATO strategy has been largely American
strategy, with which in the end, notwithstanding prior consultation, other
members have had to fit in as best they can'.

One is forced to wonder in what sense Britain is in control of its own
defence policy and is a truly sovereign state in this situation. Moreover,
there are surely important constitutional implications caught up in
allowing the USA, an independent sovereign state answerable to another
electorate, to operate nuclear weapons from British soil. The actual terms
and conditions upon which US military bases operate in this country are
closely guarded secrets. Vague suggestions that the British government
would be 'consulted' in the event of Cruise missiles being used do not
eliminate the threat to national sovereignty and they give scant comfort to
Britons facing the prospect of a retaliatory nuclear attack.

The self-generating momentum of military expenditure. So far we have provided information which contradicts the traditional and comfortable picture of civil–military relationships in the field of defence policy: the civilian government is not truly in control; the military are not really apolitical and indifferent to policy outcomes, and together with the arms industry they have an impact on the defence posture of the state which goes way beyond the exertion of mere influence; and the USA assumes a role in the defence of the West which means that they do much to dominate domestic decision-making in Britain.

This perspective in fact makes rather too much of people, institutions, and the impact of the United States. We have rather ignored the *impersonal,* self-generating, momentum of military expenditure and the arms race – a momentum which almost leads us to suggest that the whole system lies beyond control. What do we mean by this?

All of us are prisoners of our past and our commitments. In the field of defence, past decisions on spending have locked government and military alike into a spiral of expenditure that cannot easily be rolled back. It can now take a decade or more to develop a major weapons system from initial research to final assembly. During that time there may be two or three changes of government and several changes of Defence Secretary. Governments and Defence Secretaries find themselves acting in a play they did not write. Moreover, they come onto the stage of defence policy-making whilst the play is already in progress. In this situation they are faced with a whole series of relatively minor decisions to carry on, but the range of commitments built up in the opening scenes before they were around preclude them from the opportunity of taking a major decision that rocks the stability of continuity. Of course, there are occasions when we do *seem* to be at the crossroads with respect to defence policy, but those in the know see only the constraints of past commitments and contracts all around them which encourages a cautious continuity and a continuance of established, but escalating, commitments.

Within countries, inter–service rivalries crank the handle of military expenditure, and between countries and power blocks mutual fear escalates the arms race. Behind all this are the weapons themselves, weapons that have acquired the power to dictate to their political masters as innovation and the struggle for 'needed improvements' has become self-generating. Defence policies have become increasingly subordinate to the technological 'pull' of the weapons and the promise of what they can do. In this situation, policy takes on the role of justification *after* the event for decisions to manufacture, taken for quite other reasons that are lost in the mist of the past, when defence circumstances and needs may have been quite different. Strategic planning on defence is an out-of-control science. Defence commitments spiral upwards according to their own self-generating logic. Nor is this momentum just a matter of weapons technology. Once the task force set sail to the Falklands in 1982 it was almost inevitable that it would come to engage in a killing war, not just because the navy needed such a war to protect and extend their budget, but because the campaign itself took on a life of its own: it was easier to follow the steady and incremental logic of action on the high seas than to call a halt to a war that has in the event done nothing to solve the long-term problem of the Falklands and the islanders.

Recruitment

Information on the background and recruitment of officers to the three armed services is hard to come by, but we do have a certain amount on the recruitment of army officers and on the career patterns and characteristics of naval officers. Much of this information is now rather dated, but the Ministry of Defence refused to give a recent researcher more up-to-date information on the grounds that 'it would not be meaningful'.

In the seventeenth and eighteenth centuries, great political significance was attached to the social position of army officers. Parliament wanted to ensure that the army was officered by men of high social position and wealth so that they would pose no challenge to the status quo and the position of those of status and wealth. To this end, to secure a commission a man had to be nominated; had to purchase entry and promotion; and had to accept a rate of pay that was too small to live on so necessitating the possession of substantial private means. In the nineteenth century, it grew increasingly difficult to justify the *overt* aristocratic grip on the officers corps. At the same time, however, a cautious establishment was reluctant to contemplate drastic changes and so was only prepared to allow access to commissions to the offspring of the new propertied and professional classes provided that they could provide proof of 'gentlemanly' status. The public schools assumed a crucial filtering and socialising role in all of this, neatly tying up social *and* educational qualifications in just one institution.

Otley has looked at the social affiliations of the British army elite over the period 1870–1959. He found that 90 per cent of elite officers were drawn from the propertied and professional strata (and 40 per cent from a military background: officers are a self-perpetuating elite); barely 3 per cent of senior officers could claim lower-middle-class origin; and not one single officer had a working-class background. Their education was at one with their origins, and virtually all of the generals, whose schooling was known, were educated in the private sector. Generals have been well connected. Overall, 46 per cent of elite officers were sons or sons-in-law of members of the economic, military, or administrative elites in this country, and Otley found that 'the incidence of well-connected officers seems to have been more or less constant throughout the entire ninety-year period under study'. As late as 1969, it is almost certain that the officers corps as a whole still contained more public-school than state-school products, whilst at the levels above the rank of captain there is no doubt about this (in 1981 80 per cent of the fifty most senior army officers had been educated in public schools).

Grusky's study of British naval officers was based on a 1967 survey. Two-thirds of those of the rank of rear admiral or above had fathers who were professionals or were in the armed forces and only 6.7 per cent had attended state schools. Lower-ranking officers, however, were less likely than their higher-ranking colleagues to have come from upper-class families and to have had a public-school education leading Grusky to conclude that 'the Royal Navy officers corps should become more socially representative...when the present elite retires'.

It is possible that the relative subordination of the military to civilian authority is actually best explained by attending to the similarity between the officer corps and the civilian governing elites in Parliament and the civil service in terms of background, education, connections, ideas, and values — a similarity which bespeaks more of a *commonality* of interest and viewpoint than of military subordination. Changes on the military or civilian front with respect to these matters, and a collapse in the all-party consensus on defence policy, could well disturb this commonality, and so the political stance of the military, leading to their wanting to intrude rather more directly into British politics. We will consider this in our concluding section.

The military and democracy

War is the high point for the military. Popular wars swell budgets and morale. At the close of the Second World War, the British army had nearly 3 million men and women in uniform, but by 1980 the army was reduced to 155 000 and there were just 330 000 in the armed forces. Since the Second World War the British military role has shrunk and changed. Despite pretensions to the contrary, Britain is no longer a world power: the military has a restricted global role and is increasingly caught up in American-determined NATO commitments, and we have had our empire taken from us. Withdrawal from empire has steadily reduced the scope of British naval deployment (although the Falklands War provided a boost for their case for more money and ships), and although the empire has come home to the 'dirty' war in Northern Ireland, the army is less involved in defending the empire against winds of change abroad. The military has had to come to terms with Britain's decline and its own declining role, and this has inevitably affected military morale.

The military is organised on the principles of hierarchy, authority and discipline, and it is officered by men (and just a few women) of a conservative disposition operating in the context of traditions tied to the preservation of times past. These principles and this disposition are hard to reconcile with the practice of democratic politics let alone the prospect of any kind of socialism via the ballot box. Two things are of significance in relation to these points.

First, if the all-party consensus on defence policy continues to crack and if Labour moves further towards a unilateral and anti-NATO stance, then the military will not only need to be increasingly politically active in order to preserve their patch and budget, but they may also need to align themselves more overtly to the political fortunes of the Conservative Party.

Second, there are the implications of the reduction of consensus within society at large and the increasing threats of disorder at home consequent upon the tumble into unemployment and social crisis. The military, in having to come to terms with a restricted world role, have had to carve out a new legitimation for their existence and they have seen political space for themselves in their availability to suppress internal dissent. Many may see these developments as benign, but they contain profound implications for democracy in Britain and for civil liberties.

In the mid-seventies, there was informed speculation as to the prospects for a military coup in Britain: the country was seen as harder to govern; the unions were 'too' powerful; a variety of new movements made for unrest on the streets; and the politicians were regarded as failing to get a grip. Men in the shadows regarded authoritarian rule with favour, and, for many, democracy went out of fashion. In fact, practice has shown us that it would not take a coup to bring British troops onto the streets and into a position of political prominence. Moreover, we should remind ourselves that no revolution can take place without the aid of at least sections of the military and no successful revolution in Britain would be left wing, for the army are the men with the guns, and, like many other parts of the secret state, they are committed to the essentials of the status quo — and to the status quo as once was at that.

CONCLUSIONS:

We have attempted to do a number of things in our consideration of the role and significance of the secret state in British politics.

First we set down the well-established orthodoxies that have traditionally been used to deal with the non-elected parts of the state. Those orthodoxies were grounded in liberal-democratic constitutional theory. They asserted that the non-elected parts of the state were neutral, impartial, unbiased, and lacking in real political power of their own because they were either controlled by government and responsible to Parliament, or else were answerable to, and held in check by, the law of the land.

Second we argued that these orthodoxies were of only limited utility in enabling us to understand the workings of the non-elected parts of the state machine, and in some cases they were misleading and just plain wrong.

Third, at a more positive level, we were concerned to demonstrate a number of things.

1   A distinction needs to be made between government and state. The government is but a *part* of the state. This being the case, the terms government and state should not be used interchangeably, and at least as much attention needs to be given to the non-elected side of the state as to the elected side and the government of the day.

2   The non-elected parts of the state are largely or wholly immune from *direct* political pressures from below precisely because they are not subject to popular election.

3   It is not the case that the government is firmly in control of the non-elected side of the state machine as liberal-democratic constitutional theory tends to assert, and the relationship between the elected and non-elected parts of the state is complicated. Some parts of the state machine (such as the civil service and the military) that are supposed to be controlled by government and accountable to Parliament do not behave in these simple ways. Some parts of the state machine that are supposed to be held in check by law (such as police and the judges) in fact sometimes break the law and often make the law. Some parts of the state machine are actually 'allowed' a measure of independence from the elected side of the state (such as security services, the Bank of England, and the nationalised industries). Still other parts of the state machine that are supposed to be independent of government and politics (such as the judges and the BBC) in fact enjoy a special relationship to the state system as a whole which effectively limits their scope for truly independent and impartial activity.

3   Because the non-elected side of the state is not simply accountable and is not simply controlled by the democratic side, and because it enjoys a goodly measure of independence and autonomy it is made up of a number of institutions that enjoy very real power.

4   Information about the workings of the non-elected side of the state is restricted by the prevalence of liberal-democratic myths and by the existence of laws and conventions. We are dealing with fairly closed institutions and it is for this reason that we refer to the non-elected side of the state as the secret state.

5   We did not, and do not, pretend to have a 'theory' to explain the workings of the secret state, but we argued that understanding would be advanced if we set aside the liberal democratic orthodoxies and set down concrete information on the background and socialisation of those influential in the institutions of the secret state; if we dealt with the organisational structure of those institutions; and if we attended to the role or function of those institutions within society as a whole.

6   We found, in fact, that those influential in the secret state were in no sense representative of the population at large in terms of social

background, education or income. Small numbers of people occupied the influential positions and (with the notable exception of the police) they were overwhelmingly drawn from the *same* kinds of upper-middle-class backgrounds. Indeed, the connections between one institution of the secret state and another, and the common backgrounds of those involved, have led some to assert that Britain is run by a self-perpetuating 'Establishment'. More than this, the fact that those influential in economy and society are often of a very similar background to those influential within the polity and the state is suggestive of a commonality of viewpoint and interest that may bespeak of the existence of a 'power elite' or even a 'ruling class'. In this chapter we pointed to the close connections between top civil servants and industry, and between the military and the arms industries which have led some to speak of the existence of a 'military industrial complex', but in the next chapter we will be dealing rather more fully with the connections between the state elite and those influential in the economic system.

7 The institutions of the secret state tend to be organised on bureaucratic or authoritarian lines. New recruits are expected to assume a quiet, learning, apprenticeship role, and power tends to go to those with service and seniority in the institutions. The combination of apprenticeship and seniority inhibits innovation and change, and encourages continuity and stability.

8 Given much of the above, it is not surprising that we suggested that most of the institutions of the secret state assume a conservative, or even a reactionary role in society in that they maintain the essentials of the status quo and so often block the impulses for change that may come from the elected side of the state and the government of the day. This tendency is encouraged by the nature of those dominant within the institutions of the secret state and by the bureaucratic or authoritarian nature of the institutions themselves. In addition, however, the conservative role of the secret state is also partly explained by recognising that the institutions are somehow 'constrained' to behave in a particular way because of the larger structural position which they occupy within economy and society: the civil service cannot suddenly throw away its files and start afresh; the nationalised industries cannot be insulated from the blast of market forces for long; most law (and therefore the activities of the police and the judges) involves the defence of established patterns of power, privilege and authority; and in a capitalist society it is practically inevitable that the security services will see subversion as a left-wing thing and so will not challenge the power of property.

All of the above is disturbing of that simple view which suggests that Britain enjoys a truly democratic system of government, and there are alarming civil-liberties implications caught up in the powers of the police, the judiciary, and the security services.

In fact, the institutions of the secret state have become an issue in

British politics: the orthodoxies are crumbling and the realities of political practice are in the limelight. On the one hand, a freedom-of-information lobby emerged in the late 1970s to press for more open government, and there are attempts to control the institutions of the secret state and to increase their accountability to the democratic side of the state system – most notably with respect to the police. On the other hand, it is clear that the proposals for change and openness have met opposition from the secret state itself and from those who are keenly attuned to the need to preserve the established economic and social order. There is, then, something of a conflict between those who seek to create a more truly democratic state in order to try to effect popular change, and those who are concerned to create a strong state (much of which they wish to see continue to exist outside of effective democratic control) in order to preserve the essentials of things and block the prospects for change.

WORKS CITED AND GUIDE TO FURTHER READING

Aubrey, C. (1981) *Who's Watching You?* Harmondsworth, Penguin.
Discussion and critique of Britain's security services and the Official Secrets Act from a man who was arrested under the act in 1977.

Box, S. (1971) *Deviance, Reality and Society,* London, Holt, Rinehart and Winston.
Wants us to look at deviance 'in a different light'. Chapter 6 is an important discussion of police discretion and power, and how and why they tend to exercise it against members of the lower strata in society.

Committee to Review the Functioning of Financial Institutions (Chairman Sir Harold Wilson) (1980) *Report,* Cmnd 1937, London, HMSO.
Mildly critical of the financial institutions, Chapter 25 is a good discussion of the position and problems of the Bank of England.

Controlling the police? Police Accountability in the UK, *State Research Bulletin,* Vol. 4, No. 23, April/May, 1981.
Critical of established procedures for control. Calls for increased accountability to democratic structures.

Devlin, Lord (1981) *The Judge,* Oxford, Oxford University Press.
Distinguished judge recognises that judges do make law. Worries about this and does not want them to do it too much.

Estimates Committee (1965) *Recruitment to the Civil Service,* London, HMSO.
Highlights the public school, upper-class background of recruits to the higher ranks of the civil service.

Expenditure Committee (1977) *The Civil Service,* London, HMSO.
Critical of recruitment into the higher ranks of the civil service and of the power of the service *vis-à-vis* ministers and Parliament.

Finer, S. E. (1970) *The Man on Horseback,* London, Allen Lane.
General discussion of the role of the military in politics.

H. H. Gerth and C.Wright Mills (1948) *From Max Weber,* London, Routledge and Kegan Paul.
Chapter 8 provides the classic discussion of bureaucracy from one of the founding fathers of modern sociology.

Gordon, P. (1983) *Whitelaw,* London, Pluto.
Points to institutionalised racism in police, courts and prisons.

Griffith, J. A. G. (1981) *The Politics of the Judiciary,* 2nd edn, London, Fontana.
Waspish essay asserting that judges act politically (not neutrally) and tend to promote 'certain political views normally associated with the Conservative Party'.

Grusky, O. (1975) Career patterns and characteristics of British naval officers, *British Journal of Sociology,* **26,** 35–51.
Documents the predominantly public school and upper class social background of senior naval officers.

Heclo, H. and Wildavsky, A. (1981) *The Private Government of Public Money* 2nd edn, London, Macmillan.
Powerful study which gets inside the 'culture' of the state machine, the civil service in general, and the Treasury in particular.

Hewitt, P. (1982) *A Fair Cop,* London, National Council for Civil Liberties.
Critique of the established procedure for handling complaints against the police. Plea for reformed, independent procedure.

Holland, P. (1981) *The Governance of Quangos,* London, Adam Smith Institute.
New Right tirade against quangos and quangocracy.

Hunt, A. (1981) The politics of law and justice, *Politics and Power,* **4,** 3–26.
Criticises left positions on law, and argues that the Left have failed to take law seriously. A plea for a 'socialist politics of law' and more rigorous approach to the question of rights and justice.

Huntington, S. P. (1957) *The Soldier and the State,* Harvard, Harvard University Press.
Discussion of the theory and practice of civil–military relations. Broadly uncritical of the situation in the West.

Kellner, P. and Crowther-Hunt Lord (1980) *The Civil Servants,* London, Macdonald.
Good general and critical study of what the authors see as 'Britain's Ruling Class'.

McCabe, S. and Sutcliffe, F. (1978) *Defining Crime,* Oxford, Blackwell.
Detailed study of police discretion in recording crimes in two police districts.

Mark, R. (1979) *In the Office of Constable,* London, Fontana.
Autobiography of the former Commissioner of the Metropolitan Police.

Marshall, G. (1965) *Police and Government,* London, Methuen.
Semi-official view of the status and accountability of the police to law.

Otley, C. B. (1968) Militarism and the social affiliations of the British army elite, in J. Van Doorn (ed.), *Armed Forces and Society,* The Hague, Mouton, 84–108.
Documents the public school, upper class social background of army officers.

Owen, D. (1972) *The Politics of Defence,* London, Cape.
Ex Labour minister turned Social Democrat casts a critical eye on the process of defence policy-making.

Paterson, A. (1982) *The Law Lords,* London, Macmillan.
Closely researched study of the law lords which argues that they have room for choice and so 'cannot avoid making law'.

Pincher, C. (1978) *Inside Story,* London, Sidgwick and Jackson.
Journalist's insights into the workings of the security services.

Policy Studies Institute (1983) *Police and People in London,* London, P.S.I.
A four-volume study of the Metropolitan Police involving a survey of Londoners; a survey of 1770 police officers; a study of young black people in a self-help hostel; and lengthy observations of police practices over 2 years in eleven divisions. Volumes 3 and 4 of particular importance and very much a warts-and-all picture.

Powis, D. (1977) *The Signs of Crime: A Field Manual for Police,* London, McGraw Hill.
The Deputy Assistant Commissioner to the Metropolitan Police advises on how to spot suspicious characters.

Prins, G. (ed.) (1983) *Defended to Death,* Harmondsworth, Penguin.
Critical of the arms race, pointing to the secrecy surrounding decision-making and the power of the 'military–academic–industrial complex' in a defence situation which has got increasingly out of control.

Pryke, R. (1981) *The Nationalised Industries: Policies and Performance Since 1968,* Oxford, Martin Robertson.
Up to date critical account of the performance of the nationalised industries.

Rees, T., Stevens, P., and Willis, C. F. (1974) Race, crime and arrests, *Home Office Research Bulletin,* No. 8, 7–13.
Evidence of arrest rates for blacks far higher than to be expected given black involvement in crime. Suggestion of police bias.

Reid, Lord (1972) The judge as lawmaker, *The Journal of the Society of Public Teachers of Law,* **12,** 22–9.
The title is self-explanatory. A judge explodes the myth that judges only 'declare' law and asserts that they 'make' it.

Roshier, B., and Teff, H. (1980) *Law and Society in England,* London, Tavistock.
Excellent discussion of the reality of law in action. Chapter 3 contains important evidence on police discretion and police power.

Royal Commission on the Police (1962) *Report* Cmnd 1728, London, HMSO.
Set up to review arrangements for control and administration of police. Recommendations did not involve any fundamental disturbance of established system, but recommended more effective central control. Complacent as to police–public relations and the problem of complaints.

Sedgemore, B. (1980) *The Secret Constitution,* London, Hodder and Stoughton.
Critique of the power of the civil service from someone who was once a top civil servant before be became a Labour MP.

Select Committee on Nationalised Industries (1968), *Ministerial Control of the Nationalised Industries,* London, HMSO.
Dated, but still the best study of the relations between ministers and Parliament and the nationalised industries.

Select Committee on Nationalised Industries (1970) *The Bank of England,* London, HMSO.
Good, hard-hitting, account that focuses on the lack of accountability of the Bank.

Smith, D. (1980) *The Defence of the Realm in the 1980s,* London, Croom Helm.
Good account of the problems of defence in the eighties.

Stevens, R. (1979) *Law and Politics,* London, Weidenfeld and Nicolson.
Massive study of the House of Lords as a judicial body since 1800 in which it is pointed out that the law lords have the important creative function of making law.

Thompson, E. P. (1980) The Secret State, in E. P. Thompson (ed.) *Writing by Candlelight,* London, Merlin, pp. 149–80.
Powerful critique of the security services and their lack of accountability.

Wilson, H. (1971) *The Labour Government 1964–70,* London, Weidenfeld and Nicolson.
The Prime Minister's account of the trials and tribulations of office.

Young, H. and Sloman, A. (1982) *No Minister,* London, BBC.
Ministers and civil servants talked about the role of the civil service in a number of radio programmes. The series concluded that the civil servants were 'the masters' because 'they are the guardians of what they're pleased to call reality'.

CHAPTER 6

Power and Domination in British Society

Power is visible only through its consequences: they are the first and the final proof of the existence of power. The continuing inequalities of wealth, income and welfare that divide the population are...the more visible manifestations of the division of power in a society such as Britain.

John Westergaard and Henrietta Resler (1975) Class in a Capitalist Society, *London, Heinemann, p. 141.*

Now that racial, ethnic and religious conflicts have moved towards the centre of the political stage in many industrial societies, any general model of class or stratification that does not fully incorporate this fact must forfeit all credibility.

Frank Parkin (1979) Marxism and Class Theory: A Bourgeois Critique, *London, Tavistock, p. 9.*

In previous chapters, we have seen that political power in Britain is not located exclusively in the formal and democratically elected institutions of government, and that the study of constitutional principles can only be a first step in understanding how decisions get taken and how policies and programmes become implemented. Thus, in addition to Parliament and the Cabinet, any analysis of contemporary British politics must also address itself to the operation of the civil-service bureaucracy, the machinations of political parties and pressure groups, the procedures followed by the police, courts and the military, the discretion enjoyed by appointed 'quangos', and so on. Such is the stuff of contemporary Western political science.

In this chapter, we extend our analysis still further by broadening our conception of what is entailed in the very term 'politics'. All too often, the assumption is made that political processes in society are confined to what goes on in formal institutions and organisations such as parliaments, parties and pressure groups. Such bodies are, of course, important, but there is more to understanding political power than just this.

Our aim in this chapter is to broaden our analysis of British politics through an examination of power and domination in society as a whole. In taking this step, we may be said to be moving from the traditional realm of political science into the related, but in our view distinct, area of political sociology.

The distinction between political science and political sociology is by no means clear cut, and some writers have argued that they are merely different labels for the same thing. Yet there is a difference, for it is noticeable that, when sociologists come to write about politics, they tend to adopt a much broader focus than the characteristic concerns of political scientists with the way government works. Such differences of approach are a function, not of any idiosyncratic differences between sociologists and political scientists as people, but of differences between sociology and political science as disciplines. While political science is interested in one particular aspect of the organisation of society – namely, the way it is governed – sociology is interested in the organisation of society as a whole.

This points to a significant difference between sociology and most of the other social sciences. While disciplines such as economics and political science focus on one specific 'slice' of social life, and can in this way be defined in terms of the particular social institutions which they study (e.g. markets or governments), sociology attempts to embrace all aspects of social life and thus concerns itself with a variety of different social institutions in terms of how they relate to each other. It is for this reason that sociologists can so often be found 'trespassing' on the terrain of other social scientists in the sense that they too are interested in the markets studied by economists, the governmental institutions studied by political scientists, the socially deviant activities studied by criminologists, the uses of language studied by linguists, and so on.

What is distinctive in the way sociology studies these things is that they are analysed in their broader social context. The sociologist, for example, is not interested in studying government for its own sake. Rather, he or she will be drawn to look at, say, the operation of the civil service or the activities of pressure groups as part of a wider concern with social structure and social change. At the very heart of such a concern lies the question of power.

The sociological analysis of power in British society is, to say the least, uneven. As is so often the case in sociology, theory has tended to run ahead of empirical research — a problem which has been exacerbated by the obvious difficulties of doing research on powerful groups, for information is often hard to come by and barriers of privacy and secrecy cannot easily be penetrated. For this, and for other reasons, we still know remarkably little about the distribution and the use of power in our society.

What we do know, however, is that power in Britain often has something to do with class and economic inequality. In asking what, in the organisation of British society, generates inequalities of power between people, most sociologists have traditionally turned, in the first instance, to an analysis of class relations. As we shall see, this can only take us so far, for power is not simply a function of class. It is however, a useful point at which to begin.

THE CLASS BASES OF POWER AND DOMINATION

Class is probably the key concept in contemporary sociology, yet there is precious little agreement over how it is to be analysed and theorised. Sometimes we find sociologists using a notion of class which has been developed in consumer marketing and government surveys, and which basically distinguishes different groups in the population according to the occupational status of the head of household. A major problem with this approach is that it leaves out altogether the importance of ownership of private property in determining class relations. At other times, sociologists have attempted to resolve such problems by adopting a concept of class found in Marxist theory (see Chapter 7) in which classes are distinguished according to whether or not they own and control the means of production in society – the land, the factories, the banks, etc. The problem with this approach is that it tends to overlook the importance of divisions between those different occupational groups which do not own the means of production yet which vary considerably from each other in terms of income and outlook on life.

Clearly, therefore, any analysis of class relations will need to address both occupational divisions arising out of the labour market and divisions based on the ownership and non-ownership of key property resources. Class power, that is, has something to do with power in the labour market and something to do with the power of property ownership.

In arguing thus, we are broadly following the work of the influential German social theorist, Max Weber, who was writing in the early years of this century. A major theme of Weber's work was concerned with understanding the nature of power and domination in human society (it was this, for example, that led him to the analysis of bureaucratic domination in modern societies, discussed in Chapter 5), and, like Marx before him, he saw that in contemporary capitalist societies, the organisation of power and domination was in large part a function of the division of the society into classes. Although Weber was careful to argue that the class system was not the only basis of power in modern society, he also recognised that power could not be understood without analysing the nature of class divisions.

Weber defined power itself as 'the probability that one actor within a social relationship will be in a position to carry out his [or her] own will, despite resistance, regardless of the basis on which this probability rests'. In other words, a powerful individual or group is one which can secure its objectives, even in the face of opposition from others who do not share them. They may achieve this in a number of different ways; e.g. through the use of physical force, through bribery, through persuasion, through devious manipulation, and so on.

In Weber's view, however, such crude and one-off examples of the use of power are neither as significant nor as interesting as those cases where people are in a position routinely to achieve their objectives by issuing orders which they know will be obeyed. Power struggles, though dramatic, are relatively unimportant when compared with the more mundane instances of people exercising power without encountering the resistance of others. Relationships of power, in other words, tend to become regularised in social life such that opposition rarely occurs, in which case powerful individuals or groups can effectively count on others to carry out their commands and thus to fulfil their objectives. In cases like this, Weber referred not to a relationship of power, which is always precarious, but to a relationship of 'domination', which is normally stable and predictable.

Analysing patterns of domination in modern societies, Weber suggested that dominant groups – those who could normally expect to get their way without resistance – were often those whose members controlled economic resources of one kind or another way; domination in societies such as modern Britain is often a function of people's economic or 'class' position.

Weber identified as a 'class' any group of people who share a broadly similar market situation. In any market there will be those who enjoy a relatively privileged position – a dominant class – and those whose market position is relatively weak – what he termed a 'negatively-privileged class'. In a situation of housing shortage, for example, the landlord with a house to let will be in a strong economic position relative to the individuals who are desperate to find somewhere to live, just as in a situation of acute labour shortage, skilled workers will collectively be in a relatively strong market position *vis-à-vis* potential employers. Landlords and skilled workers are thus two examples of 'classes', the members of which share a broadly comparable market situation and thus enjoy similar life chances.

There are, according to Weber, two main sources of economic or class power. One is ownership of particular types of property which can be used to generate income – examples include landlord ownership of rental housing, ownership of stocks and shares generating dividends, ownership of bank deposits producing interest and so on. The other is the possession of particular kinds of skills which are in short supply and for which there is a high demand (and which, therefore, command high remuneration). It is, therefore, possible to identify two main sources of class domination. On the one hand, there are relations of domination which arise out of the property market, and the privileged class of property-owners will include people such as private bankers, industrial magnates and large landlords and landowners. On the other there are relations of domination which arise out of the market for labour, and here the privileged class will consist of those, such as top managers and established professional people in fields like law and medicine, whose qualifications and aptitudes enable them to command high salaries. Let us consider each in turn.

The power of property ownership

The distribution of property wealth in Britain remains, as it has always been, remarkably skewed. Indeed, the persistence of these inequalities through the twentieth century may itself be taken as strongly indicative of the power enjoyed by the 'positively privileged property class' in the sense that a very small number of people have seemingly succeeded in maintaining their hold over a large proportion of the nation's total wealth while excluding others from it.

Statistics on the distribution of wealth are notoriously difficult to compile, for very different patterns emerge according to the method used for gathering information and the types of resources included or excluded in the calculation. People are, for example, generally reluctant to disclose all their wealth holdings to official agencies such as the tax authorities, and legal titles to ownership may in any case not reflect the actual ownership and control of resources. Furthermore, decisions such as whether or not to include rights to a state pension in an individual's portfolio of personal wealth will obviously have a marked effect on any research into the degree of concentration or dispersal of wealth. The various figures on the distribution of wealth in Britain must therefore be treated with extreme caution.

According to Lord Diamond's Royal Commission on the distribution of income and wealth, which reported in 1975, the wealthiest 1 per cent of the population in Britain owned 24 per cent of the wealth in 1974. When these figures were adjusted to take account of state and private pension schemes, however, the proportion of wealth owned by the top 1 per cent fell to 13 per cent. Furthermore, the Commission was convinced that inequalities of wealth had dropped dramatically over the preceding 60 years from a point before the First World War when the richest 1 per cent had owned no less than 69 per cent of the nation's total wealth.

The Diamond Commission's findings have, however, been questioned and criticised by a number of academics, for various studies have suggested that the fall in the concentration of wealth has been much less dramatic. Atkinson, for example, calculates that the top 1 per cent saw its share of total wealth drop from 69 per cent in 1911 to around 30 per cent in the 1970s, while (more significantly) the share of the top 5 per cent remained relatively stable over this period. Comparing figures for 1911 with those for 1960, for example, he shows that, while the share of the top 1 per cent fell from 69 per cent to 42 per cent, that of the next 4 per cent rose from 18 per cent to 33 per cent! According to these figures, there has been a redistribution 'not between the rich and the poor, but between the very rich and the rich', and this has probably been brought about by a spreading of wealth within families in attempt to avoid estate duties.

Whichever figures we accept, however, it is clear that the wealth of the nation is still today concentrated in relatively few hands. Britain is a remarkably unequal society. But what, if anything, does this tell us about the distribution of power?

In one sense, any form of private-property ownership increases an individual's power in relation to others and improves that individual's life chances as a result. To establish a property right in something, whether it be a teddy bear or an office block, is to exclude others from the right to use and enjoy its benefits. To own property is to claim exclusive rights of use, benefit, control and disposal, and such rights are crucial when it comes to achieving one's objectives in the world.

Having said this, however, it is obvious that many forms of property, including most of those enjoyed by large sections of the population, are of little significance for an analysis of economic or 'class' domination in society as a whole. The owner of a house or a car, for example, may certainly enjoy a better quality of life than the individual who rents a few rooms and is obliged to stand in the rain waiting for a bus, but such ownership is hardly enough to enable that individual to achieve much impact in society as a whole. How I use my house and whether or not I choose to sell my car is of precious little interest to anybody beyond my immediate circle of family, friends and neighbours.

How the banks use the money invested with them, and whether or not a multinational corporation chooses to close down its factories in Britain and move to Germany, are, by contrast, crucial questions for millions of people, for on such decisions rest the employment prospects of workers, the success of government economic policies and the future standard of living of virtually everybody in Britain. It is, in other words, power over productive resources such as land, factories and money investments – in short, over capital – which appears as potentially the most significant form of property ownership in our society.

Ownership of capital has changed in two significant ways during the twentieth century. First, ownership has become centralised and concentrated in the sense that an ever-smaller number of companies is producing an ever-larger proportion of national output. In manufacturing, for example, the 100 largest companies in Britain accounted for 20 per cent of total manufacturing output in 1950, yet by the early 1970s this had risen to 50 per cent. In many sectors of the economy – motor cars, pharmaceuticals, computers, glass – there are now effective oligopolies or even monopolies which render talk of competitive market capitalism problematic, and even where competition does exist it turns out that different products are being made and marketed by different subsidiaries of the same multi-national company. Nor is this concentration limited to manufacturing companies, for in the financial sector too, mergers and take-overs have reduced substantially the number of banks and finance companies which between them channel billions of pounds into investments at home or abroad.

The second trend has been a progressive formal separation between those who own capital and those who direct its use. Although not entirely a thing of the past, the large company which is owned and managed by a single family has tended to be replaced by the joint-stock company in which ownership is vested in a variety of shareholders while effective decision-making is left to salaried managers and directors. This would seem to suggest that economic power has not only become concentrated in a relatively small number of giant corporations, many of which are controlled ultimately from overseas, but also that the locus of power within these companies has shifted from those who own them to those who manage them.

Much has been said in the sociological literature about the significance of this division between ownership and control, for it has often been suggested that the 'managerial revolution' of the twentieth century has rendered obsolete the image of the capitalist entrepreneur wielding great power in pursuit of great profit. The new managerial class, it is said, consists of highly educated 'organisation men' (for they are nearly always male) whose concerns are with stability rather than turning a quick buck and whose influence has humanised the harsher aspects of tooth-and-claw capitalism. As one proponent of this view, Ralph Dahrendorf, expressed it in 1959: 'Never has the imputation of a profit motive been further from the real motives of men than it is for modern bureaucratic managers.'

Such arguments have, however, been challenged. It has been found, for example, that the top managers and directors of the large companies tend to act in much the same sort of ways as the old family owners did. They share the same values, they have been educated at the same schools and universities, they move in the same social circles and they are subject to the same constraints in that they must put profits above all other considerations if their companies are to survive.

Equally significant is the evidence that the effective division between ownership and control has been exaggerated. It is certainly true that most large companies in Britain today are owned by shareholders rather than by single individuals or families, but it is important to recognise that effective control can often be achieved through ownership of a relatively small proportion of total shares, especially if the remaining shares are distributed among a large number of small and unrelated owners. A block holding of, say 20 per cent of voting shares in a company will often be enough to secure a majority if the remaining 80 per cent is scattered among thousands of other people whose votes are likely to be distributed randomly. In this context, it is worth noting that of the 250 biggest, non-financial, companies in Britain in the mid-1970s, one-third were dominated by a single block ownership of 10 per cent or more. Furthermore, directors and their families are often major shareholders – 62 of the biggest 250 companies were run by directors who themselves held 5 per cent or more of the shares.

The relationship between property ownership and economic power is thus far from broken, but it has become more complex. Ownership of British companies today falls into two main categories – personal ownership and institutional ownership. Personal ownershp (i.e. shareholding owned directly by wealthy individuals and families) is of decreasing significance when compared with institutional ownership (i.e. shareholding owned by financial institutions such as pension funds, insurance companies and unit trusts). In 1963, for example, 54 per cent of all shares were personally owned compared with 18 per cent of shares held by insurance companies, pension funds and unit trusts. By 1975, the respective figures were 38 per cent and 37 per cent, and the proportion of shares owned by the financial insitutions has continued to rise quite dramatically ever since. What appears to be happening, therefore, is that individuals are increasingly investing their wealth indirectly, through the financial institutions, rather than directly in company shares themselves.

When we analyse the pattern of the personal shareholdings which do still exist, it is clear that ownership is concentrated in very few hands. The most wealthy 5 per cent of the population owns virtually all personally-held shares, and within this select group, the very richest stratum owns the great majority of shares. As we have already seen, company managers and directors are often to be found in this stratum, although their holdings will often be in a range of different companies rather than concentrated in those companies which they themselves manage.

The financial institutions, on the other hand, today invest millions of pounds every year on behalf of a wide range of ordinary people in Britain, for everybody who pays into an occupational pension fund or takes out a life assurance policy invests indirectly in shares floated on the London Stock Exchange, as well as in other investments such as farm land, office blocks and even works of art. That this represents some diffusion of ownership, minimally defined, is undeniable. It does not, however, represent any diffusion of economic power, for most of us have no idea how our money is being invested and we certainly have no control over such decisions.

Given the increasing significance of the financial institutions in the British economy, it is important to determine who is exercising this crucial economic power. Who decides how our money will be invested? And who decides how the power of these institutions will be wielded within those companies which they do invest in?

The obvious answer is again the managers. The financial institutions are owned by millions of virtually powerless individuals but are controlled by directors and managers who clearly enjoy considerable autonomy. But things are not quite this simple, for when we investigate who these managers and directors are, we find that they are generally drawn from the ranks of bank directors, directors of large companies and so on – the very people who, as we have already seen, are themselves often major personal shareholders!

The picture which emerges is one of a system of interlocking directorships. No one individual or set of individuals can be said to control the fate of the major British companies, but there is a recognisable stratum of individuals which collectively accounts for the great bulk of personal shareholdings, which occupies the boardrooms of the major companies and which directs the investment decisions of the major banks and financial institutions. This stratum is generally self-perpetuating in that vacancies on boards of directors will usually be filled from within its ranks or the ranks of its children, and it represents a network of contacts and influence through which information passes which forms the basis for its investment decisions. It is impossible to disentangle this corporate web in order to identify a distinct 'ruling group' directing the British economy from behind the scenes, for the system does not work like that. What we can say, however, is that major economic decisions with implications for millions of ordinary people in Britain now emanate from a relatively small network of generally wealthy and powerful people who, between them, own and control a substantial proportion of the productive resources of this country. As Max Weber was well aware, no analysis of domination in society can afford to ignore the power which springs from ownership and control of private property.

Power in the labour market

Weber, it will be recalled, identified two bases of economic power in society. One of these was the ownership and control of strategic property resources. The other was the ability to monopolise opportunities in the labour market.

Power in the labour market may to some extent be gauged through an analysis of the distribution of income as between different groups of workers in that a group which can monopolise and control market opportunities should succeed in maintaining a substantially higher return from the sale of its labour than a group which cannot. Income distribution is an indicator of economic power in the labour market, just as wealth distribution is an indicator of economic power in the property market, although it should be remembered that the two are related in that wealth generates unearned income, and high incomes generate wealth.

As with data on wealth distribution, statistics on income distribution are hotly contested, although all commentators agree that the inequalities between top and bottom, while large, are nowhere near as gross as those revealed by wealth data. At the best available estimate, it seems that the top 1 per cent earn some 5 or 6 per cent of total net income (i.e. after tax) while the top 10 per cent take around 25 per cent. Most commentators, including Lord Diamond's Royal Commission, also agree that, despite the effects of progressive direct taxation, the distribution of take-home income has remained remarkably stable over time, although the pattern has fluctuated according to the state of the economy and the nature of government policies (e.g. on income restraint), and the top 1 per cent of earners has probably seen its real income reduced somewhat (although companies have increasingly topped up the earnings of top and middle management with payments in kind such as company cars and business-account luncheons).

Not surprisingly, income levels are closely associated with different types of occupations. On average, professional workers earn nearly two-and-a-half times as much as skilled workers who themselves earn nearly half as much again as unskilled manual workers. When the analysis is broadened to include fringe benefits and to take account of total household income (including the earnings of spouses), the gap between manual and professional workers widens still further. When considering these figures, it should also be borne in mind that variations of income within the professional group are themselves considerable such that averages tend to conceal the substantial income advantages of the highest-earning professional groups such as lawyers and doctors. It is also important to note that income inequalities spin off into inequalities in other areas of life. A high income, for example, brings with it the availability of mortgage funding to buy a house, the opportunity to send one's children to private schools, the chance to buy into privileged medical treatment, and so on. The inequalities of life chances represented in unequal incomes are thus cumulative, and this helps to perpetuate patterns of inequality right across the generations. On the government's own figures, published in 1983, 3 million people now live on or below the official poverty line while a further 12 million hover just above it.

Statistics on income distribution reflect the differential power of the different occupational groups in the labour market. Such power is exercised in one of two ways which can be identified as a strategy of 'exclusion' and a strategy of 'usurpation'. An exclusionary strategy will tend to be adopted by relatively powerful and privileged groups which seek to limit entry into the occupation and thus to maintain scarcity and high remuneration. A usurpationary strategy is more characteristic of less powerful and privileged groups whose members come together in an attempt to improve their material situation through collective pressure and organisation.

In some cases, exclusionary strategies may be operated by identifying particular groups in the population as eligible or ineligible for entry. In Northern Ireland, for example, certain jobs are effectively reserved for members of one or another of the two religious communities, and in London it is virtually impossible to gain entry to the Fleet Street print unions without some kinship connection with an existing member. More commonly, however, exclusion operates on individualistic criteria of formal credentials and paper qualifications, and there has been a tendency in many jobs for the necessary level of qualifications to increase over time as the number of potentially qualified applicants has risen with the expansion of educational opportunities.

Professionalism is the classic example of such an exclusionary strategy, for what is entailed here is the enforcement of strict rules of eligibility governing entry into the profession. The most successful – and hence in general the most highly paid – professions are those which have managed to secure the endorsement of the state for their monopoly to practice through some form of licensing provision. Obvious examples of such legally-enforceable monopolistic practices include the law, where even the simplest activities such as house conveyancing are strictly regulated by governments in order to exclude those whom the profession does not recognise as technically qualified, and medicine. In these and in other professions, the monopolization of market opportunities is achieved through a strategy of 'credentialism' involving lengthy and sometimes costly periods of training for potential entrants. The number of vacancies on training courses is strictly controlled and credentials to practice are only issued after various criteria of eligibility (e.g. completion of a period of articled apprenticeship with a practising solicitor, accountant, etc.) have successfully been negotiated. In a class-stratified society such as Britain, where (as we can see in Chapter 10) educational performance and qualification is still strongly influenced by one's class of origin and where a public school and Oxbridge education remains an enormous advantage in gaining entry to top managerial and professional occupations, exclusion through credentialism can be a most effective way of perpetuating inequalities across the generations.

In contrast to a strategy of exclusion, a strategy of usurpation tends to be characteristic of those occupational groups which are less privileged in material terms and which thus have less advantages to defend against the potential claims of others. The obvious example of a usurpationary mode of social closure is that of the trade union movement in Britain.

Like the professions, the trade unions have enlisted the support of the state for their closure strategy in that the unions enjoy certain legal rights and immunities, although some of these (e.g. the right to picket and to enforce a 'closed shop') have increasingly come under attack by recent governments. Where their strategy differs from that of the professions is that they are engaged in an attempt to force concessions from more privileged groups in the population whereas the exclusionary practices of the professions are designed to maintain an existing pattern of privilege and domination.

The effect of this difference is that the market power of organised labour depends crucially on its collective cohesion. In the modern period, trade unions are probably potentially more powerful than ever before, for the complexity of the British economy is now such that relatively small groups of strategically-located workers can, by withdrawing their labour, cause enormous and costly disruption throughout the economy. In 1966, for example, the seamen's strike disrupted crucial exports; in 1974, the miners' strike reduced production throughout British industry to a 3-day week; and in 1978/9, industrial action by local-authority manual workers led to the deployment of troops to clear piles of refuse in city streets, to maintain water and sewage services, and so on. But in all such cases, industrial action involves cost to the workers themselves as well as to employers, and these costs inevitably generate internal fragmentation and dissension. Unlike an exclusionary strategy, a usurpationary strategy is always likely to be undermined by a tension between collective and individual interests. This tension will be all the greater where workers are called upon to take action in support of their 'brothers and sisters' in another sector of the economy, or where industrial action is used to pursue broader objectives than merely wages or immediate conditions of service.

None of this is to deny that organised labour remains a potentially powerful interest in British society. But its power is essentially limited in two important ways. First, it is a negative power – the power not to work, not to cooperate, not to agree. In Weber's terminology, it is always power, never domination, in the sense that it is exercised in situations of conflict, against the resistance of others. The ability to dominate – to secure the compliance of others without encountering resistance – is an ability the unions simply do not have.

Secondly, it is a power whose scope is limited in that it is generally exercised only in particular industries over particular issues. Trade union leaders have, throughout the twentieth century, interpreted their role very narrowly and have left the pursuit of broader social and economic objectives to the Labour Party in Parliament. The division between the 'industrial' and 'political' wings of the labour movement is the institutionalised expression of the limited objectives of the union movement.

Within these constraints, much has been achieved through the collective organisation of working people. The gap in earnings between strongly-unionised, skilled, manual workers and unorganised, routine, white-collar workers has narrowed and in some cases closed over the years; indeed, many sections of the lower-middle-class have themselves come to recognise the benefits which can be gained through unionisation with the result that the fastest growing area of trade unionism has for some years been among white-collar workers. Groups like school teachers, for example, are today engaged in an uneasy combination of both exclusionary and usurpationary strategies, pressing for professional closure on the one hand while mobilising collectively through unions affiliated to the TUC on the other.

The power of organised labour has also resulted, directly or indirectly, in a long history of social and economic reform in the interests of working people and their families. As we shall see in Chapter 9, pressure from the labour movement and the fear of that movement on the part of those groups who dominate British society were often major factors in the development of welfare policy through the twentieth century. Less grand, but still significant, was the spate of legislation introduced in the 1974–79 Parliament on questions such as equal pay, the right to maternity leave, industrial injury and sickness, all of which was a product of the so-called 'social contract' between the Labour Government and the TUC (see Chapter 8).

Having said all that, however, it is nevertheless clearly fallacious to argue, as so many people do, that the trade unions rule the country today, for they are a powerful group but not a dominant one. No trade unionist has yet been able to sack his or her employer, nor has any trade union yet taken on the Government of the country and won. (In both 1926, during the 10-day general strike, and in 1974, during the miners' strike, Conservative Governments defined the conflicts in constitutional terms as an illegitimate challenge to an elected government, yet the general strike was seen by most trade union leaders in purely industrial terms, while the fall of the Heath Government in 1974 was brought about, not by the muscle of the miners but by the result of the general election which Mr Heath himself chose to call.) It is also important to note that the growth of union power since the 1950s was premissed upon the commitment of successive governments to a policy of full employment. From the mid-1970s onwards, the commitment disappeared, and there is no doubt that the mass unemployment of the 1980s has severely weakened the power of organised labour. The Conservative Government elected in 1979, and subsequently re-elected in 1983, succeeded in driving down wages, dismantling major areas of welfare provision, reducing trade union rights and pushing unemployment to its highest levels since the Great Depression of the 1930s, and there was apparently very little that the trade unions could do about it. These are hardly the outcomes which one would expect were the unions as dominant a group in British society as they are so frequently made out to be.

THE NON-CLASS BASES OF POWER AND DOMINATION

So far, we have focused only on the question of how far different groups in British society may be said to be powerful by virtue of their monopolistic control of property or labour-market opportunities. Drawing this discussion together, we may say that those who enjoy the greatest economic power in our society and who may thus be said to constitute the dominant class are those who enjoy the exclusive right to use, control, dispose of and benefit from crucial resources which bear directly on the distribution of life chances in society. Basically, this refers to those who own and control major capital assets and to those who are able to sustain high incomes through monopolistic control over the supply of labour. As Frank Parkin puts it: 'The dominant class under modern capitalism can be thought of as comprising those who possess or control productive capital and those who possess a legal monopoly of professional services. These groups represent the core body of the dominant or exploiting class by virtue of their exclusionary powers.'

While such class inequalities are certainly pervasive and enduring, they are clearly not the only basis of power and domination in contemporary British society. It is certainly true that power is to a large degree a function of class, yet it is also the case that other patterns of domination exist which may cut across class divisions.

Returning briefly to Weber, we find an important distinction in his work between what he termed 'classes' and 'status groups', both of which were important expressions of the distribution of power in society. Classes, as we have seen, are distinguished on the basis of their market power. Status groups on the other hand, are distinguished on the basis of what Weber termed 'social honour'. What he meant by this is that different groups may be held in different degrees of esteem on the basis of the personal characteristics of their members and the styles of life which they follow.

The importance of status groups is clearest when we consider power inequalities in pre-industrial and pre-capitalist societies. In feudal Europe, for example, power was primarily a function not of wealth, but of noble birth (although the two usually went together), and the rulers of society were drawn from a select stratum of families which passed on their privileges through inheritance. Indeed, a major reason for the upheavals in Europe, such as the French revolution in 1789, was precisely that the new wealthy class of industrialists and merchants was systematically excluded from effective power by the *ancien regime* of the landed aristocracy. In Britain, it was not until 1832 that mere wealth came to be admitted as a credential for political participation in the public affairs of society, and for a long time after that, the pretensions of money were held in low esteem by the traditional ruling stratum which continued to stress the importance of high birth and aristocratic manners.

In modern Britain, of course, the significance of aristocratic status, though still present, has waned. What has not waned, however, is the importance of other types of status in structuring people's lives. Of particular significance in this respect is the importance of both gender and ethnicity as bases of domination.

Women and blacks are the clearest examples in contemporary Britain of social groups which are subject to routinised patterns of domination, not on the basis of their market situation (although this is often very weak), but on the basis of their status characteristics. Domination on the basis of gender and ethnicity cannot, in other words, be passed off as in some way an aspect of a 'more fundamental' class domination in society, for, although discrimination by sex and colour is clearly related to the way in which economic power is organised, it is a distinct phenomenon of the distribution of power. We can, in other words, control for the effects of class and still see the independent effects of gender-based and ethnicity-based domination, for even those women and blacks who have managed to achieve dominant positions in labour and property markets still experience subordination on the basis of their status. To put the same point a different way, there are different, though related, systems of domination in our society, and the capitalist system of private property and wage labour is only one of them. Any analysis of power and domination must, therefore, be alive to the others, and in particular to the systems of domination organised through patriarchy and racism.

Domination on the basis of gender

It is important to stress at the outset that the subordination of women by men in our society is not necessarily a conscious and deliberate process. Not all men are sexist, just as not all whites are racist, and not all capitalists are intent on squeezing the last drop of life blood from the veins of the workers. The point about all of these examples of domination is that they are *systemic* as well as personal. In other words, our society has developed in such a way that certain patterns of domination have become established and inscribed within many different areas of social organisation such that they tend to operate in a sense, 'behind our backs', even where conscious intent on the part of individuals is lacking (this is a point which we shall discuss in more detail later in this chapter). The clearest example of this systemic character of domination as regards gender relations concerns the traditional domestic role of women.

A major legacy of the development of capitalist industrialization in Britain has been the separation between 'work' and 'home'. Paid employment now overwhelmingly (though not exclusively) takes place outside the home in factories, offices, building sites, schools and so on, such that distinctions between 'work' and 'leisure' or 'production' and 'consumption' have in large part become synonymous with the division between 'workplace' and 'home', and derivatively, with that between 'male' and 'female'.

The dominant image of the 'home' in our culture is one which stresses emotional comfort, privacy and security – a refuge to which the worker can return each day and which offers autonomy in contrast to the subordination experienced at work. However, the 'home' clearly carries different meanings for men and women, for this dominant image of the home as refuge is actually grounded in the male experience. For most women in our society, irrespective of whether they are also in paid employment outside the home, the home is a place of work rather than an escape from it. This is because most mature women are ascribed a particular role on the basis of their status – the role of 'housewife'.

The role of housewife is in reality a combination of roles which includes that of wife, mother and domestic worker. Seen in this way, the housewife role is inextricably bound up with the differentiation of roles within the family, for it is as a member of a family unit that the woman is allocated her duties as a child-rearer, emotional prop, sexual partner and house worker. If women's role as housewives is grounded in gender differentiation, then this is in turn grounded in the structure of the family. The 'home' and the 'family' have become virtually interchangeable terms in our society, and women's role in the former follows almost automatically from their role in the latter. To put it crudely, to be a 'wife' in contemporary Britain is also to be a 'housewife'.

The identity as a 'housewife' is, for most women, their primary identity, even if they also work outside the home in paid employment. In other words, the roles of wife, mother and domestic worker are the major elements that go to establish what a woman is in her own eyes and in the eyes of others. For most men and women, the husband's job comes before the wife's and the husband's primary life activity lies outside the home while the wife's lies within it.

The demarcation of gender roles is reinforced by various values and beliefs which many men and women share regarding the presumed genetic basis of sex differences. Women, for example, are assumed in our culture to be emotional while men are governed more by the intellect; women are expressive while men are rational. It then follows from this that women are 'naturally' best-equipped for domestic pursuits – notably, raising children and soothing their menfolk – and this assumption is reinforced by the biological differences between the sexes regarding the ability to succour infants, the physical ability to undertake hard manual labour, and so on. Gender roles, in other words, are underpinned by a strong and pervasive ideology regarding the 'natural' inclinations of men and women towards different kinds of tasks, even though anthropological and historical evidence reveals that the pattern of tasks undertaken by males and females is in large part specific to particular cultures at particular times.

The main importance of the strong association in our culture between femininity and the home is, from our present perspective, that it creates and reinforces a system of dependency of women on men. In a society where money is the main basis of power and independence and where work in the home does not attract payment, the association of women with a domestic role must inevitably result in a dependency upon males and hence in the perpetuation of a system of domination based on gender. Such a system of domination (sometimes termed 'patriarchy') is then reflected in and institutionalised throughout the organisation of the society.

For example, there are many ways in which the state underpins patriarchal domination. The organisation of tax collection is premissed on the assumption that the husband is the main earner and, as such, is head of the household. Social benefits are normally tied to national insurance payments in such a way that women must depend on eligibility established through their husbands, and for women who are not married, benefits are subject to regulations such as the cohabitation rule which assumes that any sexual relationship with a man may be taken as indicative of financial dependence on him. Various Factory Acts preclude the employment of women (together with children) in certain industries, and divorce laws enshrine traditional gender roles through provisions for maintenance and child custody.

Many such interventions are, of course, defended on the grounds that they assert women's rights to expect support from men, yet such arguments only make sense in the context of a system which assumes women's dependency on male support in the first place. It is only in a patriachal society, for instance that the law will deem it necessary to enforce maintenance payments from men to their estranged wives, for this is in effect a legal expression of the obligation which a social superior generally feels towards his dependent social inferior. Similarly, it is only in a partriarchal society that domestic violence within the home could routinely be treated by the police as a private matter into which the law should not normally intrude.

A major expression of patriarchy within British society is also found in the organisation of the economy. The significance of women's primary role as housewives is perhaps most keenly felt when they attempt to break out of it and to enter the 'male' world of paid employment outside the home.

Since the war, female employment in the formal economy has expanded enormously; where one in four women had paid employment in 1950, the proportion today is one in two. What is not revealed by such figures, however, is the way in which the housewife identity spills over into the other areas of women's work and lives. Three points in particular can be made about this.

First, the overwhelming majority of women who have paid employment are also still 'housewives' – around 40 per cent of the labour force is female, and three-quarters of these women also perform the housewife role. It has been calculated that housework takes up an average of some 80 hours every week, and, although there has been some reorganisation of the domestic division of tasks by some couples, it remains the case that most of this work in the house is still done by women, even where they also work outside the home.

This overburdening domestic role clearly limits women's freedom to seek paid work even where there are no other restrictions on their doing so. It is likely to disrupt a career pattern, for example, for the characteristic of most women's career patterns is of lengthy breaks for child-rearing as well as more intermittent breaks by illness in the family, a move to a new area prompted by a change in the husband's job, and so on. Similarly, many women are obliged to seek part-time work in order to accommodate their domestic responsibilities (nearly nine in every ten part-time workers are female), and such part-time employment is generally low-paid and offers little prospect of career advancement. Other women have little choice but to 'take in' work, and employment of this nature is notoriously badly paid.

Second, precisely because women's role is still defined primarily in terms of the home and family, women in the labour force are often seen and treated as expendable. With the onset of recession, it is generally women who are the first to be expelled from paid work and forced back into the home (a pattern which male-dominated trade unions have done little to counter). Indeed, as we shall see in Chapter 10, the deepening recession in Britain from the 1920s onwards culminated in a deliberate strategy by the Thatcher Government to reemphasise the 'traditional' domestic role of women within the family and to discourage women from holding jobs outside the home.

Third, the sort of employment to which women gravitate is specific to their conventional image as domestic workers. Labour markets are to an amazing extent segregated by gender, and more than 90 per cent of employed women work in jobs which are only done by women (a degree of labour-market separation and exclusion matched only by the South African Apartheid System). There are, in fact, just five key occupational sectors in which women can be found in any numbers – nursing, teaching, unskilled factory work, domestic employment and clerical work – and most of these are characterised by notionally 'feminine' attributes (e.g. the so-called 'caring professions'), or by low pay, or both. Furthermore, when an occupation becomes identified as 'female' – e.g. nursing or routine assembly work in the new electronics industries – its status falls and the level of remuneration falls with it.

Such a situation of employment segregation makes a nonsense of legislation such as the Equal Pay Act, 1975, for if men and women generally do different jobs, the issue of equal pay for the same job rarely arises. There is still the assumption in this country that men must earn a living wage on which to support their families while women's pay is in some way merely a supplement to the household income (although for many families, two incomes are in fact a necessity).

A further example of patriarchal domination in British society is the operation of the educational system. Here too, the role of women as housewives has left its mark, both in levels of female take-up of education beyond the minimum school-leaving age, and in the sorts of subjects in which girls typically specialise, for in both cases the assumption is still made (though less, perhaps, than in the past) that the woman's principal role in life will be as wife-mother within the family unit. At school, despite the fact that girls tend to perform academically marginally better than boys, girls take a narrower range of subjects (e.g. only half as many girls as boys take maths examinations and in science, girls are over-represented in biology and under-represented in physics and chemistry), and less girls than boys stay on to age 18. At university level, only one-quarter of the intake is female, and this is overwhelmingly concentrated in arts subjects characterised by a minimum of vocational content. At a time when government is intent on placing greater emphasis on technical education at all levels, this pattern of gender bias seems more likely to become exaggerated than narrowed.

In every nook and cranny of British society, then, gender plays a crucial role in organising patterns of domination and subordination. Clearly these patterns of domination cannot entirely be divorced from the fact that British society is also class-stratified, for the situation of women is to some extent a product of a capitalist mode of social organisation. For example, the fact that women are pushed out of employment when the economy goes into recession cannot be explained without first understanding the vulnerability of wage labour as a whole within a capitalist economy. The woman who loses her job, in other words, is as much a victim of the domination of labour by capital as of the domination of women by men. Similarly, the woman who performs unpaid housework for her husband is also, in a sense, performing unpaid labour for her husband's employer as well, for her unpaid work enables the employer to pay less in wages than he (or she) would have to do if the husband himself were obliged to buy domestic services such as cooking, child-minding and laundry on the open market.

Gender domination cannot, therefore, be understood entirely in isolation from class domination. Nevertheless, it is also true, as many radical feminists point out, that the exploitation of women by men pre-dates the exploitation of labour by capital by several thousand years and that there is no guarantee that the transcendence of a capitalist system of organising the economy would automatically entail the transcendence of a patriarchal mode of domination.

It was this recognition that women's subordination was a distinct feature of domination in society which led, in the 1960s, to the growth of a separate women's movement in Britain and in many other countries. As it has developed, the women's movement (which is actually nowhere near as homogenous or cohesive as this singular term implies) has adopted the classical features of what was termed in the previous section of this chapter a 'usurpationary strategy'. Faced in other words with a system of domination resulting in the exclusion of women from privileges and power enjoyed by men, the women's movement has set about demanding social changes designed to break down gender-specificity and bias across a wide range of social institutions.

Some of the main demands have related to the world of employment where women have organised against discriminatory practices and in favour of provisions such as crèches and day nurseries which would help loosen the constraints of the traditional domestic role. Demands for 'positive discrimination' in favour of women have been pressed in relation to job selection in traditionally male preserves, as well as in other areas (e.g. selection of parliamentary candidates).

Feminist demands have, however, gone beyond this to take in issues which relate directly to women's personal and everyday experiences. The link between the personal and the political – between private troubles and public issues – has always been central to feminist organisation and is revealed in the significance of campaigns designed to confront and challenge traditional conceptions of 'femininity' in our society. Thus, for example, the movement has protested loud and long (and not without effect) about the portrayal of women in advertising, in beauty contests, in pornography and so on where women's bodies are presented as depersonalised commodities, usually for the enjoyment of men. Similarly the pro-abortion campaign, fought on the slogan of 'A woman's right to choose', was central to the movement's objective in asserting the autonomy of women to direct and control their own bodies and their own lives in accordance with their own values and choices. Associated with this has been an offensive against male violence both within the family and outside it, and various women's groups have developed initiatives such as hostels for battered wives, rape crisis centres and so on as well as launching campaigns to 'reclaim the night'. In some sections of the movement, the usurpationary closing of ranks against the exclusionary practices of patriarchy has been taken to the point where female sexuality itself has been questioned and redefined in such a way as to attack heterosexual relations in favour of lesbian activity.

As the movement has strengthened and as confidence has grown, so the scope of its activities and concerns has broadened. By the early 1980s, for example, the women's movement and the peace movement had become inextricably bound up with one another as a result of the establishment at Greenham Common and other US Air Force bases of women's 'peace camps' protesting at the siting of Cruise missiles. The Greenham Common women in particular achieved considerable media coverage which helped to reinforce the message that there was a distinct 'women's perspective' on major political issues. The women's movement, in other words, was beginning to move centre stage in British politics, for no longer could it be confined to traditional 'women's issues' such as the provision of crèches or action against sexual harassment at work. With the traditional labour movement in disarray at this time, the women's movement began to assume the mantle of radical leadership and innovative opposition to the Conservative Government.

This increased scope of women's politics is, of course, of major significance for an understanding of British politics as a whole. However, two points should be noted in conclusion.

First, it is important that we keep sight of the difference between women in politics and women's politics. While issues such as equal pay, aborton on demand, and sexism in schools are inherently 'women's issues', in the sense that they pertain specifically to women's situation as women, broader issues such as the siting of American Cruise missiles on British soil, or the future of the National Health Service, are not. After all, men as well as women are vulnerable to a nuclear holocaust and men as well as women die because of hospital closures and cuts in investment in kidney machines.

When issues like these come to be defined in gender terms, there is not only likely to be some confusion and muddying of waters (many women supported the deployment of Cruise missiles, just as many men opposed it), but there is also a clear danger that familiar gender sterotypes will re-emerge in order to clarify matters. In the early days of the Greenham Common peace camp, for example, the exclusion of males was frequently explained publicly through arguments which suggested, implicity or explicity, that men were warmongers while women were peaceable, that men were concerned to maintain a quantitative balance of terror in the world while women were more attuned to the qualitative aspects of life for themselves and their children, and so on. Such assertions have a familiar sexist ring about them, and this is perhaps an inevitable consequence of any attempt to develop a distinctive 'women's perspective' on those political issues which cannot be confined to women's interests alone.

Paradoxically, then, the broadening in the scope of the women's movement may result in increased fragmentation of radical politics (because of the exclusion of other groups from campaigns) and in a dilution of the support base among women themselves (because there is no necessary relation between gender and, say, opposition to nuclear weapons). This is a classic problem of all usurpationary groups, for labour unions, the black movement, the student movement and other such groups all face the problem that, when they try to expand their focus beyond the immediate concerns of their support base, they increase the likelihood of dissension within it.

The second point to make is that, although it has grown in significance in recent years, the women's movement remains relatively small, and its impact on British politics in particular, and on patterns of domination in British society in general, is still somewhat marginal. As in so many other radical movements, the activists in the women's movement are overwhelmingly middle class and have largely failed to mobilise any significant degree of female working-class support. The major institutions and strategies of male domination and exclusion have survived intact so far, and this is not perhaps surprising since gender domination in one form or another has been a fact of British society for thousands of years. We do not seek to belittle what has been achieved in a remarkably short time, nor to suggest that much more may not be achieved in the future. People's assumptions about gender are now being challenged and institutional practices are slowly changing. But as the activists in the movement would be the first to admit, there is still a long, long, way to go, and for most women in Britain, gender remains a major axis along which relations of domination continue to be organised.

Domination on the basis of ethnicity and race

A second major dimension of non-class-based domination in British society is that organised around racial and ethnic identity. The parallels between gender-based and ethnicity-based patterns of domination are striking (as John Lennon observed in one of his songs, 'Woman is the nigger of the world') although, as we shall see, the two do also diverge in certain important respects.

One obvious parallel is that, like sexism, racism is a long-established feature of human societies and in one form or another it pre-dates the rise of capitalism, although in Britain it seems to have developed mainly in the wake of colonial conquest. Black immigration into Britain from former colonial territories in the West Indies, East Africa and the Indian sub-continent is, on the whole, a post-war phenomenon, but immigration from other countries involving other ethnic groups – e.g. Irish, Jews and Poles – has a much longer history. Like the post-war black immigration, these earlier migrations often provoked hostility which was expressed in racial/ethnic terms, and there is a long tradition in Britain of a nationalistic chauvinism which has readily been translated at various times into a populist sentiment of racial superiority coupled with fears of a 'threat' from 'alien' groups with their 'alien' cultures. The peculiar significance of the post-war black immigration has been that the immigrants have come from precisely those countries which Britain had once conquered and controlled, and this, together with the stark visibility of differences of skin colour, has given an added impetus to indigenous white hostility and fears. Thus today, the major dimension of ethnic/racial domination is that organised around the polarity of black and white.

This leads us to a second obvious parallel with the case of gender, and that is that domination through racial exclusion is based on the identification of certain physical characteristics as crucial in distinguishing the dominant from the subordinate group. It is in principle possible to change one's social class, but it is not ordinarily possible to change one's gender or one's race.

This physical basis of relations of domination organised around characteristics such as gender or race has reinforced and legitimated assumptions and arguments regarding the 'natural' bases of social and economic inequalities. Just as women's subordination to men is justified through arguments about their physical weakness and 'emotional nature', so too the subordination of blacks to whites is commonly explained with reference to 'natural' inequalities between the races. West Indians are stereotyped as 'spontaneous', 'musical', 'fun-loving' but basically indolent; Asians as hard-working but also as secretive, devious and subservient; whites as sober, intelligent and industrious. Such racist assertions may then be backed up in various ways by academic research which purports to show, for example, that the average measured intelligence of blacks is lower than that of whites (such findings being based on tests devised by white researchers and reflecting white culture).

A third parallel is that, like women, blacks tend to play a marginal role within the formal economy. They tend to be concentrated in certain sectors of the economy just as women are (there is, for example, a striking over-representation of Pakistanis in the textile industry), and within those sectors they are found mainly in the lowest paid, least skilled and most insecure positions. As Britain slid into recession during the 1970s, so, not surprisingly, blacks were among the first to swell the growing numbers of the unemployed. For some years now, the plight of black youth in particular has been desperate.

Blacks and women together make up the most easily expendable parts of the workforce. They are today's equivalent of what Marx referred to in the nineteenth century as 'the reserve army of labour' – i.e. that section of the population which can be sucked into employment when the economy is expanding (thus helping to keep wages down by increasing the supply of labour as demand increases) and which can be pushed out again when it collapses back into recession. Where women and blacks have managed to resist this and to hang on to their jobs, they have become easy scapegoats to be offered up to white male workers who are all too often ready to accept that unemployment is caused by increased numbers of blacks and women in the labour force. Where they have failed to resist it, they may still be scapegoated as 'scroungers' living off social security while white workers pay taxes to support them. Either way, their employment situation is unenviable.

A fourth parallel, related to this, is that both women and blacks are subject to exclusion practices in various crucial areas of social life (and as we shall see later, they have both responded to this through the development of a usurpationary strategy). Employment is one obvious case in point, for like women, blacks are not only concentrated in the poorest jobs, but they also tend to earn less money for doing an equivalent job (despite provisions of three Race Relations Acts since the mid-1960s). This weak employment situation then spills over into other areas – notably in the case of blacks, housing and education.

Low-paid and insecure employment renders house purchase difficult. Those black families who have bought their homes (and many have, especially in the Asian community) have often been obliged to buy short-life housing in run-down inner-city areas, where the only loans available are those on offer from finance companies at crippling rates of interest. Those who have not been able to buy have either rented in the dwindling private sector (often from black landlords who have to take in tenants to pay off their housing loans) or have had to rely on local authorities for a council house or flat (and have often been allocated the worst-quality housing in the least-desirable estates).

In education too, blacks are systematically disadvantaged (although again, Asians seem to suffer less in this respect than West Indians). Black children, like white girls, underachieve in school. Part of the reason for this is that schools in black areas are often those which experience the most severe staff shortages, the most rapid staff turnovers and the lowest morale. Partly too it has to do with the clash between a white school culture and a black pupil culture. This problem is obvious in the case of language use; a survey in 1983 found that no fewer than 147 foreign languages were being spoken in inner-London schools and that almost one child in six in these schools spoke a language other than English when at home. But cultural divergence extends beyond language, for it is now clear that many black children not only experience racism from teachers and pupils from a very early age, but also are confronted daily at school with a culture and curriculum which makes few concessions to their experiences in the world outside. Most black children thus leave school at the earliest opportunity with few or no qualifications and go straight into the dole queue.

There are, then, many parallels between gender-based and ethnicity-based systems of domination in Britain. Nevertheless, there are also at least two important differences. One is that blacks are not native to Britain as white women are (the question of citizenship). The other is that blacks are a small minority, accounting for less than 4 per cent of the total population. Both of these differences are very significant both for the way in which exclusion practices come to be operated and for the way in which the groups themselves have responded to such exclusion.

Citizenship has become an important instrument of racial domination in Britain. By 'citizenship' we mean the rights which individuals can legally claim by virtue of their membership of the nation state. One important difference between the situation of (white) women and that of blacks of either gender, is that women's struggle for full citizenship (e.g. in the fight for voting rights in the early part of this century) has taken place from a position of security within the boundaries of the nation state. On the other hand, for over 20 years, blacks have been in the position of having to assert and defend citizenship rights for themselves and for their relations from a position of insecurity. Ever since 1962, Parliament has presided over an increasingly restrictive series of legislative measures designed to limit citizenship rights enjoyed by blacks who had previously had the same rights of entry to, and abode in, Britain as those enjoyed by white natives of the country. The problem of citizenship is in this sense a problem women have never had to confront – the problem of how to get into, and stay in, the country.

The withdrawal of black citizenship rights began with the passing of the Commonwealth Immigration Act, 1962. Until then, members of the British Commonwealth in the various ex-colonial possessions had enjoyed the right of entry into Britain. Indeed, during the 1950s many, especially in the Caribbean countries, had been encouraged to migrate to Britain in order to swell the labour force during the post-war boom. The 1962 act modified this right of entry by placing an annual quota on the number of immigrants who would be accepted and by introducing a selective voucher system which distinguished between different grades of workers. Despite the Labour Party's commitment when in opposition to repeal this act, the Wilson Labour Government at first strengthened it (when in 1965 it reduced the quota and abolished vouchers for unskilled workers), and then supplemented it with its own Commonwealth Immigration Act, 1968 (which basically stripped Kenyan Asians with British passports of automatic rights of entry despite assurances which had been given in the 1950s at the time of Kenyan independence).

The years of the Wilson Government were crucial in institutionalising racial qualification as a criterion of citizenship, for despite the ameliorative introduction of two Race Relations Acts in 1965 and 1968, it became clear in this period that no major political party would or could resist the growing pressures of white racism. Indeed, the abject capitulation of the Labour Government to these pressures simply hastened the flow of ever-more extreme racist demands, for, as the decade went on, so the bounds of 'legitimate' and 'respectable' racism were pushed wider and wider (notably by the right-wing Conservative MP, Enoch Powell, whose famous 'rivers of blood' speech in 1968 gave further sustenance to white racism in general, and to the activities of the newly formed National Front in particular). The Labour Government thus became locked into a vicious spiral of its own making, for tougher immigration controls vindicated those who argued that the black presence in Britain was harmful, and the louder this was argued, the stronger became the case for further controls.

The legislative history since 1968 has simply continued along this predictable spiral. The Immigration Act, 1971 drawn up by the Heath Conservative Government, introduced an explicitly racist distinction between 'patrials', who had a right of abode in Britain, and 'non-patrials' who from then on did not, and thus effectively ended all black immigration except for that of dependents. Ten years later, another Conservative Prime Minister, Margaret Thatcher, justified a new Nationality Act, in which three different classes of citizenship were established (which in practice distinguished between people already resident in Britain, whites abroad who could claim British ancestry, and who retained the right of entry, and blacks abroad who could not and did not) by referring to the danger of Britain being 'swamped' by alien people with an alien culture. By the 1980s, then, official racism had become fully established both in law and in 'respectable' political rhetoric.

It has, of course, to be recognised that none of this legislation has so far withdrawn the right of abode from black people who have already established a legal right of residence (though there is an increasingly insistent body of opinion within the Tory Party which seeks government assistance for the voluntary 'repatriation' of black families). This does not mean, however, that these Acts of Parliament have left such people untouched, for not only have they hindered the rights of their families to join them in Britain, but they have also reinforced through law the popular belief that blacks represent a 'problem' and that they are here on sufferance. Such legislation, in other words, implicitly justifies racism within Britain by applying racist criteria to keep people out.

An obvious example of how this works is in relation to the activities of the police. Together with immigration officers at ports of entry into Britain, the police have the task of identifying 'illegal immigrants' who have outstayed their right of residence and who are therefore liable for summary deportation with no right of appeal. Any and every black person in Britain is a potential suspect and may be stopped and interrogated as such while whites can safely be left alone. Racism in police practices goes beyond this, however, for as we saw in Chapter 5, the police operate in their everyday practice on the basis of certain sterotypical assumptions, and these systematically generate a racial bias in the way they perform their duties. Certain crimes, for example, are commonsensically associated with certain types of people, and street crimes – handbag snatching, assaults and the like – are closely associated in the minds of most police officers with young male blacks with the result that their efforts came to be concentrated on precisely this group in the population. This then generates what sociologists term a 'self-fulfilling prophecy', for the assumption (right or wrong) that young blacks are disproportionately responsible for street crimes such as 'mugging' (a term which was imported into Britain from America in the early 1970s and which carries with it an inherent racial association) leads to increased surveillance of blacks, which then in turn results in higher detection and conviction rates. All this culminated in 1982 in the controversial publication by the Metropolitan Police of statistics purporting to demonstrate a clear connection between race and crimes against property and the person in London – statistics which were then cited to justify the continued heavy police presence in mainly black areas.

It was this police presence which led directly to the riots in various cities in the Spring and Summer of 1981. While it is almost certainly the case in at least some of these incidents that other factors such as high rates of unemployment contributed to the explosion of violence on the streets, there is little doubt that the factor which triggered them off was the rising level of tension between the white police force and the black community consequent upon the increased use of police stop-and-search powers and the increased deployment of the para-military police units, the 'Special Patrol Groups'. For many young blacks the police came to represent the organised expression of white racist domination and they responded accordingly with violent counter-attacks against police forces which were initially taken by surprise.

The riots of 1981 were simply the most vivid expression of the recent growth of a black consiousness, especially among second-generation black youth. There has developed over the last 20 years a distinct stratum – what one observer has termed a 'black underclass' – in British society which is increasingly marginalised in its relation to mainstream white society. It is economically marginalised in respect of access to jobs, housing and education; it is culturally marginalised in its attachment to, for example, Rasta Farian symbols of dreadlocks, ganja, West Indian music; and it is politically marginalised in its rejection of white parties and white liberal institutions. The hopes of many whites and blacks alike during the 1950s that the races would become 'assimilated' are now dead. Instead, young blacks have retreated into their defensible areas in the large cities and have to a large extent rejected the white society ('Babylon') outside.

In the face of this, government measures (such as the establishment of the Merseyside 'Task Force' in 1982) designed to improve job prospects and living conditions in the inner cities, represent too little too late. The possibility of assimilation is long gone, and as the British economy continues its slide into deindustrialisation (see Chapter 8), so the disillusionment, resentment and alienation of the black minority, concentrated in specific areas and excluded from white privileges, is likely to grow.

Other dimensions of domination

Class, gender and race are the three principal axes along which domination and exclusion in contemporary British society is organised, but they are not the only ones.

Age, for example, is one further factor which is perhaps becoming increasingly significant in this respect, for as the economy weakens, so those at both ends of the age spectrum tend to suffer. This is true as regards access to employment, for, by 1983, school-leaver unemployment was running at a staggering 50 per cent while people in late middle age also found it virtually impossible to get work once they had been declared redundant. It is also true as regards access to other social resources such as health care (where services for the elderly have consistently been deprived of vital finance) and housing (where young and old alike have often to rely on the relatively squalid private rented sector since they fail to qualify either for mortgage loans or for local-authority tenancies). The scandal of inadequate pensions should also be cited as a further indication of the way in which age may be crucial in the determination of life chances, although here it should also be noted that retirement tends to blight the lives of working-class people much more than the middle class who often have other sources of income to supplement a grossly inadequate state pension.

Another dimension of domination and exclusion which is more pertinent in some parts of the United Kingdom than in others is religion. The obvious example here is the plight of many Catholics in Northern Ireland, and we discuss this specifically in Chapter 11, but the problem is not limited to that province. In parts of Scotland, and in some cities such as Liverpool, the division between Protestants and Catholics remains pertinent in many aspects of life including employment, schooling and leisure pursuits, while elsewhere religion also often reinforces exclusionary practices based upon ethnicity (e.g. as in the case of anti-semitism).

Finally, we should also note here the significance of what may be termed 'sectoral cleavages' in the organisation of relations of power and domination. The notion of sectoral cleavages is one which we discuss in more detail in the next section. Basically it refers to divisions both at work and outside it between those who are dependent on the public sector for their employment or for provision of their consumption requirements, and those who rely on the private sector. Thus, the major production-sector divisions, which cut across class lines, are those between state-sector workers and private-sector workers (who may themselves be further differentiated into those in large companies and workers in small firms), for these groupings differ in security of employment, wage levels and so on, even controlling for class, and the income of the former is derived from compulsory taxation on the latter. Similarly, the main consumption divisions (which again cut across class lines) are those between people who own key resources such as housing, cars or private medical insurance, and those who do not. As we shall see, such sectoral cleavages have become increasingly significant in recent years in determining both patterns of material privilege and disadvantage and patterns of political alignment.

SOCIAL CLEAVAGES AND POLITICAL ALIGNMENTS

We have seen that relations of domination in contemporary British society are not simple and clear cut. There is no single dimension of power and inequality, but several, and these to some extent cut across each other and make it very difficult to identify one dominant group and another subordinate group.

Class is, of course, a crucial aspect of domination, but even here we have to distinguish between class divisions arising out of ownership of property and those arising out of monopolistic closure in labour markets. There are, as we have seen, two privileged classes – those who own and control capital, and those, such as the traditional professions, who control labour-market opportunities. Overlaid upon these divisions are other relations of domination arising out of gender, ethnicity and other status distinctions, for we have seen that in our society, males are often able to claim privileges denied to females, whites can maintain exclusive access to life chances which are generally denied to blacks, and so on. Thus, although class and status divisions may, and often do, overlap (most bankers, company directors, lawyers and hospital consultants, for example, are male and white), the picture which emerges is one of a society divided vertically by class and horizontally by status.

The question which now arises is how far these various divisions in society come to be expressed in the political arena. To what extent, in other words, are patterns of domination in the society as a whole reflected and reinforced in political relations?

In addressing this question, it is again useful to return in the first instance to the work of Max Weber. Having distinguished between classes and status groups as two phenomena of the distribution of power in society, Weber then identified a third which he termed 'parties'. His notion of 'parties' was much broader than merely formal political parties, for it referred to any group which organised itself in an attempt to gain control of, or influence, the power of the state. Parties, in other words, are groups, such as the Campaign for Nuclear Disarmament, or the Confederation of British Industry or the women's movement which attempt to gain or influence the use of power in the public domain of government and state administration.

What was essential to Weber's analysis (and, as we shall see in Chapter 7, what separated him most markedly from Marx) was his view that domination arising out of market power (i.e. class domination) or out of the distribution of social honour (i.e. status group domination) did not necessarily lead to political domination arising out of control of the state (i.e. domination by parties). Put another way, money and prestige, though often significant, do not necessarily lead to political power and influence. Or, in more technical language, the relation between power in society and power in the state is a contingent rather than a necessary one.

Thus far in this chapter, we have limited our consideration of power and domination to an analysis of civil society – to the way in which some groups are able to dominate others by closing off opportunities to others and by maintaining privileges for themselves. It is obvious, however, that such patterns of domination are only part of the story, for the state may and does intervene in this process, either to reinforce it or to modify it in some way. State policies with regard to taxation, welfare support and the like are obviously potentially crucial in influencing prevailing patterns of inequality and privilege. So too are the laws which are passed by Parliament and implemented in the courts – e.g. laws relating to the right of companies to sack their workers, or the right of professions to licence practice and limit entry, or the right of whites to exclude blacks from housing and jobs or of males to prevent females from gaining entry into certain spheres of activity. The question which arises from all of this is, how far political relations of domination mirror relations of domination in the society as a whole? How far is organisation around the power of the state merely an expression of existing cleavages in other areas of social life?

There are two related ways of approaching this question. One is to ask to what extent the divisions which arise in the political process reflect class- and status-group divisions in Britain as a whole. The other is to ask to what extent those who come out on top in respect of class power and status power also come out on top in respect of political power. We shall address the first of these questions in this section, leaving the second for consideration in the following section and in the following chapter.

Voting and political alignment

Perhaps the principal theme to have emerged throughout this book so far is that power is by no means concentrated exclusively in government. Thus, we have seen in this, and in earlier chapters, that government has to share its power both with other agencies within the state (e.g. the civil service, the police force, the judiciary and the military) and with other groups and institutions outside it (e.g. the banks, the major commercial and industrial companies, the big unions). It follows from this that the act of voting is by no means the only, or even the most important, aspect of political activity in British society. As we saw in Chapter 3, many commentators who are themselves sympathetic to the liberal-democratic system have recognised that government is subject to many influences other than those exercised periodically through the ballot box, and as we shall go on to see in Chapter 7, other less sympathetic analysts have argued that voting has little more than symbolic significance since the choice of a governing party has precious little effect on the way British society is actually run.

Given all this, it may be suggested that the central importance which British political science has traditionally accorded to the study of voting ('psephology') appears to be out of all proportion to its actual political significance. However, the significance of voting cannot be judged simply in terms of its effectiveness in determining public policy, for in analysing British politics, voting is perhaps most significant for what it tells us about political alignments generally. The point is that for most people, voting once every 4 or 5 years is the only active political intervention they ever make. Most people do not belong to political parties, do not attend trade union branch meetings, do not demonstrate against nuclear weapons and do not riot on the streets. Around one-quarter of them, it has to be said, do not vote in general elections either, but as an indication of political orientation, national voting patterns are the best information we have.

We do, however, have to take considerable care in interpreting voting data. There is, in particular, a danger that we read too much into how people vote, for there is now considerable evidence to suggest that voting is not such a calculated and rational act as has sometimes been imagined. As we saw in Chapter 2, most people do not apparently coolly weigh up competing party programmes and deliver their solemn verdict at the polling station, for many factors – party image, the personal charisma of party leaders, a negative reaction to alternative parties, a barely thought-through desire for a change, and the dull force of habit – may affect how people vote, and many of us register a vote despite, rather than because of, the policies advocated by the party of our choice.

This is important because it means we cannot deduce from a person's position in society how he or she will (still less 'should') vote. There is no direct connection between class, or gender, or ethnicity, or age or any other factor or combination of factors and political alignment based on voting. The act of voting, in other words, is a meaningful act but not necessarily a rational one, and the meaning that it has for different people may have as much to do with a desire to please or spite one's spouse, or a judgement on Margaret Thatcher's accent, as with a sober assessment of which party programme will be best for oneself or for the country.

Nevertheless, it is possible to come to some generalizations about how people tend to vote, and thus to come to some conclusions about the patterns of political division in British society. This is because groups do differ politically according to factors such as class, age, gender and race – i.e. social cleavages *are* reflected to some extent in political alignment. The way in which these cleavages are reflected is, however, changing, as we shall see.

Traditionally, political sociologists have identified class (by which they normally mean simply occupational class) as the single most important factor associated with variations in voting patterns. This is not perhaps surprising given that one of the major political parties through most of this century has been one whose very name – Labour – indicates not an attachment to a political philosophy (as in conservatism or liberalism) but a commitment to a class (wage-labour), and whose origins lie in the organised trade union movement. Ever since the end of the First World War, the Labour Party has seen itself, and has usually been seen by others, as the party standing for the working class (defined in its Constitution somewhat broadly as 'workers by hand or by brain'), and although various attempts have been made (with varying degrees of success) to broaden its appeal to other classes (as in the early 1960s when the 'cloth cap' image was deliberately abandoned) and other subordinate groups (as in the early 1980s when the party tried to appeal to women, blacks, youth, gays and any other disadvantaged groups it could lay its eyes on), it has remained the case for most of this period that the backbone of Labour Party support has been the manual working class.

There are three points which have immediately to be noted about this, however. One is that this traditional support base has been getting smaller. Due mainly to the combined impact of technological change (which has swollen the size of the service sector at the expense of the industrial sector, and the size of the routine non-manual workforce relative to manual workers), and of the long-term relative decline of the British economy (which has shrunk many industries such as steel-making, car manufacture, ship-building, coal mining and the like which have been unable to withstand competition from abroad – see Chapter 8), the manual working class has been dwindling in numbers and has been changing its character. It is no longer the case (if indeed it ever really was) that solid proletarian support for the Labour Party is sufficient to win office.

This was first recognised in the 1950s when three successive

Conservative general-election victories led to much speculation over whether Labour would ever again be able to muster a parliamentary majority. The vogue word among analysts at this time was 'embourgeoisement' which basically meant that the working class was becoming more like the 'middle class' (generally taken to mean non-manual workers) in terms of its level of income, its life experience and its life style, in which case it was also likely that it was becoming more like the middle class in its political behaviour too. Such speculation came to an end in the mid-sixties when Harold Wilson's revamped Labour Party won two general elections in the space of 18 months, and when sociologists began to realise that economically and culturally, most manual workers were still a long way from a middle-class income and life style. We shall, however, have cause to return to the question of embourgeoisement presently.

The second point is that, although most Labour Party support has always come from manual workers, it is not the case that the manual working class has ever voted solidly for the Labour Party. Through the 1950s and 1960s, the conventional wisdom among analysts was that, although class was a key to voting behaviour, some people would always be 'deviant'. In particular, much interest was channelled into explaining why around one-third of manual workers voted for the Conservatives (with rather less interest in why around one-tenth of middle-class electors voted Labour). Explanations for this working-class Toryism tended to emphasise either the notion of working-class deference or that of inherited party loyalties.

The idea of deference as an explanation for the working-class Tory looked back to Bagehot, Disraeli and the nineteenth century. Bagehot had seen England as a deferential country, as one in which 'the numerous unwiser part wishes to be ruled by the less numerous wiser part' so that the majority abdicates in favour of an elite of superior persons. Numerous commentators during the 1950s picked up on this idea to suggest that Britain enjoyed a deferential (and therefore a stable) political culture and that working-class Tories were those who manifested a strong preference for high-status people as the governmental leaders, and who viewed society not in terms of class conflict but in terms of an hierarchy of status in which it was seen as right for better people to run the show. The theory did not, however, fare well in the face of survey evidence, for various studies suggested that only about a quarter of working-class Tories could be classified as deferentials and that deference was in any case declining as a basis for working-class Conservatism.

The alternative explanation for working-class Tory support was advanced in the 1960s in an influential book by David Butler and Donald Stokes entitled *Political Change in Britain*. They argued that party loyalties are acquired early in the childhood home; the Labour Party has only been a serious contender for power since the First World War; and so many of those voting in the 60s were socialised into politics and partisanship by parents who themselves had been socialised into a party system in which Labour had no major part. Put another way, the home passes on and 'protects' old partisan loyalties. In consequence, changes in partisan identification tend to lag behind developments in the party system itself. Time is needed for historic attachments to the older parties to weaken and realignment to take place. Given this kind of perspective, Butler and Stokes expected to see 'the progressive conversion of the working class to the Labour Party'; the decay of working-class Conservatism; and Labour coming 'much closer to a full seizure of its "natural" class base'.

As things have turned out, of course, this explanation has proved no more successful that that couched in terms of deference, for during the 1970s and 1980s, traditional party loyalties have been eroded and working class desertion from the Labour Party has escalated. Indeed, as we shall see, the very notion that working-class Toryism is a political deviation in need of special explanation now looks rather curious, for in the 1983 general election, the Labour Party managed to win just 38 per cent of the manual working-class vote. The party never has commanded the solid support of the entire working class, but now it seems that it cannot even win a majority among it.

The third point to note about traditional political science assumptions regarding the association between class and voting concerns the electoral significance of non-class cleavages. As we have seen, factors such as gender and ethnicity are crucial in the organisation of domination in British society as a whole. Political analysis has generally recognised this in its analyses of voting patterns while at the same time arguing that class remains the major determinant of political alignment. In other words, it has generally been recognised that these other factors may influence voting – men have traditionally voted Labour more than women have; the young have supported Labour in larger numbers than the elderly; blacks have overwhelmingly voted Labour when they have bothered to vote at all – but such factors have generally been seen as additive or secondary variables. In effect a whole range of things from religion to region, and from age to sex, were somehow seen as so inextricably tangled up with the phenomenon of class that they were regarded as embellishments that could either be *reduced* to class, or else *added* to the basics of occupational class so as to provide explanations (or rather predictions) of voting behaviour of still greater precision. Tell a psephologist that you were a manual worker, and she or he would reply that you probably voted Labour. Add to this the additional information that you were also male, young, black or Catholic and the odds would shorten still further.

Such predictive confidence has today, however, all but disappeared, for not only has the influence of class on voting been weakened, but so too has the influence of most of the other familiar variables of psephological analysis. At the 1983 general election, for example, not only did Labour's lead over the Conservatives among manual workers fall to just 5 per cent, but its lead among trade union members (traditionally a strong predictive variable) fell to just 7 per cent, and its lead among young voters and men was actually reversed.

What this means is that neither class nor other factors such as age and gender now seem to explain political alignment. Nor can it be suggested that the 1983 election was in some way a 'freak', for the tendencies which became manifest there had been developing more or less rapidly throughout the 1970s. Something fundamental and quite dramatic has been happening to restructure traditional patterns of political alignment, and the old political science nostrums now lie in tatters as political scientists and sociologists attempt to make sense of the changes which are taking place.

One possible explanation for all this is that voters are becoming more rational in their decision to support one or other party. Such an explanation would suggest that people are no longer prepared to vote habitually, but rather weigh up party programmes and cast their votes accordingly. On this view, the decline of the Labour Party is largely a function of its commitment to policies such as unilateral nuclear disarmament and public ownership which are massively unpopular and which its traditional supporters are no longer prepared to swallow uncritically.

There is probably some truth in this explanation, for opinion polls before and during the 1983 election demonstrated the widespread popular support for Conservative policies on issues such as law and order, defence, trade union reform and privatisation of nationalised industries, while the issues dear to the hearts of predominantly young and middle-class Labour Party activists evidently held little appeal for the electorate as a whole. As we shall see in Chapter 7, the Labour Party has itself been changing over the last 10 years and it would be foolish to deny the possibility that it is therefore the Party which has moved away from its traditional working-class supporters rather than the other way round (an argument voiced in 1981 by those Labour MPs who left the Labour Party to form the SDP).

In our view, however, the changes run deeper than this, for they reflect changes in the pattern of inequality and domination in British society as a whole. Our argument, in a nutshell, is that shifts in voting patterns over the last 15 or 20 years reflect the increasing saliency in society as a whole of divisions which have largely been neglected in both sociological and political analysis. These are what we termed at the end of the previous section of this chapter 'sectoral cleavages'.

Sectoral cleavages, it will be recalled, are divisions based neither on class nor status but on the split between those who rely on the public sector for employment and/or for consumption provisions such as housing, and those who work in or rely on the private sector. There are, in other words, production-sector cleavages between public-sector and private-sector workers (the latter in a sense paying for the wages of the former through their taxes), and consumption sector cleavages between those who are dependent upon state provision of key resources such as housing, transport or medical care, and those who achieve access to such resources through the market (the latter again paying, at least in part, for the provisions of the former through state subsidies, although private consumption too is often subsidised through taxation as in the case of tax relief on mortgages).

As we suggested at the end of the previous section, these divisions can be and often are of major significance in the distribution of life chances. Wage settlements, conditions of work and job security often vary markedly between similar occupations according to whether they are located in the public or private sectors. Similarly, the costs, standards and privileges associated with private consumption (e.g. pay beds, public schools, private-car ownership or owner-occupied housing) tend to differ substantially from those of public-sector provision, and cut-backs in welfare provision since the mid-seventies (see Chapter 9) have exacerbated these inequalities.

What we are suggesting (and here we broadly follow recent arguments developed by a British political scientist, Patrick Dunleavy) is that such cleavages are not only important for determining people's quality of life, but are also crucial in influencing their political orientation as manifested in the way they vote. Basically, those who depend on the state for employment or for substantial consumption provision tend to subscribe to a 'statist' ideology which has become associated with the Labour Party, while private-sector workers and those who buy their key consumption requirements in the private market tend towards an 'anti-statist' ideology which has become associated with the Conservatives. Seen in this way, the main reason why working-class Labour support has declined is that the party has been deserted by that sector of the working class which stands to benefit least from an extension of state activity involving increased public expenditure and administration.

The evidence for this, though not extensive, is impressive. In his analysis of the 1979 election, for example, Dunleavy shows that the Conservatives polled significantly better among private- than public-sector workers (especially when they were non-unionised). This was subsequently borne out at the 1983 election, where private sector manual workers split evenly (36 per cent to 37 per cent) between Conservative and Labour while comparable public-sector workers remained far more loyal to Labour (46 per cent voting Labour compared with 29 per cent Conservative and 25 per cent Alliance).

The same pattern emerges in respect of consumption cleavages. Dunleavy shows that, in 1979, workers who were reliant on state provision for their housing, transport and health care voted by a margin of 29 per cent for Labour over the Conservatives. Among those who had bought one of these provisions (e.g. a private house or car), this margin was reduced to 24 per cent and among those who had bought two, the

Conservatives enjoyed a lead over Labour of 10 per cent. This lead was extended to 40 per cent among workers (albeit a very small number) who had a car, house and private medical care. Again, these findings were later reinforced by the 1983 election, notably in respect of housing, for 47 per cent of manual-worker owner-occupiers voted Conservative (compared with just 25 per cent for Labour and 28 per cent for the Liberals or SDP), while only 19 per cent of manual worker council tenants did so (compared with 57 per cent for Labour and 24 per cent for the Alliance).

What all this amounts to is that we are dealing in both sociological and political terms with two distinct sectors of the working class (and, for that matter, of the middle class as well). There is, on the one hand, that sector of the manual working class which works in the private sector, which owns its own house, car and (increasingly) may have access to private health care (e.g. in 1982 the Electricians Trade Union offered its members private health insurance) and which tends to be located in the South of the country (where 42 per cent of manual workers voted Conservative in 1983). There is, on the other hand, that sector of this same class which works in the public sector, which rents its housing from the local authority and relies on the state for public transport and health care, and which tends to be located in the North (where 42 per cent of manual workers voted Labour).

In suggesting this, there is an obvious temptation to dust off the old embourgoisement thesis from the 1950s and to suggest that, although it may not have held water 30 years ago, it does so today. This, however, would be to misunderstand the evidence. It is not that the working class is in some way becoming middle class and is therefore turning away from Labourism; such an argument rests on the fundamental misconception which holds that class is still the key to understanding political alignment. It is rather that the working class is becoming increasingly fragmented, not only by status divisions surrounding gender and race domination, but also, and just as significantly, by sectoral cleavages reflecting the basic division between those who stand to gain from increased levels of state activity and those who do not.

What this analysis of voting behaviour has shown therefore, is two things. First, political divisions *do* to a large extent reflect divisions within British society as a whole. Second, these divisions cut across each other, and relations of class domination are only one aspect of them. In addition to *class,* we must also consider divisions of *status,* such as gender and ethnicity, and divisions of *sectors,* both in relation to production and consumption. Domination in British society is organised around all three of these axes, and political alignments and political struggles may equally develop around any one or all of them. When women mobilise (whether through voting or more active and collective campaigns) to break down the exclusivity of male perserves, or when public-sector workers mobilise to defend their jobs, even in the face of demands by private-sector workers for tax cuts, or when home-owners mobilise to reduce the rate subsidy to council tenants, we cannot simply close our eyes and continue to assert the singular primacy of class as the basis of social and political domination. It is in this sense that we may agree with those theorists, discussed in Chapters 2 and 3, who assert that British politics and British society are 'pluralistic', for many of us are in one context strong and in another weak, and it is this very complexity of power in contemporary British society which renders simple class theories of politics (such as some of those to be discussed in Chapter 7) highly problematic.

THE MANAGEMENT OF DOMINATION

We have arrived at a curious position in our argument. Having pointed to, and agreed with, major criticisms of pluralist interpretations of British politics in Chapter 3, we now find ourselves apparently endorsing such interpretations! Power, it seems, *is* to some extent, dispersed, fragmented and cross-cutting, and people who are at the top of one pile may find themselves at the bottom of another. There is no single overarching system of power and domination through which any one group can exert overall control and direction. Or is there?

Political sociologists in Britain have long devoted much of their energies to the study of elites. In their work they have been influenced by classical nineteenth-century European elite theorists who argued that power in society is (and always will be) concentrated in the hands of a small group of people acting more or less in unison to dominate the masses. These ideas were subsequently taken up in the United States in the 1950s by C. Wright Mills whose influential book, *The Power Elite*, suggested that the apparent pluralism of American society and politics was in fact misleading, and that the USA was actually run by a combination of three different elites which interacted closely with each other. These were the political elite (which ran the government), the business elite (which dominated the economy) and the military elite, and Mills argued that together they constituted a single 'power elite' whose members were recruited from the wealthiest families and were linked with each other socially and through common memberships of the same committees, boards and organisations.

Mills's book had an enormous impact in Britain as well as in America, and although both his arguments and his evidence were subsequently questioned and thrown into some doubt, it led to a wave of studies by British researchers intent on identifying and tracing the links between different elite groups in an attempt to discover a power elite operating behind the scenes in British society as well as in the USA.

A British power elite?

On the face of it, the evidence for a single cohesive power elite operating in Britain seemed slim. Groups which are active and influential in one area of policy tend not to be active in others – teachers' unions, for example, may play a significant role in educational policy-making, but they tend to be insignificant in affecting defence policy, just as military chiefs do not have much to say in determining the content of school curricula.

Undismayed by such considerations, elite researchers asserted four major arguments to back up their belief that a power elite could (or did) operate in Britain.

1 The existence of open political conflict between different groups over different issues does not rule out the possibility that a single unified elite is operating behind the scenes.
2 We cannot rely on evidence taken from public sources such as newspaper reports or government documents as a test of the existence of a power elite since such sources will not report the activities of a relatively secretive elite whose influence is exerted informally.
3 A power elite will not be interested in dictating the outcome of all issues, for many areas of political controversy are of little concern for its members.
4 Given that a power elite should be expected to maintain a low profile, it is a mistake to focus analysis on major issues of public concern. A power elite, if it exists, will be most effective in crucial yet routine areas of policy where (to use Weber's distinction) it can achieve dominance without becoming involved in open power struggles.

These are legitimate points to raise against pluralistic conceptions of power which tend to be grounded in the analysis of public issues, but they also indicate a major problem in research on the question of elites. This is the problem of 'infinite regress', and it is a problem which can all too easily render elitist models immune from any empirical tests. Basically, the problem is that critics of elite theory can never actually prove that hidden elites do not exist, for no matter how carefully they document the political process, it is always possible to assert that they have failed to discover the group behind the scenes (or, indeed, the group behind that group) which is 'really' running things, albeit in a secretive and invisible way. Just as we can never actually prove to somebody who is convinced otherwise that witches do not exist, or that international world Jewish conspiracies do not exist, so too it seems ultimately impossible to prove that elites operating through hidden channels of influence and control do not exist.

Given this problem, the burden of proof must arguably lie with those who assert the existence of a power elite rather than with those who deny it. This challenge was taken up by a number of researchers from the 1950s onwards, and over the years, three main types of evidence have been collected in order to back up their case.

The first has been the evidence relating to the social backgrounds and patterns of interaction of different elites. The second, which has in fact only rarely been employed in British studies but which became for a time very popular in America, has been the study of reputations for power as indicators of hidden influence. The third and most fruitful has involved the study of patterns of benefit which are seen to arise from the routine exercise of elite domination.

Backgrounds and inter-connections

There have been numerous studies of elite recruitment, and although the exact figures and proportions vary from group to group and from study to study, the overall message is clear; in Britain, top positions, whether they be those of bishops or businessmen, politicians or press barons, are filled overwhelmingly by people (usually men) from the same sorts of class backgrounds who have attended the same sorts of schools, gone to the same Oxbridge colleges and frequent the same London clubs. What is more, there is considerable evidence to show that these different elite groups are connected quite closely with each other through kinship, friendship and overlapping memberships.

The main reason for gathering evidence like this on the social background of elites is to establish the existence of a common pattern of experience which, it is assumed, may foster a common set of values among top people in different walks of life in our society. The existence of such a shared set of values – a common elite consciousness – has never been demonstrated directly, for there are no opinion polls or attitude surveys to show that bankers, Cabinet ministers, top civil servants and the like do in fact think along the same lines, subscribe to the same commonsense beliefs and see things in much the same way. The difficulties involved in collecting such evidence are clearly immense, and we are left only with indirect evidence and with inferences drawn from what we know about the importance of childhood socialisation in shaping adult views of the world. Nevertheless, we are probably justified in assuming that the similarities in the backgrounds of these people may contribute in some way to a common outlook and perhaps even a shared consciousness of themselves as a group.

Elitist interpretations of power in British society do not rest solely on data on recruitment, for it can also be shown that different elite groups are often in close social contact with each other. Such evidence has been used to support the argument that elites may not only share the same sorts of values, but also constitute a relatively coherent single social entity. Thus, while data on backgrounds and recruitment has been used as evidence of common *consciousness,* that on linkages between elites has been used to demonstrate group *coherence.*

Various studies have successfully traced quite intricate networks which tie together different members of different elites. Evidence on the business backgrounds of MPs, for example, shows that on average, each

Conservative Member of Parliament holds two company chairmanships and four company directorships. It is common practice for ex-ministers to join the boards of private companies and, increasingly, for retired civil servants to do likewise. There is, in other words, a circulation of personnel between different elite positions, and the cross-fertilization which this fosters is underpinned both by kinship connections and club memberships (one study, for example, found that 75 per cent of elite members in government, the civil service, private enterprise, the armed forces, the judiciary, the media and the aristocracy belonged to a small number of exclusive clubs). The problem, however, is that such findings tell us nothing about the quality of the relationships between different elite members – it is quite possible, for example, to interact regularly and informally with somebody without liking them or agreeing with them. Just as evidence on top people's backgrounds cannot prove that they share the same values, so too evidence on their interconnectedness cannot prove that they act coherently as a single group.

Neither of these problems would matter too much for an elitist interpretation of the British power structure if researchers were able to demonstrate the existence of collective action on the part of elite members. The acid test for modern elite theory is not whether elites exist (clearly they do), nor whether they are exclusive in origin and relatively cohesive in their interrelations (as they appear to be), but whether their existence is significant in determining political outcomes on which the fate of the country depends. It is on this third criterion that sociological work on elites in Britain has been found most wanting.

Reputations

The basic problem confronted by researchers who seek to demonstrate that a cohesive elite actually does run the country is that their view of power is one which emphasises the secrecy and informality of elite actions. If a power elite exists, its members' activities are not likely to be recorded in *The Times,* nor are they to be found leading delegations to Downing Street. The more powerful you are, the less visible you need be. It follows from this that the most powerful people of all – the power elite – are likely to be largely invisible to outsiders, in which case some indirect method for studying them is called for.

What is entailed in such a method is the use of visible indicators of the invisible use of power in society. Just as a jet skimming across the sky may not itself be visible to the naked eye but can readily be detected by the trace of white vapour which it leaves in its wake, so too elites may not themselves be seen directly but may be detected by the traces left by their effective use of power. One such trace is the reputations which certain people have as influential individuals; another is the pattern of benefits which accrues out of the perpetuation of the routines of ruling.

The analysis of reputations for power (the so-called 'reputational method') was pioneered in studies of local power structures during the 1950s, mainly in the United States. The technique was fairly complex but the idea behind it was simple – namely, to discover hidden influentials by asking those who are visibly active in political affairs whom they thought to be powerful. Whenever this procedure has been followed – in Britain as well as in North America – the same sorts of results have been achieved; namely, the 'discovery' of a small and cohesive elite group behind the formal façade of democratic politics and public administration.

The problems with these studies are, however, enormous. The choice of individuals whose opinions are sought is inevitably arbitrary. The restriction on the size of the 'elite' which is eventually identified is unwarranted. There are no grounds for assuming that reputations are an accurate reflection of the real relations of domination in society, for reputations may, quite simply, be unfounded (the example of trade union power, discussed earlier in this chapter, would appear to be a case in point, for the widespread belief that the unions run Britain seems to have little basis). None of this is to deny that reputations for power are interesting data in their own right, for the individual who is seen as powerful by others may well be able to use that reputation to his or her own benefit. Such cases, however, do nothing to change the fundamental objection to a reputational method that people's opinions about power are a very limited basis from which to generalise about the complexities of power.

The pattern of benefits

Today, the reputational method is rarely if ever employed in studies of power. Instead, it has been replaced in the analysis of elites by an altogether more sophisticated method for tracing power and domination in society which involves investigation of patterns of benefit arising out of everyday routines of ruling.

The basis of this approach lies in the work of two American political scientists, Peter Bachrach and Morton Baratz, in the early 1960s in which they introduced the notion of 'non-decision-making'. According to Bachrach and Baratz, power involves not simply the ability to make decisions and thereby shape policy outcomes, but also the ability to dominate the political process in such a way that certain types of issues never arise and certain kinds of decisions never get made with the result that existing patterns of benefit are never challenged. When researchers study decision-making and conclude that power in society is dispersed, they are in this view studying merely those issues which have been allowed to surface in the political system and are ignoring crucial questions of power at a much earlier stage where a power elite may have been able to determine what will and will not be discussed thereby preventing any effective challenge to its privileges.

From the work of Bachrach and Baratz, it is possible to identify three ways in which issues may be stifled by a powerful elite before they emerge into the political arena.

1   Such an elite may be able to ignore political demands and thus avert the need for making a decision one way or the other. There are many different ways in which this may be achieved. In some cases, like Nelson at Trafalgar, an elite may simply place a telescope to its blind eye and insist that nothing is happening. Alternatively, it may define those who are raising demands as 'unrepresentative' or as unworthy of serious consideration. If pushed, it may agree to consult with those who are leading a campaign in the hope of coopting them, or to establish an enquiry into their grievances in an attempt to defuse opposition and thus avoid having to deal with it. In all such cases, the strategy is the same – to maintain the current pattern of privileges in society while averting the need to take what may well turn out to be unpopular decisions.

2   A powerful elite may be able to ensure that awkward political demands are never raised. This may be achieved through the phenomenon of 'anticipated reactions' – i.e. disadvantaged and less powerful groups may anticipate that it would do no good to raise demands, that it is not worth their time and effort to organise when they know that they will be ignored, or even that any opposition on their part would be met by force or other negative sanctions. The existing pattern of power and privilege may in this way be maintained by virtue of a fatalistic recognition on the part of those who suffer from it that there is little they can do to challenge it, and such fatalism may be encouraged by the powerful (e.g. as in the early 1980s when Margaret Thatcher constantly repeated that there was no alternative to her economic policies, even though they were leading to despairing levels of unemployment – see Chapter 8).

3   A power elite may be able to prevent people from formulating grievances in any clear or coherent way. Thus, if it controls the media, the schools and so on (see Chapter 10), it may be able to shape people's perceptions of the political process and of their place within it and thus engineer a degree of consensus or acquiescence which is sufficient to maintain its own position virtually unchallenged. In this way, the issues which do emerge for public debate will be confined to a very narrow range of options and will never threaten the fundamental basis of political and economic organisation in society. Put another way people will argue about the means for achieving a particular goal (e.g. how best to run a capitalist economy) but the possibility of disputing the end (e.g. the maintenance of capitalism) will rarely if ever cross their minds.

The obvious question raised by all this, of course, is how non-decisions can be studied in empirical research. On the face of it, this is a tall order, for it is difficult enough gathering evidence about decisions which have been taken without having to study those which have not. There is, after all, an infinity of things that do not happen in our society, so where is the analyst to start?

Bachrach and Baratz themselves went some way to resolving such problems, for they and other writers noted that some aspects of non-decision-making are visible. The first strategy – the ability to ignore demands – is the easiest to study, for if the researcher is alert to the various grievances which different groups are expressing, she or he can simply follow up what does or does not happen in response to them. One example is the government response to the inner-city riots of 1981, discussed earlier in this chapter. Those involved were predominantly young, black and/or unemployed, and the main reasons for these riots appeared to involve resentment against what was felt by many young blacks to be oppressive and discriminatory police procedures, and a festering disillusionment about the prospects of finding employment in areas where rates of school-leaver unemployment were in excess of 50 per cent. The issues raised, but never resolved, by these riots were thus those of racism and unemployment. The government responded by setting up an inquiry whose findings had little impact on subsequent policy, by pumping a little more money into inner-city areas with one hand while removing it through a new system of financing local government (discussed in Chapter 11) with the other, and by calling for more police officers and firmer sentences against those convicted of street crimes. Thus, although the issues were raised in particularly dramatic form, precious little was done by way of response.

The second strategy – the ability to prevent people from airing their grievances – is less easily studied. There may, of course, be cases where people float an idea and then hastily withdraw it. Shortly after the Social Democratic Party was formed in 1981, for example, one of its leading members proposed that tax relief on mortgage interest payments should be abolished, but this idea was soon dropped and not heard of again as the SDP prepared itself for an election in which it anticipated the power of the owner-occupier vote (a good example, incidentally of the political significance of consumption cleavages). Usually, however, anticipated reactions are routinized in the sense that people generally 'know' what they can and cannot achieve, and in these cases, empirical research into why particular demands have not been raised is likely to be very difficult.

Most difficult of all, of course, is research on the third strategy which basically involves the ability of elite groups to influence the ways in which people come to formulate grievances and to conceive of their interests. Critics have argued, not only that it is impossible to demonstrate through empirical research that one group has effectively shaped the values, goals and beliefs of another, but also that elite theory has here again fallen foul of the familiar tendency to predetermine its findings in that it starts off with the assumption that a powerful elite group exists which is capable of shaping people's political ideas and then cites the lack of popular opposition as evidence for this.

Elite theorists have never been able to counter this criticism satisfactorily. As with the reputational method before it, most political sociologists have now come to accept that analysis of persistent patterns of benefit is simply not enough to demonstrate that the beneficiaries constitute a hidden power elite which uses its power to suppress and prevent challenges to its privileges. Britain is, as we have seen throughout this chapter, a highly unequal society, but this fact alone is an insufficient basis for the assertion that the country must therefore in some way be controlled by a cohesive and conspiratorial elite group operating behind the scenes to prevent any challenge emerging to its power. Despite all the effort which has been directed into this area of research over the years, there is no evidence to suggest that such a power elite exists in Britain, and in recent years, even the most cynical political analysts have, perhaps with some degree of reluctance, come to accept this.

The fact that the power elite thesis is today widely regarded as at best unproven and at worst discredited does not, however, lead automatically back into an acceptance of pluralist interpretations of power. Rather, sociologists have moved away from the notion of a power elite and have begun to develop an altogether more subtle and more compelling analysis of power in society in which power is seen to be located, not so much in particular groups of individuals, but in systems of domination. In this way, the sort of evidence we have been discussing in this chapter has come to be seen as supporting neither a pluralist nor an elitist interpretation of power, but rather as indicating the existence of pervasive relations of domination inscribed in social systems themselves.

Systems of domination

What is involved in this rethinking of the sociological analysis of power is basically a return to the distinction drawn by Weber between 'power' – the ability of an actor to gain his or her will even against the resistance of others – and 'domination' – the probability that a particular command will be obeyed. Domination is, as we saw earlier, a power relationship which has become regularised, for it involves sets of social relations in which one party has established routine command over another such that he or she is rarely challenged. Orders, that is, are obeyed as a matter of course.

Sociological work on the power exercised by elite groups has tended to focus more on the ability of particular individuals to impose their will even against resistance than on regularised relations of domination. It is for this reason that such work has run into problems in explaining non-decision-making, for this is precisely an aspect of power which is regularised and routinised. The essence of the non-decision-making concept is that dominant groups are not challenged and hence that issues do not arise and conflict does not occur. What this suggests is that we should be paying much less attention to the question of power (i.e. the question of who tends to prevail in a range of different issues) and much more attention to the question of domination.

Once the question is reformulated in this way, it becomes obvious that attempts to identify particular groups as powerful are based on a misconception, for domination involves the exercise of power through a system. Relations of domination, in other words, are to a large extent inscribed in social systems. Whites in South Africa, for example, are clearly a powerful group – a power elite if you like – in that they can usually achieve their will even against the resistance of the majority black population, but this 'power' clearly derives in large part from the fact that they are the beneficiaries of a system of domination which is inherently biased in their favour and which is organised in the very fabric of South African society through the system of Apartheid. Similarly, Protestants in Northern Ireland may be said to be 'powerful' relative to the Catholic population, mainly because Orange supremacy is built into the very foundations of the Northern Ireland state as a sectarian political unit with a built-in Protestant majority. Domination and bias are thus socially organised, and although individual white South Africans and individual Protestant Ulstermen clearly help to maintain the systems of domination from which they benefit through their actions, they are equally clearly not the sole cause of that bias.

It follows from this that we need to shift from a purely individualistic conception of power, such as characterises traditional elite studies, to an understanding of power in the context of the social organisation of domination in which no one individual or group of individuals is alone responsible for what happens. We need to recognise that people may be dominant over others without intentionally bringing about the bias which operates in their favour (a point which we also made earlier in our discussion of gender domination). It is therefore quite possible to talk of non-decision-making operating within political systems without having to demonstrate that a particular elite has intentionally brought this about.

We need to be cautious at this point, however, for, as the pluralist theorist, Nelson Polsby, has argued, we cannot simply attribute power to people on the basis of an analysis which shows that they benefit from existing political or social arrangements. Polsby himself cites the example of taxi-drivers benefiting when it rains. The fact that more people take cabs when it is raining does not allow us to argue that taxi-drivers are part of a system of domination which causes it to rain. Equally, however, we are surely justified in asking whether there is a system of domination, of which taxi-drivers, private motorists, road haulage companies, car manufacturers and so on all form a part, which has created and maintained a situation where public transport is inadequate such that, when it rains, people have little option but to take a cab since there are rarely any buses around. In Los Angeles, for example, a consortium of oil, car and tyre manufacturing companies bought up and ran down the public transport system in the 1930s with the result that today, the private car is virtually the only viable form of personal transport in the city. Less dramatically, in London, in 1981/2, a cheap-fares policy on buses and tube trains was reversed by a House of Lords decision with the result that many people found it cheaper and more convenient to use private forms of transport. Neither in Los Angeles nor London can it be said that taxi-drivers intentionally and individually caused these policies, but in both cases it can be said that they constitute a very small part of a dominant private-sector interest which has routinely prevailed over alternative public-sector strategies, many of which (e.g. a free public transport option) never even reach the political agenda. This is precisely what is entailed in the notion of non-decision-making.

Many of these theoretical issues were brought together by the British political theorist Steven Lukes in his short but influential book on power, published in 1974. He begins by criticising both the pluralist conception of power, which he dismisses as 'one-dimensional' in the sense that it studies only observable behaviour, and Bachrach and Baratz's 'two-dimensional' view of power which studies both what people do and the ways in which they may prevent others from doing anything. He then develops a 'three-dimensional' view which focuses not simply on what people do and do not do, but also on the systems of domination in which they exercise their power. Such an approach, he suggests, offers 'the prospect of a serious sociological and not merely personalised explanation of how political systems prevent demands from becoming political issues or even from being made'.

According to this 'three-dimensional' view of power, the analysis of relations of power and domination in society must achieve two things. First, it must show that those subject to the exercise of power would have thought or acted differently in the absence of such power. Secondly, it must identify the mechanism by which they have been prevented from thinking or acting differently. According to Lukes, both criteria will be difficult to meet in empirical research, but they are in principle realisable.

On the first of these criteria, Lukes argues that it is sometimes possible to show that people would have thought or acted differently by studying what happens when relations of power and domination change over time or vary between different places. In Poland, for example, workers formed a free trade union, Solidarity, for a short period in the early 1980s, when state controls were briefly relaxed and challenged, and this may be taken as evidence that the more established system of unions controlled by the Central Communist Party in that country represents a system of domination in which workers are generally prevented from organising themselves as they would wish. Similarly, it can be shown that, in countries with cheap and plentiful public transport, people will often choose to travel by bus or train rather than by private car or taxi, and this may be taken as evidence that the domination of the public sector by the private sector represents a system of domination in which people are generally prevented from travelling as they might otherwise wish.

Suppose, however, that in Poland following the suppression of Solidarity, an opinion poll of workers showed a majority in favour of the official trade unions, or that in London following the House of Lords ruling, a majority of commuters was found to favour the newly enforced higher fares. The obvious response to such findings would be to suggest that these people are not being dominated after all since their expressed wishes are in fact being reflected in government policy. Such a conclusion would, however, ignore the possibility that people's views are being influenced, coerced or otherwise shaped by, for example, fear of the military in Poland or exposure to propaganda in London. We need to know, in other words, why it is that people may apparently accept systems of domination from which other people benefit.

This is probably the most difficult issue of all in contemporary power analysis. Weber in his work never explicitly confronted it, for although he noted that there may be all sorts of reasons why people come to obey commands and to see systems of domination as legitimate, he did not think it important to investigate these reasons – all that mattered for him was that, for whatever reason, leaders could count on their subordinates to heed their commands. Yet it clearly is important to understand why people obey – why people accept or even support particular policies or particular systems even when they do not benefit from them.

What is at issue in such a question is how to define people's 'real interests'. If, for example, we decide that it is in Londoners' real interests to have cheap public transport fares, and yet we find that most commuters express a preference for the new higher-fares policy, then we may take this as evidence that power or domination has been exerted to change these people's views from what they could otherwise have been. But how are we to determine that it is in fact in their interests to have lower fares – especially when this means higher subsidies to London Transport paid for by higher rate bills for all those living in London?

Lukes's own answer to this is inadequate. He suggests that we can identify people's 'real interests' by assessing what they would want if they were able to make choices relatively free of domination by others. The problem with this is that we can never know whether an individual is in fact making a relatively free choice. Indeed, the pervasive influence of socialisation (discussed in Chapter 10), whereby individuals in any society are brought up to accept certain beliefs, to endorse certain values and to behave in particular ways in particular situations, is such as to raise the question of whether we are ever in a position to make relatively autonomous judgements. How can we escape the influences of our home backgrounds, our teachers, the newspapers we read and the television programmes we watch?

The problem of how to identify people's 'real interests' can never be resolved to everybody's satisfaction, for as Lukes himself recognises the concept of interests is an irreducible evaluative one. In other words, the judgement that some policy is or is not in somebody's interests ultimately rests on personal opinion. Many of us would agree, for example, that it is not in the interests of the British people to be obliterated by a nuclear holocaust, but there are intense disagreements over whether it is therefore in our interests to disarm unilaterally or to maintain an effective nuclear deterrent. As Weber was well aware, science cannot legislate on moral questions – i.e. questions about what people 'ought' to want. This appears to be a major stumbling block in the sociological analysis of power and domination, for if we cannot determine what people's interests are, then we cannot judge whether their expressed wants and preferences have been distorted as a result of the exercise of ideological power over them.

Lukes's second criterion for demonstrating the existence of a power relationship is that we must be able to show, not only that people's thoughts or actions are different than they would otherwise have been, but also how this change has been brought about. He makes two points about this.

First, he emphasises that power is not necessarily exercised intentionally. To say that a powerful group has caused others to do, or not to do, something is not to say that this was deliberate. As we have already noted, power is generally exercised routinely as domination, and neither party to a relation of domination may be particularly aware of it. In Lukes's view, all that is necessary in order to identify some group as powerful is to show that it has brought about some change and that its members could in principle find out that they were responsible for this.

Second, he emphasises that power is not necessarily exercised by indentifiable individuals but may rather be exerted by social groups, organisations or even social classes. Again we came across this point earlier when we saw that individuals may be powerful by virtue of their location in a system of domination. Whites in South Africa may not be particularly powerful as individuals, but they derive their power from a *system* of Apartheid which they collectively perpetuate and benefit from. Similarly, individual factory owners or property developers may not be especially powerful, but they derive their power from a capitalist *system* to which they belong and from which they gain as owners of productive property.

This recognition that power may be collectively organised raises an additional problem for the sociological analysis of power, for at what point does it cease to make sense to identify particular individuals as powerful? Was the Nazi concentration camp commander powerful, or was he simply a passive part of a crushing system of domination over which he had no control and about which he could do nothing? Is the managing director of BL Cars powerful given that he can declare thousands of workers redundant at the stroke of a pen, or is he basically powerless in the face of a system of world capitalism which leaves him no choice but to close down his factories and replace workers with robots? Clearly, it makes no sense to identify some individual or group as powerful unless we assume that they could have acted differently despite the constraints of the system in which they operate.

Like the identification of people's interests, the judgement that people enjoy scope for effective action within the constraints of the system in which they live poses enormous problems for the sociological analysis of power, problems which we shall need to consider in more detail in Chapter 7. Here we may simply note that the analysis of power in British society is by no means as simple as may have been thought, for it clearly involves much more than merely analysing decision-making by governments or the recruitment of elites. Inevitably, it seems, we are drawn into philosophical and theoretical disputes concerning the relation between the individual and society – disputes which have divided social theorists for centuries and to which there is no single, incontrovertible solution. Given this, it follows that the sociological analysis of power will always involve controversial and personal judgements about what power is and how it is to be analysed. In recognising this, we have obviously left the cosy world of traditional political science a long way back and have entered in to a much less certain, but perhaps more challenging, terrain.

CONCLUSION

Britain is a highly unequal society. The extent of inequality is revealed in the distribution of private property such as land and shareholdings, in the distribution of earned and unearned incomes, and in the overall distribution of life chances – access to decent housing or education, security of employment, quality of life – which is associated with factors such as gender and ethnicity as much as with class.

Sociologists have long recognised that such material inequalities are both the basis for, and the product of, unequal relationships of power and domination in society. Those who are materially privileged tend to enjoy much more potential for shaping the pattern of their lives and the lives of others than those who are not. Such a potential is revealed, not only in economic relations where certain groups are able to exclude others from the privileges they enjoy, but also in public affairs where social cleavages are revealed in political alignments (e.g. in voting) and where definable elite groups appear to dominate all major areas of life and to perpetuate their domination across the generations by means of their exclusive access to channels of recruitment such as the public schools and the ancient universities. All of this has been well and consistently documented by sociologists over the years, and to the extent that it is possible to talk of undeniable 'facts' in social science, all of this is fact.

Where the problems arise, however, is in analysing how, if at all, these relatively exclusive strata in British society actually use the power which is apparently located in the positions they occupy. We know, for example, that a small number of people collectively controls the major command posts of the British economy through their common memberships of the boards of the big banks, financial institutions and industrial companies. We also know that these people tend to be drawn from the same class backgrounds, that they interact regularly with each other formally and informally, and that they are much the same sort of people as also control the command posts of government, the civil service, the armed forces and so on. What we do not know, however, is what these people do and how they do it.

Part of the reason for this paucity of empirical research findings lies in the difficulties encountered in studying elite groups. We are not even sure where we should look, and the difficulties of gaining access to the exclusive preserves of British elites in order to oberve these people in action are daunting. We are left, therefore, with reading *Who's Who*, culling what we can from biographies, diaries and official reports, and drawing our own uncertain conclusions.

We have seen in this chapter, however, that the problems go beyond simply the difficulties of studying top people, for more basically, the analysis of power has confronted problems of a philosophical and theoretical nature concerning the very notion of power itself. The theoretical sophistication of recent work on power and domination represents a tremendous advance on what, in retrospect, seem the rather naive concerns of political sociologists in the 1950s and 1960s with identifying ruling groups or a power elite. Our theoretical reflections have led to a transcendence of the old disputes between pluralists and elitists over whether power is basically dispersed or concentrated in a few hands, for we now see that power cannot be understood except in the context of a system of domination which no one group totally controls or consciously manipulates.

Such theoretical insights have not, however, been matched by empirical research, and in recent years, theory has undoubtedly run way ahead of our empirical knowledge. Part of the reason for this is that it is undoubtedly a lot easier to sit in an armchair and theorise than it is to apply theories to an analysis of relations of domination as they are revealed in contemporary British society. But partly, this growing disjuncture between increasingly sophisticated theories and increasingly inadequate empirical data is also due to the nature of the theories themselves. When our theories, be they pluralist or elitist, told us simply that this or that group is powerful there was an obvious incentive to go and find out whether there was any evidence to support such assertions. But the more our theories have moved from a focus on the actions of individuals to one on the bias inherent in social systems, the less incentive there has been to go and study the actions of anybody. There is, therefore, a real and paradoxical danger in recent theories of power that, by shifting the emphasis from powerful individuals to systems of domination, we end up losing sight of power altogether. As we shall see in the next chapter, this is a danger which was fully realised by certain developments in Marxist political theory in the 1970s.

WORKS CITED AND GUIDE TO FURTHER READING

Atkinson, A. (1972) *Unequal Shares: Wealth in Britain*, Harmondsworth, Penguin.
Although now somewhat dated, an important investigation into the distribution of income and wealth in Britain.

Bachrach, P. and Baratz, M. (1970) *Power and Poverty*, London, Oxford University Press.
The first two chapters (originally published as journal articles in the early 1960s) set out the basic idea of non-decision-making; later chapters provide a rather disappointing application of the idea to a study of poverty in Baltimore.

Butler and Stokes, D. (1969) *Political Change in Britain*, London, Macmillan.
See page 54.

Centre for Contemporary Cultural Studies (1982) *The Empire Strikes Back*, London, Hutchinson.
A collection of articles from the Birmingham-based centre presenting a Marxist analysis of race and racism in contemporary Britain.

Dahrendorf, R. (1959) *Class and Class Conflict in Industrial Society*, London, Routledge & Kegan Paul.
A major statement of the 'managerialism thesis' which tries (rather unconvincingly) to retheorise classes in terms of authority relations rather than property ownership.

Dunleavy, P. (1983) Voting and the electorate, in H. Druker *et al.* (eds.) *Developments in British Politics*, London, Macmillan, pp. 30–58.
A brief but useful introduction to the issue of class dealignment in voting and to Dunleavy's own explanation for it in terms of sectoral cleavages.

Lukes, S. (1974) *Power: A Radical View*, London, Macmillan.
An important little book, though perhaps ultimately flawed, which attempts to redirect the sociological analysis of power away from the study of elites to take account of structural features of power relationships.

Mitchell, J. (1971) *Women's Estate*, Harmondsworth, Penguin.
An early statement by one of Britain's most prominent feminist writers which details the nature of women's oppression and considers the relation between feminism and socialism.

Oakley, A. (1974) *Housewife*, Harmondsworth, Allen Lane.
Discusses the role of 'housewife' and how it affects women's position in contemporary society.

Parkin, F. (1979) *Marxism and Class Theory: A Bourgeois Critique*, London, Tavistock.
A very readable and highly stimulating discussion of class and other sources of domination. Most significant, perhaps, for its pioneering analysis of modes of social closure (exclusion and usurpation).

Parry, G. (1969) *Political Elites,* London, Allen and Unwin.
A useful review of elite theory. Particularly good on the early elite theorists such as Pareto, Mosca and Michels.

Polsby, N. (1980) *Community Power and Political Theory,* 2nd edn, London, Yale University Press.
A re-issue of a pluralist classic first published in the late fifties. Half of the book is newly written to take account of (and to criticise) neo-elitist approaches such as those of Bachrach and Baratz and Lukes.

Rex, J. and Tomlinson, S. (1979) *Colonial Immigrants in a British City,* London, Routledge and Kegan Paul.
In 1967, Rex published an influential study of blacks in the Sparkbrook area of Birmingham. In this follow-up, based on nearby Handsworth, he documents the systematic exclusion of blacks from jobs, housing and education and concludes, in far more pessimistic tones than in the earlier study, that a distinct 'black underclass' has formed which must now directly challenge white domination if its situation is to improve.

Scott, J. (1979) *Corporations, Classes and Capitalism,* London, Hutchinson.
Contains an informed critique of the notion that a managerial revolution has transformed British capitalism and backs up its arguments with much useful evidence on the composition and operation of major industrial and financial sectors of the economy.

Smith, D. (1977) *Racial Disadvantage in Britain,* Harmondsworth, Penguin.
The report on major research undertaken by the independent Political and Economic Planning Institute, into racial discrimination, particularly in employment and housing. Somewhat dry, but none the less important for that.

Stanworth, P. and Giddens, A. (eds) (1974) *Elites and Power in British Society,* London, Cambridge University Press.
Contains studies of various elite groups, all introduced by a useful general discussion of elites by Giddens.

Weber, M. (1946) *The Theory of Social and Economic Organisation,* New York, Macmillan.
A not-always-accurate, but readily available, translation of Volume I of Weber's major work, *Economy and Society.* Contains important extracts on class, power and bureaucracy, but the reader is advised to go to *Economy and Society* itself (if it is available) for a more faithful translation and for a more extensive presentation of Weber's work.

Wright Mills, C. (1956) *The Power Elite,* London, Oxford University Press.
Now something of a classic in American sociological studies of power, though the evidence is often flimsy and Mills' interpretation of that evidence is certainly questionable.

CHAPTER 7

Capitalism, Labourism, and the State

The capitalist class rules but does not govern

Karl Kautsky (1902) The Social Revolution, *London, Twentieth Century Press, p. 13*

Taken together, as they need to be, these three modes of explanation of the nature of the state – the character of its leading personnel, the pressures exercised by the economically dominant class, and the structural constraints imposed by the mode of production – constitute the Marxist answer to the question why the state should be considered as the 'instrument' of the 'ruling class'.

Ralph Miliband (1977) Marxism and Politics, *Oxford, Oxford University Press pp. 73–4.*

State power is not a machine or an instrument, a simple object coveted by the various classes; nor is it divided into parts which, if not in the hands of some, must automatically be in the hands of others: rather it is an ensemble of structures

Nicos Poulantzas (1973) Political Power and Social Classes, *London, New Left Books, p. 288.*

Marxism has represented one strand of thinking within the social sciences for over 100 years, yet for most of that time it has been a relatively minor and insignificant body of thought for most social scientists. Indeed, there have been periods when Marxism has almost slipped from sight altogether in Western social science. During the 1950s, for example, the 'Cold War', the McCarthy purges in the USA and an unprecedented period of growing and unbroken economic expansion and affluence all combined to convince most social scientists that Marxist theory had little left to offer to an analysis of mature capitalist societies. A spate of books was published at this time arguing that the crushing poverty and naked class exploitation which had been so apparent in European capitalist societies at the time when Marx was writing had been transcended following the Second World War, and even that capitalism itself was now giving way to a 'post-capitalist' era founded on full employment, a 'mixed economy' and a comprehensive welfare state. There was, it seemed, a new post-war consensus in society which was reflected in British politics in an accommodation between the two main political parties and which made all talk of 'class struggle' and 'class exploitation' appear anachronistic if not ludicrous.

From the mid-1960s onwards, however, such complacency was shattered, initially by a wave of civil unrest in virtually all major Western countries which culminated in massive demonstrations against the Vietnam war in America and in street battles in Paris in 1968 between the armed forces and radical workers and students, and later by the onset of an economic recession which swiftly reversed the growth and affluence of the previous decade and which defied all efforts by governments to reverse it.

Just as social science in the 1950s reflected the optimism of the societies it studied, so from the late 1960s it came to reflect the new problems which those societies were confronting. In discipline after discipline, theoretical orthodoxies which had become established in the post-war years were re-examined and found wanting. In political science, liberal-democratic theories of representative government came under sustained attack; in sociology, the cosy and generally conservative assumptions of functionalist theory crumbled under a widespread critical onslaught; and in economics, Keynesian strategies for fine-tuning the economy were increasingly questioned as both inflation and unemployment soared though the 1970s.

In all these disciplines, the new critics searched for alternatives to the theoretical orthodoxies which had failed them. Sometimes, as in the case of the 'overloaded government' thesis in political science (discussed in Chapter 3) or the rediscovery of monetarism in economics (discussed in Chapter 8) this involved a marked shift to the 'right' and the development of a hard-nosed 'realism' which attacked various aspects of liberal democracy and welfare capitalism as the basic causes of the problem. Others, however, developed a 'left' critique which involved the rediscovery and further refinement of Marxist theory. So it was that, by the early 1980s, the major social science disciplines had polarised just as British society itself had polarised, and at one of these polarities was to be found the long-neglected influence of Marxism.

MARXIST THEORY: ECONOMICS, POLITICS AND CLASS STRUGGLE

Like sociology, Marxism is concerned to analyse the ways in which different aspects of social organisation relate to each other. Although there are, of course, Marxist theories of politics, Marxist theories of economics and so on, Marxists themselves tend to deny the relevance of disciplinary labels, arguing that we can never understand any particular process in society unless we locate it within a broader analysis of the society as a whole. Disciplines such as political science and economics are therefore criticised on the grounds that it is impossible to explain policy-making by governments or economic decision-making by individuals and firms except through an analysis of the wider society in which governments and firms have to operate.

As we saw in Chapter 6, many sociologists make much the same sort of claim, and it is apparent from this that Marxist theories and sociological theorists are often to be found contesting the same terrain. Some Marxists argue that, in its approach to analysing society as a whole, sociology is fundamentally incompatible with Marxism and that Marxism alone can provide a 'scientific' analysis of how capitalist societies operate. Others, however, suggest that Marxism has, to a large extent, become fused with sociology in the sense that most sociological theorists are today influenced by Marx's writings (e.g. on the theory of social classes), and most serious Marxist works are similarly influenced by a broader sociological perspective.

It is not necessary here to enter into this debate about whether sociology and Marxism are or are not compatible, but it is important to note two points on which they do diverge in significant ways.

The first is that, unlike sociology or any other academic discipline, Marxism is both a claim to knowledge and a recipe for action. This is not to deny that the various social sciences may also reflect a desire for change on the part of those who research, write and teach within them, for most social scientists hold strong personal views about the sort of society they would wish to live in and the various ways in which this might be brought about. What is distinctive about Marxism is, however, that it is both a mode of scientific analysis of society and a political movement to change it. From Marx onwards, Marxist intellectuals have consistently sought to relate their theories and ideas to the current practices and strategies of working-class (generally Communist Party) movements. As Marx himself put it: 'The philosophers have only *interpreted* the word, in various ways; the point, however is to *change* it.' In this commitment to what Marxists themselves term 'praxis' (i.e. the fusion of theory and practice, and hence of intellectuals and workers), Marxism is distinctive, for none of the social sciences share this belief that a scientific analysis of society only has point in the context of a political struggle to transcend it.

The second way in which sociology and Marxism diverge is in the way in which they analyse society. What is distinctive about Marxism in this respect is that, notwithstanding the many different varieties and nuances of contemporary Marxist thought, it holds to the fundamental assertion that the way in which any society is organised and operates must reflect in some sense the way in which it organises its productive activities. If we are to understand contemporary Marxist analyses of British politics, we must begin by considering what is entailed in this basic axiom of Marx's theory.

Marx arrived at his conclusion that an understanding of the social organisation of production is the key to understanding the organisation of the rest of society by means of a two-step argument. First, he made the 'obvious' point that production is a prerequisite of social organisation. In other words, before a group of people can develop a means of governing themselves, systems of law by which to regulate themselves, religious practices, artistic forms or any other aspect of social organisation, they must first organise themselves to produce from their environment the basic necessities of life – the food, clothing, shelter and so on, which are necessary if they are to reproduce themselves. Indeed, Marx argued that what makes human beings unique in the animal world is their capacity consciously to work upon and change their environment. Beavers may build dams and birds their nests, but these activities are simply repeated across the generations. Human beings, by contrast, develop and change their world through their labour, as is evident in the fact that we no longer live in caves, eat our meat raw or rely on clubs and stones as our tools.

The second stage of the argument is that the way in which a group of people organise production will leave its imprint on the way in which they organise other aspects of their collective existence. Production, that is, is not simply prior to other activities but is fundamental in shaping these other activities. This idea has sometimes been expressed by means of an architectural metaphor, for just as the foundation of a building limits and affects the style and dimensions of the construction which is developed upon it, so too the organisation of production in a society constitutes a 'base' which limits and affects the 'superstructure' of government, law, religion, arts and so on which can develop from it.

The organisation of production in any society will, of course, depend to a great extent on the materials which are available in the environment and on the tools, skills and know-how which the members of that society have developed over the generations. It is hardly possible for a society to develop a factory system of production, for example, if it has not developed the tools and knowledge necessary for mining coal, smelting iron, generating power, and so on. Marx's argument goes much further than this, however, for he suggests that the productive forces which are available in any society at any one time will tend to shape the way in which productive activity is socially organised. In virtually all human societies up to the present, this organisation has involved a basic division between two classes of people; those who own the means of production and those who provide labour. The nature of the relationship between these two classes has, however, changed as the productive forces have been developed. On the great estates of ancient Rome, for example, the relationship was that of master and slave; in feudal Europe it was that between lord and serf; in contemporary capitalist societies it is that between capitalist and wage-labourer. As the productive forces have developed, so new relations of production have arisen.

Taken together, the 'productive forces' (i.e. the technology and materials used in production) and the 'relations of production' (i.e. the way in which productive activity is organised through a division between those who own the technology and materials and those who provide the labour) constitute the foundation or 'base' of any society. The 'superstructure' of law, politics and so on which then arises in that society will, in essence, reflect the character of this base. The argument is summarised in a famous passage written by Marx in 1859:

In the social production of their life, men [sic] enter into definite relations of production which . . . correspond to a definite stage of development of the material productive forces. The sum total of these relations of production constitutes the economic structure of society, the real foundation on which rises a legal and political superstructure and to which correspond definite forms of social consciousness.

Marx is, of course, aware that societies with a similar material base may develop different forms of government, different types of law, different cultural characteristics, and so on. Societies organised on the basis of capitalist relations of production, for example, have often varied in their forms of government – Britain has retained a constitutional monarchy, the USA has a Federal republic, Sweden exhibits an advanced form of social democracy, Germany under the Third Reich was dominated by a Fascist dictatorship, and so on. What is entailed in this claim, however, is first, that certain forms of government are not possible given a capitalist system of production, and second, that those forms that are possible are, in essence, variations on the same theme.

The argument that certain forms of government are ruled out by a particular system of production is based on the claim that no political system can survive for very long which fundamentally contradicts the essential requirements of the economic system on which it is based. For example, the feudal system of politics and law is essentially incompatible with a developed capitalist economy since capitalism is organised around a contractual relationship between employer and worker, in which both sides are in principle 'free' to seek alternatives in the market, while feudalism sought to bind lord and serf together through a legally enforceable system of mutual obligation. Neither capitalists nor workers would for long put up with a political system which denied the right of the former to lay off workers or the right of the latter to change their source of employment.

The argument that the forms of government which are possible in any mode of production all represent different variations on the same basic pattern, is based on the claim that the political system must reflect and sustain the prevailing relations of production in society. Thus, in a capitalist society, the role of the state – whether it takes the form of a constitutional monarchy, a Federal republic, a social democracy or a Fascist dictatorship – must always be the same; namely, to safeguard and promote capitalist production. If, over the long term, the state does not do this, then the economy itself will collapse and the state will collapse with it to be replaced by a new political system which better reflects the requirements of the economy at that time. It therefore follows that, in a capitalist society, the state must attempt to maintain the conditions in which capitalists can make profits, for without profits they cannot invest and without investment they cannot produce. So it is that, whether they be fascists, democrats or monarchists, those who run the machinery of government will in different ways (e.g. by shooting trade union leaders or by coming to agreements with them) be obliged to pursue policies which are in the long-term interests of the capitalist class.

The political system (and, indeed, the rest of the 'superstructure') of any society thus reflects the character of its economic organisation. Yet this economic organisation itself undergoes change over time. The mainspring of this change is the development of the productive forces. In feudal Europe, for example, the mode of production was based primarily on a labour-intensive system of agriculture which was organised through the system of serfdom by which those who owned the land allowed those who did not to farm a strip of land for their own subsistence in return for which they were obliged to render a specified amount of labour on the land retained by their overlord. This system was reinforced by a political system through which the landed nobility ruled the country in conjunction with the monarch, by a legal system through which the landed class was able to enforce the obligations owed them by the serfs, by a religious system which taught that such a mode of social organisation had been ordained by God, and so on. All of this was, however, gradually undermined from within by the development of new productive forces. New machines enabled the gradual development of a manufacturing sector. New forms of transport enabled the growth of markets for manufactures. Innovations in agricultural techniques reduced the reliance on human labour-power in the fields. These and other developments slowly brought about a new system of production based, not on the relation between lord and serf, but on that between industrial capitalist and wage-labourer. A new pattern of capitalist-production relations thus grew up side-by-side with the old system of feudal-production relations.

As the new capitalist mode of production matured within feudal society, so the old feudal relations of production, expressed through the feudal state, came to represent an intolerable blockage to its further development. The rising capitalist class required a free labour force but this was hindered by feudal relations of serfdom; they required venture capital yet usury was prohibited under feudal law and religion; they demanded a say in running the country but found their paths blocked by an hereditary system of government. Thus, a system which had at one time reinforced the old system of production was now holding the new one back, and revolution became inevitable. In country after country, whether peacefully or by violent means, the old ruling class of feudal landowners was overthrown to be replaced by a new political system which better reflected the requirements of the new dominant class of capitalists.

According to Marx, much the same process is now under way in capitalist societies. Indeed, the process has speeded up because capitalism has developed the productive forces much faster than in any previous period. This is because capitalism is based on competition for markets between different producers, each of whom is keen to undercut his or her competitors by investing in the newest labour-saving technology, and this provides an enormous stimulus to technological innovation. Yet, as in the feudal era, the more the productive forces are developed, the more they encounter the limits of the existing relations of production, and the more quickly they bring into existence the class (in this case, the proletariat) which will eventually lead the revolution against the dominant class. Thus today, our productive capacity is truly staggering yet a system of production in which nothing can be produced unless a profit can be realised from it has created a situation in which much of this capacity lies idle while basic human needs remain unfulfilled. Millions of workers in Britain are unemployed at the same time as desperate housing need goes unmet, the hospital service is crippled by lack of staff and factories containing millions of pounds worth of machinery are left to rot. For present-day Marxists, such evidence is indicative of the growing contradiction between the productive forces (which, they suggest, have developed to a point where we could meet the basic needs of everybody in society) and capitalist social relations (which prevent this technology from being used to bring about such a result), and this contradiction will, it is felt, eventually result in the revolutionary overthrow of the entire capitalist system by the proletariat.

The role of the state in all this is to attempt to safeguard the interests of the capitalist class (the 'bourgeoisie') as a whole, just as the feudal state represented the interests of the feudal landowners right up to the point at which it was overthrown. This does not mean that the state is simply manipulated by capitalists. Indeed, this would not be possible since the capitalist class is internally fragmented (individual producers compete with each other and there are fundamental conflicts of interest between different types of capitalists such as industrialists and financiers). The state, therefore, must act as the representative of the capitalist class as a whole, even if this means that at times it follows a course of action of which particular sections of the capitalist class strongly disapprove. The state is, in this sense, 'a committee for managing the *common* affairs of the *whole* bourgeoisie'.

As for the proletariat, it follows from this analysis that little can be achieved through the pursuit of political demands within the existing state system. Both Marx and Engels recognised that concessions could be won by the working class within a capitalist system of parliamentary democracy, and Engels even went so far as to suggest that an eventual socialist revolution in Britain could possibly come about through the electoral process, but in general both writers were adamant that the very nature of the capitalist state was such as to render parliamentary action largely ineffective. However it comes about, a proletarian revolution must involve the abolition of the state in its present form and its replacement by a form of political organisation, such as that of the ill-fated Paris Commune in 1871, which will be consistent with the development of socialist relations of production in which all producers own in common the productive resources of their society. Just as the capitalist class had to replace the feudal state apparatus with a 'bourgeois' system of representative government which would safeguard its class interests, so the proletariat must replace the capitalist state with a form of political organisation which expresses and reinforces the new socialised mode of production.

CAPITALIST DOMINATION OF THE BRITISH STATE

The obvious question to arise out of Marx's theory is how the state in a society such as that of Britain manages to safeguard the interests of the capitalist class. What is the mechanism by which this is achieved (assuming, of course, that it is achieved)? There is, in fact, considerable dispute within Marxism about how to answer this question, and as in the sociological work on power discussed in Chapter 6, so too, in Marxist work on the British state, there has been an unfortunate tendency for theoretical innovation to race ahead of our empirical knowledge about how the political system actually operates. Having said that, however, it is probably fair to suggest that Marxist work in this area has gone somewhat further than the elite studies managed to go.

Most Marxist analyses begin by drawing two important distinctions. The first (which we have already noted in earlier chapters) is that between the 'state' and the 'government'. The second is that between the 'state' and 'civil society'.

In his, by now, classic study of the British state (*The State in Capitalist Society*), Ralph Miliband warns against any confusion between the terms 'state' and 'government'. The government, he says, is just one among several institutions which together make up the system of state power, and while the government is the public face and official voice of the state, it is not necessarily its most powerful or significant element. To gain control of the government (e.g. by winning a general election) is no guarantee of gaining control of the state. Thus, in addition to government, the state system also comprises what we have termed the 'secret state': a vast system of administration (including the civil service, the public corporations and nationalised industries, the Bank of England etc.), the military and the police force, and the judiciary, as well as the system of local and regional authorities, and the representative assemblies such as the Houses of Parliament. Any analysis of the operation of the British state must, therefore, encompass all of these interrelated institutions.

What such an analysis must also accomplish, however, is the identification of the relationship between these state institutions and the wider society from which they are, in a sense, 'set apart'. As we saw in Chapter 6 in the discussion of Weber's work, there is no necessary and direct relationship in capitalist societies between economic power and state power. In earlier societies such as those of feudal Europe or ancient Rome, those who owned the means of production also 'owned' the state in that there was a direct relationship between one's social position (e.g. as a member of the landed aristocracy) and one's political position. In these societies, the state was in the hands of just one class whose members alone enjoyed the right to develop policies and make laws. The relation between economic and political domination was thus clear and unambiguous, for the two were synonymous. This is not the case, however, in modern capitalist societies such as Britain where there is a formal separation between state power and 'civil society' and where political representation is organised, not on the basis of one's class membership, but according to a principle of one citizen, one vote.

Taken together, these distinctions between 'government', 'state' and 'society' help to define the basic problem to which all Marxist analyses of British politics have been addressed: how does the capitalist class in Britain ensure that the state operates in its collective long-term interests when the state itself is made up of a number of different and partially autonomous institutions, and when those institutions are formally set apart from any exclusive control by those who own the means of production? How can a single class, the members of which represent only a small minority of the total population, ensure that popularly-elected governments pursue policies which favour it, that appointed 'independent' judges interpret laws in its favour, that administrators adopt practices which take account of it, that the police and armed forces are used to protect it and so on?

Some of the 'classical' statements of Marxist political theory suggest that the capitalist class in some way directly controls the various arms of the state in just the same way as earlier ruling classes have controlled earlier forms of states. There are traces of such an argument in Engels' view that: 'The state is nothing but a machine for the oppression of one class by another.' And in Lenin's assertion that: 'The state is a particular form of organisation of force; it is the organisation of violence for the purpose of holding down some class.' Such stark statements are, however, less common in the contemporary Marxist literature where it is recognised that the state is not simply a tool to be manipulated at will by those who own the means of production, but rather operates to some extent autonomously while at the same time safeguarding the fundamental interests of the capitalist class.

Perhaps the clearest exposition of this rather more subtle position is that provided by Miliband who suggests: 'While the state does act, in Marxist terms, *on behalf* of the ruling class, it does not for the most part act *at its behest.*' He identifies three basic mechanisms by which this comes about.

The occupancy of key state positions

Drawing on much of the literature discussed in Chapters 5 and 6, Miliband argues that one reason why a formally autonomous state generally operates on behalf of the capitalist class is that its key positions are held by members of that class or by others whose outlooks are broadly compatible with the interests of capitalists.

This argument is perhaps at its weakest when applied to the elected institutions of the state – Parliament, government and local councils – for the growth of the Labour Party during the twentieth century has brought into leading political positions men and women who, if not fully representative of the mass of the population in terms of their backgrounds, are hardly drawn from traditional capitalist families either. Miliband, of course, is aware of this, but argues that at least three factors can be identified which suggest that representation of non-capitalist interests in elected agencies of the state has done little to undermine capitalist interests.

The first is that Parliament, and elected assemblies at the local level, are weak and have become progressively weaker as time has gone on such that very little power is vested in ordinary elected members. The second is that radicals have successfully been held in check within these assemblies and within government – the radical MP at Westminster finds herself or himself cut off from the support of rank and file activists and subject to the intense pressures towards conforming with established parliamentary procedures and ways of thinking, while left-wing socialists in local authorities are more in touch with radical activists but find themselves at the mercy of central government dictates and financing (see Chapter 11). The third is that one major political party (the Conservatives) is generally predisposed to favour the interests of capital while the other (the Labour Party) has been reluctant to confront them and has preferred to pursue a mildly reformist strategy in which the continuation of capitalism is never seriously questioned. The result has been that the alternation of governments between different parties has had little fundamental impact on capitalist relations of production.

Nevertheless, Miliband does recognise that the elected agencies of the state do sometimes respond to popular pressures and aspirations expressed through the ballot box or through lobbying and other organised activities. Indeed, he suggests that the stability of the system as a whole depends upon this ability of governments to make concessions to groups other than the capitalist class in that this helps to contain pressure from below and to keep it within manageable limits. The other institutions of the state, of course, are not subject to these diverse and competing pressures, and he suggests that it is their task to ensure that elected governments do not stray too far from an orthodox pro-capitalist line:

'Universal suffrage brings a government to office: the rest of the state system sees to it that the consequences are not so drastic as to affect conservative continuity.'

Drawing on various sociological studies of elite recruitment, he shows that the top civil servants, the police and military leaders, the judiciary and other groups such as those in control of the media who are in a position to influence public opinion all are drawn from bourgeois backgrounds or else are socialised into bourgeois values through their schooling and their advancement up the career hierarchies. His argument here, of course, is only as strong as the data on which he relies, and as we have seen in Chapter 6, these studies are severely limited in that they have rarely provided evidence to show what Miliband claims they show – namely, that all these people subscribe to a 'narrow' range of political values from 'moderate Labour' at one extreme to 'reactionary Conservative' at the other. Nevertheless, we can probably safely assume that for most of them this is indeed the case, if only because most people in the country as a whole fit into much the same continuum, which is perhaps not as 'narrow' as Miliband tries to make out.

Miliband's first argument, then, is that governments generally seek to support capitalist interests and that, when there is the slightest danger that popular pressure might blow them off course, the remainder of the state apparatus, staffed by solidly conservative individuals, will bring them back into line. Disappointingly, he gives little actual evidence for such assertions, but this perhaps does not matter too much since this first argument is probably the least significant of the three he develops to support his thesis.

The political power of business interests

We saw in Chapter 3 that pluralist interpretations of British politics emphasise the range of diverse pressures, organised through shifting alliances and coalitions of interests, to which the government and other elected agencies, such as local authorities, are constantly subject. Miliband does not deny this. Nor, indeed, does he deny that organised labour is often prominent among pressure groups in Britain, for he notes that no government can afford simply to ignore organisations such as the trade unions and the TUC which claim to represent the interests of millions of workers. What he does deny, however, is the assumption which is often implicit in pluralist theories that the different interests which pressure government and other state agencies are of comparable power, and the assertion in such theories that no one interest routinely prevails over a range of policy issues. There is, he suggests, a competition for the ear of government, but it is a one-sided competition in which the rules are biased, the referee is biased and the favoured side – big business – enjoys a goal start. Big business, in other words, is a uniquely influential pressure group in Britain.

The arguments and evidence which Miliband puts forward to support this view are mostly familiar. Business, he points out, is the wealthiest of all organised interests in society, and this has at times enabled it to mount very expensive campaigns such as those in the 1950s against steel nationalisation and in the 1970s against rather half-hearted Labour Party proposals to take the major banks into public ownership. It is also a major source of funding for the Conservative Party and can generally rely on the strong support of many MPs, a substantial majority in the House of Lords, most of the national and provincial press and even the Royal Family whose members have increasingly taken to making pronouncements in favour of private enterprise. Business also exerts a pervasive yet virtually invisible influence over state institutions by virtue of its strategic importance in controlling production, for all governments know that their programmes and their survival depend on continued investment and growth in the private sector. No government can single-mindedly pursue policies which result in a loss of business confidence; a run on the pound, a shift in the balance of payments and a quiet word of advice from the Governor of the Bank of England will normally suffice to encourage governments to drop those policies which threaten to undermine capitalist profitability. Where this is not enough, British capitalists can always rely on pressures from overseas to bring British Governments to heel; the International Monetary Fund effectively buried the Labour Government's social programme in 1976 by imposing conditions of financial orthodoxy on a loan which it granted at that time, and together with other international agencies such as the European Economic Community (discussed in Chapter 11), pressures from other governments, and the impact of decisions taken by international currency speculators, multi-national corporations and the like, such external influence and control works strongly against any moves which are liable to threaten levels of profitability or the sanctity of private property.

Such arguments are indeed strong ones and, paradoxically perhaps, they appear all the stronger at times of economic recession when the power of organised labour is weakened by unemployment (as unemployment grew through 1981, for example, male trade union membership fell by a staggering 8 per cent) and the pressure to 'revitalise the economy' by adopting policies favourable to big business is almost irresistible. As the influential Marxist and Labour Party activist Harold Laski noted during the Great Depression of the 1930s, popular pressures for social reform and improved living standards can often be accommodated during periods of economic growth, but at times of economic contraction, governments' responsiveness to democratically articulated demands must take second place to the need to increase private-sector profits.

For many Marxists, however, the clearest evidence for the continued and highly successful pressure brought to bear by big business upon the state concerns the fiscal policies of successive British Governments. In a book published in 1961, Sam Aaronovitch argued that 'finance capital' (by which he meant the major banking and industrial companies which he saw as fused through their interlocking directorships) constituted the British 'ruling class', and as evidence for this he pointed to the long-standing commitment of both Conservative and Labour administrations to maintaining the overseas value of the pound sterling and keeping a strong overall balance of payments. Finance capital, he suggested, seeks to invest in areas of highest potential return, and these have often been overseas in countries where labour is cheaper and pickings are richer. In order to pursue such investments, big business desires first, full convertibility of currencies to allow it to change its pounds into whatever local currency is needed for its overseas investments; second, a liberal system of exchange controls to allow it to export as much money as it wishes; third, a strong pound so that its profits do not decrease in value when it converts its overseas earnings back into sterling; and fourth, an equilibrium or surplus on the balance of payments to cover the drain of money going overseas and thereby avoid any devaluation of the currency. 'In all this', he concludes, 'it has been evident that the state apparatus has been occupied with furthering the aims of finance capital. The Treasury, the Board of Trade and Cabinet have shared the same views as "the City".'

Subsequent events and later analyses have both supported Aaronovitch's basic argument. As we shall see in Chapter 8, for example, the Labour Government elected in 1964 was so committed to maintaining the value of the pound that it struggled for 3 years to avoid the devaluation which had to come given the declining competitiveness of British industry in overseas markets, and during this time, most of its social and economic programme was sacrificed to this end. Throughout the post-war period, governments have confronted balance of payments crises which have been caused by massive outflows of money to finance overseas investments, and invariably they have responded by cutting domestic demand in an attempt to reduce imports rather than by cutting overseas spending.

This predisposition on the part of British Governments to support major financial interests has never been clearer than under the Conservative Governments from 1979 onwards. One of the government's first acts following its election in 1979 was to abolish all exchange controls, and this resulted in a flood of money overseas (overseas investment increased ten-fold in 4 years). Throughout most of its early years in office, it also pursued a policy of high interest rates which attracted overseas money into London and thus maintained a relatively strong pound, but at the cost of reducing domestic demand (since people could not afford credit to buy goods) and domestic investment (since small- and medium-sized firms could not afford to borrow to finance new developments), and thereby causing a wave of bankruptcies among smaller entrepreneurs and a massive increase in the rate of unemployment.

Those who have benefited from such policies have been the big companies which can seize overseas investment opportunities and which do not need to borrow on the British market. Those who have lost have been the smaller companies whose products have been priced out of world markets by an over-valued pound and who rely on domestic borrowing to finance their expansion. Such evidence points strongly to the validity of Miliband's assertion that big business has generally been able to secure from government commitments which support its financial interests, even at the cost of further weakening an already crippled home economy.

The constraints of a capitalist system

The third and final factor cited by Miliband to explain why and how the state in Britain comes to be subordinated to the requirements of major capitalist interests echoes the argument concerning 'non-decision-making' introduced at the end of Chapter 6. It is also the most significant of the three factors he discusses, for even if the people who occupy the key positions in the state system were radicalised overnight and big business pressure were to cease, this third factor alone would ensure a continuing bias towards capital, for the main reason that the interests of big capital are safeguarded by the state is simply that the state is charged with administering a system which itself generates a continuing advantage to those who own the means of production. For as long as those who control the state take as given the continuation of a system based on the capitalist organisation of production, capitalist interests will continue to be the main beneficiaries.

Miliband notes that political leaders, media commentators and others often tacitly equate business interests with the 'national interest', assuming that what is good for business is also good for Britain as a whole. This, he suggests, is no simple delusion, for, given a capitalist system, the whole society does indeed depend on the vitality of the private sector. If capital does not continue to make profit, then investment will fall away, unemployment will rise and government will lose the tax revenue on which it depends in order to finance schools, hospitals, defence and all other policies. When politicians and others tell the electorate that we must 'tighten our belts', accept cuts in public services, see our wages reduced and curb the tendency to strike in order that business may increase its profits, they are simply expressing the logic of a system of production in which profits must be sustained if economic activity is to continue. When Mrs Thatcher repeated time and again to the unemployed, and to those reliant on declining public services and provisions, that there was no alternative to her policies, she was appealing to this same logic, for if business must make profit before it will produce, and if profits are being eroded by 'high' wages, 'high' taxes and a surplus of 'inefficient' labour, then it does indeed follow that wages must be driven down, government spending must be reduced and workers must be made redundant – if the system itself is taken as given.

Clearly, the question of who is in control of the state and of which groups are most able to pressurise them will make some difference to how governments respond to the requirements of capital. Labour and Conservative administrations for example, may be expected to respond more or less enthusiastically and with lesser or greater coercion to the dictates of capitalist profitability. At the end of the day, however, it seems that the values, wishes and concerns of those who run the state count for very little: as Miliband concludes: 'The trouble does not lie in the wishes and intentions of power-holders, but in the fact that the reformers...are the prisoners, and usually the willing prisoners, of an economic and social framework which necessarily turns their reforming proclamations, however sincerely meant, into verbiage.'

It is in the analysis of this system of constraints that Marxist work is most distinctive. Miliband's first two factors – the identity of those who run the system and the relative power of different organised interests which influence it from the outside – have also been examined in work which is by no means Marxist in its orientation. One does not have to accept any of Marx's arguments concerning the inevitability of class struggle and the primacy of the economy to recognise the significance of the narrowness of recruitment into key state positions or of the wealth and contacts enjoyed by business organisations. As we have seen in earlier chapters, such issues have been thoroughly chewed over by sociologists and political scientists, and the disagreements between elitists and pluralists revolve around the question of how significant such factors are in shaping government policies. Where Marxist political analysis makes its major contribution (and where it also moves right away from the assumptions on which both elitists and pluralists develop their arguments) in in the recognition that the major explanation for what happens in the political system may lie, not in what individuals in that system do, but in the economic constraints which a capitalist system of production places on their actions. In this way, the focus of analysis shifts from politics to the economy and from individual actions to system constraints – a shift which reflects Marx's argument that the political 'superstructure' is in some way dependent upon the economic 'base' which sustains it and from which it derives.

Such a shift of focus raises again the problem first identified at the end of Chapter 6 concerning the point at which the power of individuals ends and the constraints of the system begin. How much scope for action does a Prime Minister, a top civil servant or the head of a nationalised industry have in shaping the future course of events? How much difference does it really make whether the country is governed by a right-wing Conservative or a reforming Labour administration? Do the requirements of a capitalist economic system effectively preclude any but the most minor of political changes? Such questions go to the very heart of Marxist analysis in that they refer to the nature of the relationship between economic and political organisation. Just how determinate is the 'determinate' relationship between economics and politics? Can the political system operate to some extent autonomously of the economic system and if so, what degree of discretion do political leaders enjoy when it comes to shaping policies?

Miliband himself is rather unclear on all this. He insists that the state is not totally constrained by the capitalist system in which it operates, that individuals in key positions do have some power to shape events independently of the compelling logic of the system in which they find themselves, and that the state cannot simply therefore be seen as the instrument of those who own the means of production. Those who control the state enjoy some degree of freedom in deciding how best to serve the interests of the capitalist class, and their decisions may not always meet with the approval of that class. They may, furthermore, sometimes pay attention to groups other than the capitalist class and make concessions to their demands even where this runs counter to the immediate interests of capital (e.g. by increasing trade union rights or by providing services which involve increased taxation on profits):

> The state and those who were acting on its behalf did not always intervene for the specific purpose of helping capitalism, much less of helping capitalists for whom power-holders...have often had much contempt and dislike. The question is not one of purpose or attitude but of 'structural constraints'; or rather that purposes and attitudes, which can make *some* difference, and in special circumstances a considerable difference, must nevertheless take careful account of the socio-economic system which forms the context of the political system and of state action.

What remains unclear in this passage, however, is how much is 'some' difference, and what are the 'special circumstances' in which 'some' difference becomes 'considerable'? How are we to recognise a situation in which power-holders may be deemed responsible for the outcomes of the policies they have pursued?

In part, the problem here reflects a confusion over the notion of 'constraints', for it is important to distinguish 'structural constraints', (about which we can literally do nothing) and 'rational constraints' (which prevent us from doing anything given the values and beliefs we hold). Rational constraints clearly do not absolve the individual of responsibility for his or her actions, for in this case a choice of action is available even though the individual concerned may consider only one alternative acceptable. The distinction between the two notions of 'constraint' is never clear in Miliband's work, however, for although he talks of political leaders as 'willing prisoners' of the capitalist system, he shrinks away from analysing the extent to which they are willing and the extent to which they are prisoners.

In part too, the problem reflects a lack of good empirical research by Marxists on what the British state actually does. Thus one way of deciding whether those who run the state are responsible for any given outcome is to investigate instances where they have attempted to fly in the face of system constraints. It may, of course, be difficult to find such instances given Miliband's assertion that no Labour Government has ever been totally committed to carrying through a socialist programme – i.e. the constraints have never been fully tested. Be this as it may, there have been governments, in Britain and abroad, which have changed capitalist societies in rather important ways – the post-war Attlee government is one example, and (albeit in a very different sense) the 1979 Thatcher Government is another. The Attlee administration nationalised large sectors of the economy while the Thatcher administration has privatised others; the former created a network of welfare provisions which the latter set about systematically dismantling; and so on. The question is whether and to what extent the condition of the British economy in 1945 and in the early 1980s necessitated such changes, and Miliband's analysis makes it almost impossible to provide an answer.

There is, in all of Miliband's books, a failure to grapple with the relationship between power and constraint, autonomy and determinism, active choices and imperatives. The result, when he does consider what particular governments have done, is that he shifts inconsistently and unpredictably between blaming the individuals and blaming the system, at one point attributing the failings of socialist governments to the 'ideological dispositions' of those who ran them, and at another denying that people's beliefs and values are of any great significance. This also means that we are left with few indications as to whether a socialist transformation of British society is possible on the basis of a parliamentary strategy. In his book on *Capitalist Democracy in Britain* for example, he recognises that no extra-parliamentary revolutionary strategy is open, asserts that a parliamentary road to socialism is 'a very unlikely prospect', yet concludes that 'a strong and unambiguous political force on the left is . . . indispensible for the achievement of great economic and social changes'. How such change is to be brought about remains a mystery, not least to Miliband himself. Marxist 'praxis', it seems, has here ground to a halt.

THE RELATIVE AUTONOMY OF THE STATE

One response to such problems from within recent Marxist theory has been to deny altogether the significance of individuals in politics. According to this view, which was most fully elaborated from the late 1960s onwards by a Greek Marxist, Nicos Poulantzas, the personalities of Prime Ministers, the club memberships of Cabinet ministers, the prejudices of judges and the maze of informal contacts between business and political leaders cannot explain the inherent class bias in the operation of the capitalist state. It is to the system, and not the individuals within it, that we should look if we seek to understand why the state operates in the long-term interests of big corporate capital. Put another way, the constraints on individuals are overwhelmingly 'structural' in character such that they can do little other than fall in line with the logic of the system.

In an intermittent, but protracted, debate with Miliband in the pages of the Marxist journal, *New Left Review,* Poulantzas suggested that the evidence cited by Miliband concerning the class backgrounds of those who run the state should be seen, not as the cause but as the effect of class bias in the state's mode of operation. It is because it is a capitalist state that it tends to be staffed by people sympathetic to the capitalist class, not vice-versa. In this way, Poulantzas echoed Marx himself when he wrote in the preface to the first volume of *Capital*

I do not by any means depict the capitalist and the landowner in rosy colours. But individuals are dealt with here only in so far as they are the personifications of economic categories, the bearers of particular class relations and interests. My standpoint...can less than any other make the individual responsible for relations whose creature he [sic] remains.

Individuals, in other words, are 'slotted into' already existing sets of social relations which they can do little to change. Capitalists, whether they be altruistic Quakers or grasping tycoons, must still act as capitalists, for they are part of a system of production which demands that they keep their labour costs down by cutting wages if they can and by investing in machines that throw their employees out of work, no matter how unhappy they may be about doing these things. Similarly, those who occupy positions within the state are also part of this same system and, whether they be tories or socialists, this means that they are obliged to follow the logic of that system in what they do.

For Poulantzas, therefore, individuals are merely agents of the system in which they find themselves. They 'personify' this system in that they are the means through which the system operates. To understand why they do what they do, it follows that we should not investigate their personal motives for action, but rather the nature of the system of which their actions are merely the expression.

Poulantzas begins his analysis of the system by distinguishing between capitalist societies as they actually exist (what he terms 'social formations') and a theoretical abstract model of a 'pure' capitalist system (which he terms a 'capitalist mode of production'). He suggests that a pure capitalist mode of production would consist of three interrelated sub-systems or 'levels' – an economic system, a political system and a system of ideology. In a purely capitalist economy there would be only two classes, capitalists and workers, for capitalism is a system of wage labour in which those who own the factories, banks, shops and offices make profits through the direct or indirect exploitation of those who sell their labour-power in return for a wage. In a capitalist political system, the role of the state would be to regulate the system as a whole in order to maintain the conditions in which this system of wage labour could function, and in the ideological system, institutions such as schools, churches and the mass media would function in order to legitimate this system of wage labour.

Now Poulantzas recognises that actual societies are more messy and confused than this model suggests. This is because different countries with different histories all represent a mixture of different 'modes of production' – no country is purely capitalist. In France, for example, there is still a substantial independent peasantry, a legacy from an earlier pre-capitalist period. Similarly in Britain there is still a landed aristocracy and a monarchy which became established during the feudal era. All countries also contain people such as independent craft workers and the self-employed – groups which arose out of the transition from feudalism to capitalism and which are neither purely capitalist nor purely proletarian. Nowhere, therefore, is the economy organised on purely capitalist lines, and this is reflected in the political and ideological systems of these countries (an obvious example in Britain being the continued existence of the House of Lords and the persistence of aristocratic festivals such as Henley and Ascot).

Although a country like Britain contains elements and traces of several different 'modes of production', Poulantzas nevertheless argues that it is predominantly capitalist in which case the abstract model of a pure capitalist mode of production is the best way of analysing how the system works.

According to this model, the three 'levels' of the system – the economic, the political and the ideological – are related in such a way that what happens in one will affect what happens in the other two. Poulantzas is keen to escape from the traditional and, in his view, over-simplistic notion in Marxist theory that the organisation of the 'economic base' determines what goes on in the 'superstructure' of the state and ideology. He recognises that the organisation of the economy will influence the way in which the three levels operate and relate to each other – in a feudal system, for example, the ideological level will have a particularly important part to play because the economic organisation of serfdom is so blatantly biased towards the landowners that institutions such as the church will be crucial in justifying this to those who suffer from it. But having said this, he insists that each of the three levels has its own autonomy. Thus, what the state does in a capitalist society will certainly be influenced by economic factors, but developments at the level of the economy will not lead directly to political responses. Furthermore, political developments themselves may to some extent take on their own momentum and this will, in turn, influence the organisation of the economy.

All of this sounds very complex, but the basic idea is simple enough. In Britain, for example, the state has, in recent years, obviously been affected by the decline of profitability in the economy, but the economic problems faced by capitalist firms have not led directly to the adoption of particular policies demanded by capitalists. From the mid-1960s onwards, British Governments have tackled economic problems in a variety of ways. We have had controls on incomes and prices, both compulsory and voluntary, and the abandonment of such controls. Firms have been nationalised and privatised, company profits have been bolstered by grants and weakened by taxation, the state has bought shares in some companies and sold shares in others, interest rates have been held down or pushed up, and so on. What all this shows is first, that the actions of the state cannot simply be deduced from the nature of the economy; second, that the state is clearly influenced by factors other than the demands of capitalists; third, that different sections of the capitalist class will be more or less pleased or displeased with what the state does at any one time; and fourth, that the actions of the state are not simply a response to economic developments but themselves influence the future course of those developments. The political system is, in other words, *relatively autonomous* of the economy and hence of the dominant economic class.

According to Poulantzas, a relationship of 'relative autonomy' between the economic and political levels, and hence between big capital and the state, is a necessary feature of capitalist societies if the state is to perform the function required of it by the system of which it forms a part. As we have already seen, the function of the political level in the capitalist mode of production is to regulate the system as a whole, to smooth out problems which may arise to threaten future profitability. The major problem, of course, arises out of the perpetual conflict between capitalists and workers. These two classes are tied together in an inherently antagonistic relationship. They need each other, for capitalists need workers to supply the labour-power to run their machines, and workers need capitalists to supply the means of production for them to work with. Yet this mutual dependency is founded on a relationship of exploitation in which capitalists try to keep wages down so as to maximise the profit which they can extract from their employees' labour, while workers will constantly seek to retain in wages as much as they can of the value which they have created for their employers through their labour. Class struggle between the two is thus inscribed in the very fabric of capitalist societies and is reflected all the time in all areas of life – in wage negotiations and strikes, in worker absenteeism and 'skiving', in political elections, in the pages of the press and the studios of the television companies, in pulpits, in classrooms, in supermarkets, in leisure pursuits.

It is the state's role, not to eliminate class struggle (for this is impossible), but to regulate it, to keep it within manageable proportions and to head off any direct challenge to the system of production. Such regulation is only possible if the state has some degree of autonomy from the dominant class, for it needs room for manoeuvre, scope for flexibility. Given this relative autonomy, the state is then able to do two things.

First, it can work in a coherent way on behalf of capitalist interests which are themselves fragmented and lacking in cohesion, and in this way ensure that the long-term interests of the class are safeguarded even if in the short-term certain members of that class are unhappy about the decisions being taken. Second, it can work to disorganise the working class, to bring about divisions where none previously existed and to wrong-foot working-class demands for change by making short-term concessions which defuse conflict and buy off those whose complaints are loudest. And precisely because the state does sometimes act against the short-term interests of one or other section of the capitalist class and does sometimes make concessions to working class demands, it is able to represent itself as neutral, as the voice of the people as a whole – in short, as a responsive liberal-democratic state in a pluralist society.

The question which all this raises, of course, is, how does it do it? We have already seen that Poulantzas dismisses as insignificant any analysis which focuses on individuals as the causes of state action, so where is the mechanism by which the state acts to ensure that the long-term conditions of capitalist profitability are safeguarded? It is one thing to identify the 'function' which the state 'must' perform in a capitalist system, but quite another to identify the mechanism which ensures that this function will in fact be discharged.

For Poulantzas, the mechanism is class struggle. Indeed, he argues, in a way which may initially seem puzzling, that the state is not a 'thing' which can be controlled by individuals, but is rather the expression of the relation between classes at any one time. In saying this, he is not of course denying that state institutions – the civil service, Parliament and the rest – exist, but is simply suggesting that what these institutions do will reflect the relative strengths of workers and capitalists in the society as a whole at any given time. Thus, at times when the working class is relatively strong and its demands cannot be ignored, state policies will reflect this strength (e.g. through the introduction of social reforms, a liberalisation of trade union law, improvements in the quality of welfare services, action to curb some of the worst excesses of landlords or employers, and so on). At times when the working class is relatively weak, however, such measures will be reversed or diluted in order to bolster capitalist profitability. By responding in this way, fundamental challenges to the capitalist system itself are headed off and the long-term security of that system is safeguarded at the cost of short-term concessions on the part of the capitalist class, or sections of it.

This argument can be illustrated with reference to the years between 1974 and 1980 in Britain. Despite a deepening recession, the working class in Britain was still relatively strong in 1974 and groups of workers (notably the miners) were able to resist government attempts to hold down wages. This resistance came to a head in the miners' strike of that year when coal deliveries to power stations were successfully disrupted to a point where the rest of industry was forced onto a 3-day working week.

The Prime Minister at that time, Edward Heath, called an election and was defeated, and for 2 years after that, the Labour administration which replaced him presided over a 'wages explosion' coupled with a spate of reforms in favour of workers in general and organised labour in particular. By 1976, however, the crisis of profitability (which was exacerbated by these reforms) had reached a point at which, pressured by the International Monetary Fund, the Labour Government began to reduce public spending and introduced a new supposedly 'voluntary' incomes policy. By this time, worker militancy had successfully been bought off, and by 1978/9, when various groups of low-paid workers attempted to force an improvement in wages through strike action, rising unemployment had severely weakened the unions to a point at which they could no longer force concessions. With the return of a Conservative Government in 1979, the resurgence of the capitalist class took on a new impetus as wages were further reduced and unemployment rose in an attempt to restore profitability while the state reduced taxation on companies by dismantling large areas of welfare provision.

This example, while illustrating Poulantzas's argument that the state is an expression of class relations rather than of the motives of those who control it, also serves to point to some of the major difficulties in applying his analysis. Four points in particular may be noted.

1   The argument is circular. If the relative power of the two main classes is held to be the cause of state actions, then we clearly need to be able to assess when the working class is strong and when it is weak. The only way in which we can do this, however, is by looking at what the state does. Thus, for example, the judgement that the working class was strong in 1974–76 depends entirely on the fact that concessions were being made to it during this period, but it could presumably equally be argued that the working class was weak and that a Labour Government chose to protect and strengthen it! It seems difficult if not impossible to find evidence to suppport the view that class struggle causes state outcomes rather than the other way round.

2   The argument is tautologous. To argue that the state is 'relatively autonomous' of the dominant economic class is to have your cake and eat it since such an argument can never be disproved. Evidence that the state has acted in the interests of the working class can be 'explained' in terms of the 'autonomy' which it enjoys, while evidence that the capitalist class has benefited can be 'explained' by the fact that this autonomy is only 'relative'. Poulantzas fails to provide any criteria by means of which his theory can be tested empirically; it is true by definition and therefore of limited use in trying to understand any given example of state action.

3   The argument is incomplete. We have seen that Poulantzas argues that the function of the state in a capitalist system must be to safeguard the interests of the dominant economic class in the long run. The mechanism by which this function comes to be carried out is class

struggle. But on what ground are we to believe that class struggle (the cause) will always lead in the end to the reassertion of capitalist interests (the effect)? It is plausible, as the example of the 1974–80 period shows, to suggest that working-class strength may lead to reforms which reduce working-class militancy and thus pave the way for the reassertion of capitalist interests. But surely it is equally plausible to suggest that working-class strength may lead to reforms which strengthen that class's resolve to go for even more reforms leading eventually to the transcendence of capitalism itself. Poulantzas fails to show any necessary connection between the cause and the effect posited by his theory. This, we would suggest, is an inevitable failing of any theory which refuses to take account of individuals' actions for 'the system' simply does not work mechanically, and the way in which the state responds to a shifting balance of class relations will depend crucially on the values and beliefs of those taking the decisions. To deny that it will make any significant difference whether Margaret Thatcher or Tony Benn is Prime Minister or whether the Cabinet and the back-benches are filled with old Etonians or Trotskyist members of the Militant Tendency is as absurd as the elitist argument that such people can do exactly what they want without taking into account the economic context in which they make their decisions. The problem with Miliband's analysis, it will be recalled, was not that he asserted the importance of both people and the system but that he failed to give any clue about how their relative importance might be assessed. To respond to this problem by denying that people have any importance is to duck the issue rather than resolve it.

4 The argument is too narrow. The causal element in political analysis is, for Poulantzas, class struggle. When we consider any particular period in British politics, however, it is immediately obvious (as we saw in Chapter 6) that many other groups, apart from capital and labour, are involved in struggle and that many issues other than questions of wages or union reform or taxation, come to dominate political argument. Poulantzas himself recognises this and attempts to argue that all political movements in some way 'represent' the major class interests in society even though they are not organised directly on class lines. Such an argument is, however, unsupportable. From the 1970s onwards in Britain, many issues have surfaced in the political system which simply cannot be analysed through the categories of Marxist class theory. The civil war in Northern Ireland has involved, not capitalists and workers, but Catholics and Protestants, Republicans and Loyalists. The resurgence of nuclear disarmament as an issue cannot be understood through an analysis of the conflict between capital and labour, nor can many issues concerning the rights of women or blacks or youth. One response by Marxists to this problem has been to assert that the state or the capitalist class has in some way engineered such divisions in order to set worker against worker and thus blind the working class as a whole to its shared interests and common political aims. Such an argument is, however,

arrogant and involves a surprisingly derogatory view of working-class people who, it is assumed, are too dulled by ruling-class ideological manipulation to see where their true interests lie. Class *is* a crucially important factor in British politics, but this does not allow us to represent all political conflicts as in some way class-based.

The major problem in Poulantzas's work stems from his refusal to accept that individuals do make a difference to the way in which the system works. Miliband is right: we cannot understand why the state does what it does unless we take account of both the system of which it forms a part and the individuals who run it and influence its decisions and day-to-day operations. The problem in Miliband's work is that he gives no indication of the extent to which 'power-holders' are constrained by the system, but this is a problem which can only be overcome through detailed analysis of different examples of state activity (such as those discussed in the chapters that follow). It is no solution at all to emphasise the constraints to such an extent that 'power-holders' disappear out of the analysis altogether as is the case in Poulantzas's writings.

CAPITALISM, SOCIALISM AND LIBERAL DEMOCRACY

The ideas and arguments developed by Marxist theorists such as Poulantzas are often very dense and very abstract – sometimes to the point where they defy understanding altogether. Clearly, work like this is unlikely to be read much outside of a small circle of like-minded intellectuals. Nevertheless, despite its opacity, such work has been important in shaping or influencing political movements, for as we saw earlier, Marxists generally claim to marry together a scientific analysis of how capitalist society operates with a political guide to transcending it. Poulantzas himself, for example, was a member of the French Communist Party and much of his writing was addressed implicitly or explicitly to debates within the Party during the 1970s concerning electoral strategy, the need to build alliances, the nature of the support base for the Party, and so on.

Seen in this light, the arguments we have been discussing in this chapter have been crucial in informing socialist and communist thinking and strategy in continental Europe and, to some extent, in Britain as well. Of particular significance here has been the issue of whether the actions of the state are best explained with reference to the individuals who run it or the wider capitalist system of which it forms a part. If you believe that the state benefits the capitalist class mainly because it is controlled on the whole by members of that class then it is perfectly plausible to suggest that the state can be used to benefit other groups once these key individuals are replaced (e.g. through elections). If, on the other hand, you believe that the state simply reflects the logic of the system of which it forms a part, then it follows that a change of personnel will achieve nothing until the wider system itself is overthrown.

These, in essence, are the two polar positions around which much of the political argument within Marxism over the last hundred years has taken place. On the one hand, there have been those (sometimes disparagingly referred to by their opponents as 'revisionists') who have argued that it is possible to change capitalism from within by using the democratic insitutions of the capitalist state to bring about a socialist transformation of the society as a whole. On the other, there have been those (such as Lenin, for example) who have argued that the capitalist state is inherently structured in such a way as to ensure domination by the capitalist class, that the institutions of liberal democracy are little more than a sham, and that effective working class power can only be achieved by smashing the 'bourgeois state' and replacing it with an altogether different kind of apparatus which will ensure domination by the proletariat (organised through the Communist Party).

As is so often the case in arguments like this, the truth of the matter probably lies somewhere between the two extremes, and most Marxists today tend to adopt a position which is rather more subtle or complex than either of these two polar opposites. Indeed, Marx himself was never entirely clear in his writings on whether or not liberal democracy could effectively be used to bring about a socialist transformation.

Marxist theory and parliamentary socialism

There are many points in Marx's works where he appears to reject the possibility of using existing state institutions to bring into being a socialist society. Such a rejection would seem to follow from his argument that the economic 'base' (i.e. the organisation of the forces and relations of production) determines the political 'superstructure' rather than the other way round, for, although he recognised that the superstructure could and did react back upon the base, it is clear from his writings that he saw the economy as the prime mover in bringing about social change, in which case the state will always tend to follow change rather than instigate it.

Overall, Marx's position appears to have been that any system of state power is a system of class power, that the state in a capitalist society will be an instrument of bourgeois domination and that in a future socialist society a socialist state form would need to be organised as a means of institutionalising working-class domination.

There is, however, another side to Marx's writings in which he appeared to recognise at least a limited role for 'bourgeois democracy'. According to his collaborator, Engels, Marx believed that in England (the country which at that time had the most developed capitalist economy and the most established system of parliamentary democracy) it may be possible to bring about a revolutionary transformation 'entirely by peaceful and legal means'. Engels elaborated on this theme on a number of occasions, arguing that 'bourgeois' political freedoms such as the right of assembly and the freedom of the press could be used to good effect by workers' movements, and that elections were themselves an important aspect of the class struggle in that they provided an opportunity to develop workers' consciousness of themselves as a strong and united political force.

This second strand in Marx's theory was never developed as forcibly as the first, however, and following the Russian Revolution, most Marxists for most of this century have tended to argue that a parliamentary socialist strategy of 'reformism' is unlikely to get very far, and that sooner or later, bourgeois domination will have to be directly confronted outside Parliament through, for example, the organisation of a general strike and the mobilisation of workers on the streets. The example of Chile, where the first and only elected Marxist Government in the world was swiftly deposed by an American-backed military coup, has often been cited in defence of such a position and as evidence that a seizure of power that stops with an electoral victory will always turn out to be hollow and precarious.

Against this, however, there has developed in recent years in many European Communist Parties a new strategy which has deliberately watered down any commitment to physical insurrection as the way to achieve socialism (this change is partly pragmatic for there has been precious little evidence that the working class in these countries is actually willing to confront the military might of the state in a direct and dramatic challenge to bourgeois rule). The development of what has been termed 'Eurocommunism' in Italy, Greece, Spain and to some extent France has led many Communist Parties in the West to weaken their ties with Moscow, to renounce the doctrine of 'the dictatorship of the proletariat', and to endorse the system of liberal parliamentary democracy. Eurocommunism is an essentially reformist version of Marxist political practice which involves an attempt to use parliamentary power to win concessions for working-class people while at the same time continuing to organise outside Parliament – especially in the trade unions. It is, in other words, a 'third road' between the two polar extremes identified earlier, for it recognises that real gains can be made within the framework of parliamentary democracy while at the same time it understands that no fundamental change can occur through parliamentary action alone.

In Britain, the Communist Party adopted its own version of Eurocommunism in the early 1970s. Unlike countries such as France and Italy, however, the British Communist Party is electorally very weak. In 1983 it had no Members of Parliament, and its membership stood at just 16,000. Although it does have an important influence in some trade unions, the Communist Party is almost totally eclipsed in Britain by the Labour Party which is much more broadly based ideologically than most socialist parties in Europe and which has therefore always been more or less open to Marxist influence of one form or another. Unlike socialist parties in Sweden, West Germany, Austria and the Netherlands, the British Labour Party has retained its commitment to public ownership of the means of production (the well-known 'clause 4' of the Party's constitution) and has never broken its historic and organic links with the trade unions. It is still, therefore, in appearance at least, a class-based party wedded in principle to bringing about a socialist transformation of British society which will shift power and wealth from one class to another. It is for this reason that Marxist debates over political strategy in Britain have always tended to revolve around the potential of the Labour Party as an instrument of Socialist revolution.

Labourism and Marxism in Britain

Most British Marxists, despite their many differences with each other, are probably agreed that a parliamentary strategy based on getting a radical Labour Party elected into Parliament is not itself enough to bring about a socialist transformation of British society. Where the arguments begin, however, is over the question of whether the Labour Party can play any effective part at all in such a transformation. Those who believe it can have become involved in the Party and have attempted to change it into an effective revolutionary political force despite the evidence of the last 80 years that such attempts have never previously succeeded. Those who believe it cannot, become involved instead in a bewildering variety of fringe left parties despite the evidence that such parties have never been able to build up a mass working-class membership. The dilemma for British Marxists, in other words, has been that the Labour Party is the only left party with any chance of gaining any significant political power, yet it also appears to be unshakeable in its commitment to parliamentary reformism which Marxist analysis believes to be inadequate for the task it has set itself.

At the heart of the problem as seen by Marxists is the Labour Party's longstanding commitment to the constitutional practices of parliamentarianism; i.e. to what was set out in the first three chapters of this book as a liberal-democratic or pluralist theory of the state. Labour's first ever Prime Minister, Ramsey MacDonald, spelt out this commitment clearly when he suggested that: 'The modern state in most civilised communities is democratic, and in spite of remaining anomalies and imperfections, if the mass of the ordinary people are agreed upon any policy neither electors, privileged peers nor reigning houses could stand in their way.'

We have seen, however, that this view is quite simply wrong! The historic commitment of the Labour Party to constitutional propriety is founded on a basic misconception of where power in British society lies. The power of the civil service, the military chiefs, the press barons, the bankers and the boards of directors or multinational companies simply cannot be dismissed as, in MacDonald's words, 'anomalies and imperfections', for it can and does prevail, even against the wishes of 'the mass of the ordinary people'.

This has long been recognised by Marxists in the Labour Party. In the 1930s, for example, Harold Laski argued in his *The State in Theory and Practice* that capitalism and democracy were fundamentally incompatible and that at times of crisis, the capitalist class would, if necessary, suppress democratic institutions rather than see its interests subordinated to those of the majority of electors. For Laski, constitutional methods could and should be followed until they are exhausted, but at that point violent revolutionary action would be necessary in order to counter the power and privilege of capital. Nowhere, he suggested, have peaceful methods successfully brought about a transfer of power and wealth from one class to another, for 'the owners of property rarely yield save what they must'.

The legacy of Laski lives on in the Left of the Labour Party today, and much of the turmoil that followed the 1979 election defeat and which culminated in 1981 in the breakaway of the 'social democrats' to form a new party revolved precisely around the battle between those (including the then leader, Michael Foot) who remained wedded to Macdonald's vision of the sovereignty of the British people in Parliament, and those (concentrated mainly among the Constituency Party activists) who sought to reduce the autonomy of parliamentary members and to develop a challenge to the government outside the Palace of Westminster as well as within it.

There is no doubt that the influence of this latter group (i.e. the Marxist-inspired Left) within the Labour Party has increased in recent years. However, the question still remains whether the Labour Party can be an effective instrument of Marxist political practice even if Marxists succeed in taking control of Constituency Parties and trade union branches and thereby achieve access to powerful positions within the Party's organisational structure.

We can only begin to answer this question if we are alert to the historical evolution of labourism in Britain. As Tony Benn has suggested, the Labour Party has its roots in a wide range of historical movements which include Marxist socialism but which also include (arguably more significantly) Christianity (especially non-conformist religions), the arguments of the Levellers during the Civil War period, the programme of the Chartists during the 1840s, and the writings of radicals of various shades of opinion including Robert Owen, Tom Paine and Sydney and Beatrice Webb. Most crucially of all, of course, the Labour Party sprang from the organisation of workers in trade unions, for it was set up in 1900 as the Labour Representation League by trade union leaders who sought to gain expression for the voice of organised labour in Parliament. Two crucial points follow from all of this.

First, the diversity of intellectual origins of Labourism gave rise to two main strands of Labour Party thinking. One, reflecting above all the

Fabian influence of the Webbs, was rationalistic and pragmatic in that it saw in the Labour Party an electoral instrument for improving the lot of ordinary working people through reform and legislative change within the context of an existing capitalist system of production. The other was more emotional and utopian in that it absorbed from the religious teachings of non-conformism a moral zeal to crusade against perceived injustice. The rationalistic element soon prevailed over the utopian one but what is most important from a Marxist point of view is that neither of these strands could alone provide a clear theoretical and philosophical basis for the development of a socialist strategy. As a result, the history of the Labour Party has been a history of muddling through based on good intentions and high ideals but precious little analysis. There has arguably never been a Labour Government which has assumed office with a clear idea of how it was going to implement its programme. The catalogue of defeats from the debacle of MacDonald's National Government in 1931, through the half-hearted nationalisation programme of the Attlee government after the war and the collapse of the Wilson Government's National Plan in 1965, to the bitter conflicts over the Callaghan Government's Social Contract in 1978/9 (all of which is discussed in Chapter 8) is indicative of the failure of all Labour administrations to understand the relation between parliamentary democracy and power in a capitalist society. Similarly, wherever a crisis has developed – the outbreak of war in 1914, the General Strike of 1926, the collapse of the Gold Standard in 1931, the appeasement of Hitler in the late 1930s, the devaluation of the pound in 1947 and 1967, the miners' strike of 1974 and the International Monetary fund loan of 1976 to cite just a few examples – Labour's parliamentary leadership has been caught wrong-footed. Labourism, in short, has been conspicuously lacking in theoretical understanding of its own position (indeed, there is a strong anti-intellectualist current within the labour movement as a whole which has militated against the fusion of political theory and political action which is entailed in the Marxist notion of 'praxis').

The second important legacy of the history of Labourism in Britain lies in the relationship between the Labour Party and the trade unions. Ever since 1900, the labour movement has been split between the industrial and the political wings, and this division has been crucial in preventing the development of a coherent socialist strategy. In part this is because the unions (or, to be more accurate, the union bosses) have always commanded a massive majority of conference votes by virtue of the block-vote system, and although some union bosses are more radical than others, this has generally operated as a brake upon Left activists in the constituency parties. The problem, however, goes deeper than this for the division between industrial issues (handled by the unions) and wider social and political issues (handled by the Labour Party in Parliament) has simply reflected and institutionalised a division which is characteristic of liberal capitalism but which is entirely inconsistent with what most

Marxists would see as socialist democracy. This is because socialist democracy, unlike liberal democracy, sees as artificial any separation between the political sphere (where government makes decisions) and the economic sphere (where owners of capital make decisions). Socialist democracy, if it means anything at all, means that working people share in making *all* decisions which affect their lives, and this is a far cry from voting once every 5 years in parliamentary elections!

What we are suggesting, therefore, is that the division of the labour movement into a Labour Party and trade unions has set up artificial barriers between the two and has fostered the limited parliamentarianism of the Party which we identified earlier. The Labour Party, to put it another way, is by its very nature the voice of organised labour *within* capitalism; it exists to represent in Parliament workers' interests as wage labourers rather than to transcend the system of wage labour itself, and for as long as it remains the political head of the trade union body, it will continue to be limited to such a role.

As the political mouthpiece of organised labour, the Labour Party exists to get the best it can for workers within the context of a capitalist system. Its job in Parliament is to express the aspirations of working-class people and of their organisations, the trade unions. As such, it has never really been interested in leading the working class, only in representing it. Political education within the Labour Party has never been a high priority, for the Party's task has always been defined in such a way that it takes people's desires as it finds them and tries to translate them into legislation. As we saw in Chapter 6 in the discussion of immigration controls, Labour Governments have generally ducked out of giving a principled lead where this conflicts with popular opinion and prejudice, and have preferred instead to adjust their conception of socialism to the non-socialist and often anti-socialist sentiments of the mass of the population. It is for this reason more than any other that socialism has never really been placed on the political agenda in Britain.

In recent years, with the resurgence of Marxism within the Party, all this has begun to change. The New Left (which is nearly always young, well-educated and middle class) has taken over many constituency parties, has won control of many local councils (see Chapter 11) and has made its influence felt in organisational and policy changes within the party (e.g. the establishment of an electoral college to choose the leader of the Parliamentary Party, the mandatory reselection of Members of Parliament, and the 1983 manifesto commitments regarding nationalisation, nuclear disarmament, withdrawal from the EEC etc). The result of this pronounced shift in the traditional role of the Party was, first, the split which gave rise to the SDP (which means that for the first time ever, there are now two major national parties in Britain committed to some form of social democracy), and second, the disastrous defeat in the 1983 general election when Labour's share of the vote fell in absolute terms to its lowest level since 1918 and in proportional terms (i.e. votes cast per Labour candidate) to its lowest level ever.

The New Left tended to shrug off this crushing defeat as a temporary set-back (indeed, Tony Benn saw it as a major victory on the grounds that 7 million people had voted for an explicitly socialist programme). As has long been common on the Left, much of the blame for the defeat was attributed to the pernicious influence of the mass media and to the treachery of leading members of the parliamentary party, and activists resolved to go and knock on even more doors and to sell even more socialist newspapers in order to 'enlighten' the working class about the true nature of its policies and to win the masses over to socialism.

It is at this point in the analysis that we reach the basic question regarding the role of the Labour Party as a vehicle of a socialist transformation of British society. The question is simply this, are Marxists and others on the Left justified in their belief that millions of ordinary working people constitute a potential support base for socialism? Is it really the case, if the socialist message is spelled out loud enough and long enough, that it will touch a nerve in the working-class collective consciousness which will spark off an irresistible popular surge for change? Or is it rather that the entire Left Labour strategy is fundamentally flawed in which case no amount of propaganda and political education will win a majority for socialist revolutionary change?

The Labour Party and the Working Class

Most Marxist political analysis – and most Left political activism for that matter – assumes that there is in a country like Britain a potential mass base for socialism, a natural in-built majority which is lying dormant and which only needs to be roused by the correct socialist strategy in order for its power to be unleashed and for capitalism to crumble. Given this assumption, the problem for the Left is simply one of strategy and organisation. The world is there to be won if only a way can be found to 'raise the workers from their slumbers'.

This mode of thinking rests on four crucial and generally unexamined premises. First, it is taken as axiomatic that all significant political struggles are in one way or another class struggles. Second, it is argued that the working class constitutes a majority of the population, which means it must be the most potent political force in the society. Third, it is taken as given that socialism is the natural political home of the working class, and that when workers embrace other ideologies they are in some way misguided as to where their true interests lie. Fourth, it is asserted that such misguidedness can be countered by socialists taking a bold lead which eventually will strike a chord in workers' consciousness as the scales fall from their eyes.

All four of these basic Left assumptions are in our view highly questionable.

'All significant political struggles are class struggles' This is patently not

the case, for as we saw in Chapter 6, class is only one dimension of inequality and domination in British society. Divisions based on gender, ethnicity and sectoral cleavages cut through and across class divisions and are clearly revealed in political struggles.

This has to some extent been recognised by some sections of the Left in Britain which have made conscious efforts to support, say, women's groups or black organisations. However, there is inherent in Marxist thinking an assumption that, even if such groups cannot be seen simply as part of the class struggle, they can be seen as secondary to it or as reinforcing it, for the 'real' struggle remains that between capital and labour. Non-class divisions, in other words, may be recognised but their significance is not, for there is generally a failure on the Left in Britain to understand or accept the *inherent* heterogeneity of the working class which follows from the fragmentation by gender, race, age, religion, income, type of employment, housing tenure, area of residence and many other factors besides.

The first problem which the Left faces but does not recognise is, therefore, that the homogeneous working class of its theory does not and cannot correspond to the working class as it exists in British society. Put another way, people have many interests other than their interests as workers and these often conflict with each other with the result that actual political alignments and struggles will always escape from the narrow confines of a class analysis and a class movement.

'The working class constitutes a majority interest' Again, this is questionable for the working class can only be seen as a majority force in British society if class divisions are identified in a very simplistic and unhelpful fashion.

We have seen that for Marx, the basic class division in a capitalist society is that between the owners of capital and those who have to sell their labour-power in order to live. We also saw in Chapter 6, however, that this 'basic' division has become very confused, for not only are there important divisions between different groups of workers (e.g. between professional and manual workers, state-sector and private-sector workers, and so on), but ownership of capital has changed as well with the growth of financial institutions such as pension funds and insurance companies, and with the division between ownership and management of capital.

Recent Marxist class theory has tried to take account of these changes. In particular, there have been various attempts to develop Marx's original theory in order to take account of the existence of a 'middle class' which is distinct from both capitalists and proletariat. Some writers, for example, suggest that only private-sector workers employed by capitalist firms can be said to be 'working class'. Others suggest that the 'real' working class be limited to those engaged in industrial production as opposed to the growing service sector. Still others suggest that the working class should be defined in such a way as to exclude employees such as managers and foremen who carry out supervisory functions on behalf of capital.

Most of these formulations remain unconvincing (even to other Marxist theorists), but what they all have in common is a recognition that the working class cannot simply be defined as all those who work, for this is to ignore the crucial economic and political differences between, say, hospital consultants and hospital porters, or university lecturers and university cleaners, or middle-level management and the shop floor. There is, in other words, an uneasy recognition that the working class – that group to which socialism is addressed and in which the hopes and aspirations of socialists are vested – may not be very big after all. Indeed, in some formulations, such as that of Poulantzas who limits the working class to non-supervisory manual workers employed in industry, this class turns out to be disconcertingly small (around one-quarter of the total employed population in this case).

The second problem for the Left, therefore, is that the belief that socialism must eventually prevail given the size of the working class appears to rest on an outdated and redundant understanding of what the shape of the British class structure actually looks like.

'Socialism is the natural political home of the working class' There are real problems with this argument, historically and theoretically.

The historical problem is quite simply that in all countries at all times, the working class divides fairly evenly in its support for the left, right and centre parties. There is no evidence here to suggest that the working class naturally inclines towards socialism.

Theoretically too, there is no reason to suppose that this should be the case. The Left's assumption that one's economic position should in some way determine one's political position derives, of course, from Marx's arguments regarding the primacy of the economic 'base' over the political 'superstructure'. However, when we consider the issue more carefully, it is obvious that there is no necessary reason for assuming that the fact of being a worker should generate a socialist commitment as opposed to any other. Different people may and do experience and interpret the same situation in different ways, and the way in which people align themselves politically will be a product, not of some automatic connection with their economic location in society, but with the way they respond to political and moral arguments. There is nothing in your class situation which will necessarily lead you to favour unilateral as opposed to multilateral disarmament, trade union autonomy as opposed to legal regulation, public ownership as opposed to privatisation of industry. People's views on these and similar issues, and their willingness to support one or other party, will reflect a host of factors, and it is a mistake, therefore, to assume any automatic predisposition on the part of one class or another towards any particular political ideology.

The third problem for the Left, then, is that its commitment to socialism has no prior claims on the sympathies of the working class. The socialist message is one among several competing philosophies, and it has no head start in this competition. Indeed, given the character of key institutions such as the mass media and the schools (discussed in Chapter 10), it may even start at a distinct disadvantage, for it is always likely to be easier to win popular acquiescence for keeping things much as they are than to generate support for changing them in dramatic and perhaps unpredictable ways.

'A bold socialist lead will eventually strike a chord in working class consciousness' As we have already seen, the failure of socialism in Britain is generally explained by the Left as a failure of strategy and in particular as a product of the faint hearts of labour leaderships over the years. It follows from this that the working class can be mobilised through a concerted and single-minded commitment by the Party to move towards full-blooded socialism with no concessions, and to drag the working class along behind it.

Any evaluation of this argument can only be tentative. However, it should be noted that in June 1983, an explicitly 'Left' manifesto which generally enjoyed the support of many constituency and trade union activists in the Labour Party failed to inspire mass support at the polls despite the dismal economic performance of the Conservative government over the previous 4 years. As we noted earlier, Labour's total vote in 1983 was the lowest since 1918, and its average vote per candidate was the lowest ever.

This crushing rejection of a socialist programme by the great majority of British people did not, however, lead to much – if any – reassessment by the Left of its policies and its basic assumptions. Rather, it was argued that the policies were right but that the working class, misled by a 'false consciousness' fostered by the media, had yet again got it wrong. The lesson which the Left learned from 1983 was not that its strategy had failed or that its message was out of tune, but that the same strategy must be followed next time with even more zeal, and that the same message must be repeated, only louder, in order to drown the propaganda emanating from 20 million television sets.

This points to what is perhaps the most serious problem in Marxist analysis and in contemporary Left activism in Britain – the capacity for self-delusion. The problem is not simply that class is not the be-all-and-end-all of politics nor that the working class is a lot smaller than it is fondly imagined to be, nor even that there is nothing in socialism which will automatically commend itself to working-class people, for above and beyond all this is the fact that contemporary Marxism is an example of a belief system which is immune to its own falsification. The more the working class turns its back on Marxism, the more Marxists become convinced that bourgeois ideology is to blame, in which case the socialist vision must be presented even more vividly in order to counter the hold of this ideology over the minds of working people. The greater the set-backs, the more convinced the Left becomes of its own mission. There is no space in such a messianic movement for the critical self-reflection which must be an essential feature of any political movement which seeks to retain its relevance in a swiftly changing world. Seen in this way, the problem for the Labour Party in the years to come is likely to have less to do with the stunted consciousness of the working class than with the tunnel vision of the socialists who seek to win that class's support.

CONCLUSION

The resurgence of interest in Marxist political theory since the 1960s has provided a valuable corrective to some of the more orthodox approaches within mainstream political science. In particular, Marxist work on the capitalist state has pointed to the inadequacies of liberal-democratic theories which seek to analyse power through an almost exclusive focus on political institutions, for Marxists have emphasised that political processes cannot be understood except in relation to the organisation of the economy.

The problem, however, is that neither traditional nor recent Marxist work has been able to demonstrate the nature of this relation. What is distinctive to Marxist political theory is the view that politics are in some way determined by economic forces, but the question of how this occurs remains unanswered.

In this chapter, we have considered two major theorists, both of whom recognise that there is some degree of autonomy between the political system and the economic system, but who differ markedly between themselves over how this autonomy is to be explained.

On the one hand, we have Miliband's position which is that, although those who run the state apparatus are generally drawn from the capitalist class, are sympathetic to its interests, are strongly pressured by big business and are constrained by the requirements of the economic system, they do retain some autonomy in deciding how best they can serve the long-term interests of capital. In this view the 'relative autonomy' of the state is a reflection of the limited autonomy enjoyed by those who run it.

There are two problems with this 'explanation', however. First, as we saw earlier in this chapter, Miliband gives no indication of the degree to which those who run the state are able to make up their own minds about the actions they deem necessary. How much scope do they have? How far can they go? How relative is 'relative' autonomy? Clearly, the 'concessions' which the British state has made over the years are by no means trifling, and their cost in terms of taxation on profits has been considerable. Indeed, as we shall see in Chapter 8, some Marxists (and non-Marxists) have argued that one major factor in the continuing slump in British capitalism has been the size of the state's budget as it has expanded its provisions for working-class people, thereby eating into capitalist profits. Such evidence would seem to suggest that the autonomy of the state may at times be considerable, but there is no way of judging this from Miliband's analysis.

This leads us into the second problem with Miliband's explanation of the relative autonomy of the state, and this is that it seems to assume a degree of canniness and foresight on the part of those who run the state which is historically highly dubious. The notion that Cabinets, Civil Servants and others carefully and correctly calculate how many concessions will need to be made in order to contain pressure from below seems faintly ludicrous in the light of what we know about the haphazard way in which British governments have responded to crises and problems, yet Miliband's argument rests on the view that these people are endowed with such a degree of political intelligence and sophistication that their actions always turn out in the end to have been exactly what capitalism as a whole required. What else, other than their supposed political acumen, can explain why they may not make disastrous decisions from the point of view of capital? To suggest that the constraints of the system prevent this from happening is to give no answer at all, for the argument that the system must be supported if it is to continue does not explain why the system is in fact supported and does continue. What is lacking in Miliband's analysis, in other words, is any explanation of what it is that has prevented the 'relatively autonomous' state leaders from using their autonomy in such a way that the system itself is fouled up or collapses.

On the other hand, there is Poulantzas's position which is that the 'relative autonomy' of the state reflects not the scope for action on the part of those who run it, but rather the shifting fortunes of class struggle such that, when the working class is in the ascendant, the state will respond with reforms. As we saw earlier, however, this is an inadequate formulation, for not only does it neglect altogether the motives of key individuals and the significance of political struggles which are not class-based, but it also fails to demonstrate why class struggle (the cause of state policies) should always result in the maintenance of the long-term interests of big capital (the necessary function of such policies). As in Miliband's formulation, so too in that of Poulantzas, there is a basic failure to identify the necessary mechanism by means of which the state responds to one class while safeguarding the interests of another.

In these, as in other Marxist approaches, the basic problem stems from the commitment of any Marxist theory to some view of politics as determined by economic organisation. That the economy influences political processes is undeniable; that it determines them, however, seems insupportable.

It is the failure of Marxist theory to resolve this problem which has led to the tangled debate within Marxism in particular, and within the Left in Britain in general, over whether or not parliamentary socialism represents a viable strategy for transforming capitalism. Clearly, if politics are simply 'determined' by economic forces, then there is no possibility of a capitalist state being used as an instrument of socialist change. But if some degree of 'autonomy' is accorded to the political system, then this self-evident 'truth' becomes rather less compelling.

In the final section of this chapter, we saw that most Marxists in Britain see a parliamentary strategy as a necessary but not sufficient condition for achieving far-reaching social change. However, it is also commonplace in the Marxist literature to express considerable doubt regarding the capacity of the Labour party to carry off such a strategy, and many writers (including Miliband) see little hope of transforming Labourism into socialism. The prognostication, therefore, seems gloomy, for Marxists doubt both the possibility of transforming capitalism though electoral victories and the possibility of transforming the Labour Party into a vehicle of socialist change.

Such intellectual pessimism is well founded, for the prospects of socialism in Britain today seem slighter than at any time in the last 50 years. The trade unions are demoralised and have been weakened by high rates of unemployment; the political Left has split, with the formation of the Social Democratic Party in 1981; and the electoral plight of the Labour Party has been underlined by the heaviest general election defeat in its history. In such a situation, old Marxist orthodoxies concerning the relationship between politics and economics, socialism and the working class, appear to require fundamental reassessment, yet there is little evidence that the Left is willing or able to take such a step.

The conclusion to be drawn from all of this is that, while Marxist political theory has been important in demonstrating the inadequacies of alternative approaches, it has itself been found wanting in certain important respects as well. The basic question of the relationship between politics and economics remains unresolved, and despite their claims to provide an overall 'total' explanation, it turns out that Marxist theories can no more provide all the answers than liberal theories can.

The obvious question raised by this conclusion is whether different theories may be applied to an explanation of different aspects of the political process. Is it possible that Marxist and liberal approaches are not as incompatible as those on both sides of this theoretical divide have made out and that a comprehensive and coherent analysis of British politics may usefully draw on aspects of both? This is a question which we address in the course of the next four chapters where we shall draw on the insights of various theoretical traditions in order to understand and explain different aspects of the state's role in British society.

WORKS CITED AND GUIDE TO FURTHER READING

Aaronovitch, S (1961) *The Ruling Class*, London, Lawrence & Wishart, especially chapter 5.

In many ways a forerunner of Miliband's more influential work. Argues stridently, but not always convincingly, that the British state is dominated by large industrial-financial interests.

Anderson, P. and Blackburn R. (eds) (1965) *Towards Socialism*, London, Fontana.
A collection of essays bemoaning the past and looking to the future in the wake of Labour's 1964 general election victory. See especially Nairn on 'The nature of the Labour Party' and Anderson on 'Problems of socialist strategy'.

Coates, D. (1980) *Labour in Power*, London, Longman.
One of many commentaries which sees the Labour Party as a means by which the working class has been politically incorporated into the capitalist system.

Gold, D., Lo, C. and Wright, E. (1976) Recent developments in Marxist theories of the capitalist state, *Monthly Review*, **27,** pp. 37–51.
A useful introductory guide to the work of Miliband and Poulantzas.

Hindess, B. (1983) *Parliamentary Democracy and Socialist Politics*, London, Routledge and Kegan Paul.
A stimulating critique by a Marxist of Marxist orthodoxies. In particular, Hindess takes issue with the view that 'the real working class is out there somewhere, patiently awaiting the socialist call'.

Jacques, M., and Mulhern, F. (eds) (1981) *The Forward March of Labour Halted?*, London, Verso.
The Marxist left agonises about the implications of Labour's electoral decline and seek all manner of solutions. See especially the essay by Eric Hobsbawm.

Laski, H. (1935) *The State in Theory and Practice*, London, Allen and Unwin.
In which one of the key figures of the British Left this century drives home his message (made all the more urgent by the rise of Nazism in Germany at that time) that capitalism and democracy are fundamentally irreconcilable at times of economic recession.

Lukes, S. (1971) Power and structure, in S. Lukes (ed.) *Essays in Social Theory*, London, Macmillan.
An interesting discussion of the constraints on the powerful. Lukes draws the distinction between 'structural' and 'rational' constraints, and then uses this to criticise Poulantzas for his over-deterministic and over-structuralist analysis of state power.

Marx, K. and Engels, F. (1968) *Selected Works in one Volume*, Moscow, Progress publishers.
Contains many of the key political essays including the Communist Manifesto and 'The Civil War in France'.

Miliband, R. (1969) *The State in Capitalist Society*, London, Weidenfeld & Nicolson.
Now becoming something of a classic. Despite its lack of theoretical subtlety and good empirical evidence, it remains the best single Marxist analysis of politics and the state in Britain.

Miliband, R. (1982) *Capitalist Democracy in Britain*, London, Oxford University Press.
Overall, a disappointing work. Thirteen years and umpteen debates after 'The

state in capitalist society', it demonstrates that Miliband still lacks theoretical subtlety and good empirical evidence.

Poulantzas, N. (1973) *Political Power and Social Classes,* London, New Left
   Books.

Appallingly written and virtually impossible to read. Those who wish to get to grips with Poulantzas might do better to approach him via his debate with Miliband in the journal *New Left Review*. This began in 1969 (no. 58) when Poulantzas reviewed Miliband's book, and continued through no. 59 (1970) when Miliband replied; number 82 (1973) in which Miliband reviewed Poulantzas's book; and no. 95 (1976) when Poulantzas replied to this and to a later critique from Laclau. A good (but again difficult) critical review of Poulantzas's theory can be found in S. Clarke (1977) 'Marxism, sociology and Poulantzas's theory of the state', *Capital and Class,* **2,** pp. 1–31.

CHAPTER 8

Managing the Economy

In the future, the Government will have to take on many duties which it has avoided in the past.

John Maynard Keynes (1952) Essays in Persuasion, *New York, Harcourt Brace, originally published 1926, p. 331.*

What we urgently need, for both economic stability and growth, is a reduction of government intervention, not an increase.

Milton Friedman (1962) Capitalism and Freedom, *Chicago, University of Chicago Press, p. 38.*

If capitalism is to be maintained, the state has to expand and contract at one and the same time.

Andrew Gamble and Paul Walton (1976) Capitalism in Crisis, *London, Macmillan, p. 189.*

The British economy has been in decline, relative to other industrial countries, for over 100 years. Sometimes the decline has been gradual and has gone virtually unnoticed, while at others the economy has lurched into slumps of alarming proportions. There have been periods – after the Second World War, for example – when living standards have consistently risen, but even in these periods Britain's growth rate has lagged behind that of her competitors. There have also been periods – such as in the 1930s and the 1970s/80s – when the economy has slumped absolutely as well as relatively, and it is at these times that factories have been closed down, wages have fallen, and millions of people have been thrown out of work.

As the decline of the British economy has become more marked, so the management of the economy has become an issue increasingly central to British politics. It is of course the case that Britain's fortunes are to some extent determined by factors beyond her shores and out of reach of any government, for as a trading nation the country has long been vulnerable to world-market trends. Nevertheless, it is also the case that, when the world economy is booming Britain lags behind, and that when it enters into recession Britain suffers more than most other countries and takes longer to recover. It does seem, therefore, that there is something peculiar to the British economy and to British society which accounts for the country's specific problems; something which successive governments have attempted to isolate and thus to remedy.

There has been no shortage of theories purporting to identify the nature of the problem and to prescribe appropriate solutions. As the country's economic decline has become more obvious and more serious, so successive governments have grasped at different theories and have pursued different strategies aimed at reversing the decline. As each theory has failed and each strategy has been found wanting, so a fresh attempt has been made to grapple with the problem until that too has been found to be inadequate and has in turn been replaced by a new orthodoxy. Indeed, it became obvious by the 1980s that governmental initiatives had gone full circle – from a strategy of minimal state intervention, through attempts to manage demand and to plan production and supply, and back again to a market strategy under the Thatcher regime. The tragedy is that throughout this period, the decline has got worse, and each new strategy has succeeded only in building up yet more problems for the next one to confront.

This record of failure of successive governments trying out different remedies suggests that the problem that they have been grappling with is fundamental and deep-rooted. Whatever the immediate causes of Britain's economic plight, and the specific mistakes made by particular governments, it seems that we can only begin to understand the problem through an historical perspective which takes us back, not simply to the last government or the one before that, but to the beginnings of the decline mid-way through the nineteenth century. In 1850, Britain was the single most powerful country on Earth. Somewhere in the 130 odd years since then lies the explanation for the country's present economic difficulties.

THE RETREAT FROM LAISSEZ FAIRE: FROM THE GREAT
EXHIBITION TO THE GREAT DEPRESSION

In 1851, Imperial Britain celebrated her domination of the world, militarily and economically, with a Great Exhibition of industrial products and innovations which was held in a magnificent structure of steel and glass erected in London's Hyde Park. At that time, Queen Victoria reigned over a quarter of the world's total population, and her Empire, which had been built on the success of British manufacturing and the supremacy of her navy, was the largest in the world's history. Furthermore, British industry produced one-third of the world's manufactured goods and accounted for a quarter of total world trade. Although, as we shall see in Chapter 9, the living conditions endured by many of Victoria's subjects in industrial towns and cities throughout Britain were appalling, the wealth of the country as a whole increased dramatically through the nineteenth century. In the 70 years from 1811, national income trebled while prices halved; in other words, national wealth increased six times in real terms.

From the mid-nineteenth century on, however, the picture began to change dramatically. By the eve of the First World War, the output of British industry had been overtaken by both Germany and the United States with the result that Britain's share of total manufactured goods had fallen from one-third to less than one-seventh. While the country retained the trappings of Empire, it was clear by 1914 that it was fast losing its role as world leader.

One factor which undoubtedly contributed to this spectacular loss of industrial advantage was the commitment of British Governments throughout this period to a policy of free trade, for this commitment was not shared by other countries. Britain's enthusiasm for a free-trade policy was understandable given her head-start in the industrialization process, for it could be seen as a recipe for maintaining her domination of world markets in manufactures; if every other country allowed British goods free entry into their domestic markets, then their own infant industries could hardly hope to compete against the already-established British industries. It was for precisely this reason, of course, that other countries did not allow free access for British manufactured goods, but instead preferred to erect high tariff walls while nurturing their own manufactures behind them.

By the outbreak of the First World War (which was itself in large part a product of the intensified rivalries between the major industrial countries), Britain's unilateral commitment to free trade had resulted, not only in the stimulation of foreign competition, but also in a marked decline in investment in home-based industries. Net investment in British industry fell from over 8 per cent of total national income in 1870 to around 5 per cent in the first decade of the twentieth century, and the amount of capital equipment per worker in British industry remained virtually constant throughout this period at a time when it was rising quickly in America and Germany. The result was that the productivity of British industry remained stagnant in marked contrast to the situation overseas where industrialists were investing in new machinery which could produce more goods more cheaply than in Britain.

The money which could have gone into re-tooling British industry went abroad instead. In the years 1905 to 1914, 7 per cent of the national income was invested overseas (compared with just 5 per cent invested at home). Foreign earnings from these investments escalated to £200 million by 1913 compared with £35 million in 1870. Put another way, at the start of the war, one-third of total profits came from abroad compared with one-eighth in 1870. These overseas earnings augmented the wealth of the country (or more accurately, they augmented the wealth of those who owned most of the country's financial assets), but at the cost of weakening the country's industrial base. British industry became less and less competitive as British financiers became more and more wealthy, for the capital needed to modernise British factories if they were to hold their own against the newer German and American industries was not being invested here.

All of this raises the question of why successive British governments failed to intervene to protect home industry from foreign competition and to encourage greater investment. There were at least three reasons for this.

First, powerful sections of British society were benefiting from free trade and from governments' commitments to *laissez faire;* these included exporters and financial institutions such as the banks. Second, the working class, whose votes were assiduously sought following the extensions of the male franchise in 1868 and 1884, were benefiting from cheap food imports, and proposals for tariff reform in the 1900s met with fierce popular resistance since they were seen as an attempt to tax workers' food. Third, the liberal ideology, of which free trade was a major feature, was deeply embedded in both British society and the British state. The economic orthodoxy and political philosophy of the time both underpinned a largely unquestioned commitment to a minimal state role in economic and social affairs.

The economic orthodoxy derived from the theories of political economists such as Adam Smith who argued that the pursuit by individuals of their own economic self-interest was the best way of ensuring continued growth and affluence for all. The free market was in this view the best available mechanism for coordinating the activities of millions of atomised individuals, for the price mechanism ensured that demand would always be balanced by supply and that goods and services would be provided at an optimal level of economic efficiency. Any 'interference' by the state could only upset the delicate equilibrium of the 'naturally' self-regulating market and any attempt to limit free trade with other nations would result in higher prices and lower efficiency of home-based industries. In Smith's view, therefore, the economic role of the state should be limited to ensuring a stable monetary and legal framework within which the free market could operate nationally and internationally.

This argument was then reinforced by political theories of the time – most notably, the utilitarian political philosophy of Jeremy Bentham and his followers who argued that any restriction of individual liberties by the state had to be considered as evil and could only be justified if it overcame an even greater evil (which in Bentham's view was rarely the case). As we saw in Chapter 1, this mode of thinking reappeared forcefully in nineteenth century liberal theory of the constitution which sought to establish the limits of state power and to find ways of preventing the propertyless masses from using their political majority in the country to undermine the rights of private property.

This potent combination of economic liberalism, utilitarian philosophy and constitutional theorising, meant that, in nineteenth-century Britain, state power was widely regarded with deep suspicion. Unlike Germany, where there was a long and strong tradition which saw the state as the expression and embodiment of the people, the Fatherland and the national spirit and identity, in England the state had, ever since the Civil War, been seen as something set apart from the society and as something to be held at arm's length. The prospect of the state actively intervening in economic life, such as occurred in Germany from the time of Bismark, was one which industrialists and financiers alike regarded in total horror, and most political leaders shared this reaction. The state neither wished to, nor was allowed to, intervene.

As time went by, however, the force of these anti-statist sentiments in British political culture came inevitably to be mediated by the practical problems posed by the erosion of British supremacy in the world economy. Following the First World War, the problem confronted by British Governments was no longer that of how to maintain Britain's lead over her industrial competitors, but was rather how to revive the country's flagging economic fortunes in order to stay in the race. Following a brief economic boom after the war, which was stimulated by the explosion of pent-up demand for capital and consumer goods, the economy slumped in 1920/1 and never really recovered again throughout the inter-war period. Although this long period of recession was in part due to external factors (notably, of course, the onset of the Great Depression triggered off by the American stock market collapse of 1929), it was also a reflection of Britain's weakened economic position in the world economy. This relative weakness was undoubtedly exacerbated by the government's decision in 1925 to return to the Gold Standard in order to preserve the value of sterling and hence the value of investors' earnings from overseas.

If free trade was one major pillar of liberal economic thought at this time, then the Gold Standard was the other. Under this system, every national currency was given a fixed price in gold, which meant that every currency exchanged with every other currency at a fixed rate, and that the domestic issue of coins and paper money within each country could not exceed its holdings of gold and other currencies. Individual governments were thus prevented from increasing the money supply in their economies unless they also increased their holdings of gold, since every note they issued had to be backed by the equivalent amount in gold.

If a country was not paying its way, and was importing more than it was exporting, then under this system it had to make good the deficit by transferring gold to its creditors. This then depleted its reserves and forced it to reduce the amount of money circulating in the economy. This then had the effect of lowering domestic demand (and hence cutting the import bill) while at the same time increasing unemployment and reducing wages until such time as its industries again became competitive in world markets. Or such was the theory.

When Britain returned to the Gold Standard after the war, the government fixed the price of sterling at its pre-war level. The reduced competitiveness of British industry, however, meant that the pound was now vastly over-valued, with the result that British exports were priced much higher in overseas markets than goods from other countries. British industry had continued to fall behind that of other countries; between 1913 and 1925, manufacturing output fell 14 per cent at a time when the United States increased its output by 40 per cent and total world manufacturing output rose by 20 per cent. Pegging the value of sterling at its 1913 level was, in this context, a recipe for massive deflation. To compete at all, British industry had to reduce its costs dramatically, and this meant cutting wages and abandoning all but the most efficient sectors of production. The immediate result was the General Strike of 1926 provoked by a wage cut imposed in the mining industry. In the longer term, the result was a stagnant economy with high rates of unemployment, low wages, low prices and falling profits. In 1931, the government was forced to abandon both free trade and the Gold Standard, but by then the world economy as a whole was in the midst of a massive recession from which there seemed little prospect of recovery.

The Great Depression of the 1930s hit all Western capitalist countries. In the United States, industrial production fell by more than half between 1929 and 1932 and unemployment climbed to 14 million as profit rates slumped into negative figures. In Germany the picture was much the same with a 40 per cent fall in industrial production and 6 million unemployed. Compared with these statistics, the British recession was relatively mild, partly because the British economy did not have so far to fall. Industrial production fell by 17 per cent and unemployment reached 3 million (representing 22 per cent of the work-force), although these gross figures are somewhat misleading in that the impact of the recession was variable across different regions and in some areas such as South Wales and the north-east of England, unemployment was much more widespread. One reason why the famous 'hunger march' from Jarrow to London made such an impression was precisely that in areas such as London and the South-East, the full horrors of the economic collapse had never been that apparent.

The British Government's response to the Great Depression was as limited as it was predictable. As we have already seen, Britain came off the Gold Standard, and this relieved pressure on exporting industries by reducing the artificially high value of sterling, although the relief was short-lived as other countries also devalued their currencies. The government also belatedly abandoned its long-standing commitment to free trade and began to enter into bi-lateral trading agreements with other countries. While this undoubtedly helped to protect the new fledgling industries (such as cars and electronics) which were then being established in the Midlands and elsewhere, it too had little lasting effect since other countries were pursuing much the same policy with the result that world markets for Britain's exports were shrinking. Finally, Ramsey MacDonald's National Government, elected in 1931, drastically cut back government spending by reducing unemployment and other benefits, thus exacerbating the plight of those out of work in an attempt to reduce taxes and stimulate investment.

The basic problem for the government at this time was that, even if it had been inclined to do more (and more positive intervention would of course have flown in the face of the long tradition of antipathy towards state involvement in the economy), it was far from clear what else it could do. Put bluntly, orthodox economic thinking at this time held that a recession on this sort of scale simply could not happen!

As Adam Smith had argued, and as most economists continued to argue, an unfettered capitalist market system should be self-regulating. Put simply, the liberal economic theory of the time suggested that supply would always generate its own demand so that prices would stabilise at the point of full employment. This theory, which was made to look rather sick in the context of the 1930s, was based on the simple argument that the prices paid by entrepreneurs to the three factors of production (rent payment to owners of land, interest payments to owners of capital and wage payments to those who sell their labour) would reappear in the economy in the form of new demand for the goods which entrepreneurs subsequently produced. Thus workers would spend their wages, landowners their rent and investors their interest on the coal, cars, clothing and other goods which industry was producing, and this would then enable industrialists to plough back their profits into a new cycle of production. The economy, in short, was self-sustaining.

Under the influence of the Treasury, British Governments of the 1930s thus sought simply to balance their budgets in the hopes that eventually the mysterious and benign operation of market forces would lead to recovery. What actually happened, however, was that high unemployment and low wages depressed domestic demand such that entrepreneurs could not find markets for their products. The economy therefore became locked into a downward spiral of falling investment, falling levels of demand and falling prices while governments looked on apparently powerless to do anything about it. It was only the onset of war which dragged the economy out of this vicious circle.

NATIONALIZATION AND NATIONAL PLANNING: THE WAR AND THE POST-WAR LABOUR GOVERNMENT

Rearmament and the mobilisation of the labour force into the military and into industry in order to support the war effort provided the stimulus to new investment which had been lacking throughout the inter-war years. Measures which had been inconceivable in peace-time were seen as necessary in time of war and the niceties of liberal economic and political theory were cast aside as the British state erected a system of economic controls and directives unprecedented in the nation's history.

By the end of the war in 1945, a staggering 60 per cent of the total national product was being consumed by the government while over one-third of national income was accounted for by taxation. Both capital and labour had been made subject to a battery of controls imposed by the coalition wartime government in its attempt to direct all available spare capacity into the war effort. Imports were regulated in order to save precious foreign currency and to release shipping for essential supplies, and this in turn necessitated rationing of consumer goods (notably foodstuffs). Labour was subjected to a system of industrial, as well as military, conscription and the right to strike was curtailed. Capital too became subject to a variety of controls involving restrictions on the use of raw materials, controls on dividends and overseas investments, a wide-ranging system of price controls covering over half of all consumer purchases, and a comprehensive system of licensing which governed virtually all new investment in building and machinery. It was almost as if the government realised that to defeat a centralized and authoritarian Nazi state, it would itself have to construct an authoritarian and centralized system of its own.

When the system of democratic elections was restored following the eventual victory of 1945, the Labour Party won a large parliamentary majority for the first time in its history, this reflecting a popular mood for change among the millions of men and women who had been drafted into the services and into industry during the previous 6 years. The Labour Party was committed to the continuation of a system of state economic planning not simply as a short-term practical expediency following the rigours of war, but as a principle by which the peace-time economy was to be managed and controlled. The old liberal orthodoxies had had their day and were to be replaced by a rational system of economic planning through which the nation's resources were to be harnessed and directed according to democratically-expressed social objectives. In 1945, in other words, the new Labour Government set out to do precisely that which nineteenth-century liberal constitutional theorists had feared; namely, to use the state as an instrument of social change by shifting power and resources away from those who had traditionally owned and enjoyed them towards those who had lived by their labour.

This restructuring of the British economy and of British society was to be accomplished partly by retaining war-time controls such as those governing imports, prices and new investment, partly by the introduction of new controls such as a comprehensive land-use planning system, and partly by the adoption of an interventionist economic planning strategy involving the nationalization of key sectors of the economy and the use of fiscal policy to maintain full employment.

Between 1945 and 1950, the Labour Government changed the face of the British economy by taking into public ownership a number of key basic industries which together employed some 2 million people and accounted for some 10 per cent of the country's total productive capacity. Most of these industries were, however, relatively unprofitable and their average rates of return on investment were just one-third of those in industry as a whole. Most of them – such as the coal mines and the railways – were also in desperate need of new investment which their dispossessed owners had long been unable or unwilling to finance. The cost of nationalization to the public purse was therefore considerable, for not only were the former owners compensated at what, in retrospect, seem often to have been over-generous terms, but the government assumed responsibility for some of the least efficient, least profitable and most under-capitalized sectors of what was already a severely weakened economy.

As we saw in Chapter 5, the nationalised industries were generally run as public corporations with little or no opportunity for democratic accountability or workers control. They did not, therefore, represent as dramatic a change in the capitalist organisation of the economy as might at first be imagined. Furthermore, as we shall see in the next section, it does seem that to a large extent public-sector industries have been run since the war to the direct or indirect advantage of many private-sector firms and that limited nationalization was by no means incompatible with an economy which was still organized predominantly on capitalist lines. Even the sober and somewhat conservative weekly journal, *The Economist,* noted in one of its editorials at the time of nationalization that the government had probably done the least that was necessary if Britain's basic industries were to be nurtured back to health following the war.

A further point to remember is that, even following the wave of nationalization by the post-war Labour Government, the vast majority of industries and services remained in private hands. It was therefore obvious that a coherent economic planning strategy aimed at achieving growth and full employment would have to entail, in addition to direct ownership, the pursuit of a fiscal policy which would influence investment outside the public sector. The post-war Labour Government found such a policy in the *General Theory* of Maynard Keynes which had been published in 1936.

Keynes had basically argued that orthodox economic theory needed to be inverted. It was not true, as economists at that time generally believed, that savings would generate new investment. Rather, new investment needed to be stimulated by rising demand which meant that far from encouraging saving at times of recession, governments would be better advised to encourage people to spend.

The conclusion to be drawn from this analysis was that, in order to regenerate the economy, it was necessary to stimulate new demand, and this was a task which must inevitably fall in the lap of government to perform, for no other agency could be used in such a way as to raise aggregate demand as a deliberate policy. Government alone could stimulate demand through its control of fiscal policy and its role as a major spender.

As we saw earlier, the British Government in 1931 actually cut its spending by reducing benefits. For Keynes, however, this was precisely the wrong policy to adopt, for he argued that public expenditure should be increased at times of recession, even though this would mean running a deliberate budget deficit. Government, in other words, should spend more than it receives (obviously there would be no point in raising government spending and financing this through increased taxation, since this would simply increase public-sector demand by reducing private-sector demand; the task was to raise demand overall, and this meant leaving money in people's pockets while at the same time raising the level of state expenditure). By pumping additional money into the economy, government could stimulate new production both directly and indirectly. A new schools building programme, for example, would lead directly to increased demand for building workers to put up the schools, teachers to instruct in them and administrators to run them. It would also stimulate production of building materials, desks and chairs, text-books, sports equipment and so on, all of which would be produced by bringing idle industrial capacity into use. Such a programme would also have further indirect effects, for the teachers, bricklayers, carpenters and other who had been brought back into employment would now have more money to spend, which means that the initial increase in demand brought about by increased public spending would be multiplied up by increased private spending. The teachers and others would begin to spend more on food, clothing, holidays and the like, and this would then stimulate new investment in agriculture, textiles and the leisure industries which would then further raise the level of employment. Before long, the economy could be pulled out of recession and a level of output could then be maintained which guaranteed full employment.

In Britain, Keynesian theory was generally resisted through the 1930s by orthodox politicians and Treasury mandarins who saw little to commend itself in a theory which criticised the traditional value of thriftiness, advocated deliberate public overspending and asserted the need for government intervention to make the market system work. Liberal economic orthodoxy was at that time still too strongly entrenched in Whitehall and Westminster to countenance a move away from a balanced budget.

By 1945, however, things had changed, for the war had in a sense been the test of Keynesian theory (Keynes himself had been recruited into the Treasury in 1941). At the end of the war, both major political parties were openly committed to the pursuit of a Keynesian demand-management strategy for maintaining full employment – a strategy which replaced the old liberal orthodoxies of laissez faire and which itself became the new orthodoxy which was to underpin state fiscal policy for the next 30 years.

DEMAND MANAGEMENT: THE MIXED ECONOMY AND THE POST-WAR BOOM

The Labour administration which had achieved office in 1945 with such high hopes and extensive aspirations eventually vacated office 6 exhausting years later. It had presided over post-war demobilisation, over the beginnings of the end of the Empire (notably with Indian independence in 1947), and over the establishment of the welfare state and the mixed economy. Its (partially successful) attempt to restructure British society had come at a time when the weakness of the British economy had never been more clear, for the war had proved immensely costly in the winning and had exacerbated the problems which had been building up in the decades before. The diversion of investment into the war effort had left much of British industry vastly undercapitalized; export industries in particular had been badly run down and new investment had been below that required even to replace worn out plant. Massive debts of £3.5 billion had been incurred to finance the war effort, and new loans had had to be negotiated from the United States after the war which had carried the condition that Empire markets be opened up to American companies thus removing one further crutch upon which the ailing British economy had come to depend.

Yet despite all this, the government did succeed in laying the basis for a sustained period of economic growth and full employment during the 1950s – a boom which many economists (including Keynes himself) had believed would never materialise. Real incomes of British workers rose by 50 per cent through the 1950s, while unemployment remained low. The new light industries which had taken root before the war flourished after it, and although economic growth in Britain lagged behind that in most of her competitors, it was at least sustained, leading Harold Macmillan to make his famous pronouncement towards the end of the decade that the British people had never had it so good. For 20 years after the war, Britain shared, albeit less than fully, in an unprecedented period of growth and affluence throughout the Western capitalist world, and this long boom helped to disguise the fact that the basic problems of the economy remained unresolved.

A number of different factors together explain the long post-war boom, of which four seem to have been paramount.

First, there was a plentiful supply of cheap imports required by Western industries. Of particular significance there was cheap oil from the Middle East, and world consumption of oil rose by a staggering 7.5 per cent per year between 1950 and 1970. Other products from the Third

World, such as food and raw materials, were also bought cheaply by the industrialized nations, and the poorer countries contributed cheap labour too, either in the form of European 'guest workers' or as permanent migrants into the former Imperial centres, such as the UK which set out to attract immigrants from the former colonies.

Second, the world monetary system was stabilised following the Bretton Woods conference of 1944. By the end of the war, it was clear to all that Britain had been replaced by the USA as the foremost Western nation, and at Bretton Woods it was agreed to establish a new system of international currencies to fill the void left by the collapse of the Gold Standard. This system was based on the convertibility of the American dollar whose price was in turn fixed in terms of gold. All currencies, in other words, were given a fixed exchange rage against the dollar and this, together with the establishment of the International Monetary Fund, the World Bank and the General Agreement on Tariffs and Trade, laid the foundation for a new era of expanding multilateral world trade.

Third, the end of the war opened up massive new investment opportunities. This had, of course, been the case after the First World War as well, but then the boom fuelled by post-war reconstruction had been all too short-lived. What was different after 1945 was that new investment was possible, not only in reconstructing and replacing assets damaged by the war, but also in whole new areas of production. Throughout the depression years, new discoveries and inventions had in a sense 'piled up' without being fully exploited because capital could not be invested at a time of falling prices and low profits. The stimulus given to the Western economies by rearmament, post-war reconstruction and (in the ex-fascist countries where the organised labour movement had been destroyed) low wages and a docile workforce, brought about an expansion of the economy which then promoted investment in these new areas of production. The post-war boom was thus built on the development of new techniques of production (automation, nuclear fission, computerisation, etc.), which unleashed onto the British public an avalanche of new consumer goods such as cars, televisions, domestic labour-saving devices and so on. Throughout the 1950s, industry cashed in on a new technology which offered high productivity and high rates of profit.

All of these products had, of course, to be sold if profits were to be realised, and this is where the fourth factor became crucial, for perhaps the major difference between the pre-war and post-war years lay in Western governments' commitment to an interventionist role in the economy based on the principles of Keynesian economics.

Following the end of the war, the long tradition of liberal economic orthodoxy which sought to limit the role of the state in economic affairs to facilitating the operation of the free market was re-established in external affairs (e.g. through the return to free trade and the support of a strong pound as an international currency), but was replaced domestically by an interventionist stance adopted by Labour and Conservative governments alike. This new interventionism formed the basis for what has often been referred to as the post-war 'compromise' or 'consensus' through which all main parties agreed on certain fundamental principles of policy – a consensus which gave rise to the term 'Butskellism' (an amalgam of the names of the Conservative Chancellor, Butler, and the Labour leader, Gaitskell).

At the heart of Butskellism were three core principles. First, both parties were committed to the maintenance of a comprehensive system of welfare support which encompassed free health care, universal education, social security, the right to a house (whether private or public), and so on. We discuss this in Chapter 9 and shall not discuss it here except to note that, as the years have gone by, so the cost of the welfare state has increased substantially in real terms, thus increasing the pressures on public expenditure.

Second, both parties were committed to the maintenance of the so-called 'mixed economy'. As we have seen, the post-war Labour Government nationalized a number of key industries and although the Conservative administration which won office in 1951 subsequently denationalised steel (which was then nationalised again in 1967), it never made any attempt to return other industries such as the coal mines and the railways to private ownership. Indeed, in later years, both Labour and Conservative Governments were instrumental in extending the size of the public sector (Rolls Royce aeroengines, for example, was nationalized by the Heath Government in 1971 when it was on the brink of collapse), and it is only since 1979 that any serious attempt has been made to sell off substantial public assets in the more profitable sectors of public enterprise such as British Petroleum, the British National Oil Corporation, British Ports, the non-postal side of British Telecom, etc.

There were a number of different reasons why governments of both main parties were prepared to support the mixed economy through the 1950s. In some cases it was recognised that the employment prospects of thousands of workers could only be safeguarded by public ownership since many of the old staple industries had become too unprofitable and uncompetitive to survive in private hands. In other cases, nationalization was seen as a strategy for maintaining cheap energy supplies for private industry (coal, gas, electricity), or for providing cheap raw-material inputs (steel), or for servicing the transportation requirements of the private sector (railways). Harold Macmillan summed up the thinking of both Conservative and Labour Governments when he argued:

The socialist remedy should be accepted in regard to industries and services where it is obvious that private enterprise has exhausted its social usefulness, or where the general welfare of the economy requires that certain basic industries and services need now to be conducted in the light of broader social considerations than the profit motive provides.

Put another way, public ownership was seen as a necessary cost which government would have to bear in order to sustain a profitable private sector. Nationalization was a strategy for maintaining production in those areas of the economy on which much of the private sector depended but which were insufficiently profitable to attract new private-sector investment.

The third main plank of Butskellism was the commitment to maintaining full employment and economic growth through the adoption of Keynesian demand-management policies. If support for the nationalized industries was primarily an attempt to maintain the supply of relatively cheap energy and raw material inputs to the private sector, then fiscal policy and increased public expenditure was oriented towards stimulating demands for the products of the private sector.

As we saw earlier, the Keynesian economic management strategy rests on the attempt by government to keep demand in the economy sufficiently buoyant so as to soak up all that industry can produce when working at full capacity. This is achieved partly through increased public spending and partly through encouragement of private spending by easing the supply of money and credit. The problem with both strategies, as Keynes himself recognised, is that they are inflationary, for if more money is made available to buy the same number of goods, then prices inevitably will rise. Keynes argued that a mild inflationary trend was the price that would have to be paid to maintain full employment, and post-war governments in Britain and elsewhere readily accepted this price, with the result that unemployment during the 1950s was generally kept at or below 2 per cent while retail prices and wages rose by a few per cent each year.

The use of this strategy rested on at least three important conditions. The first was the assumption that, when the government stimulated demand in the economy, this would increase domestic investment and raise the output of home-based industries. This did occur to some extent, but such a response was increasingly hindered by the continuing haemorrhaging of British capital into overseas investments once currency controls were relaxed after the war (private investment abroad rose from an average of £180 million in the early fifties to £320 million 10 years later). This, together with the greater competitiveness of German, Japanese and other overseas manufacturers, meant that stimulation of demand was met increasingly by rising imports and a deterioration in the balance of payments. A rising deficit on the balance of payments, which was exacerbated by continued government spending overseas (particularly military expenditure in Aden, Cyprus, Germany and elsewhere), then inevitably led governments to reverse their policies and cut demand by imposing a credit squeeze designed to reduce domestic demand for imported goods. Thus developed the familiar 'stop-go' cycles of the later 1950s and 1960s in which spending would be encouraged by a relaxation of credit controls at one point, only to be squeezed as soon as it led to a balance-of-payments crisis. The uncertainty that this caused further contributed in no small way to the country's economic problems since it discouraged long-term investment, leading industrialists to hesitate before investing in response to a government-induced boom and financiers to look overseas for more stable and profitable places to invest their money.

These consequences could perhaps have been avoided had governments chosen to react to inflationary pressures and balance of payments deficits with measures such as devaluation or import controls. For 20 years, the pound sterling was pegged at a rate of $2.80, and it was not until 1967 that the government eventually devalued, this reflecting the customary concern with maintaining a strong currency, even at the expense of home-based industry whose products were overpriced in overseas markets and undercut by imports in the domestic market. By making British exports cheaper and foreign imports more expensive, devaluation could have eased balance-of-payments problems, but this was strongly resisted by financial interests seeking to maintain the sterling value of their overseas earnings. So it was that a relatively weak industrial base was made even weaker by a commitment to a strong pound and hence to a policy of domestic deflation whenever the balance of payments ran into deficit.

The second assumption on which a Keynesian strategy necessarily rested was that governments would resist the temptation to stimulate the economy at the 'wrong time'. Demand-management appeared as a useful tool for manipulating the economy for electoral purposes, for it enabled a government to induce a mini-boom prior to an election in the knowledge that the inflationary effects would not work through until some time after the election had been won. As we saw in Chapter 2, some commentators believe that governments generally did not resist this temptation, with the result that a series of 'political business cycles' came to be overlaid upon the existing stop-go cycles, with the economy being primed during the lead-up to an election and then slammed into reverse gear immediately afterwards. To the extent that this occurred, it not only exacerbated the decline in business confidence, fuelled wage demands and sent even more investors scurrying overseas with their cash, but it also built up a long-term inflationary pressure, for each politically-engineered boom built on the last and made it that much more difficult to bring the money supply back under control.

This leads us to consider the third assumption of a Keynesian strategy which was that, all that was required to maintain full employment and avert a serious recession was periodic 'fine-tuning' of the economy, raising demand at one point, dampening it down at another. It was this assumption that was challenged by the publication in 1966 of *Monopoly Capital* by two American Marxist political economists, Paul Baran and Paul Sweezy.

In their book, Baran and Sweezy accepted Keynes's argument that the basic problem in advanced capitalist economies was that of engineering sufficient demand to enable private firms to operate at full capacity, but they argued that, in the long term, this could not be achieved. The reason for this lay in a tendency in modern capitalist societies for effective demand to fall short of a rising productive capacity. The basic problem as they saw it was that the economy was increasingly dominated by a small number of large firms which have effectively reached a tacit agreement not to cut each others' throats by aggressive price competition. With the virtual eclipse of price competition in this 'monopoly sector' of the economy, each firm is able to fix prices at a level which guarantees an acceptable level of profit, provided that it can sell its goods. In order to raise this level of profit, each firm also seeks to reduce its costs by investing in new technology which raises productivity and hence increases the amount of goods that can be produced by each worker. The result is that more and more can be produced, and even greater profits can be achieved, but this expansion depends upon an ever increasing market. Monopoly capitalism, in other words, finds itself in a perpetual spiral of increasing capacity which demands that more and more goods be sold at a fixed price if the system as a whole is not to collapse into recession. The problem confronting monopoly capitalism is the problem of how to absorb an ever-expanding surplus.

Baran and Sweezy discussed various strategies which have been adopted in an attempt to increase the markets for the goods produced in the monopoly sector, and they stressed the importance of state expenditure (particularly military expenditure) as the major source of new demand. In their view, however, even massive military budgets are unlikely to prove sufficient to absorb this continually rising surplus. The long post-war boom was fuelled by enormous military spending, plus private spending on new consumer goods (e.g. cars) which was underpinned by a vast expansion of credit, but such a boom could not continue indefinitely. Neither the state nor private individuals could perpetually increase their purchasing of goods, for the expansion of credit and the growth of indebtedness would eventually reach its limits.

Seen in this light, recession was being postponed, not averted. Keynesian demand-management was an important factor underlying the continued growth of all Western economies for the 20 years after the war, but in retrospect it can be seen as having stored up problems for later. Certainly in Britain, it was becoming clear, even by the late fifties, that certain fundamental problems remained unresolved and that Keynesian fine-tuning was not going to be enough to overcome them. Particularly worrying was the evidence that Britain was still falling further behind her main competitors; throughout the boom years, wages increased much faster than productivity with the result that British industry became less and less competitive on world markets. From a share of world trade of 21 per cent in 1953, Britain experienced a dramatic fall to under 14 per cent in 1964. The British people may never have had it so good, but the British economy was evidently sick and becoming sicker. Something new had to be tried.

CORPORATIST PLANNING: 1962–79

We have seen that during the long period of British economic decline up to the outbreak of the Second World War, governments remained committed to liberal orthodoxies of minimal state intervention. During this period, the role of the state *vis-à-vis* the private sector may be termed 'facilitative'. Following the war, however, we have seen that domestic economic policy became more interventionist as a result of the adoption of demand-management strategies aimed at maintaining full employment. The relation between the state and the private sector in these years may therefore be more accurately described as 'supportive'. From the early 1960s onwards, governments took a further step away from liberal orthodoxy by attempting to plan economic growth. In this sense, the years between 1961 and 1979 may be seen in terms of an increasingly 'directive' role of the state in economic affairs.

It is important to note that this progressive shift away from a facilitative towards a directive role occurred primarily in respect of domestic economic intervention. Throughout this period, British governments remained reluctant to extend planning and direction to Britain's relations with other countries. Some attempt was made during the 1960s to restrict imports through the imposition of a temporary system of selective surcharges, and the commitment to free trade was modified through the eventually successful attempt to join the European Common Market which permitted free trade within its boundaries while erecting a high tariff wall against non-members. The commitment of successive governments to the principle of free trade nevertheless remained strong, as did their commitment to the balance of payments and a strong pound. The new interventionism of the 1960s had much more to do with the planning of investment, incomes and industrial relations than it did with the planning of trade.

The move towards economic planning began under a Conservative Government with the establishment of the National Economic Development Council ('Neddy') in 1962. This represented the first formal attempt to establish an institution for economic planning which would bring together the state and the two sides of industry on a regular basis in an attempt to monitor the country's economic performance and to develop government initiatives which would stimulate growth. It was also hoped that formal trade union involvement on the National Economic Development Committee would win the support of organised labour for some form of wage regulation or restraint and thus avoid the need for dramatic measures such as the 6-month pay freeze which the government had imposed in 1961 following the latest in a series of sterling crises.

It was with the election of the Wilson Labour Government in 1964, however, that the marked shift towards a planning strategy occurred. At the 1964 election, Labour projected itself as a modern technocratic party. Harold Wilson himself bemoaned the 'thirteen wasted years' of tory rule and spoke of regenerating British industry through the planned introduction of new technology. The image of the Labour Party which fought and won the 1964 election was more that of the white coat than the cloth cap, while the image of defeated Conservatives under the leadership of Lord Home was that of the deerstalker hat.

The new Labour Government retained the NEDC as part of a new ministry – the Department of Economic Affairs – which was run by the party's deputy leader, George Brown. The principal task of the new department was to develop Britain's first National Plan which was published in 1965. This envisaged a growth rate in the economy as a whole of nearly 4 per cent per year until 1970, to be achieved on the basis of a 3.4 per cent annual growth in productivity and a substantial rise in rates of investment (this required rate of productivity increase was by no means unrealistic, for productivity in British industry actually rose by more than 4 per cent per year between 1962 and 1975). As part of its planning strategy, the government also established a National Prices and Incomes Board which scrutinised all wage and price increases before they came into effect and put considerable pressure on trade unions to enter into productivity agreements as the means for raising real wages, and this helped to create the conditions in which growth could be fostered.

The increased investment which was necessary was left to the private sector. Growth targets were published for each industry in the hope that investment would increase in a new climate of long-term predictability. In fact, investment did begin to pick up, but not for long. In the summer of 1966, the government was rocked by another balance-of-payments crisis accompanied by the familiar run on sterling. George Brown and his Department argued for a devaluation but they were over-ruled. Instead, the government abandoned its National Plan and its growth targets by introducing severe cuts in public expenditure and a statutory 6-months pay freeze. The familiar stop-go pattern had returned and Britain's first attempt at national economic planning had been jettisoned in favour of a massive deflation. Those businesses which had stepped up investment in response to the government's assurances of sustained growth were left to contemplate the prospects of a dramatically reduced market for their goods. Business confidence, never strong, had received another bad knock.

The 1966 deflation had an immmediate impact on unemployment which rose in just 6 months from 250 000 to 600 000; a new post-war high. This trend to rising unemployment continued through the remainder of the government's term of office and marks the first decisive break with the post-war commitment to a Keynesian policy of using public spending to maintain full employment.

With its National Plan in tatters, the government came increasingly to rely on pay controls as its major level of economic management. Statutory controls on income were renewed following the 1966 pay freeze, but although ministers were still able to count on the support or acquiesence of most union leaders, it was evident that large sections of the rank and file union members were becoming restive. The growth of power of shop stewards became manifest in the rise in the proportion of unofficial to official disputes, and government attempts to restrain incomes were increasingly challenged by the growth of shop-floor militancy. Eventually, in 1969, the government responded to these challenges by issuing a White Paper designed to reduce official stoppages by enforcing strike ballots and a 28-day delay on unofficial strikes. The proposals sparked off a storm of protest in both the industrial and political wings of the labour movement, and the government was eventually obliged to back down.

In June 1970, Labour lost a general election which it had been widely expected to win. The government had succeeded in at last bringing the balance of payments into surplus (in this it had been aided by a long-overdue devaluation of the pound later in 1967), but this had been achieved at the cost of rising unemployment, slow growth, accelerating inflation and falling rates of industrial investment.

The evident failure of Labour's attempt at economic planning had had its impact on Conservative thinking, and the Heath government that came to office in 1970 was determined to have no more to do with either Keynesian demand-management or state planning. Government was to return to its traditional facilitative role and economic growth was to be fostered through minimal interference with market processes. The trappings of state planning such as the National Board for Prices and Incomes and the Industrial Reorganisation Corporation (which Labour had established in 1966 to aid company mergers in the hope that this would increase industrial efficiency) were scrapped. The NEDC survived but the government effectively ended any close consultation with the unions. Indeed, one of its first priorities was to introduce the Industrial Relations Act, 1971, which outlawed the closed shop, made provision for legally-enforceable agreements in industry, introduced Labour's earlier proposals for strike ballots and 'cooling-off periods', and established a register of trade unions, all of which was interpreted by the unions themselves as an unprecedented attack on their power. The government also insisted that there would be no more state aid for ailing industries ('lame ducks'), no more legislation on prices and incomes (although state employees were made subject to tight government controls on public-sector wage rises), and no more increases in public expenditure to maintain full employment. Public spending was to be cut back, taxes were to be reduced and the economy was to boom under the influence of pure market forces and a return of the entrepreneurial spirit.

By 1972, the government had executed a famous 'U-turn'. Confronted by rapidly rising unemployment, increasing closures, escalating industrial unrest and spiralling inflation, the government abandoned its free-market strategy and returned to large-scale intervention. In 1972, it nationalized that symbol of British free enterprise, Rolls Royce, in order to avert its imminent closure. In the same year it introduced a new and highly interventionist Industry Act which allowed the Secretary of State for Industry to purchase shares in companies in order to improve output and efficiency. A new Pay Board and Price Commission was established as the government introduced statutory incomes regulation, and negotiations were opened with the CBI and TUC as union leaders were brought back in from the cold. This remarkable turn-around was completed by a 'dash for growth' on the part of the Chancellor, Anthony Barber, who abandoned the earlier tight monetary controls in favour of a swift and huge injection of money into the economy designed to stimulate new investment. The effect of this last policy was to suck in imports at an unprecedented rate (imports rose by 44 per cent in volume between 1971 and 1973) thereby turning Labour's hard-won balance of payments surplus into a resounding deficit, and to raise public spending by nearly 20 per cent in a year. Unemployment continued to climb and passed the million mark while inflation climbed with it, thereby demonstrating that the Keynesian trade-off between inflation and employment was no longer operative in a situation where both were rising simultaneously. And on top of all this, oil prices quadrupled as a result of the 1973 Middle East war, the Gold Exchange Standard worked out at Bretton Woods collapsed following the devaluation of the dollar in 1971 and the subsequent floating of all the world's major currencies, and the whole of the Western capitalist world slumped into recession in 1974 as world trade contracted on a scale not seen since before the war. In Britain, a miners' strike against the government's pay policy put most of industry on a 3-day week as electricity supplies from coal-powered generating stations dwindled. The government called an election on the specific issue of the miners' strike and the unions, and in February 1974, Harold Wilson was back in Downing Street as leader of a minority Labour Government.

By now, the crisis of the British economy was becoming acute. Industrial output in Britain had risen by 18 per cent in eight years compared with increases of 40 and 50 per cent by Britain's major European trading partners. Profit rates were falling steeply; returns on capital invested had fallen from 12 per cent in 1960 to under 4 per cent by 1975. This, not surprisingly, was deterring new investment. The proportion of earnings reinvested had fallen from 78 per cent in 1967 to 63 per cent in 1974 as companies attempted to maintain the level of dividend paid to their shareholders, yet dividends continued to fall and the value of shares fell with them. In desperate need of new investment, most companies found that their low profitability made it impossible for them to attract funds. The proportion of new investment funded by shares fell from 12 per cent in the late fifties to just 4 per cent in 1972. This meant that companies were forced to finance new investment through borrowing, yet the financial institutions were increasingly reluctant to lend except at crippling high rates of interest over very short periods. The result of all this was that investment was drying up, even in the more viable firms. British manufacturing industry had become vastly under-capitalized with investment per worker amounting to just one-third of that in West Germany and one-quarter of that in Japan. Given these disparities, it is hardly surprising that goods from Germany, Japan and elsewhere were flooding the British market, undercutting British producers, and laying waste large sectors of British industry including both the old staples such as textiles and the newer light industries such as cars, motor cycles and television tubes.

Faced with such dramatic evidence of Britain's economic decline, the newly-elected Labour Government resorted once again to state planning. This time, however, it attempted to intervene directly in the investment policy of key companies rather than simply trying to create a climate in which the companies themselves could choose to invest. It also tried to target its interventions on specific companies and specified industries rather than developing policies designed to stimulate growth in the economy as a whole as had been the case in the 1965 National Plan. The instrument for this fresh attempt at planning economic growth was the Industry Act, 1975.

Labour's Industry Act introduced two major innovations. The first was a system of 'planning agreements'. By the mid-1970s, a series of mergers and take-overs had produced a situation where just 100 firms accounted for half of Britain's manufacturing output. Given that most other firms depended directly or indirectly on these 100 giants (e.g. by supplying them with components or raw materials), it seemed that it would be possible to plan the overall course of the British economy by influencing the future investment plans of these biggest companies. This did not require wholesale nationalization which was unpopular and extremely expensive. Rather, the big firms could be left in private hands but could be encouraged to cooperate with government, pooling information and expertise and drawing on public funds where necessary in order to develop a future growth strategy which would secure both the profitability of the company and a planned growth of the economy as a whole.

As things turned out, however, the system of planning agreements was virtually stillborn. Only one company – Chrysler in 1977 – ever entered into such an agreement with the government, and this was in return for a massive injection of public funds which was necessary to avert imminent closure. The idea of planning agreements as a principal tool of economic management is still very much alive in the Labour Party today despite this failure, although many advocates of such agreements now argue that they cannot operate successfully on a voluntary basis, and that only some form of state compulsion will ensure the involvement of most large companies.

The second major innovation of the 1975 act was the establishment of the National Enterprise Board. This was more successful, though more limited; indeed, it even managed to survive the election of the Thatcher Government in 1979 (albeit in a much scaled-down form).

The purpose of the NEB was to provide investment funds to viable firms which were struggling to survive due to lack of liquidity. As we have seen, by the mid-seventies, many companies were finding it impossible to invest since they could not attract new shareholders and the terms imposed by the banks for new loans were prohibitive. The NEB (which inherited government shareholdings in various companies which had been bought as a result of the Heath Government's Industry Act) sought to overcome this problem by buying shares in such companies as well as advancing grants and low-cost loans.

State shareholding through the NEB obviously increased the ability of the government to influence decision-making in the private sector, but it was far from the 'creeping nationalization' which some Conservative critics saw in it. The state often only took a minority holding, and when and as companies were restored to economic health, even these holdings could be sold off. The NEB was, therefore, a flexible instrument of economic planning, buying and selling shares whenever it seemed appropriate with little direct control from Paliament. And, in a limited way, it worked; firms such as Sinclair Electronics, for example, were undoubtedly saved, later to prosper, as a result of its interventions. Together with various regional bodies such as the Scottish, Welsh and Northern Ireland Development Agencies, which were also established in 1975 with power to buy shares in potentially viable firms, it represented an important innovation aimed directly at the major problem confronting British industry for the last 100 years – lack of investment. However, its impact was inevitably limited given the failure of the planning agreements system, for it was bailing out medium-sized firms while the investment decisions of the largest and most crucial companies remained virtually unaffected by government influence.

The Industry Act, 1975 was one leg of the government's economic strategy. The other related not to capital but to labour and involved the attempt to regulate incomes. Wary after its own experiences of statutory incomes controls during the sixties and the Heath Government's downfall in 1974, the government applied the voluntary principle to incomes just as it did on the other side of industry to planning agreements. Following a spate of legislation in the early years of the government designed to shift the balance of power in industry back towards organised labour (e.g. through repeal of the Industrial Relations Act, 1971, introduction of new rights of unions to gain recognition, run a closed shop and secure immunities from certain common law actions, and introduction of new rights for individual workers pertaining to redundancy pay, protection against arbitrary dismissal and maternity leave), the TUC entered into an agreement with the government in 1975 whereby its member unions would accept a flat-rate pay rise in return for price controls and improvements in the 'social wage' (i.e. welfare and social security provisions). This agreement (which was also endorsed by the employers' organisation, the CBI), formed the basis for what became known as the 'Social Contract' by which, each year, union leaders agreed to voluntary limits on wage rises in return for social provisions or tax reductions from government.

For 2 years, this voluntary system of pay restraint operated very successfully in that wage increases generally conformed to those that had been agreed while the number and duration of strikes fell considerably. The unions had effectively been coopted as junior partners in government, being directly involved in the development of policy and carrying the responsibility themselves for implementing agreements on wages. The government's broader economic policy was operating rather less successfully, however, and the inflation which had been stoked up by the Heath Government's dash for growth was now spiralling beyond 20 per cent per year, fuelled by the government's commitment to increased industrial and welfare spending. The result, predictably, was a sterling crisis in the autumn of 1976 which was triggered off by a continuing balance-of-payments deficit and the falling value of the pound. As investors scrambled to exchange their sterling holdings into other currencies, the government turned to the International Monetary Fund for assistance. The Fund granted credit to pay off foreign debts and stabilise the currency, but it imposed severe conditions on this loan which effectively undermined the whole basis of the government's economic strategy by insisting on tight monetary controls which inevitably meant substantial cuts in public spending and a massive reduction of demand in the economy. As in 1966, so in 1976, a Labour Government was blown off course by international pressure on sterling which in turn reflected the weakness of the country's industrial base.

The 'Social Contract' remained only in name as living standards were reduced and unemployment rose in an attempt to bring inflation under control. In 1977, the government imposed a 10 per cent ceiling on wage rises without the consent of the TUC, since this represented a real cut in wages at a time when prices were increasing by more than twice that figure. In 1978, the government chanced its arm on a fourth round of pay restraint, this time insisting on a norm of just 5 per cent. Through the winter of 1978/9, strikes among low-paid public-sector workers caused massive disruption throughout the public services, and in May 1979, the Conservative Party was swept back into office on a wave of popular anti-union and anti-government sentiment.

Reviewing the years from 1962 to 1979, it is apparent that an important change took place in the relation between the state and the private sector.

With the exception of just two years (during the period 1970–72) when the Heath Government attempted to revert to a market strategy, governments of both main parties presided over a growth in state involvement which entailed increased planning together with increased participation in policy-making by the repesentatives of capital (the CBI) and organised labour (the TUC). The fact that Heath had tried and failed to break this trend lent credence to the view that direct state involvement in the economy was becoming established and in some way necessary as a feature of economic life in the last quarter of the twentieth century in Britain. The theory which developed to identify and explain this change was the theory of corporatism (see Chapter 3).

For some observers writing in the 1970s, corporatism was to be understood as a new type of social and economic system, distinct from both capitalism and socialism but containing within it elements of both. The clearest example of such a view is found in the work of Jack Winkler who detected a trend towards ever-increasing state direction of the economy and who argued that the state was gradually replacing the owners and managers of capitalist firms as the driving force in the economy. Thus he suggested that, under the new corporatist system which he believed was emerging, those who owned capital would continue to pocket their (strictly-controlled) profits, but they would have less and less say over how their productive resources were to be used. Just as in the war the state had subordinated traditional capitalist concerns with profit maximisation and free enterprise to its own greater objectives, so 30 years further on, the state was once again, in Winkler's view, directing the economy in accordance with its own concerns to ensure unity, order, efficiency and the 'national interest'. Winkler argued that the way in which the state sought to impose these principles was by means of flexible, relatively informal and non-bureaucratic modes of organisation such as the 'Quangos' which enabled technical experts to come together with company and union leaders away from the public gaze and relatively insulated from the political battleground of the parliamentary system. The deals which were worked out there were then administered, not by the state itself, but by the participating organisations. Agreements reached with the TUC over wages, for example, were to be implemented by the TUC itself, while agreements reached with big companies over future investment strategies were carried through by the companies working cooperatively with the government on the basis of planning agreements, price codes and the like. Corporatism thus entailed a flexible and hierarchical system of state economic control characterised above all by the cooption of the organised interests of capital and labour into the heart of the policy-making and implementation process.

The main problem with Winkler's thesis, of course, is that even in the context of the mid-1970s, it does not stand up to empirical examination. For a start, the state's control over capital is over-emphasised. Winkler placed considerable weight on the development of planning agreements and the use of price controls, yet as we have seen, only one planning agreement was ever signed (and even this proved toothless), while price controls have rarely been effective for more than a short period precisely because they actually undermine the profitability of companies which the state is supposed to be sustaining. State control over organised labour is also over-emphasised in Winkler's model, for although there is no doubt that union leaders have successfully been incorporated into government as junior partners, there is considerable evidence to suggest that their rank-and-file members have remained wilfully antagonistic to many of the deals struck on their behalf. The period identified by Winkler as an era of growing corporatism was in fact a period characterised by the continual break-down of wages policies and by various efforts by governments and union bureaucracies to control unofficial action at the level of the shop floor.

None of this necessarily means that the concept of corporatism is without value in understanding recent economic policy in Britain, but it does mean that the concept needs to be narrowed down from Winkler's sweepingly broad application of it in ways we suggest in Chapter 3. In particular, it makes little sense to argue that, during the sixties and seventies, Britain was changing from a capitalist to a corporatist society for as many critics have pointed out, the country remained capitalist in the sense that those who owned and managed the means of production continued to direct their use and that the economy continued to function according to the overriding principle of the search for profitability. What happened during these years was not that the state took over control of the economy and began to run it according to its own objectives, but that it searched in a somewhat haphazard way for new solutions to Britain's long-term economic decline. This search led it to develop new modes of operation, new strategies for attaining its long-standing objective of maintaining the profitability of private-sector firms.

Essentially, what happened from the 1960s onwards was that governments tried to involve key economic interests directly in economic policy-making. They did this by developing a form of political representation based not on geographical constituencies but on functional interests. In other words, side by side with the elected parliamentary system of representation there grew up a non-elected corporatist system of representation in which the leaders of particular sections of the population were invited to participate according to their role in the division of labour. Seen in this way, corporatism involved the selective incorporation of particular producer interests within the political system with the aim of developing policies and managing economic growth according to the specific requirements of these groups.

The principal interests represented in this corporatist strategy were, of course, industrial firms (represented by the CBI and other industrial employer groups such as the Engineering Employers' Federation and the

National Federation of Building Trades Employers) and organised labour (represented by the TUC). These two blocks remained in regular and close contact with government through their participation in private political forums such as the NEDC, and in return for the opportunity to help shape government policy, they undertook the responsibility for ensuring that the agreed policies were actually implemented (e.g. as in the case of the TUC policing government incomes policies). In this way, big capital and organised labour evolved as appendages of the state, as new 'governing institutions' collaborating with the state rather than simply pressuring it from outside.

Now, it is important to emphasise that such a corporatist system of interest representation was not new in Britain in that governments have been more or less willing to share their power with capital and organised labour, and to include these groups within the policy-making process, since the 1930s. What happened from the 1960s onwards was simply that consultation and participation became institutionalised through the establishment of formal organs of economic planning. It is also important to recognise that corporatism was not limited exclusively to governments' relations with industry and the unions; in agriculture, for example, the National Farmers' Union has long enjoyed the fruits of a close and exclusive partnership with government through which farm prices, farm workers' wages and many aspects of investment and marketing policy are determined away from the public gaze, while various professional bodies such as the British Medical Association have similarly developed close consultative relations with the relevant departments of state.

What is common to all these cases is that corporatism can be seen as a strategy of exclusion. While certain key producer groups – major industrial employers, the principal unions, the farmers, the doctors and so on – became integrated and incorporated into the process of state policy-making, other interests in British society – consumers, small business people, the self-employed, non-unionised labour, old age pensioners, single parents etc. – were left out and unincorporated. There developed from the 1960s on a bifurcation of British politics between, on the one hand, the traditional arena of competitive electoral politics as represented by Parliament and local authorities, and on the other, a corporatist system of interest representation wherein participation was selective and exclusive. While a wide variety of different groups could attempt to get their views heard in the electoral arena, this was not the case in the corporatist sector where participation was limited to particular economic interests. Seen in this way, corporatism developed as the antithesis to pluralism. Indeed, corporatism may be understood as a response to the problems of pluralism in that it enables governments to insulate themselves from the clutter of competing opinions and diverging demands and to concentrate instead on responding to those groups which are most strategically important as regards the future development of the economy.

By the late 1970s, however, it had become apparent that this corporatist strategy for managing the economy was not working. The so-called 'winter of discontent' in 1978/9, when millions of low-paid public-sector workers rebelled against continued income restraint, demonstrated that the close cooperative relationship between government and unions had broken down and that union leaders could no longer deliver on their side of the bargain. Furthermore, the continuing rise in unemployment and fall in the profitability of large sections of British industry showed that the economic policies developed within the corporatist sector of the economy were failing to resolve the country's basic economic difficulties. There was a growing and festering resentment among large sections of the population against what was seen as the privileged position of organised labour and the remoteness and non-responsiveness of big government. In 1964, Harold Wilson had been able to rally support with his call for a new technocratic politics involving an extension of state planning, and in 1974, when the country was on its knees as a result of the miners' strike, he had still been able to win an election on the basis of his promise that Labour could work with the unions to manage the economy. By 1979, however, the electorate had evidently had enough, and voters turned in their millions to Margaret Thatcher's new Tory Party which held out the promise of an end to government 'interference' and a return to the principles of the free market. Twenty years of corporatist economic planning had come to an end, and the wheel was about to come full circle.

THE RETURN TO A MARKET STRATEGY: THATCHERISM AND
ECONOMIC POLICY IN THE 1980s

The Conservative Government elected in 1979 has a claim to be regarded as the most radical administration since the 1945–50 Labour Government in that it challenged all the orthodoxies which had been accepted with lesser or greater enthusiasm by all post-war governments. The three main planks of Butskellism – the mixed economy, the welfare state and the use of Keynesian demand-management to ensure full employment – all came under sustained attack. It is true that the outgoing Labour Government had itself eroded welfare spending and abandoned any pretence at achieving full employment following the 1976 International Monetary Fund loan, but the Thatcher administration went much further and attacked such policies as a matter of principle.

It is impossible to understand what happened after 1979 without first understanding what was entailed in 'Thatcherism'. Thatcherism was not simply an economic policy, although the commitment to a free-market strategy was certainly a key component of it. The important point is that the market was supported as a principle in its own right rather than as merely a means for overcoming Britain's economic problems. Thus, in the years following 1979, the government aggressively pursued a market strategy even where this entailed increased economic costs: profitable state industries were privatised, for example, thereby reducing public revenues, just as council houses were sold off at large discounts thereby increasing the burdens on the public purse (see Chapter 9). Thatcherism in this sense represented a return to the nineteenth-century emphasis on the liberal aspects of liberal-democracy.

This principled support of the free market reflected an individualistic philosophy which held that economic freedom was a condition of political freedom. Milton Friedman, an American economist whose ideas played a crucial role in the development of Thatcherite philosophy, expressed this argument with deceptive simplicity when he wrote:

Fundamentally, there are only two ways of co-ordinating the economic activities of millions. One is central direction involving the use of coercion – the technique of the army and of the modern totalitarian state. The other is voluntary cooperation of individuals – the technique of the market place.

The government's promotion of the market was thus a function of its commitment to a classical liberal philosophy (resurrected in the work of writers like Friedman and F. A. Hayek) in which individuals should be left to make their own choices while the state's role is to be limited to ensuring that the conditions under which free choice can be exercised are maintained. This is a philosophy which has a long pedigree in Britain, going back to the nineteenth-century utilitarians and beyond, yet it is a philosophy which represents a fundamental break with the paternalism of the traditional Tory Party. It is also probably true to say that Thatcher's original appeal was to the 'small people' – the self-employed, the independent professionals, the skilled artisans – rather than to big business. As she often reminded her audiences, she was herself a humble grocer's daughter made good.

This appeal to the very people who had felt themselves excluded from the corporatist planning of the previous two decades was reinforced by a potent mixture of political nationalism, populism and authoritarianism. The nationalism, which had been nurtured by Enoch Powell and others on the extreme right of the Conservative Party through the 1960s and 1970s, took the form of a latent racism (Thatcher, for example, spoke of Britain as having been 'swamped' by black immigrants) a single-minded pursuit of British interests within the European Community, an uncompromising stand against Irish republicanism and Scottish and Welsh separatism (discussed in Chapter 11), and a general reassertion of patriotic sentiment which swelled to a peak in 1982 during the successful war waged to recapture the Falkland Islands from Argentina. This was then combined with the populist campaign against 'big unions' and 'big government', and with a new authoritarian ideology which stressed the need for strong state which would stand up to Britain's enemies abroad (by a massive increase in spending on conventional and nuclear forces) and at home (by strengthening the police force, imposing stiffer sentences through the courts, and confronting the power of 'anti-social' elements in British society – notably the trade unions).

All of this was the context within which the government's economic strategy was pursued – a strategy which was designed to bury neo-Keynesianism and break up old-style corporatism. It was a strategy which deliberately removed the props and crutches on which so much of British industry had come to lean over the previous 20 or 30 years, and which sought instead to expose British firms to the full cleansing blast of international competition. It was, in a sense, a Darwinian strategy of survival of the fittest; companies would either adapt to these changed circumstances by reducing their costs and improving efficiency, or they would die. As we shall see, many died.

The strategy itself was based on an analysis of the manifold ills of the British economy which emphasised the deleterious effects of at least four main factors: powerful unions, weak government, an over-burdened private sector and, most important of all, profligate public spending.

The argument that *strong unions* have been one important factor in Britain's more recent economic difficulties is by no means peculiar to right-wing theorists, for some Marxist theorists too have suggested that private-sector profits have been squeezed over the years by a combination of intense foreign competition (which has prevented companies from increasing prices) and a strong union movement (which has forced them to increase wages). This is, however, a view which is more often heard on the right where there is, in any case, a marked antipathy towards the principle of unionism in so far as it is seen as intruding on individual rights (e.g. through the imposition of closed shops) and as undermining the operation of a free market. For the New Right, trade unions are the modern equivalent of the feudal barons, and they have used their monopolistic control over the supply of labour and their coercive powers such as the right to picket in order to force up wages beyond their 'natural' market level, thereby crippling the profitability of British industry.

Seen in this light, trade union power represents an obstacle to any attempt to force companies to become more competitive since it prevents firms from reducing their costs by cutting wages and shedding surplus labour. From the point of view of the Thatcher Government, successive post-war administrations in Britain had exacerbated this problem through the pursuit of Keynesian full-employment policies, which had strengthened the bargaining power of the unions, and through the adoption of corporatist management strategies which included union leaders within the policy-making process. Just as the old nineteenth-century liberals were concerned that the extension of the franchise would subordinate state power to the sectional demands of the working class, so their new twentieth-century counterparts now argued that this had indeed occurred and that Keynesianism and corporatism had been the instruments of this unwarranted increase in the power of organised labour.

What was required therefore was a weakening of union power rather than compromises with it, and from 1979 onwards, the government set out to do just this by allowing unemployment to rise, by legislating on issues such as the right to picket, by reducing union involvement in policy-making bodies, and by standing firm against workers in the public sector (such as health service workers, the water workers and others) who attempted to breach the government's tight 'cash limits' on public-sector wage rises. To a large extent, the policy worked. Wages fell in real terms and as unemployment rose above 3 million, unions lost members and rank-and-file union members lost any enthusiasm for costly and protracted strikes; even the miners, who had crippled the Heath Government in 1974, were split over their leaders' calls for strike action against pit closures. Yet the attack on the unions could only represent one aspect of the government's economic policy, for the available statistics demonstrate that take-home wages had not risen by any significant extent as a proportion of the nation's domestic product, and that, compared with other industrial nations, wage rates in Britain were among the lowest and had been for many years.

The second element in the government's strategy rested on the view that *weak government* had been a further factor in Britain's economic decline. This view derived from the thesis, discussed in Chapter 3, which held that government had become 'overloaded', and that there had developed a 'bias of excessive expectation in democracy', which had been fuelled by the continuing expansion of state spending from the 1950s onwards. A whole post-war generation had been reared in the belief that it had a right to expect comprehensive welfare support in housing, health care, education and so on, and no government had been strong enough to stand up against the escalating demands from various different sections of the population for more spending on more and improved services. The result had been an ever-widening gap between the level of state spending and the total revenues collected in taxation, even though taxes had increased. This gap had been filled by government borrowing and by 'printing money' – hence the inflation spiral of the 1970s.

This analysis rests on the argument that various groups have been able to use the state for their own selfish ends in that they have been able to push successfully for expensive programmes whose cost must be shared by everybody else. Industrialists, for example, have pushed for increased aids to industry, professional groups such as teachers, social workers and doctors have pushed for more spending on education, welfare and health, trade unions have pushed for increases in the 'social wage', and so on. While there is undoubtedly some truth in this analysis, the question which it fails to address is why the government has generally caved in to such pressures. To explain this simply in terms of governmental 'weakness' is hardly adequate since it involves a tautology; after all, governments that 'give in' to pressures are by definition weak. What we need to know is why governments have apparently been so 'weak' in the face of demands for increased spending for which there are no additional sources of revenue.

One answer, advanced in the Marxist literature of the 1970s, is that governments have had little choice but to given in, for a refusal to increase spending would have led to a massive fall in company profits and to an erosion of working people's living standards to a point at which they began to question the very legitimacy of the capitalist system. Such is the argument developed in a very influential book by the American political scientist, James O'Connor, who suggested in the early seventies that Western governments were running up frighteningly large fiscal crises precisely because they were obliged at one and the same time to increase direct and indirect subsidies to the private sector and to supplement people's incomes through expanded social security provisions, while they were unable to meet these escalating costs through increased taxation. Government borrowing was spiralling out of control as a result.

This is in many ways a powerful argument, and we shall need to return to its implications in our discussion of welfare policy in Chapter 9. For our present purposes, however, we do need to query the assumption that governments effectively had no option but to increase spending. After all, from 1979, the Thatcher Government set out to do precisely the opposite; it reduced aid to industry, privatised large sectors of state enterprise, imposed tough cash limits throughout the public sector, drastically reduced welfare spending in areas such as housing, held social security payments such as pensions and unemployment benefits below the rate of inflation, and pinned its sail to the mast of monetary controls. It is true that even this government proved incapable of cutting public expenditure to the extent that it desired, partly because the massive rise in unemployment increased gross spending on unemployment and other benefits despite cuts in the value of these benefits. It is also true that these policies had a devastating impact on the profitability of British industry, contributed to a break-down in social order such as occurred in the wave of inner city riots during the summer of 1981, and eroded people's motivation to the extent that a general air of fatalism settled upon much of the country. None of this, however, was sufficient to deflect the government from its chosen course, and this indicates that the constraints on governments which led them to expand public spending through the sixties and seventies were more 'rational' than 'structural' (see our discussion of the question of constraints, pages 236-8). Governments clearly did have the option to refuse to 'give in' to the various demands for more public expenditure, and this was an option which was exercised from 1979 onwards.

The fact that previous administrations had not felt able to take such a course reflects their belief that massive cuts in government spending would prove highly unpopular and electorally disastrous. From 1979, however, the Thatcher Government set out to change this climate of opinion by asserting a new set of values based on individualism and given that it won the subsequent election of 1983 it evidently succeeded. The old political catchwords to which previous generations of politicians had felt obliged to pay lip-service – words like 'compassion' and notions of 'social rights' – were replaced with new ones – the importance of 'standing on one's own two feet' and of rewarding individual effort, initiative and hard work. This new message brought little comfort to the unemployed, but as Margaret Thatcher herself pointed out when unemployment first breeched 10 per cent, nine out of ten people were still in work, and even at a level of 14 per cent and rising, six in seven were still working. For those in employment, particularly those in the less-devastated southern parts of the country, the recession did not generally entail any great reduction in living standards, and it was to them that the Thatcher message was addressed. When the Prime Minister told them that there was no alternative to her unpleasant medicine, those who did not have to take it believed her, and when she called for 'sacrifices', those who remained unaffected applauded her. She was widely admired for her 'resolution' among those were were not called upon to bear the costs of it, and her government's crusades against 'selfish' trade unions, welfare 'spongers', 'cossetted' public-sector workers, black 'muggers' and the rest, struck a popular chord in the minds of millions of skilled manual workers and middle-class professionals who had for years fondly imagined themselves as a beseiged and hard-working minority who were carrying the rest of the country on their backs. The Thatcher message rode the waves of a new hard-nosed intolerance bred by years of economic decline; even her colleagues within the Tory Party who were less than enthusiastic about cuts in welfare spending and rising levels of unemployment were disparagingly dismissed as 'wets'.

One group which had for some time been singled out as social parasites was the public-sector workforce, and in particular civil servants and local authority employees, who were widely seen as inefficient and over-paid. An attack on them was entirely consistent with the government's anti-statist, anti-bureaucratic ideology, and it was underpinned by a third element in the Thatcherite explanation of Britain's economic decline involving the assertion of an *overburdened private sector*. British industry, it was believed, had been held back by an unproductive and burgeoning public-sector workforce.

The intellectual rationale for this belief came in the form of a book written by two economists which summarised the country's problems as due to 'too few producers'. What the authors, Robert Bacon and Walter Eltis, meant by this was not simply that the private sector had shrunk in comparison with the public (although it had), nor that industry had shrunk in comparison with services (although this again was true), but most crucially that the proportion of marketed to non-marketed output of goods and services had fallen. Through the 1960s and 1970s, the number of workers employed in producing profitable goods and services, whether in the private or public sector, had fallen while the numbers employed by the state and engaged in non-profitable activities such as administration, teaching or production of loss-making outputs such as coal or Concorde, had correspondingly risen. The consequence of this was that a declining marketed sector was increasingly called upon to finance an expanding non-marketed sector.

One obvious solution to this problem of too few producers having to sustain too many non-producers was to cut back the size of the non-marketed sector by cutting public spending and by ending state subsidies to loss-making public-sector industries such as BL Cars and the National Coal Board. This is precisely what the Thatcher Government set out to do by selling off public assets, closing down 'inefficient' pits, ending subsidies on council houses and selling houses wherever tenants expressed a desire to buy, laying off thousands of steel workers, teachers and other public-sector employees, cutting financial grants to local authorities, and so on.

It is worth noting, however, that Bacon and Eltis had themselves warned of 'the certainty of disaster' if a Conservative pro-market-sector government came to power and just sat back, balanced the budget, and let unemployment mount waiting for the market to solve its problems. In their view, the problem of the British economy was so severe that any shift back towards the market sector would have to proceed slowly and in conjunction with a battery of government controls, akin to those adopted in war time, which would gradually be lifted as the economy strengthened. This clearly did not happen after 1979, for the other elements of the Thatcherite strategy ruled out the use of government economic controls, with the result that the 'disaster' forecast by Bacon and Eltis was indeed unleashed in the form of the biggest slump in industrial production since the 1930s.

The fourth and most central element in the Thatcher Government's economic strategy was the commitment to monetarism, and this reflected the view that the major cause of Britain's economic ills lay in *profligate government spending*. It is this, of course, that lies behind the other three factors, for the pursuit of full employment to appease the unions, the weakness in the face of demands for greater expenditure, and the growing size of the public-sector workforce have all been possible only because governments have been willing to increase the supply of money. It was here, above all else, that the Thatcher Government sought to break with the past. Influenced by its economic guru, Professor Milton Friedman, it published monetary targets (which referred to the amount of money in circulation, plus bank deposits, plus money 'created' through credit) which sought to reduce the amount of money in the economy so as to reduce price inflation. In this way, the government tried to return to the old monetary discipline of the pre-Keynesian years before the war when the money supply had automatically been held in check through the operation of the Gold Standard. In the 1980s, with no such external controls on spendthrift governments, this meant self-imposed monetary discipline.

This doctrine of sound money had first been imposed during the Labour Government's term of office in 1976 as a condition of the International Monetary Fund loan, but from 1979 it was adopted freely and enthusiastically, almost as a matter of faith. Monetarism represented the antithesis of Keynesianism in that it stressed the need to control the money supply in order to avoid inflation rather than the manipulation of the money supply in order to avoid unemployment. Thus, for monetarists such as Friedman, the main (and in some views the only) economic responsibility of government is to ensure price stability.

The thinking behind this was that for years, Britain had been living in a fool's paradise in which an increasingly necessary restructuring of the country's economic base had been put off by stoking up inflation in the hope that higher and higher spending could avert the inevitable and painful process of readjustment to new world markets. Vast unprofitable and uncompetitive areas of industry had been propped up at ever increasing costs in order to put off the evil hour when they would have to be closed down, yet this had only made things worse since it had not only fuelled inflation, which priced British goods even further out of overseas and home markets, but had also diverted human and financial resources away from more viable sectors of the economy thereby crippling those firms which could hold their own against foreign competition. Britain, it was argued, could not hope to compete with the manufactures of countries like Taiwan, South Korea and Singapore which enjoyed a natural 'comparative advantage' in trade given their very low labour costs, and it was thus a policy of folly to continue to support traditional industries which had been in decline for years at the expense of new, high-technology firms which (it was hoped) could compete successfully in world markets.

Monetarism, then, was the means to bring about a long-overdue purging of the British economy involving the collapse of unprofitable industries whose day had passed and a shift of productive resources into more viable sectors. So it was that the government deliberately engineered a massive deflation by cutting public expenditure, winding up subsidies to industry, and reducing demand through the imposition of cash limits and the maintenance of high interest rates designed to squeeze the supply of credit.

Pre-war policies brought about pre-war consequences, and the country soon crashed into a recession of 1930s proportions. Between 1979 and 1983, industrial output fell by a staggering 13 per cent as viable and non-viable firms alike went to the wall. Manufacturing output fell even further, by 19 per cent, thus more than wiping out the previous 10 years hesitant growth. Unemployment rose at an unprecedented rate reaching 14 per cent (3.25 million) on the official figures by 1983. Investment stagnated, for the high interest rates which had been designed to control the growth of credit also had the effect of rendering loans too expensive for companies to contemplate. The removal of exchange controls resulted, predictably, in a flood of money going abroad – overseas investment increased ten-fold in just 4 years. Only the happy accident of North Sea oil kept the economy afloat and the balance of payments within bounds, but even the oil revenues could not disguise the fact that, for the first time in British industrial history, the import of manufactured goods outweighed manufacturing exports. Surveying the ruins, the government was able to claim, with some justification, that it had succeeded in reducing inflation to around 5 per cent, but to many, this appeared a Pyrrhic victory.

CONCLUSION

We have noted several times in this and earlier chapters that a key function of the state must be to maintain the conditions in which production can continue and expand. It is, however, one thing to say what the state 'must' do, and quite another to say what it actually achieves. It is clear from the evidence reviewed in this chapter that the British state over the last 100 years or so has failed to discharge this key function adequately, for the economy has been in a long and steady decline relative to other industrial countries, and this decline shows no sign of coming to an end. Clearly, we need to ask why the state has failed to reverse this trend. It seems that at least three factors need to be taken into account.

First, the state has not been an autonomous agent; policy choices have been hemmed in by economic constraints. Economic factors have not, of course, determined political strategy – government leaders, Treasury mandarins, Bank of England chiefs and the rest have always enjoyed some discretion in determining their policies. Indeed, as the radicalism of the Thatcher Government makes clear, governments may enjoy considerable leeway and are certainly not all constrained to follow the same path. The constraints under which they operate are as much rational as structural: the Wilson Government did not have to abandon the National Plan in 1966 (it could have devalued instead); the Heath Government did not have to execute its famous U-turn in 1972 (it could have let unemployment rise and companies go to the wall as Thatcher has done); and so on.

Nevertheless, the discretion which governments have enjoyed has been a discretion within limits imposed by factors beyond their control – governments are not free agents. One major source of constraint upon their actions has been the operation of world markets, for ever since the abolition of the Corn Laws, the British economy has been dependent upon, and thus vulnerable to, the international economy, and this dependency and vulnerability has increased as the cushion of the colonies has been lost. When Harold Wilson blamed the faceless 'gnomes of Zurich' for the eventual devaluation of the pound in 1967, there was some truth in the charge, just as Edward Heath's complaint about the impact of a quadrupling of oil prices in 1973, or James Callaghan's plea of impotence in relation to the International Monetary Fund in 1976, or Margaret Thatcher's identification of the world slump as a major factor in Britain's recession in the 1980s, all contained more than a germ of truth. Furthermore, it seems that these external constraints are likely to have most impact on reformist rather than reactionary governments in that a government which is committed to moving away from the capitalist system in some way is most likely to come up against the harsh logic of an international capitalist economy. Socialism in one country seems no less difficult now than it did in the years following the Russian Revolution, for it is a lot easier for governments to float with the tide than to struggle to swim against it. This, of course, is the major reason why Thatcher was able to introduce a radical shift back towards a market strategy when successive Labour Governments had found it so difficult to introduce any radical shift forward towards socialist planning.

A second factor which helps to explain the relative impotence of the state in correcting Britain's economic decline is that it is by no means clear what policies need to be adopted. The picture which suggests itself as a result of the last three decades of muddled and incoherent responses is that the state finds itself on the horns of a dilemma. On the one hand, there is a strong case to be made that direct state intervention is required if the economy is to be nurtured back to something approaching 'health', for the Thatcher experiment has demonstrated that an abdication of government responsibility is likely to knock out vast sections of productive enterprise whether or not the firms concerned are viable and efficient. In particular, the fundamental problem of a shortfall in new investment has now reached such a point that it is difficult to see how industry can be expected to recover without massive injections of publicly directed funds and stringent controls on the flow of capital overseas. Yet on the other hand, the Thatcher government was surely right to argue that high levels of state spending had themselves contributed to the fall in profitability in the private sector over the years, in which case a new interventionist strategy is likely to create fresh problems as it resolves old ones. As Gamble and Walton suggest in the passage cited at the start of this chapter, it seems that what is required is both an expansion and contraction of state involvement in the economy – both Keynes and Friedman.

This paradoxical conclusion is reinforced by evidence relating to the contradictory outcomes of both market and interventionist strategies. As we have seen, a monetarist policy appears almost self-defeating, for cuts in public expenditure which are designed to reduce the money supply result in steeply rising unemployment which increases public expenditure as millions of people are forced to depend upon state hand-outs.

Alternatively, attempts to control inflation through planning of prices and incomes have invariably come unstuck, not only through the wages explosion which builds up with each successive year of restraint, but also because price controls hamper the growth of profits and investment which the policy is supposed to stimulate. There is, in short, no single or obvious solution for governments to adopt in the face of the country's continuing economic decline, and those policies which are adopted seem to have a nasty habit of recreating the very problems they are designed to overcome.

The third factor inhibiting effective policy responses to the country's economic decline has, in our view, been the influence (some would say stranglehold) of financial interests over government policy. We have seen in this chapter that, while governments have blown hot and cold over the pursuit of a liberal domestic economic policy, they have never fundamentally challenged the old liberal orthodoxies in respect of overseas trade. A common thread running through the last 100 years of economic policy has been the concern to support free trade, to support the overseas value of sterling, to permit the continuing flow of British capital overseas and to subordinate the pursuit of economic growth at home to the need to rectify recurring balances of payments deficits. In all of this, home-based industry would seem to have been sacrificed in the interests of the City of London: free trade has allowed foreign imports to undercut domestic producers; an over-valued pound has priced British exports out of foreign markets; the flood of capital overseas has starved home industry of new investment; and support of the balance of payments (which has often gone into deficit largely as a result of overseas spending by financial interests and by governments) has necessitated deflationary measures which have brought a halt to the growth of demand for industry's products.

In arguing thus, we do not seek to paint too simple or conspiratorial a picture. It is true that financial and industrial interests cannot be clearly separated in modern Britain, for mergers and overlapping directorships (discussed in Chapter 6) have resulted to some extent in a fusion of the two. It is also true that interests other than finance capital have achieved a considerable input over the years into economic policy-making; the evidence of the development of corporatist strategies involving the CBI and the TUC demonstrates that the state can in no way be seen simply as the captive of the City of London (indeed, the Bank of England was only included in the NEDC meetings as late as 1980 – until then, the NEDC was very much a forum for industrial rather than financial interests, although its discussions were always limited by the Treasury's refusal to allow it to interfere with budgetary policy). Nor do we have much firm empirical evidence on how financial interests have exerted influence over governments, for although it is often argued that the Treasury and the Bank of England function almost as the voice of the City of London within Whitehall, we have little beyond the diaries of Cabinet ministers to tell us how these institutions actually operate. But having entered all these caveats, it does seem from an analysis of successive governments' policies, dating right back into the nineteenth century, that finance capital has generally prevailed in those areas of economic policy which most directly impinge on its interests, and that its success has often been won at the expense of both industrial capital and labour. While much more research is needed on this issue, we would therefore tentatively conclude that the evidence supports the arguments of those such as Aaronovich and Miliband (discussed in Chapter 7) who argue that, in economic policy at least, the state in Britain has functioned almost as an 'instrument' of powerful financial interests. Whether or not this conclusion is accepted, it is clear that the state's support of these interests has been one factor inhibiting its ability to resuscitate the country's industrial base.

The combination of these three factors– the constraints on action, the contradictory requirements of any action which is taken, and the influence of finance capital – go a long way to explain the characteristic features of state economic policy over the years. Governments, it seems have lacked any coherent strategy for modernising the economy. Sometimes they have functioned almost as passive onlookers, denying either their responsibility of their capacity to intervene. At other times, they have reacted to short-term crises with pragmatic avoidance strategies with little thought for their long-term consequences. The rule, for the most part, has been one of muddling through, responding to problems as and when they arise, and attempting to make the country's decline as gentle as possible.

This decline may be reversed at some time in the future, although writing in the mid-1980s, such a possibility seems remote. Britain's economic decline has gone on for so long, and has now become so serious, that it is difficult to see how or when it may be reversed. Governments have shifted from a non-interventionist market strategy, through management of consumer demand and management of production and then, almost in desperation, back again to a social market policy, and with each shift, the problems have been exacerbated. It remains to be seen whether two full terms of a Conservative government committed to what is essentially a nineteenth-century stance can turn the economy around, but it has to be said that this seems unlikely.

The costs of failure may be high. A continuing economic decline may be expected to generate quite traumatic social effects, for just as the early period of industrialization wrought fundamental changes in the social and political life of the country, so the prospect of deindustrialization may be expected to have an equally dramatic impact. We cannot predict the future, but we can suggest with some confidence that not even British society can expect to maintain its familiar pattern for very long in the face of falling living standards and swelling numbers of people whose relation to mainstream economic activity is minimal and precarious. Indeed, as we shall see in Chapter 10, the price of economic failure is already being paid in the increasing use of state coercive powers to maintain social order.

WORKS CITED AND GUIDE TO FURTHER READING

Bacon, R. and Eltis, W. (1978) *Britain's Economic Problem: Too Few Producers,* 2nd edn, London, Macmillan.
An influential analysis which traces the post-war decline of the British economy to the growing imbalance between marketed and non-marketed production of goods and services, and which documents the sadly missed opportunities in the 1960s and 1970s to put this right.

Baran, P. and Sweezy, P. (1968) *Monopoly Capital,* Harmondworth, Penguin.
From a broadly Marxist position, the authors seek to argue that American capitalism in particular, and the world capitalist system in general, faces a mounting problem of absorbing a growing surplus capacity generated by the small number of large multinational companies which now dominate the market. In identifying the problem as one of 'underconsumption', Baran and Sweezy were clearly influenced by Keynes as well as by Marx, and their book has often been criticised by other Marxist economists who suggest that the problem is not so much how to absorb a surplus as how to generate it in the first place.

Friedman, M. (1962) *Capitalism and Freedom,* Chicago, University of Chicago Press.
The classic statement of the New Right's economic liberalism. Friedman argues that any attempt by the state to manage economic life is fundamentally incompatible with the maintenance of individual liberties, and that such attempts have in any case contributed to economic problems by disrupting the natural equilibrium of the market. In his view, the primary responsibility of the state is to maintain a balanced budget by ensuring strict regulation over the supply of money. When it was published, the book received the Nobel Prize, but Friedman's ideas have not been conspicuously successful in countries such as Chile and Israel where governments took them to heart, often with disastrous effects.

Gamble, A. (1981) *Britain in Decline,* London, Macmillan.
A stimulating analysis by a Marxist political economist of Britain's long-term economic decline. This is explained in terms of the international role of the British state and of British finance capital, the peculiar relationship between the state and society which has prevented any effective direction of the economy by governments, and the incomplete incorporation of the working class into the institutions of British society. The book also considers the extent to which the Thatcherite social market strategy and a socialist 'alternative economic strategy' may be expected to reverse the decline. A gloomy yet largely persuasive analysis.

Glyn, A. and Sutcliffe, B. (1972) *British Capitalism, Workers and the Profits Squeeze,* Harmondsworth, Penguin.
An interesting analysis from a 'left' position which attributes Britain's economic problems to the squeeze on profitability brought about by a combination of strong trade unions (which have forced up wages) and intense foreign competition (which has forced down prices).

Hall, S. and Jacques, M. (1983) *The Politics of Thatcherism,* London, Lawrence & Wishart.
A collection of articles, many of which first appeared in the journal *Marxism Today,* in which socialist theorists attempt to grapple with the nature of Thatcherism – the basis of its popular appeal, the problems which beset it, and the possibilities of developing a viable alternative to it.

O'Connor, J. (1972) *The Fiscal Crisis of the State,* New York, St Martin's Press.
An influential book by a radical American political scientist who argues that Western states have been obliged to run up dauntingly-large debts in order to support private-sector profitability. According to O'Connor, this support has taken the form of both 'social capital' expenditures, through which governments have reduced the price paid by private-sector firms for raw materials and infrastructure, and 'social consumption' expenditures, such as housing and health care which have reduced the level of wages which firms have had to pay. In addition to all this, governments have also had to increase spending on social control items such as police and social security, and such 'social expenses' have represented a massive drain on the public purse. These three categories of state spending have all increased in ever more desperate attempts to stave off recession with the result that expenditure has far out-run revenue. Hence the onset of 'fiscal crisis' in the 1970s.

Schmitter, P. (1979) Still the century of corporatism? in P. Schmitter and G. Lembruch (eds), *Trends Towards Corporatist Intermediation,* London, Sage.
See page 79.

Stewart, M. (1972) *Keynes and After,* 2nd edn, Harmondsworth, Penguin.
A standard and readable work which outlines the major elements of Keynes's ideas, sets them in the context of their time, and considers the success of their application over the first 25 years after the war. Chapter 4 is a particularly useful exposition of Keynes's theory of how savings and investment determine the level of employment. The book also contains a timely chapter on monetarist economics.

Winkler, J. (1975) Corporatism, *European Journal of Sociology,* **17,** pp. 100–136.
In which Winkler most clearly sets out his argument that, by the end of the 1980s, Britain will have developed into a fully fledged corporatist society based on private ownership and state control. An object lesson in the perils of social science prediction!

CHAPTER 9

Providing for Social Need

It is clear that, in the twentieth century, citizenship and the capitalist class system have been at war

T. H. Marshall (1950) Citizenship and Social Class, *London, Cambridge University Press p. 29.*

The translation of a want or need into a right is one of the most widespread and dangerous of modern heresies.

Enoch Powell (1972) Still to Decide, *London, Elliot Right Way Books, p. 12.*

The embarrassing secret of the welfare state is that, while its impact upon capitalist accumulation may well become destructive (as the conservative analysis so emphatically demonstrates), its abolition would be plainly disruptive (a fact that is systematically ignored by the conservative critics). The contradiction is that while capitalism cannot coexist with the welfare state, neither can it exist without the welfare state.

Claus Offe (1982) Some contradictions of the modern welfare state Critical Social Policy, *2, p. 11.*

Social policy is probably the most politicised area of state activity in the contemporary period. To most of us, questions of economic policy seem remote, but this is not the case with social policy. Most of us are directly affected in personal ways by the state's role in organising social welfare. The vast majority of people in Britain rely on state provision for their medical care and for the education of their children, and they experience changes in the quality of service first-hand. Every family in the land regularly visits the Post Office to draw family allowance and every one of us who lives to retirement age will draw a state pension.

Given this personal interest in the welfare state, it is not surprising that myths abound in popular consciousness concerning the way in which welfare policy operates. Some of these myths are positive in their evaluation – e.g. that the British welfare state is the 'envy of the world', that it has succeeded in abolishing poverty, and so on. Others – such as the myth that there exists a veritable legion of welfare 'scroungers', that life is easier on the dole than it is for those in work, that the council estates are creaking under the weight of Jaguar cars and colour television sets – are negative and reflect the fear and indignation which stem from the sense that one is being taken for a ride by an anonymous and parasitical bunch of freeloaders.

Most myths are not entirely without foundation. There was a time, for a few years after the war, when welfare provisions in Britain were probably in advance of those in many other Western countries, and it is true that welfare benefits are subject to some abuse by a small minority of claimants (although relative to the scale of tax evasion, such abuse appears trifling). Yet by and large, these are myths, not truths. It is not true, for example, that the problem of poverty has been overcome, for something approaching 25 per cent of households enjoy insufficient incomes to enable them to partake of social activities regarded as 'normal' in our society. Nor is it true that welfare provision in Britain is more extensive than in other comparable countries, for even in the early 1970s (i.e. after a considerable expansion of state welfare provision and before the cuts which began in 1976), spending on pensions, child allowances and unemployment and sickness benefits amounted to just 7.7 per cent of gross domestic product in Britain (less even than in the United States and nearly 5 per cent below that of France and Germany), while total welfare expenditure at 12.6 per cent of GDP was lower than the average of eighteen Western countries and was surpassed by ten of them. As for 'dole scroungers' the facts are that a married man's unemployment benefit in Britain in 1983 stood at just 29 per cent of average earnings, compared with 70 per cent in West Germany and 80 per cent in France. In recent years, welfare spending in Britain has been systematically cut back, partly as a response to the worsening economic plight of the country discussed in Chapter 8, and partly as a function of the resurgence of an individualist and anti-statist ideology in the form of Thatcherism.

In this two-part chapter we shall first attempt to explain why and how the state came to be increasingly involved in the provision of welfare from the nineteenth century onwards. We will then explore two contemporary critiques of state welfare provision. Both the left critique and the right critique challenge the rosey perspective on the welfare state, and they both have a bearing on the current reversal of the trend to increased state involvement in this field of public policy and provision.

THE DEVELOPMENT OF STATE WELFARE PROVISIONS

Laissez faire: self help and provision by the market in the nineteenth century

The provision of welfare services by the national state is a comparatively recent phenomenon. In 1860 there was no system of income security, no state medical care apart from lunatic asylums, vaccination and environmental health regulations, no state education apart from grants to religious schools, and no system of state housing. A century later, the state was operating a battery of income support schemes (old age and invalidity pensions, sickness, maternity, work injury and unemployment benefits, family allowances and national assistance), a comprehensive and largely free health service, free and compulsory primary and secondary education and grant-aided higher education, and was landlord to over a quarter of all the nation's households. Over the same period, welfare spending as a proportion of GNP increased seventeen times. Over 7 million people are today employed by the state, many of them in administering or providing welfare and social services.

The relative lack of state welfare provision in the mid-nineteenth century did not of course mean that there was no system of social support. In the main, however, this was a period when people's basic consumption requirements – the need for accommodation, for medical treatment and so on – were met, to the extent that they were met at all, through the market rather than by the state. Private landlords provided housing in return for rents, private tutors provided education in return for fees, private doctors charged for elementary medical treatment. Those who could not afford to pay went without, or relied on private charity and the benevolence of a hard-nosed Victorian middle class, or banded together into friendly societies to provide mutual aid in times of unemployment or sickness.

Not surprisingly, the quality of provision for most people was patchy and in many respects inadequate: Engels, for example, painted a vivid picture of the squalor, overcrowding, disease and ignorance which afflicted the English working class in town and country alike in the 1840s, and more rigorous poverty surveys at the turn of the century, by Booth in London and Rowntree in York, confirmed that even on the strictest criteria of need and deprivation, poverty in Britain was widespread. Indeed, as army recruitment at the time of the Boer War demonstrated, many young working-class males were not even fit and healthy enough to offer their lives in the service of their country, for thousands had to be turned away on grounds of ill-health. The prosperity of Victorian Britain was built to a large extent on a combination of exploitation of the colonies abroad and through the pitiful poverty of millions of working-class people at home. The profits of the new industrial bourgeoisie were achieved at the cost of wages which were often too low to provide for the basic physical necessities of life and conditions of work which themselves gave rise to disease and crippling disablement.

Government thinking about the relief of poverty and distress during the nineteenth century was shaped by the Poor Law reforms of 1834 which sought to distinguish the 'deserving' and 'undeserving' poor. The former category included those, such as widows, orphans and the chronically sick, who had fallen upon hard times which made it difficult or impossible for them to work. The latter encompassed the able-bodied who, it was assumed, were idle and feckless and were happy, given half the chance, to subsist on the charity and pity of others. In both cases, poverty was seen as an individual problem rather than as the product of the way in which society was organised. The problem, therefore, was how to aid the genuinely deserving without at the same time giving comfort to the work-shy and the shiftless.

The solution to this problem was found in the extension of the workhouse system. This entailed a deliberate policy of deterrence in the provision of aid; the conditions of poor relief were to be made so bad that only those who were in genuine and desperate need would turn to the state for help. This was achieved by fixing the level of relief at a point lower than the lowest wage, and by curtailing 'outdoor relief' in favour of the workhouse where families were split up and conditions of life and work were kept intentionally harsh. As the 1833 Report of the Poor Law Commissioners explained; 'Into such a house none will enter voluntarily; work confinement and discipline will deter the indolent and vicious; and nothing but extreme necessity will induce any to accept the comfort which must be obtained by the surrender of their free agency.' The British state has inflicted many horrors on its people over the centuries, but the barbarism of the workhouse system must rank as among the least forgiveable.

Forgiveable or not, this cold-comfort policy was remarkably effective, for the workhouse represented a symbol of popular dread and hatred throughout the nineteenth century. Its deterrent value was undoubtedly high. Yet in another respect, the policy was an obvious failure in that thousands of people continued to rely on poor relief despite the conditions which were attached to it. Every down-turn in the economy brought more destitute people to the workhouse door and served to demonstrate that widespread poverty had less to do with individual pathology than with the evident failings of a free-market economy. Within 10 years of the introduction of the new Poor Law, the workhouses were crammed with nearly 200 000 people.

The basic problem with leaving provision for people's needs to the operation of the market was, quite simply, that at that time large numbers of people could not afford to buy what even then was generally considered to be the basic necessities of life. The problem was particularly acute, of course, for those who could not find work or were not capable of working, but it did not end there, for many of those in employment similarly suffered immense deprivation.

The inability to pay for crucial items of consumption was due above all else to low wages. In the ninteenth century, labour represented a major cost of production in most industries – not only in the primary sectors such as agriculture and mining, but in manufacturing as well. This meant that labour costs had to be kept to a minimum if profits were to be maintained, yet low wages meant that workers could not provide for themselves and their families by buying the services which they so desperately required. The problem is clearly illustrated with reference to the housing question in nineteenth-century Britain.

Working class housing at this time was built as an investment. Landlords bought whole streets of houses in order to rent them out to working-class tenants, and they did so in the expectation that they would be able to receive a level of rent which, after deductions for repairs, interest payments and running costs, would at least be comparable to the rate of return they could achieve by investing their capital elsewhere. The working-class tenants themselves, however, were in receipt of very low wages which prevented landlords from charging high rents. The result was that housing was built as cheaply as possible, maintenance was kept to a minimum and tenants were crowded into insanitary rooms and cellars in order to raise the total rental income to an acceptable market level. This in turn led to disease which spread virtually unchecked because the tenants could not afford to pay for medical treatment either. The problems and deprivations were thus compounded, and for as long as consumption was organised primarily through the market, there was no way out of the vicious circle.

From this example, it can be seen that the basic problem which lay behind the efforts of governments, philanthropists and working-class people themselves to improve conditions during the nineteenth century was the contradiction between the operation of the market for labour, which led to low wages, and the operation of the market for consumption goods and services, which led to high rents and other living costs. It was the evidence of this contradiction which gradually led government to temper their principled commitment to *laissez-faire* with a pragmatic acceptance of the need to do something to alleviate the worst and most unpalatable aspects of working-class living conditions, even if this meant treading on the toes of those with property. Nobody planned it, but gradually the extreme self-help philosophy of the early Victorian period was eroded by piecemeal social reform.

At first, governments restricted themselves to regulating conditions at work and at home. As early as 1833, for example, Parliament legislated to limit the length of the working day and to restrict the use of child labour in certain industries, and further Factory Acts in the 1840s and 1850s imposed tighter restrictions, closed loopholes and increased surveillance by factory inspectors. From the 1850s onwards, locally elected Boards of Health began to regulate Britain's towns and cities in an attempt to eradicate the insanitary conditions, and middle-class concern about the spread of diseases from working-class slum areas led to a programme of compulsory vaccination (which was fiercely resisted by the advocates of old-style liberalism).

Later in the century, however, state intervention was stepped up from mere regulation. A succession of Housing Acts, for example, permitted local authorities to purchase and clear slum areas and to provide alternative rental housing for the tenants who were made homeless as a result. Because this legislation was permissive rather than mandatory, its effectiveness remained limited, but from 1890, local authorities did begin to build new dwellings as well as to demolish old ones. This was also the period when the state began to take on responsibility for educating the children of the working class. A series of Education Acts, in 1870, 1880 and 1891, culminated in the provision of free, universal and compulsory elementary education designed, in the words of Matthew Arnold (the headmaster of Rugby school) to spread 'sweetness and light' and to counter the 'barbarism' of the newly enfranchised proletariat. By the turn of the century, therefore, the commitment to *laissez faire* and to Benthamite principles of utilitarianism had been undermined in practice by 50 or 60 years of hesitant and sometimes grudging social reform. The question, of course, is why did it happen?

There is no doubt that the potential threat to capitalist social order posed by the concentration of millions of working-class families in the slums of the new industrial cities loomed large in the consciousness of many reformers and many politicians throughout the nineteenth century. The spectre of the 1789 revolution in France and of later upheavals in Europe in 1830 and 1848, coupled with the agitation at home during the Chartist years and the later growth of trade unions among skilled artisans and unskilled workers, was clearly one factor which helped focus political attention on the question of reform and social policy. The extension of the franchise to the working class also led to increased political concern with working class living conditions (Disraeli, for example, saw the provision of elementary education as crucial in 'gentling' the new political majority), and middle-class philanthropists did much to publicise the squalor, ignorance and disease which existed at the very heart of the Empire. Yet having said all this, it does not seem to have been the case that the working class *itself* was instrumental in pressuring the state for reforms in this period, but policy was made in the *presence* of that class and there was a consciousness of its *potential* for disruption and disorder that prompted action if only to block the threat of more fundamental changes coming from below.

There is considerable controversy among nineteenth-century historians on these points and it may be that certain sections of the working class did press for certain types of reform. In general terms, however, it seems that the hostility towards the state, fostered by the operation of the Poor Law, and sustained by a widespread view of the state as the preserve of a wealthy few, led many working-class people and their leaders (e.g. in the trade union movement) to suspect and distrust most attempts to extend state regulation through new welfare provisions. The Housing Acts, for example, resulted all too often in the displacement of working-class people from their homes rather than in the provision of new housing, and overcrowding actually increased as a result. The early Education Acts made it compulsory for working-class people to send their children to school yet levied fees which many could not afford or were unwilling to pay. Even the various Factory Acts were often unpopular since they prevented working-class families from increasing their income through the extensive use of the labour of their children. Much of the nineteenth-century legislation, therefore, was unpopular not only among those with property, but also among those without, and it is notable that the extension of the franchise in 1886 did not thrust social reform into the mainstream of political argument, for none of the elections between then and the turn of the century were fought on issues of social policy.

Such evidence suggests caution is necessary in explaining the nineteenth-century origins of the centralised, interventionist welfare state. Indeed, it raises something of a puzzle, for if reform was far from popular, then it is difficult to understand why it ever came about. In retrospect, we may be justified in arguing that social policy in this period was introduced in a rather paternalistic way on behalf of the working class, and was certainly pursued out of a concern with the working class and a fear of the threat which it represented, but most of this legislation cannot be said to have been achieved through working-class agitation or struggle.

The welfare state: cradle to grave and provision by the state in the twentieth century

Much the same point may be made of the period up to the outbreak of the First World War despite the fact that the 1906–14 Liberal Government is often seen as having laid the basis of the modern welfare state. For a start, this government was not elected, as was the Labour Government following the Second World War, on a popular programme of social reform (the general election of 1906 turned more on the issue of free trade than on domestic social policy). Furthermore, with just one exception, the government introduced precious little social reform until Asquith replaced Campbell-Bannerman in 1908 (the one exception being the introduction of school meals in 1906 which was largely a response to the horrifying evidence of working-class malnutrition thrown up by recruitment for the Boer War).

The two major items of social legislation introduced under Asquith were the provision of old age pensions in 1908 and the introduction of selective compulsory sickness and unemployment insurance in 1911. The first of these was undeniably popular, although even here it seems that the government was responding as much to the demands of middle-class and bourgeois reformers, such as Charles Booth and the Cadbury family, as it was to working-class pressure through the trade unions and the sprinkling of newly-elected Labour MPs. As with so much of the nineteenth-century legislation, the introduction of pensions seems almost to have been in advance of popular aspirations.

As for the National Insurance Act, 1911, the popular response seems at best to have been muted. The scope of the legislation was in any case limited; unemployment insurance, for example, covered only 2.25 million workers in industries where jobs were thought to be reasonably secure and provided benefit for only 15 weeks, while the health insurance scheme was whittled down following pressure from the big insurance companies (widows and orphans, for example were removed from the scope of the act) and the British Medical Association (which succeeded in bringing the operation of the scheme more under the control of doctors and in raising charges for medical treatment under the act to nearly double those prevailing in 1906). Furthermore, compulsory insurance was financed by regressive flat-rate contributions, the level of sickness benefit was little better than that provided by the voluntary friendly societies to which many workers already belonged, and the creation of a virtual state monopoly on health insurance represented a defeat for the various agencies of mutual aid (such as the friendly societies and medical clubs) which had developed among skilled workers in the nineteenth century and which had offered their members a greater degree of control over their doctors than could be offered under the new scheme. The act did, however, represent a positive step away from the ethos of the Poor Law, in that it established a right to benefit, and it did cover groups of workers who had not previously been able to afford medical treatment. It was, in short, a mixed blessing, and it brought forth an equally mixed reaction.

Taken together, reforms such as the introduction of school meals, the provision of old age pensions and the enforcement of a state-run system of health and unemployment insurance have to be seen as the product of a number of different factors. These include: the influence of pressure groups, top civil servants and middle class reformers (e.g. as in the case of old age pensions); the concern of leading Liberals such as Lloyd-George, Churchill and Asquith himself with alleviating poverty and improving the efficiency of the workforce (e.g. by providing school meals to counter malnutrition); a desire to head-off the possibility of socialism by incorporating the working class within the capitalist system (e.g. a major motive behind the introduction of national insurance in 1911 was to emulate Bismark's example in Germany where such a scheme had deliberately been introduced in order to counter the appeal of socialist propoganda), and, in virtually every case, the consideration of short-term tactical electoral advantage in response to the emergence of what was to become the Labour Party. Whatever the particular explanation for particular reforms, however, it is noticeable that in most cases, the government was in advance of popular opinion and aspirations; in the period to 1914, changes in social policy originated more from above than from below.

The 4 years of war which followed did much to change this. The First World War was the first war in British history in which millions of working class people were conscripted to fight for their country, and the government was well aware that the massive tragedy of their sacrifices demanded some reward. The war had also seen a massive mobilisation of the country's economic resources by the state – the size of the budget in

1918 was five times that of 1914 – and this effectively countered any argument that the country could not afford to expand social provisions. But on top of all this, the war years had been politically traumatic, both at home, where labour militancy had produced a wave of industrial unrest, which continued after hostilities had ended, and even spread to groups such as the police and the troops, and abroad, where revolutionary movements had succeeded in toppling the Tsar in Russia and threatened to sweep through Germany as well.

There was an air of popular expectation, if not militancy, in the immediate post-war years in Britain, and unrest was fuelled by the sudden slump which trebled unemployment within just 6 months in 1920. The government was haunted by the spectre of the Bolsheviks in Russia; the Cabinet received weekly intelligence reports on 'revolutionary organisations' such as the National Unemployed Workers' Movement (founded by the Communist Party in 1921) and these seem to have convinced most leading politicians and civil servants that concessions would have to be made if the security of the realm was to be guaranteed.

The major issue which dominated social policy at this time and throughout the inter-war years was, of course, unemployment. The problem for the government was that neither the system of Poor Law relief, nor that of unemployment insurance, established in 1911, were adequate in making provision for mass unemployment, for both were premissed on the assumption that, for most people, lack of work was a temporary problem. An insurance-based scheme, for example, could only work if most of those contributing to it did not need to draw benefit from it. From 1920 onwards, however, this proved not to be the case, and gradually successive governments were obliged to resort increasingly to state funding in order to support the unemployed. In 1920, state contributions to the unemployment insurance fund amounted to just over £3 million at 3.4 per cent of total social services expenditure; by 1930, this had risen to £37 million (37 per cent of total spending on social provisions).

This break with the strict insurance principle resuscitated the fears expressed by thinkers a century earlier that state aid to the unemployed would deter people from working and would thus encourage malingering. In order to avoid this, the government introduced the infamous 'means test' and enforced a 'genuinely seeking work' condition.

The means test was widely seen by those who were subjected to it as a return to the methods of the nineteenth-century Poor Law. Applied to all those who were claiming benefits to which their contributions did not fully entitle them, it entailed a thorough investigation of the assets and income of both the individual concerned and the household. Benefit could be, and was, withheld where a spouse or children were found to be earning or where the household still owned assets which could be sold to realise income. This pernicious and despised system was eventually ended in 1927.

The 'genuinely seeking work' condition was, as its name implies, intended to ensure that those in receipt of benefit were actively searching for employment. In many ways, the effect of this condition was even harsher than that of the means test, for the burden of proof lay on the claimant who had to provide evidence to show that each day of the previous week had been spent walking the streets in search of non-existent jobs. Unlike the means test, this condition was not the subject of any great political opposition; indeed, in 1924, it was extended to all claimants, irrespective of whether or not they had full entitlement to benefit.

The use of the means test and the genuinely seeking work condition reveal the way in which, during the 1920s, governments were obliged to extend unemployment relief yet at the same time attempted to avoid the erosion of individual responsibility which this seemed to entail. Throughout this period, unemployment-relief policies emerged in a haphazard, trial-and-error fashion as pragmatic responses to a worsening situation which demanded actions which governments were reluctant to take. Eventually, in 1934, Ramsey MacDonald's National Government did at last come to terms with the fact of long-term structural unemployment by establishing the Unemployment Assistance Board which provided benefits as of right to those without work and without entitlement by virtue of contributions paid. The stigma of the dole still remained, but at least the philosophy of the Poor Law had finally been abandoned.

These changes, together with various other piecemeal reforms affecting state provision of housing, education and pension benefits, meant that, by the outbreak of the Second World War, Britain had a *de facto* welfare state in the sense that the state was committed to providing a 'safety net' and a minimum level of support as of right to all those in need. The unemployed, the elderly and the sick were covered by state-administered insurance schemes. All children were entitled to free state education up to the age of 14. Those in desperate housing need were entitled to rent a house built and subsidised by the state. None of this, of course, had in any final sense overcome the problem of poverty, for the provisions were in most cases minimal and largely inadequate. It was a 'sticking plaster' system of welfare aid in which the state attempted to bandage up the worst wounds inflicted by a capitalist economy in long-term recession. Nevertheless, the nature and scale of state intervention was such that the Poor Law had been buried as governments accepted responsibility for alleviating need and recognised the principle of free provision.

Between 1942 and 1948, this system of social support and provision was extended and overhauled as war again revolutionised popular aspirations and overturned conventional thinking about the acceptable and tolerable limits to state activity. In 1942, Beveridge published his report on the future organisation of social security schemes in which he outlined a system of national insurance which would provide protection 'from the cradle to the grave' in return for a weekly compulsory payment by all workers. In fact, these proposals, which formed the basis of the National Insurance Act 1946, did not represent any radical departure from the situation pertaining before the war, but rather brought unemployment, sickness, retirement and maternity benefits together under a single system while retaining the National Assistance Board with its means-tested benefits as an additional resource of last resort for those whose incomes still fell below a minimal subsistence line. This unified system of national insurance was still to be financed out of insurance payments rather than taxation; as Beveridge himself emphasised: 'The plan for Britain is based on the contributory principle of giving not free allowances to all from the state, but giving benefits as of right in virtue of contributions made by the insured persons themselves.' Like all previous insurance schemes since 1911, it involved a regressive system of flat-rate payments in which all workers paid the same premiums irrespective of their income; and because the level of payments had to be fixed at a point which the lowest-paid workers could afford, the scheme necessarily provided only subsistence levels of benefit. It was never intended that national insurance should provide anything more than a minimal 'safety net' for those in need; the main achievement of the National Insurance Act was simply to weave such a 'net' more tightly.

Other social reforms introduced during and immediately after the war did, however, represent a more radical break from the 1930s. In 1944, for example, Parliament passed a Town and Country Planning Act, later consolidated in 1947, which enabled local authorities to acquire land for housing at a price reflecting current use rather than future speculative value, and this was followed in 1949 by a Housing Act which empowered local authorites to build housing for all members of the community and not simply for those in proven housing need (this reflecting the assumption of the Labour Government at that time that public renting would gradually become the main form of housing provision). Throughout the late forties and early fifties, local authority house building far outstripped that in the private sector, and it was only from 1958 onwards that this pattern began to be reversed.

Also in 1944, Parliament passed the Butler Education Act which not only raised the school leaving age to 15, but also introduced the tripartite system of grammar, technical and 'modern' schools, which was designed to increase working-class educational opportunity. As things turned out, many working-class and lower-middle-class children did benefit from this system, but research through the 1950s and 1960s also demonstrated that many others were falling foul of the class discrimination which was implicit in the system, and gradually, from the mid-sixties onwards, selective secondary schooling came to be replaced in most parts of the country by comprehensive systems.

Perhaps the most important piece of social legislation introduced during this period, however, was the National Health Service Act, 1946.

This established the principle of free and universal medical care and treatment, although the effective veto power of the British Medical Association forced considerable concessions (e.g. to permit pay beds in NHS hospitals) in favour of the doctors just as it had when health insurance had first been introduced back in 1911. The principle of free treatment was also eroded soon after the act was passed when prescription charges were introduced in an attempt to reduce the high cost of the service by dampening down popular demand for medicines and appliances such as spectacles.

In 1948, the modern welfare state had been fully established. It stood on two pillars. The first was the system of national insurance which guaranteed a minimum income in the event of sickness, accident, unemployment and old age and was financed out of individual contributions. The second was the system of assistance and services financed wholly or partly out of taxation and including free and universal health and school systems, income assistance through family allowances and doles, and specific provisions such as rental housing and child welfare clinics. Although the pre-war insurance principle was retained as part of the new welfare state, the major part of the system entailed free services paid for out of general taxation. Indeed, as time went on, the 'insurance' component became increasingly fictitious as the cost of pensions and other benefits far outstripped revenues collected from insurance contributions. Today, the two parts of the welfare system have effectively fused although the notional separation between national insurance and income tax payments has been retained.

Through the 1950s and 1960s, governments of both major parties administered and developed this comprehensive system of welfare with little basic disagreement between them. On some issues, they did diverge in their relative emphases; the Conservatives, for example, were always somewhat less enthusiastic about the spread of public-rented housing than was the Labour Party, although by the early sixties, both parties were committed to encouraging owner-occupation while at the same time continuing to subsidise public rental for those who could not afford or did not wish to buy. In general then, there was a broad degree of consensus between them, and changes introduced in these years (e.g. the development of earnings-related contributions and benefits) met with the tacit support of both parties. As in economic policy, so too in social policy, the years of post-war affluence underpinned a remarkable degree of bi-partisanship in British politics.

The mixed economy of welfare: attacking the welfare state

There are two main reasons why this bi-partisan consensus on welfare was eventually undermined during the 1970s. The first was that, as the years went by, it became increasingly apparent that the state welfare system had not achieved the greater degree of equality which those on the left had sought from it. As we saw in Chapter 6, there were only slight shifts in the distribution of income in the years after 1945, and the problem of poverty remained largely unresolved. Indeed, Beveridge's fond hope that the need for national assistance (which later became supplementary benefit) would gradually disappear proved totally unfounded, for the number of people reliant on non-contributory cash benefits to raise their total income to the minimum deemed necessary for susbsistence actually rose from 1 million in 1948 to 2 million in 1965 and reached 3 million by 1978. Groups such as pensioners, one-parent families and the low-paid were clearly slipping through the national insurance net in alarming proportions, and this led to increasingly vociferous demands within the Labour Party and the new crop of welfare pressure groups (e.g. the Child Poverty Action Group and Age Concern) for more radical redistributive measures financed out of increased progressive taxation. This was a prospect regarded with deep suspicion by many conservatives, and those on the right of the party (notably Enoch Powell and later Keith Joseph and Margaret Thatcher) began to express their sense of unease at the continuing increases in personal taxation levied to finance welfare measures.

The second factor which was linked to this was that the welfare state became more and more expensive at a time when the British economy was again revealing its fundamental weaknesses. Government spending on social security, personal social services, health care, education and housing increased dramatically from the 1960s onwards – from 16 per cent of the country's Gross National Product in 1951, to 24 per cent in 1971 and to 29 per cent in 1975 when it was accounting for half of all public expenditure. By 1977, a staggering 14 million people were in receipt of benefits (nearly double the figure for 1951), while the public-sector services had grown much faster than any other sector of the workforce. Gradually, the New Right of the Tory Party began to question whether the country could afford to underwrite this increasingly heavy financial burden, and familiar arguments about the need to re-establish work incentives and to discourage 'scrounging' and indolence began once more to find a voice.

During the 1970s, therefore, both Left and Right began to reappraise their support for the welfare state. On the Left, it was increasingly argued that the welfare state, as it had evolved in Britain, was an inadequate response to the problems generated by capitalism, and even that it was of greater benefit to dominant groups than to ordinary working people and their families. On the Right, by contrast, the welfare state came increasingly to be seen as a major source of the problems which were once again besetting British capitalism, for provision as a right was seen to be undermining individual initiative and the work ethic while the cost of universal provision was identified as a crippling drain of private-sector profitability. The Right was concerned to roll back the state in this field of policy and saw a place for private and voluntary provision in a mixed economy of welfare approach which challenged the cradle-to-grave ethic of the welfare state. If we are to understand contemporary changes in and arguments over the question of social welfare, it is necessary to consider each of these two positions in turn.

CRITIQUES OF THE WELFARE STATE

The left critique of social welfare

What is distinctive to the left critique of social welfare as it developed through the 1970s is the view that, despite appearances, the British Welfare State has functioned as much, if not more, in the interests of dominant groups as of the working class. At first sight, of course, this seems paradoxical, for bankers and industrial magnates are not generally found living in council houses or drawing social security benefits, yet they have had to pay increased taxes to finance the ever-increasing welfare budget. How, then, can they be said to have been the principal beneficiaries of increased state welfare spending?

Many Marxist analysts have suggested that the capitalist class in general has benefited from such spending in three main ways.

The first and most indirect benefit has come from the increased markets which the welfare state has created for many private-sector producers. This is a point which was fully discussed in Chapter 8 where we saw that state spending has been used in part to raise the level of effective demand in the economy, and thus to help private companies to find a market for their products. Building firms have often relied on government contracts for their very survival; drugs companies have made super-profits by supplying the NHS; and many enterprises, large and small, have benefited from the custom of the 7 million people employed by the state to administer or carry out its various services. Such benefits have often been important for private firms (and they are perhaps now becoming more important as various welfare-related services such as school and hospital cleaning are put out to private tender), but they are not themselves enough to warrant the conclusion that the welfare state aids capitalists more than it does their workers.

A second and more important benefit for capital has, according to many writers, derived from the way in which social provisions have helped to co-opt the working class into the capitalist system by legitimating that system in the eyes of those who benefit least from it. Seen in this way, the welfare state represents the 'human face' of capitalism, for it has succeeded in overcoming the most brutal effects of the capitalist industrial system and therefore tends to reduce levels of popular discontent and to stifle revolutionary fervour. Slums still exist in Britain, but housing conditions for most of the population are undeniably far superior to those of, say, a century ago. Old people still die of hyperthermia as a result of inadequate heating and poor nutrition, but such cases do not represent the norm. Many parents still cannot afford to feed and clothe their children properly, but we no longer see children begging on street corners or wending their way to school with no shoes on their feet. Council housing, old age pensions, child allowances and all the other paraphernalia of the modern welfare state can thus be said to represent the 'necessary overhead expenses' of running a capitalist system; they are, in a sense, an alternative to further expenditure on more formal agencies of social control such as the police and the army, for they help to dampen down unrest. In this sense, welfare policies have sometimes been seen as an insurance policy for the privileged, as a way of smoothing out the conflict-laden relationship between capital and labour (an argument which we consider in more detail in Chapter 10).

Such a motive for supporting reform has often been openly and surprisingly acknowledged by politicians over the years. During the nineteenth century in particular, political philosophers such as John Stuart Mill, educationalists such as Matthew Arnold and political leaders such as Benjamin Disraeli all argued openly about the therapeutic effects of social policy for the 'health' of a capitalist society. As we saw earlier, the introduction of unemployment insurance by the Liberals in 1911 represented a deliberate application of Bismark's thinking in Germany to the effect that the working class could be incorporated within capitalist society through such measures, and this strategy was endorsed by the Conservative Prime Minister at the turn of the century (Balfour) who argued that: 'Social legislation... is not merely to be distinguished from socialist legislation, but is its most direct opposite and its most effective antidote.' Socialists and revolutionaries of the time also agreed with this, and their argument with the Fabians was largely based on the view that support of reform within a capitalist framework would make a future transition to socialism all the more difficult to bring about (an argument which continues to this day on the left of British politics). What all of these people were arguing, therefore, was that social policy represented a most effective instrument for 'buying off' the working class; exploitation of wage labour in the world of work could be maintained by ameliorating the worse effects of such exploitation in the world beyond the factory gates. Or, to put it another way, concessions in the sphere of consumption (housing, health, education, etc.) were the price to pay to avoid more fundamental changes in the sphere of production.

Such arguments carried particular force during and immediately after the two world wars. War has often been a forcing agent of radical change, for the widespread disruption of 'ordinary life' which it causes brings about a considerable upheaval in people's taken for-granted expectations about what their world has to offer. The desire for a 'new start', a fundamental break with the past, was widespread and pervasive in Britain in 1918 (when the fledgling revolution in Russia seemed to offer new hope to many working-class people) and in 1945 (when the Labour Party was swept into office in a wave of popular support for radical change). In both cases, this appetite for far-reaching social change was sated by welfare reform. Following the First World War, this took the form mainly of housing legislation (reports to cabinet at this time stressed the significance of poor housing conditions in fermenting popular unrest) although subsequent reforms of the unemployment insurance system can also, to a large extent, be explained in terms of governmental fear of the prospect of millions of poverty-stricken unemployed workers turning to a revolutionary solution to their problems. Following the Second World War, it took the form of a comprehensive reshaping of welfare policies under the Labour Government, although most of these changes had been planned during the war years by Churchill's National Government which was well aware of the importance of the promise of a 'new Britain' in maintaining war-time morale and damping down unrest.

There is no doubt that fear of unrest and a desire to incorporate the working class within the capitalist system have been crucially important motives behind the growth of the welfare state in Britain. Indeed, they have clearly continued to be so; the 'social contract' of the 1974–79 Labour Government represented a deliberate attempt to reduce working-class militancy in the face of real wage cuts by promising improvements in welfare services. Yet such arguments can be over-emphasised. In particular, those who seek to explain the development of social reform purely or even primarily in these terms run the twin dangers of exaggerating the conspiratorial canniness of ruling groups while ignoring the active role of the working class in forcing concessions. While it is true that political leaders have often consciously used welfare policies in an attempt to control the working class, it is also true that they have often been most reluctant to extend state provision and have attempted to resist popular demands for improved support and better services. The 'ruling class' has never been so clever as to manipulate social policy on its own initiative to further its own ends without at least some degree of prompting from below. Similarly, the working class has never been so inert as to have merely played the role of meek recipient without also flexing its political muscle. To explain the growth of the welfare state purely in terms of the desire of powerful groups to co-opt the working class is to exaggerate the foresight of the powerful and to strip the working class itself of its history.

The third and perhaps most crucial way in which the welfare state is said to have aided the capitalist class is that it has lowered the production and reproduction costs of human labour-power and has thereby raised the rate of profit. In other words, the state has assumed responsibility for providing many of the resources which workers need to consume if they are to provide labour-power for the factories and offices of capitalist firms. This has meant that employers have been able to pay lower wages than would otherwise have to be paid.

The logic of this argument is fairly simple (although the detailed theoretical arguments which it throws up are often highly complex). Basically, it is argued that human labour-power, whether that of muscles or of brains, gets used up in the process of production. This is true in two senses. First, it is used up during the course of the working day – people return home tired and weakened by their expenditure of labour-power in factory or office. Secondly, it is used up over the years – each generation of workers gradually gets worn out as it gets older, just as machines do. This means that, in the absence of state intervention, employers must pay sufficient wages to enable workers first to replenish their energies on a day-to-day basis (i.e. by consuming food, housing, leisure, and so on), and second, to raise a new generation of workers which will eventually replace them (i.e. by feeding and clothing their children, paying others to educate them up to the standard required by employers, and so on).

If, however, the state steps in and begins to provide some of the items which workers need to reproduce their labour-power and to raise a new generation of workers, then employers will no longer have to cover all these expenses in the wage packet. Provision of council housing at subsidised rents, for example, means that workers no longer have to spend so much on their housing, and, other things being equal, this will enable wages to fall. Similarly, free state schooling removes the burden of school fees, free medical care removes the costs of 'repairing' labour-power when it is sick or damaged, and so on. In this way, provisions which appear to be in the interests of workers actually turn out to be in the interests of their employers.

Indeed, this argument can be carried further, for it can be suggested that state provision of welfare services not only lowers the cost of reproducing labour-power, but also increases the efficiency of that labour-power. Workers who live in slum housing will often fall ill, those who are poorly-educated will be slow in adapting to the rigours of work, those who cannot afford decent medical treatment will have to take a lot of time off from work. Furthermore, as Marx himself suggested in his discussion of the nineteenth-century Factory Acts, workers become less efficient if they are over-worked and over-exploited. Thus, social provision (e.g. of health and housing) and state regulation (e.g. of hours of work or of safety standards at work) both function in the long-term interests of the capitalist class by raising the productivity of labour and thereby increasing profitability.

One obvious objection to this suspiciously neat argument is that all these provisions still have to be paid for in some way. If capitalists are no longer paying for the reproduction of their workforce through the wage-packet, are they not, nevertheless, still paying for it through their taxes?

The response to this objection from those who argue for this explanation of the welfare state is that it all depends on the relative power of the two main classes at any point in time. If the working class is strong, then it will usually be able to shift the burden of paying for the welfare state onto capitalists – this seems to have happened during the 1960s. But if the working class is weak, then attempts will be made to reduce the tax burden on capital and to finance welfare spending through taxes on wages. If neither of these options is politically or economically feasible – as in Britain from the late sixties onwards when organised labour was still strong enough to resist any erosion of real wages but the profitability of capital was too low to support additional taxation – then such provisions are likely to be financed by mounting deficits (i.e. increased public borrowing and inflation). This is a point to which we shall return in the next section of this chapter.

There are, however, other objections to this attempt to explain the growth of the welfare state in terms of the requirements of the capitalist class. Three in particular deserve comment.

First, it is important to distinguish between the question of who benefits from welfare provision and that of who causes it to be provided in the first place. In other words, even if we accept that the welfare state has aided capital by reproducing labour-power more cheaply and efficiently than before, this does not explain its origins. Policies which are brought into existence through the actions of one group may turn out to benefit another; the fact that the capitalist class may have benefited from welfare policies does not therefore justify the conclusion that it was this class, acting in its own interests, which generated such policies. Furthermore, the simple identification of a functional 'need' tells us nothing of whether or how this need comes to be met (e.g. to say that capital 'needs' labour-power to be reproduced as cheaply and efficiently as possible is undoubtedly true, but whether this has actually happened or not remains an open question). The first objection to this sort of argument, therefore, is that it focuses on outcomes, not causes, and we cannot deduce a cause from an effect.

Second, the argument would seem to be grossly over-stated. It may be, for example, that capitalists 'need' their workers to be housed in reasonable accommodation, and 'need' future generations of workers to be schooled to a reasonable standard, but the post-war welfare state in Britain would seem in many respects to have exceeded these 'requirements'. It simply makes no sense, for example, to suggest that capital 'requires' its workers to be housed in centrally-heated council houses with garages, or 'needs' future generations of workers to be educated for at least 11 years in subjects such as the geography of Africa, the literature of France, the history of Greece or even the political science of modern Britain. There is an enormous gap between the level of provision which capitalists may deem 'necessary' for reproducing labour-power or ensuring legitimacy, and that which has actually been provided over the years.

Third, the argument has to some extent been overtaken by events, for since the mid to late seventies, welfare provisions in Britain have been cut back quite dramatically to a point where we may validly begin to question whether such provisions are as important to capital as many Marxist writers during the 1970s assumed. Widespread provision of council housing, for example, has often been cited as crucial in ensuring the reproduction of labour-power, yet in the period following 1979, the Thatcher Government virtually put an end to new building, sold off as much housing as it could to existing tenants, and raised the rents of the remainder by around 160 per cent in just 3 years. It may be responded to this that such a policy is doomed in the long-run, and that state subsidies to housing provision were in any case retained in respect of owner-occupied stock (where tax relief on mortgage interest repayments now far exceed subsidies on public-sector rents), but the fact remains that a key area of provision has been the subject of unprecedented cuts and that employers do not seem that worried about it.

There is an additional point to be made about the period from the late seventies onwards, and that concerns the rising level of unemployment. With upwards of 3.5 million people out of work, the need to reproduce labour-power seems somewhat less pressing than it once did. The standard response to this is to suggest that welfare provisions are still necessary, not so much to reproduce labour power, but to maintain legitimacy and social order. Even this argument, however, seems weak in the context of the mid-1980s, for there has been no generalised break-down in legitimacy, nor any coherent threat to social order, despite the apparently potent combination of high unemployment and reduced welfare spending (much the same observation, incidentally, may be made of the 1930s).

None of this is to deny that certain types of welfare provision at certain times in Britain's recent history have probably benefited certain sections of the capitalist class as much if not more than the direct recipients. The important point which is made forcibly in this literature is that welfare expenditure is not necessarily a 'drain' on capitalist profitability, for it may aid the pursuit of profits by helping to relieve capital of some of the costs of investing in labour-power. It is also doubtless the case that certain pieces of legislation have at particular times been supported or even sponsored by capitalist interests, in which case we should be wary of interpreting the development of the welfare state in terms of a glorious history of working-class struggle.

Yet when all of this has been said, we are still left with the fact that the welfare state has been, and continues to be, an arena of political conflict in which dominant groups in British society have more often been concerned to limit than to extend the scope of state provision. In our view, the welfare state is first and foremost a manifestation of the growing power of labour in British politics in the twentieth century.

One obvious way in which the working class in Britain has actively contributed to the growth of the welfare state is through its electoral influence over governments. The extension of the franchise to working class men in 1868 and in 1884 obliged the Liberal and Conservative Parties to court the working-class vote, and led eventually to the emergence of the Labour Party during the first 20 years of this century. Working-class aspirations were thus to some extent transmitted to government through the electoral process in the way in which liberal-democratic theories of politics and the constitution suggest (see Chapters 1 and 2), although the representation of working-class interests by the various political parties was by no means always obvious or direct. Indeed, beginning with Ramsey MacDonald (who cut unemployment benefit by 10 per cent in 1931 and precipitated a disastrous split in the Labour Party in the process), Labour leaders have not shown themselves averse to subordinating working-class interests to the pursuit of capitalist profitability by enforcing wage reductions (e.g. through incomes policies) and trimming welfare expenditure.

Despite the set-backs, however, it is undeniable that the extension of political rights to the working class in the nineteenth and early twentieth centuries (women were given the vote after the First World War) has been a major factor in the subsequent extension of 'social rights'. The development of such social rights has not brought about social equality, but they have made inroads into the traditional rights of private property and they do represent a constant threat and challenge to the continuing system of class inequality. Put another way, the welfare state is a real gain by the working class and the principle of free social provision as of right does represent (as various right-wing politicians have warned) a real challenge to the basic principles on which a capitalist society is founded.

This is a crucial point and one which is often overlooked in left critiques of the welfare state which tend to emphasise the usefulness of social policy to the capitalist class while ignoring the challenge which it represents to that class. It is not in our view any exaggeration to suggest that the existence of a comprehensive system of universal welfare provision within a capitalist society represents an element of socialism in the very heart of capitalism, for it breaks the link, on which capitalism depends, between work and material sustenance and establishes the right to enjoy services on the basis of need rather than ability to pay. This is not to deny that the principle of the work ethic has often been reasserted by governments, just as the notion of social rights has often been eroded, for ever since 1834, governments have been concerned to make welfare beneficiaries work for their benefits (e.g. through the workhouse system of the nineteenth century, the 'genuinely seeking work' condition of 1920s unemployment relief, and the so-called 'Youth Opportunities Programme' and 'Youth Training Scheme' of the 1980s) and welfare services are to this day linked to the importance of wage labour (e.g. in the condition that the unemployed must be 'available for work', in the definition of sickness, as 'inability to work', in the concern to orient schooling to the 'demands of work', and so on). Nevertheless, the welfare state still represents a 'Trojan horse' within the citadels of capitalism in that it rests firmly on a set of values which are fundamentally opposed to those of capitalism. If capitalism entails a system of allocating power and resources according to the ownership of private property, welfare services entail a system of allocating society's resources according to the right of all citizens to share in the common wealth of the society according to their need. There is, therefore, a fundamental ideological contradiction – that between property rights and citizenship or social rights – built into the very foundations of any advanced welfare-capitalist society.

This is a contradiction which can be, and has been, exploited by those who do not benefit from ownership of the means of production. During the 1960s and early 1970s, for example, there is little doubt that one reason why the profitability of capitalist industry fell so dramatically was precisely because non-owners of capital – ordinary workers, the professional middle classes, old age pensioners, claimants of supplementary benefit and others – were able to lay claim to a greater proportion of the country's wealth through an extension of welfare provisions, and it was this that led to a 'fiscal crisis' of the state as governments attempted to expand social spending while defending the private sector against crippling rises in taxation.

Seen in this way, it is clear that social reforms have not simply been 'ceeded' by dominant groups as a way of maintaining order and legitimacy, but have been struggled over. Sometimes – as in the two periods of war and again in the 1960s – these struggles have resulted in real gains for working class people. At other times – as in the inter-war years and the period from the mid-1970s – they have resulted in real losses as wages have been cut back and welfare provisions curtailed. It is only in certain historical situations, therefore, that the less-privileged strata in British society have been able to 'usurp' resources controlled by the more-privileged strata.

The first type of situation in which real gains have been secured relates to periods of war. This is because government and other powerful groups in society have been obliged at times of war to subordinate all other concerns to the pursuit of victory over the external enemy, and this has enabled working-class people, organised through trade unions, tenants associations and other such organisations to secure concessions in return for their continued co-operation in the war effort. Furthermore, with the economy operating at full capacity, the industrial strength of workers (especially those employed in strategic sectors such as the production of munitions) has been maximised, and this has been reflected not only in increased wages, but also in social reforms which might otherwise have been unthinkable in peace-time.

The second situation in which working people have been able to secure real gains in their standard of living through improved state provision of services is at times of economic growth. In a thriving economy such as that of Britain in the 1950s, full employment and even labour shortages strengthen the hand of organised labour in bargaining with both employers and governments. Indeed, government may itself take the lead in developing social provisions, for at times of economic prosperity it is possible to extend provisions to the working class without eroding to any great extent the existing material privileges of the wealthier sections of the population. To revert to an analogy much beloved by politicians, if the national 'cake' is getting larger, then it is possible to give working people larger and larger slices without necessarily changing the proportionate shares going to different social groups. Put another way, it is possible in such situations for the working class to win without anybody else actually losing. As we saw in Chapter 6 in relation to statistics on the distribution of income and wealth, this does seem to have been largely the case over the years in Britain.

This being the case, the end of a period of economic boom clearly marks a crucial point in the development of social provisions, for as the boom turns into recession, organised labour becomes weakened as unemployment rises, and the scramble to maintain existing shares of a dwindling cake may be expected to intensify. As Harold Laski observed some 50 years ago:

The concessions that the government can [offer in times of prosperity] do not seriously invade the established expectations of those who control the means of production. They are prepared to pay the price...But the situation is wholly different when capitalism is in a phase of contraction. The price of concessions expected by democracy then appears too high. The assumptions of capitalism then contradict the implications of democracy. If the phase of contraction is prolonged, it becomes necessary either to abrogate the democratic process or to change the economic assumptions upon which the society rests.

The right critique of social welfare and the privatisation of the welfare state

The critique of the welfare state which emerged from the New Right of the Conservative Party during the latter half of the 1970s was in part a response to the growing problems of the British economy and in part a product of the neo-liberal theories and philosophies which were beginning to spread through the party at that time. When the Conservatives returned to power in 1979 and set about cutting social expenditure, they did so not only because they saw this as necessary in order to regenerate private-sector profitability (something which the Labour Government had itself reluctantly come to accept during the last years of its tenure of office), but also because they believed in reducing public reliance on state provision as a matter of principle. As in its economic strategy (discussed in Chapter 8), so too in its social policy, the Thatcher Government was thus inspired both by what it saw as a pragmatic necessity, and by what it believed to be its moral duty. By cutting welfare provisions, in other words, it was also intent on liberating the British people from what it saw as the stifling yoke of years of social-democratic paternalism.

Paradoxically, perhaps, this libertarian strand of New Right philosophy tended to agree with many of those on the left who were arguing that the welfare state was not benefiting those whom it had originally been intended to benefit, although different explanations were advanced for why this was the case. In particular, Friedman and others who provided much of the inspiration for the resurgent right-wing of the Tory Party argued that such a failing was inherent to any attempt to use the state to bring about social objectives, no matter how laudable such objectives may at first appear.

There is considerable evidence to suggest that, notwithstanding the dramatic increase in expenditure by the state on welfare provisions, poverty has not been eliminated and a good case can be made to the effect that the major beneficiaries of much of this expenditure have been middle-income groups. One indication of this is that the middle class tends to make greatest use of the most expensive services: education is an obvious example, for students from middle-class backgrounds are greatly over-represented in further and higher education, but the same is also true of the health services where the greatest provision is centred on the most affluent parts of the country. A second factor (which the New Right tends to ignore) is that there has developed alongside the visible welfare state an 'invisible' one in the form of tax allowances to the better off; those who can afford to take out a mortgage for house purchase, to contribute to private pension schemes or to purchase private life assurance have been able to claim tax relief on their payments, and the cost of this (which amounts to something like twice that of all state cash benefits) has been met through higher taxes on those with lower incomes.

As things have turned out, therefore, the welfare state has tended to benefit the middle class at least as much as the poor, and it has been paid for largely out of the pockets of ordinary working people. This was probably never intended by the legislators and reformers of the last 150 years, so why has it happened?

According to Friedman, Hayek, and other right-wing critics of the welfare state, such an outcome may be seen as almost the inevitable result of the pursuit of social objectives through the use of state power. In their view, such a strategy inevitably ends up by sacrificing the general interest to the particular interests of relatively small groups which are able to direct the use of the monopoly coercive power of the state to their own ends. In other words, once the principle of forcing individuals to make provisions which they would not otherwise freely make is accepted, it becomes possible for sectional interests to mobilise to force others to subsidise them. This, according to the New Right, is precisely what has happened with the development of welfare policies.

A further related point can be made about this, and that concerns the people who administer or service the welfare state. The doctors, organised through the BMA, have for example been major beneficiaries of the extension of state power in the area of health care, for, as we saw earlier, they have been able (in 1911 and again after the Second World

War) to exact considerable concessions from governments as the price of their co-operation. The same has been true, to a greater or lesser extent, of various groups of public-sector workers whose numbers have swollen over the years and who, through their unions, have sought to secure their own interests as producers of services without necessarily improving the quality or quantity of service provision to consumers. Thus it is argued that those who are directly employed by the state in the administration and delivery of welfare services have been able to direct state expenditures in their own interests; much of the additional spending on welfare during the 1960s, for example, went on building up the bureaucracy and extending the career prospects of social workers, teachers and others rather than on materially improving the services received by the clients of welfare bureacracies.

For the New Right, then, a major explanation for the spiralling cost of the welfare state could be found in the power of certain groups who saw that it was in their interests to perpetually expand spending on public services. The task, therefore, was to reduce the power of these groups by cutting state spending, thereby reducing taxation and enabling consumers to make their own choices based on the money in their own pockets. The liberty of the individual was thus to be extended through a reduction of state compulsion.

The problem with such a strategy, as the more perceptive analysts recognised, was that, as in the nineteenth century, many people could not afford to pay for their basic consumption requirements. True, wages have increased enormously in real terms in the last 100 years, but it remains the case that millions of people still cannot possibly afford to pay market rates for their housing, or their medical needs, or their children's education. As we saw earlier in this chapter, there was, and to a considerable extent still is, a fundamental contradiction between the need to keep wages down in order to ensure profitability and the need on the other hand to ensure that people can gain access to necessary, yet inherently costly, means of subsistence.

The development of the welfare state through the twentieth century was one response to this problem. For all its faults – the spiralling costs, the lengthening waiting lists, the lack of consumer choice and the unresponsive public bureaucracies which it brought into being – the socialisation of consumption through state welfare provisions did at least succeed in improving the living standards of working-class people. The housing built for rent by local authorities far surpassed that offered by the private landlords; medical treatment was brought within reach of millions of people who had not previously been able to afford it; working-class children received at least a basic education and some were able to seize this opportunity to move out of the working class altogether.

It is also evident, however, that the basic contradiction was displaced, not resolved, by increasing state welfare provision, for the houses, hospitals, schools and home helps which the state now provided itself, still had to be paid for. If ordinary working people could not afford to pay, then somebody else would have to. The state, in short, had to pick up the bill. This meant that the contradiction, far from being resolved, was simply shifted from the market place to the public sector.

The problem is well illustrated by the development of unemployment relief between 1911 and 1934. We saw that, in 1911, the government tried to provide some measure of benefit for the unemployed, but that this was limited to workers who represented a good risk in actuarial terms and was to be financed strictly out of contributions rather than taxation. During the inter-war years, however, the scheme came under pressure as a result of mass unemployment, and this led both to its extension to workers who represented a greater risk, and to the eventual establishment of the Unemployment Assistance Board which paid benefits as of right even in those cases where there was no entitlement on the basis of contributions. By 1934, in other words, it had been recognised that workers could not pay for their own benefits and that unemployment relief would have to be financed out of taxation. Despite the attempt to retain an insurance system, financed out of contributions, after the war, benefits have continued to be paid increasingly out of taxation, and the burden on the central exchequer has correspondingly risen.

This financial 'burden' on the state has increased in similar fashion as a result of the expansion of other welfare services. Once established, the scale of the provisions has grown, and the real cost has grown with it. The problem has therefore arisen of how to finance these increasing commitments.

Throughout the 1960s and 1970s, this massive expansion in state spending was paid for to some extent by wage-earners – mainly through direct taxation and national insurance contributions – and the number of people liable to pay income tax increased in the 30 years after 1948 from 15 to 21 million. There was, however, a limit to how far the working class could be called upon to finance welfare provisions – after all, it was their inability to pay the full cost of such services which had led the state to take over responsibility in the first place. Capital too, therefore, had to contribute, and by 1975, companies were paying 18 per cent of the state's total tax revenue (not including local authority rates). Yet there was a limit here as well, for rising taxes represented a drain on profitability which threatened future levels of investment.

The original contradiction, therefore, reappeared, but in a new guise. By the 1970s, the problem was no longer that the working class could not afford to pay for its key consumption requirements, but was rather that the state could not afford to pay for them. If it continued to increase taxation on workers, then this would either drive large sections of the working class back into poverty or would result in higher wage claims to compensate. But if it continued to raise taxes on capital, this would reduce profits, drive many companies out of business, and further increase demand for social security and other benefits as unemployment rose.

Until the late 1970s, government's response to this dilemma was to attempt to maintain the level of provision and to finance this through increased borrowing. Between 1971 and 1975, the gap between state revenues and state expenditures widened to 11 per cent of GNP and government borrowing increased to £11 billion per year. Such a policy could not be pursued for long, and in 1976 the mounting 'fiscal crisis', which was most clearly manifest in an inflation rate in excess of 20 per cent, led the then Labour Government to accept an International Monetary Fund loan which stipulated that public expenditure had to be cut back.

When the Conservatives were returned to power in 1979, they were determined to embark on an entirely different strategy. Rather than providing a wide range of services free or at low subsidised prices, they would attempt to increase the ability of people to pay for services provided from within the private sector. Whereas before, governments had acted to reduce the cost of social provisions, now the government was to pursue the logical alternative strategy of enhancing people's ability to pay while leaving the supply of services to the market. The problem to be addressed was thus how to put more money back into people's pockets.

In principle, this could be done first of all by reducing personal taxation consequent upon a radical reduction in the scale of state spending. This, however, would probably be insufficient and would not in any case help those people who were not in work and were not therefore paying tax on incomes. Something else was therefore required. According to writers such as Friedman, for example, the problem could in principle be overcome through the introduction of a system of negative income tax (in which those in receipt of income below a specified level would receive a 'top-up' cash supplement from the state) and by the development of various voucher schemes (through which people would receive vouchers which they could spend in whichever way they chose on education, or medical treatment, or whatever other service was covered by the scheme).

It was this radical 'libertarian' thinking, as much as the pressing need to cut public expenditure in the fact of a fiscal crisis, which lay behind the Thatcher Government's assault on the welfare state. The government never got so far as to introduce negative income tax, and its support for education vouchers proved impossible to put into practice. Nevertheless, the aim was to return as much as possible state provision to the private market (e.g. by selling council houses, encouraging private health insurance, and so on) while supporting people's incomes by reducing direct taxation, increasing tax relief on items such as mortgages and private pension contributions, and maintaining the value of cash benefits such as family allowances. This was not a return to the nineteenth-century market mode (as many of the government's critics made out) because it involved considerable state subsidisation. The point was, however, that the subsidies were to be directed to incomes rather than to providing services.

Now it may be suggested at this point that such a strategy was unlikely to prove any more successful than had the socialised mode of consumption, for both involved high levels of state expenditure but on different things. Surely, if government could no longer afford to subsidise the provision of education, housing and so on, nor could it afford to subsidise people's incomes to a point where they could themselves afford to buy such services? Was not the shift from a socialised to a privatised mode merely a shift from the swings to the roundabouts?

In one sense, this was indeed the case, for the Thatcher Government found that it simply could not afford to reduce its demands for revenue. Personal taxation, for example, actually increased by 9 per cent between 1979 and 1983, and the real value of cash benefits such as pensions and family allowances (i.e. benefits which needed to increase substantially if people were to be able to buy housing, health care and so on)failed to rise. Apart from the very rich, most people in Britain were worse off as a result of government policies at the end of the Thatcher administration's first term of office than they had been at the start of it.

The failure of the government to support people's incomes did not, however, mean the total failure of its privatisation strategy, for unlike the situation in the nineteenth century or even that between the wars, many people could now afford to begin to buy at least some of the basic items of consumption. This was due to the fact that the old contradiction between low wages and high consumption costs had to some extent resolved itself without any help from government, for over the preceeding 30 years, the real incomes of most households in Britain had risen substantially. Real wages rose continually through the long post-war boom and through most of the 1960s and 1970s, and the increased participation of women in the labour market meant that many households were in receipt of two incomes. By the time the Thatcher government came to office in 1979, many people in Britain could already afford at least some of the services which their parents or grandparents could never have paid for and private provision in areas such as personal transportation (through car ownership) and housing (through owner-occupation subsidised in most cases by mortgage-related tax relief) had already become widespread, even among the working class (over half of all households, for example, were buying or owned their homes, and 40 per cent of manual workers were home-owners).

What the Thatcher Government did was to encourage this existing trend towards private-sector provision. It did this by first raising various welfare user charges in order to reduce or eliminate the element of subsidy, and then by encouraging private producers to take over responsibility from the state for provision of these services. Prices of school meals, for example, were raised to a point at which private catering firms could be invited to tender to provide them. Health service charges were raised and, together with the continuing deterioration of NHS health care, this led to a considerable increase in the use of private health insurance (even some trade unions such as the Electricians' took out health insurance subscriptions for their members). Higher education fees were raised at the same time as the 'independent' university at Buckingham was awarded a Royal Charter, and the government began to consider ways of replacing student grants with bank loans and reintroducing scholarships. Most dramatically of all, council-house rents were pushed up to notional 'market levels' at the same time as council tenants were offered the right to buy their homes at discounts of up to 50 per cent.

This trend to private provision, which was set in motion long before 1979 but which achieved official blessing and encouragement from that year onwards, is not in principle irreversible. Even in the 1980s, the socialised mode remains the principal form of provision, and the future balance between this and the developing privatised mode will depend upon the relative impact of diverse pressures and influences exerted by groups such as state employees, professional organisations of teachers, doctors etc., civil servants at central and local government levels, voters, pressure groups, welfare clients such as council house tenants, lawyers and judges, ratepayer organisations and all the other interests which will help to shape the future pattern of welfare provision. All that can be said at this point is that it is by no means impossible that the state's role in the direct provision of welfare will continue to dwindle and to be replaced by the private sector.

We would therefore reject the arguments of those on the left who suggest that the functional importance of the welfare state within capitalism means that no fundamental shift away from state provision of services such as health, housing and education is possible. Privatisation (e.g. in the case of council-house sales) has often proved popular, for many people have become disenchanted and disillusioned with the inefficiency and impersonality of big welfare bureaucracies and they may well welcome the opportunity to reassert more control over their lives by freeing themselves from dependency upon the state. Furthermore, many households can now afford to pay for at least some of their consumption needs. Private housing is, as we have seen, now well established among the working class, and private health care is now also just beginning to become more widely available than it has been in the past.

This is not to suggest, of course, that privatisation of consumption is universally welcomed, nor that a private solution is possible for everybody. Some crucially significant sections of the population continue to have a personal vested interest in the welfare state as it is presently constituted; there are, for a start, 7 million people employed by the state in Britain, and many of these would be threatened by any sustained and fundamental shift in the nature of provision. There are also millions of working-class people who cannot and will probably never be able to afford to pay private-sector rates for their vital services; working-class home-owners, though numerous, are still in a minority of their class, and the number of working-class people covered by private health insurance, though increasing, remains tiny in absolute terms. It is obvious that the Thatcherite privatisation strategy can never extend effective choice to everybody and that some sections of the population can only suffer as a result of it.

What we are suggesting then, is that powerful forces are ranged on each side of the socialised versus privatised division, and the future of the welfare state remains to be determined (just as its origins were) by the outcome of political struggles. What is crucially important about all this as regards an analysis of contemporary British politics is that consumption issues – housing, health, education, pensions and so on – have increasingly come to the forefront of political argument and conflict as the welfare state has come under attack from government cuts and the move to privatisation. The question of how vital areas of consumption are to be socially organised and managed has become a highly charged and highly politicised one, and it has thrown up new patterns of political alignment and conflict which do not correspond to the conventional lines of class cleavage on which so much of British politics has traditionally been fought out.

As we saw in Chapter 6 political struggles around issues of consumption cut across class lines. Sometimes, this results in the formation of new and strange alliances between people who more often find themselves on opposing sides. Middle-class teachers join with working-class parents to fight school closures; local 'anti-cuts' movements are formed which bring together members of public-sector unions threatened by job losses, welfare state clients threatened by an erosion of services, radical intellectuals committed to an extension of socialism, and so on; community activism draws together members of the women's movement, of ethnic groups, of gay rights campaigns and of the Labour movement in a common cause of, say, campaigning for a community centre.

At other times, however, this redrawing of political alignments results in a hopeless fragmentation among people who more often find themselves on the same side. Council-house rent rises, for example, may be fought by working-class tenants, yet may be welcomed by working-class owner-occupiers who see such a policy in positive terms as reducing the burden on their rates. Low-wage earners may ally themselves with prosperous professional and business interests in demanding tighter restrictions on welfare benefits claimed by the unemployed, one-parent families and others who are popularly seen as parasitical and 'scroungers'. The politics of consumption, in other words, are often divisive and entail struggles and conflicts between sectors of the population which cut across social classes.

The conventional wisdom in the Conservative Party and elsewhere that an extension of private-property rights to the working class is a sure way of undermining the appeal of socialism is not without foundation. If the extension of state provision in the early part of this century was seen by politicians at the time as a way of maintaining political stability and social order, then the erosion of state provision in the later part of the century has, paradoxically, also come to be seen in the same way.

The momentum of the shift to privatised forms of provision is considerable. Should it continue, then it may be that not only private housing and private pension schemes, but also private medicine and perhaps even private education may eventually come to represent the majority form of consumption provision (subsidised, where necessary, through state support by means of tax relief and other income-support measures). If this should come about, then the implications for British politics – and for British society as a whole – would be enormous.

Sociologists have become accustomed to representing the social structure of modern Britain in the form of a pyramid with a small upper class at the pinnacle and a large working class at the base. This has, for some time now, been a less than perfect metaphor – the growth of the middle class, for example, has led to a considerable 'bulge' mid-way up the pyramid, and the break-down in the relation between social class and voting (discussed in Chapter 6) has made such a model increasingly useless for political scientists interested in explaining patterns of political alignment. A major problem with this pyramidal model, however, is that it relates solely to social class – to the question of how production is socially organised. It therefore ignores the equally important question of other sources of inequality and other bases of political alignment – notably those concerning the social organisation of consumption.

If the question of consumption is taken into account, then we may have to end up inverting our pyramid model. As more and more people find themselves able to buy vital services, so those who cannot will become an increasingly marginalised minority reliant on a dwindling and deteriorating state sector. The signs are already present in housing and, to some extent, in health care. The initial responses of this marginalised minority are also present, and they range from violent explosions of unrest (such as the 1981 inner-city riots) to a return to mutual aid strategies in some more stable working-class communities. Just as, in Chapter 8, we saw that the decline of the British economy was creating a division between a majority of people in reasonably secure and well-paid employment and a minority of unemployed and low-paid insecure workers, so now we see that much the same division is emerging with the decline of the welfare state. The time is coming when we may need to re-examine our traditional 'them-and-us' conceptions of British society, for the tendency in relation to both production (the world of work) and consumption (the world outside the factory gates) is towards an increasingly large 'them' and an increasingly marginalised and desperate 'us' (though still, of course, with a tiny 'them' at the very top of the heap!)

CONCLUSION

In the conclusion to our discussion of economic policy in Chapter 8, we suggested that there was considerable evidence to support the view that particular powerful interests – notably those of finance capital – had done much to shape political outcomes over the years. This evidence was such as to lend credence to those Marxist interpretations of British politics which explain policies as the product of the influence or even domination achieved by certain capitalist interests over the state.

The evidence discussed in this chapter in respect of social policy cannot, however, support the same conclusion. The interests of capital have certainly played some part in the development of some policies on some occasions and – more importantly – governments' concerns with maintaining profitability in the private sector of the economy have certainly represented an important check on the expansion of welfare spending (e.g. as in the 1930s when real spending on welfare services was cut in order to reduce the tax burden on capital, and again in the period since 1976 when the renewed crisis of profitability in the economy again led to a reversal in the upward trend of social services expenditure).

What this evidence suggests, however, is not that capitalist interests have been instrumental in controlling or directing social policy, but rather that a concern with maintaining private sector profitability has represented an important *constraint* on the development of welfare policy. As we stressed in Chapter 8, it is important to distinguish between factors which determine political outcomes and factors which constrain the range of outcomes which are possible. The over-riding interests of capital with maintaining profits have in this sense constrained social policy, but they have not *determined* it. Only rarely in the history of British social policy since the nineteenth century has the state responded directly to the demands of capital for this or that piece of legislation.

We have seen in this chapter that the determinants or causes of social policy over the years have been many and varied. Sometimes governments have acted on their own initiative in response to some perceived problem. At other times, policies have been introduced as a result of pressure from particular interest groups or individual reformers. The organised working class has loomed large as a factor in social reform, but much of the earlier legislation was introduced despite working-class antipathy and resistance, and sometimes social policy has represented an attempt to head-off anticipated working-class militancy rather than as a response to working-class pressure itself. Middle class and professional groups have also played an important part in shaping the development of the welfare state, and policies initially designed to benefit one group have sometimes been re-moulded to suit the interests of another. Even today, struggles continue over the issue of welfare, and the groups engaged in these struggles are as disparate and varied as ever. Clearly, there is no one group or class which has dominated or controlled social policy, and different alliances of different interest groups tend to form around different specific issues.

All of this lends support, not to a simple Marxist theory of the state, but to some kind of pluralist theory, for it is in the work of pluralist theorists (discussed in Chapters 2 and 3) that we find the emphasis on political competition between shifting groups of alliances and it is this pattern of politics which seems to characterise the history of the development of social policy in Britain. Having said that, qualifying points must quickly be made. First, the build up of the welfare state has carried within itself the fact that it is now a substantial employer of labour. The professionals employed in health and social service provision have enjoyed an inside track with respect to their influence over policy-making and this is suggestive of a corporatist, closed style of policy-making rather than the open, pluralist pattern. Second, and as we have already made clear, it is important to make a distinction between who causes welfare provision and who benefits from that provision. To say that welfare policy is made in response to a variety of pressures from many interests does not lead us to say that everyone in society benefits equally from the provision that results: the left argues that welfare provision is to the ultimate benefit of the capitalist class, and the right is not unmindful of the benefits which the welfare state brings to the middle class. In many ways identifying who benefits from welfare policy is more fundamental than identifying who makes that policy although it has to be recognised that reform is necessarily ambiguous in terms of whom it advantages. Third, and on the policy-making front, it is important to recognise that the responsiveness of government to pressures is constrained, and, in the context of economic recession, it is constrained by the need to take account of the implications of different policies for future private sector profitability. In other words, political competition has been imperfect and unbalanced and the government and the state has not been the neutral referee between competing interests but an active and involved participant.

When we look at the evidence on welfare policy-making as compared to the evidence on economic policy-making set down in the last chapter, then we see it as reasonable to suggest that certain areas of state activity seem to be more open to pressure and influence by competing groups than others. Economic policy-making is a relatively exclusive business in a way which is less evident with respect to policy-making in the field of welfare provision. Indeed, the determination of social policy cannot be achieved exclusively given its direct and obvious impact on a wide range of people and the popular concern and political activity which it arouses. Furthermore, social policy is developed and implemented at many different levels and in many different agencies of the state which would make it difficult to insulate it from popular pressure – elected local authorities, for example, play a key role in the organisation of public housing, schooling and personal social services, and the fierce battles which developed from 1979 onwards, between Labour-controlled authorities intent on defending the welfare state and a central government intent on weakening it, bear eloquent testimony to the diversity of interests which come to be represented in the struggles over such policies (the relation between different agencies of the state is discussed in Chapter 11).

This being the case, we are now in a position to draw a tentative but significant theoretical conclusion based on the evidence of this and the previous chapter. This is that the state appears to operate in different ways and is subject to different determinations in different areas of its interventions. As regards economic policy, it seems to be strongly influenced by one particular sectional interest (that of finance capital) and any conflict which does take place occurs between large, class-based organisations within state agencies such as the NEDC. As regards social policy, however, state policy-making appears to be subject to many different and competing influences and pressures, and the conflicts which take place occur relatively more openly and in a diversity of contexts. A broadly Marxist interpretation of British politics would seem appropriate to the first situation, but is clearly less appropriate to the second. Policy making in the field of welfare provision *is* increasingly constrained by the demands and requirements of capitalist interests, but within these limits it reflects competing pressures.

WORKS CITED AND GUIDE TO FURTHER READING

Barratt Brown, M. (1971) The welfare state in Britain, *Socialist Register* London, Merlin Press. or reprinted in his (1972) *From Labourism to Socialism,* Nottingham, Spokesman Books.
Quite a good example of New Left analysis of the welfare state at a time when the cuts and Thatcherism were still some way off. Concludes, unlike most Marxist approaches, that free welfare services represent 'a bastion of socialist conception' within capitalist Britain.

Deacon, A. (1977) Concession and coercion: the politics of unemployment insurance in the twenties, in A. Briggs and J. Saville (eds), *Essays in Labour History,* London, Croom Helm.
Not only an excellent guide to government policy on unemployment in the twenties, but also a careful analysis showing how pressure from below brought about concessions which were then limited as far as possible in order to prevent any erosion of the work ethic.

Fraser, D. (1973) *The Evolution of the British Welfare State,* London, Macmillan. Has become a standard text on the development of welfare policy in Britain – perhaps a bit weak on explanation, but strong on detail.

George, V. and Wilding, P. (1976) *Ideology and Social Welfare,* London, Routledge & Kegan Paul.
A useful if slightly superficial account of four contrasting ideological approaches to the questions of welfare – those of the 'anti-collectivists', the 'reluctant collectivists', the 'Fabian socialists' and the 'Marxists'.

Gough, I. (1979) *The Political Economy of the Welfare State,* London, Macmillan.
Probably still the best of what has become a very large literature analysing the question of welfare from a Marxist perspective. Gough's analysis is careful and coherent in showing how social expenditure has benefited capital as well as labour, and he shows himself adept at distinguishing the causes of particular policies from the functions which they have come to perform.

Green, D. (1982) *The Welfare State: For Rich or For Poor?* Institute of Economic Affairs, Occasional Paper, number 63.
A nice example of an application of the ideas of Hayek and Friedman to historical analysis; in this case, to an analysis of how the medical profession was able to secure its own position through the introduction of compulsory state health insurance in 1911.

Hay, J. (1975) *The Origins of the Liberal Welfare Reforms, 1906–14,* London, Macmillan.
A slim but useful volume which traces the diverse pressures – from within and outside the state – which resulted in the spate of welfare reforms before the First World War. Hay argues that different pieces of legislation had different origins, and his book is therefore a useful corrective to those – on the right and the left – who seek to explain the growth of state intervention through monocausal theories.

Hayek, F. (1960) *The Constitution of Liberty,* London, Routledge and Kegan Paul.
In many ways the most comprehensive and compelling development of the neo-liberal position including its relevance to contemporary problems of welfare provision. In a very readable way, Hayek traces the dangers for individual liberties which he sees as emanating from the growth of state intervention, and thus poses a series of uncomfortable problems which defenders of the welfare state will ignore at their peril.

Laski, H. (1935) *The State in Theory and Practice,* London, Allen & Unwin.
See guide to further reading at the end of Chapter 8.

Marshall, T. (1950) Citizenship and social class, in T. Marshall (ed.) *Citizenship and Social Class, and other essays,* London, Cambridge University Press.
A classic essay in which it is argued that the development of legal rights in the eighteenth century led inexorably to the extension of political rights in the nineteenth and thence to the establishment of social rights of citizenship in the twentieth. Particularly insightful in pointing to the growing tension between rights of private property and rights of citizenship – i.e. to the conflict between a capitalist system of production and a collective system of welfare provision.

Marx, K. (1976) *Capital, Volume I.* Harmondsworth, Penguin, Chapters 10 and 15.

In which Marx analyses the nineteenth-century Factory Acts in the context of his theory of exploitation. The analysis is more subtle than is sometimes imagined, for while state regulation is seen as a product of class struggle, it is also seen as having aided capital by safeguarding the quality of labour-power and stimulating investment in new capital-intensive means of production. A standard reference for later marxist analyses of social policy.

Mishra, R. (1977) *Society and Social Policy*, London, Macmillan.
Considers various different theoretical explanations for the growth of state intervention in welfare.

Offe, C. (1984) *Contradictions of the welfare state*, London, Hutchinson.
A collection of essays by an important contemporary left writer. Argues forcefully that capitalism can live neither with nor without the welfare state, and that the state itself thus confronts recurring problems which it cannot resolve.

Pelling, H. (1968) *Popular Politics and Society in Late Victorian Britain*, London, Macmillan, Chapter 1.
An important analysis of the growth of state intervention in the nineteenth century which suggest that, far from being a response to working-class demands, many policies were introduced in the face of working-class antipathy or even opposition.

CHAPTER 10

Securing the Social Order

Quite clearly, the greatest of all dangers to the capitalist system is that more and more people...should come to think as both possible and desirable an entirely different social order

Ralph Miliband (1969) The State in Capitalist Society, *London, Weidenfeld & Nicolson, pp. 260–2*

We are surely heading for a situation in which stricter measures of social control may have to be applied to stabilise society and secure our democratic system

James Anderton, Chief Constable of Greater Manchester (1977), Annual Report.

Britain is a very unequal society. As we saw in Chapter 6, the distribution of wealth and income remains remarkably skewed. Such inequalities have been exacerbated by the economic recession of the 1970s and 1980s. As unemployment has spiralled, so a substantial minority of the population has found itself unable to participate in the 'normal' life of our society. Furthermore, the erosion of welfare services (discussed in Chapter 9) has heightened inequalities, for those who depend most on the services and benefits which have been cut are those who earn the lowest wages (if they are earning at all) and who own the fewest assets.

On the face of it, a society which is divided by gross inequalities between top and bottom; which is being squeezed by a sustained economic decline; and which is being governed by a party which makes no secret of its desire to stretch these inequalities still further, would seem to be in a rather precarious position. Yet Britain in the 1980s does not appear to be perched on the brink of the revolutionary abyss. In 1983, with unemployment at 14 per cent and no sign of an economic recovery, Margaret Thatcher's Conservative Party won a massive parliamentary majority (albeit on a minority of the popular vote) on a manifesto which simply promised more of the same.

In this chapter we shall consider the extent to which Britain's core economic and political institutions are in fact secure against any significant groundswell of popular fury or discontent. As in the previous two chapters, our focus will again be mainly on the activities of the state, for it is a major responsibility of the modern state to secure stable social conditions so that the economy can continue to function. Thus we shall see that tasks which two or three hundred years ago were performed by agencies such as the church or the family are today the province of state agencies, for as with the management of economic affairs and the provision for social need, the maintenance of social order in the contemporary period is first and foremost a state function.

In Britain, as in most other countries of the world, the state is involved in maintaining social order in two ways. First, it attempts to engineer and sustain widespread social and political consensus. In other words, various agencies such as state schools and the state broadcasting corporation are crucially involved in reinforcing particular 'norms' (i.e. acceptable ways of behaving), and particular values (i.e. things held in high regard) which are compatible with existing social arrangements. Second, the state is also involved in organising physical coercion to be used against those who do not comply with the standards which it lays down.

In this chapter, then, we consider the ways in which the state in Britain has been involved in maintaining social order and political stability through both the management of consensus and the organisation of instruments of coercion. Although, as in previous chapters, we adopt an historical perspective, our analysis is directed mainly at the problem of social control in the 1980s at a time when mass loyalty appears to be under strain and when new cleavages are opening up between those sections of the population for whom the system is still working and those for whom it patently is not.

THE 'VELVET GLOVE': MANAGING CONSENT

Over the years, it has often been suggested by observers of British politics and society that the country exhibits a peculiarly 'deferential' political culture. Probably the best known statement of this view came in the nineteenth century with the publication of Walter Bagehot's influential study of the English constitution (see Chapter 1), but the idea has persisted in various guises through twentieth-century political sociology as well. As we saw in Chapter 6, for example, many analyses of voting behaviour have suggested that deferential attitudes may explain the apparently puzzling phenomenon of working-class Conservatism, and sociologists too have devoted considerable time and energy to studies of groups such as farm workers or employees in small, family-owned companies whose behaviour and attitudes seem to result in a rather passive endorsement of their own subordination and relative powerlessness.

Such views of British political culture and of large sections of the British working class as deferential must be treated with some caution. The society has never been as calm and well-ordered as these accounts seem to assume, and there are obvious dangers in taking behaviour which appears to be deferential as indicative of genuine belief in the right of social and political elites to rule. Often we may find, for example, that the farm workers tugging their forelocks with one hand may be giving a 'V'-sign behind their backs with the other, and workers who vote Conservative may do so for a variety of reasons which have nothing to do with a belief in the political wisdom of their social superiors.

While rejecting the concept of a deferential political culture, we would nevertheless emphasise that, notwithstanding the various explosions of unrest and rumblings of discontent which from time to time have threatened political order, Britain does seem to have been peculiarly stable when compared with many other Western capitalist nations. Even when we take account of such manifestations of popular unrest as the Peterloo massacre, the great Chartist demonstrations, the Captain Swing riots, or the 1926 General strike, it does seem that ever since the upheavals of the Civil War in the seventeenth century, the political order has never come under the sustained and real threat of revolution. Britain in the nineteenth century was shielded from the waves of revolutionary change which ebbed and flowed across much of continental Europe, and in the twentieth century it has stood relatively immune from Communist uprisings and Fascist coups alike. In short, those who tell us that liberal-democracy is as deeply embedded and as secure in Britain as in any other country on this globe may be guilty of chauvinism but should not lightly be accused of hyperbole.

Explanation of this relatively enduring stability of the political and social order in Britain is no simple task, and there are obviously many different factors which would need to be taken into account. Britain's geographical location as an island off the coast of mainland Europe is undoubtedly one factor, for the Channel has, on more than one occasion, provided a physical barrier against the wars of conquest which have done so much to shape the present character of other major European countries. The legacy of the Civil War is a second important factor, for the restoration of the monarchy in 1688 effectively sealed a truce between the old ruling class of landowners and the new rising class of industrialists and financiers and thereby avoided the bloody turmoils and struggles for power which took place between these classes in France, Germany and elsewhere through the ninteenth century. Britain's history as the world's first industrial capitalist country is a further element in the explanation, for the working class reached maturity here long before the development of socialist and Marxist ideology on a world scale with the result that revolutionary Marxist ideas have never really taken root in the Labour movement. Add to all this the impact on British society of an Empire which was systematically exploited to the advantage of (among others) the working class at home, and which unleashed a jingoistic and nationalistic strand of popular sentiment which resonates throughout the class structure to this day, and we have identified some of the major factors which any explanation of British political stability would need to address.

Whatever the explanation, it is apparent that this relative stability has meant that the balance between coercion and consensus, the iron fist and the velvet glove, has tended over most of this period to emphasise the latter more than the former. It has, in other words, been the 'soft' agencies of social control rather than the 'hard' ones which seem to have played the major role in maintaining order over the last 300 years.

By 'soft' agencies of control, we mean those institutions which have contributed to social and political order by supplying, maintaining or reinforcing particular beliefs, values, standards of behaviour and understandings of the world which are consistent with the contemporary organisation of the society. According to which theory you read, or which ideology you subscribe to, their function may be identified as that of 'socialization' or 'legitimation'. The term 'legitimation' is one which is more often found in radical and Marxist literature (but which is not exclusive to left political positions) and which refers to the process whereby a particular organisation of state, economy and society comes to be seen by the members of that society, including those in subordinate positions, as morally correct or legitimate. For our purposes, socialization and legitimation may be taken to refer to essentially the same thing – the direct or indirect control over people's ways of thinking and acting other than through the use of physical force.

Traditionally in Britain, the three most important institutions involved in socialising individuals and in legitimating the existing social and political order were the family, the church and the local community. While all three retain some significance today, it is clear that each of them has declined in importance and has to some extent been replaced by other agencies, among which welfare institutions, the educational system and the mass media are probably the most important. As we shall see, these more 'modern' agencies have not generally achieved the same degree of cohesion and power which the more traditional agencies once enjoyed, and this has led in recent years to an attempt by Conservative Governments in particular to reinforce the moral bind of family, church and community as a response to what has been seen as a growing crisis of social control and of morality in the contemporary period.

Before considering all this in more detail, it is important to stress one point at the outset. Socialisation into particular norms, values and beliefs never has been and never can be total, and legitimation is thus always more or less but never completely successfully achieved. Human beings are not empty receptacles into which can be poured those ways of thinking and action which dominant groups or their agents in the pulpits, the classrooms and the editorial offices of Fleet Street wish people to accept. Both Marxism and political sociology have often forgotten or ignored this. Much of the sociological theory of the 1950s, for example, was guilty of assuming an 'oversocialised' conception of human beings in which individuals came to be seen as little more than puppets reacting to situations according to preprogrammed internalised role responses.

Similarly, Marxist thinking has long been bedevilled by the concept of 'false class consciousness' bequeathed by Engels as a label to be applied whenever working class people failed to embrace a Marxist revolutionary ideology. Neither right nor left should assume that the 'soft' agencies of social control are, or ever could be, all-pervasive in their impact on our customary ways of thinking and modes of understanding the world in which we live, for we are all conscious, acting subjects, and we all reflect on the world not only through the cognitive tools handed to us by schools, the church or whatever, but also through our immediate, everyday-life experiences. As we shall see, these experiences may often conflict with the images handed down through soft control agencies, and in cases like this received ideologies may well be questioned or even rejected.

Traditional 'soft' control agencies

The Family. Of the three traditional soft agencies of social control, the family was – and remains – the most important. This is because the family is the principal agency by means of which newly born members of the society come to learn what their world is like and how they are expected to behave within it. Even today (and even more so in the past) the first and most crucial years of childhood are spent almost exclusively within the family unit with the result that the family enjoys extensive control over how infants develop. It is in these years that the child learns what its parents expect as 'normal' and 'correct' behaviour in various situations; 'normal' ways of thinking and 'normal' assumptions about the way the social world works are taken in with the mother's milk. It is similarly in these early formative years that the child will learn, from those with whom it is in closest and most regular contact, the difference between 'good' and 'bad', the distinction between what it is in its power to control and what is controlled by others, the differentiation of the world into 'people like us' and 'people like them', and so on. It is, and has long been, overwhelmingly the task of the family to equip the new members of our society with the basic social skills and 'cookbook recipes' by which they will go on to live their lives, and it is for this reason that the family was, and is, a crucial agency in the transmission of social values and normative standards across the generations.

Having said that, however, it has also immediately to be recognised that the family in Britain no longer plays so central a role in the maintenance of order as once it did. The shape and nature of the family has changed and is still changing. Although the historical evidence is to some extent debated in details, it is the case that in pre-industrial Britain, before the dawn of capitalism had transformed the country and its people in the most dramatic and far-reaching of social changes the world has witnessed, the family unit was typically based on a close network of extended kinship ties. Especially where they were living off the land (where the family functioned as much as a unit of production as anything else), families often consisted not simply of the nuclear unit (comprising husband, wife and immature offspring) but also of grandparents, siblings, aunts, uncles, nephews, nieces and cousins, all living in close proximity and all contributing in one way or another to the many different tasks which the family as a whole was called upon to perform. Thus, in addition to working the land, it was typically the responsibility of this extended family unit to rear and educate its young, to tend to its sick, to care for its aged, to protect its members and so on. It was, in short, the basic and most crucial unit of social organisation at that time, for it was in the family that the individual found a role and identity, and it was through the family that the individual was integrated into the wider society.

With the onset of capitalist industrialization, all this changed. As people were displaced from the land and propelled into the squalid housing and bleak factories of the new industrial cities, so it became increasingly difficult for households based on extended kinship to stay together. Young people left their families to find work and the basis of employment in the factories and the mines was the individual rather than the family unit. Although wives and children were often recruited into the labour force, more extended kin ties were progressively broken or weakened. Today, most sociologists suggest that the 'typical' family form has changed from the extended to the nuclear (or in some views, 'modified-extended') type whose members rely only occasionally and tangentially for aid on more distant kin (e.g. for services such as child-minding or for financial support in the case of more affluent families).

Even this nuclear family type is, moreover, still changing. In a shifting moral climate, for example, the number of single-parent families is increasing quite rapidly. Improved financial autonomy for women has meant that increasing numbers of women today enjoy a real choice as to whether to marry and whether to raise children themselves or with a partner. Liberalised divorce laws mean that marriage is less and less a contract for life, and some observers have detected a phenomenon of 'serial marriage' in which individuals move from one relatively stable monogamous relationship to another, taking some or all of their children with them as they go. What is clear, therefore, is that literally millions of children in Britain today are being brought up either by a single parent or by at least one adult who is not their natural parent.

Not only has the form of the family changed over the last two or three hundred years, but so too have the functions which it is called upon to perform. With the exception of the small family firm, the family is no longer a significant producer unit, and its consumption functions too have been whittled down. Where once the extended family educated its young, there now exist state schools, nurseries and colleges. Where once the extended family catered for its sick and its elderly, there now exist state hospitals, state nursing homes and state-employed home helps. There is, however, still one key area where the state has not, as yet, assumed responsibility from the family, and that is in the socialisation of the infant.

The importance of this continuing socialisation function is recognised by government in the battery of supports it provides for the nuclear family with young children. These include family allowances, tax concessions, family income supplements, child clinics, home nursing services, family casework and so on. Yet despite such supports, it has become increasingly clear that the family is not discharging its socialisation function in such a way as to contribute to social order as it once did. Over recent years, it has become commonplace among many commentators and politicians to attribute manifestations of social malaise such as vandalism, street crime, soccer hooliganism and other forms of anti-social behaviour to the weakness of the family. Family discipline, it is suggested, has been eroded, the emotional security of children has been weakened by mothers working, and there has been a general laxity in moral standards.

Since 1979, Conservative Governments under Mrs Thatcher have attempted to reverse this 'decline' and to reassert the traditional 'strengths' and functions of the family unit. In a drive to disinter what Thatcher herself called 'Victorian values', these governments set about expelling married women from the workforce back into the home and at the same time transferring responsibility for child care, care of the elderly and so on from state welfare institutions to private families. While such moves were in part motivated by a desire to reduce the unemployment figures and to cut back on welfare spending (see Chapter 9), they were also a response to what the government and its supporters saw as a growing threat of breakdown in the social and moral order. One response to such a threat was to employ more police officers; another was to strengthen the moral bind of the family by re-emphasising the traditional role of women as emotional props for their husbands, children and parents to lean on. Such a strategy was, however, almost certainly doomed from the start, not simply because of the resistance which it encountered from feminists and others, but also because it failed to understand the significance of what we may term 'moral pluralism' in the contemporary period. The 'problem' with the family as an agency of social control today is not so much that it is failing to socialise the young, as that different families are bringing their children up according to *different* sets of values and normative standards. There is no longer (if indeed there ever was) a single core value system which is transmitted through the family to successive generations, for the old certainties have vapourised in an age of doubt and ethical divergence. While the state has done something to try to control this (e.g. by defining certain groups as 'problem families' and applying intense case work to them in an attempt to shift their ways of thinking and acting, or by taking children into 'care' where it is felt that they are not receiving an appropriate upbringing), it cannot hope to achieve any significant impact, for the decline of the family as an agency of social control is directly related to the decline of traditional morality in the society as a whole. The main manifestation of this, of course, is the reduced social and political significance of the church.

The Church. The significance of the Church as a 'soft' agency of control in pre-industrial England lay in the virtual monopoly which it enjoyed as the source of authoritative explanations and justifications of the world as people experienced it in their everyday lives. Religion was, in other words, integrated into everyday life as a taken for-granted reality, and there was little dispute or even conscious reflection over its moral content. The Church thus played a crucial legitimating role in that it provided explanations for the harsh conditions in which most people lived and worked, and these explanations usually stressed the role of divine will such that mere mortals could and should do very little to change them;

> *The rich man in his castle,*
> *the poor man at his gate,*
> *God made them high and lowly*
> *and ordered their estate.*

It was precisely this legitimatory role of religion which led Marx to his well-known formulation of religion as 'the sigh of the oppressed creature, the soul of soulless conditions... the opium of the people', for in his view, organised religion served the interest of the ruling class by obscuring people's understanding of the 'real' causes of their misery and by providing a social safety valve through which ordinary people could be offered the compensation of salvation in the next world in return for material damnation in this one.

When considering this traditional role of the Church as the cement which held an aggressively exploitative social order together, we should not lose sight of the fact that religion did – and in some countries still does – also function in some circumstances as a medium of radical critique of existing material conditions. As Tony Benn has pointed out, an important strand in the British socialist tradition can be traced back to the importance of non-conformist religions in the Celtic fringe areas such as Wales, Scotland and the south-west of England, and in many South American countries today, radical worker-priests are prominent in the socialist opposition to extreme right-wing authoritarian regimes. As with all other agencies of socialisation and legitimation, the Church never has and never could exert a total control of people's minds. Nevertheless, it is clear that for centuries, the Church has played a major role in maintaining social control, and in England at least, this was institutionalised through the formal establishment of the Church of England which effectively fused together Church and State with the monarch as the head of both.

Today, the Church of England is still the established Church. The monarch appoints the bishops and archbishops and is in turn crowned in Westminster Abbey by the Archbishop of Canterbury, and the bishops still occupy seats in the House of Lords. Under the terms of the Education Act, 1944, religious instruction remains a compulsory subject on every school curriculum. Yet having said this, it is also apparent that the political significance of the Church in particular, and of religion in general, is today very slight. The reason for this lies in the secularisation of British society over the last 100 years or so.

One obvious indicator of secularisation is formal participation in the activities of the Church – e.g. the number of christenings and baptisms, the rate of attendance at key services such as Easter communion, the number of church weddings, and so on. On all such indicators, the Church has declined in significance since the mid-nineteenth century. However, secularisation goes much deeper than this, for statistics on christenings, weddings and the like are to some extent misleading. This is because for most people, most of these religious rituals retain importance for their form rather than their content. The church wedding is important not so much for the solemn sanctification of the marriage vows in the eyes of God as for the display of the wedding dress, the carnations and the confetti in the eyes of friends and relatives. Religious ceremonies for many people play a secular role as what anthropologists term 'rites de passage'; i.e. as rituals designed to mark a change in status. We thus use the Church to mark important stages of our lives – notably, to mark our entry into this world, our transition from single to married status and our exit from the world – but for little else.

Britain is today without any doubt a secular society, and the fact that the schools set aside a particular period for religious instruction and that the broadcasting media isolate a special 'God slot' within their weekly programming is, paradoxically, strong evidence in support of this view. It is precisely the hallmark of a secular society that religion is marginalised and compartmentalised in this way, for the Church has lost its monopolistic position as the all-embracing source of moral influence and knowledge. Thus Bryan Wilson, the author of a classic text on secularisation, suggests that: 'There has been a compartmentalizing of life; religion which once had a general presidency over the concerns of men [sic], and endowed their activities with a sense of sacredness, has increasingly lost this pre-eminence and influence.' In Britain today, the voice of the Church is simply one point of view being expressed among a cacophony of other points of view, many of which conflict with it. Few people today look to the Church for moral guidance, and fewer still rely on the Church for explanations of world events. The Church, then, is of only marginal significance as an agency of social order, and the vacuum which has been created by the loss of its 'general presidency' has been filled by a plurality of groups and institutions expressing different values, different beliefs and different orientations to the world. Social order has thus been problematised precisely because there is no longer any one powerful institution through which a set of 'core values' can consistently be expressed and reinforced.

Community. This 'problem' has simply been exacerbated by the erosion of the third traditional agency of social cohesion and control, the local community. In pre-industrial Britain, most people lived in settlements of such a size that personal relationships based on face-to-face interaction could be sustained between most or all inhabitants. Furthermore, the difficulties entailed in travel, together with the lack of opportunities outside of the home village or town meant that most people spent most of their lives in the same place, thus reinforcing the strength of neighbourhood ties. None of this should be taken to imply that, because people tended to know each other, they therefore necessarily liked each other, but it does mean that they were constantly aware of each other's actions across virtually all aspects of their lives. Precisely because there was little or no opportunity for the individual to carve out a separate and private existence, overall behaviour could easily be monitored and any deviation from the shared expected norms would swiftly incur sanctions in the form of gossip, ostracism, family shame, and so on. Because the individual was known, the scope for individualism was limited and pressures of collective standards and conformity was intense.

Just as capitalist industrialization undermined the traditional strength of the extended family, so too it disrupted these moral ties of localism. Urbanisation broke down face-to-face modes of social control, for in the relative anonymity of the large industrial city, individuals could carve out discrete areas of their lives and could move through a series of different and unrelated social worlds in which associates in one area of activity had little or no contact with those in another. In such a setting, the old informal sanctions of gossip, ostracism and dishonour lost their grip, and the symbolic and material significance of neighbourhood was weakened.

As in our earlier discussions of the family and the Church, these changes should not be exaggerated. Relatively cohesive neighbourhoods can still be found even in the heart of the large metropolises, and for many of us, the place in which we live still retains some significance. Furthermore, even though community based on residence and locality has been weakened, it has to some extent been replaced by communities formed around other axes – e.g. the sense of community which we experience as members of an occupational group, or a voluntary organisation or a trade union or political party. Informal social control has not, therefore, collapsed entirely, for, to the extent that the people we mix with are important to us (irrespective of whether or not they live near us), we are likely to take their expectations into account in the way in which we think and behave.

The important point, however, is that these expectations are likely to be partial and fragmented and may not in any case be consistent with the sort of behaviour required to support existing social institutions. Peer group pressure among adolescents, for example, can undoubtedly be every bit as strong as ever the old traditional village pressures to conformity were, but they may well result in the development of 'deviant' subcultures which confront rather than reinforce the norms and values of mainstream society. Furthermore, the pressures we experience in one area of our lives (e.g. among workmates) may to a greater or lesser extent be inconsistent with those we experience in another (e.g. among fellow members of the bowls club).

What this means is that the cohesion of the traditional agencies of control has been lost even where the extent of their influence remains strong. Traditionally, the individual stood at the centre of a series of concentric circles of control, each of which reinforced the other. Thus, the individual was a member of a family, which was itself part of a wider local community which was integrated through the Church into the society beyond. Today, however, the individual stands at a point where many different circles of control intersect but do not overlap. As such, the individual is still subject to what we have termed 'soft' agencies of control, but each one impacts on her or him only partially, and taken together they may well pull in different directions. The erosion of the three key traditional agencies of social control has thus resulted in a situation where there is no longer any single set of values or any single institution which can be relied upon to guide people's thoughts and actions. In the modern period, there is only one institution which could possibly fulfil such a central and co-ordinating role, and that is the state. Increasingly, therefore, the state in Britain has been sucked into the vacuum left by the erosion of the family, the Church and the local community in an attempt to reassert conformity in the face of diversity.

Modern 'soft' control agencies

The educational system. Without doubt, the most important of the state's activities as regards socialisation and legitimation is its responsibility for providing and managing the educational system. From our present perspective, the education system in general, and schooling in particular, is important in two principal ways. First, it is the way in which most people come to be selected for different positions in society while at the same time learning to accept if not endorse their fate. Second, it is the principal agency through which stocks of knowledge which dominant groups in our society deem to be fundamental come to be transmitted to new generations. We shall consider each of these points in turn.

As we saw in Chapter 6, Britain is a remarkably unequal society. To a considerable extent, inequalities of wealth, income, prestige and power are perpetuated through the occupational system, for some jobs provide access to key components of life chances which are effectively closed off to others. Although family connections and wealth are still often important in determining entry to the most favoured positions (e.g. in business and the old professions), educational qualifications have for most people become the single most important criterion by which individuals are evaluated for entry into the occupational system.

For some 30 years now, sociologists have been reporting on studies which show that success in the educational system is dependent as much on social as on educational factors. The more socially disadvantaged the background from which a child comes, the less likely it is that that child will succeed at school, irrespective of his or her innate intelligence. The schools, it seems, hold up a mirror to our society, for those who experience relative deprivation or discrimination in the society are also those who 'under-achieve' in the educational system. This is particularly true of racial minorities and of children from relatively unskilled working-class backgrounds, although there is also considerable evidence of a bias operating on the basis of gender and of geographical location as well.

The reasons for this are many and varied. Some undoubtedly have to do with the home environment from which different children come, for parents who are themselves well educated can pass on a crucial legacy of 'cultural capital' to their children, and the level of parental interest and encouragement has often been found to be a significant factor as well in influencing children's performance in school. Other factors seem to have something to do with the children themselves, peer-group pressures can be very strong, and the development of an anti-school subculture (especially among working-class adolescent boys for whom manual labour may have a positive symbolic significance) can function as a virtually impenetrable barrier against learning in the class room. The major explanation, however, probably lies in the schools themselves, for given that schools are essentially middle-class institutions, we should not perhaps be surprised that it is middle-class children who derive most benefit from them.

There is now an enormous literature on the way in which working-class children experience the middle-class language and culture of the school, and from this it seems that some children at least encounter school as an alien environment in which modes of behaviour, assumptions about the world and even styles of language are strange. Before they can begin to learn the formal skills which they are being taught, they have therefore first to re-learn the social skills with which they have been imbued since birth and which continue to conflict each time they go home at night.

For whatever reasons, the fact that the educational system is class-biased cannot be denied. The importance of this is that the schools therefore function in practice as means of transmitting class privileges from one generation to the next while at the same time legitimating this perpetuation of class inequality through an individualistic ideology of merit. It is rather like an Aesop's fable of the fox who invited the stork to dinner. The fox provided the stork with food, but on a platter from which no creature with a large bill could be expected to eat, with the result that the fox ended up eating both portions on the grounds that the stork was obviously not hungry. So it is in our schools that all children are offered the same chances but in a form which some are better equipped to take advantage of than others. In this way, middle-class children generally (although not of course always) end up with middle-class jobs, working-class children end up with working class jobs (if they can find a job at all), and most people assume that these results are a reflection of different individual abilities and aptitudes. In short, what is in fact a system of class selection appears as a system of meritocratic selection and is thus widely accepted as legitimate.

Particularly important in all of this is the process of 'labelling'. Even though the infamous eleven-plus examination has now been abolished in most parts of Britain, academic selection, through streaming and setting, still takes place relatively early in most children's school careers. Experiments have shown that teachers and pupils alike to a large extent internalise the labels which are applied through selective systems such as streaming. In other words, once a child has been identified as 'bright', or 'average' or 'dull', she or he will tend to behave accordingly, while teachers too will treat children with different 'labels' differently, even if there is in fact no academic difference between them. Unlike the American school system, where sifting and selection is usually delayed until late on in the school career (often with traumatic effects for those who eventually fail), in Britain, selection occurs relatively early with the result that children spend much of their secondary education learning to come to terms with the label which has authoritatively been applied to them. By the age of 13 or 14, the working-class child who is destined for a working-class job will have shed former illusions about becoming a brain surgeon or an airline pilot and, in many cases, will have accepted that he or she is 'not bright enough' for anything other than a routine manual or clerical occupation. When you fail in what everybody believes to be a fair competition, there is no-one to blame but yourself.

This, then, is the first important way in which schools aid the legitimation of the social order, for whether they intend it or not they train future generations of the working class and other disadvantaged groups for their own subordination.

The second aspect of the schools' legitmatory role lies in what actually gets taught. Although Britain is somewhat unusual in the lack of any substantial and formal degree of 'civics' or political education in its school syllabi, it would be naïve in the extreme to assume that the content of education is politically neutral. As various 'content analyses' of school books have demonstrated, there is a consistent hidden message in many standard texts, be they advanced-level history books (in which history is written from a one-sided perspective which concentrates on the great and the good to the almost total neglect of those unnamed masses who actually died in the wars, laboured in the factories, built the cities and so on) or infant reading schemes (in which middle-class boys climb trees, middle-class girls stand by and watch admiringly, and working-class people, or people with black faces, are nowhere to be found). It is not only in South Africa and the Soviet Union that history gets rewritten or that certain views and interpretations are expunged from the literature which children are allowed to read.

The significance of the knowledge which schools transmit to our young goes beyond this, however, for beneath the formal curriculum of science, geography and religious instruction there is a 'hidden curriculum' which never appears on the timetable but is none the less significant for that. What we learn in school – though are rarely taught – is how to sit still, to speak when addressed, to stand in rows, to divide our time into 'work' and 'play' or 'free time', to be punctual, to treat learning as a means to an end (i.e. passing an examination), to control our exuberance and channel our aggression, to respect authority, to be passive, to be subordinate. When most of us at 16 come to exchange our school uniform for blue overalls or a grey suit, and to exchange our school desk for an office desk or a factory bench, we are already well equipped with all the unwritten yet crucial knowledge which we are required to have if the economic system and the social order which rests upon it are not to crumble under the strain of an undisciplined workforce and an active citizenry. The school, in other words, is an agency of socialisation second in importance only to the family itself. It really does not need 11 years to teach most of the elementary maths, the smattering of geography and the rudimentary English grammar with which we eventually pass out of school, but it needs all of 11 years to mould individuals into a largely unthinking and non-reflexive orientation to the world around them in which the present mode of organising our society is taken as given.

Is it really the case, though, that schooling is as powerful an influence on our lives as this analysis suggests? We would argue that it is, although it has immediately to be recognised that, like all the other agencies discussed in this section, the educational system is never as total in its impact as may be imagined. As places of learning and enquiry, schools and colleges must to some extent open themselves up to competing definitions of reality. Furthermore, many teachers do not themselves endorse the values which they are expected to transmit, nor accept the role which they are called upon to play. Schools are in this sense cumbersome instruments of control for it is difficult to monitor what teachers actually teach inside the classroom, and central government direction of syllabus content is limited (although there have been recent moves to strengthen it).

One indication of the problems which government has encountered in trying to direct schooling according to its objectives is the difficulty which successive administrations since the mid-1970s have had in making course contents more appropriate to the expressed demands of the employers. In addition to this, government also has the problem that many teachers do not share its philosophy or its objectives, while increasing problems of discipline in many areas have in any case reduced schooling, in some instances, to a question of maintaining physical control with little time or opportunity for developing the finer aspects of social control.

For all of these reasons, it is important not to exaggerate the significance of schooling as a soft control institution. Nevertheless, it is apparent that schools are as close as we have come in the contemporary period to finding a functional equivalent of and replacement for the traditional role of the Church. They are, in other words, the major source of knowledge and moral guidance in modern society, and although the teacher's word will never carry the power and conviction that the priest's once did, we should not forget that, unlike the Church of old, schools today are compulsory institutions which enjoy the right to control the flow of ideas to young people as they grow from infancy to adulthood. Seen in this way, their potential power to shape our understanding of the world is staggering.

The Press. The educational system is to some extent aided in this respect by the various organs of the mass media. This is because socialisation – and, for that matter, legitimation – is a continuous process. The beliefs, norms, values and taken for-granted assumptions which we develop in childhood through the family and the school do not remain rigid and fixed for all time, for in a rapidly changing world we constantly encounter new situations and competing interpretations of reality which may throw some of our most basic assumptions into question. In modern Britain, the media – notably the newspapers which we read and the television programmes which are channelled into virtually every household in the country every night in the week – have come to play an important role in informing us about our world and in providing ready-made frameworks through which to understand and evaluate it.

Two points should be made at the outset in relation to both the press and the broadcasting media. One is that they are overwhelmingly national institutions, for most people in Britain who read a newspaper (and newspaper readership per head of population is the highest in the world) read a national paper produced from London, while both the BBC and Independent Television, although organised through a regional structure, are also overwhelmingly nationally oriented and centrally controlled. Although recent developments such as local radio and cable television may represent some challenge and alternative to this London-dominated focus, it remains the case that our media are remarkably centralised and homogenous when compared with most other countries.

The second point is that both press and broadcasting are formally free of government control. The state is, of course, involved in broadcasting through its funding of the BBC and its licensing of the Independent Broadcasting Authority, but both of these bodies are legally and constitutionally independent of government and are required by statute to ensure 'balance' in their output as between different views and opinions. As for the press, all newspapers are privately owned and there are no legal restrictions on the rights of any individual to publish a newspaper.

So much for the theory. Turning first to the press, it is well known that, in practice, newspapers are very costly to set up and are even more costly to run such that the number of people who could realistically expect to own a national newspaper is minute. It is also well-known that most Fleet Street proprietors are more or less Conservative in their political orientation and that this is reflected in the balance of editorial opinion in the national press. The *Morning Star* is the daily mouthpiece of the Communist Party and has a circulation to match; the *Daily Mirror* has for 30 years been a consistent supporter of the right-wing of the Labour Party; the *Guardian* takes a liberal, left-of-centre line; and the rest range along a continuum from Conservative to ultra-Conservative. Ever since the labour movement's own newspaper, the *Daily Herald*, collapsed in 1961 (due to a shortage of advertising revenue), both the Labour Party and the unions have been toying with the idea of starting up another, and as we write, proposals for such a venture are under active consideration. Even if such a paper could be launched and successfully financed (which seems unlikely), it would not go far in correcting the imbalance of our 'free' press.

Nobody seriously doubts that both national and local newspapers (for the provincial press exhibits much the same pattern and is in any case mainly owned by national chains) are overwhelmingly biased towards the right in both their editorial columns (where such bias is made manifest) and in their manner of reporting news events (where it is less so). What is less clear, however, is how significant this is in shaping people's political views and in influencing the way they think about their society. After all, if the influence of the press were as direct and strong as some left-wing critics have sometimes suggested, it would be difficult to see how the Labour Party has ever managed to win popular support.

It is notoriously difficult to assess the impact which years of exposure to, say, the *Daily Mail* has on people's beliefs and ways of thinking. A number of points may, however, be noted. First, people freely choose which newspaper to buy; they are not forced or constrained to read a right-wing paper, for although most papers are right-wing, there is in principle no reason why they should not choose to read the *Mirror,* the *Morning Star* or even *Newsline* (the daily paper produced by the Workers Revolutionary Party). Second, most people are probably aware of the bias of the paper they read (although there is evidence that some readers of papers such as the *Sun* and the *Express* believe them to be Labour papers; this could suggest either that the bias is insidious and has become routinised to the point where readers do not notice it, or that the bias is ineffective and that readers are immune to it). Third, people tend to read newspapers selectively; there is a healthy scepticism which holds that 'you cannot believe everything you read in the papers', and it seems that readers tend to ignore or shrug off opinions which do not accord with their own position. Finally, there is in much of Britain's press precious little news anyway, for in the so-called 'popular papers', presentation and analysis of domestic economic and political affairs tends to be brief while treatment of foreign affairs is generally derisory. Readers of newspapers such as the *Sun* and the *Daily Star* are likely to learn far more about the sacking of football managers, their latest bingo numbers, the week's special offers at Tescos and the bust measurements of 19-year-old beauties from Bognor than they are about parliamentary exchanges or the latest diplomatic moves in the Middle East. As a former head of the *Mirror* group once candidly observed: 'You have got to give the public what it wants...it is only the people who conduct newspapers and similar organisations who have any idea quite how indifferent, quite how stupid, quite how uninterested in education of any kind the great bulk of the British public are.'

In our view, the significance of the press as an agency of social control lies not so much in what it says as in how it says it and what it does not say. Put another way, its importance derives, first from its selection as to what is to count as 'news', and second from the assumptions about the world which are reinforced (often unconsciously) through the way in which the 'news' which has been selected is presented and interpreted.

The selection of news is obviously crucial and reflects both tacit journalistic criteria of what constitutes a 'good story' and external constraints on the gathering of information. Criteria of a good story are, among other things, that it should be personalised (thus much of the treatment of politics, for example, revolves around what key political leaders say or do rather than around questions of policy), that it should be near to home (hence the remarkable lack of foreign news coverage in most papers), that it should be readily understandable in terms of familiar stereotypes and categories of thought (the machinations of city financial institutions are, for example, much less newsworthy than strikes in the car industry) and that it should be dramatic (such that unusual events of little significance tend to achieve greater prominence than recurring events of considerable significance – the 'man bites dog' syndrome). The emphasis on news as drama is particularly important since it tends to rule out reporting on 'everyday' aspects of economic and political life – another factory closure in the north-east, another sectarian murder in Northern Ireland – which may have a crucial bearing on people's lives but which do not readily lend themselves to the banner headlines which sell popular papers.

Reinforcing these selective tendencies are pressures from the environment in which the news media operate. The popular image of news gathering as investigative journalism is largely a myth, for all papers rely to a great extent on 'feeding' from agencies and from official sources. Much of the political news which appears in the papers, for example, is little more than repetition (sometimes word for word) of government press releases, official briefings, press conferences and carefully-managed 'leaks' from Whitehall. When journalists do take a more active role than that of the government's ventriloquist's dummy, they find that material is difficult to dig up, that there are enormous constraints on what they are allowed to write (libel laws, contempt of court, D-notices, etc.), and even that transmission of copy may be hindered (as during the 1982 Falklands war when correspondents were often kept away from the fighting, had their dispatches censored and delayed and were sometimes unable even to get to a transmitter). 'All the news that's fit to print' thus all too often turns out to be very little news at all.

What is also crucial is the way in which this 'news' is reported. Just as there is a 'hidden curriculum' in the schools, so there is a 'hidden agenda' in the newspapers. News is presented through the use of a language which derives from a particular interpretive framework in which certain 'obvious' 'facts' about the world are taken as given. One example is the use of words such as 'militant' and 'moderate' to describe trade unionists and politicians. We are never explicitly told what these words mean (moderate by whose standards?), nor are we ever told that 'militancy' is a bad thing and that moderation is to be commended. We do not have to be told, for these are inherently evaluative words which are used in a matter-of-fact way in order to structure our reading of particular reports. When we are told that 'the militant miners' leader' has said one thing, or that a 'leading moderate in the Labour Party' has done another, we are being presented with 'facts' which are inextricably tied up with opinion. The choice of such words (and of many others – 'terrorist' as against 'freedom fighter'; 'disruption of production' as against 'industrial dispute'; 'invasion' as against 'liberation') is crucial in signifying to us how we the readers should understand and evaluate a particular event. They are a cue for us to delve into our store of 'cookbook knowledge' and to dust off the appropriate 'recipe' through which we are to respond.

It is too crude to suggest that the papers tell us what to think; but they do to a large extent tell us how to think it, for they furnish us with the relevant mental tools which today are so often taken from the New Right toolkit of theories and world views which we explored in earlier chapters. It is too crude to argue that the barons of Fleet Street impose their values on us, but they do constantly reinforce certain sets of values as against others. The press functions as a soft social control agency to the extent that its partial view of social reality emphasises a dominant conception of the world while marginalising others.

The broadcasting media. The same is true of the broadcasting media. Television, in particular, is almost certainly more significant than the press in this respect, for the degree of exposure to television is for most people greater than that to the newspapers, the impact of this exposure is also greater due to the power of visual images, and – most significantly of all – television and radio are seen as more 'trustworthy' and 'reliable' sources of news given the legal requirement that they maintain balance and impartiality. This faith is particularly marked in popular attitudes towards the BBC.

Ever since 1927, the BBC has been run as a public corporation by a board of governors who are appointed as 'trustees of the public interest' to shield public-service broadcasting from both commercial and political pressures. In theory, the Board of Governors *is* the BBC. They take responsibility for policy and for the oversight of management, and they assume a position of special significance in that they make the senior appointments to the permanent professional staff. By Royal Charter, the Board is accountable to parliament, not to government or to a particular department of state, although it has faced the problem of trying to work out independently (as the Charter enjoins it to do) how it can best establish the accountability of the corporation. Inevitably, the Board has to display trust in the people who plan and make programmes, and the government has an interest in the material produced by the BBC. The relations between the Board of Governors, the professional and creative staff, and the government of the day are potentially fraught with problems. For the most part, however, conflict tends not to occur for reasons that bear on the nature of the Board and the organisation of programme making.

The Board itself, in spite of its independence, tends to be drawn from the ranks of the 'great and the good' and to mirror the predominance of the upper middle classes in the ranks of political life in elected and non-elected positions of power. Of the eighty-five governors who have served during the first 50 years of the BBC's history, fifty-six had a university education (forty at Oxford or Cambridge), and twenty were products of Eton, Harrow or Winchester. The political experience of Board members has come mainly from the House of Lords, although there have been nineteen former MPs, of whom eight were Labour. By convention, from 1956 one governor has had a trade union background, but in no sense can the Board be said to be representative of the population at large.

For their part, programme makers, in spite of the fact that they do enjoy an independence in that the government does not tell them what to do, nevertheless tend to produce programmes that do not seriously offend the views, still less the interests, of the Board or the government. This tends to be the case because what is acceptable is internalised, and potentially hostile reactions are anticipated and avoided in the interests of personal and organisational survival. Programme makers are socialised into an awareness of what will and will not 'go', and if they wish to get on the air (and stay on the air) then they 'choose' to operate within the confines of acceptability.

As with the press, we are not suggesting that the broadcasting media directly shape people's beliefs, values and opinions, but rather that they help to establish one set of views as 'normal' and others as marginal. Paradoxically, perhaps, this tendency is reinforced by the legal need to

ensure 'balance', for this has led the BBC and ITV to equate
'impartiality' with majority or middle-of-the-road opinion and to seek
'balance' in the safe middle ground of consensus politics. The
broadcasting authorities could, of course, reply to this charge (and with
some justification) that to provide equal air time for the views of
Communists (or indeed Fascists) as for mainstream political party
orthodoxy would be the epitome of imbalance since it would distort the
balance of opinion in the country as a whole. In one sense this is true, but
it raises familiar 'chicken and egg' problems, for it is at least plausible to
suggest that one reason why mainstream opinion remains mainstream is
precisely because it is treated as such in the nightly output of the
broadcasting media.

This immediately raises a further related issue, and that is whether
there is a discernible 'mainstream' political culture in Britain any more.
As we have suggested throughout this chapter so far, the old certainties
have been eroded and it is difficult to argue that in Britain today there is a
single 'core' value system to which virtually everybody is committed. On
most major issues, the nation often turns out to be deeply divided, in
which case the search for balance in the middle ground is a recipe for bias.
There is, to put it another way, an obvious danger that in seeking to
express 'mainstream' values, the media actually express merely
establishment values (a danger which is clearly exacerbated given the
nature of recruitment into such bodies as the BBC). Be that as it may, it
should be obvious that the political 'centre' (however that is identified) is
no less a political and partial position than what the media themselves
tend to designate as the political 'extremes'. With the growth in electoral
significance of the 'centre parties' (the Liberals and the SDP) in the early
1980s, this problem is now clearer than it has ever been before.

The question of bias and partiality goes deeper than this, however, for
as with the press, it is as much the form as the explicit content of output
which has given rise to concern. Of particular importance here has been a
series of studies of television news carried out by the Glasgow University
Media Group since the mid-1970s. This, together with other similar
research, has shown that television news is a remarkably homogeneous
product across all channels and that its treatment of events such as
industrial disputes consistently rests upon taken for-granted assumptions
which turn out to be the assumptions of dominant groups in our society.
Strikes, for example, are treated as irrational acts, usually provoked by a
small number of 'militant' leaders, which disturb what is taken to be the
'normal' state of 'harmonious' joint endeavour by capital and labour.
Their negative impact on customers and on the ailing British economy is
emphasised, and this is brought out in the way in which representatives of
the two sides to the dispute are interviewed. Strikers' leaders are
invariably interviewed in the street or on the picket line and the tone of
questioning is aggressive, while managers are sat in the calm of the
television studio and are subjected to a passive line of interviewing in

which they are invited and encouraged to spell out in eminently 'reasonable' language the negative implications of this latest stoppage for the future of the company and of the workers' jobs. Add to this the systematic message that strikes lie at the heart of Britain's economic problems, that wage rises are the cause of inflation, that workers have priced British industry out of world markets, together with the equally systematic exclusion of other items of economic news from any meaningful coverage at all (e.g. the massive flow of capital overseas, the 'stoppages' caused by machine failure or by shortage of parts due to management miscalculation, and so on), and it is little wonder that so many workers in this country are prepared to believe that trade unions are the cause of the country's economic ills even though they go on to argue in the same breath that their own union has done precious little to safeguard their own living standards and working conditions.

Research such as that at Glasgow University stands as a well-documented and generally damning indictment of the broadcasting media as neutral agencies of news dissemination. It is, of course, true that, just as there are radical teachers in the schools, so there are radical journalists in the media, and their views do receive a somewhat ritual airing from time to time (e.g. in special reports, usually on some aspect of foreign affairs such as the exploitation of black labour in South Africa or covert US military involvement in South America). It is also true that radical playwrights have had their work broadcast and that such plays (beginning with *Cathy Come Home* in the mid-1960s and continuing with plays such as *The Price of Coal, Law and Order, United Kingdom, Days of Hope* and *The Nation's Health*) have often had a marked impact on popular opinion and political argument, not least because they are so unusual that they come as a bolt out of the faint blue hue of broadcasting orthodoxy. The BBC and ITV are not totally closed to alternative opinions and their statutory independence from direct government control is to be prized. However, the reality of that independence is limited because views are shared and external control is rendered unnecessary (and too obvious) in a situation in which the objectives of control are roughly internalised in practice and convention. John Reith, the first Director-General of the BBC, put it all very nicely when he wrote to the Prime Minister at the time of the General Strike in 1926: 'assuming the BBC is for the people and that the government is for the people, it follows that the BBC must be for the government in this crisis too.' The initials BBC advise those within the corporation to Be Bloody Careful: they can enjoy independence but only if they exercise it with care in cautious programmes that operate within the consensus of the 'common-sense' of 'reasonable' men and women.

Like the press, therefore, the broadcasting media are important in confirming certain values and beliefs as the norm and in relegating others to the sidelines. Precisely because socialisation is not a once and for all process which ends when we reach adulthood, socially accepted ways of thinking and acting have constantly to be reinforced through 'secondary' agencies of socialisation if they are to maintain their hold in a world which is in perpetual change. The media are today the most important institutions by means of which this process of reaffirmation may be accomplished. In this sense, the nine o'clock news has replaced the confessional as the major source of guidance on what to believe and how to live in the increasingly confused and confusing world of the late twentieth century.

Social work agencies. There is one final soft agency of control which must be mentioned before closing this section, and that is social work. Understood through the concerns of this chapter, social work stands on the borderline between 'soft' and 'hard' control agencies, for it is the first line of defence against those who in one way or another step out of line. The social worker, that is, steps in when the family, the schools and the media have failed.

In Chapter 9, we discussed the view, common on the left, that the welfare state can be understood as an agency of control and class domination. This is a view which in general we reject, for the historical causes of the growth in state welfare provision are too varied, and the beneficiaries of such provision too diverse, to permit of such a singular interpretation of the welfare state's role and function. However, there is one aspect of the welfare state where it is useful to interpret state intervention in such terms, and that is the casework undertaken by various types of social workers and, of course, probation officers.

Now it is true that social work as a profession has undoubtedly been radicalised over the last 20 years, and more than any of the other agencies discussed in this chapter, local authority social-work departments contain many employees whose values run counter to those of dominant groups in our society. Nevertheless, it is also true that the *nature* of social work is such that, notwithstanding the views and opinions of those engaged in it, it identifies as 'deviant' those whose way of life fails to conform in some ways to standards laid down by the state, and then goes on to explain such deviancy as the outcome of individual pathology which must be 'treated'. In this way, it functions as an important control agency by identifying those who are not conforming in various ways and by prescribing methods of changing their behaviour.

One clear example of this is in the designation of 'problem families'. They are said to be those who, for reasons of personal inadequacy, cannot manage their money properly or cannot look after their homes properly, or cannot raise their children properly. Once identified by a social worker, a problem family may lose many of the social rights which most of us take for granted. Problem families find themselves re-housed in 'dumping' estates along with other problem cases; their privacy is invaded by social workers who come to look through their rent books, to inspect their children or to counsel them on how to spend their money;

their children may forcibly be taken from them and placed in the 'care' of a state-run children's home or of state-approved foster parents who can manage their money properly, look after their homes properly and raise children properly.

Similar points have been made from time to time about other social-work client groups. It has been suggested, for example, that psychiatric social work similarly identifies non-comforming people, sticks a negative label onto them (in this case that of 'mental illness') and then uses this label to justify various state-enforced measures such as therapy or electric-shock treatment in an attempt to bring their behaviour more into line.

What is common to social work interventions is that they are premissed on the assumption that problems experienced by individuals are individual problems and can thus be treated as such. Put another way, the essence of social work is that it individualises social problems and privatises public issues. The social problem of unemployment, poor housing and low pay thus becomes translated into the individual or family problem of an inability to manage money or a failure to bring up the children properly. Not only does this encourage the individual to look to his or her own personal character as the cause of his or her problem (in much the same way as selection in schools teaches children that failure is a result of their own intellectual disabilities), but it also casts the social worker in the role as helper, the client's friend. Children are forcibly placed into the care of the local authority for their own good and for the good of the family, even if the parents and children concerned 'cannot' see it that way; depressed houswives are incarcerated in mental institutions and subjected to psychiatric treatment for their own good even if they may suspect that the 'problem' has more to do with the domestic role which they are expected to play; and so on. None of this is to deny that children may sometimes 'objectively' benefit by being removed from their home environment (especially where domestic violence is rife), nor that people may respond to anti-depressant drugs or psychoanalysis, nor even that social workers may genuinely have the best interests (as they define them) of their clients at heart. What we are suggesting, however, is that social work also functions as an agency of social control which uses the power of the state to intervene in people's lives where behaviour is deemed to fall short of, and thus in some way to threaten, certain standards which the state itself identifies as acceptable. Seen in this light, social work represents the soft face of the coercive state.

THE 'IRON FIST': ORGANISING COERCION

Social control has become one of the problem areas in British politics. As the soft agencies stumble in their task of mobilising people into behaviour and sentiments supportive of the established system of politics and power, so law is increasingly becoming the primary mechanism of social order. Behind the law are the hard and overtly controlling agencies of 'justice' that are part of the secret state we discussed in Chapter 5. The police, the judges, the courts, and ultimately the prisons to contain convicted law breakers, all are involved as are the military and the security services. In fact, social control is no new problem and law has often been central to the maintenance of social order at moments of crisis and change.

From old to new policing. The rules of eighteenth-century England cherished the death sentence and supported a system of criminal law crudely but effectively based on terror. The number of capital statutes grew from about 50 to over 200 between the years 1688 and 1820 and almost all of them concerned offences against the established division of property. In these times the suppression of crime was still a simple community affair. 'Civic responsibility' was a sufficient spur to action for the apprehension and punishment of offenders. There was little call for specialised agents and facilities. True, the office of constable was established in the late thirteenth century, but officials went without pay and their duties were to be discharged out of civic rather than pecuniary motives.

With the decline of feudalism, so the informal and voluntary system of social control through family, church, and community became increasingly problematic. Public spirit was no longer enough. Private interests came to replace social obligations as the mainspring of the control system. Fear and greed went hand in hand. The fear of capital punishment and transportation was designed to hold potential wrongdoers in check, whilst greed was appealed to through a network of incentives and rewards in a way which called into being a privately organised system of crime control. Policing was conducted for profit. Constables were able to demand rewards and portions of recovered goods in exchange for their services, and imprisonment provided an opportunity for private gain as fees were paid to those who provided a crude lock-up. The wealthy paid gamekeepers to protect their property and middle-class traders formed voluntary protection societies. These private and ill-organised solutions were always of limited effectiveness unless solidly buttressed by the soft agencies of control. The system was poorly co-ordinated, irrational and inefficient, and because those enforcing the law were paid by results there was every incentive for them to instigate crime just as it made good sense for them to sell to prisoners the chance to escape.

As the market system developed and as trade grew so a stable public order became a crucial prerequisite for further development and yet private solutions were of limited value in securing this. The use of the army was inevitable at moments of major unrest. However, this too was problematic. The army was not popular in the late eighteenth century and neither the officers nor the men liked riot duty; it took time to get a detachment of troops to a riot area and once there they had very limited local knowledge; and, more fundamentally, the fact that army training was mechanistic and geared to the fighting of set-piece battles meant that the military lacked any capacity to develop a flexible response geared to the control of unarmed protesters but instead engaged in an unlimited offensive. The vicious military control of crowds reached a climax in August 1819 when local yeomanry on horseback killed eleven people and injured several hundred more in the Peterloo massacre. It was some kind of turning point in the control of public order. The moral consensus of the nation outlawed the riding down of an unarmed crowd and so there was the need to create a system of 'new policing' that would secure public order and hold down the 'dangerous classes', *and* solve the related problem of crime and criminality all of which was increasingly beyond the capacity of the soft agencies of family, church and community and the informality of the 'old policing' system based on parish constables and justices of the peace.

The country's first public professional police force was founded in 1829 when Sir Robert Peel persuaded the unreformed House of Commons to set up the Metropolitan Police for London. The County and Borough Police Act, 1856 made the recruitment of a regular police force obligatory, and by 1860 there were some 259 separate forces in England and Wales. So, instead of the old combination of low-profile policing in ordinary times mixed with brutal suppression by the military in extraordinary ones, the police were to establish a regime of permanent surveillance attempting to win consent and public acceptance for their controlling work through tact, discretion, benevolent prevention, and the minimum use of unarmed force.

Establishing the police as bureaucratic organisations of permanently employed professionals relieved the ordinary citizen of the need to perform police duties (and the urban middle classes were never keen on this); made the all-or-nothing use of the military in internal peace-keeping less necessary; and drew attacks onto the police so that they served as buffers insulating the wealthy from the more direct threats of popular violence for change. Professional policing and the Rule of Law together created a situation in which constitutional authority and law were seemingly separated from the reality of social and economic dominance. Ideas developed (and came to assume a position of dominating orthodoxy) suggesting that the law was neutral and in the public interest, and that the police were simple servants of the community as a whole. We criticised some of these orthodoxies in Chapter 5, and we will attend to the orthodoxies surrounding law later in this chapter, but for the moment it is sufficient to note that ideas of this kind have fulfilled a crucial function, both legitimating the role of law and policing, and sustaining (by concealing) a particular system, of social and economic power. Having said that, it would be quite wrong to suggest that the law and the police are *only* about the preservation of capitalism and the power of the wealthy since they are also involved in protecting the basic conditions of existence of individuals in all classes. In any known society, some of the functions of the police are as necessary as those of the fire and ambulance services, and these include crimes against the person and the enforcement of the law protecting citizens against offenders. Thompson is right to remind us that 'a wholly indiscriminate attitude of "bash the fuzz" is...sentimental...self-indulgent, and counter-productive' because it fails to recognise that the police are in an ambiguous position preserving both society and individuals in ways which may pose challenges to those of power.

In Chapter 5 we pointed out that the police have the task of preserving peace and public order, and the task of preventing crime and trying to catch those who break the criminal law. In that chapter we only dealt with the role of the police with respect to crime, but when we turn to the public order role of the police then the social and political aspect of their work is more keenly revealed – at least in times of political unrest. In periods of relative economic prosperity, when societal consensus and cohesion may more easily be attained, the need for the rough exercise of the public order function does not push to the fore and it is hard even to 'see' the police preserving the peace. However, when the consensus cracks; when the soft agencies of control fail to mobilise support and control behaviour; and when interests and groups are pushing for social change against established interests, then politics quickly burst outside of Parliament and onto the streets. In this kind of situation the police's public order role pushes to the fore (and crime prevention takes a backseat) and preserving the peace has a hard political edge to it that involves the police in containing group pressures from below. The more privileged sections of society rarely, if ever, take to the politics of the streets; they do not pose a threat to the prevailing social order (why on earth should they when they benefit from it?); and so they just do not come up against the police in their public order role. But where there is a strike, there are also the police and behind the police are laws to assist them in their work. Where blacks and youth gather on street corners, there are also the police backed up by laws giving them the right to 'stop and search'. And where there are demonstrations against nuclear weapons, there are also the police, police photographers, and the special branch who have a brief to combat 'subversion' which takes them way beyond the policing of the unlawful alone since the Home Secretary defined subversion in 1978 as 'activities which threatened the safety and well-being of the state, and are intended to undermine or overthrow parliamentary democracy by political, industrial or violent means'. Far from the police being outside of politics, the exercise of their public order function means that they are always at the sharp end constraining social and political change. Indeed, the ex-Commissioner of the Metropolitan Police, in his book *Policing a Perplexed Society,* firmly placed the role of the police in the context of opposing socialism: 'the police are very much on their own in attempting to preserve order in an increasingly turbulent society in which socialist philosophy has changed from raising standards of the poor and deprived to reducing the standards of the wealthy, the skilled and the deserving to the lowest common denominator.' The Chief Constable of Greater Manchester, James Anderton, put the purely criminal aspect of police work firmly in its place when he told a *Question Time* audience in 1979:

I think that from a police point of view...that the basic crimes such as theft, burglary, even violent crime, will not be the predominant police feature. What will be the matter of the greatest concern to me will be the covert, and ultimately overt, attempts to overthrow democracy, to subvert the authority of the state and, in fact, to involve themselves in acts of sedition designed to destroy our parliamentary system and the democratic government of this country.

The police, then, are not just a thin blue line against (and occasionally in) crime, since they are also against a different kind of political order as well: they are at the hard front line acting as guardians of the social order as a whole. We will attend to the problem of policing the eighties and the drift into a law-and-order society shortly, but for the moment we need to attend to the signficance of law itself. Law is central to the work of the police (even though they may break it) and it is also central to the maintenance of particular patterns of 'proper' behaviour since the law defines certain types of acts as illegal and prescribes the penalties which will be exacted against those found guilty of such acts.

The law. Law is important, but it is not equally important in all societies. In simple societies, where custom and traditional norms are well-established, there is little need for a systematised and officially enforced code of law to order relations and regulate behaviour in predictable ways. As societies become more complex and subject to change and conflict, and as custom and tradition decline in importance, so law comes to assume a place of central significance offering a kind of social regulation distinct from that provided by religious taboos, established conventions, or naked violence and arbitrary power. Social regulation under capitalism is typically conducted through law and it is not difficult to see that the law of property and the law of contract are basic to the effective and smooth functioning of this particular economic system.

1 Law, then, guarantees and protects existing productive relationships and ways of distributing resources and serves as some kind of guarantor of 'business as usual'. Law also fulfils other functions.
2 In seeking to establish certain simple fundamental rules for living together it assumes a peace-keeping and social harmonising function.
3 In providing principles and procedures for settling conflicts between individuals and groups its fulfils a conflict resolution function.
4 Law also criminalises certain kinds of social action and although it is

invariably presented as neutral and remote from particular interests, in reality it bears very unevenly on different interests. The law may forbid rich and poor alike from stealing bread, and it may forbid both employers and workers from engaging in certain kinds of picketing in the furtherance of an industrial dispute, but in reality it is not difficult to appreciate the true significance of laws of this kind.

5 Law is also important because it mobilises symbols and encourages the formation of popular views about, for example, the 'necessity' for private property and the problem of mugging (and its connection to black youth), and this is crucial because all day-to-day politics occurs within the constraining context of these views.

6 Law is a crucial arena for political struggle because politics often revolve around the claim for rights, and because rights really need to be entrenched in law to be secure. Indeed, much statute law 'made' by parliament is developed in response to organised pressures and is designed to change and replace the judge-made common law that is often just the embellished codification of old customs and traditional ways of doing things.

7 Finally, and of particular importance in this chapter, we should not forget that law is increasingly becoming a primary mechanism of social control or social order.

When we looked at the political significance of the judiciary in Chapter 5, we made it clear that a certain mystery needs to attach to the nature of law in order that it can secure the kind of public support and larger legitimacy that will ensure that obedience is secured with the minimum of force, coercion, and political dispute. Put another way, law needs to be *presented* in a particular way if it is to work effectively in controlling behaviour. In Britain, the orthodox view sees law as in the public interest; as above political conflict; and as remote from the control of particular groups or classes. In fact, views of this kind, whilst helping to sustain the mystery and legitimacy of law, do not get us very far in understanding the precise place and real significance of law in ordering behaviour and contributing to the stability and cohesion of contemporary Britain. Indeed, the orthodoxies are actually wrong since law is not above society; it is not outside of conflict; and it is not neutral, impartial, or blind, as to the ways in which particular conflicts are resolved.

Now it is one thing to assert that law is important and that the orthodox views do not make good sense of its significance and position in society, but it is quite another thing to provide a more adequate and realistic perspective. If the orthodox views supportive of the prevailing order and legal system are wrong then it is always tempting to think that those social theories critical of the capitalist system will provide the key to understanding. In fact, there is no coherent or systematic theory of law in the works of Marx and Engels. Moreover, law has not been a central focus of concern for later Marxists, and only a few have troubled themselves to examine law in the kind of detail that is necessary. The left have failed to take law seriously as something worthy of study in its own right. They have been content to simply deduce the nature of law from larger views and general theories as to the nature of capitalist society. The limits of Marxist theories of the state were explored in Chapter 7, where we saw that Marxists tend to view law in capitalist society as but an instrument of the needs and will of the capitalist class. Law and state are run together, and both are tied down to the all-determining economic base and to the power of the capitalist class in the economy. The capitalist class is seen as in control of the state; the state makes laws; and so laws inevitably reflect the interest of the economically dominant class. From this kind of pessimistic determinism there is no possibility of a progressive politics of law and little significance is attached to struggle in the legal field because the nature of the law is crisply determined by the need to maintain the system.

Although this perspective is too general to enable us to analyse the nature of law in Britain, it does at least thrust to the fore the need for us to see law in the context of the larger society and in the context of competing interests struggling for advantage through the entrenchment of political victories in the solidity of law itself. In fact, we do not see it as possible to provide a general theory of law, but we can say that law needs to be seen as an arena of struggle and that the nature of particular laws is not predetermined according to the narrow controlling interests of dominant classes but is some kind of register of the balance of competing interests around issues in question. Gains and losses can, therefore, be made by all contending interests, and legislation consolidating the rights of workers to combine in unions or reducing the length of the working day represents a positive gain for labour. Some laws, then, favour specific classes; some laws cut across class boundaries and protect the basic conditions of existence for all individuals; and some laws have little or nothing to do with class and class struggles. We cannot escape the fact that law is a complex, contradictory, and ambiguous phenomenon.

E. P. Thompson is an English Marxist historian who has attempted to tease out the ambiguities surrounding law and policing. In his analysis of law in eighteenth-century England he recognised that law did organise class relations to the advantage of the rulers, but at the same time the law *also* mediated those relations through legal forms and the entrenchment of civil liberties which imposed, again and again, inhibitions upon the actions of the rulers. In this sense, Thompson argues that the Rule of Law does matter; is not just a legitimating ideology and a mask for class power; and does actually inhibit, curb, and check the exercise of arbitrary power and direct unmediated force to the advantage of those subject to rule. More than this, any realistic account of law needs to recognise that there is a world of difference between law in the books and law in action. Law needs to be enforced to impact on behaviour and as we saw in Chapter 5 the police exercise discretion and discriminate in the way in which particular laws are enforced over particular groups and individuals. Law, then, is important in effecting control, but it is limited by the stance of the enforcing agencies *and* by the stance of those subject to it since mass disobedience stretches the capacity of the hard agencies of control no matter what the level of their enthusiasm for enforcing a particular act.

Although it is important to see law as a political battleground fought over by different interests, it is also necessary to recognise that the *context* of struggle has an impact on the outcome. The extension of the franchise mattered and did something to change the context of law making. After the Second World War the commitment to full employment reflected the wishes of ordinary people *and* further strengthened the economic and political hand of the trade unions in law making. Much legislation through to the 1970s has to be regarded as some kind of grudging gain for many disadvantaged and discriminated groups in society. Landlord-and-tenant law challenged the private landlords' freedom to dictate the terms on which property was let, and set rent levels, provided for security of tenure, and made it a criminal offence for a landlord to evict a tenant unlawfully; Race Relations law sought to protect racial minorities from discrimination in the fields of housing and employment; women secured the right to legal abortions and the establishment of the Equal Opportunities Commission sought to counter discrimination against them in the field of employment; the law came to allow consenting adults to engage in their preferred sexual behaviour in private so freeing homosexuals over the age of 21 from the restraint of the law; the legislative floor of rights for the individual worker was radically extended by the Employment Protection Act 1975; and so on and so on across a swathe of concerns.

If the soft agencies of social control were loosing their grip and capacity to shape behaviour then it should be no surprise that the law was developing in ways which reflected the new mood of permissiveness. But behind this, there was the increased power of working people as they enjoyed economic and political advantages based upon full employment and the fact that they were needed and in demand. Put another way the moral pluralism discussed in the first part of this chapter spilled over into the field of law which came to bear less heavily on many minority and disadvantaged groups in society at the same time as it also came to advantage particular sections of society including organised labour.

The loosening of social control and the extension of concessions through law could be coped with whilst the economic system possessed sufficient slack to enable the politicians to respond. From the mid-1970s onwards, however, the onset of recession cut into the slack and policing the eighties has become a problem.

Policing the eighties: the drift to a 'law-and-order' society: Just a few years ago the phrase 'law and order' had no political ring to it, but by the 1980s it had become a contentious issue in British politics, with the

Conservatives on the effective offensive. A decade of New Right concern about ungovernability, overload, adversary politics, and the problem of unlimited democracy within our constitution (discussed and assessed in Chapters 2, 3 and 4) had reached political bursting point, and was buttressed by a concern about crime, permissiveness, falling standards (in just about everything), and the whole problem of order and control. The Conservative electoral victories of 1979 and 1983 provided an opportunity for the New Right to fight back against trends of change by using the law and the police to create a more disciplined kind of society. In this section we want to deal with contemporary developments with respect to the role of law and the place of the police in keeping the lid on social change in Britain in the 1980s.

In Chapter 4 we set down the views of the constitutional authorities who wanted to limit politics by law and who sought to limit the role of the state through limits on the sovereignty of Parliament to create law. Less is heard of this perspective on constitutional change in the 1980s because the Conservative Government is actually committed to rolling back the state at the same time as it is committed to backing off from the trend to permissive legislation with an emphasis on the need to return to Victorian values and pass a spate of disciplinary legislation designed to restrict established legal rights and back up the discipline provided by the market.

A number of things are central to this political and social control offensive through law.

First, there is the law on industrial relations that we discussed in Chapter 8. For most of this century, British labour law 'abstained' from this field and the system was dominated by voluntary collective bargaining. The Employment Acts, 1980 and 1982, however, do legalise many aspects of industrial relations and tip the legal scales against workers and in favour of employers. The right to strike is restricted; the right to picket is limited; the closed shop is challenged; it is easier for workers to be sacked; rights to a decent wage have been eroded; and trade unions can be sued for damages by anyone who can claim to have suffered a financial loss from any trade union activities. Plans for 'trade union democracy' propose compulsory ballots before strikes, no-strike clauses for workers in 'essential' public services, and a switch to a 'contracting in' system for trade union contributions to political activity that would cut funds for the Labour Party whilst business contributions to the Conservative Party were left untouched.

Second, and discussed more fully in Chapter 9, there is the attack on the welfare state, not just through a reduction in funding, but through an undermining of the whole philosophy of welfare rights consequent upon a steady dribble of stories about 'scroungers'. The welfare state is coming to be represented as *the* institutional embodiment of the scrounger who is lazy and eats into the income and wealth of the deserving better-off. This development, alongside the implications of recession and unemployment, places a particular burden on many women and drives them back into the home to support, not just the nuclear family of children and husband, but the extended family of grandparents as well.

Third, the British Nationality Act, 1981, severely restricts the acquisition and transmission of British citizenship in a way that hits at women (the right of men settled here to marry foreign women and to bring them to this country has never been questioned) and men from the Asian sub-continent in order to appease racist opinion bent on trying to swim against the tide and resecure a white Britain (on this, see Chapter 6).

Fourth, there are the attacks on a broad mass of democratic rights manifested in the concern to abolish the elected metropolitan counties in favour of a reliance on a variety of non-elected boards (see Chapter 11 for a fuller discussion of this); in the opposition to a Freedom of Information bill that would provide for more open government (and in the abortive attempt to strengthen secrecy through a Protection of Official Information Bill in 1980 that was only dropped because of a spy fiasco); in the blocking of attempts to make the security services more accountable to the democratic side of the state machine; in the concern to reduce the effective freedom of the media, and especially the independence of the BBC, from the pressures, concerns, and interests of government; and in the restriction of rights to peaceful assembly and protest as a result of the Employment Acts and the use of the Public Order Act, not to mention the flirtation with a Riot Act to give the police power to clear the streets, and a possible law on domestic trespass.

Fifth, the fact that the Commons voted against the reintroduction of the death penalty yet again in 1983 against the clear wishes of the Conservative Party in the country put pressure on the Home Secretary to 'do something' about crime and adopt a 'tough' line with offenders: minimum sentences were recommended, there was the idea of giving young offenders a 'short sharp shock', and plans were set in motion for a net increase in new and refurbished prison places.

Finally, there is the whole issue of extending police powers and the implications of this for civil liberties and rights, but this needs to be seen in the larger context of developments in British policing over the last 10 years.

In theory, we have a system of policing by consent by an unarmed force that is close to the people. The police are seen as bound by law and as outside of politics. When people talk of Britain as having the best police in the world then this is the image in their minds backed up by a smiling bobby on his beat. In fact, this characterisation has always been somewhat at odds with the reality of policing for, as we saw in Chapter 5, the police are only partly bound by law and they are in politics. Moreover, a steady trend to an increasingly centralised force backed up by sophisticated hardware has taken police officers off the streets and made them more remote. In the more recent past, however, a series of developments has made for a crisis in policing, and practice has moved in ways very sharply at odds with the traditional picture.

The crisis of policing in terms of their success, image, and relationship to the public, has been made up of a number of components. First, there has been the running sore of police corruption. Between 1969 and 1972, a score of London detectives went to prison, hundreds more left the force in disgrace, and the old CID hierarchy was savagely restructured. We are not just dealing with a few cases of individual police malpractice, but with an ethic of detective work that prevailed among wide sections of the London CID. The issue, then, was about more than rotten apples, and the problem was not confined to London alone. Second, there is the problem of police complaints (discussed in Chapter 5) and the related problem of police violence. For example, over the period 1970–79, 143 of the 245 deaths in police custody were from other than natural causes. Third (and again discussed in Chapter 5), there is anxiety about the fact that the police are not accountable to any democratically elected body. Fourth, the police have not been conspicuously successful in dealing with crime. In 1981 only 30 per cent of the burglaries in England and Wales were solved, and in the Metropolitan police district just 9 per cent were solved. Fifth, the police have experienced difficulties in controlling demonstrations and the inner-city riots of the eighties. The police actually withdrew for a while from St Pauls in Bristol in 1980 thereby conceding victory to the rioters. More aggressive policing in Brixton did not stop (and may well have helped to cause) the rioting there in 1981, and the police could do little to stop the riots spreading to some thirty urban centres in July of that year with damage estimated at £45 million. Simply expressed, traditional methods of policing were just not up to scratch with respect to crime and public order, and the police were losing the support of the public. Taken together, these elements of crisis meant that the time was ripe for a fundamental change of policing practice in order to try and enhance both effectiveness *and* public credibility. What, then, has happened over the past 10 years?

Policing by consent has given way to policing by coercion and confrontation. Preventive policing by the patrolling bobby has been replaced by reactive, 'fire brigade', policing – by a system of quick co-ordinated response to reported incidents that relies on the technological cop in which the car, the radio, and the computer dominate the police scene. The use of computerised command and control systems dates from 1972 with the Home Office assuming a co-ordinating role of great importance. During the 1970s, the police brought the application of scientific knowledge to many different aspects of their work. This included the use of closed-circuit television; the creation of specialist Technical Support Units; the use of helicopters for surveillance; and the back-up provided by the Police National Computer at Hendon that in addition to filing away the 23.25 million adults registered as keepers and owners of vehicles also contains an undisclosed amount of political intelligence.

As back-up to the 'quick response' system provided by computerised command and control, many police forces have also set up Special Patrol Groups. The first group was set up in London in 1965 as an anti-crime unit to go to the aid of local divisions and provide saturation policing in areas of high crime. Similar groups were formed in the 1970s outside of London. By 1974, about half the forces in England and Wales had such groups and they rapidly came to adopt a para-military role in relation to public order and anti-terrorism to the detriment of a substantive involvement in crime fighting. Politicians may debate whether or not Britain should have a 'third force' standing between the army and regular police to deal with strikes, demonstrations, and terrorists, but in practice that debate has been resolved. 'Mutual aid', whereby officers from one force go to the aid of another, has been long-established, but in the 1970s this has been extended to providing riot-trained police through special Police Support Units. By 1981, it was estimated that there were at least 11 000 specially trained riot police in Great Britain, and this figure leaves aside the 27 known Special Patrol Groups and the Shield Trained Units existing in London and West Yorkshire.

Nor can the British police any longer be viewed as an unarmed force. First, some 12 000 rank-and-file officers are now trained in the use of firearms, and all newly recruited police officers receive firearms 'familiarisation' training. Second, many forces have formed Firearms Support Units as specialist firearms squads. The police are reluctant to talk about guns, but to put this development of practice into perspective we should remember that between 1970 and 1979 the police in England and Wales only fired their guns on persons on about twenty occasions resulting in six deaths and five injuries. The weapons held by the police go beyond truncheons and guns, however, as since the mid-1960s every police force has maintained stocks of CS gas. This gas has been used extensively in Northern Ireland since 1969 (over the period 1970–75 some 5359 cartridges and 22 602 grenades were fired) and was used to control the Toxteth riots in Liverpool in 1981 in defiance of manufacturers, instructions and at a cost of four serious injuries. In the immediate aftermath of the summer of riots in 1981, the government made the provision of new anti-riot weapons a top priority including the provision of CS gas, rubber bullets, and water cannon wherever the police wished to employ them. Merseyside's chief constable, Ken Oxford, said that he would be reluctant to use water cannon but he would like armoured personnel carriers.

In addition to these developments with respect to the public police, we also need to attend to the developing role of the private police and to the role of the military in matters of internal security.

In Chapter 5 we pointed out that in 1971 there were some 105 000 private police in the whole of the United Kingdom. Securicor by itself accounted for more than 20 000 of these. In effect, boring tasks, like enforcing parking restrictions or searching hand baggage at airports have been hived off to traffic wardens and private firms, and dangerous jobs like guarding bank shipments have been hived off to private security firms. An old boy network ensures 'co-operation' between the public police and ex-colleagues in the private sector with the exchange of information and the leakage of confidential official records to those prepared to pay the going rate.

The role of the army in matters of internal order and security is a complicated matter that has been subject to change over the years *and* to mystification as to the true extent of its involvement. Earlier in this chapter, when we dealt with the development of the police force, we saw that prior to the formation of modern forces in the nineteenth century the army was regularly called in to quell mob disorders. Since that time, however, the police have supposedly been in sole control. In fact, in between 1910 and 1914, and 1918 and 1926, military interest and involvement in civil order generally and industrial unrest in particular grew steadily in intensity. To a large extent the military came not only to supplement but almost to supersede the role of the police in these matters. Having said that, between 1926 and 1970, the police reasserted themselves and regained overall control – thanks partly to the process of militarisation and professionalisation within the regular police force instigated in 1919. Of course, the military were not entirely absent from the domestic scene in this period (some 10 000 troops were used to discharge ships during the 1945 dock strike), but after the Second World War the army was preoccupied with anti-colonialist struggles overseas and the long post-war boom of the fifties and sixties did not push public order questions to the fore at home. The demise of Britain as a world power and the loss of empire, and the problem of disorder at home (manifested most forcefully in the onset of the 'troubles' in Northern Ireland in 1969) encouraged the military to see a new role for themselves geared to subversion and insurgency in Britain. Brigadier Frank Kitson wrote *Low Intensity Operations* in 1971 specifically to draw attention to the steps that needed to be taken 'in order to make the army ready to deal with subversion, insurrection, and peacekeeping operations during the second half of the 1970s'. Moreover, Kitson made it clear that he did not see the army's role in these matters confined to Northern Ireland alone since 'there are other potential trouble spots within the UK which might involve the army in operations of a sort against political extremists who are prepared to resort to a considerable degree of violence to achieve their ends'. In a speech in 1980, 'The place of the British army in public order', General Sir Edwin Bramall, the head of the army, made it clear that 'the police will never have to turn in vain to us for help'. By now most infantry units have served for a tour of duty in Northern Ireland. In 1974, the army *and* the police jointly occupied London airport and the surrounding areas in four successive exercises, and in August 1978 they carried out a similar operation . The army has also come to assume a substantial and significant role in industrial disputes: in 1970 they were used in the Tower Hamlets refuse collection strike; in 1973 they were used in a fire service strike in Glasgow and in that city again in 1975 to cope with a refuse collection strike; they provided fire-fighting facilities during the fire service strike of 1977–78; and they have guarded prisoners during industrial action by prison warders in 1980. Given these developments in military strike breaking it was hardly surprising that the Ministry of Defence sought to change the Queen's Regulations in 1978 so as to legitimate the use of troops in national strikes in a way that gave the military powers beyond those intended by Parliament when it passed the Emergency Powers Act, 1964. In fact, the increasing centrality of the military and the private police in matters of order and security today takes us back to the situation of the eighteenth century when the forces of the public police were backed up by these agencies precisely because the public police could not cope.

Many of these 'hard' policing developments have occurred beneath the skin of public debate in response to the 'need' for an iron fist in troubled times. They have, however, been buttressed in law by the Police and Criminal Evidence Act, 1983 which extends police powers in such matters as stop and search; arrest; searches of bodies, houses, and workplaces; detention; fingerprinting; and so on. Now, many of these developments do little to respond to that aspect of the police crisis that bears on the problem of public confidence and support, and so it is no real surprise that much publicity has been given to the virtues of reinvigorating traditional 'community policing' – of putting bobbies back onto the beat in a preventive role. In reality, however, only limited resources are being put into community policing which is less a policing strategy than it is a publicity device for winning back public support. In Chapter 5 we made it clear that there is no official sympathy for increasing the community control *of* the police through democratic structures and in the absence of this community policing can best be construed as a technique for harnessing the community to help the police in achieving the goals set *by* the police and those who are their real masters outside of the intensely policed high-crime communities.

In broad terms, how can we best characterise and explain these developments with respect to law and policing, and what are their significance for civil liberties and democracy in Britain today?

We agree with Stuart Hall that 'we are now in the middle of a deep and decisive movement towards a more disciplinary, authoritarian kind of society' in which law and police are at the heart of order and control. In order to make sense of this drift into a law-and-order society we need to attend to a number of things.

First, we need to see the drive for more law and order as some kind of backlash against the permissive 'excesses' of the 1960s by those who were never part of the trend for change but who were silent or went unheard in their opposition to it at the time it was occurring.

Second, it is important to recognise that the concern of the Conservative Governments of 1979 and 1983 to create a free-market economy and to stop the state meddling in economic management (discussed in Chapter 8) actually requires a strong state with the police in the frontline to manage the social and economic effects of rising levels of unemployment and the inevitable fall-out in terms of social conflict and class polarisation. The state may well be doing *less* in the 'modern' fields of economic management and welfare provision but it is being forced to do *more* in the 'traditional' areas of state activity. It is no coincidence that attempts are being made to cut back on welfare spending at the same time as funding is willingly increased for the police and for the building of prisons. If the market is to be free then the people need to be disciplined in its support, not just through the rigours of unemployment in the market itself, but through the full force of the law as well.

Third, and pushing beyond the immediate politics of personalities, governments, and Thatcherism, we need to attend to the significance of the structural backwardness of the British economy. In the 1950s and 1960s, the economics of growth and affluence led to a politics of prosperity, permissiveness, and concessions, and to a loosening of social control both informally and through law. It was, however, a peaceful and successful interlude in a history of decline dating back to the last century. The onset of recession in the 1970s has, once again, cut into the economic slack from which politicians give and so has pushed the problem of social order and control to the fore. Recession has, at the same time, also weakened the political power of organised labour and contributed to a decline in expectations and to a new mood of (system supporting) 'realism'. Simply expressed, by the late 1970s, the time was ripe to reassert the power of the iron fist in British politics: it was *needed* to resecure productive relations, and it was *possible* because of the weakened position of labour to resist and because of the electoral victories of the Conservative Party in both 1979 and 1983.

Naturally enough, the move towards a stronger state and a more controlled and disciplined society has profound implications for civil liberties and democracy. In Chapter 5 we pointed to the power of the secret state, but now, in crisis, we are seeing attempts to strengthen the power of the policing side of the secret state at the same time as there is profound hostility to introducing a measure of democratic control over the activities of the police. The police (an unaccountable force) are being given extended powers, and these together with other innovations in the law, are eating into the established rights and liberties that have traditionally been regarded as of central significance within a democratic polity. We may be drifting into the tighter control of law-and-order society in defence of the free economy, but at what cost in terms of democratic politics?

CONCLUSION: A CRISIS OF LEGITIMATION?

We have seen that the traditional soft agencies of social control – the family, the Church and the local community – have to some extent been weakened over the years while the newer agencies which have developed to replace or complement them are generally not as powerful in their influence over the way people think and behave. Nor does their combined influence necessarily always run in the same direction. And internally, the existence of radical teachers, socialist social workers and left-wing journalists means that these newer agencies are never fully reliable in the way that the Church of old was, for the growing numbers of people who are 'in and against the state' pose a constant potential threat of subversion on a small or a grand scale.

When an economy is growing, legitimation by means of soft control agencies is unlikely to be a major problem because in a situation of expansion and rising general levels of affluence, a capitalist system will, in a sense, look after its own legitimation with little help from government, for it will be *seen* to be working. People have more money in their pockets, the shops are full of the latest consumer goods which many people can realistically aspire to buy, home ownership (which is generally recognised as having a conservatising influence) is expanded, and although people may feel that there is something missing in their lives, and that a new car, a dishwasher and home video do not entirely compensate for this, they are unlikely to begin fundamentally questioning whether the system in which they live is the most appropriate to their needs.

When the economy slumps, as it has in Britain since the 1970s, all this changes. Rising popular material aspirations can no longer be met which means that some attempt has to be made to justify the system, even though it is no longer producing the goods. In this situation, the state's role in securing legitimation becomes central, and if the soft agencies begin to fail, then the more coercive agencies such as the police and the army will come into prominence.

The argument that economic problems exacerbate legitimation problems is one that became familiar in both New Left and New Right thinking from the 1970s onwards. While the Left saw the worsening recession as a potential trigger for a radical break from the status quo, the Right saw in it a dangerous threat requiring a firm and steadfast response.

The reasoning of the Left was best revealed in a book written in the mid-1970s by a German Marxist, Jurgen Habermas, and entitled *Legitimation Crisis*. The book is a dense and complex piece of writing, but the essence of its argument is that advanced capitalist societies such as Britain suffer from four related tendencies towards crisis and breakdown.

The first of these is a tendency towards economic crisis – a tendency which became ever more apparent in Britain from the mid-1970s onwards.

The second is the tendency to what Habermas termed a 'rationality crisis', or an inability to find the means for bringing about desired objectives. What he meant by this was that governments in capitalist societies seek to support economic growth yet do not control the means for achieving this goal since control over investment is generally in private hands. As we saw in Chapter 8, worsening economic problems thus tend to provoke ever-more frantic political responses, none of which succeeds in turning the economy around.

The third crisis tendency, which emerges as a result of such governmental failures, is the development of a 'legitimation crisis'. Thus Habermas argues that intervention in the economy by the state politicises the operation of the market and raises popular expectations. Whereas in the nineteenth century people tended to accept slumps and recessions as in some way natural and unavoidable, today they look to government to manage the economy in such a way that dramatic economic downturns are avoided, or at least to make provision through welfare support, job creation and so on for those who are hit by them. If, however, government lacks the tools to manage the economy, then it will fail to fulfil the expectations which people have of it. This then creates a situation in which mass loyalty to the state, the government and the capitalist system itself may easily be undermined.

The fourth and final tendency to crisis involves the development of a 'crisis of motivation' in which the erosion of legitimacy leads people to question traditional values, re-examine conventional ideologies and reject ways of life which have hitherto been taken as 'normal'. When and if crisis reaches this fourth level, then consensus in society has finally broken down and all that remains for securing the future of the state and the capitalist system is the explicit use of force.

There is much in Habermas's thesis which makes sense and which strikes a familiar chord in the context of contemporary British government and society. Certainly we would agree with him that the root cause of legitimation problems is economic, and that the deeper the economic difficulties, the more strain we should expect to be placed on both traditional and newer agencies of socialization and legitimation.

Yet having said that, it does not seem to have been the case that the country's continuing economic slump and successive governments' failures to halt it has resulted in a real crisis of legitimation or motivation. In order to understand why this is, we need to consider the response of the New Right to the growing threat of social breakdown from the mid-1970s onwards.

We saw in the previous two chapters that Thatcherism was much more than simply an economic doctrine. Viewed against Habermas's four crisis tendencies, it is now apparent that Thatcherism was in effect a fresh assault, not only on economic problems, but on rationality, legitimation and motivation problems as well.

The New Right tackled the problem of motivation by attempting to reassert traditional 'Victorian' values. Of particular importance here was the Falklands war in 1982, for this provided the opportunity for mobilising all the nationalistic and jingoistic sentiments which had been laid down in the popular consciousness during the age of Empire but which had to some extent lain dormant during the post-war years when the Empire had been lost, military expeditions (notably Suez in 1956) had ended in farce and Britain had been consigned to a walk-on role in the theatre of world affairs. Coupled with the Falklands hysteria (ably whipped up by most of the popular press) went a new emphasis on traditional values stressing the family, individual self-help and self-reliance and discipline, all of which was contrasted with the shallow trendiness of permissiveness and the sloppy and easy assumption that the world owed you a living. Tendencies to motivation crisis, in other words, were countered by dusting off the well-worn and trusted values of a by-gone age in the hope that the classes which had embraced them once would readily embrace them again.

The assault on the tendency to legitimation crisis followed from this. Habermas, it will be recalled, saw a crisis of legitimation as the product of a situation in which people have been led to expect effective resolution of problems by government at a time when government actually fails to carry this off. The Thatcher governments' answer to this was to tell people that the problems from which they were suffereing were problems of their own making and that they should look to themselves rather than to government for their solution. Government, we were told time and again, could actually do very little. If people were losing their jobs, this was because they had driven up wages to such a point that they had priced themselves out of a job. If British manufacturing was collapsing, this was because people were not working hard enough to compete with the industrious Germans, Japanese, South Koreans and the rest. If the welfare state was crumbling, this was because for years the country had been taking more out of the economy than it had been putting in and the day of reckoning had to come sooner or later. The same message was proclaimed loud and long: there is no point in blaming government (still less capitalism), the answer lay in the people themselves.

This denial of responsibility was then carried over into the New Right's response to tendencies to rationality crisis, for rather than trying to find new ways in which the economy could be managed, the government claimed that it had been precisely these attempts in the past which had prevented the capitalist system from functioning properly. From now on, government would step aside and let market forces do the job which they are so good at. There was, we were told, no alternative to this, for, as every housewife knows, you cannot spend more than you earn; thus a government cannot spend its way out of slump. In the post-Keynesian age, these were the economics of the simpleton, but such arguments had an immediate commonsense appeal and, judged in electoral terms, they paid off in 1983 when the government was returned for a second term in office. So it was that people continued to 'tighten their belts', sure in the knowledge that sacrifices today would bring their rewards in the form of 'real jobs' and a sound economy tomorrow – or maybe the day after that.

The problem with all this, of course, was that sooner or later the economy would have to show some signs of recovery and unemployment would have to start going down. If the analysis presented in Chapter 8 is correct, then any such sustained recovery seems most unlikely. This being the case, the government's juggling of motivation, legitimation and rationality problems could not be expected to continue indefinitely, for the fundamental economic problems which lay at the heart of the other three crisis tendencies would eventually re-emerge. The unemployed person, can after all, get on a bike to look for work (as the unemployed were recommended to do by the Employment Secretary in 1982) only so many times before coming to the conclusion that it is the economic system rather than his or her own character which is at fault. You can try to 'pull yourself up by your bootstraps' only so many times before recognising that you are not actually getting any higher. You can turn out to wave flags welcoming home the victorious Falklands fleet only so many times before you begin to ask why these ships are then turning round again to be refitted in overseas dockyards. The Thatcherite solution to the problem of legitimation was, in other words, only ever a temporary solution, a holding operation whose success, like all legitimation strategies, still depended ultimately on the performance of the economy.

It was for this reason that the coercive apparatus of the state had to be strengthened, for the soft agencies could not be expected to hold up for ever under increasing pressures. People are not simply passive receivers of wisdom transmitted from above, and no matter how persuasive the ideology, there will eventually come a time when it will lose its power if it fails to relate to people's everyday-life experiences. As we have suggested at a number of points in this chapter, there is no single, all-embracing value system, no one, cohesive and authoritative view of the world which is endorsed across all classes and all regions at all times. In an age of compulsory universal education and pervasive instruments of mass communication, we may all be subject to much the same ideological pressures from above, but our different life situations – the sorts of work we do, the types of areas we live in, the kind of people we interact with on a day-to-day basis – mean that there are other influences which help to shape our values, beliefs and assumptions, and that these may not be consistent with the messages which we hear from school teachers, newsreaders and social workers. If we know that our take-home pay has dropped dramatically in real terms in recent years, then our credulity may be stretched when we hear that we have priced ourselves out of a job. If we know that the pace of work has intensified, then we may doubt that it is our laziness which has brought the economy to its knees.

What this means is that what may be termed a 'dominant value system' is unlikely to have things all its own way, for it must compete with other sets of values and other understandings of how the world works which arise out of people's life experiences and which may be reinforced by what we hear from, for example, shop stewards on the factory floor, radical local councillors or even disaffected teachers and journalists. Legitimation and the construction of a social consensus is, in short, always a precarious business and always a contested terrain. Where ideological messages transmitted from above come constantly into conflict with commonsense wisdoms generated through the process of living one's everyday life, social control becomes problematic. In such a situation, people are likely to become at best (from the point of view of system order) ambivalent in their attachment to dominant norms and values, and at worst they may come to reject these norms and values altogether and turn to an alternative ideology which seems to make more sense in accounting for their everyday experiences.

In Britain in the mid-1980s, we would suggest that few people have become totally detached from the dominant value system, but that many have become more or less ambivalent towards it. Such a mood of ambivalence and fatalism is an unsure foundation on which to base an aggressively capitalist economic and social order, and the government itself seems to have recognised this. Increasingly over recent years, it has become clear that the government has recognised the dangers of an over-reliance on legitimation strategies as the major means of ensuring social control. It is for this reason that, within the velvet glove, the iron fist has been re-cast.

WORKS CITED AND GUIDE TO FURTHER READING

Anderson, P. (1965) The origins of the present crisis, in P. Anderson and R. Blackburn (eds) *Towards Socialism,* London, Fontana.
Argues that capitalist hegemony is more secure in Britain than in any other Western country and explains this in terms of various peculiarities of British history – its early and incomplete bourgeois revolution, its early industrialization, its huge nineteenth-century Empire and its escape from conquest for a thousand years. Interesting.

Bierne, P. and Quinney, R. (eds) (1982) *Marxism and Law*, New York, Wiley.
Well-edited collection of material reflecting the new interest of Marxists in a serious analysis of law in capitalist society.

The Brixton Disorders 10–12 April 1981, (The Scarman Report), Cmnd. 8427, London, HMSO, 1981.
Liberal and balanced, but compelled to conclude that 'a significant cause' of the riots in Brixton was a loss of local confidence in the police. Recommendations challenge many 'hard' developments in police practice over the past 10 years but

supports saturation policing and the Special Patrol Group, and rejects police accountability to democratically elected bodies.

Critchley, T. A. (1978) *A History of Police in England and Wales,* 2nd edn, London, Constable.
Thorough, standard, but fairly uncritical account by the former head of the Home Office Police Department.

Gamble, A. (1979) The free economy and the strong state: The rise of the social market economy, in Ralph Miliband and J. Saville (eds) *The Socialist Register, 1979,* London, Merlin, pp. 1–25.
Explores the connections between the moves to a free economy and the trend to a stronger state through a particular emphasis on the writings of F. A. Hayek.

Glasgow University Media Group (1983) *Really Bad News,* London, Routledge and Kegan Paul.
The third in the series of 'bad news' studies monitoring and analysing the news output of the BBC and ITN and demonstrating a systematic bias of presentation and interpretation. These studies have attracted considerable criticism from government and the broadcasting agencies, but the evidence they contain is impressive.

Habermas, J. (1976) *Legitimation Crisis,* London, Heinemann.
An important but exceedingly difficult book. Somewhat easier to digest is Habermas's short paper on 'Legitimation problems in late capitalism' which is included in P. Connerton, (ed) (1976) *Critical Sociology,* Harmondsworth, Penguin.

Hall, S. (1980) Drifting into a law and order society, London, Cobden Trust.
Powerful analysis, and critique, of the trend to a more disciplinary society based on an 'authoritative populism'.

Hunt, A. (1981) The politics of law and justice, *Politics and Power,* **4,** 3–26.
Criticises various left positions on law and argues that the left have failed to take law seriously. A plea for a 'socialist politics of law' and a more rigorous approach to the question of rights and justice.

Illich, I. (1971) *Deschooling Society,* London, Calder and Boyars.
A radical attack on schooling by one of America's most innovative and libertarian social thinkers. Important, among other things, for its discussion of the hidden curriculum.

Kitson, F. (1971) *Low Intensity Operations,* London, Faber.
Frank statement by a leading army officer urging the army to prepare itself for a role in keeping the lid on domestic disorder.

Mark, R. (1977) *Policing a Perplexed Society,* London, Allen and Unwin.
Ex Chief Commissionerof the Metropolitan Police agonises about the problems of maintaining law and order in difficult times.

Morgan, D. (1971) *Social Theory and the Family,* London, Routledge and Kegan Paul.
A useful guide to key literature – includes a discussion of those theorists, such as Talcott Parsons, who emphasise the changing structure and functions of the family consequent upon industrialisation.

Piven, F. and Cloward, R. (1972) *Regulating the Poor,* London, Tavistock.
An American study of how social welfare functions as a method of maintaining social control.

Royal Commission on Criminal Procedure (1981) *Report,* Cmnd 8092, London.
Established in 1977 as a result of the outcome of years of conflicting pressures. The report, which advocates a widening of police powers, was viewed by most of the left as a triumph for the law and order lobby.

State Research Pamphlet No 2 (1981) *Policing the 80s: The Iron Fist,* London, State Research.
Full and well-documented account of developments in British policing over the past 10 years from an organisation which is *the* source of information on police and security matters.

Taylor, I., Walton, P. and Young, J. (1973) *The New Criminology,* London, Routledge and Kegan Paul.
Three neo-Marxists concerned to advance a 'fully social theory of deviance' which involves their asking, 'Who makes the rules and why?'

Thompson, E. P. (1975) *Whigs and Hunters: The Origin of the Black Act,* London, Allen Lane.
In the conclusion, this Marxist historian criticises those Marxists who persist in seeing law as the simple outgrowth of the power of the economically dominant.

Thompson, E. P. (1980) The Secret State, in E. P. Thompson (ed.) *Writing by Candlelight,* London, Merlin.
See page 168.

Westergaard, J. & Resler, H. (1975) *Class in a Capitalist Society,* London, Heinemann.
The chapters in Part IV deal with the inequalities of opportunity in Britain and focus specifically on the ways in which the education system operates selectively on social-class lines.

Willis, P. (1977) *Learning to Labour,* Farnborough, Hants., Saxon House.
An influential study of how working-class children rub up against the culture of school and end up desiring working-class jobs.

Wilson, B. (1966) *Religion in Secular Society,* London, Watts.
A classic and readable study of secularisation. Full of useful (though now slightly dated) statistics woven together by an insightful text which makes clear the decline in the significance of religion and the Church in modern Britain.

CHAPTER 11

The Organisation of the United Kingdom State

The question whether a nation is to be free depends upon the creation of the opportunity and habit of local self-government.

T. Burgess and T. Travers (1980) Ten Billion Pounds: Whitehall's take-over of the town halls, *London, Grant McIntyre, p. 5.*

How central governments and their territorial sub-units are linked politically is not only a problem of intergovernmental relations but also one of managing the class and interest conflicts of modern societies.

S. Tarrow (1978) Introduction, in S. Tarrow, P. Katzenstein and L. Graziano (eds), Territorial Politics in Industrial Nations, *New York, Praeger, pp. 1–2.*

One of the motives for the British establishment wanting us so strongly to go into Europe was that they believed that the British people armed with the ballot box were going to become unmanageable, and the only power structure strong enough to control us would be an international power structure.

T. Benn (1979) Arguments for Socialism, *London, Jonathan Cape, p. 163.*

The United Kingdom state is not some unitary monolith. Although political theorists often talk about 'the state' as if it were a single or homogenous entity, the modern British state actually consists of a bewildering array of different agencies. Some of these are elected, although most are not. Some are subject to direct control or supervision by elected governments while others enjoy considerable autonomy. Some are single-purpose bodies while others may be responsible for a wide range of different functions. Some are organised horizontally on the basis of function while others are organised along a vertical dimension entailing different geographical or territorial levels of operation. Indeed some are organised at national or even international level while others have a limited regional or local basis.

As the state has taken on more responsibilities so, inevitably, its organisation has become more complex. In this chapter, we turn to the way in which the state organises its vastly expanded field of activities paying particular attention to the different geographical or territorial levels of operation and noting the strains and conflicts between them.

Just as the central level of the state contains many institutions run by people whose name has never appeared on any ballot paper, so too at local level we find a plethora of non-elected state agencies. The local level of the state includes, in addition to elected local councils, police forces over which there is very little local democratic control, Justices of the Peace whose appointment is generally shrouded in mystery, district health authorities which are not directly elected by the populations they exist to serve, boards of school governors staffed entirely by appointees, local offices of central departments such as the Department of Health and Social Security and, of course a bureaucratic system of local administration which services local councils and which functions much like a mini-civil service. Not surprisingly, then, many of the decisions which are taken locally and which impact directly on people's everyday lives – the allocation of council housing, cuts in hospital beds, delays in social security payments, allocation of children to state schools, saturation policing of black neighbourhoods – are not taken by the councillors whom we (or to be more accurate, around one-third of us) elect, and local councils very often have little or no opportunity to influence or change them. There is, in short, much more to the local state than simply local government, and it is a stunning weakness of much of the literature on local politics in this country that we still know very little about how these other agencies operate. Having said that, however, local government does have a peculiar significance by virtue of the fact that it is elected as well as locally based. Indeed, it is the only centre of political power in the whole state system outside of Parliament itself which can claim legitimacy for its actions on the basis of a popular vote. Local councils are, therefore, in a unique position to challenge the centre and they provide a potentially crucial medium through which groups excluded from representation at the centre can mobilise to express their interests. This, as we shall see, is precisely what has been happening in recent years in Britain.

The local government system

The local government system as it exists in Britain today has its origins in legislation in the late nineteenth century which first set up a system of local, elected, multi-purpose authorities. Before that, cities, towns and rural areas were run locally by a confusing melée of different functional authorities. Under the Local Government Acts, 1888 and 1894, most functions were reallocated to new elected councils. A two-tier system of local government was adopted consisting of county councils (for mainly rural counties) and county borough councils (in major towns and cities) at the higher level, and borough, urban district and rural district councils at the lower level. All of these bodies were democratically elected – much to the consternation of traditional local elites throughout the country who saw these reforms as striking at their power. In town and country alike, the working class for the first time was given the opportunity to wrest political control away from the businessmen, landowners and gentry who had for so long dictated the course of local affairs. Although traditional elites often succeeded in winning election to the new councils (and many were able to retain their position through the non-elected aldermanic system), by the 1920s, many local authorities were controlled by Labour or (as in parts of South Wales) Communist members.

Not only were the new councils elected, but they were also given a considerable range of new powers which grew over the years as the state extended its activities into ever more areas of civil society. By 1929, when the Boards of Guardians were at last disbanded and control of poor relief and hospitals was transferred to local councils, local government had become wholly or partly responsible for a wide variety of functions including both social provisions (e.g. health, housing and education) and economic management (e.g. of municipal enterprises and public utilities such as water supply, town gas and electricity distribution).

This was, however, to prove the high point of municipal power and local autonomy. From the 1930s onwards, Conservative and Labour Governments alike have stripped local authorities of many of their most significant functions. The process began in 1934 when local councils lost control over local poor relief, thus clearing the way for central government to impose cuts in the level of relief without encountering the sort of local resistance which had occurred a few years earlier in Poplar where the socialist-controlled Board of Guardians had raised the level of payments in the face of central demands that they be reduced. This was then followed by a flurry of legislation removing local responsibility for trunk roads (1936), administration of supplementary benefits (1940), hospitals (1946), electricity supply (1947) and gas (1948). While local councils did gain some new powers during this period (notably in respect of land-use planning after 1947), the clear trend was one of erosion of their responsibilities, and this has continued ever since. More recently, for example, local councils have ceded control over water supply and sewage treatment (1974), community health care (1974) and provision of sewers (1983), and at the time of writing, legislation is being introduced to remove control of London Transport from the Greater London Council (GLC).

Although the functions of local government changed dramatically from the 1930s onwards, its organisation remained largely undisturbed until the 1960s. The first major organisational reform of the system which had been established towards the end of the nineteenth century came in 1965 when the local government system in London was fundamentally restructured as a result of the London Government Act, 1963, passed by the Douglas-Home Conservative Government. This was then followed by further reforms in the rest of Britain as a result of the Heath Government's Local Government Act, 1972, which came into effect in April, 1974. Taken together, these two pieces of Conservative legislation form the basis of the present local government system, although further changes are now being introduced as we shall see later.

The 1965 and 1974 reforms basically aimed to 'rationalise' the local government system by creating a smaller number of larger, 'efficient' authorities. These changes proved very expensive to implement (partly because local bureaucrats up and down the country seized the opportunity to extend their 'empires' by massively expanding staffing and building new offices), yet they perpetuated many of the weaknesses of the system they were designed to replace. In particular, the government retained a two-tier system of local government which has proved cumbersome in its operation, and it preserved the archaic distinction between 'urban' and 'rural' authorities. In both instances, the motive was political.

The retention of a two-tier system in England and Wales (though not in Scotland where a new system of regional councils was introduced) flew in the face of the recommendations of a Royal Commission under the chairmanship of Lord Redcliffe-Maud which had argued strongly for a unitary system based on city regions. This idea was rejected, partly due to pressure from the Tory-dominated shire counties which bitterly opposed any move to legislate them out of existence, and partly out of a fear that councils based on city regions would swamp the rural and suburban Conservative interests by urban-based Labour representation.

The answer to this problem was to retain the shire counties (with some adjustment of boundaries and names) as higher-tier authorities, to create new district councils at the lower tier, and to create six new 'metropolitan counties' (each presiding over a number of 'metropolitan district councils') for the major urban conurbations such as Merseyside, the West Midlands and Tyne and Wear. Although this system created all sorts of problems in terms of overlapping functions between district and county level and lack of co-ordination between major cities and their hinterlands, it had the political merit of maintaining a Conservative stranglehold over wide stretches of the country.

Given the geographical pattern of traditional party voting in Britain, it was assumed (rightly) that the shire counties would remain overwhelmingly Conservative. What was less certain was what would happen to the GLC and the six metropolitan counties, for these massive authorities (the population of the GLC area alone was around 7.5 million) straddled the inner urban Labour heartlands and leafy middle-class suburbs alike. The hope was that Labour's traditional hegemony in the cities could be eroded by a leavening of deep blue suburban influence; the risk was that the new powerful metropolitan authorities would fall under the control of the Left, providing socialists with a local power base without parallel in the pre-1965/74 local government system.

As things have turned out, some of the metropolitan counties (e.g. the GLC, the West Midlands and Merseyside) have been won by the Conservatives in some election years, while others have been controlled by traditional Labour Party machines. However, through the 1970s, the growing influence of the Left within local Labour Parties began to make itself felt in the metropolitan counties, and by 1981 when the Radical Left won control in London, the West Midlands, South Yorkshire and elsewhere, it was clear that the blatant gerrymandering of boundaries in the 1963 and 1972 acts had badly misfired. From 1981 onwards, the Thatcher Government encountered fierce local resistance to many of its policies, and this eventually led to further proposals for organisational change involving the abolition of the GLC and the metropolitan counties.

The growth of central control

Elected local government has often proved a thorn in the side of central government. Although Labour Governments have certainly had their problems with Tory-controlled councils (notably between 1964 and 1970 over the comprehensive reorganisation of secondary education), the boot has more often been on the other foot – especially at times of recession and public expenditure cut-backs when Conservative Governments have often come under challenge from militant socialist councils. Thus, it was a Conservative Government under Baldwin which hounded the Poplar Guardians to jail in the 1920s for their refusal to cut poor relief; it was a Conservative Government under Heath which sacked and surcharged a dozen Labour councillors in the Derbyshire mining village of Clay Cross in the early 1970s following their refusal to increase council-house rents; and it has been Conservative Governments since 1979 under Thatcher which have come into head-on confrontation with a variety of Labour councils in Scotland (e.g. Lothian) and England (e.g. Greater London, Camden, Norwich, Sheffield) which have resisted cut-backs in welfare provision and attempts to privatise welfare services.

It is precisely because of the peculiar difficulties in controlling local government from the centre that so many functions have been taken away from local councils since the 1930s and this also goes a long way in explaining the organisational reforms of the 1960s and 1970s. This is clearly seen, for example, in the regular complaints voiced by central government in this period about the 'inefficiency' of local councils and the declining 'calibre' of local councillors, for such phrases indicated central government's concern to make local government more controllable by delivering it into the hands of 'efficient' bureaucrats and 'high calibre' councillors drawn from the ranks of business and the professions. Damaging political confrontations, such as that at Clay Cross, could, it was thought, be avoided in the future by making local councils bigger and more remote from local electoral pressure, for the bigger the council, the more difficult it would be for working-class militants to gain control of it, and the easier it would be to shift effective power from amateur part-time elected members to professional full-time appointed bureaucratic 'experts' who would toe the central government line.

The attempt to emasculate local democratic government has thus involved a number of related strategies. One has been to reduce the number of functions for which local government is responsible. Another has been to reorganise the structure of local government so as to increase its immunity to local pressures. But in addition, central government has increasingly developed at least five further strategies designed to extend its ability to control and regulate local authorities which stray out of line. Let us look at each of these in turn.

Increased bureaucratic power. Concomitant with the 1972 reorganisation, the government issued comprehensive guidelines (the Bains report) advising the new authorities on how to set up their internal administrative apparatus. The recommendation was basically that 'corporate management teams' consisting of chief officers under the chairmanship of a Chief Executive should be established to increase efficiency and 'effectiveness' by facilitating inter-departmental co-operation. These teams were then to liaise closely with an 'inner cabinet' of elected members drawn exclusively from the majority party group on the council and headed by the group leader. In this way, Bains argued for the creation of a small, specialist exclusive stratum of officers and councillors who would between them be in a position to develop policies and to push them through the full council. Virtually all the new authorities adopted these proposals in one form or another shortly after they came into being in 1974.

The 'corporate management' idea was not, of course, original to Bains, for it was first developed by American management consultants for use in private-enterprise firms. This itself led critics to wonder whether a management system designed to maximise profits was necessarily appropriate to a democratic system designed to deliver services to meet people's individual and collective needs. Certainly there is little doubt that the logic of Bains' recommendations reflected a technical rather than political view of the future role of local government – a concern which had more to do with efficiency than democracy and which took the 'ends' as given while devising rational methods for attaining them. This is all very well in a business context where the end – profitability – can indeed be taken as given, but in an elected governmental system, it is precisely the ends which must always be open to argument and debate. The adoption of corporate management in British local government since 1974 has effectively limited such debate, for it has held most councillors at arms length from the effective centres of power in town halls while leaving cabals of leading councillors and officers free to develop policy objectives away from the public gaze.

This then raises the question of how these inner groups of political and bureaucratic leaders determine policy objectives. One factor here, according to the critics, is that popular demands may come to be ignored as corporate management teams come to liaise more closely with central government departments (see 'Increased formal controls' below) and with large private-sector interests. In other words, the development of corporate management has been seen as a possible recipe for the development of corporatist modes of interest representation at local level. Whatever the truth of these claims, it is clear that, as in Whitehall, so too in the town halls, bureaucratic power tends to be a conservatising influence over policy development and implementation, and that central government finds it easier to deal with 'responsible' local bureaucrats than with radical local politicians. It is precisely for these reasons that some left-wing local authorities have recently begun to make explicitly political appointments to key jobs in the local authority bureaucracy or have developed an alternative set of advisers of their own to counter the influence of their chief officers.

The growth of non-elected local bodies. An important example of this strategy was the establishment after the Second World War of New Town Corporations to direct the development of housing and physical infrastructure in designated areas of population growth. Members of these corporations were appointed by central government, and they took over planning and housing powers from existing local councils in their areas, thus making them far more responsive to both central government and local private-sector firms than the local councils would ever have been.

Most of the New Town Corporations have now been wound up by the Thatcher Government, but they have recently spawned new off-shoots in the form of Urban Development Corporations set up to foster commercial redevelopment in the run-down inner city areas of Merseyside and London's docklands. Again, these corporations have assumed powers from local councils in their areas, and they have liaised closely with private-sector firms while keeping the elected representatives of the local population out of their deliberations. As with the development of corporate management within local authorities, the growth of development corporations outside them has thus had the effect of insulating local policy-making from the potentially disruptive pressures of democratic local government while at the same time increasing the responsiveness of the decision-making process to private-sector interests and to central departments.

Increased informal controls. Local authorities are subject to various pressures from the centre which fall short of direct control but which can nevertheless have an enormous influence on what they do and how they do it. The use of circulars, for example, is a traditional method whereby central departments 'inform' local council bureaucrats of the requirements and implications of government policy.

Probably more important than pieces of paper, however, are informal personal contacts. There has developed in Britain what has been termed a 'national local government system' or a system of 'policy communities' by which the centre can exert pressure while at the same time getting local feedback on its policies. Such a liaison takes place, for example, through local government professional associations (e.g. associations of municipal engineers, town planners, municipal accountants and so on) and through the local government associations (the Association of County Councils, the Assocation of Metropolitan Authorities, the Association of District Councils and the London Boroughs Association), for bodies such as these function as effective forums through which advice, influence and cajoling can be effected. Such pressures do not always work, of course in which case openly coercive measures may be called for.

Use of legal sanctions. In recent years, informal persuasion of local authorities by the centre has increasingly given way to coercion by means of new legislation. Local government in Britain has always been hemmed in by the doctrine of *ultra vires,* which basically means that it is illegal for a local council to do anything which it has not specifically been authorised to do by Parliament. Not content with restricting what local authorities may do, however, central government has increasingly prescribed in law what they must do. The law governing local government has become less permissive and more mandatory as the years have gone by. A recent example of this was the Housing Act, 1980, which obliged councils to sell their houses to sitting tenants at considerable discounts irrespective of whether they considered this wise or acceptable. Where, as in Norwich, local councils dragged their feet, the government stepped in directly by appointing its own commissioner to supervise the sales programme.

The tightening of legal restrictions on local councils has resulted in recent years in court proceedings against various local authorities which have tried to resist various aspects of central government policy. In 1981 for example, Labour won control of the GLC on a manifesto which promised as one of its main objectives to reduce public transport fares in the capital. Following litigation by the Conservative-controlled London Borough of Bromley (fully supported by the Thatcher Government at Westminster), the courts ruled that the fares reduction was illegal under the London Transport Act, 1969, and in an extraordinary judgement with profound implications for the future of local democracy, ruled that local manifestoes were merely instruments of election propaganda and that the GLC could not reduce fares even though it had won an election on precisely that platform.

The GLC subsequently found and exploited a legal loophole which enabled it to introduce a revised cheap fares policy, and this seems to have worked fairly successfully. The government's response was to resort once again to a legislative battering ram by introducing a new act which was aimed at ending altogether the GLC's responsibility for public transport in London. This example shows the way in which law has increasingly become an instrument of central government domination of the local authorities, and how it can be used to by-pass troublesome elected councils, for under the terms of the new act, control of London Transport passes to a new independent and non-elected body answerable directly to the minister. No longer are the people of London to be allowed to determine their own public transport policies.

Increased Financial controls. Without doubt, the most significant and effective way in which central government has been able to control local authorities is through controlling their sources of revenue.

There are four main sources of local government revenue – user charges (e.g. rents paid by council tenants and entrance fees paid by those using municipal facilities); rates (a local tax levied on all domestic and commercial properties); central government grants (paid to local councils annually from the central exchequer); and loans (which are normally raised on the City of London finance market). Increasingly, central government has moved to control or influence all four.

Local authority *borrowing* to finance new capital works projects was until 1981 subject to central government approval in that councils had to seek 'loan sanction' before they could borrow. This system of control was replaced in 1981 by the more simple expedient of fixing 'cash limits' on annual local capital expenditure (local councils are not permitted to borrow to finance current expenditure). Under this new system, the central government sets a ceiling each year on what each council can spend on new projects but does not stipulate how the money for these projects is to be raised. This apparent liberalisation of controls was, however, largely cosmetic since few councils since 1981 have been able to afford to borrow, and most have failed to spend up to their ceiling. Effectively what has happened is that high interest rates have made it unnecessary for central government to control local government borrowing, for most local authorities are already burdened with massive debt charges which absorb the lion's share of their annual revenue and which make further large-scale borrowing a fiscal impossibility.

Nor is local government free any longer to fix its own *user charges* (notably rents on its housing stock). Conservative Governments in 1972 and again in 1980 introduced legislation compelling councils to raise rents to notional market levels irrespective of whether they wanted to or needed to. This, of course, has increased local authority revenue, often to the point where tenants are now subsidising other items in local authority budgets, but has reduced the ability of local authorities to cater for their own housing needs.

The method of funding *central government grants* to local authorities has also changed in recent years. Local councils have always relied to some extent on grants from the centre, but the trend over the last 50 years has been towards ever-increasing dependency. Immediately after the war for example, central government paid for just 29 per cent of local spending. By 1952, when this figure had swollen to 35 per cent, central government was for the first time ever paying more in grants than local authorities were receiving in local rates. By 1976, this gap had widened to a point where grants made up no less than half of all local council revenue (compared with just 24 per cent coming from the rates).

As the size of the central grant has grown, so the system for administering it has changed. The most significant in a long line of reforms came in 1980 when the Thatcher Government adopted a system of 'block grant' which had been devised but never implemented by the preceeding Labour administration.

The basic difference between the new 'block-grant' system and the old 'rate support grant' which it replaced was that, whereas under the old system the centre increased its grant to match increases in local spending, under the new one it actually reduces the amount paid to councils as their expenditure increases. Thus, since 1980, central government decides each year how much a local council needs to spend in order to maintain an adequate level of services, how much of this it can be expected to raise for itself in rates and charges, and how much therefore remains to be provided from central funds. These calculations are, of course, influenced by the government's own desire to cut public expenditure, and each year the Department of the Environment (DoE) has tended to reduce the amount which it considers as 'necessary' for local authorities to spend (the so-called 'Grant Related Expenditure' level). Those local councils which wish to spend above this level have until recently been free to do so by raising their rates, but have then been penalised by a loss of grant. The more they spend, the less grant they get. Local councils which have sought to maintain or improve services have therefore been put in the position where they have had to raise their rates, thereby incurring grant penalties, thereby necessitating a further rate increase.

When it introduced the block-grant system, the government assumed that local authorities would be reluctant to risk the wrath of their ratepayers by jacking up the rates to cover increased spending plus swingeing penalties. Such an assumption turned out to be ill-founded, however, and by 1983 some Labour-controlled authorities (including the GLC) had reached the point where they were no longer receiving any central grant at all and where central government penalties no longer carried any form of sanction.

It was in this context that the centre moved to control the fourth source of local government revenue – *the rates* themselves. The first step was to abolish the right of local councils to levy a supplementary rate mid-way through the financial year. This, however, had little effect since those councils which were intent on maintaining services simply fixed a higher rate each April than they would otherwise have done, thus anticipating block-grant penalties before they were actually applied. The government then toyed with the idea of enforcing local referenda on large rate rises, but this proposal was eventually dropped following considerable opposition from the local authority associations and from Tory back-benchers who were concerned about the constitutional implications of such a measure. At last, in 1983, the government settled on a scheme which came to be known as 'rate-capping'.

Of all the controls over local government which we have discussed in this section, rate-capping is the most significant and far-reaching. What it entails is the right of central government to limit by law any rate increase proposed by any local council. It thus represents a fundamental and unprecedented intrusion into the taxation powers of local councils, for under this system, local populations no longer have the right to vote for a political programme which aims to support council services at the cost of increasing rates.

The imminent demise of local government as a democratic and reasonably accountable system has been forecast many times before. Rate-capping makes such forecasts a reality, for it totally constrains a local council to follow the line being laid down at the centre by removing its one autonomous sphere of revenue. Effectively stripped of the power to raise taxes beyond a level determined by the centre, local authorities cease in any meaningful sense to function as systems of government and are reduced to the status of local outposts of the government in Westminster. Like the wicked queen in the story of Snow White, the centre has administered a poisoned apple to its one competitor and can now be reassured that it has no challengers. Unlike Snow White, however the local authorities are likely to find that the dose does indeed prove fatal.

The hidden agenda of central–local conflicts

Local government in Britain has today become a political battleground. Huge local authorities are to be found locking horns with central departments or being dragged through the courts. The basis of local government financing has been turned upside down, the metropolitan authorities are being legislated out of existence, councillors have been replaced by government commissioners and local democracy itself has cracked under the strain of a series of frontal assaults without parallel in modern times. The obvious question is why?

One factor, as we have already seen in our discussion of local government reorganisation, is *political*. Since 1979, Britain has been governed centrally by a Radical-Right Conservative Government which has deliberately abandoned the old post-war consensus on the welfare state and the mixed economy and which has set out to transform the major institutions of British society. In this context, the New Left of the Labour Party has seized upon local government as one arena in which a fight-back can be mobilised, and both sides have become preoccupied with fighting and if possible defeating each other. Indeed, the greatest single challenge to Tory governments since 1979 has come not from parliamentary opposition, nor even from the trade union movement, but from radical (and often middle-class) socialists who have won control of the town halls in the major conurbations and who have used their power base to challenge Thatcherism. Seen in this way, the abolition of the metropolitan counties just 12 years after they came into being, the establishment of new corporate agencies beyond the reach of elected local councils, and the financial crippling of local government are all part of the response by conservatism at the centre to socialist challenges at the periphery.

Yet there is more to all this than simply a clash between two radical and opposing movements, for underlying the battles between central and local government are two other factors.

The first of these is the state of the economy. As we saw in Chapters 8 and 9, the sustained crisis of the British economy has given rise to a strategy of public expenditure cut-backs in an attempt to reduce taxation on private companies and hence to restore profitability. These cuts have fallen mainly on consumption-oriented expenditure – e.g. spending on council housing, the health services, social services, education and so on. Despite the removal of many local government responsibilities since the 1930s, local councils are still today strategically involved in the provision of many of these services. It follows from this that the Treasury's concern to limit overall expenditure has depended to a large extent on the ability of the DoE to control the local authorities. The battle between central and local government in recent years has thus reflected the tension between private-sector profitability and welfare provision at a time of deep economic recession.

Having said this, however, it has also to be recognised that in recent years, it is not local government but central government which has failed to keep spending under control. It is true that during the late sixties and early to mid seventies, local council expenditure spiralled to a point in 1975/76 when it accounted for 30 per cent of total state spending and soaked up over 13 per cent of the country's Gross Domestic Product. Following the International Monetary Fund intervention of 1976 and the subsequent election of the Thatcher Government in 1979, however, it fell back in real terms. By 1981/82, local government's share of total state spending had dropped to under 25 per cent and the proportion of GDP going on local council spending had fallen to just over 10 per cent. Despite the barrage of government propaganda over this period suggesting that local councils show a wanton disregard for ratepayers' money, the continuing rise in public expenditure has mainly been a product of escalating central government spending, especially on law and order, defence and financing unemployment.

This leads us to consider the second underlying factor which has been involved in struggles between central government and local authorities, namely an ideological battle. The fact that the centre has continued to press home its attack on local council spending at a time when such spending has fallen quite dramatically suggests that the concern is less with how much is being spent than with what it is being spent on. What the Thatcher Government has really objected to is that radical local authorities have been engaged in a series of innovations which are not especially expensive but which do fundamentally challenge the ethos of a market system of provision. We have already seen one example of this with the GLC over its cheap fares policy, for the development of a successful cheap, or even free, public-transport system provides a visible challenge to an orthodoxy that holds that public subsidies are wasteful, that state bureaucracies are inefficient and that the only rational way of organising social affairs is by leaving everything to the operation of the free market. Similarly, the growth of new economic initiatives by some of the big Labour-controlled authorities such as London, Sheffield and the West Midlands – e.g. the establishment of Co-operative Development Agencies or of municipal enterprise boards – does much to undermine the fatalistic message of the government that there is 'no alternative' to its policy of allowing companies to go to the wall and unemployment to rise. Every time a firm is saved by the intervention of a local council's enterprise board, or a group of workers is supported in setting up a producer co-operative, the potentiality of a socialised system of production is raised in people's minds while a doubt is sown regarding the inevitability of the market solution.

Local government, then, has been used by the Left in an attempt to demonstrate that there is a viable alternative to the Thatcherite social-market strategy. Social planning at local level has in this way directly confronted privatisation and the support of the free market at the centre. As we saw in Chapter 10, central government has been engaged since 1979 on an ideological crusade designed to reassert traditional capitalistic values of individualism, privatism, and anti-statism. The activities of Radical Left local authorities threaten constantly to undermine this crusade. It is for this reason above all others that local government has continued to come under such bitter and sustained attack from the centre.

Conclusions

It is of course true that local authorities are not entirely the creatures of central government. Nevertheless, the relationship between the two levels of government has been changing very rapidly over the last few years such that the view of local government as little more than the local branch of the central state is becoming more rather than less appropriate as time goes by. It may well be, for example, that local authorities can be used to express the interests and aspirations of local working-class people, but this is of little account if the authorities themselves are then legislated out of existence as is now the case with the metropolitan counties. It may well be that the centre depends upon local councils for a minimal degree of co-operation, but this seems insignificant if it takes for itself the power to control their finances such that they have little choice whether or not to comply.

We have suggested earlier that local government occupies a potentially crucial place in the overall organisation of the state due to the fact that its scale of organisation makes it relatively accessible to ordinary people while its mode of organisation ensures some degree of democratic accountability. Today, however, the effectiveness of local government is at an all-time low. The system is still relatively accessible, but the loss of functions and autonomy means that there is less point in gaining access to it. The system is still relatively accountable, but the constraints on what councils can do are now such that there may be little point in voting for or pressurising local representatives who will be prevented from implementing their policies and programmes. We are free to vote in any local council we want, but our choice is unlikely to make much difference to what that council actually does. Local democracy in Britain has in this sense all but disappeared. Precisely because it has in the past represented (to some extent) a democratic enclave within the state system, and has thus proved a constant irritant to those in positions of power elsewhere in the system, local government has been neutered. The emaciation, restriction and, ultimately, abolition of troublesome local councils has been nothing less than a deliberate attempt to close up the one democratic chink in the state's armour, the Achilles heel of the state apparatus.

THE REGIONAL LEVEL

The available literature on the regional level of the state in Britain (i.e. those institutions which operate at an intermediate point between local and national administration) is remarkable for its paucity. The main reason is that there is no regional level of elected government. Unlike federal political systems such as those in the USA, West Germany or Australia, the United Kingdom state has developed in such a way that there are but two tiers of elected government, and there is in this country no equivalent to the state Parliaments and Legislatures which figure so prominently in most Federal systems. To the extent that political commentators and academics have discussed the intermediate level of the state at all, they have tended to limit their observations to this contrast between Unitary and Federal systems. In consequence, they have tended to overlook the fact that there is already an extensive system of regional state administration in Britain. Regional state institutions do exist and are powerful, yet few people seem to be aware of, or interested in, their existence. In this sense, the regional level of the state forms part of the 'secret state' discussed in Chapter 5, for not only is it non-elected, but precious little is known about it.

The growth of regional state institutions

The development of a regional level of the state dates from the 1930s. It is no coincidence that regional agencies should have begun to grow at the same time as local councils began to lose their powers, for many of the responsibilities which were taken out of local hands were passed over to newly-created regional offices. When local government lost control of trunk roads in 1936, for example, the Ministry of Transport set up a new regional organisation of offices to administer them. When gas and electricity were nationalised after the Second World War, new regional boards were appointed to run them. When hospitals were taken out of municipal hands in 1948, they were given to newly created Regional Hospital Boards, and the removal of water services from local government at the time of reorganisation in 1974 led the government to establish Regional Water Authorities to take them over. One major factor in the growth of regional state institutions has therefore been the attack on democratic local government.

A second factor was the onset of the Great depression in the inter-war years, for this highlighted the plight of the traditional heavy industrial regions of Scotland, south Wales and the north-east of England, and led the government to take its first reluctant steps towards a regional planning policy. Under the Special Areas (Development and Improvement) Act, 1934, two Regional Commissioners were appointed with the task of stimulating economic growth in four designated 'special areas', thus marking the beginning of a long and largely unsuccessful history of governmental support for the declining regions involving the creation of various different types of regional agencies.

A third factor in the growth of the regional state from the 1930s onwards was the government's growing concern at that time with threats to social order from within, and to national security from without. As part of its meticulous preparations for the general strike, the government in 1925 divided England and Wales into ten regions and appointed a Civil Commissioner to each whose job it was to maintain communications, food supplies, power and public health services in the event of a breakdown following strike action or civil unrest. Similarly, though with rather less perspicacity, the government responded to the external threat of war in 1938 by appointing ten Regional Commissioners for civil defence who remained in office, much to the chagrin of local authorities, until the end of hostilities in 1945.

During the war, most government departments set up regional offices based on the 1938 civil defence regional boundaries so as to establish a devolved system of administration which could survive if the centre came under attack. These offices were then co-ordinated by ten Area Boards, set up by the ministry of Supply in 1940, and consisting of the heads of the various government offices in the region together with three employers' and three trade union representatives. At the end of the war, these Area Boards were replaced by similarly constituted Regional Boards for Industry under the auspices of the Board of Trade. Like the wartime Area Boards, the Regional Boards included representatives of government, industry and organised labour in their memberships, thus perpetuating a system of functional representation which has remained a characteristic of many regional state institutions to this day.

By 1945, then, there was already a well-established regional framework of state administration. Most government departments in Whitehall had set up regional offices in the provinces, there was a rudimentary system of regional aid and planning, and economic policy was being mediated through the new Regional Boards for Industry. The post-war Labour Government then strengthened the regional level by adopting a statutory regional structure for the new public-sector industries and services such as the railways, gas and electricity, and the health service, and by developing eleven Regional Physical Planning Committees as a result of the Town and Country Planning Act, 1947. A regional strategy was thus seen as fundamental to the post-war reconstruction programme.

In the years that followed, however, much of this regional machinery fell into disuse, largely because the Conservative Governments of the 1950s set about deregulating the battery of controls which had grown up during the war and its immediate aftermath and saw little need for special regional policies at a time of relatively full employment. Between 1953 and 1958, most government departments closed down or cut back their regional offices and many of the special regional agencies which had been set up by the Atlee Government were wound up.

The Regional Boards for Industry did survive, however, and in the early 1960s, the government once again began to recognise the need to do something about the declining industrial regions as the post-war boom began to peter out. The National Economic Development Council, which was established in 1962 (see Chapter 8), pressed for regional development as a major objective of any national growth strategy, and in 1965, when the new Labour Government published its National Plan and set up the Department of Economic Affairs, eleven economic planning regions were created (eight in England plus one each for Scotland, Wales and Northern Ireland) as the means for ensuring a geographically balanced and co-ordinated national economic strategy.

The establishment of these economic planning regions is as near as the United Kingdom has ever come to developing a regional system of government. Each region had its own Economic Planning Board, consisting of civil servants drawn from different regional offices of government whose job was to advise the Regional Economic Planning Councils consisting of members recruited from employers, trade unionists, local government councillors and officers and academics living and working in each region. The Planning Boards were often referred to as 'regional Whitehalls' and the Planning Councils as 'regional cabinets', but the latter designation was somewhat misleading given that the council members were not directly elected but were appointed by central government. The Planning Councils, in other words, were not democratic bodies but were corporatist agencies organised in much the same way (though on a grander scale) as the Regional Boards for Industry which they replaced. Seen in this way, they served as forums within which representatives of government, capital and labour could come together undisturbed by the glare of electoral politics.

This new system of regional economic planning boards and councils was to survive for 14 years, but its political significance and effectiveness lasted for barely more than two. In 1966 the National Plan was abandoned, thereby leaving the boards and councils in the curious position of having to plan their regional economies in the absence of any national economic strategy. They pressed on with drawing up regional plans in the hope that local authorities in their regions would pay some attention to them, but this was always a vain hope given that most local councils were suspicious of and hostile to the entire regional planning machinery. The plight of the regional boards and councils was effectively sealed in 1969 when the Department of Economic Affairs was itself closed down, for this virtually ended their influence in Whitehall as well. They struggled on through the 1970s, attempting to influence both local authorities and central government departments but making little headway with either, until in 1979, the newly elected Thatcher Government abolished the Planning Councils and scaled down the Planning Boards into 'Interdepartmental Regional Boards' of which little has been heard ever since.

The regional planning machinery has not entirely disappeared – agencies such as the Welsh Development Agency and the Highlands and Islands Development Board have survived and continue to have some effect in attracting new industrial investment into their areas. However, the demise of the economic planning boards and councils means that today regional state institutions are less significant in economic planning than in the organisation of specific services. Of particular importance here are the health and water services, both of which were reorganised when the local government system was reformed in 1974 and both of which are now the responsibility of particular regional authorities.

Regional Health and Water Authorities

The fourteen Regional Health Authorities (RHAs) and ten Regional

Water Authorities (RWAs) which came into being in April, 1974 are probably the most significant state institutions currently operating at the regional level. They are significant both in terms of their size and their political autonomy.

As regards their size, the water authorities control the second-largest industry in the country with 80 000 employees and well over £3000 million worth of capital assets (most of them under the ground in the form of a maze of sewer and water pipes) at 1979 prices. The health authorities employ, directly or indirectly, around 1 million people (over 4 per cent of the country's total workforce) and account for over 10 per cent of total public expenditure. Figures like these underline the importance of the regional level of the state in the contemporary period.

The RHAs and RWAs are also important for their autonomy. Unlike the regional boards of the nationalised industries or the regional offices of central government departments such as the Department of Industry or the Department of the Environment, these authorities enjoy a major responsibility for making policy and for allocating resources in the areas they administer. They are much more than merely provincial outposts of central government or public corporations, for as their name implies, they are authorities at the regional level (just as local councils are authorities at the local level). The difference between them and local authorities, however, is that the latter are elected whereas the people who run the RHAs and RWAs are appointed.

Health. Ever since it was set up in 1948, the National Health Service has consisted of three elements; the hospital sector, general practice and community health care. Until 1974, these were run by different agencies; the hospitals by Regional Hospital Boards and Hospital Management Committees, general practice by Executive Councils, and community services by local authorities. The 1974 reorganisation brought all three under the one umbrella of the new RHAs in an attempt to improve 'efficiency' and increase co-ordination between the various branches of health care.

What actually came to be established was a three-tier system with fourteen RHAs at the top and accountable to the central Department of Health and Social Security, ninety Area Health Authorities below them, and over two-hundred District Management Teams at the bottom. The details of how this triple-tier system was meant to work need not concern us, partly because the blueprint for Health Service planning was never fully implemented, and partly because the system was overhauled again in 1982 when the middle 'Area' level was abolished and the District Management Teams became District Health Authorities answerable directly to the Regional Authority. The main point to note about the system as a whole is that it was (and since 1982 has continued to be) informed from top to bottom by the same managerial ethos which lay behind the 1974 local government reorganisation.

Where local government had the Bains report, the reorganised National Health Service had what came to be known as the 'Grey Book' which advised the new RHAs on how they should operate. Like Bains, the Grey Book called for the establishment at each level of corporate management teams of officers who were expected to reach a consensus on all major policy decisions. They were to work closely with appointed members of the Regional and Area (after 1982, District) Authorities who were similarly expected to achieve a consensus. In other words, the emphasis right from the start was on the achievement of managerial efficiency by officers and members alike. The whole process of decision-making was seen as apolitical, the task being simply to arrive at the technically defined 'best' solution to problems within overall guidelines laid down by the centre.

How then has this system operated in practice? We may consider this by tracing the relation between the RHAs and the three major sets of interests with which they interact – central government, the medical professions, and the consumers of health services.

When the system came into operation in 1974, it was hoped that RHAs would develop plans by liaising upwards, with the DHSS, and downwards, with their Area and District bodies. In particular, central government was keen to redress the imbalance which had been inherent in the NHS ever since 1948 between different parts of the country (the north generally suffering a lower level of service than the south) and between different sectors of the service (hospitals being disproportionately funded relative to the so-called 'Cinderella services' such as care for the elderly). Such a laudable objective was blown off course right from the start, however, due partly to resistance from the more prosperous regions and from the powerful hospital consultants, and partly to the deteriorating economic situation which meant that any reallocation of resources would have had to occur without any additional funds being made available. The result was that the grandiose planning system was effectively stillborn, and when the Thatcher Government won office in 1979, it abandoned planning in favour of a system of cash limits similar to that applied to local authorities. Today, in other words, the RHAs enjoy considerable autonomy to determine their own priorities within the financial limits imposed by the centre, and the centre's concern to achieve a more equitable distribution of resources has receded. The main priority of central government has increasingly been to cut health expenditure rather than to direct it, and in this it has been fairly successful. In 1983, for example, the newly re-elected Thatcher Government announced Health Service cuts which it was able to impose on Regional and District Authorities with little difficulty, for unlike cuts affecting local councils, there was no elected body in a position to resist them.

Within the financial limits set by the centre, then, the RHAs can determine how to spend the money allocated to them. The major influence over such decisions is undoubtedly that of the medical profession.

The doctors are able to control the system in three ways. First, they enjoy strong and effective representation within it through the Medical Advisory Committees which are consulted at both regional and district level. Second, the managers of the system at each level are themselves often doctors (i.e. doctors on the advisory committees are often to be found advising doctors on the management teams!). And third, decisions at all levels from the DHSS downwards are informed by a taken-for-granted assumption that health care is about curing patients of disease rather than preventing people from becoming ill or maimed in the first place, and this assumption is entirely consistent with the interests of hospital consultants and family practitioners who make their livelihoods by doing operations, treating the sick, dispensing prescriptions and so on.

The power of the medical profession is in theory counter-balanced by the influence of consumers' representatives. The consumer voice within the NHS since 1974 has, however, been muted, mainly because the vast technobureaucracy of health service management has no place in it for elected members.

The consumer interest is ostensibly organised in three ways. First, through lay members (including a minority of local authority nominees) appointed at each level. Their role, however, is very limited, partly because they are appointed not as representatives but as managers, partly because they are part-time amateurs up against full-time 'experts' in the medical profession, and partly because they are by no stretch of the imagination representative of the population as a whole (e.g. of 210 appointments made to the new RHAs in 1974, 56 were drawn from the medical profession, 79 were company directors, managers or professional and business people, 12 were trade unionists and just 3 were manual workers). Second, there is an indirect elected local authority input via Joint Consultative Committees, but this mode of influence has always been weak and was made weaker still by the 1982 changes which abolished the Area Health Authorities whose boundaries were coterminous with those of local authority social services departments, thus leaving local councils to make such arrangements as they could with the various District Authorities operating in their area. Third, each district has its own Community Health Council which is meant to function as a consumer 'watchdog'. However, like other consumer councils such as those in the nationalised industries, the Councils are pathetically weak, they have no executive powers and most people are not even aware of their existence. The Thatcher Government would ideally like to abolish the Councils altogether, although so far it has limited itself to cutting their budgets and reducing their size.

The organisation of the Health Service is, therefore, remarkably immune to popular pressure or control. Within cash limits imposed by the centre, the RHAs can effectively determine their own health priorities without having to worry too much about consumer opinion, and this effectively lays them open to the sustained influence of the medical profession in general and the hospital consultants in particular. As we saw in Chapter 9 in our discussion of the welfare services as a whole, policy-making in the welfare state is peculiarly susceptible to the influence of professional groups, and this tendency is especially marked in health care where elected local control has been abolished and where decision-making is concentrated in regional structures which are inaccessible and non-accountable to the populations they administer.

Water. As in the health services, the 1974 reorganisation of the water industry brought together various different but related functions which had previously been the responsibility of different agencies. The supply of water itself had previously been undertaken by local councils (singly or jointly) and by various water companies whose activities were (and still are) closely controlled by statute. Provision of sewers and treatment of sewage was also a local council responsibility, although the system here was much more fragmented with nearly 1400 different authorities (compared with just 187 water undertakings) still operating at the time of reorganisation. Finally, responsibility for rivers and land drainage had been vested in twenty-nine River Authorities which were autonomous of local councils but which included a majority of local authority nominees in their memberships. Various other bodies – e.g. the British Waterways Board which runs the canal system – remained outside of the 1974 reorganisation, but with just one or two exceptions, the new RWAs took over full responsibility for the management of water from the sea to the tap and back again.

Just as local government had its Bains and the NHS its Grey Book, so the new RWAs had the Ogden report. Ogden's recommendations were strikingly familiar – the establishment of corporate management teams of officers at both regional and divisional level to 'advise' the appointed members of the RWAs who were themselves cast in a managerial role and expected to reach a consensus on all major policy decisions. The emphasis throughout was on technical efficiency, and the result was to enhance the power of the water engineers who were freed from the political control of local councils and who enjoyed considerable professional autonomy under the new system.

As in our discussion on the new health authorities, we may consider the way in which the RWAs have used this autonomy by tracing their relations with central government, local councils and those who consume their services.

The RWAs are accountable upwards to two different departments – the DoE (or in the case of the Welsh Water Authority, the Welsh Office) and the Ministry of Agriculture, Fisheries and Food (MAFF). The reasons for this divided central control lie in the influence of the farming and landowning lobby, which campaigned successfully in the early 1970s to retain land drainage functions as part of MAFF's responsibilities, thereby ensuring for themselves a continuing friendly ear in Whitehall.

Leaving the organisation of land drainage on one side for a moment, it is clear that the centre exercises little direct control over the RWAs. Like the RHAs, they are subject to central government cash limits on new capital spending, but unlike the RHAs, they are totally self-financing and do not depend upon the centre for any of their revenue. Financially, therefore the RWAs appear stronger even than elected local councils. Like local authorities, they enjoy the right to levy rates, but unlike local councils, they are not subject to central government rate-capping, they do not depend on central government grants, and they are totally immune to electoral control or influence. They enjoy absolute discretion on fixing their charges and they represent an extraordinary example within the state system of taxation without representation.

The total lack of representation dates from 1983. In the 9 years before that, local authorities had the right to nominate a minority of water authority members, but even this very limited and indirect form of popular control was ended by the Water Act, 1983, which reduced the size of RWA memberships to between nine and fifteen, all of whom are appointed by central government.

The RWAs and local authorities do liaise informally at member and officer level, but local council influence tends to be weak. The main issue of concern to local councils in their dealings with water authorities is future industrial and housing development, for plans to develop a new site cannot go ahead unless the RWA agrees to lay down water mains and sewers. Before 1983, local councils could at least provide their own sewers (even though they no longer treated the effluent that passed through them), but this power finally disappeared in the Water Act, 1983, leaving them totally dependent upon the future investment decisions of the Water Authority on which they no longer enjoy any right of representation. Precisely because the RWAs are dominated by water engineers who are wedded to an ethos of technical efficiency and cost-effectiveness, they have tended to reject local authority proposals for what they see as 'speculative developments' – e.g. proposals by left-wing councils to develop new factory estates in an attempt to attract new employers into their areas. Put another way, the RWAs are generally conservative institutions which have acted as a brake on the aspirations of various 'progressive' local councils.

With the final abolition of local authority representation on the RWAs in 1983, consumer representation has passed to newly established 'Consumer Consultative Committees'. The arrangements for these committees vary between different authorities, but most are organised at divisional (i.e. county) level and include representatives from local authorities and from organisations such as the Confederation of British Industry, and National Farmers Union, Chambers of Commerce, the tourist industry and various recreational groups. Like the Community

Health Councils in the health services, these bodies have no executive power and appear to all intents and purposes to be an irrelevance in terms of policy formation.

Some groups, however, have managed to achieve considerable influence within the RWAs, and foremost among these are farmers and landowners. Their principal concern is with agricultural land drainage, which alone among all RWA functions is controlled at the centre by the MAFF. Not only do the National Farmers Union and Country Landowners Association enjoy close consultative links with MAFF, but they have also established a notable degree of hegemony over the Regional Land Drainage Committees (which operate virtually independently of the RWA of which they are formally a part) which are dominated by farmers and landowners nominated by county councils and by MAFF, and which enjoy the right to levy rates, borrow money and (again uniquely in the reorganised water industry) receive grants from central government. Farmers also dominate the local Land Drainage Committees while their exclusive control over Internal Drainage Boards (through which they are able to claim public money to help finance their own field drainage with virtually no check on them from any outside body) is little short of scandalous.

The picture which emerges, therefore, is in most respects similar to that of Regional Health Authorities only more so! In both cases, local authority representation has been weakened, but in the water industry it has now disappeared altogether. In both cases, consumer representation is little more than token, but in the water industry key private-sector interests have established exclusive modes of access and influence. In both cases, central control is mainly limited to the imposition of limits on spending, but in the water industry there is the right to levy taxes, thus establishing effective financial autonomy. And in both cases, a bureaucratic system has evolved in which service professionals (the hospital consultants and water engineers respectively) have been able to secure their own interests and to impose their own technocratic ideologies in the vacuum left by the erosion of local political control.

Conclusions

There is today a strong and growing regional level of the state, and there is every likelihood that it will continue to grow in the future. The various regional agencies are organised in different ways, are responsible for different kinds of services, and often do not even share common territorial boundaries. This makes it difficult to discern a distinct or cohesive regional stratum and generalisation appears hazardous. Nevertheless, it is possible to draw three broad conclusions about the significance of regional institutions in the United Kingdom state system.

1   We are dealing in every case with non-elected bodies. In none of these

cases is it possible for those who consume (and ultimately pay for) the product or service to elect or dismiss those who are responsible for providing it. Even where, as in the case of the water authorities, these agencies levy their own taxes, there is no electoral check other than that most tenuous and indirect channel of accountability which runs from the agency to a central department to a minister to Parliament and thence to the electorate as a whole.

2   These are political agencies charged with making politically crucial and contentious decisions. In most cases they attempt to disguise this political function through the assiduous cultivation of a technocratic image, but this cannot obscure the fact that they decide how millions of pounds will be spent and that these decisions inevitably reflect particular values which perforce go unchallenged in any open political argument or debate. In the absence of any effective democratic control, they tend to make their decisions according to the influence enjoyed by professional interests within them and/or powerful private sector interests outside them.

3   Regional institutions are less likely and less able to confront central government than are elected local authorities. While the degree of central control over regional bodies varies between different agencies, all of them are immediately susceptible to central government's concern to limit public expenditure. Even the health and water authorities, which are probably the most autonomous of all regional bodies, have easily been controlled in their spending by the centre. One has only to imagine how the 1983 health cuts would have been resisted had health services still been in the hands of local councils to see the significance of the growth of the regional level in a context of economic recession and cuts in consumption provision by the state.

The importance of this third point cannot be overemphasised, for it indicates why regional agencies now appear so attractive to central government. Some degree of decentralisation of responsibility is necessary in most areas of public policy-making in order to take account of the varying circumstances of different areas and to monitor the implementation of central policies on the ground. Decentralization, however, can be dangerous since it opens up the possibility of resistance from below. The solution it seems, lies in the further extension of non-elected peripheral agencies which can be kept out of the reach of potentially troublesome opponents. Regional agencies such as those discussed in this chapter fit the bill perfectly.

THE NATIONAL LEVEL

In the previous section, we took 'regionalism' to refer simply to the existence of an intermediate level of the state. The essence of such a definition is that regional institutions, or indeed regional political movements and identities, form part of a larger territorial unity to which they are both loyal and subordinate.

When we consider the organisation of the United Kingdom state, however, it is immediately apparent that it encompasses certain territorial units which, while occupying an intermediate position between central and local agencies, are more than merely 'regional'. England, Scotland, Wales and Northern Ireland are four separate 'nations' within a single-state system, and in different ways they retain a certain distinctiveness historically, culturally, legally and politically. Sometimes this distinctiveness has become blurred (e.g. in the tendency among many English people to equate 'England' with 'Britain' and 'the British Isles') but at others it has formed the focus for political struggles based on sentiments of nationhood and the assertion of a national interest opposed to that of the unitary United Kingdom state. Such nationalist movements derive their strength from a shared sentiment which goes beyond anything associated with mere regionalism, and since the 1960s, they have represented a real threat to the continuing integrity of the United Kingdom.

In order to understand the significance of nationalism within the contemporary United Kingdom state, it is therefore important to clarify the distinction between 'state', 'nation' and 'region'. A region is nothing more than a geographical sub-division of a larger territorial unit. A nation, by contrast, is a sociological entity which is territorially bounded and whose members share in common certain sentiments by which they recognise in each other a common identity. A state, which may or may not be based on one nation, is a political unit which reserves for itself the right to use force within a given territory. It is in this sense that the United Kingdom consists of one state, four nations and an indefinite number of regions.

The growth of the union

The nation which became England has its roots in the Roman conquest which subjugated England itself but failed to take control of the rest of the British isles, contenting itself with driving the Celts out of the area it controlled. By the time of the Norman invasion, the south-eastern core around London had fused into a single kingdom which was gradually extended, over the next 500 years, to encompass first Wessex, East Anglia and the Midlands, and later Cornwall and the North of England.

Wales came under English domination in 1277 when the English Crown claimed half the land in that country, leaving the other half to powerful lords who ruled (as in the North of England at that time) as semi-sovereign magnates. Before then, Wales had been controlled by various warring chiefs, and it is important to emphasise that even before the English arrived, there had never been a Welsh state as such.

Wales was not made subject to English parliamentary laws until 1536 when it was formally absorbed into the English state following fears of possible foreign invasion along the Welsh coastline. Under acts of 1536 and 1542, Wales was granted representation at the Westminster Parliament, was made subject to English law, and had the Anglican Church imposed upon it as the established church (disestablishment did not come until 1920).

Unlike Wales, Scotland did develop as an independent state before it unified with England in 1707, although the effective power of the Scottish Crown in the Highlands was always limited. Furthermore, union with England came not as a result of conquest and annexation, as in Wales, but as a result of negotiation and treaty between two sovereign states. The reasons for this agreement were partly economic (in that powerful Scottish interests felt that they could do better as a junior partner in an emerging imperial state south of the border) and partly constitutional (in that both countries had shared the same monarch since 1603, and with the establishment of a constitutional monarchy in England following the restoration of 1689, the king became accountable to the London Parliament thus necessitating some sort of accommodation on the part of Edinburgh).

While the Act of Union, 1707, put an end to the separate Scottish state, it recognised and perpetuated the existence of a separate Scottish nation. The Scots, for example, were never subjected to the imposition of an established Anglican Church in the way that the Welsh had been, for the act safeguarded the Presbyterian kirk for all time. Similarly, Scotland retained its own courts and its own distinctive legal system which remains in force to this day.

The fourth nation to enter the union was Ireland. Ireland, of course, was physically separated from the other three countries by the sea. It was also separated by a religious gulf, for while England, Scotland and Wales were predominantly Protestant countries (albeit with different denominations – Anglicanism, Presbyterianism and Nonconformism), Ireland was indigenously Roman Catholic.

Some English settlement in Ireland had begun as early as the twelfth century but the major migration took place when the country was annexed by Elizabeth I. The Catholic lords, especially in the northern province of Ulster, lost their lands and fled to France, and a plantation policy was put into effect whereby estates were handed over to English and Scottish Protestant landowners. In 1641, Irish Catholics rebelled against the immigrant landlords and set in motion a series of bloody events which culminated in the arrival of Cromwell's army in 1649 which ruthlessly quashed Catholic peasant resistance. By 1690, when William of Orange defeated the deposed Catholic king, James II, at the Battle of the Boyne, thereby securing Protestantism in both Ireland and Britain, nearly 80 per cent of all Irish land was owned by English and Scottish migrants.

Following the military victory of 1690, a Parliament was established in Dublin from which all Roman Catholics were excluded. This Parliament ran Ireland on behalf of the Protestant landowners until 1800, but it came under increasing pressure as a result of the enfranchisement of Catholics in 1793 and the French-backed rebellion of 1798. It was as a result of this pressure that Anglo-Scottish interests in Dublin hurriedly agreed an Act of Union with Britain in 1800 which was to hold for the next 120 years.

Throughout the nineteenth century and into the twentieth, the union brought considerable economic benefits for lowland Scotland, South Wales and the Protestant-dominated north-eastern counties of Ireland, for all three areas developed large-scale industries and reaped the harvest of the empire. The Scottish Highlands (where people were driven from their crofts), North and Central Wales (where the population dwindled as labour was attracted to the South and the English Midlands) and the great bulk of Ireland (where, what remained effectively a backward peasantry, was left to scrape a living from the soil and where a million died in the potato famine of the 1840s) were, however, left behind in this wave of industrial expansion, and all three areas experienced dramatic depopulation in this period.

It was in Ireland that popular resistance developed in the face of this systematic exploitation, for it was in that country alone that effective nationalist aspiration had been kept alive. A history of forcible sequestration of land, bloody coercion of people, religious persecution of the majority and extreme rural deprivation resulted in a nationalist challenge being mounted on the basis of the popular religion – Catholicism. In other words, because the domination of the Irish had been organised culturally (through exclusion of Catholics) as well as economically, the reaction was organised in these terms as well. Through the nineteenth century, Irish nationalism thus became intertwined with Catholicism, just as in the north-east, loyalty to the union with Britain became the hallmark of Protestantism.

The rising tide of Irish resistance to continuing British domination forced itself onto the agenda of parliamentary politics in 1885 when, following the extension of the franchise to all adult males, eighty-five Irish members were returned to the Westminster Parliament on a 'home rule' ticket. The Liberal Prime Minister, Gladstone, proved willing to cede a limited degree of Irish home rule, but neither Parliament nor the Protestants in the north of Ireland agreed with him. The Liberal Party split on the issue and the bill was thrown out by the Commons.

A second Home Rule bill was introduced in 1893 but, having passed through the Commons, was defeated in the Lords. In 1912 a third attempt was made, and this eventually became law in 1914. In the north of Ireland, the Protestants prepared for an armed struggle against what they saw as the inevitability of eventual Irish independence, but civil war was averted by the outbreak of the First World War which resulted in the suspension of the Home Rule Act. In the north, the Protestants breathed again, but elsewhere in Ireland, the nationalists were furious at seeing power snatched from their grasp. In 1916, Sinn Fein organised an uprising in Dublin which was soon quelled and which led to the execution of fifteen of the ringleaders. Anti-British sentiment was fanned by the executions, and in the post-war general election, Sinn Fein candidates swept the board in most Catholic constituencies and proceeded to boycott Westminster by setting up their own assembly in Dublin. This, together with attacks on the police and the infamous 'black and tans' who were sent in to Ireland as reinforcements, increased the pressure on the British Government to grant some form of Irish independence.

The government responded with the Government of Ireland Act, 1920. This set up separate Parliaments in Dublin, to administer twenty-six counties, and in Belfast, to administer the remaining six where Protestants were in the majority. This partition was readily accepted in the north where the establishment of a devolved assembly in Stormont Castle was seen as a way of guaranteeing a continuing link with Britain and independence from the south, but was rejected by Sinn Fein which demanded dominion status for Ireland within the British Commonwealth. Following an escalation of political violence, this demand was partially granted in 1922 with the establishment of the Irish Free State in the south, and Eire's secession was finally completed in 1949 when it left the Commonwealth and became an independent republic. Meanwhile, the six counties in the north continued to be administered under the provisions of the 1920 Act which granted considerable powers to the Stormont assembly, reserving foreign affairs, external trade and responsibility for the armed forces for determination by Westminster. From 1921 until 1972, the new nation of Northern Ireland was therefore run to all intents and purposes like a Federal province, thereby enabling the Protestant majority to perpetuate a sectarian hegemony over the Catholics who still represented one-third of its population and who still harboured nationalist and republican aspirations.

The fracturing of the United Kingdom in Ireland had little impact on the union in Great Britain. Although demands for Irish home rule over the previous 40 years had stirred nationalist consciousness in Scotland (no less than thirteen Scottish devolution bills were presented to Parliament between 1885 and 1914), this had little lasting significance beyond the establishment of the Scottish Office in 1885 and the appointment within the cabinet of a Secretary of State for Scotland from 1926 onwards. As for Wales, the nationalist party, Plaid Cymru, was formed in 1925 more in an attempt to salvage the Welsh language (which was by then spoken by less than one-quarter of the population) than as a genuinely secessionist movement. As the United Kingdom emerged into the long boom of the post-war years, so the union seemed as, if not more, secure as it had ever been. Even the Irish question seemed to have been settled if not resolved. As with so many aspects of British politics, it was only with the end of the boom in the 1960s that old problems began once again to reappear.

The re-emergence of nationalism: Scotland and Wales

We have already seen that Scotland and Wales, though both peripheral and long-neglected nations within the United Kingdom, are very different countries with very different histories. It is misleading to suggest (as one influential thesis has it) that both have been subject to a process of 'internal colonialism' in which their distinctive Celtic cultures have been ravaged by English imperialism, for this not only neglects the fact that Celtic culture in Scotland has for many centuries effectively been limited to the Highlands (the Gaelic language, for example, was virtually absent in the lowland areas from the end of the Middle Ages), but it also exaggerates the eclipse of Scottish nationhood. We are not referring here to 'tartanism' as revealed in the aggressively male chauvinism unleashed each year in football matches against the 'auld enemy', but to the survival and assertion of a distinctively Scottish set of national institutions such as the autonomous legal system, the separate educational system, the Scottish Presbyterian church and so on, all of which remains from the days of statehood before the Act of Union. Scotland, in other words, is an 'historic nation' in a way that Wales never was.

This, together with the crucial discovery of North Sea oil in the 1960s and the investment and development by multinational companies which followed, meant that the resurgence of nationalism in Scotland took a very different form than in Wales. Welsh nationalism had no institutional structure of nationhood on which to build; it was born of a desperation on the part of some of the Welsh intellectuals who saw an old culture disappearing. This was the culture of the Welsh language, the chapel and the rural way of life based on the land, and the movement which grew up to defend it was essentially backward-looking. Plaid Cymru has never succeeded in winning and holding the allegiance of the industrial English-speaking population whose radicalism has always been channelled through the mainstream parties (first the Liberals, then the Labour Party), for it has little basis other than cultural nostalgia.

Scottish nationalism, by contrast, did not have to create and foster a cultural nationhood, for it was already there. The problem faced by the Scottish National Party was rather how to wean Scottish voters away from two-and-a-half centuries of economic dependence on England and to convince them that Scottish independence would actually benefit them. This task was facilitated by the discovery of oil and by the all too realistic fear that the revenues would be dissipated in propping up the English economy rather than being used for new investment to replace Scotland's declining traditional industrial base. It was not, however, the oil *per se* which stimulated the resurgence of nationalism in Scotland from the mid-1960s, but rather the clear evidence that the British economy was failing.

In both Wales and Scotland, it seems clear that nationalism was fostered by the end of the long post-war boom. Industry in both countries was hit earlier and harder than in most of England, and this was reflected in the growth of the nationalist vote at by-elections during the 1964–70 Labour Government's terms of office. The Labour Party had never been keen on devolution of power (although its opposition to loosening the union has never been as resolute as that of the Conservatives), but sheer pragmatism suggested that some token response was necessary if electoral support in the party's traditional heartlands was not to ebb away. Only twice in its history (in 1945 and 1966) has the Labour Party ever managed to win a majority of English seats in Parliament, and the growing nationalist challenge in Scotland and Wales was in this sense more of a threat to it than to the tories.

The answer to the problem was sought in establishing a Royal Commission on the constitution in 1969 under the chairmanship of Lord Kilbrandon. This eventually reported 4 years later. The Commission was unanimous in rejecting both national independence and federation, but its members split three ways over devolution. Some wanted to restrict any change to the establishment of a Scottish assembly; some wanted to include Wales; and some wanted to extend decentralization to England as well by setting up elected regional assemblies. The Heath Government ignored all of them.

In the February 1974 General Election, the Scottish National Party (SNP) won seven seats with 22 per cent of the Scottish vote, and together with Plaid Cymru and the Liberals (who have remained advocates of devolution since Gladstone's time) held the balance of power in Parliament. Eight months later, the SNP increased its vote to 30 per cent and eleven seats, making it the second largest party in Scotland (Plaid Cymru's vote over this period stayed relatively constant at around 10 per cent). After issuing three White Papers in two years, the Labour Government eventually brought forward a devolution bill in 1976 which was defeated by an alliance of Conservatives and Labour rebels. The government then produced separate bills for Scotland and Wales, and in order to win a parliamentary majority, agreed to a provision that each should be subjected to a referendum in which at least 40 per cent of the total electorate in the two countries would have to vote for devolution in order for the acts to be ratified. In the event, 52 per cent of those voting in Scotland voted for the proposed Scottish assembly, but this only amounted to 33 per cent of the total electorate (in Wales the respective figures were just 20 per cent and 12 per cent). The SNP Members of Parliament demanded that the Scottish Act be implemented, but the government refused and was then defeated on a vote of confidence, thereby opening the way for the election of the new Thatcher government.

The events of 1979 marked the end of a unique period in British politics. Twenty years earlier, nobody would have thought it possible that a government would fall over the issue of the union, for the union simply was not an issue. Through the 1960s and 1970s, however, it became an issue until eventually it dominated the political agenda. With the set-back of the referenda results and the electoral reverse which followed (Plaid Cymru and the SNP won just two seats each in the new Parliament), the nationalist cause in Scotland and Wales has once again faded, and there is little prospect of any progress being made under a strongly unionist Conservative Government at Westminster. Nevertheless, the economic problems which arguably triggered the revival of nationalism show no sign of abating, and in Scotland at least, the economic advantages of the union are becoming ever less apparent. The nationalist advance has been repelled for the moment, but it would be foolhardy to believe that it has been overcome.

The re-emergence of the Irish question

The people of Scotland and Wales have never known devolved government within the United Kingdom context. The people of Northern Ireland, by contrast, have experienced it for 50 years following the establishment of the province. It was the way this power was used which eventually led to the present 'troubles' which date from the late 1960s.

The republic in the south has never formally renounced its traditional claim to sovereignty over the whole of Ireland, and the IRA remained in existence after 1922 with units both north and south of the border with the long-term aim of bringing this about. However, the origins of the present troubles lay not in any struggle for Irish unification but in the demands of the Catholic population in the north for better treatment within the existing constitutional arrangements.

Ever since the settlement of 1920–22, the Protestants in the north had used their majority position to continue the 300-year tradition of excluding Catholics from those civil and political rights which are taken for granted elsewhere in the Kingdom. This was achieved by abolishing proportional representation in 1929 and by retaining a property qualification in elections which disenfranchised one-quarter of the population, most of whom were Catholics. Most effectively of all, however, it was achieved by gerrymandering electoral boundaries. In the south-western county of Fermanagh, for example, county council ward boundaries were drawn in such a way that a roughly 50 per cent Catholic population was able to win just one-third of the seats, while in the city known to Protestants as Londonderry and to Catholics as Derry, 14 000 Catholics and 9000 Protestants were represented on the borough council by eighteen members, twelve of whom represented Protestant-dominated wards!

This gerrymandering was crucial in perpetuating discrimination in public-sector employment (in Fermanagh, for example, 332 out of 370 council employees were Protestant) and in housing (Protestant councils allocating the worst houses to Catholics, building more houses for

Protestants, and refusing to admit Catholic families to housing located in traditionally Protestant areas). This discrimination was often openly acknowledged and defended on the grounds that Catholics owed alliegance to the Papist state in the south and were therefore enemies of the state in the north, and under the 1920 and 1949 acts, there was little that the Westminster Parliament could apparently do about it.

In 1967, the Northern Ireland Civil Rights Association was formed by a group of middle-class Catholics to campaign on these and similar abuses. The Association was seen by many Protestants as a veiled attack on the state, although following the collapse of an IRA offensive in the north between 1956 and 1962, it is apparent that most northern Catholics were at that time reconciled to the separate existence of Northern Ireland as part of the United Kingdom while the IRA itself had been virtually extinguished. The Northern Ireland Prime Minister, Captain O'Neill, was more conciliatory, but he came under growing pressure from Protestant militants such as Ian Paisley to resist the civil rights movement. In 1968, civil rights marches were attacked by loyalists and rioting broke out in several cities as Catholic communities came under physical attack from Protestant groups aided all too often by the Protestant-dominated Royal Ulster Constabulary and the part-time 'B-specials'. The Westminster Government's reluctance to intervene was eventually strained to breaking point, and in 1969 British troops were deployed to defend the minority population while constitutional changes were put into effect to remove housing from the hands of the Protestant councils. It was too little too late.

The troops, who were at first welcomed by most Catholics, soon became identified in the eyes of the minority with Protestant oppression, and following 'Bloody Sunday' in 1972, when thirteen people in Derry were shot by soldiers, they were never again to win Catholic trust. As the conflict intensified (over 10 000 shootings in 1972 compared with 200 in 1970; 322 civilian deaths and 146 army and police deaths in 1972 compared with 23 and 2 just 2 years earlier), the government in London suspended the Stormont assembly and imposed direct rule over the province for the first time in its history.

There then followed the most important single constitutional initiative to have occurred in the recent history of Ireland. Under the so-called 'Sunningdale agreement', representatives of both communities agreed to establish a system of 'power sharing' in the north involving an assembly elected on proportional representation from which would be chosen a Northern Ireland Executive consisting of six unionists, four members of the mainly Catholic Social Democratic and Labour Party and one member of the non-sectarian Alliance Party. The elections took place, the Executive was set up, and for 2 weeks in May 1974, the province was crippled by a general strike called by the Ulster Workers Council which eventually forced the unionists to resign from the Executive, thus bringing it to an end.

Various initiatives have been tried and failed since then, but there has never been any sign that either London or Dublin could impose an effective solution. British Government propaganda which seeks to suggest that the warring factions are made up of fanatical minorities with no support in the mass of the population is quite simply false, for Northern Ireland society is split irrevocably into two camps, organised around religious affiliation, nurturing incompatible aspirations, and identifying with legal and illegal political and military organisations which see it as their task to defend 'their people' against the threat of the other side. In this situation, the British Government can do little more than attempt to keep the violence within bounds, for it is governing a society where there is no consensus. Armoured cars trundle through council estates, armed soldiers peer nervously from barbed wire enclaves on street corners, shopping centres are fenced off and patrolled by sentries, suspects are interrogated in army barracks and tried in courts without juries, and still people are shot in broad daylight and buildings are bombed as the conflict grinds on with no apparent prospect of final victory on either side.

Northern Ireland has reached stalemate. The Protestant majority emphasises the historic union with Britain out of a fear of being subordinated to what is still a relatively under-developed and Catholic-dominated Irish state. It has developed a frontier mentality through which it sees itself threatened from the south and betrayed by Britain, and it knows that the only thing that will ensure a continuing British presence is the real threat of the often-predicted 'bloodbath' should the troops pull out. Yet for as long as the British presence remains, there can be no solution to the problem of Ulster.

Many different 'solutions' have, of course, been proposed over the years. Some, such as the Left's dream of a united socialist Ireland ('neither orange nor green but red') totally ignore the fact that politics in the north are structured around the historic division between Protestant unionism and Catholic republicanism and that all other political movements and alignments are subordinate to this. The Irish conflict is not a class conflict but is a civil war between two nations. Others, such as the various federal schemes which have been put forward from time to time (a Federal Ireland, a Federal British Isles, a Federal Europe) can only be envisaged realistically in the very long term following the development of some degree of trust (which is totally absent at present) between the republic in the south and the Protestant majority in the north. Perhaps the most realistic 'solution' (if indeed there is one) lies in the establishment of an independent Northern Ireland state based on four of the existing six counties and involving massive population shifts such as occurred with the partition of India and Pakistan in 1947. Even this, however, seems unlikely (notwithstanding the human misery which would be involved in the transition) until the northern Protestants develop a nationalist ideology (such as that in Scotland) which leads to a demand for severance from, rather than stronger union with, the rest of the United Kingdom.

Conclusions

In Chapter 6, we suggested that British society is shot through with many different kinds of cleavages – class, certainly, but also race and ethnicity, gender, production and consumption sectors, and so on. We should now add nationality to this list, for in this section we have seen how national identity may cut across and even eclipse other divisions.

Struggles around historic national identities within the United Kingdom are often dismissed by (mainly English) progressive opinion as anachronistic and many critics on the Left go even further, preferring to dismiss nationalist sentiments as in some way 'displaced' or 'deformed' versions of the 'real' class interests around which people 'should' be mobilising, and suggesting that nationalist ideology has in some way been manufactured or sustained as a cunning ploy by the ruling class to divide and confuse the masses.

Such arguments are not only arrogant; they are fundamentally misconceived. If any one interest is more 'basic' than any other, then surely this is the interest which people have in living in a state which corresponds to their national identity and aspirations. The pursuit of the other interests which they have as members of a particular class, gender or whatever is entirely dependent on this; the Scots cannot defend their economy, nor the Welsh their culture, nor the northern Irish their religion or their homes for as long as they remain a minority within a wider state system which can afford systematically to ignore them. All the political institutions and processes which we have discussed in this book – government, the courts, the police, the media and the rest – are organised on the basis of the territorial boundaries of the United Kingdom state. If these boundaries are themselves disputed, then settlement of the national question must be prior to any other social or political innovation.

THE INTERNATIONAL LEVEL

Most analyses of British politics treat the United Kingdom state as though it were a self-contained system untouched by the implications of our being part of an international political and economic order. This is a nonsense. No account of British politics and public policy-making is complete which does not attend to the external constraints on government action – constraints which have their contemporary origins in the international settlement effected at the end of the Second World War.

The Second World War confronted its survivors with both a challenge and an opportunity. A challenge because it had been allowed to happen, and an opportunity because it had demolished the old international order and thereby created space for a new one, hopefully built upon more stable principles. On the economic front, world trade was devastated and the European nations were faced with the problem of their own recovery, and on the more political front, the Western nations were concerned to secure their common defence. Old ways were recognised as inadequate, but new ways were feared. A return to the regulation of world trade through the free-market system and a *laissez-faire* international order was not a politically acceptable option to the industrial nations that had been distorted and disrupted by war since they had economies that were too weak to cope with the blast of an open world economy. At the same time, however, there was the fear that, in the absence of this commitment to an open world economy, nations would retreat into national planning and managed trade involving the full use of all the protectionist economic mechanisms which had predominated in the 1930s where the economic nationalism of each-country-for-itself-and-the-devil-take-the-weakest had led to the breakdown of the international monetary system itself.

If national solutions were feared with respect to the problem of economic trade, then they were recognised as inadequate with respect to the problem of defence. The war itself stood as some kind of testament to the disasters of a rampant nationalism, but, regardless of this lesson of history, the size of the Soviet bloc seemed to defy the possibility of purely national defence arrangements in Europe. At the same time, however, the strength of national identities and fears meant that the conditions were not ripe for a fully international solution to the problem of world security, anymore than they lent support to a fully fledged system of international co-operation *and* government to manage the world economy for the advantage of all. Compromise, then, was to be the order of the day with respect to the problems of economic recovery and world trade, and Western defence. In both cases, however, the fact that the USA controlled almost 70 per cent of the world's gold and foreign exchange reserves and more than 40 per cent of industrial output meant that it was to be the leader in fashioning new arrangements for the international political and economic order.

Britain depends on international trade for its living and through the Western Alliance it hopes to secure some kind of security in the face of the external threats. It follows from this that much British policy-making must be conducted multilaterally from within the framework of international organisations. In previous chapters we have seen that the twentieth century has witnessed the rise in state intervention at home, but in this section we are concerned to attend to the rise of international organisations and to the ways in which they come to have a decisive impact in constraining choice in British politics. The International Monetary Fund (IMF), the North Atlantic Treaty Organisation (NATO), and the European Community (EC), are all international organisations that emerged out of the post-war settlement, and it is particularly important to outline the ways in which these organisations have come to constrain and control crucial aspects of British politics and state activity.

The International Monetary Fund

In July 1944, forty-four nations met at Bretton Woods in America to try and create a new international monetary order as a crucial basis for the revival of international trade. There was a concern to modify the system of national and international competition that had prevailed in the 1930s. The national principle came to be challenged through the creation of a number of international agreements and organisations all of which established the basis for a substantial degree of multilateralism, though without making any frontal attack on the principle of national sovereignty itself.

For international trade to flourish an international monetary system is necessary to resolve a number of key problems to do with exchange rates between different currencies, the finance of balance of payments deficits, and the integrity of the system as a whole. The Bretton Woods conference created two international organisations that were to fulfil central bank functions for the world system. The International Bank for Reconstruction and Development – the World Bank – was created to provide loans and developmental assistance to speed the recovery of the weaker countries in the system, although its role was limited in practice because it came to operate in a very conservative way charging commercial rates and terms as restrictive as would be imposed by private bankers. The International Monetary Fund was to be the keeper of the rules, but under a system of weighted voting that enabled the USA to exert the preponderant influence within that body. Member countries wishing to adjust the exchange rate of their currency needed to secure the permission of the IMF; the fund was available to advise countries on policies affecting the monetary system; and it could advance credit to countries with serious balance-of-payments deficits but would do so only on the understanding that they adopted policies which the IMF considered appropriate. This imposition of conditions before loans are granted gives the IMF power to intervene in the domestic policy-making of individual countries and has been of decisive importance at particular moments of British history as we shall now see.

As we saw in Chapter 8, the British economy ended a period of rapid expansion in 1963. Imports increased much more rapidly than exports and as a result the balance of payments shifted from a surplus of more than $600 million in 1962 to a deficit of almost $650 million in 1964. Beginning in the summer of 1964 sterling weakened in the foreign-exchange markets (that is its value fell against the dollar). In consequence, British reserves began to be used and so a standby credit of $1 billion from the IMF had to be renewed. Because a general election was due some time in 1964, the Conservative Government was reluctant to act to stem the deteriorating balance of payments position but instead adopted short-term, coping solutions.

Labour was elected to office in October on the promise of a 'New Britain'. Economic growth through 'socialist planning' and a strong pound was to be the priority, but the manifesto was also committed to full employment and to a series of social reforms ranging from a capital gains tax through to a guaranteed income for the retired and widows, and the abolition of charges within the National Health Service. Electoral promises are one thing; the economic realities of office are quite another. The Labour Government was immediately confronted with a balance-of-payments deficit on current and long-term capital account of $2.25 billion for 1964. There was also widespread uncertainty in the international money markets as to the government's intentions, especially on the question of devaluation. The fateful decision for the new government was whether or not to devalue sterling and fix a new exchange rate. The decision was quickly taken to defend the existing parity of sterling, in part because Prime Minister Wilson did not want his party to be identified as the 'devaluation party', and in part because the Americans were known to be strongly opposed to British devaluation – and this at a time when Harold Wilson was anxious to strengthen his relationship with that country. In the event, the government imposed a temporary surcharge of 15 per cent on imported goods. However, the November budget, which promised increased pensions and the introduction of a corporation tax and capital gains tax, inspired a massive movement of foreign and domestic investors out of sterling. Labour ministers were forced to respond by increasing the bank rate by 2 per cent; by arranging a substantial standby credit of $3000 million with the central banks; and by going to the IMF in December for a further $1000 million. This credit package seemed to do the trick of persuading foreign-exchange markets that the sterling exchange rate would be held and sterling recovered.

Reflecting on this experience in his 'personal record' of the Labour Government, Harold Wilson noted how in the early days of office

We were soon to learn that decisions on pensions and taxation were no longer to be regarded, as in the past, as decisions for Parliament alone. The combination of tax increases with increased social security benefits provoked the first of a series of attacks on sterling, by speculators and others, which beset almost every action of the government for the next five years.

In more concrete terms, Wilson notes how the Governor of the Bank of England demanded all round cuts in public expenditure which led Wilson to write that

not for the first time, I said that we had now reached a situation where a newly elected government with a mandate from the people was being told, not so much by the Governor of the Bank of England but by international speculators, that the policies on which we had fought the election could not be implemented; that the government was to be forced into the adoption of Tory policies to which it was fundamentally opposed. The Governor confirmed that that was, in fact, the case. I asked him if this meant that it was impossible for any government, whatever its party label, whatever its manifesto or the policies on which it fought an election, to continue unless it reverted to full-scale Tory policies. He had to admit that this is what his argument meant, because of the sheer compulsion of the economic dictation of those who exercised decisive economic power.

In fact, the respite of sterling was shortlived, and it weakened again in March 1965. In May the government drew the remainder of its quota from the IMF. Behind the scenes an active discussion was taking place both within the British Government and between British and American officials on the need for a more stringent incomes policy. Gradually a programme was formulated involving an incomes policy 'with teeth' on the British side and, on the American, leadership in assembling an additional rescue package for sterling by the USA and other countries. Notwithstanding a series of budgets and packages cutting public expenditure in ways which curbed the radical edges of Labour's election pledges, sterling remained under international pressure and by the end of 1967 the issue of devaluation was again on the political agenda. If Britain was to hold the parity of the pound then the IMF made it clear that it would lend its support, and its dollars, only on the basis of 'rigid restrictions' that Prime Minister Wilson saw as leading to 'the most searching intrusions not only into our privacy, but even into our economic independence'. The government took the decision to devalue and the chancellor of the exchequer sent a *Letter of Intent* to the IMF outlining the proposals that had been hammered out in secret between the government and the IMF to restore a healthy balance of payments. On the basis of a promise to cut public expenditure on health, education, and housing, the government secured an IMF standby in support of the new exchange rate.

Despite the devaluation and the stringent monetary and fiscal measures designed to shift resources to improve the British balance of payments, sterling remained weak on the foreign exchange markets during much of 1968. In his diary entries for March 1968, Richard Crossman, a leading figure in the Labour Cabinet, describes how he was told by the chancellor that he was under 'the pressure of the IMF' and that 'a second devaluation would occur within the next three months if the budget didn't restore confidence in sterling...This was the big stick with which he decided to beat the cabinet into accepting a tremendous budget and also accepting the prices and incomes policy.'

Labour in office between 1964 and 1970 discovered the truth of Harold Wilson's insight when in opposition that

you can get into pawn, but don't then talk about an independent foreign policy or an independent defence policy...If you borrow from some of the world's bankers you will quickly find that you lose another kind of independence because of the deflationary policies and the cuts in social services that will be imposed on a government that has got itself into that position.

Labour lost the election of 1970, but was returned to government in 1974 with a series of clear policy commitments more radical in tone and in aspiration than any that the party had endorsed since 1945. In his 1975 budget speech, Denis Healey had said that 'we in Britain must keep control of our own policy', but in December 1975 the government had to borrow from the IMF. This loan did not stop the pound falling sharply against the dollar through the spring of 1976 and, under pressure, the government announced a set of public spending cuts. By Septermber, the government's reserves of foreign currency stood at their lowest level since 1971 and the government was again forced to accept an IMF investigation into its policies. The loan was negotiated but, naturally, the lending institution set down certain terms as a condition of the loan – terms that were roughly spelled out in the chancellor's *Letter of Intent* to the IMF. After December 1976, the financial constraints on government policy eased somewhat although the government was under close IMF scrutiny throughout 1977. Eventually, the pound stabilised, the balance of payments improved, and even inflation began to fall.

Any assessment of the precise impact of the IMF on domestic policy-making in Britain demands an appreciation of the policies which it seeks to impose as a condition of any loan. In essence the IMF seeks to restore a balance-of-payments surplus in a country to which it offers a loan on the basis of that country avoiding protectionist measures and going instead for policies which reduce consumption and increase private capitalist investment. A standard IMF package, therefore, involves a reduction in state expenditure (particularly in the provision of subsidies for the consumption of goods by low-income groups); some mechanism for reducing wages; and the dismantling of controls on the activities of private capitalists either domestic or foreign. The effect of these policies is designed to reduce the level of consumption and therefore the level of imports, and to boost the rate of profit and the level of exports through reductions in taxes and wages. Accepting an IMF loan involves accepting a massive international intrusion into domestic policy-making in a way that hits at progressive taxation and policies for income and wealth redistribution, as well as policies involving state intervention in the economy.

The North Atlantic Treaty Organisation (NATO)

Following the coup in Czechoslovakia in early 1948, Britain, Belgium, Holland, Luxembourg, and France, all signed the Brussels Treaty promising that all countries would come to the aid of any one of them that was attacked. The ink was scarcely dry when the Russians blockaded Berlin. The Canadian Prime Minister suggested that the Brussels powers look beyond Europe for their defence and merge in a single defence system with North America. Following negtiations in Washington, NATO was formed in August 1949.

The American Government recognised that economic recovery in Europe was keenly related to the problem of Western defence, because the domestic need to give priority to reconstruction precluded those nations being able to afford their own defence. In order to meet the challenge of Communism, the American Government provided a programme of overseas assistance that was made up of a number of elements. The Marshall Plan committed substantial resources to rebuilding the European economies on very generous terms; expansion in America's overseas defence spending turned a surplus on their balance of trade into a deficit on their balance of payments; and NATO was a vehicle through which the USA became entangled in the affairs of Europe and active in military collaboration.

There have been changes in NATO over the years (and whilst America was preoccupied with the Vietnam war, NATO was consigned to some kind of limbo) but two things have been constant. First, the USSR has served as a unifying presence for the NATO powers, and second, the USA has been the leader and dominant force within the Alliance because it provides the nuclear 'umbrella' and the major part of the combined defence budget. Notwithstanding Britain's 'special relationship' with America, NATO strategy has been largely American strategy and Britain has had to fit in. Britain's foreign policy is geared to our membership of NATO (we 'know' our friends and our enemies) and American missiles are located on British soil on the basis of a decision by a 'high-level group' in NATO and with scant regard to the wishes of the British public. The only serious option for a major cut in Britain's defence expenditure (at 4.7 per cent of GDP in 1979, larger than all other Western countries excluding the USA) would be to withdraw from NATO. Whilst we stay in NATO, it is doubtful whether anyone in Britain can be said to make a defence policy. Our troops are fully integrated into NATO, and apart from considering the future of our 'independent' nuclear deterrent and determining policy with regard to remnants of the Empire such as Ulster, the Falklands and Hong Kong, there are no major political decisions to be made. Policy questions tend, therefore, to boil down to considerations about equipment but, even here, the fact of our increasing involvement in co-operative ventures with other countries cuts into British autonomy to decide on these matters.

The essence of national sovereignty has to do with a nation deciding to go to war or to make peace, but whilst we are members of the NATO alliance, that sovereign right has been effectively passed over to the USA which enjoys the capacity to use nuclear missiles based on British soil (thereby inviting a retaliatory attack on Britain rather than the USA) without even the constraint of a British finger on the trigger.

The European Community

When the United Kingdom joined the European Community in 1973 she was already a member of several other international organisations such as the United Nations, NATO, the IMF, the Commonwealth, the Organisation for Economic Co-operation and Development, the European Free Trade Area, and so on. All these organisations involve the British Government in commitments that impose constraints on the making of British public policy, but they are all *intergovernmental* organisations with no formal authority over the autonomy of the British state and, in theory at least, no British Government is legally bound to agree to a policy that it does not accept. The European Community is in a different league, however, because it is a *supranational* organisation which enjoys legal authority over the British state in a way that sharply constrains the sovereignty of Parliament to make and unmake laws as it sees fit in accord with the will of the people as expressed at a general election.

When Prime Minister Edward Heath signed the Treaty of Accession which bound Britain to the Treaty of Rome, Britain was accepting a body of law which formally committed government to certain European policies, and to defined procedures for reaching decisions on those policies and enforcing their implementation. European laws take precedence over laws passed by the British Parliament where the two conflict. European laws are also enforceable by the British courts even to the point of the courts declaring the actions of an elected British Government illegal. Having stated the implications of membership in bold legal terms it is important to recognise that the actual impact of the European Community on British policy-making varies as between different areas of policy. Central to the whole ethos of the European community, however, is the entrenchment of a system of liberal capitalism involving the elimination of barriers to trade between member states and the erection of a common external tariff to non-members. Under the terms of the Treaty of Rome, therefore, the British Government has ceded its authority to fix quotas or taxes on imported goods and to subsidise exports independently. In consequence what was once an area of British national competence has become an area of European competence and control: it is doubtful whether any future Labour Government would be able to implement those aspects of its alternative economic strategy that bore on import controls whilst we continued to remain within the Community. In agriculture, too, issues which were once dealt with at national level are now almost exclusively handled at the community level through the Common Agricultural Policy. This policy accounts for some 70 per cent of the Community budget and it works against British interests in favour of those Community countries that are net agricultural exporters with a large percentage of their population in agriculture. In few other areas have EC policies effectively replaced British policies, but Community competence covers an extremely wide range of government activity nonetheless, for Britain is not free to decide its own fate with respect to industrial policy, regional policy, or energy policy.

Whilst we continue to remain in the EC (and the Labour Party leadership now recognises the problem of effecting a withdrawal) then in order to explain the factors shaping many of the public policies affecting the British people it is as important to attend to the play of politics in Brussels and Strasbourg as it is to study the antics in Westminster and Whitehall.

Conclusion

A number of things stand out from this brief statement as to the significance of the international level of politics for the British political system.

1   In crucial areas of policy, Britain just cannot be seen as self governing or in control but is rather constrained by the implications that flow from alliances, treaties, and an involvement in a host of international organisations. In a very real sense Tony Benn is right to characterise 'Britain as a colony' which enjoys a subordinate role within the American defence system; is subject to the 'economic imperialism' of the IMF; and which engaged in a 'formal surrender to the Common Market'.

2   In so far as international organisations bear onto British politics then they bear very unevenly on the policies and programmes of the different political parties. International organisations constrain the aspirations of Labour Governments more than they do those of a conservative persuasion be it with respect to policies for economic management, welfare provision, or defence.

3   Having pointed to the constraining significance of international organisations for British politics it is wrong to conceive of those organisations outside of the larger economic context within which they themselves operate and take their being. For example, although it is tempting to suggest that the Labour Governments of the sixties and seventies were 'dictated to by the IMF' it is important to recognise that the Fund itself was not a free agent but was subject to processes at work in the world economy to do with trade cycles, monetary instability, the concentration of capital into the hands of ever fewer multinational corporations, and the increase in international competition – processes which both the IMF and the British Government were having to respond to in the absence of their capacity to simply control them. Even if the IMF were to have vanished overnight it is still probable that cuts would have

been made in public expenditure because it was the weakness of the pound rather than the power of the IMF that constrained government policy and this was a function of Britain's economic decline relative to that of her trading competitors.

CONCLUSION

Because the United Kingdom state is not some kind of unitary monolith it seems highly unlikely that the range of different agencies which compromise it will all operate in exactly the same way or could all be subject to exactly the same influences. To put it another way, it is unlikely that any single theory can explain the different activities of the different levels of the British state, and it is hardly plausible to suggest that the state as a whole is controlled or directed by any single group, be it the Cabinet (as in orthodox liberal democratic constitutional theory discussed in Chapter 1) or the capitalist class (as in orthodox Marxist theories discussed in Chapter 7). The divisions *within* every level of the state system, and the conflicts *between* the levels, render it virtually impossible for any one group successfully to impose its interests across the board. The state is not and cannot be cohesive, for inscribed in every nook and cranny of the system is the possibility of resistance in and against the centre of the state. Having said that, we need to go on to make a number of qualifying points.

First, when we considered the local level of the state, we pointed out how functions had been lost to the centre and to non-elected bodies (often at regional level), and we also noted how the central state has come to exert a tighter control over elected local authorities in a number of ways that substantially reduce their autonomy and so erode their established constitutional position within the British system of government. In other words, to explain what happens at the local level of the state we now need to know rather more about the balance of power at the central level and rather less about the nature of conflicts and interests at the local level precisely because the centre is intruding very effectively into the workings of local democracy.

Second, recognising that no one group controls all the levels of the state should not excuse us from attending to the implications which flow from how the various levels operate, and to what interests are, and are not, effectively involved and advantaged. The elective principle only holds good with respect to local government. All other local bodies, all regional bodies, and all national bodies (outside of Parliament itself) are non-elected. They are controlled by experts and appointed bureaucrats who operate according to managerial criteria and are rather responsive to the intrusions of the central state and to particular (and powerful) private interests in a situation in which the popular, consumer, interest is weakly organised and unrepresented in policy-making.

Third, we stop short if we are content to point to the central challenge to local democracy, and to the power of experts and professionals at other levels of the state, because we present British politics as closed and self-contained. It may well be that the centre is now more in control of local government than was once the case and that both local and regional bodies are constrained by the pressing concerns of the central state, but to say this rather ignores the extent to which the central state is *itself* less in control in the context of a complex and pressing international political and economic order where a need to rely on the IMF and decisions taken by NATO and the EC effectively constrain the scope of central state policy making.

In this chapter on the organisation of the United Kingdom state we have concentrated on the geographical or territorial dimension of British politics and in this way we have complemented the emphasis in earlier chapters on functional divisions within the state system (e.g. divisions between the executive, the legislature, and the judiciary discussed in our first chapter on constitutional theory, and divisions between different agencies discharging different functions such as law enforcement, internal and external security, economic management, welfare policy, and so on). It is important to recognise that political representation tends to be organised on a territorial basis in that both national and local elections are fought on the basis of constituencies and wards which are geographically determined. When we vote for a Member of Parliament to represent us, we are obliged to choose someone who will act as a representative of the small part of the country in which we happen to live, even though this area may actually have little significance for us and may include a variety of different types of people who actually share precious little in common other than the fact that they reside within a few miles of each other.

Given the long history of territorial representation it is perhaps not surprising that we tend to take this very much for granted as the 'obvious' way of organising a political system. On further reflection, however, it seems rather strange that territory should still play so central a role in the organisation of political life when it significance in most other areas of social life has declined quite dramatically. In fact, representation by area is not the only way in which diverse interests may be expressed in national assemblies, and the alternative to territorial representation is one in which different interests come to be expressed on the basis of people's social location as opposed to their geographical one. We have already encountered this idea in Chapters 3 and 8 where we discussed the growth of a 'corporatist' system of interest representation in which groups such as the Confederation of British Industry, the National Farmers Union, the Trades Union Congress and various professional associations (e.g. the British Medical Association) have, during this century, developed close and relatively informal relations with appropriate government departments through which they have been able to defend and further the specific economic interests of their members as these are affected by government policy.

Political representation in the United Kingdom state today is thus organised around two axes – territorial interests and functional interests. The origins of territorial representation lie in the growth of nationalism, while the origins of functional representation lie in the later growth of industrial capitalism, for it was this that gave rise to organised groupings of employers, workers and professions in the modern period. Over the last 50 years or so, these groups have tended to increase in political significance with the result that the system of territorial representation has declined in effective significance as forms of functional representation have strengthened. Put another way, something of a split has occurred within the political system between the electoral sphere, based on geographical representation, and the interest-group sphere, based on functional representation. Furthermore, we would argue that the impact of the latter has grown at the expense of the former.

The development of functional representation at the centre has, of course, excluded many different groups in the population. For those who are excluded, all that remains is the more traditional territorial system for expressing their grievances. The bargains and compromises which are reached at central level as a result of closed negotiations between state agencies and corporate interests today increasingly come under challenge from below (notably through radical local councils and nationalist movements at the periphery) as a result of the mobilisation of non-incorporated interests through territorial strategies and alliances. Functional and territorial organisation constantly clash precisely because territory remains important as the basis for opposition to centrally determined policy-making. The point has been made succinctly by Tarrow who concludes his excellent analysis of these issues by suggesting:

If functional centralization has had one single effect, it has been to lead citizens at the periphery to turn more and more to the local, regional and primordial identities around them . . . In the long run, therefore, the functional cleavages that earlier scholars saw displacing the territorial dimension in politics may actually reinforce it, channelling electorally bolstered demands to the national state, which may then come into conflict with the functional demands of national and international interest groups.

British politics, then, are bifurcated. On the one hand, there is a system of functional representation of corporate groupings operating mainly at central level. On the other, there is a system of territorial representation of many different types of interests operating mainly at sub-central level. The two systems constantly come into conflict, and this conflict is generally expressed through different political agencies operating at different levels of the state apparatus. Far from being a unitary monolith, the United Kingdom state is thus subject to all sorts of internal cross-cutting pressures, and this in turn suggests that no single political theory is likely to be able to explain every aspect of British politics. This is a theme which we take up in the following conclusions.

WORKS CITED AND GUIDE TO FURTHER READING

Bains, M. (1972) *The New Local Authorities: Management and structure,* London, HMSO.
The blueprint for corporate management methods within the reorganised local government system.

Benn, T. (1981) *Arguments for Democracy,* Harmondsworth, Penguin.
Chapter One – 'Britain as a colony' provides a powerful, if polemical, statement as to Britain's loss of self-government to America, the IMF and the EEC.

Birch, A. (1971) *Political Integration and Disintegration in the British Isles,* London, Allen and Unwin.
A useful and sobre discussion of the national question within the United Kingdom, written at a time when political controversy was at its height and when it seemed certain that something in the centralised United Kingdom state would have to give.

Boddy, M. and Fudge, C. (eds) (1984) *Local Socialism,* London, Macmillan.
A collection of articles discussing the changing pattern of central–local relations in Britain and focusing in particular on the strategies adopted by the New Left at the local level. Includes interesting interviews with the socialist leaders of the Greater London and Sheffield councils.

Coates, D. (1980) *Labour in Power? A study of the Labour Government 1974–79,* London, Longman.
Powerful, left-wing, critique of the record of the Labour Government together with an explanation of the record and lessons for a future Labour Government. Interesting on the way Labour handled sterling crises, and on the intrusions of the IMF.

Cockburn, C. (1977) *The Local State,* London, Pluto Press.
Cockburn's Marxist analysis of local state activity and of the responses to it by local people in Lambeth has often been criticised as over-simplistic, yet recent developments have perhaps made her basic thesis more sustainable.

Crossman, R. H. S. (1979) *The Crossman Diaries: Condensed version,* edited by Anthony Howard, London, Magnum Books.
Covers the same period as that covered by the Wilson record but rather more critical and incisive into the workings of Cabinet government. Seen by *The Times* as 'the most important book on British government to have appeared since the war'.

Hogwood, B. and Keating, M. (eds) (1982) *Regional Government in England,* Oxford, Clarendon Press.
The title is a bit of a misnomer, for as the editors admit, there is a lot government activity in the regions, but there is no regional government. Nevertheless, this is virtually the only up-to-date review of regional state agencies in England (the rest

of the United Kingdom is omitted, as are a number of English regional authorities such as the boards of the nationalised industries), and it contains several useful pieces on different agencies and on the role of regional bodies in the contemporary period.

Holland, S. (1980) *Uncommon Market,* London, Macmillan.
Left-Labour Member of Parliament and ex-university economics lecturer lays into the European Community with a vengeance. Tends to be turgid at times, but best of a big boring bunch of books on the Community.

Jones, G. (ed.) (1980) *New Approaches to the Study of Central–Local Government Relations,* Farnborough, Gower Press.
Well not that new you understand, but it does contain interesting contributions by Rod Rhodes (see also his *Control and Power in Central–Local Government Relations,* published by Gower in 1981) whose framework has been very influential in recent writing on this topic, and by Patrick Dunleavy, who injects a welcome dose of radical scepticism and critique into what is otherwise a rather dry book.

Kilbrandon, Lord (1973) *Report on the Royal Commission on the Constitution,* Cmnd 5460–1, London, HMSO.
Unanimous in rejecting Scottish and Welsh independence or any Federal solution to the national question, but deeply divided over the question of devolution, its proposals came to nothing in 1978 when Scottish and Welsh referenda failed to endorse the Labour Government's devolution strategy.

Nairn, T. (1981) *The Break-up of Britain,* 2nd edn, London, Verso.
By far the best Marxist analysis of the national question written by an old member of the New Left who is himself a Scottish nationalist. The book is important not only for its insights into Wales, Scotland and Northern Ireland, but also for its analysis of the links between the decline of British capitalism and the nature of the United Kingdom state.

Redcliffe-Maud, J. (1969) *Royal Commission on Local Government in England,* Cmnd 4040, London, HMSO.
The report which recommended a system of unitary local authorities and which was subsequently ignored by the Heath Government.

Solomon, R. (1982) *The International Monetary System,* Rev. edn., New York, Harper.
The chapter on 'The travail of sterling, 1964-1968' provides a crisp statement as to the international economic constraints on Labour policy at this time.

Tarrow, S. (1978) Introduction, in S. Tarrow, P. Katzenstein and L. Graziano, (eds) *Territorial Politics in Industrial Nations,* New York, Praeger.
A short and insightful analysis of the nature of territorially organised conflict between core centres and their peripheries.

Wilson. H. (1971) *The Labour Government 1964–1970: A personal record,* London, Weidenfeld and Nicolson.
A massive and self-justifying record, but in the context of the concerns of this chapter check out all the references to the IMF that are cited in the index.

Conclusions

It is widely believed that politics and economics are separate and largely unconnected; that individual freedom is a political problem and material welfare an economic problem; and that any kind of political arrangements can be combined with any kind of economic arrangements... Such a view is a delusion... There is an intimate connection between economics and politics... The kind of economic organisation that provides economic freedom directly, namely competitive capitalism, also promotes political freedom because it separates economic power from political power and in this way enables the one to offset the other.

Milton Friedman (1962) Capitalism and Freedom, *Chicago, Chicago University Press, pp. 7–9.*

A democratic republic is the best possible political shell for capitalism, and, therefore, once capital has grasped this very best shell... it establishes its power so securely, so surely, that no *change, either of persons, of institutions, or of parties in the bourgeois-democratic republic, can shake this power.*

V. I. Lenin (1976) The State and Revolution, *Peking, Foreign Languages Press, pp. 17–18.*

The term 'capitalist democracy' is... intended to denote a permanent and fundamental contradiction or tension, in a capitalist society such as Britain, between the promise of popular power, enshrined in universal suffrage, and the curbing or denial of that promise in practice.

R. Miliband (1982) Capitalist Democracy in Britain, *London, Oxford University Press, p. 1.*

We shall not in these conclusions be providing a summary of the contents of the last eleven chapters, for each contains its own summary together with a suggested list of further reading. Nor shall we be attempting to draw all the loose threads together into some grand and unified single generalisation about British politics in the contemporary period, for (as we noted in the Introduction) the complexity of politics is such that any broad and sweeping statement is almost certain to be partial and should, therefore, be regarded with healthy scepticism. What we shall attempt in these last few pages, however, is to identify the three principal themes which have rippled through the book as a whole, and we shall consider these in the light of the arguments and the evidence reviewed in the preceeding chapters.

The three themes which together constitute the core concerns of this book have been :

1 The question of where power lies and how power is used. More particularly, the relation between the distribution of power in British society and the organisation and power of state institutions.
2 The question of the adequacy of different theories and perspectives to deal with these issues of where power lies and how it is used. This has involved our exploring mainstream political science, New Right accounts, political sociology, and the several strands of Marxism.
3 The question of the relationship between political organisation on the one hand and economic and social organisation on the other. In bald terms this involves an exploration of the relationship between democracy and capitalism in Britain.

In a sense, of course, all three of these questions are but variations on the same basic theme – namely, *what* is happening to the British system of government and politics at a time of sustained economic problems, and *how* to understand these developments when many of the orthodoxies through which we have traditionally understood our politics no longer seem adequate. Although this has been the fundamental concern of this book, it is nevertheless useful to break the problem down into its three component parts in order to develop a clearer focus on what we believe are quite dramatic changes which are now taking place.

POWER AND POLITICS

In the Introduction, we introduced the reader to Steinbeck's tragic tenant farmer faced with eviction from his land by people or forces whom he was unable to identify. In the last eleven chapters, we have left the poor man standing, gun in hand, confused and bewildered, still waiting for an answer to his question, 'Who can I shoot?'

It is a question which (metaphorically at least) is resonating through British society today. Who are the 3 million plus unemployed to blame for the blighting of their lives, their hopes and their self-respect? Who is to be held responsible for the deaths of thousands of people affected by kidney disease which could be treated were resources made available? Whose fault is it that so many people are being deprived of the education from which they could so richly benefit, or that old people die in their hundreds every winter for lack of warmth, or that so many families seem trapped in a vicious cycle of poverty from which there is little prospect of escape?

Until the mid-nineteenth century, the response of most people to their problems would have been limited to a hopeless shrug of the shoulders and a blank gaze, for the pitiful conditions endured by the majority of the population at that time were seen as something which nobody (save the individuals themselves or God Himself) could or should be expected to do anything about. The 'hidden hand' of the market moved in mysterious ways, and it made no more sense to blame the government for the poverty and squalor over which it presided than it did to blame it for the weather.

As we saw in Chapters 8 and 9, however, governments have over the last 150 years assumed increasing responsibility for mediating the effects of the market through both economic and social-policy interventions. This has in turn fed through into popular expectations and aspirations such that today (despite the repeated protestation by Conservative administrations since 1979 that there is actually little that they can do even if they wanted to) most people are likely to blame 'the government' or 'the politicians' for failing to resolve the problems of economic decline and social malaise which are now so marked and so pressing in Britain.

Is it in fact the case, that power, and hence responsibility, lies in the hands of the government? Throughout this book, we have deliberately expanded our focus so as to adopt a broad view of politics and this has led us beyond any simple institutional definition of power. We began in Chapter 1 where most accounts of British politics begin – with a discussion of the constitution. We soon saw, however, that the established constitutional arrangements were themselves under challenge and that, far from being inscribed in tablets of stone (or any other written form for that matter), the constitutional framework of politics is itself subject to political argument and political struggle (e.g. over methods of electoral representation, the powers of the second chamber, the question of a bill of rights, and so on). The constitution, in other words, is as much a *reflection* of political power as a constraint upon it – the constitution is in politics as well as about politics.

We also swiftly saw that crucial aspects of political organisation refer to processes and agencies which are extra-constitutional. The organisation of political parties and the representation of interests through direct or indirect pressures and negotiation involving government and outside groupings are both central to an understanding of how and why the country is governed. Yet even when we extended our analysis to include a discussion of parties and pressures, it was apparent that there were still other agencies operating whose impact on the direction of public policy and the allocation of resources was enormous. In Chapter 5 we discussed some of these – the civil service, the military, the police, the security services, and so on – which together comprise a 'secret state' apparatus over which elected politicians often seem to have little control and about which most of us have virtually no knowledge or understanding.

Having lifted the lid off democracy and discovered forms of life in murky non-elected state institutions, we could be excused for believing that we had at last identified the end-point in our quest for the receding locus of power. Clearly we had established that there would be little point in 'shooting' politicians and government leaders if we did not at the same time line up against the wall an array of party bosses, interest group leaders, civil servants, military chiefs, media controllers, quango members and others as well. But was that really the end of our quest?

In Chapter 6, we extended the scope of our investigations further still by recognising that power in British society is not contained within the state system, open or secret, elected or non-elected. The organisation of power through the state is but an *aspect* of relations of domination in British society for another crucial aspect of power and the determination of people's life chances derives from the ownership and control of the country's productive assets and from the closing off of labour market opportunities by various privileged and powerful groups such as the 'independent' professions and some trade unions. Nor was that all, for the 'class power' which reflects patterns of economic ownership and control is overlaid and cross-cut by other relations of domination such as those based on ethnicity and gender. By the end of Chapter 6, the task of identifying a distinct group of powerful people was beginning to look like an impossible one (as we saw in our critique of elite theories), for lined up against the wall alongside the politicians, civil servants and others were private-sector managers and major shareholders, the professions, whites, and males – and we had still to consider the power of the International Monetary Fund, NATO, and the European Community! Facing this array of apparently powerful or dominant people and institutions were the marginalised minorities of British society – blacks, unemployed youth, single-parent families, the low-paid, and those in insecure employment or no employment at all.

In the face of all this, what conclusions can we draw regarding the distribution of power in our society? Two points (neither of which may provide much comfort for Steinbeck's tenant farmer) stand out.

The first is that power is not crisply organised along any single dimension. This is not to endorse the pluralist claim that power is fragmented and dispersed, still less to accept Freidman's argument (quoted at the start of this chapter) that economic power and political power in some way balance each other out. But it is to recognise that there is no one power elite or ruling class in Britain despite the fact that power on each dimension tends to be concentrated and that those who are positively privileged on one dimension are often positively privileged on others as well. It is also to recognise that there is no necessary relationship (as Marxist theorists so often try to argue) between the different dimensions. Although those who control the various agencies of the state often have connections to those with power outside the state system (as we saw in Chapter 5), the tie-up is not complete and state functionaries will not always (or even 'in the last instance') pursue policies which are in the interests of dominant economic classes. Indeed were that to be the case then we would be forever in a static, no change, situation.

Having said that, it is vital to recognise that Britain *is* a highly unequal society, politically as well as economically. However, lines of political and economic cleavage are often drawn at *different* points in *different* circumstances and it is grossly misleading to imagine that there is a very small group of 'up-people' dominating the mass of 'down-people' right across the board – if this really were the case, then would it be possible to secure the social order through either legitimation or coercion for any length of time?

Our first concluding point about power in British society, therefore, is that we need to look at several different though related dimensions of domination. We cannot, as so many traditional political scientists have done, concentrate simply on the organisation of political power through the state (still less merely through government) to the neglect of economic and social relations. Nor can we adopt the classical Marxist position of assuming that political domination can simply be 'read off' from an analysis of class power in the organisation of the economy. Such simple recipes for knowledge are no longer (and probably never were) adequate, and if, by extending our analysis to embrace different dimensions of power we end up with a confused picture in which comfortable liberal myths about democratic government and exciting radical myths about the ruling class are left behind us, then complexity and the lack of simple answers is the price that has to be paid for enhancing our understanding of the world in which we live. The reality of power is messy, and in this sense there is no straight-forward response which can honestly be offered to Steinbeck's frustrated tenant farmer.

The second point to make concerns the nature of power itself. In Chapters 6 and 7 we saw that individuals make decisions within a context of constraints. Sometimes certain courses of action are simply not possible. At other times, actions designed to achieve an objective turn out, through circumstances beyond the control of any individual or group, to have very different and often totally unanticipated results. Very often, people benefit from situations which they neither sought nor desired. Given this, it is clearly fatuous to limit an analysis of politics and power to a consideration of what people do and achieve, for we need also to consider the systems of social relations within which they are operating and over which they may have very little direct control.

Having said this, it is no more justifiable to develop a 'structuralist' analysis of politics (in which acting individuals disappear from view altogether) than it is to concentrate on people's actions to the exclusion of any consideration of their structural context. We need, obviously, to take account of both action and constraint, although this is easier said than done.

One step forward in this respect lies in the distinction emphasised in Chapter 6 between 'power' and domination'. Power – the pursuit and achievement of a given objective even against the resistance of others – is clearly important for our analysis, but arguably more significant is domination which involves routinised relationships through which particular interests benefit on a day-to-day basis in a relatively unquestioned manner. Domination, in other words, is systematised, institutionalised, and often beyond view. In our society, for example, whites routinely achieve access to life chances which tend to be denied to most blacks, even though many may not intend this and do nothing themselves to bring it about. Similarly, the relations between employers and employees, males and females, the state and its citizens, are all characteristically relations of domination in which super- and subordination has become institutionalised in social and legal forms which are often taken for granted by both parties to the relationship (e.g. the form of the wage contract through which workers routinely cede control over large slices of their waking hours to another person; the housewife role through which women are expected to perform unpaid labour in the home; and the system of liberal democracy itself in which millions of us apparently endorse our subordination to the state in return for the right to cast a vote once every 4 or 5 years).

Now, it is exceedingly difficult to analyse such relations of domination, partly because they are generally taken for-granted (and are to this extent virtually 'invisible' in the sense of being able to 'see' one group controlling another's actions), and partly because it is never entirely clear whether any given outcome is a product of an individual's will or of the working out of institutionalised relationships of which she or he is, in a sense, an involuntary member. Men most certainly benefit from patriarchal relations of domination, but are they to blame for the existence of such relations? Similarly whites benefit from institutionalised racism but does that make them culpable? And, most crucially of all from the standpoint of the present discussion, the class that owns and controls the major slice of the British economy clearly benefits from the perpetuation of a capitalist system of production which the British state has done much to underpin, but does this justify the conclusion that the individuals who run the economy and/or the individuals who run the state apparatus (including, from time to time, socialist politicians, trade union leaders and the like) are personally responsible for the inequalities and exploitation that results?

In posing such questions, we are in our view, pushing against the limits of social and political theory. By the end of Chapter 7, we had chewed over these issues and pointed to the various weaknesses of the theoretical attempts to resolve them, but we had reached an impasse. This was because the questions which we were posing were essentially *empirical* and *historical* questions as much as theoretical ones. We cannot answer in the abstract questions which relate to particular relations of domination in particular places at particular times. The only way in which we can judge the extent to which any one group – government, big business, the working class, or whatever – has power is by considering specific examples of political organisation and outcome. This we did in Chapters 8 to 11, and it is to a consideration of the light which this evidence throws on theories that we now turn.

THEORY AND PRACTICE

Our examination of different areas of state intervention served two main purposes. The first was to set contemporary political change in its historical context, thereby to identify some of the factors which have contributed to it. In these chapters we saw that, while the state is being 'rolled back' in some areas (e.g. the antipathy to economic planning and the privatisation of many aspects of social welfare), it is being 'rolled forward' in others (e.g. the steady chipping away of civil liberties and the sustained attack on local democracy), and that there is a sense in which the traditional nineteenth century, *laissez-faire,* view of the role and functions of the state is now being reasserted in a new guise. However, history never really repeats itself, for the context in which the British state must operate today is very different from that of the Victorian period or the inter-war years. British politics have changed dramatically during this century as economic and social conditions have changed. In particular, the British economy has become locked into a downward spiral which has had profound implications for political change – a point which we explore further in the final section of these conclusions.

The second rationale behind our historical analysis of various aspects of state activity was that it enabled us to put empirical flesh on the bare bones of the theories discussed earlier in the book. In particular, our review of the different ways in which the British state, organised at different levels, has attempted to manage the economy, make provision for social need, and maintain social order has allowed us to evaluate different theories against each other and to assess the extent to which various perspectives may complement each other.

In the Introduction, we suggested that no one theory should or could be expected to enjoy a monopoly of explanatory wisdom and that theories which are often pitched against each other as alternatives may better be seen as in some ways complementary. However, we also warned against simply mixing theories together in the hope that a bit of this and a dash of that will result in a coherent picture of the whole. The task, therefore, has been to identify which questions are best answered by which theories.

Our discussion of the relative applicability of different theories in the later chapters has been premised on two basic points.

First, the social world can never be totally predictable. The aim of theory is to develop causal generalisations about the world in which we live, yet social scientific generalisations must always be limited and hedged around with qualifications and doubts since human affairs will always be the product of peculiar combinations of unique events. Factors which can never be built into theoretical generalities can and do have an enormous impact on the course of human history, and the explanation of any one event will thus involve an exploration of a plethora of factors which together helped to bring it about. Theoretical explanation thus entails the development of generalisations while *also* recognising the significance of historical contingencies and chance events.

The second point follows from this, for, given the complexity of historical causality, it is clear that no one theory can hope to encompass all the factors which may together explain a particular phenomenon. When they develop their generalisations, different theorists inevitably focus on particular kinds of factors to the exclusion of others. All theories, therefore, are partial in their scope and focus. There is in principle an infinite number of causes which *could* be identified to explain any one phenomenon; mass unemployment, for example, can be explained in terms of the activities of the City of London in sending capital abroad, the poor management record of industrialists, the rise in the world price of oil, the restrictive practices of the unions, the fiscal policies of successive governments, Margaret Thatcher's psychological make-up, the legacy of empire for British political culture, and so on, and so on. Different theories tend to emphasise different factors, and it does not follow that if one is in some sense 'right' that another must therefore be 'wrong'.

This does not mean that all theories are valid, for despite the enormous problems of testing theories in the social sciences, it can sometimes be shown that a particular theory does not stand up in the face of empirical and historical evidence. Nor does it mean that all theories are of equal value, for some are able to explain more than others. In evaluating different theories, therefore, we have needed to ask both whether the theory in question helps to explain the 'facts' and the extent to which it is able to do so. We have been interested, that is, in validity and generality. Theories which can be empirically supported may still tell us very little (as we noted in our discussion of pluralism in Chapter 3), for in addition we need theories of sufficient *scope* to encompass some of the most important factors which give rise to the phenomenon which we seek to understand (hence our concern to develop a broad view of power and politics.)

Now, when we considered some of the theoretical perspectives discussed in the earlier chapters of this book, we saw that they were often valid in their own terms yet limited. To say, for example, that governments have become 'overloaded' with varying demands from different groups in the population may well be true, but the explanatory power of New Right theories of overloaded government seems very limited unless they are set in a broader context which enables us to understand *why* there has been an inflationary spiral of political demands and *why* the state has been obliged to respond to them in the way that it has. To answer these broader questions, it is obviously necessary to look beyond the political arena to a wider social and economic context that is often taken for granted by theorists of the New Right.

So it is with other political theories as well. Constitutional theorists are not 'wrong' when they point to the various powers and responsibilities vested in the formal institutions of government. Such a focus is valid but it does not take us very far in understanding *why* these institutions act in the way they do or *how* they actually relate to concrete forces in society. Mainstream political science has not been 'wrong' in asserting the importance of elections as a mechanism for translating popular preferences into policy outputs, but its focus has proved too narrow for any significant understanding of political processes and relations of power and domination in the rest of the state, still less in society and economy. What all this amounts to is that to understand British politics we need to look beyond what is conventionally defined as politics. Political processes form part of a much wider set of social processes, and a political theory which focusses on 'politics' alone will always be limited in its analytical capacity and trapped within the system it needs to explore.

The two traditions which do explicitly attempt to explain political phenomena with reference to broader social and economic relations are political sociology (discussed in Chapter 6) and Marxism (discussed specifically in Chapter 7). What is common to both of these approaches is their concern with politics as an *aspect* of social organisation rather than as a discrete topic of study in its own right. Both are therefore attuned to the way in which political change and social change interrelate, and in this way they are in principle capable of developing theories which recognise the constraints imposed upon state agencies by the context in which they have to operate.

Neither of these approaches, however, seemed entirely adequate for discharging the tasks they had set themselves. The political sociology tradition has been valuable in pointing to the significance of power and inequality in society as a whole and thus in identifying the inevitable weaknesses in political science approaches which attempt to theorise power through an exclusive focus on domination organised through the state. In particular, this work is important in alerting us to the fact that power is not merely control or influence over state institutions, but it is also embodied in the ownership of capital, control of labour-market opportunities, exclusion through gender and race, and so on. It is also important in pointing to the ways in which such relations of power become institutionalised in forms of domination which are inscribed within the very framework of contemporary British society. Yet this work has generally failed to explain the *relation* between state power and other forms of domination, and its understanding of how structures of domination may constrain individual actions is very underdeveloped.

Much the same can be said of the Marxist literature. Unlike the sociological tradition, Marxist theories tend to emphasise the importance of relations of economic domination in determining other patterns of social relations, yet this has given rise to a large number of unresolved problems. What is the relationship between economic power and political power in liberal democratic systems where there is no one-to-one correspondence between them? To what extent does the fact of a capitalist form of economic organisation determine the form of the state and the way it operates? And how are the others sources of inequality and other patterns of cleavage – e.g. divisions between men and women, blacks and whites, public-sector and private-sector employees, welfare-state clients and private consumers – to be explained through a theory which asserts the primacy of class struggle in politics?

We are left, then, with on the one hand political theories – those of mainstream political science as well as aspects of the New Right – which are useful in explaining facets of British politics but which fail to understand the broader context in which these politics occurs, and on the other the much broader theories of political sociology and Marxism which attempt to relate political domination to the wider organisation of British society yet which leave all sorts of loose ends in their overall mode of explanation. The strengths of the former are the weaknesses of the latter, and vice versa. The obvious task for future work is to explore the possibility of bringing them together so as to combine their strengths while hopefully side-stepping their weaknesses.

Such an endeavour will need to recognise that *different* kinds of theory may be appropriate to the analysis of *different* kinds of politics at *different* levels of generality. If this idea of theoretical 'horses for courses' is accepted, then we may begin to see how different perspectives and theories which have often been regarded as incompatible may in fact be complementary because they deal with different things *all* of which are of some importance if we are to take in the complexity of British politics today. Having said that, we noted in our introduction that any broad and coherent analysis of British politics needs to take both capitalism and liberal democracy seriously. Our complaint about mainstream political science is that it has tended to focus almost exclusively on the latter; Marxist theories have suffered from the opposite tendency; and New Right accounts have blamed democracy in their concern to defend a capitalist economic order that they have chosen to define in simple and rosey terms.

If the task for the future is to relate different theories which hitherto have focused on different aspects of the world, then we shall need to begin by tracing the connections between those aspects. More specifically, we need to tease out the nature of the relationship between the democratic polity theorised by mainstream political science and the capitalist economy theorised by Marxist and other broader perspectives. Not until we are sensitive to the tensions between democracy and capitalism in the real world can we begin, in the world of theory, to overcome the tensions between perspectives which only focus on one or the other.

Throughout this book we have made it clear that making good sense of British politics demands that we 'see' politics, not as a self-contained activity that only occurs in officially designated 'political' organisations and institutions, but in the round and in the larger context of economy and society. Nineteenth-century theorists recognised this; they did not write about politics *or* economics but explored the total political economy and the complex intermeshing of governments and markets, public power and private power. Sides were taken on the appropriate balance between governments and markets. Defenders of free-market capitalism supported a *laissez-faire,* limited state and were anxious as to the implications that might flow from a state based on unfettered mass democracy: would public power eat into private power, and would the voting many use the state to pillage the wealthy few who were dominant in the market? From the other side, those critical of the privilege and power of private property saw, in a popularly controlled public power, the possibility of fundamental change and the emancipation of the masses.

These, then were the questions that were the stuff of theoretical political economy, and they were at the core of politics and political action as well. If you were 'for' the market then you were probably against democracy, and if you were against the market and the power of private interests then you were likely to be optimistic as to what might come from the extension of the franchise to the working class. Simply expressed, prior to the extension of the franchise to the urban working class, theorists explored politics and economics in relation to each other, and most informed commentators saw a polity based on democracy and an economy based on capitalism as in many ways incompatible.

Since those days assessments as to the 'fit' between democracy and capitalism have changed. The extension of the franchise in England did not bring the immediate disasters and transformations that opponents (and even liberals) feared. Indeed, supporters of the free market gradually came to praise liberal democracy as a good in its own right and as posing little challenge to the survival of the economy of capitalism. The point was not lost on Marxists. Marx himself expressed high hopes as to what democracy *could* bring, claiming that universal suffrage was a 'socialistic measure' and its 'inevitable result' would be the 'political supremacy of the working class'. However, he also recognised the limitations of *bourgeois* democracy which he believed simply served to incorporate the working class within the prevailing economic order. It was this idea of democracy as a concession that helped to legitimise the system whilst leaving the fundamentals unchallenged which was later to inform Lenin's argument that 'a democratic republic is the best possible political shell for capitalism'.

So, as the practice of liberal, or bourgeois, democratic politics unfolded, reassessments were made as to its implications for the prospects of stability or change on the larger canvas of society. There were intellectual about-turns. The kind of people who once feared democracy learned to love it, whereas critics of capitalism who had once held out high hopes for deomcracy found them dashed so that the Marxist tradition came to see revolution as the only viable road leading to transformation and socialism. All in all, by the beginning of the twentieth century a new and fudgy consensus had emerged between supporters and critics of both capitalism and democracy. That consensus overturned the view which suggested that democracy and capitalism were in conflict, and held instead that capitalism and democracy were in fact mutually supportive. Defenders of capitalism and democracy argued that they fitted together because freedom, competition, and power dispersal were the essential hallmarks and guarantees of both. Critics of capitalism and democracy argued that they fitted together because a formal democracy of citizens actually served to sustain the economic inequality of the market: workers accepted political rights in return for a general sacrifice of economic ones, and the fairness central to the ideology of liberal democracy legitimised the total system in the eyes of the majority whilst still allowing dominant minority interests sufficient scope to rule from behind the scenes.

Having highlighted the extent to which democracy and capitalism came to be seen as compatible (albeit for very different reasons) it is also important to recognise that the connections between the two have not been really seriously explored. The social sciences split into their separate disciplines at the end of the nineteenth century and the problems of political economy fell between the two stools of political science and economics with each discipline considering questions of secondary significance. Moreover, as we have already made clear, Marxists have failed to take liberal democracy seriously, while those who have come to see liberal democracy in entirely positive terms – those, that is, who have provided the mainstream perspective on British politics – have failed to locate democracy within the framework of the capitalist system. From one side, inadequate attention to democratic politics; from the other, inadequate attention to capitalism, and from all perspectives and disciplines no attention to capitalism and democracy considered together so that nineteenth-century insights into the strains and tensions between them have been lost.

Now, there is a problem in exploring the relationship between democracy and capitalism in Britain because the terms themselves are contested. Mainstream and liberal opinion is content to see democracy in *procedural* terms – e.g. in the existence of formally free elections and certain civil liberties. Left opinion, by contrast is concerned to define democracy in *substantive* terms – e.g. as involving popular participation in decision-making in both the polity and the economy with that participation inevitably leading to a rough equality of results in terms of the distribution of material benefits. Similarly, apologists for capitalism are concerned to define it in terms of freedoms and opportunities where the bulk of economic activity is organised through private enterprise in a free market, whereas critics of this mode of production (whilst recognising the importance of private ownership and the market) are concerned to assert the lack of freedom and opportunity which follows from the exploitation and subordination of those who only have their labour power to sell to the owners of capital.

Given the disagreement concerning the definition of capitalism and democracy, it is perhaps not surprising that there are also disputes as to whether Britain is any longer 'really' democratic or 'really' capitalist. Mainstream and liberal opinion would certainly see Britain as democratic – indeed, as too democratic – but tends to see the growth of nationalisation and state economic activity as having produced a 'mixed' economy in place of a purely capitalist one. Left opinion, by contrast, generally sees British democracy as partial and crushingly constrained by economic power and the institutions of the secret state, but insists that the economy is still unremittingly tied to capitalist essentials despite the many changes which have occurred since the nineteenth century.

Now, even allowing for the intellectual uncertainty that is part and parcel of these contests and disputes, there is surely something of a paradox in the coexistence of democratic institutions within capitalist societies since the principles of majority rule and political equality (one person one vote) seem inconsistent with the economic reality of minority power and the persistence of marked inequalities with respect to material advantages and benefits that are a feature of all capitalist economies. In our view, it is by no means self-evident that democracy is the 'best possible political shell' for capitalism, nor that capitalism is a necessary condition for the full realisation of democracy. Doubts about the supposed 'fit' between the two are reinforced once we realise that capitalism is by no means universally associated with formal political democracy. The burgeoning capitalist economies of Latin America for example, could be cited to support a contrary hypothesis of a 'natural' fit between capitalism and authoritarian and military regimes with limited political freedoms.

Nearer to home, it is important to consider the challenging implications of contemporary New Right thinking on these matters. Here is a body of work vehemently opposed to socialism and centrally concerned to defend capitalism and revive the flagging economies of the West. In Chapters 2 and 3 we outlined their critique of developments in British democracy. Interest groups and trade unions are accused of contributing to an overload of demands that has made for ungovernability, political parties are criticised as too adversarial, and both these tendencies are said to have made for unstable public policies and to have led to 'too much' state intervention and public spending which has served to provide an unstable base for capitalist development. High taxation has, we are told, crowded out opportunities for economic growth in the private sphere because resources have been pre-empted by the state in order to provide uneconomic social benefits. In Chapter 4, moreover, we outlined the contemporary disputes as to what should be the nature of the British constitution, and pointed to an influential body of opinion which has sought to create a new constitution for Britain better attuned to the needs of the market. Under such new constitutional arrangements, the sovereignty of a democratic Parliament and the scope for state intervention would be limited by law; the power of the judges would be extended; and the significance of the unelected House of Lords would be revived. Here, then is a body of work that is making the running with respect to contemporary political debates and which underpins much of the thinking of the Conservative Governments of 1979 and 1983. The fact that it criticises British democracy and proposes a new constitution of *limited* democracy, and the fact that it justifies these criticisms and proposals in the name of an active and aggressive defence of the virtues of free-market capitalism, surely provides still further grounds for our wondering whether capitalism and democracy have come to the parting of the ways.

What all this suggests is that we should be wary of seeing a tight fit between democracy and capitalism. No absolute and general relation can be constructed between them. It is true that a democracy is a *possible* form of capitalist state, but it is less certain that mass democracy is the *best* or most adequate form of capitalist state (especially when we see it in the context of an increasingly monopolised economy where huge multi-national companies need to manage governments in the way in which they manage and manipulate their markets). Democracy, then, is indeterminate in so far as its relationship to capitalism is concerned. Put another way, certain conditions must be satisfied if it is to function in a way that is supportive of continued capitalist development. What are these conditions?

1 Harking back to the ideas of Bagehot in 1872 when he was forced to ponder the implications of working-class suffrage, the population as a whole must be 'deferential' and modest in their expectation of politics and of change through politics so that they accept the 'natural' order and inequalities of the market. A deferential politics limits the popular role in the political process at the same time as it limits the claim for rights through the public power of the state.

2 The precise type of democracy should itself be limited to a representative and parliamentary form. If this prevails and secures a

legitimacy then the scope for a more participatory democracy involving intra-party democracy and extra-parliamentary action is restricted. Furthermore, pivotal positions within the state system and crucial institutional centres of state power should not be based on the elective principle; should be beyond the effective reach of the elected side of the state; and should enjoy close links to those dominant in the market system of private power.

3   The capitalist economy should be buoyant and subject to steady growth so that there is sufficient 'slack' within the economic system to enable elected politicians to respond to popular pressures for more and better public services and to fund those services through an ability to draw increasing tax revenues from an expanding economy without crowding out opportunities for further growth, and squeezing the economically powerful.

4   Because the danger is ever present that political power will be employed to undermine individual economic freedoms in the market if the 'wrong' people and parties employ the power of the state for the 'wrong' purposes, it is vital that interests sensitive to the need to maintain the essential disciplines of a capitalist economy are politically and ideologically dominant. This occurs if the electorate is firmly attached to political parties that are committed to the rules of parliamentary democracy (with all the limitations this implies) and if the parties are content to develop programmes that are 'realistic' (in that they work within the dominant ideology and accept that certain crucial aspects of economic life lie beyond the bounds of political control).

It should be clear that all these conditions serve to box democracy in to a narrow formalism of particular procedures which fall far short of participatory democracy and which represent a mere shadow of a substantive democracy in which all citizens have relatively equal chances to influence and control the making of decisions that affect them be they in politics or the market. Having said that, it is nevertheless clear that the four conditions relate each to the other and the importance of any one condition for sustaining capitalism varies at particular points in time. For example, if there is substantial slack in the system (condition 3) then there is scope to concede to demands from below. In this state of affairs, deference (condition 1) is less needed to ensure that democratic demands do not press up against the limits of capitalist concession because the limits are themselves expanding. However, if both slack and deference are lacking, then popular politics need to be constrained by a particular kind of public ideology (condition 4), and if that too is a problem, and the limits of the form of democracy are insufficient to restrain people's demands and aspirations, then public power needs to be successfully and legitimately transferred to the secret side of the state (condition 2). Attending to the relationship between democracy and capitalism in contemporary Britain thus involves consideration of the extent to which these four general conditions are satisfied in practice and whether they pull together (or compensate each other) in support of a free economy. What, then, can we say about each condition today?

1   A lot has happened since Bagehot wrote *The English Constitution* over 100 years ago. He feared that the established political parties would bid for the support of the working class, and he feared still more the possibility that the 'lower classes' might combine to form their own political party to advance their own interests ('an evil of the first magnitude that...would make them...supreme in the country'). He feared, in other words, the breakdown of deference which he saw as the key holding democratic excesses in check. Much has been written about the significance of deference in British politics but there is little doubt that deference is less a force than was once the case (reflected in the changing balance of forces securing the social order and discussed in Chapter 10) and popular expectations of the state have risen in the period since Bagehot. Moreover, those who write about adversary politics today are right to remind us that political parties do bid for popular support, and elections have often been auctions of popular policies where the problem of paying for the promises is only faced after the event of victory. In addition, the 'political combination of the lower classes' that Bagehot so feared came into being with the formation of the Labour Party at the beginning of this century. Although the extent to which the party has 'really' transformed Britain when in government is still hotly debated, there is little doubt that elements within the party have always held to an ethic of provision that is challenging of capitalism and market power, and aspects of the welfare state are a concrete embodiment of the ethic of provision according to need rather than according to ability to pay. So, the conditions that Bagehot saw as vital to make democracy compatible with 'property' have largely evaporated.

2   It is true that democracy in Britain is mainly restricted to the representative and parliamentary form but this has not stopped moments of participation which have fallen outside, and challenged, those procedures. Working people, organised in trade unions, have taken action on the streets and in their workplaces. In the period since the 1960s, many people have begun to take local democracy seriously, participating in locally based campaigns of 'community action' in a way that has asserted the legitimacy and credibility of a more participatory democracy, and attempting (as in the Greater London Council and some of the metropolitan counties in the early 1980s) to use local authorities to challenge the power of the centre and to assert an alternative set of values to those of private property and the market system. Again in the 1970s, sections of the Left in British politics were active in an extra-parliamentary politics that often tumbled into anti-parliamentary politics as well. Notwithstanding these challenging developments, however, it continues to be the case that crucial centres of state power are beyond

democratic control and in Chapter 5 we saw how many of the pivotal positions within the secret state are still occupied by those of an upper-middle-class social background with dispositions to match.

3   Democracy is a fragile flower. It is always likely to push up against the confines set by the pattern of social and economic power based on the ownership of property and the control of economic opportunities by privileged groups. The survival of democracy requires tolerance, the inclusion of all classes in the exercise of political power, and a fundamental unity on the part of the people. The problem is that the unity between the classes is contingent on economic success. Harold Laski has not been the only person to wonder 'whether the uneasy marriage between capitalism and democracy is psychologically possible in the period of capitalism's decline' when the 'better classes' no longer feel able to concede. In the 20 years of relative affluence following the Second World War, slow but sustained economic growth provided slack, constraints on public policy-making were comparatively loose, and much could be achieved through parties and pressures and the democratic process. But at times of economic recession, the constraints on popular politics and the democratic process tighten as dominant economic interests look to their profit margins and exert pressures on the state to reduce the cost of the concessions made in the democratic round of politics. At times like this (and Britain has been going through one such period since the early 1970s) capitalism and democracy come into sharp conflict.

However, it is important to remember that recession does not *create* the problem of the fit between capitalism and democracy since it simply serves to *exacerbate* the endemic problem which faces the state in a capitalist economy where democracy entrenches popular expectations and the means to press them that cannot easily be ignored, repressed, or left to be satisfied in the market. In bald outline, the state has to encourage economic growth because if it fails to do so it does not have an expanding base to tax, and tax is the source of its own power. At the same time as the state encourages economic growth through the market it also has to secure social harmony and legitimise its role in the eyes of the larger public whose actions do not directly make for growth. So, the state has to assist in the making of profits and so support the few who can contribute in vital ways to economic growth. But in helping one class at the expense of other classes and in limiting its role in the provision of social benefit, it risks losing its legitimacy as a neutral, fair, and caring agency and so undermines the basis of its loyalty and support. With recession, the Catch 22 problem is heightened as the capitalist economy is unable to deliver the goods as promised and so state efforts at social amelioration become increasingly urgent as popular pressures escalate. However, at the very moment when the state is most pressed to provide social support services it is least able to do so because the surplus is not there and those concerned with the preservation of a lean and fit capitalism see these services as expensive deductions from profits and an obstacle to further growth. Something has to give. Recession seems to highlight many of the problems integral to maintaining a capitalist democracy.

4 So far we have highlighted problems with respect to the fulfilment of the conditions resolving the paradox of the fit between capitalism and democracy. Deference is not what it was; popular politics frequently challenge established democratic procedures; and most profoundly, recession cuts into the slack that gives democracy room to move within the confines of capitalism. This being the case, sustaining the connection between capitalism and democracy at the present time seems to depend on the fulfilment of the fourth condition – the political and ideological supremacy within democracy of those interests attuned to the need to protect the essentials of the capitalist economy. What, then, can we say about this?

The Conservative Party won the election of 1979 and won again in 1983. The Labour Party was routed in the 1983 election and the Liberal-SDP Alliance secured the support of over a quarter of the voters. Two things are significant about these events. First, the ideological tendency that is supreme within the Conservative Party and that has been endorsed twice at the polls is keenly pro-market and anti-state and so is active in attempting to create the conditions to revive a viable system of capitalism in Britain. Second, the Labour Party is the only mass party committed in principle to an alternative mode of organising the economy, and yet it failed to secure substantial popular support even in 1983 at a time of mass unemployment when the individualistic philosophy of the market should be vulnerable to challenge. So, the fourth condition *is* roughly fulfilled at the present time, but is this enough to sustain the fit between capitalism and democracy?

Observing contemporary politics rather suggests that rights and freedoms that have been at the core of the democratic tradition are under challenge. The repressive side of the state is being strengthened in support of the free economy while civil liberties are being eroded; trade union powers are being curbed and certain government employees are banned from union membership altogether; popular movements are attacked when they dare to move outside the tight limitations of established procedures and the cost of working within these procedures is itself increased by, for example, raising the candidate's deposit at elections from £150 to £1000; moves to open government are resisted and the powers of the secret state are strengthened and defended; the significance of elected local authorities is being massively eroded and those authorities most vulnerable to control by non- or anti-capitalist interests are being abolished; and those in positions of constitutional authority advocate limiting democracy by law and strengthening the power of the judges.

Writing on the allegedly supportive connection between capitalism and democracy has been casual. What our review suggests is that conditions need to be met if capitalism and democracy are not to come into conflict and those conditions all involve limitations on democracy and limitations on the ends to be pressed on the state by democracy. It is not so much capitalism and democracy that go together but capitalism and *liberal* democracy – the democracy, that is of *limited* participation by a *limited* section of the population which sees the principal role of the state itself as *limited* to the traditional sphere of law and order that does not involve it intervening in the operation of the free market. The trouble is that democracy is not easily contained within the liberal political straitjacket, and it seeks by its own inner impulses to be more and become a social and economic democracy as well. It finds the road barred by the capitalist foundations upon which the political democracy is built and thus inevitably represents a constant threat, now hidden, now manifest, to these very foundations. It is for this reason that we agree with Laski that 'a political democracy which rests upon capitalist foundations has war, open or secret, in its midst.'.

One last point needs to be made about all this. To assert, as we have, that capitalism and democracy are locked into a relationship of perpetual tension does not imply that socialism fits democracy any better. With the short and notable exception of Allende's Chile, no country in the world has yet been able to reconcile a socialist system of collective and centralised economic planning with the protection and development of individual civil rights and political freedoms. Socialists themselves tend to argue that, while genuine economic and political democracy is impossible in capitalism, it is possible in socialism since the power of private property has been removed. We doubt this, for it is difficult to see how the detailed planning of a modern complex economy and the power of the planners can be reconciled with an extension of individual liberties and local self-determination.

In pointing to the contradictions between capitalism and democracy, therefore, we should be wary of drawing the all-too-easy conclusion that socialism and democracy go together any better. When we move from the cosy world of studying British politics to the chilly and uncertain world of acting within them, it may well be that, as conservatives or as socialists, we will be called upon to make some very uncomfortable choices between values that we cherish.

Index

Note: Authors are indexed only where they are cited in the main text. Authors cited in guides to further reading at the end of each chapter are not included here.